GODSFALL

GODSFALL

STRANGER THAN FICTION
— BOOK 1 —

T. B. MARE

Podium

Podium

GODSFALL

To travel to the Great Below was to traverse a path of no return.

It was a known tale, one that every mother told her child. A tale of caution shared amongst one's brethren, a wise old saying that prevented men of spirit from under- taking journeys that would consume their very souls.

Such tales meant nothing to her. Caution, after all, was merely an excuse. One used by vermin when faced with that which transcended them.

For this was the domain of the Underworld. The Blackness of the Grave. Her sister's dominion.

Turns out . . . those mothers?

They had it right.

PROLOGUE

Inanna was bound in chains.

Three sets of shadow-forged metal entwined her waist, the cold, poisonous links tearing into her flesh. They pried at her back and kept her upright while the collar around her neck constantly pulled her head down. Four more chains wrung around her wrist and ankles, holding her spread-eagled, leaving her breasts to dangle freely as she hung in midair.

All the while, countless spectators—denizens of the Great Below, fallen gods, creatures of the night and the grave, and even wraiths whose names had been lost to time—gathered around to watch her heinous degradation. Jackals howling at the sight of a wounded lioness.

"I do hope you are enjoying the royal treatment, dear sister."

Inanna raised her head, ignoring the accursed metal that dug into her neck. Her shadowed eyes took in the audience, feasting upon their hesitant features as her gaze passed over them. *Vermin.* Even in this state, she made them cower in fear of her.

It made her smile.

She glanced up at the towering spine of basalt that rose like a cruel peak, with a magnificent throne of bones at the top. Seated upon it was a tall, willowy woman wearing robes of pitch black belted with joined fragments of bone. A tall crown of more bones rested upon her head, framed by white hair that spilled over her shoulders. Distant and cold, she looked as lovely and merciless as moonlit snow.

Ereshkigal. Empress of the Dead. Queen of the Great Below.

Her eyes were illusion. Her touch, death.

And yet, Inanna thought, *merely an imitation.* A soft chuckle escaped her throat.

"Laughing, are you?" the empress's voice boomed from her throne, throaty and suggestive. "Even in such a state, you think yourself my better?"

"I *am* your better, Ereshkigal," Inanna softly chided, as if talking to a slow child. "But then, you have always known that. Have you not, little sister?"

The Empress of the Dead stood up from her throne, her robes billowing in the harsh winds of the Underworld. At once, every single entity in the chamber knelt, their heads bowed in quiet reverence. Inanna felt her legs being pulled on either side. Yet, not a single sound escaped her throat. Her sister's righteous fury was met with casual indifference.

The message was sent. Silent, but loud and clear.

Ereshkigal heard it all too well.

You will not break me.

"Enough," the empress rumbled. The monsters of the night near her drew back, leaving nothing between the dangling Inanna and the Stone Table beneath her. A single golden chain erupted out of the polished surface, its tip spearing into her navel. Precious, crimson lifeblood oozed down the chain into the table below, and the sigils on its surface glowed with maleficent power.

Inanna glanced down at the construction—no, *conduit*. One that dragged everything from the victim and gave it to . . . something else. But what? She could not say. If she'd had her pendant with her, she could have read its Truths, seen its concept of creation.

The golden chain pulled, and Inanna fell spread-eagled upon the table, her jaw dislocated from the fall.

She looked like a wasted slave.

Debased.

Demeaned.

Gleeful laughter rang in her ears. The squealers and climbers howled like mad dogs at her disgrace. The specters soon showed their conceited joy, joined by hordes of fallen gods, bestial abominations that lived on as symbionts, and other existences she had slain with her bare hands.

They will pay for it, Inanna promised. *Over and over.*

"How the mighty have fallen!" Ereshkigal declared. "Supreme Queen of An and Ki. Daughter of the stars themselves! Destroyer of civilizations and plunderer of pantheons! How does it feel to be reviled by so many?"

"Like you wouldn't believe, sweet sister," Inanna replied, licking her lips. Her thin smile could pierce through solid stone. "I could have you fucked on all fours for weeks on end and you would not feel what I feel." Her eyes shone with mirth. "Orgasmic, I tell you."

That sparked a reaction. Not from her sister, but from the surrounding vermin. Another rabisu, one of the rabid spirits that followed her sister, leaped up on the pedestal and drove a spear through her shoulder.

"Do not insult our queen!" it snarled, its tentacular maw quivering.

"Step away," Ereshkigal ordered, walking down the hill of basalt. With a flick of her fingers, the spear disintegrated, though the injury remained fresh.

Still the same. She could never stand anyone else being so close to me.

Her thoughts were interrupted by a sudden pull on her neck. She was thrown atop the Stone Table, a painful mix of blood and drool dripping from the corners of her lips as she rested upon her injured knees and palms.

Like a dog.

"You were saying?" her younger sister offered, her head slightly tilted. She always did have the best expressions. Even now, as Ereshkigal stood tall, Inanna noticed the slight whitening of her sister's knuckles. It reminded her of back then, at—

Inanna drew in a rusty, painful breath. The constant drain of her life blood was affecting her. Her mind ran in odd directions. Splotches of darkness began to invade her sight.

"I was saying that it is the prerogative of vermin, Ereshkigal," she continued, uncaring of the slow tightening of the chains binding her. "To stand in a herd, untrusting of one's own might, acting in unison against an opponent like a pack of angry dogs. Barking is something you are intimately familiar with, after all."

The chains constricted further.

Her smile only widened.

"Do not fool yourself. You did not force me down here. You are nothing but a filthy thief of power, a snake priding herself on collecting the scraps I discarded on my path to power. A back-biting coward who assembles has-beens and hustlers, standing on my shoulders and calling herself tall."

"And yet, chains can be forged," Ereshkigal softly, but firmly, replied. "And clearly, predators can be bound. Call me a backstabber. Call me a traitor. But today, I will see to it that justice prevails."

Inanna began to laugh. She laughed and laughed and *laughed* at the sheer hilarity, at the hypocrisy of it all. "Justice?" she spat. "Is that what they call it these days? Very well, begin this farce! Make me stand in judgment of my many grievous sins."

The collar around her neck was yanked to the right by an unseen force, compelling her to look upon the hordes of rabisu. Their fangs were bared, bodily fluids dripping from their maws as they gazed upon her with hunger.

"Do you remember them? Priests of the fallen god Marduk. You tore him apart, obliterated his kingdom, usurped his Truths. You violated all that these people held dear, even their right to exist."

"And what of it?" Inanna demanded. "When titans clash, the grass will suffer."

Ereshkigal stiffened. "As my parents did?"

Inanna's expression twisted into a sneer.

"Why did you do it?" A slight tremor entered the empress's voice. "Why did you spare me? Train me to fight? What—what was I to you? Nothing more than a *puppet* to entertain yourself?"

"Precisely." Inanna grinned. "I took you in. I made you everything you are today, Empress of the Dead. Perhaps I should have left you there, lying in that ditch."

"But why?" Ereshkigal repeated. "Why even bother? Why not just kill us? Why make us the way we are? We stood by you through every trial imaginable. We faced gods for you. Yet you treat us like slaves. You took away everything I valued! My parents. My husband. *Everything.* You made me suffer alone." She staggered forward. "Why?!"

"Why do you pick flowers?" Inanna asked mockingly. "Everything I did, it was simply because I could. You may have me in chains, but do not pretend, *girl.* Killing me is a feat beyond your ability."

Ereshkigal recoiled.

"There exists no curse that can taint me, nothing sacred I cannot violate. You seek my remorse, yet I have none to share. Try me, Ereshkigal. I am willing," Inanna said. "You may steal my power. Bind me away in the depths of the Underworld. Tear me down for the rabble to feed on." Her voice lowered to an icy whisper. "But you will never get what you truly want. You will never. Become. Me."

"I have already become you!" her sister roared. "Do not forget which of us sits on a throne, while the other lies defeated, shackled by chains."

"Come, now. Even you cannot be so deluded as to believe your chains will hold me forever." Inanna's shackles clinked, as if acknowledging her words. "And without your trickery or your bindings, do you truly think you can face me?" Inanna swiveled her head to stare at her audience. "I *will* tear my way out of this prison and destroy everything you hold dear. Your power, your Truths, your sacred relics—I will take everything. And upon the hill of your corpses, I will build a new world. Those by my side will become the new gods."

She looked toward Neti, the gatekeeper of the Underworld, who flinched away.

"And if you are foolish enough to not fear my vengeance, ask yourself this." She pulled at her chains. "Who does? Who is the weakest? The most afraid? Who will break first? Is there still time for it to be you?"

Uncertain, hesitant eyes glanced around the room. Quite a few stepped back. Some even fell to their knees.

"Kill everything that moved!" came the order, cold and unforgiving. The rabisu leaped upon the hapless crowd and tore the offenders to pieces before they could plead for mercy.

Utter silence shocked the chamber.

"Now then." Ereshkigal darkly smiled, her icy blue eyes gleaming. "Who else is willing to stand by my sister?"

Inanna could not help herself. She chuckled. "To think you would learn to use fear as a weapon now of all times. Even in your betrayal, you find ways to emulate me. You make me proud."

The Empress of the Dead strode forward, her robes smoothly gliding across the stone floor. Inanna stared back at her, devoid of hatred, allowing her younger sister to see a defiant, uncaring queen. The tables were turned against her, but she would prevail. She had done so in the past several times.

This would be no different.

Ereshkigal's right hand came up and caressed Inanna's bloodied cheek. It felt warm, familial, and welcoming. "In my heart of hearts, I knew this would not work," she lamented. "Agony does not faze you. Death does not frighten you. You will never succumb to mortal wounds. But you raise a fair point."

She gently cupped Inanna's chin.

"The Supreme Queen cannot die. But she can suffer."

Suddenly, the chains binding Inanna disappeared, and she weakly fell onto the floor like a sack of flesh. Ereshkigal swooped down and lifted her head up by the neck. She brought Inanna's face close to her own, until she was able to whisper in her ears.

"You were right. You made me what I am. You are my Creator. And for that . . . I will always respect you. And now, I will take your place."

And the Underworld *changed.*

A massive stone archway rose out of the ground like an eerie tombstone. Even through the red haze of her vision, Inanna could not miss the sigils engraved upon it, glowing with a bright, silvery sheen.

And there were six others behind it, forming a long, narrow passage for someone to walk through.

"Welcome, sister," Ereshkigal's voice boomed, "to the Seven Gates of the Underworld!"

Seven gates. Seven archways. The edifices standing before her were the gates that drew the line between the living and the dead. Each Gate held authority over one of the seven fundamental tenets of existence itself. Passing through them would mean an absolute suppression of each one.

This was no judgment. It was an eternal prison. A manifestation of isolationism in its truest form. An existence neither alive nor dead. The soul would remain, but all else would fade.

For the first time since she entered the Underworld, Inanna felt her heart tremble.

"*YOU, WHO HAVE ALWAYS TAKEN, SHALL FEEL WHAT IT MEANS TO BE DEPRIVED.*"

As Ereshkigal's voice echoed around her, Inanna felt an unseen might drag her to her feet. Chains, unseen and unbreakable, formed around her fists, her waist, her ankles, and her neck, unhurriedly dragging her through the First Gate.

The Trap of Opulence, Inanna quietly recognized. Everything that was her and hers would stay. Everything that was not, ceased to be hers. Her blazing connection to the divine Ax of Marduk faded. Her opal ring, the symbol of her victory over the Goddess of the Night, slid down her finger. Her necklace and her divine bracelets, smidgens of Truth that once belonged to Gula, now dropped onto the floor.

"MY HUSBAND WAS LOST TO YOUR UNABATED LUSTS. LIVE AN ETERNITY BEREFT OF THEM."

The Second Gate, the Trap of Passion, tore at her sacral knot. Once the Goddess of Lust, Inanna would no longer feel pleasure. Her body shriveled like a prune and her breasts sagged. Her cheeks wrinkled as every bit of her sensuality and charm faded away, leaving a twisted, ugly caricature of herself behind. One that would forever be unable to feel another's touch.

"WARS HAVE FOLLOWED YOUR FOOTSTEPS. CIVILI-ZATIONS BURNED AND LIVES TORN APART, ALL FOR YOUR PRIDE. FOREVER LOSE YOUR DOMINANCE AND CONVICTION."

The Trap of Self-Esteem revoked her authority as the Monarch of the Heavens. Her golden crown appeared in an earthen heap on the floor as she was flung through the Third Gate. No longer would she hold the title of queen.

"YOU WHO HAVE COMMANDED LEGIONS TO BRING FORTH DESTRUCTION SHALL BE CURSED WITH ETER-NAL SILENCE."

Her lips were sealed together, not allowing even the slightest murmur to escape as the chains dragged her through the Fourth Gate: the Trap of Expression.

"YOUR MIGHT RISES WITH FEAR. BE ISOLATED FROM ALL EXISTENCE. YOUR THRONE, YOUR RELICS, YOUR TEMPLES, YOUR WORSHIPPERS. MAY YOUR FAITH BE ENTIRELY LOST."

The Fifth Gate, the Trap of Connectivity, untethered the memories of her temples and the collective faith of her worshippers. Once aware of everything on Heaven and Earth, Inanna could no longer see past the archway that stood before her.

"QUEEN. CONQUEROR. PLUNDERER. YOU WHO CONSIDER YOURSELF ABOVE ALL ELSE SHALL BREED NO THOUGHT. LIVE AS WOULD A PEBBLE."

Inanna turned around, her dry, parched lips wanting to speak to her sister. To explain, to—

To do what?

She no longer knew as she was dragged through the Trap of—

Of—

"LET THE MEMORIES OF THE RUTHLESS GODDESS FADE AWAY. LET HER DOMAIN BE BURIED IN TIME. NO LONGER SHALL YOU BE ONE OF US. I CAST YOU ... OUT!"

Inanna trembled before the Seventh and final Gate's power as it drank from her very soul, etching upon it a curse that marked her as a denizen of the Underworld. The world above lost its meaning to her, as she dropped like a marionette with its strings severed.

Naked and unmoving, she lay on the cold floor. Her glassy eyes stared lifelessly ahead at her sister, a single tear trickling down her cheek.

"Always remember, dear sister," Ereshkigal murmured fondly. "Whatever I do, I do for love."

She flicked her hand, and Inanna's limp body was carelessly tossed against the wall. At the last moment, a rocky spike erupted outwards, piercing her through the chest.

Straight through her heart.

PART I

THE CRYPT OF FIENDISH WORMS

C H A P T E R   1

─────────

Waking Up to an Apocalypse

The arrival of the twin-tailed ball of dust shalt signal the end
of the crust.
Some will fight, some will reason, some will find hope in religion.
The bane of worlds shall be unbound.
Only in death shall respite be found.
In the flames—

Flames . . . ?" Lukas Aguilar hummed. His fingers flew across the keyboard as he scoured the online thesaurus. "Flames" and "fire" were a little too generic, with the whole *Pit of Hell* theme in Christianity. What he needed was something more uncommon. Something archaic.

Banefire?

That felt better.

Nodding to himself, he began typing again.

In the banefire of—

Lukas paused. Rubbing the tip of his nose, he pushed his chair away from the computer screen. Even from a distance, the Word document gazed back at him, the poetic prose making him feel stupider with every passing second.

Something was missing. Something . . . something . . .

"This sucks!" he groaned, raking his fingers through his hair. "What the hell am I doing?"

It was the third night in a row he'd stayed up late working on this nonsense. With less than a month left until the end of the semester, he should've been preparing for his finals, not writing shitty poetry. Yet here he was.

How can anyone take this crap seriously?

Lukas's current task was to edit an article about an ancient Akkadian prophecy for a sensational news site. *Edit* being the keyword. Somewhere along the way, Emma had him not only research the whole thing but also write it down and rework the translated prophecy so that it rhymed.

As if translating the gibberish into readable English wasn't Herculean enough of a task.

DING!

Frowning, Lukas grabbed his phone. It was a text from Emma.

Speak of the devil, and she would text you like a jilted lover. Or so the saying went.

[Where the hell are you? I've been trying to reach you for the last hour.]

With everything going on, Emma's constant phone calls were exactly the sort of distraction he didn't need. One would think that after fifteen missed calls, she'd finally get the memo. Instead, she, in a strictly Emma-like fashion, wouldn't rest until she got what she wanted.

The screen blinked again.

[I need the article before noon tomorrow. Coming over.]

What the—

Lukas speed dialed her number. Emma picked it up on the first ring.

"So," came a rich, feminine voice, laden with condescension, *"your phone does work after all."*

"I was supposed to get until the end of the week for this, Emma," he flatly replied, pushing himself off of the chair. From the sound of it, she was walking. Furiously. Maybe even climbing the stairs. He really hoped she was just joking about coming over. Hurricane Emma distracting him over the phone was one thing, but being in the same room as him?

He'd never be able to get any work done.

"What can I say? Things change. I fired the other guy, and we need this by tomorrow evening. You're all I've got."

"Listen, Emma, you don't need to—"

KNOCK! KNOCK!

"Open the door," she said.

Lukas disconnected the call and hurled the phone at his bed. Deciding to take his sweet time, he walked over to his refrigerator and grabbed an apple first. Red Delicious, his favorite. He then went over to his laptop and saved the document. Twice. Ignoring the increasingly frantic knocks, he took a bite out of the fruit and stared patiently at his screen. Only minutes later did he finally walk to the door and crack it ajar.

He was greeted with a strained smile and a glare that could melt steel.

"Hey, Emma," he offered, opening the door all the way.

Emma took a few calming breaths, though her fingers were still twitching. "I was wondering if you were going to let me in at all."

Lukas shrugged. "A part of me hoped you'd get tired of knocking. Turn around and go home. Maybe let me get a good night's sleep for once."

She wrinkled her nose. "You need it. You look like a hundred miles of bad road."

Lukas glanced toward the mirror in the corner. As he had pretty much confined himself to his room, his skin was pale and dark circles hung heavy beneath his eyes from one too many late nights working his ass off for a conspiracy website. It was hardly respectable work by any means, but his bills wouldn't pay themselves.

"Still, that's not enough to chase me away," she exclaimed. "I still want the manuscript."

He groaned and trudged back toward his desk, the half-eaten apple still in his hand. He'd known Emma ever since he began working for the website where she worked as an assistant manager. They'd recently begun seeing each other outside of the workplace, though both of them agreed not to label it.

Of course, that hadn't stopped her from being a complete ass when it came to managing people.

"But I'm serious, Luke," Emma said, stepping beside him. "You look like a radish."

She wasn't trying to piss him off. It was Emma-speak for *I have so much regard for you that I went out of my way to create this insult so we could have a mildly adversarial but fun conversation. See how much I care?*

"And you're a massive pain in my ass." Lukas sighed. "Come on in." He held the door open as she stepped inside. She threw her handbag on the couch and crossed her legs, leaning against the fridge.

"So, what gives?" he asked. "Why is this article being tossed onto my shoulders?"

Emma sighed. "Chris quit last minute—"

"I thought you said you fired him."

"—and you're the only guy in like a thousand miles who's a genius when it comes to mythology. How you manage that while pursuing a law degree, I'll never understand. Seriously, look around you!" she exclaimed. "This room feels more like an anthropology museum than a college student's apartment."

"It's not that bad," he weakly retorted, wincing as he followed her gaze. One of the perils of growing up with his dotty grandfather was not batting an eye at seeing all sorts of worldly relics lying around the home. The man had been a collector of bizarre objects, most of which Lukas had taken possession of post his demise—an opal necklace from India, a talisman from the Native Americans, an actual human skull from Louisiana, and more. The wall of mahogany bookshelves contained over two hundred limited edition books, from modern law to mysticism. *Color of Law* and *Hutchinson's Case Histories* stood next to *Kybalion* and *Zohar*.

His favorite item, however, was the grainy polaroid photo hanging above his desk. It was a picture of him and his grandfather, taken after they'd visited a local museum when he was a kid. The caption underneath was simple, and something the old man used to parrot from time to time.

"THE KEY TO OUR FUTURE IS HIDDEN IN OUR PAST."

"Lukas?"

" . . . Sorry, just lost in thought." He softly sighed. Memories of his grandfather made him oddly conscious of the familiar presence on his chest. It was a pendant—tendrils of blended gold and copper converged around a lapis lazuli orb in the center, ending in a blunt tip at the bottom. It was a most curious thing to wear as a pendant, but it had been a gift from the old man for his thirteenth birthday.

His fingers slid up and touched the pendant. It felt cold as always.

"Eccentricity comes with the territory, I suppose." Lukas grinned, turning toward his . . . friend. "And don't think I've forgotten. I have yet to hear one good reason for this rush job. I've got exams, you know."

Emma smirked. He liked her smirk. It did interesting things to her lips. Letting her purse slide off of her arm, she sauntered toward him. "Perhaps a favor?" she offered. "Something shared between two people who are attracted to one another?"

"Oh? Like what?"

She plopped down onto his bed and propped her chin in her hand, studying him through long lashes. Her skirt rode up to her knee, revealing the soft, pale skin hidden underneath. Her other hand played with an errant lock of hair, twirling it around a finger.

Lukas took another bite out of his apple.

"Oh, come on!" she complained. "Most men would be putty by now."

She wasn't wrong. Emma was someone who used her charm relentlessly to get things done her way.

"I guess I'm just pure of heart and mind." He half shrugged, ignoring her loud scoff. "Now if you're quite finished, I've got some exams to prepare for. Those cases aren't gonna read themselves."

Emma stared at him in frustration for a moment—

Before tilting her head back and laughing. It was a good laugh, rich and refined.

Emma was a known quantity. She was attractive, bright, and appealing. Her motivations were simple, and she was honest in pursuing them. She spent her free nights attending Instagrammable parties with her friends downtown. He hadn't been joking when he'd called her a hurricane.

"Tell you what, Luke," she said. "You get this done for me, and I'll take you to a new Japanese place I found. The teriyaki there is to *die* for."

"And you get me a raise. A good one."

Her eyes glittered with cheerfully malicious ambition. "Sure. If you take over Chris's work for the rest of the month."

"Nope."

"Just this month!" she pouted. "I'll get you your raise and even some paid time off during your semester exams. No work then, I promise."

"No," he stubbornly repeated.

"I have two tickets for Saturday night. Maybe we can share a joint afterward?"

"No—" He paused. "Wait, what? Yes, but that's—"

"Super!" Emma kissed him on the cheek, dangerously close to his lips. "It's a date. Now get this article done and email me by noon tomorrow. See you on Saturday."

With that, she grabbed her purse and walked out the door, leaving him staring in her wake.

Sighing, Lukas closed his laptop screen. It was late, and his bed was looking far too inviting for him to do anything but sleep. Life could wait until morning to kick him in the pants.

The floor is shaking.

There is no fire, simply heat and wispy fumes. The earth beneath his feet parts open. Alien images and sensations overwhelm him, along with the presence of heat—so, so much heat—but no light. Only darkness, accompanied by the groans of something titanic, yet . . . aware. Conscious. It's like—

Like what?

In a single moment, he sees the ponderous dance of continents clashing against one another to form mountains. He feels everything slowly seep into the deepness of the crust, feels the waves rise and fall and heavenly bodies move and twist and smash into each other while blades of grass—

Grass?

He sees gold. Minerals. Lava. A potted plant. Ants marching.

What is—what is happening? What is all this?

Images overwhelm him like the unstoppable force of a raging river. They come and go, flickering across his eyes. There is light, darkness, and brown, dewy soil. He sees lightning in a sky of stars, with the moon utterly black and opening a hole into the molten stone atop the—

Lukas's eyes snapped open.

His heart pounded within his ribcage. His eyes were teary, and gooseflesh had erupted all over his body. *What a weird dream,* he told himself, trying to calm himself down.

It didn't help.

His body felt cold and clammy, and he was shaking.

The glass of water on his table fell to the floor and shattered.

And then he realized. It wasn't him who was shaking. It was the bed. And the floor. And the room. And every other freaking thing in it. As if on cue, the tremors intensified.

That got him moving.

Jumping off the bed, Lukas quickly tossed on a shirt and grabbed his shoes. He almost fell over as the large grandfather clock came off the wall and broke into pieces right in front of him.

A fucking earthquake?! Now—this is just—

Everything around him began to tremble. Dust and debris fell to the floor in solid clumps as the tremors became unbearably violent. What was going on? There hadn't been any warnings of earthquakes.

Just as he dove underneath his desk, his laptop slipped to the ground. Lukas reached for it, but a broken piece of plaster from the ceiling fell right onto it, breaking the screen apart from the bottom half. He howled at the loss of his precious data, about to reach for the broken pieces in hopes of getting at least the hard drive out, when—

Cracks appeared along the walls, and shelves crashed to the floor, followed by dozens of *Thumps!* This—this couldn't be happening. This had to be some dream. It had to be.

The ground beneath his feet roared to life like an enraged animal. Any more, and what remained of his room would fall upon him. He wasn't safe. He wasn't safe. He wasn't—

Lukas lost it and bolted for the door—

And all he knew was darkness.

CHAPTER 2

———

WIGGLE WIGGLE

*W*iggle.
Wiggle wiggle.

"Get off," Lukas complained, feeling something heavy on his chest. His eyes were still closed, but a growing wakefulness began to spread throughout his lethargic body. Everything was so disorienting, what with that odd dream about earthquakes and a building crashing down around him and—

Wiggle wiggle.

What was that feeling? He rolled over onto his back, his eyes stubbornly shut. Normally, he would've woken up by now with all the ruckus, but his muscles felt heavy and he wanted to sleep for just a few more minutes.

Wiggle wiggle.

"Stop!" Lukas groaned. Who was bothering him so early in the morning? Emma?

Sighing, he reached toward his nightstand to grab his phone but found nothing but empty air. He blearily opened his eyes and—

Stared.

And kept on staring.

At the strange, utterly out-of-place line of text floating in front of him.

You have entered the Crypt of Fiendish Worms.

It was as if someone had dumped a bucket of ice water on his head—like that, he was awake and alert. He blinked his eyes once, twice, then several more times, but the thing floating in front of him did not waver.

It was a screen of some sort. A semi-transparent screen.

Lukas reached out a tentative hand and poked it, but his finger simply passed through, like it was some sort of illusion or a projection.

He looked around—

And froze.

No longer was he in his bed. In fact, he wasn't even in his room.

Lukas vigorously rubbed his eyes, hoping something would change.

His surroundings stayed the same. Reality still remained broken. Gone was his familiar room, replaced by rocks. Lots and lots of rocks. There were rocks on the floor, rocks on the wall, rocks on the ceiling, tapering down into stalactites with tiny droplets of water dripping from their tips. On either side were large stone walls with ferny outgrowths, each of which exuded a soft green luminescence, the only respite against the oppressive darkness of his surroundings.

Most importantly, there was an odd shape wiggling inside his shirt. As he shifted in place, it squirmed at the sudden movement and raised its tiny head out.

Lukas stared at it.

The transgressor, a tiny, furry, ugly rat with beady black eyes, stared back.

"GAAAHHH!"

The rodent let out a small squeak before jumping out of his shirt and skittering into the darkness. The screen of text, on the other hand, remained unmoved. No, unmoved was not an apt description. Rather, it stayed relative to his line of vision. Lukas looked to the left, right, up, down, backward, and forward, but the stubborn thing simply followed his movements.

"You've got to be kidding me!" Lukas cursed, pushing himself off the ground. His shoes were the very same pair of sneakers he'd put on before bolting past his door. Had the earthquake really happened? Was this place underneath all the rubble?

So many questions . . .

And a stupid screen that kept distracting him with that gibberish headline.

You have entered the Crypt of Fiendish Worms.

What is this thing?

Information.

Lukas froze.

Did it read my mind? No, that couldn't possibly . . .

Where am I?

The Crypt of Fiendish Worms.

His brows furrowed. So this thing could actually read his mind. More and more, this whole thing felt like a bizarre lucid dream that he couldn't wake up from.

Just what the hell was in that apple?

And what is the Crypt of Fiendish Worms? he thought as clearly as possible.

Insufficient local data.

Lukas cupped his chin. This thing seemed to behave like an artificial intelligence with a twisted sense of logic—probably a bug or some programming tweak. But how had he gotten it? Why did it have access to his mind? Where was this place? And how had he gotten here?

Insufficient local data.

. . . This mind-reading thing was beginning to annoy him. Not to mention, it was capable of distinguishing questions and random thought, which was both interesting and frightening on so many levels. The idea of any kind of technology capable of plucking thoughts out of one's mind with such precision was horrifying. It could mean—

A cold shudder ran through him.

He looked around. At his hands. At his legs. At the floating screen that followed him around.

Is this . . . real?

"What are you?"

The Screen flickered for half a second before new information appeared.

Status Report.

"Status report?" He frowned. "Of what?"

Host.

"And . . . who is this host?"

Lukas Aguilar.

Lukas ran his fingers through his hair, sighing to himself. He figured as much. But he didn't know what it meant yet.

"How do I leave this place?"

Insufficient local data.

"How did I come here?"

> **Insufficient local data.**

"What's your name?"

"Exit."

"Alt+F4!"

But nothing seemed to work. Each question only triggered the same response. *Insufficient local data.* How could anyone have designed an AI with such functionality, yet render it incapable of answering even basic questions?

> **Insufficient local data.**

"THAT WASN'T A QUESTION!"

> **Acknowledged.**

Lukas groaned, gripping his head with both hands in frustration. "You know what? Thank you, but I don't need your help anymore. Go away."

Nothing happened. Strange. The Screen had responded to his thoughts earlier, so he was sure it could understand his intentions. But no matter what he did, it continued to float before him. It was like dealing with a stubborn puppy.

Alright. Lukas exhaled, squaring his shoulders. *This thing can give me answers to things it knows about. Anything else will only give me an insufficient local data notification.*

But what did that actually mean?

"How do I get local data?"

> **By consuming prey.**

"And you want me to hunt this . . . prey down?"

> **Yes.**

"And I'm in . . . ?"

> **The Crypt of Fiendish Worms.**

"Which is . . . ?"

> **An anomaly.**

Lukas wrung his hands, but it didn't help. Asking specific questions was no help at all if a bunch of unfamiliar terms was thrown back at his face. What the hell was an anomaly anyway?

> **Cracks in the fabric of Reality by the superimposition of an omphalos's will upon the environment.**

"In English, please."

The Screen flickered for a moment, but the words remained unchanged.

"Great," he groaned, looking around again. This cave was a crack in the *fabric of reality?* What was going on?

"Is . . . is anyone else around?"

Displaying Omphalos Functions	
FUNCTION	**LEVEL**
Scan	1
Analyze	1

He knew what it was. A skill chart, identical to the ones found in the video games he used to play as a kid. Though what kind of bizarre, twisted mind would conjure something like this was beyond him. He paused as he realized that it was probably his mind he was disparaging.

Lukas considered the information it provided.

A Scan *and* an Analyze function.

If only the Screen could provide him with a little more detail, it would be—

> **Active Scanning and Analysis of prey within Scan Radius.**

—nice.

"Okay. Uh, scan . . . me."

More windows opened.

FUNCTION - Scan	Level 1
Fetching Details . . .	
NAME	Lukas Aguilar
Type	Prototype Host
Level	1
Experience	0
Current Threshold	40
Utilized Soul Capacity	0/1000

OMPHALOS ATTRIBUTES	
Energy Reservoir Capacity	∞
Current Energy Level	**722,457,716 units**
OMPHALOS FUNCTIONS	
Scan	**Level 1**
Analyze	**Level 1**

"This is such bullshit!" he bellowed at the new screen. "Levels? Experience? Is this actually a damn game?!"

It is a Scan of Host's attributes.

"I give up!" Lukas threw both hands in the air and began walking forward. Surely if he kept moving, there would eventually be something in the vicinity that could classify as *prey* and get this damn thing to start giving him relevant information.

He paused at that. If there were, in fact, other life-forms around, then there had to be a source of water. That was great since he would die without water. But also, water sources were connected to larger bodies of water. If he could find a tunnel or drain or something, it'd mean a way out of—

Why was the Screen blinking like that?

Prey found within Scan Radius: 1

Lukas looked around but found nothing. His vision kept zooming in and out of focus, and his head was starting to spin. Everything was going woozy. What was happening? Was this—

He spotted something large, furry, and black, out of the corner of his eye.

It was on him. Biting into his *neck*.

"What the—?"

Lukas's knees wobbled like jelly, and he fell face-first onto the ground, unable to hold himself up. He tried to move, but his body simply refused to obey him. He tried to scream, but no sound escaped his throat.

Is this . . . it?

As his world went black, a new window popped up, its words darkly humorous.

Prey found you.

Hours later, Lukas slowly stirred.

His body felt as heavy as lead, and an acute sense of lightheadedness made it difficult to think. Rubbing his head, he forced himself to sit up. Oddly enough, his neck felt strangely numb.

BLURP!

Lukas jolted from the sudden noise, and he gawked in unreal fascination at the scene playing out before him. Lying against the nearby wall was a bat, its wings splayed out in a leisurely manner. It looked perfectly content where it sat, completely ignoring his presence.

"Uh . . ."

Fragments of memories started coming back to him. Was—was this the large black thing that had bitten him on the neck? His fingers instinctively reached for the spot in question and brushed against two narrow grooves. They were subtle—if he hadn't been feeling around for them, he never would've realized they were even there.

His eyes flickered toward the bat's inflated stomach.

Is that . . . from sucking my blood?

The bat was tilting its head and moaning pleasurably. It obviously did not consider him a threat. Back when it bit him, he hadn't been able to move at all, and even now, the numbness in his system hadn't fully faded.

A powerful paralytic. Or poison.

The bat burped a second time.

As what he was seeing sank in, Lukas began to pale. Animal bites were threatening not only because of toxins, but also because they carried a litany of diseases. He didn't know where he was or where he could find the nearest doctor, but he could count himself lucky that he wasn't experiencing any ill symptoms yet.

Lukas had half a mind to just strangle the damn thing to death but decided to just get as far away from it as possible. Grappling with a bat wasn't exactly his ideal start to the morning, nor did he want to get any more scratches and earn himself an infection.

Getting to his feet, he backed away carefully, his gaze never wavering from the happily snoring bat lying on the floor. The creature's ears twitched, and it sat up groggily.

Lukas stared at the bat.

The bat stared back. And then it growled.

"Easy there, Furry," he soothed, backing away faster. "Go back to sleep."

The now-named Furry ignored his well-intentioned advice and, faster than he could react, spread its wings and pounced upon him.

Lukas yelped as he tussled with the monster, slapping it as hard as he could on the wings. The bloated bat dropped to the floor, prompting him to kick it in its belly as hard as he could. Furry squealed loudly and blood dribbled from the corners of its mouth as it began flapping its wings angrily.

"Some bats just don't know when to give up!" he huffed, grabbing it by the wing and hurling it against the stone wall. Furry bounced off like it was made of rubber and zoomed into the air, as if preparing for another round.

Lukas warily looked around, cautious and more than a little afraid. If this thing was here, then maybe more of its kin were around. One on one, he would be fine. But two? Three? A dozen?

Analyze the bat.

Insufficient local data.

Odd. it had worked on him, so didn't it work on this thing? What was he missing?

Lack of nexus with the realm.
Kill prey to establish a nexus.

More gibberish, but some of it was useful. Even he knew what *kill prey* meant.

As Furry let out a furious war cry and zoomed toward him, Lukas clenched his fists and punched it in the face, slashing his knuckles against its sharp fangs in the process. That one was definitely earning him an infection.

Just what did bats eat in this place to become so resistant to damage?

Insufficient local data.

"I wasn't asking you!" Lukas yelled, quickly following up his attack with a kick. Furry screeched and spat out something black and purple from its mouth. "Screen, if you really want to help, tell me how to kill this thing."

Try harder.

It was official. The Screen was deliberately being a wiseass. But no matter, for he was Lukas Aguilar. No cave-dwelling bat was going to get the better of him. He began railing kicks against the creature, pouring out all of his frustrations into his motions. Another kick. Then another. And another.

Furry squealed, belching out more blood.

And then it stilled. Lukas silently stared at its grotesque, bloodied form. At his own bruised, blood-covered fists and feet. At the gore covering his pants and shoes. The entire experience left him feeling . . .

What did he feel?

Remorse? Definitely not. This thing had tried to kill him—or suck his blood, or something along those lines.

Joy? No, none of that either.

Satisfaction? Precious little, now that the deed was done.

Mostly, he just felt cold, and perhaps a bit shaken that it had happened at all. It wasn't long ago that he was a simple law student writing poetry as a means to get by. How did one go from that to . . . this?

Prey eliminated.

"Yeah, I noticed that too."

And then, Lukas noticed something odd happening.

A wave of *something* flooded into him, making his body feel like its weight increased by three thousand pounds. His skin began to perspire, his muscles spasmed in place, and his bones could not stop vibrating. Gooseflesh erupted all over his body as a rush of alien images sandblasted his mind.

It was like it had a presence of its own. An alien consciousness with its own awareness.

Lukas could see clouds racing across a red sky, tendrils of flames twisting around one another like DNA. He jerked into a brief, violent contortion, like the plucked string of a guitar. It was as if every muscle was trying to tear itself away from his bones. Lukas helplessly struggled, with no control whatsoever over his own body. His throat felt inexplicably sore, and it took a while before he realized it was his scream.

And then, a second cry joined his. It sounded feminine, but he was in too much pain to give it another thought. Power flooded through him as his lips moved by their own accord, hissing—

"MINE!"

Before he could fathom it, it was gone. Vanished. Like it had never happened.

Absorption of local data: Confirmed

Nexus to Realm: Established

Autonomy of Self: Established

Initiating calibration of facilities . . .

"English, please." Lukas yawned. Why was he so tired again? Was it the blood loss? Unlike before, the Screen paid him no mind, and instead, more windows kept opening. His eyes drooped as the sudden adrenaline rush from the skirmish began to fade.

Soulscape: Initialized

Host analysis: Complete

Soul Capacity generated.

Soulscape, Soul Capacity . . . Anything with the word "soul" in it made him uncomfortable. He hadn't even finished reading through it all before the screen flickered once more.

Enabling Skill Creation.

Enabling Experience Absorption.

. . .

. . .

Soulscape: Acknowledged

And then, all of the windows vanished.

The annoying screen that had hovered in front of him ever since he'd woken up in this godforsaken place had finally disappeared. It was jarring enough to make him feel slightly autophobic.

"Er . . . Screen?" he called out warily. "Are you still there?"

An empty window flickered in front of him, before vanishing. Despite it no longer being present, Lukas could sense its existence in the back of his mind, as if it was eagerly waiting to be called upon.

What just happened?

Nexus to the Realm: Established

Relevant information has been acquired.

All sensory receptors are active.

A small part of Lukas genuinely considered whether he'd been magically turned into a robot.

"Where the hell am I?"

The Crypt of Fiendish Worms.

And what is the Crypt of Fiendish Worms?

An anomaly.

Somehow, Lukas knew he should have expected this.

Okay. Where is the Crypt of Fiendish Worms located?

On a realm.

He palmed his face. Still nothing useful. "How far is Los Angeles from here?"

Insufficient data.

That was weird, really weird. Where the hell had he ended up that the Screen couldn't even map the distance from LA? The only possibility that came to mind was if—

No.

Lukas banished the thought before it even fully formed. It wasn't—it couldn't be true. This was still somewhere around his place. Underground, most likely. It was an earthquake, after all. Maybe he fell through the cracks, and this Screen was some elaborate prank being played upon him.

His eyes brightened as an idea came to him.

Where on Earth am I?

Host is not on Earth.

He wheezed. This had to be a joke.

How far from Earth am I?

Insufficient data.

How do I get to Earth?

Insufficient data.

Lukas staggered. It couldn't really be telling him the truth, could it? His clothes were the same as what he woke up with, and this couldn't just be a large, vivid dream. Even for a lucid dream, he was able to think too clearly and act too freely. That only left one option, no matter how fantastical it seemed.

Either he was stuck in a coma with a dreamscape that was impossible to break out, or . . .

Or this is an actual location. And it's not on Earth.

A cold feeling rolled down his spine, spread across his chest, and swallowed him whole. His breath fell short and his knees wobbled as an immense nausea gripped his stomach. Unable to stay standing, Lukas fell to the rocky floor. His hands were shaking. He'd bitten his tongue.

Rock. Pebble. Screen.

He looked around some more.

Trousers. Fingers. Toes. Bat. Blood.

When he ran out of things to name, he started counting prime numbers.

Two. Three. Five. Seven. Eleven. Thirteen. Seventeen . . .

"Come on," he told himself. "Get over it! *Get over it!*" His throat felt raw. He shook even harder. "You're—you're alive! You're *alive!* Stop panicking! You can breathe, so there's oxygen. You can read English off this screen, so there's tech around. There'll be people too."

He couldn't stay here. Not like this. He needed something else. Something to focus on. He continued to count—*ninety-seven*—as he staggered through the cavernous labyrinth.

CHAPTER 3

THE FIRST CHALLENGE

S*MACK!*

> **34 prey eliminated.**

SMACK!

> **19 prey eliminated.**

"Oh, come on! These aren't prey!" He glared at the Screen. "They're plants, you hear me? *Plants!*"

As always, the Screen ignored his words.

> **27 prey eliminated.**

Lukas sighed. The dichotomy of the Screen was mind-boggling. On one hand, the technology claimed to quantify the *soul*. On the other hand, he was having a tough time explaining to it the difference between animals and plants. Design flaw or programming error, it seemed like he was stuck with it.

> **Accurate deduction!**

At least he wasn't awarded with something ludicrous like a *+1 INT*. He wouldn't know what to do if he suddenly found out that his life had become an actual game.

Not that mine is currently too far off.

From what Lukas had observed, the Screen classified every inch of bryophytic outgrowth as prey. If being alive was criteria enough to be labeled as such, then even things as small as bacteria and other microscopic organisms should fall under the category too. They were also technically alive.

And yet, they weren't considered prey.

Chalking it all up to the Screen's idiosyncrasies, he dropped the issue, no longer willing to play twenty thousand questions with a stubborn AI. Besides, he had better things to do, like—

SMACK!

---

31 prey eliminated.
+1 Experience

Yeah. Not far off at all.

Every time he managed to kill a certain number of mosses—roughly 130 eliminations, if his math was right—he was awarded a single point in Experience. It would keep rising until it reached the threshold of forty, but what about then?

This was his latest distraction. It had been an entire day since he'd found himself in the anomaly, and multiple times, he'd gone crazy. Just an hour ago, purely by accident, he'd sat on a piece of moss and got the strange Experience notification from the Screen.

"How many have I eliminated so far?" he asked aloud.

3,380 prey eliminated.
+39 Experience

Soon, he would reach the threshold and find out. Maybe he'd be able to unlock some more of those omphalos functions? It sounded silly, but there was a dearth of interesting things to do inside this place. Maybe something cool would come out of it.

It did in the games.

Rubbing his palms together, Lukas proceeded to smack the life out of his prey. It only took a few more minutes of smacking before something of note happened.

Accumulated Experience crossed Threshold!	
LEVEL UP!	
ATTRIBUTE	**CHANGE IN PARAMETERS**
Level	+1
Soul Capacity	+27

As expected, it was similar to any rudimentary gaming interface: accumulation of Experience led to a Level Up when crossing a certain threshold value. The newly refreshed Soulscape now looked different too.

SOULSCAPE	
NAME	Lukas Aguilar
Type	Base Host
Level	2
Experience	0
Current Threshold	160
Utilized Soul Capacity	0/1027
OMPHALOS ATTRIBUTES	
Energy Reservoir Capacity	∞
Current Energy Level	722,457,341 units
OMPHALOS FUNCTIONS	
Scan	Level 1
Analyze	Level 1

His Experience was back to 0, while his new threshold sat at a significantly higher 160. That meant smacking his way through . . . how much moss?

20800 prey

Right. No thanks.

Lukas was bored, but not *that* bored.

He'd need to look for something else to hunt, something that qualified as a better food source than moss. Other than that, his Soul Capacity—whatever that meant—had jumped by twenty-seven points, but he felt no real change in himself. What did leveling up mean, anyway?

Reflection of gained attributes on the Host Soul.

Vague, as usual. From what he could understand, Soul Capacity was the intrinsic capacity of the Host Soul to hold information. Information was synonymous with the word *skill*, which was . . .

An ability engraved upon the Soul.

It was as if the Screen had a university degree in providing circular answers. But no matter how you sliced it, the very concept was morbid. Souls were esoteric, metaphysical concepts, not pizza. They weren't supposed to be calculated in mathematical terms.

A blank screen greeted his inner turmoil. Fitting, considering Lukas had no proper question to begin with.

Still, at least he had made some progress. Apparently, he had a soul, skills were engraved on that soul, and he could develop more skills by . . . doing things. If the concepts were anything like fantasy literature, then maybe he could smash buildings, or shoot fire and lightning from his fingertips. That and more, especially when he got creative about it. But first—

His stomach growled.

With one final smack, Lukas frowned down at his new collection. This . . . wasn't food. It wasn't even a proper substitute for food. No, it was something to keep his stomach filled until he found more appetizing options.

Appetizing options in a cave of moss and bats. Yeah, right.

He shook his head.

Analyze the moss.

MOSS
Bright green plant with deep roots.
Grows on moist, porous rocks. Brown pigmentation indicates rot.

For a change, the Screen's information was very useful. The moss in front of him was entirely bright green in pigmentation rather than brown, which meant fresh.

But still . . . Moss?

His stomach—the traitorous thing—chose that moment to grumble again.

Lukas sighed.

Might as well.

Picking up the cleanest of the moss, he separated it into its composite parts: the roots and the leaves. Then he brought it to his nose and took a whiff. It wasn't unpleasant or overtly pungent, which meant there probably wasn't any bacterial growth.

Tearing off a piece of the moss leaf, he crushed it and rubbed it on his wrist. A few minutes later, there were still no bumps or rashes forming. Another point in its favor.

Very carefully, Lukas rolled the same leaf piece into a tiny cylinder and rubbed it over the edge of his lips. With several more minutes yielding no reaction, he sharply inhaled and plopped the piece in his mouth, chewing more and more rapidly as his confidence rose.

It was sweet, which meant sugar. A lack of bitterness and soapiness hopefully meant it wasn't poisonous, either. Still, Lukas held the food in his mouth for a full fifteen minutes before finally deciding it was safe enough to swallow.

Eyeing the rest of the moss, he decided he could manage his hunger. For now. Somewhat.

But what about thirst?

He took another cursory look around him. The walls were damp with moss growing off of them in various places, both signs of a nearby source of water. As long as he found it quickly, he wouldn't need to worry about succumbing to his own thirst. Maybe there was a running stream or lake nearby? He wasn't having any breathing issues, so he couldn't be too deep underground. Or maybe he was in a mountain.

Well, he'd figure a way out. But first, he sat down to chow on some lunch. He picked up another fresh piece of moss and stared at it with distaste. Beggars couldn't be choosers, sure, but he really hoped this was a one-time thing. He spent the next few minutes demolishing his green pile of food.

Prey found you.

Frowning, he looked around, but there was nothing. The Screen had already registered the moss on the wall behind him earlier, so it couldn't be that. And he'd smacked all the rest. Maybe some fly flew into his Scan Radius and sparked a reaction?

His stomach growled again.

Whatever it was, he'd deal with it later.

Prey found you.

You've got to be kidding me.

Instinctively, Lukas's hand reached into his pocket and gripped the rock he was using to cut down moss. It was a jagged little thing, with a sharp edge on one end, perfect for slashing flora, but also for defending against enemies. He wasn't excited about having to revert to the Stone Age, but it was better than being empty-handed.

After a few more seconds of looking around, his eyes began to droop. His stomach was full, so he supposed a quick nap wouldn't hurt.

"Screen," he murmured, "if you find anything worthwhile, let me know."

Acknowledged.

And like that, he was out like a light once again.

. . .

. . .

. . .

Prey found you.

This was starting to get old. How would he get more than a few minutes of shut-eye if the damn thing kept beeping at him? Keeping his eyes closed didn't help either, since he could still *see* the Screen in his mind like it was floating right in front of him.

Blinking his eyes open, he wiped them clear. Feeling something strange on his body, he looked down at himself and—

Froze.

There was moss on his body.

Lots and lots of moss.

It was crawling all over him, forming almost a floral blanket across his knees and legs. There were entire bryophytic outgrowths, pale, spongy fern-like structures secreting something wet and colorless onto his trousers. And then there was something different, thicker and more gelatinous, entwined around his waist like a thick belt, trapping him to the wall behind him.

What the fuck *was* this?

Lukas tried extracting himself from the mess, but the thing around his waist only grew tighter. The vines pulled him back against the wall until he was practically cemented against it, while the gel continued to be secreted onto him. How he hadn't woken up immediately, he had no idea.

A dull throbbing sound attracted his attention. He craned his head to the left and stared at the wall.

It was like looking into another world. Green and blue light slithered up the walls, eerie and subtly unsettling, each color moving in waves of differing widths and speeds. The strange scent of water and dead fish assaulted his olfactory senses. There were growths lining the walls, ugly patches of some lumpy, rough substance he could not recognize. Neon-green gel-like things too lively to be plant sap crawled up his shoulders, rolled off his shirt, and seeped down to his abdomen.

Lukas yawned, feeling an urge to close his eyes.

Prey found you.

No. No no nonono—

He had to stay awake! He had to stay awake! *Focus!*

FORMLESS GHOL
Amorphous living units formed out of malleable protoplasm.
The presence of Formless Ghol indicates Ghol Monsters within the vicinity.

Lukas pushed his knees against the vines, but they constricted further. More and more gathered around his legs, thorns digging into his trousers and making him grunt in pain. He gathered the jagged rock and severed through several vines in a straight blow.

1 prey eliminated.

That was a mistake. The vines furiously hissed and struck back at him, constricting his shoulders and scraping against his chin. Panic rising within him, he tore at his neck and chest, ripping the tendrils off of him with as much strength as he could muster. He struck and struck, but more vines replaced what he tore off.

No, not vines, his delirious mind pointed out. *They look like vines, but they're all this formless crap.*

Lukas slashed the rock against the gelatinous thing covering his chest. Hard. The shredded tubules hissed and twisted around each other, contorting into weird shapes. The growths reforged into something thicker, with a mouthlike opening on one end and the rest tapering into a tail. A cold pit began to form in his stomach as fangs protruded out of the membranous thing, forming something—

Ugly.

Horrible.

Wrong.

FANG-WORM
Chimeric spawn of formless ghol. Always found in clusters.

Lukas didn't wait. He thrust the rock straight into the worm's mouth, pushing it through the creature's tubular body. He felt its tendrils grab his neck and squeeze, but he kept on pushing, vainly trying to drive the rock in farther. The worm hissed, vicious drops of colorless liquid dripping from its fangs onto the rock, corroding its surface. Time seemed to slow down as it did.

That could have been my hand.

The tendrils tightened, galvanizing him further. He was *not* going to become food for this beast. He was going to survive. He grabbed the tendrils closest to his fingers and twisted his waist, using them to anchor his own movement. But before he could get enough moving space, more green goo grabbed him by the neck and pulled him back against the rock wall.

Lukas froze for a half second as the tendril pulled against his neck harder, shutting off his air. Then the fear took over. He struggled, but his arms and legs felt as if they'd been coated in lead.

Meanwhile, the worm slowly crawled toward him, as if drawing sick amusement from watching him try to escape its murderous clutches. Using the floor as support, he pushed his body up against the wall in one last-ditch effort of blinding panic.

Something shifted within him, pulsing with his valiant heart. Maybe it was the panic, or perhaps the sheer defiance of wanting to survive this creature, or even actual body heat. Whatever it was, it made him feel hotter, like a smoldering ball of fire hovered in the pit of his stomach. It grew hotter and hotter and *hotter—*

Before exploding.

The tendrils couldn't hold him. With a strength he did not possess, Lukas tore through his bindings. The fang-worm fell down, still hanging onto the rest of the gelatinous goo from its tapering tip. He scraped another off of his shoes and pushed himself forward, tearing through the ones around his waist as he did. As he fell forward, he squashed the fang-worm with his knee.

Any feelings of satisfaction he had felt from the subsequent squelching sound were lost in the feeling of precious, blessed oxygen rushing into his lungs once more.

> **You have used lifeforce for the first time!**

And it didn't end there.

> **Adding Essence attributes to Soulscape . . .**
> **Modifying Host stats to enable configuration by lifeforce skills . . .**
>
> **Body alteration delayed until Level Up.**

New SKILL Created!		
SKILL	**LEVEL**	**SOUL CAPACITY CONSUMED**
Raw Lifeforce Manipulation	1	50
DESCRIPTION Allows for modulating the amount, motion, and application of lifeforce within the host's skeletomuscular system.		

He could feel it, this energy, pulsing within him. Like warm coffee trickling down his throat on a cold evening, or drinking water after a long marathon on the beach. His blood brimmed, the energy within him *yearning* to be released.

Lukas gave it a much-needed exit. Clenching his fist, he gathered every bit of the warmth and pummeled it into the worm. The ground cracked as the worm was pushed into it, now shredded and torn, with colorless goo oozing out of it.

---

1 prey eliminated.
+1 Experience

And wasn't that interesting . . . He'd killed that tendril earlier, and now with this, it was enough to score an Experience point. With this, leveling up a second time wouldn't take as long as it did with smacking moss. Lukas took a step forward.

SNAP!

A thick tendril shot out of the wall and grabbed his right leg, throwing him off-balance. He fell face-first onto the ground, his nose flattening painfully. Before he knew it, more of them enveloped his feet and dragged him across the rocky terrain to the wall, where the rest of the monsters awaited him.

There was no time for forethought. Instinctively, Lukas twisted his body around and yanked the tendrils off with his left hand. His right hand slashed through the air, coming down upon the gelatinous thing with extreme prejudice. They snapped in two.

He didn't bother to wait, pushing himself away and rolling on the ground in the opposite direction until he was far away. He then stood and hacked into the gel coating his legs. Maybe cutting them off from the root was enough to disable them, if not outright kill—

The gelatinous growths morphed, turning inside out, and became two fang-worms, spitting more of that acidic secretion at him. As Lukas hastily backed away, more worms fell off from the wall and ceiling, joining the ones on the ground. All of them hissed in a frenzy as they crawled toward his person.

Always found in clusters. Clearly, the Screen wasn't joking around.

Pummeling them was not an option—he would be drenched with acid before he was even halfway done. He searched the tunnel for anything that could help but found nothing. He considered running, but he had lifeforce surging through his system. *He was strong. He didn't need to run away in fear of a few worms.*

A savage grin tore at his lips as Lukas grabbed the tendrils he'd hacked into earlier. As expected, the gel-like things cloaked his entire fist, but that was just what he wanted. Pushing a leg backward, he wrung the gooey appendages around his arms and *yanked*—

Power surged through him. Something shifted within the walls. A single pebble fell to the floor.

The tendrils stretched.

Lukas pulled even harder, pouring forth all of his might.

It began as a murmur. Next came a slow snap. Finally, a large chunk of green exploded out of the wall, shattering past the layers of stone. Cracks spread across the hole in all directions. And then, everything began to fall.

23 prey eliminated.
3,127 prey eliminated.
+47 Experience

3,127?

Fallen on the floor amidst the debris were giant chunks of moss. The wall crashing down had effectively killed them, but then why did he get that experience? Did the Screen comprehend the intent and circumstances of something being killed?

It was something to keep in mind for the future, but for now, he was safe. *Safe.*

Then why was his heart throbbing madly like it was about to beat out of his chest?

"That was lovely!"

Lukas spun around but found no one. He had definitely heard it. It hadn't been an illusion. That voice—feminine, no doubt—had felt like a rumble of heavy rocks scraping together. Like someone crafting a melodious song out of thunder. *Loud* did not do it justice. It came from everywhere, all at once, and was all-encompassing.

The same voice let out a silvery laugh. **"Brutal. Vicious. But . . . lovely."**

"Glad I could entertain you," Lukas replied, peering at the upper corners of the cavern. Had he been right all along? Was he still on Earth, playing the sadistic game of someone with too much power at their fingertips? Was this all one giant illusion, with him a lab rat running the gauntlet?

Whoever it was, the player was finally out in the open.

"One can only wonder how it is possible to be so right, yet so wrong at the same time."

"So this *is* a test." Lukas gritted his teeth. The utterly casual tone of the speaker was getting on his nerves. "Who the hell are you? What do you want?"

"Do not bother yourself with questions beyond your comprehension, mortal."

Mortal? Lukas narrowed his eyes. Was he dealing with someone with a massive god complex? Or was it a reference to his own chances of success in this . . . *game?* He was still unable to figure out where the voice was coming from. The sound was everywhere, and covering his ears did nothing. If he didn't know better, he'd think she was speaking directly into his ears.

"Yeah, you're right," he said, toning down the venom in his tone. "I don't really care who you are. Just get me out of this damn place, and we can go our separate ways."

"After all the effort I put into bringing you here?"

"Oh yeah? And why did you do that?"

"What would you like to hear?" The sheer indifference in her tone made him want to tear his hair out. **"I could say I did it on a whim. Or that I planned it. Or that it is for war. Or perhaps for peace."**

Whoever this woman was, she was not ordinary. She possessed technologies like this Screen, as well as the resources and money to create things as sinister as the slime-worm creatures. But why? Was he a part of some godforsaken reality show where people were murdered? Some program that let psychos on the Dark Web get themselves off?

"Alright," he replied, calming himself with a few deep breaths. If this was a game, he could play along. "Tell me this, at least. What do I need to do to get out of here?"

"Out of here . . ."

"Home. My city."

She laughed. The sound made the lifeforce inside him squirm uneasily. *Weird. How is she influencing it? Drugs? Nanotech?* With the world getting smaller and technology evolving faster, it was difficult to say what was possible and what wasn't.

"Finding your way back to your world is an exercise in futility. At the moment, you have far more worrisome matters at hand."

Lukas frowned. "Like what?"

As if on cue, the stones littering the ground trembled in place, and a furious hissing sound filled the cavern.

"That."

CHAPTER 4

BARGAIN

Something stirred in the darkness.

An eerie, grating sound, like hundreds of pieces of chalk dragging across a chalkboard, permeated the cavern air. A long, slender shadow twisted and turned, chitinous scales of poisonous green rubbing together, languidly fusing and segmenting into one another. The more they contorted, the more they morphed into a kaleidoscope of fragmented colors. Tiny sharp, white protrusions tore their way out of the gelatinous, tubular forms, expanding into an endless spiral.

Its mouth came into full focus, and Lukas could feel a cold sweat passing over him. The stomach-churning, nightmare-inducing mass bared its hundred-fanged mouth, releasing a gust of hot, putrid breath, the stench of rotting fish, and *roared*.

Someone screamed, and Lukas dimly registered that he was the only one there. He flinched and squeezed his eyes shut, trying to cut out the sight of this hideous terror before him. He'd bitten his tongue, his throat felt raw, and his body shook from head to toe.

KHORKHOI
Ultimate offensive morph of Formless Ghol. This worm is enormous in size with tail-like protrusions. The number of tails indicates growth. Capable of near-endless regeneration and reforming appendages.

Had he been a little less terrified, Lukas would have realized that he hadn't called for the analysis. As he read over the information, a part of him wanted to count the number of tails the so-called khorkhoi had, as if doing so would reduce his chances of contributing to this monster's appetite. But there was something else he needed to do. Something that could possibly avoid a most horrible death. But what was it? What *was it?*

"Run."

Right. That was it. He needed to run.

As several thousand pounds of angry monster charged at him with reckless abandon, Lukas did the only reasonable thing anyone in his place could have done.

Holding back a terrified shriek, he leaped, crouched, and rolled his way through an unending maze of tunnels. But no matter how far he ran or how relentlessly he pushed his legs to keep moving forward, he could not outrun the never-ending sound of falling rocks and creaking walls that seemed to creep closer and closer every time he slowed down.

The Screen called it a worm, but Lukas assumed this was in the same way a shark was a fish, or a tiger a cat. Spanning over thirty feet in length and easily half of that in width, the monster looked like a supersized fang-worm, covered with scales so massive they looked like charred bricks. As Lukas struggled to stumble forward, the monster casually swam through the floor, digging through the rocky terrain without so much as a scratch.

Lukas ran and ran, doing his best to ignore the burning in his lungs. He turned his head just in time to see the monster gather itself for a leap and threw himself down, bruising half his body in the process. The khorkhoi soared over him and buried itself into the floor once more. Lukas spun and ran back in the direction he'd come from, but he wasn't sure how long he could keep this up. Unless he thought of something else, he was going to have to turn and take his chances.

"What chance do you have?"

A chunk of rock, easily the size of a garbage can, flew across the air and collided with the floor, shattering it into a cloud of debris. He tried to hit the ground in a roll and come up running but tripped on a rock and fell. A massive tail, laden with rock-hard scales covering solid protoplasm, sliced through the air toward him.

"It will pounce from the left."

In that moment, it didn't matter if the voice was responsible for getting him there. It didn't matter if she was a psychopath with a god complex. She seemed human, and in a cavern full of monsters, that alone was reason enough to listen to her.

Lukas pushed everything he had into rolling to the left. Just as the voice had told him, the tail came slashing from the left and tore through the ground several feet to his right. The wall fractured and came down, and with it, *thousands* of moss and other floral outgrowths.

3,972 prey eliminated.
+41 Experience

The Screen displayed it all while Lukas continued to run. Like before, it added the Experience from the devastation caused by the khorkhoi to him. He barely had a moment to check the number before it vanished, replaced by another message.

Accumulated experience crossed Threshold!	
LEVEL UP!	
ATTRIBUTE	**CHANGE IN PARAMETERS**
Level	+1
Soul Capacity	+108
Maximum Lifeforce Output	+225
Replenishment Rate	100 / hour

Lukas rolled a second time and pushed himself up, sprinting off as fast as he could. The feeling of warm coffee down his throat was still there, only this time, it was stronger. Like sitting in front of a fire during a cold winter, wrapped in a blanket and watching the snowfall. The burning pain in his muscles slowly receded, and the agony in his chest was replaced *by a sense of warm confidence as he took in deep, powerful breaths, leaving the stupid monster behind—*

A gooey tendril wrapped around his leg, and Lukas fell face-first against the ground. For a second, there was nothing but a high-pitched ringing in his ears. His muscles felt strangely unresponsive, and there was a wetness on his face and slight reddening in his vision. It took him another second to realize that it might be blood. His blood. He needed to get up, but it was difficult figuring out which way was down and how to get up in the first place. Lights darted in and out of his vision, and his eyes weren't fast enough to track them.

A loud howl tore through the air, more beast than man, and something speared him in his left bicep. A wave of thick, heavy energy exploded out of him, shattering whatever pierced his body. The sudden heat filled Lukas with a sense of control that seemed to reboot his mind.

NEW SKILL CREATED!		
SKILL	**LEVEL**	**SOUL CAPACITY CONSUMED**
Momentum Manipulation	1	50
DESCRIPTION Direct ejection of raw lifeforce out of the body.		

Lukas was now back on his feet. He was fairly certain one of his shoulders had been dislocated, and given how blood kept oozing down his lips, his nose was broken. His knees wobbled, but he gathered support from the wall next to him. Spitting blood out his mouth, he stared at his predator.

The burst of energy had caused several stalactites to fall from the roof, stabbing the khorkhoi below. The monster made sounds like an angry boar as it tried to wriggle out of the wreckage and heal itself. Given its endless regeneration capacity, there was no doubt it wouldn't be delayed for long by this.

Enough time for me to run. Or at least try to.

His vision was fading; the constant blood loss and the pain were beginning to take their toll on him. He—he needed to do something.

But what?

"An admirable resistance, as ephemeral as it was."

Lukas spat out more blood but said nothing. He wouldn't dignify her with a response.

"You cannot outrun it forever."

As if he didn't know that already.

"I can help you against this creature. I can save you. For a price."

"Fuck off!" He was done with the voice's sanctimonious attitude. If he was going to keel over, he'd do so on his own terms rather than by bending backward for some sadistic bitch hell-bent on making his life miserable.

He lifted his palms, gritting his teeth as he felt his shoulder bones move in strange ways. Staggering forward, he aimed for the ceiling. His fingers shook and stars danced in front of his eyes, but he persevered. Splaying his fingers as wide as he could, Lukas took that burning heat within him and pushed it out again.

A lance of white-hot energy crashed against the ceiling, bringing it down with a deafening crash on top of the khorkhoi.

Lukas laboriously panted, a mix of blood and drool rolling off his chin. "That should do it." And just in time, too. He doubted he could keep his eyes open for another five minutes. He turned around—

"Do you truly wish for your existence to end here?"

It was like a subwoofer went off in his brain. She just wouldn't stop, would she? Some people were just gluttons for rejection.

"You can sit there in your invisible room and play God all you want, thinking yourself merciful for your exchange of favors. But guess what? You're not a savior. You're a *vulture*. A sadistic bitch who brought me here to take advantage of my desperation." Lukas spat a red wad of blood and phlegm onto the ground, his head pounding with rage. "I'll die, but I *will not bend*. You won't get the satisfaction from me."

A part of him wondered whether he'd already pushed things too far. He was a fairly rational individual . . . until he wasn't.

"How utterly unusual. After such an affront, I would not take you as my dog even if you were the last mortal remaining."

Lukas scoffed, his eyes never leaving the khorkhoi. Standing was a pain. He was sure to collapse if he even tried to walk at this stage. For better or worse, he'd have to stay there and keep trying to suppress the monster with Bursts.

That, or die.

"Yet," the voice continued, **"that wild, independent streak of yours is exquisite. It beckons me to come forward and crush it. I find this dilemma utterly vexing."**

"I don't care."

"You should care, mortal. You may serve, or you may be served as a meal. Do you not wish to survive?"

"Obviously I do. But that doesn't change the fact that you're the one who put me here."

"I removed you from your collapsing planet and brought you to a place where you can hone your potential. If anything, you should prostrate yourself and pledge to me your undying gratitude."

"Right, because every word that leaves your mouth must be gospel."

"Do not confuse me with a mewling mortal such as yourself. I am a queen. Truth is all I know."

The massive worm had been dispersed back into its formless ghol state, which meant it was still healing from the stalactites impaling it. Hundreds of tendrils were spreading out, establishing anchors to the surrounding rocks and walls as the creature constantly reformed itself around them, slowly making its way through the rocks that held it paralyzed.

But it wouldn't be that way for long, and the ceiling held no more stalactites for another attack. The strange woman gave him the impression of a particularly vicious credit card company trying to suck him into a bad deal, but she was also the only choice he had left.

"Fine," he spat. "I'm listening."

"I offer a bargain. Something precious of mine has been stolen. I wish for you to recover it for me."

Recovering stolen goods? That's it? Lukas narrowed his eyes. There was no way she had set all of this up for a simple recovery mission. "I don't think a random guy like me is going to be much help for whatever it is you're looking for."

"On the contrary, you will suit my needs perfectly."

"If you're so powerful, why not do it yourself?"

"Circumstances prohibit me from acting wholly alone. If it were possible, I would have done it aeons ago instead of wasting my precious time and efforts on a meaningless, insouciant vermin such as yourself."

"And what do I get in return?"

"Your prolonged survival should be more than satisfactory payment."

She had a point. However, this person had termed it a bargain, not an act of coercion. Sure, she couldn't act alone, but there had to be some reason why she had chosen to save him, assuming that was even the case. Which meant he was important. Being important was equivalent to being in power. Being in power meant he could put forward his own demands.

"Making it out of this alive is something I would naturally need to complete your task in the first place," Lukas countered. Maybe he was pushing his luck, but something told him that this was a make it or break it moment, that a bad deal here could ruin his life forever.

"You are playing a dangerous game, mortal. I do not have patience for your kind."

"But you need someone to recover your lost property. And if I'm to fulfill that deal, I need to be able to do that. As in, I need to be out of this place with my body unharmed and in working order. I'll also need any and all information you can provide about where I am, along with how to get out of here."

"Dear child." There was an edge to her voice now. **"You are truly naive if you think you can put forth your own conditions in this opportunity. If you do not accept my offer, you will perish."**

As if on cue, one of the last remaining stalactites holding the khorkhoi down began to crack. Thick tubules rose into the air, entwining around the fallen rocks. The chitinous coverings began to reform, and the fangs were starting to show.

Lukas felt his belly go cold.

"Your borrowed time draws to an end."

He clenched his fists. Clearly, the person behind the voice was trying to psych him out, and if he were honest with himself, it was working. "What exactly do you want recovered?"

"Something I cannot tell you without us forming an accord."

He frowned. A verbal pact meant nothing without the means to enforce it. Which meant that she either didn't care about the bargain or was supremely confident in being able to force him to follow through.

"Alright. You help me get out of this mess, alive and unharmed, and tell me everything I need to know. In exchange, I'll help you with recovering whatever it is you want."

It was far from the best deal he could've made, but beggars couldn't be choosers. And being within ten feet of certain death wasn't exactly the best circumstance for world-class negotiation.

She laughed, and it sounded as merry and clear as jingling bells. **"Then, have we a bargain?"**

"Yeah," Lukas confirmed, sighing. "We have a bargain."

"Then brace yourself, mortal. For you shall witness something the universe has forgotten."

"What's that?"

"Me at war."

The khorkhoi, now almost reformed, raised one of its massive tails and swung.

. . .

. . .

It felt like ages had passed before Lukas realized he wasn't actually dead. In fact, the pain he was feeling was practically nonexistent. He then noticed his right arm raised up in a useless endeavor to save himself. Not only would that present no obstacle to the gargantuan living weapon, but it would also crush his hand along with the rest of his body like a sledgehammer taken to a watermelon.

And yet, he was unsquashed and in perfect functioning order. The khorkhoi's tail was inches away from his face, with his arm holding it at bay.

Except it wasn't actually touching his arm. There was a tiny, nearly imperceptible gap between his skin and the monster, a void of empty air that merrily functioned as an interface between the two. More importantly, Lukas could feel the telltale thrum of power. So much power brimming through his body.

If using lifeforce was like warm coffee, this felt like sitting in sweltering African heat on a midsummer day.

POTENTIAL SKILL DETECTED!		
SKILL	**LEVEL**	**SOUL CAPACITY REQUIRED**
Kinetomancy (FRAGMENTED)	**APEX**	**177764**
DESCRIPTION **Absolute Manipulation of magnitude and direction of Momentum Vectors.**		

POTENTIAL SKILL DETECTED!		
SKILL	**LEVEL**	**SOUL CAPACITY REQUIRED**
Alleviation	**3**	**5000**
DESCRIPTION **Removal of any and all unreasonableness of the Body to return it to its calculated original format.**		

"Pathetic!" A sense of abject disappointment flooded through him as if he were worse than a cockroach. His lips thinned dangerously as he looked down at the fallen monster still trying to crawl its way out of the ground like a measly rat. A twitching insect, awaiting its death.

As was its place.

Why his thoughts were suddenly so morbid, he had no idea. But the mind-set felt completely natural, and along with it came a dangerous arrogance. A feeling of natural superiority. It was an absolute belief. *No matter what stood in his path, victory was a foregone conclusion.*

For he was . . .

He was . . .

"I had forgotten the frailty of mortal flesh. Even the meanest of skills risks the body's destruction." She paused as if considering something. **"No matter."**

And then his hand began to move on its own accord. There was a sudden surge of power within him, power so dense and intense that the debris from the ground spiraled into the air, forming a helical wave around him. Both of his hands moved in what his grandfather would have called a *mudra*, with both palms meeting each other at the bases.

The khorkhoi was bodily lifted from the floor by what looked like invisible strings. Lukas felt his palms cross each other aggressively, almost like they were squeezing something invisible held between them. At the same time, the creature let out a whimper as it was squashed, like an old car getting crushed under a hydraulic press. In the blink of an eye, the beast was no more, in its place a thousand droplets of formless ghol, splattered all over the cavern. And yet, Lukas noticed, none of the droplets had come remotely closer to his immediate vicinity.

1 prey eliminated.
+362 Experience

As if a switch was flipped, Lukas felt like he was back in control. His visage filled with shock and awe, he stared dumbly at the remains of the massive beast, the same one that had given him enough Experience to probably push through to the next Level Up. And it had happened without him so much as touching the creature even once.

"Such a waste! It perished before I could savor my first kill after aeons. Could you not have provoked a creature far more worthy? Perhaps a real wyrm, or a drake?"

Lukas didn't have a comeback for her. He was too busy gaping at the crushed remains of the creature, at the impossible power that had committed the deed, and at his own hands through which the power had enacted its influence. It had been too fast, faster than his eyes could follow, much less understand.

It was the sort of power that demanded his respect and fear by virtue of its existence. Suddenly, Lukas wasn't so sure about his position. When he spoke next, his voice was utterly mollified, the demonstration having brought him down from a rageful child to a position of affable curiosity, if not outright docility.

"Who are you?"

The woman laughed, her voice somehow managing to sound both sensual and alien at the same time.

"Who am . . . I?"

Lukas staggered in place as he was suddenly hit by a rush of impressions. Gone was the cavern around him, the shattered walls, the putrid remains of the monster on the floor; in its place was a cloudy landscape setting with pure power and things Lukas wasn't sure he *wanted* to understand. He could see hills from which rivers of golden light spilled, while crimson lightning streaked across a night sky bejeweled with countless stars. The landscape looked like a gigantic throne room built into a translucent garden. There were vines of green, flowers of gold, and flashes of other colors clawing at the gentle ground. Anchored here and there were points of light so vibrant that he could not look directly at them.

A different time. A different place. A different era began to superimpose itself upon the present.

Before him stood a royal throne amidst the shining stars, an enormous ax lying bare beside it. Seated upon it was a woman who possessed the kind of beauty that one sang odes to and waged wars over. Her hair was blacker than the darkest of nights, her skin as white as the finest alabaster. Her lips were the color of frozen mulberries, fitting perfectly onto a smooth, lovely face that had the most beautiful green eyes he had ever seen. And yet, no matter how much he tried, no matter how perfect each one of her facial features was individually, he could not behold her perfection in its entirety.

It was something beyond the superficial beauty of a supermodel. Rather, it was the beauty found between the heavens and the earth. It was majesty made manifest, the kind you saw when you beheld the depth of a valley from the top of a mountain, or the rising sun emerging from the vastness of the sea.

She wasn't old. Wasn't young. Wasn't anything but stunning.

Her lips slightly twitched, a barely formed smirk directed at him as he gawked. All around her were hundreds of entities—real and phantasmal, human and not, creatures of myth and history—all genuflecting in reverence.

Lukas looked around, finally realizing that he too was on his knees.

"Wh-who *are* you?" he asked again, his lips trembling.

She smiled. It was a beautiful and terrible thing.

"I have many names, but you may call me Inanna. Goddess of War and Lust. Monarch of the Akkadian pantheon, and the Supreme Queen of An and Ki."

CHAPTER 5

———

HERE BE GODS

Mortal. That should have been his first clue. It was what she had called him from the very start—not human, but *mortal*, as if she wasn't one in the first place. She wasn't someone with a god complex, but a literal goddess herself.

Inanna.

It was a name Lukas recognized all too well. The primary goddess of Akkad and Babylon, Inanna was the patron deity in Sumer during the reign of King Gilgamesh. She was called Annunit, daughter of the Annunaki, the titans of Sumerian mythology. The morning star. The lust-driven, spoiled daughter of the heavens. The sister of Ereshkigal. The one scorned by Gilgamesh. She descended to the Underworld, only to be resurrected once more.

Could the voice he'd been speaking to all this time be that same Inanna?

More and more realizations pelted his mind like bullets. The impossibly advanced technology that was the Screen. The power of lifeforce brimming within him. The earthquake. The monsters in the cavern. The invisible voice. Every bit of it was from the realm of fantasy, but Lukas, in his obstinance, forcibly adhered to the impossible idea of being a guest star in some sci-fi reality show.

He couldn't have been more wrong. She was a goddess. A real, live goddess. He was talking to a goddess. He had *bargained* with a goddess.

His insides did a nasty flip.

"You are wise to be afraid, mortal," Inanna commended. Her voice was like honey and hot soup on a winter night. It was a voice that promised things, one that you listened to with unrelenting interest and intensity. **"How does it feel to encounter that which you did not believe to exist?"**

Lukas swallowed a mouthful of fear. Not fear of being judged on his atheism, but because she knew something about him. Something she couldn't possibly have known unless—

Unless she could read his thoughts.

The rational cynic within him waged war against his reality, claiming everything from it being a very elaborate dream to being dosed on psychedelics. Maybe he had hit his head really hard from the falling plaster and all this was an illusion crafted by his myth-obsessed mind. He had been working on that Akkadian prophecy right before bed, right? What were the chances that he'd find an ancient Akkadian Goddess in his mind?

Hah! No way this was real. He was lying in some hospital bed. Comatose.

. . . Or maybe not.

The power exuding from this being was beyond his comprehension. And she'd implied it was a mere sliver of her strength. Whether it was truth or hyperbole was inconsequential; the limited experience he'd been shown could not be explained by any science or laws of nature. And it felt so *real*.

Real enough that he believed it to be true. That this being—Inanna was the real deal.

He was standing before a freaking *goddess*.

His expression made her smile.

"Mortals," Inanna murmured. **"Always so sure, so confident in your perception of reality. I can hear the cogs turning, spinning the little wheels."**

He took a step toward the throne. Everything he had read about her swam to the forefront of his mind. Inanna was the real deal, even for the titans of the old world. A barbaric war goddess who represented the darker qualities of beauty and lust.

Lukas's eyes met hers. It was like time itself had frozen.

"Calm yourself, mortal," she said. **"You are safe from my wrath. I find you quite amusing. And I cannot have you fulfill your side of the bargain if you are soot on the floor."**

He looked away. Maybe keeping his eyes off of her would shield his thoughts? He needed to tread carefully. He was in uncharted territory.

"Perhaps," she said, utterly uncaring that she had just confirmed his worst fear. **"I would argue you are right where you should be."**

"What do you mean I'm—"

She snapped her fingers, and the celestial throne room was gone. He was standing in his very own room, with everything just as he remembered—the shelves, his bed, the familiar table with his laptop sitting on top, switched on and displaying a random page about dishwashers of all things. He felt an urge to look out his window and see if he was back in his own world. To confirm that it was all just a nightmare.

Then, he saw *her*.

Inanna, still dressed in her celestial attire, sat in his revolving chair with her legs crossed. She was sipping on something from the coffee mug he had gifted his grandfather last year. Amusingly enough, that wasn't even the most surreal thing he had seen that day.

"It is a litter, like a rat's nest. How do mortals breathe in here?" She took another sip.

Lukas tilted his head in bemusement. "We try, I guess."

She continued to sip.

"So, uh, you're a goddess," he lamely began. It wasn't the most eloquent conversation starter, but in his defense, he'd crossed his threshold of comfort a long time ago. Inanna looked up, a little smidgen of something—*is that a latte?*—stuck on the right side of her upper lip, and cocked an eyebrow at him, her forest-green eyes shining with naked amusement.

"Do I not look the part?"

"Uh . . ." Truly, there had to be something more than grunts in the English language. At this rate, he would strike her as an ignorant fool. "I'm—" He cleared his throat. "I just, well, I've never had a conversation with a real goddess before"—or fake ones, for that matter—"and, um, you have something there. On your face." He gestured toward his own lips.

"Ah," her voice rumbled, still somehow managing to sound pleasant to his ears. She licked the smidgen off with her tongue. A tiny speck still remained right below her nose, but he didn't point it out. It looked rather cute. **"What is this drink? We did not have this delicacy in Sumer."**

"It's called a latte. Gently steamed milk with a bit of foam on top, though I tend to overdo the foam capping when I order." He paused. "Don't take this the wrong way, but is any of this real, or is it all some grand illusion?"

She laughed, and it sounded as merry, clear, and lovely as bells. **"This is your memory, mortal. Or rather, figments of them drawn together. You have been in this place for so long that it is easy to add nearly anything without shattering the illusion."**

Lukas gave himself a second to wish he was less tired. Or less in pain. Or less overwhelmed by the day's events. But one thing he did understand— he needed to stay calm. Which was kind of difficult, because the rest of him wanted to throw up and start crying.

He looked around. Everything was just as he remembered: the books on his desk, a half-eaten apple next to his laptop, its screen displaying his law school assignments, with a separate window for his shitty poetry.

Emma, he thought with a pang.

"I sense the turmoil in your mind." Inanna smiled condescendingly. **"It is understandable to have questions. I shall endeavor to quench some of it. You should be grateful."**

He didn't want answers. He wanted out of this nightmare. So naturally, he opened his mouth and said—

" . . . Sure."

"Color me impressed. Your faith in your disbelief contends with that of my fanatic acolytes. It is both fascinating and disturbing. I wonder how imprudent the gods of your era have become to let disbelief fester such."

"Gods?"

"Surely there is some demented divine entity with whom your species holds favor?"

"Actually, most people I know are atheists. Or closet atheists."

Inanna slowly blinked. **"You do not believe in your gods? In Sumer, we tortured such people until they believed in our existence, before killing them. Surely you have seen them exert their influence upon your realm?"**

Lukas shook his head. "No human has ever actually seen a god." Televangelists didn't count. "Not where I come from."

"What do you mean?" For the first time since their conversation began, Lukas felt an emotion other than arrogance bleed off of the goddess. Discomfort.

"There are no gods on Earth."

"No gods . . . You are certain?"

It's not like there are any listed in the yellow pages . . . "To my knowledge, yes."

Inanna stared at him with an inscrutable expression, looking like she'd just swallowed a bitter pill. Lukas had the oddest feeling of being X-rayed, like she was looking *through* him rather than at him.

"I suppose if there are no gods left in your miserable world, it does explain some things."

"I could always try to get more information when I get back."

"Get back?" She cocked her head. **"To where?"**

"My home. Where else? I mean, this place does have an exit, right? You told me you—" Lukas froze midway, as a sudden realization hit him.

"I removed you from your collapsing planet . . . " she had said. His collapsing planet. *The earthquake. It was just—*

His knees hit the ground. "You-you're saying that my planet is . . . gone? And everyone on it is—"

"Do not misconstrue my words to suit your imaginations," Inanna chided. **"I only said that your world was collapsing. Whether it heralded the end of your species and your civilization is beneath me."**

Her utter apathy rankled at him. He wasn't sure if he should be insulted or bewildered by the utter lack of condescension in her tone. The goddess didn't give two fucks whether humanity survived or not. All she cared about was the recovery of her lost property. To her, Lukas Aguilar the human was no different from a random fly perched upon the wall. You did not demean a fly; you simply swatted it off without a second thought.

As she was a divine being, Lukas could understand where she was coming from. But that didn't mean he had to like it.

"Why me?"

The goddess arched an eyebrow.

"Earth has billions of people. You could have saved anyone. So why was I chosen?"

"Chosen?" The incredulity in her tone was vivid. **"Is that some mortal way of escalating your self-worth?"**

Lukas spluttered at her look of utter disappointment.

"You believe you were chosen because you are smart? Talented? Special somehow? How vain!" He felt her disdainful gaze on him. **"You were *chosen* simply because you bore my relic."**

He looked down at the little ornament hanging around his neck. "This pendant?" he inquired, holding up the souvenir that had been part of his attire for a long, long time. Only now, it was shining with an ethereal luster—no, *pulsing* with power. Was this where she came from?

"The relic in your hands has been my abode for aeons. When the Cosmic Consciousness of your world shattered, I was able to attract one of its shards to myself. I used its power to open a path to . . . here. But it would not bind to me, not in my correct state. So it settled for the next available option."

"Me," Lukas realized. He hadn't known that Earth even had a consciousness, but given who was saying it, he took it in stride. Both that the Earth's consciousness had shattered, and that he had a shard of it within him. Whatever the hell that meant.

"Correct. Though, power of that magnitude should have destroyed you. At the very least, your mind should have been addled and replaced by the Cosmic Consciousness of the shard. Yet here you are."

"Is that why I have these things? The Screen, this lifeforce, all of it?"

Inanna's lips twitched as she stared at him in amusement. To her, he probably looked like a child who was just learning how to walk. **"The Screen is merely a representation of your soul. A quantitative representation of your smidgen of Potential."**

Lukas wanted to point out that he had never so much as *heard* of someone having a Screen, let alone a concept like potential made manifest. Every person, every creature, had the potential to become something. To grow, evolve, and ascend. Evolution, after all, was part and parcel of any civilization. But *quantifying* that potential, especially with such detail, was absurd.

It was what a—a *game world* would have.

"Pitiful." Inanna pinned him with a scrutinizing stare. **"Not only are you blind to such a fundamental impairment, but your faith also demeans you**

for having it. Perhaps some of your kind were enlightened enough to realize it and created this so-called *game world* as a faithful impersonation?"

His insides twisted a little. The casual way in which she picked thoughts out of his head made him feel naked and vulnerable. Violated, even. It was a surprise he still maintained his cool. Apparently, standing in front of a being of titanic strength could make even the most stubborn person see reason.

"I have suffered through some of the vilest curses the universe could conceive, and not even I could comprehend living in a world without Potential. The very idea of living in such an accursed state makes me flinch. You have something far greater than a mortal can possibly comprehend within you, yet somehow, you retain your mortal mind. What a curious paradox. Perhaps you *are* special after all."

Now Lukas didn't know what to think anymore.

"Take it as a compliment," Inanna advised. "You have something great inside you, and you also carry the vigil of the Monarch of the Akkadian Pantheon. Greater beings than you would commit genocide to be in your position."

He grabbed at the pendant again with sweaty fingers. This was where Inanna had been trapped for eons. Though, trapped meant the pendant was a prison of sorts. Inanna had called it her abode. Home. A word with an undeniably positive connotation. But then . . .

"It matters not," the goddess replied, waving away his concerns.

"Not to you, maybe. It does to me."

"Perhaps. But now is not the time. You and I have far more pressing concerns."

"Like recovering your lost property."

"Precisely."

The goddess snapped her fingers again, and everything changed once more. Lukas was no longer standing, but sitting on his imaginary couch inside his imaginary room. Meanwhile, Inanna continued to sit on an imaginary chair, drinking an imaginary mug of latte. There was an imaginary glass table between them—if he remembered correctly, it had fractured around a year ago—that stood pristine and spotless. Upon it was a single cup, crafted out of copper or brass by the look of it, filled with a brown, semi-transparent liquid that resembled whiskey. The really expensive kind.

"Drink."

Lukas dug into his ear with his pinky. "I beg your pardon?"

"I said, *drink*."

He stared at the cup with a crooked eye. After a moment of hesitation, he grabbed it and sniffed at the contents. It smelled delicious.

"What is this?"

"Tenemu. The wine of Sumer. Drink of heroes. Drink of gods. It is tradition to drink it while a bargain is being struck."

Something from her memories, then.

Lukas touched the cup to his lips, slowly savoring the wine's flavor as it trickled down his throat. It tasted sweet, terribly so, yet it was smooth on the tongue and burned his insides. Everything began to feel livelier, more vivid, like his senses had been dialed all the way to eleven. And for the first time, he felt like he could truly *see* Inanna. See the pale skin on her cheekbones all the way to her neck, hear the soft sounds of her heart beating, carrying a melody that could drive all honest men to Sin—

He shook his head, breaking out of whatever trance he had been in.

What was that?

Inanna's lips quirked.

"Are you reading my mind again?"

"I have no need for it, mortal. Your face is rather transparent."

He finished the drink and put down the empty cup. "Look, this has all been lovely, really, but I'd really like to get to the point. Why am I here?"

The wispiest shade of a smile graced the corners of her eyes. **"Very well. As we agreed, I will endeavor to aid your survival in this den of monsters. However, do not expect me to fight your battles for you. I shall provide you with information that I deem necessary to your task, and nothing else. In return, you shall do your best to survive and fulfill this task for me."**

"And what if I need to know something that you think is unnecessary?"

"Then you shall have to pay the appropriate price."

Lukas stared at her, his gaze unwavering from her misty green eyes. It was an intoxicating feeling, as if he would lose a part of him if he dared look away.

"A word of warning, mortal. Do not so casually gaze into the eyes of another. They say the eyes are the window to the soul, and it is for good reason."

With those enigmatic words, the gaze broke. The illusion flickered. And the world changed once more. His room shattered into brilliant motes of light, and a moment later, Lukas found himself back inside the cavern, next to the remains of the dead khorkhoi. Droplets of formless ghol were all over the walls, still trickling down to the floor. The Screen chose that moment to appear in front of him. Only this time, it was flashing madly, and instead of its normal blue, it was an angry, searing red.

URGENT!!!			
DETECTED SKILL	**LEVEL**	**SOUL CAPACITY**	**ISSUE**
Kinetomancy (FRAGMENTED)	**APEX**	**177764**	**Insufficient Soul Capacity**

Alleviation	3	5000	Insufficient Soul Capacity
Host Body requires calibration!			

These weren't his skills. They were *hers*. But if skills were acts of lifeforce performed in specific ways to ensure specific results, and it had been his body that had performed them, then by all logic, he had performed those skills. Thus, they could be his.

Skills like that would be really useful in surviving a cavern full of unknown, dangerous monsters.

There was just one small problem.

Insufficient Soul Capacity.

"What's my current Soul Capacity?"

Soul Capacity Consumed	100/1379

Lukas wheezed. He didn't know what was worse: that his Soul Capacity was so low that even the most meager of her skills dwarfed it, or that the APEX skill Kinetomancy required close to a hundred and eighty thousand units of Soul Capacity, and that was when it was fragmented.

"Careful," she admonished. **"Do not liken Kinetomancy to a mortal technique. It is a culmination of what allowed me to butcher gods and demons alike. You have no more chance of bearing it than an ant can bear the weight of a mountain."**

Yeah, Lukas mused. No wonder the Screen was being so testy. He could get the Alleviation skill—well, sort of, assuming he could acquire the skill in fragments.

He checked it out.

SKILL	LEVEL	SOUL CAPACITY REQUIRED
Alleviation	3	5000
DESCRIPTION		
Removal of any and all unreasonableness of the Body to return it to its calculated original format.		

Lukas blinked. Alleviation very much sounded like installing a backup. A skill that compared the injured state of the body with the latest "backup" and repaired it. And maybe new backups were made every time he gained a Level Up to keep up with the body changes.

Such a skill would be supremely useful in this dangerous environment. Unfortunately, he didn't have the required Soul Capacity for it.

He checked the next, and the most outrageous one.

SKILL	LEVEL	SOUL CAPACITY REQUIRED
Kinetomancy (FRAGMENTED)	APEX	177764
DESCRIPTION **Absolute manipulation of physical vectors.**		

Lukas stared at the Screen for a long moment, forcing himself to breathe slowly. The absolute manipulation of physical vectors? That meant force, friction, momentum, vibration and pretty much any and all kinds of motions he could find inside and outside. This skill—this *power*, it would render every single thing—living or inanimate, into puppets for the user. Briefly he remembered how She had frozen the khorkhoi midair, then squashed it inside out without so much as touching it. This—

This was—

Oh, hell. This was bad. Or good. Or good with a ton of bad thrown in. And at the same time, this was real Power. With a capital P, and all that it entailed. Not just a heap of fancy physics-defying things one could do with lifeforce, but the real deal. Even a fraction of a fraction of this thing could change everything for him.

A lone, bitter bark of laughter escaped him. "What's the point? It's not like I can use this . . ." He paused as a weird thought came to him. ". . . Or can I?"

Estimated Soul Capacity to be consumed: 1279

"But can I *use* this?"

"**Yes,**" Inanna answered before the Screen could respond. "**My Kinetomancy is an APEX skill. It means every bit of it, even the tiniest fraction of a fraction, is complete in itself. That is what you gain by accepting it.**" Her soft mouth turned into a firm line. "**A fair warning, mortal. This skill holds a deadly legacy. If you crave it, you must accept what comes with it.**"

"Like what?"

She shrugged. "**The skill is power beyond what you are built for. My own belief is that it will destroy you. But accept it or reject it, the choice must be yours.**"

Lukas knew she wasn't kidding. One didn't need to be a physics student to understand what could go wrong with manipulating motion. He could utterly wreck his own nervous system. He could tear himself apart. He could impose a death upon himself so horrible that being crushed by the khorkhoi would seem like a mercy.

But this could help him survive. It didn't matter if it was a fraction of a fraction, it was still Kinetomancy.

"This world is built on potential and unlimited growth. This skill can bring me both."

Inanna never took her eyes off him. **"Such ambition is pleasing to my eyes. Unfortunately, the most basic tenet of gaining a skill eludes you."**

"Which is?"

"Once you gain it, you will always perform it properly. Never an error, not even in your sleep. Once you gain a skill, it is engraved upon your soul. Like your heartbeat, it is a part of you."

"But my body still performed it. So it's my skill, right?"

"Your body was merely a conduit. Unless, of course, you can replicate the way I manipulated the motion of every single granule of the worm's body?"

It took several seconds for her words to sink in.

"What you're telling me is, unless you perform it for me, and I have *a hundred and seventy-seven thousand* Soul Capacity ready to use, I can't do what you just did."

"Precisely."

"And would you?"

"I am willing to act within the constraints of our bargain."

Lukas tensed. If he accepted this, he'd get a tiniest fragment of the most awesome power he'd ever seen. However, he would also exhaust all of his remaining Soul Capacity, losing his chance to gain any other skill until he leveled up again.

A quote rose to his mind unbidden . . .

"Once you have tasted flight, you will forever walk the earth with your eyes turned skyward, for there you have been, and there you will always long to return."

Damned if he did. Damned if he didn't. The game was rigged against him from the very start.

"Is that not the best kind of game there is?"

Lukas sighed, facing his Screen, and came to a decision.

"Kinetomancy. Assimilate it."

CHAPTER 6

RULES OF THE GAME

3 prey eliminated.
+49 Experience

Lukas Aguilar, Level-4 Base Host, and current vessel to an ancient goddess, stared at his schema with a mix of amusement and exasperation. He was crouched atop a rocky outcropping jutting from the wall, looking down at a pair of lizards no more than seven feet below. About as tall as the average hen, the creatures had bright crimson heads and neon-green protoplasm covering them from the base of their maws to the tips of their elongated tails.

Three others of their kind lay decapitated nearby. Lukas had watched as the furry lizards—*azolgs*, according to the Screen—viciously brawled among themselves, ending the fight when only two remained. Then one of them spat out a dark, rancid substance over the others' remains, causing their flesh to slowly hiss and melt.

What was it with these monsters and acid?

But most importantly, although Lukas had done nothing but crouch on a nearby wall and observe, his schema had registered both kills as prey eliminations and awarded him with Experience. Not that he was complaining, but whoever had designed this system clearly had no qualms over stealing others' credit.

"All that is guaranteed equally to all is an unfair reality. Only fools become involved in meaningless squabbles over right and wrong. Victors use what is given and push forward."

Lukas wanted to claim otherwise, but his own arguments felt hollow in the face of his reality. If he wanted to survive this place, he'd need to claw his way out using every dirty trick in the book. This was a jungle. And morals had no place in a fight for survival.

He glanced down at the azolgs. They had tremendous reflexes, were capable of extremely fast short sprints, and could spit corrosive acid. As if that wasn't enough, their tails were lined with thin metal ridges sharp enough to hack through flesh.

In short, they were the perfect specimens to test his newfound powers against.

SOULSCAPE	
NAME	Lukas Aguilar
Type	Base Host
Level	4
Experience	107
Current Threshold	640
Utilized Soul Capacity	1379/1379
ESSENCE	
Maximum Lifeforce Output	725
Replenishment Rate	180 / hour

SKILL ATTRIBUTES		
SKILL	LEVEL	CONSUMED SOUL CAPACITY
Raw Lifeforce Manipulation	1	50
Momentum Manipulation	1	50
Kinetomancy (FRAGMENTED)	APEX	1279

OMPHALOS ATTRIBUTES	
Energy Reservoir Capacity	∞
Current Energy Level	722,437,311 units
OMPHALOS FUNCTIONS	
Scan	Level 1
Analyze	Level 1

Only a fifth of the way to the next level?

Lukas looked at his Experience and cursed. He had spent several . . . hours? Days? He'd spent a long time busting his ass, hunting down small monsters and the like. Keeping track of time was difficult without the sun in the sky or a watch on his wrist. Even his biological clock had gone awry. Between the constant anxiety, a near-continuous discharge of lifeforce, and body pains from trying out experimental techniques, sleep had evaded him completely. It was difficult when a single whisper of the breeze or the slightest shifting of rocks made his eyes snap open.

"Sleep will continue to elude you the longer your lifeforce burns within you."

Lukas frowned. *Does that mean if I keep using lifeforce, I won't need to sleep at all?*

"Let me rephrase my earlier statement," Inanna harrumphed. **"Sleep will continue to elude you so long as you keep burning lifeforce, or until your body becomes brittle from accumulated damage, or until your mind descends into madness."**

You say the sweetest things.

"The faster you level up, the quicker you will gain access to more Soul Capacity to gain skills. Until then . . . "

Until then, Lukas would be a squishy human being. The implication was not lost on him. He rolled his eyes and looked down at the azolgs he needed to hunt down. There were a few things he had picked up during his recent experiments. Having the power to blast things away with invisible walls of force like Darth Vader was awesome, but not so much if you read the fine print that came along with it.

Point number one: Lifeforce was weird, whacky, and absolutely dangerous as hell.

It was real, yet it wasn't. There was no scientific basis behind its existence, but it could be manifested as—among other things—a physical force far more powerful than what a human body could normally produce. It could hit you like a baseball bat to the head, and it could be as subtle as a shift in your adrenaline levels. And, if he didn't pay close attention, it was easy to mistake one for the other.

Point number two: Having a skill only ensured its successful casting. It did nothing to protect him from any untoward side effects.

Lukas could easily use Momentum Manipulation to throw a concussive blast of raw force. But if he couldn't guide it out properly, or made it too powerful, he'd end up with more than *just* a broken wrist or fingers bent backward.

Yeah, he was saying from experience.

Point number three, and perhaps the most dangerous of them all: Lifeforce fiddled with the pain threshold.

Lifeforce didn't make Lukas any more indestructible, but it made him feel like he was. It was mostly an advantage since it allowed him to go Superman on his prey. It made him feel great, powerful, and confident. *Reckless*, even. But in reality, it would take his body days to put itself back together. The moment he shut it down, the aches arose and his agony spiked, and the only way to escape it was to use lifeforce again. It was a vicious cycle that would sooner than later render him crippled if he didn't develop a healing ability.

And that was without considering the impossibly dangerous Kinetomancy.

Shaking his head, Lukas leaped down from his vantage point, a cloud of lifeforce coalescing in the center of his palm. Something invisible tore through the air and struck true at the unsuspecting azolg's posterior. Before the monster could register any pain, the wave of kinetic energy drove deep, tearing through flesh, shattering bone, and rending through every ligament in the sinewy appendage.

The de-tailed azolg screeched in pain and sprinted ahead, narrowly escaping further amputation by digging into the rocky floor. Meanwhile, the detached tail flailed madly, as if unwilling to accept it had been severed from its owner's body.

At exactly the same time, the second azolg opened its maw and spat acid toward him. The spurting liquid crossed the distance between and *stopped* in midair.

Lukas grinned. Raw force exuded out of his palms and splattered the acid back onto the surprised azolg. The rodent hissed as the viscous liquid burned through its fur, but before it could react, Lukas already had. A second wave of motion smacked it in the face like a sledgehammer, hurling it across the cavern floor.

"Adequate performance," Inanna congratulated. **"A seamless combination of motion negation and force."**

I sense a "but" coming . . .

"It is a waste of energy and momentum, yours as well as your prey's."

Lukas frowned. *You mean—*

The rest of his thoughts were drowned out as the first azolg erupted out of the floor behind him, fangs and claws bared. He whirled around, feeling his lifeforce exude out of his arm and *grab* the motion of the azolg, and yanked it down. The azolg's eyes bulged from the sudden shift of momentum, throwing it into complete disarray. Lukas pushed ahead with his left fist and punched a kinetic burst into its face, shattering its jaw.

He lightly panted. *Well, that went well—*

"Behind you."

It probably said something about his experience surviving this monster-infested den that Lukas didn't turn around like an amateur to check what was behind him. Instead, he threw himself into a forward dive, rolled over his shoulder, and came to his feet already moving laterally, just in time to avoid getting slashed by something sharp and metallic. Lukas aimed his fist at the culprit and fired off another round of energy, blasting it out of the air and hurling it away.

"Take that!" he snarled, feeling fierce approval at his own success.

But it faded rather rapidly as something behind him slammed into the small of his back like a tiny locomotive. The impact knocked the wind out of him, snapped his head back sharply, and flung him to the ground. Everything became disoriented for a second. Lukas whirled around once more, only to find three new participants staring at him like he was a piece of succulent meat.

Which, come to think of it, was true in a sense.

"Three more of you damn things," Lukas spat.

All three pounced toward him, and before he knew it, he was in motion once more, having decided that waiting on his brain was counterproductive to survival.

"TAKE THAT!"

Unseen force lashed out of him and hammered the three in front. With a level of skill that surprised even him, Lukas grabbed a fourth, one of the two from before, out of the air from behind him and smashed it against the floor, before charging an angry, adrenaline-fueled knee upon its face.

---

1 prey eliminated.
+13 Experience

With indigo blood covering his tattered shirt and parts of his face, Lukas whirled around and stared at the other three—one among them had decided to call it quits and flee. Even the three that remained looked like they were reconsidering a second attempt.

"What?" Lukas taunted. "Scared already?"

One of the creatures let out a furious squeak and lunged at him, but this time, he was ready. Enveloping his arm with lifeforce, he smacked it on the head. It was dead before it hit the floor.

---

1 prey eliminated.
+13 Experience

The other two took the opportunity to sprint away.

"What?!" he yelled, smacking his bloodied palms onto his knees. "You're done already? YOU PRISSY LITTLE FU—"

"**Mortal,**" Inanna warned, "**control yourself.**"

Lukas felt a sudden surge of anger within him. Goddess or not, she was a renter in his mind-space who wasn't helping him deal with any of this shit. Instead, she had the gall to warn him like he was a fucking child? A growl escaped his throat, and his hands balled into tight fists. He opened his mouth to tell her exactly what she could do with her suggestion when—

The anger vanished as if it were never there. And in its absence rushed in fatigue and pain, the consequences of constant lifeforce exertion. His ribs felt weak, and his torso was wet. The azolgs had drawn blood. His knees gave way, and Lukas collapsed onto the floor.

"Ow!"

"Your power is an extension of yourself. A tool for you to wield. You must learn to control it lest you be controlled."

The truth of her statement rang harshly. Had he really been that close to acting like a seedy drug addict? All because he'd used a lot of lifeforce? As if he didn't have enough problems to deal with.

"How did you bring me back?"

"I cut off your connection to your lifeforce."

"How did you—you know what? Never mind." He already had a truckload of common-sense-defying things happening around him. Whatever bit of new insanity Inanna wanted to throw onto his shoulders could wait for another time.

Pushing himself back up, Lukas crawled toward a wall and rested with his back against it. A scratchy, hollow scream escaped his throat, barely louder than a whimper. He kept it up until he was out of breath.

Fuck. This hurts.

He needed to breathe. In and out. In and out. Lukas forced himself into silence, holding back the pain by focusing on his breath. The steady flow of cool air into his lungs. But the raw pain was still there. It wanted him to find a hole and crawl into it. But there wasn't one.

He could feel every injury marring his body. There were bruises on his left elbow and scratches on his back and right arm, just below the wrist. His knuckles were battered as well from all the smacking, and his jaw felt a bit stuck. And how it ached! Letting out a chagrined groan, Lukas reopened the flow of lifeforce and let it trickle back into his system.

This was his weapon. His medicine and his poison. It would keep him safe from the monsters as it tore his sanity apart from the inside. It would make him feel *invincible* and *under control*, while slowly letting him splinter his own body apart.

Until—

Until I find a way out.

"Is there?" he croaked.

"Is there . . . what?"

He rolled his eyes. Even that minute action was painful. "Is there a way to use lifeforce to heal my body? You know, like *actual* healing, not just vanishing the pain?"

"Such trivialities do not interest me."

"It's not trivial," Lukas retorted. "I need to know if there's a way. I won't be able to find your property if my back is broken, now will I?"

Inanna let out a long-suffering sigh. **"You are already aware that such a skill exists. I alleviated your body's damage when I possessed you."**

He bit his lip. "Okay, yeah, I know the skill exists, but is it the only one? I mean, I've seen lifeforce do plenty of stuff I can't explain otherwise. Can I learn to use it to heal myself?"

"Lifeforce can be used in all sorts of ways, mortal."

"But can you, or rather, will you teach me how to heal myself with lifeforce?"

"For a price."

"We had a deal!" he exclaimed.

"To provide you with information strictly relevant to your task."

"My continued existence *is* relevant to my task. I can't fulfill it if I'm dead!"

"Fear not, mortal. So long as you follow my directives, you shall survive. Accompanied by unrelenting throes of agony, perhaps, but alive nonetheless."

Lukas clenched his teeth. This was getting him nowhere. "Look, we can do this in one of two ways. Either you just tell me how to heal myself, or I can experiment with it on my own. But then maybe I'll accidentally blow my heart up or something, and you'll be left with a bloody corpse to help you find your lost property."

The goddess was silent for a moment. **"Nothing but a bluff."**

"Is it?" he challenged. "You can read my mind. You have access to my thoughts. Am I bluffing?"

"Merciless winds, you would hold your own life hostage to attain your desires?"

Lukas shrugged. "Me being alive is the only thing about me that's worth anything in your eyes. That also means it's the only bargaining chip I have."

"And so you would force me into this farce of a bargain to comply with your unreasonable demands?"

"I'm working for a goddess in a den full of monsters." Lukas snorted. "I can hardly afford to live in fear. Come on, it's not like you're performing the skill for me or anything."

"Merely ensuring that you don't do anything wrong."

"Exactly."

The goddess hummed noncommittally. **"I find myself at a crossroads, mortal. On the one hand, I am suitably impressed with your bold play,** following a precedent I myself set. An outrageous feat, but one worthy of notice. Perhaps there is some hope for you. However . . ."

Lukas patiently waited for the other shoe to drop.

"You have proven willing to destroy yourself in the past to force me into catering to your demands. Should you attempt that again, it will be the last thing you do."

Lukas could taste the raw acidity in her tone.

"You have my word. I'm here to deal in good faith."

Silence pervaded for two long seconds, but to him, it seemed like an entire hour.

"Be warned. Even if you manage to perform what I impart, your soul will still be denied the skills unless you gain the Soul Capacity for it." She paused. "Since I am already teaching you, I shall take this opportunity to begin imparting the knowledge you will need to fulfill your end of our bargain."

"Like what?" he asked curiously.

He could practically feel Inanna's smile as she spoke. "It is time you understood your reality. About the Origin, anomalies, and your true place in the World."

CHAPTER 7

ANOMALOUS ORIGINS

S tep forward."

Lukas was back inside his mindscape. Only this time, the locale had shifted from the inside of his apartment to the outside. The building looked just as derelict as he remembered, with concrete slowly breaking off the outer walls in chunks and a half-weeded lawn next to the left entrance. The outer door was covered in moldy growths and stripped paint. A single step forward, a small twist of the knob, and he could step inside.

Into his apartment. Back to normalcy.

His fingers trembled as he grasped the doorknob. Touching the solid shape with his fingers, feeling its icy cold texture within his palm, seeing it with his own eyes made it impossible to believe that they were merely illusions. His mind kept telling him that it was all real, yet his heart hung on a single question.

Is this really home?

What was true? What was real? Did it even matter? In that single moment, he was back in his own world, in front of his apartment. Everything else—the anomaly, the worms, the monsters, Inanna . . .

It would be so easy to pretend it was all just a dream.

"Step forward," Inanna repeated, her words rumbling like thunder.

"All right," Lukas whispered. He felt something heavy drop in his stomach. With a will of iron, he stepped off the pavement and into his apartment. Almost immediately, his knees wobbled and his body felt weak. An intense wave of disorientation scrambled his sense of direction. A powerful gale brushed his face, but there was blazing heat too, along with the feeling of being drowned in ice-cold water.

It was maddening. Lukas could no longer understand his own existence. His eyes shut tightly, unable to comprehend whether he was standing or falling, or if he could even fall at all. Any reaches of gravity deserted him, leaving him in some kind of multichromatic vacuum that shattered him into a million pieces, only to be reformed into countless permutations in all sorts of dimensions—

"We are here."

Lukas opened his eyes. And stared. And kept on staring.

But nothing around him made a lick of sense.

What the fuck is that?

His brain felt frozen, as if someone had shoved bars of solid ice into each individual lobe. It was as if the thing in front of him had all the colors of the world sucked out of it—no, that wasn't it. It was colorless to begin with. Or was it transparent? He genuinely could not tell.

The base was spherical, like a bulb with a single shoot rising out of it, contorting into itself in ways that defied basic Euclidean geometry. The entire thing was twisted into some kind of loop, then coiled back onto itself, as if there was nothing there. Yet there was something . . . something he couldn't truly comprehend despite his best efforts.

It was hot, it was cold. It was up, it was down. It was still, it was moving. Sideways went upward, and inward vanished into nowhere. It was biological, mechanical, alive, ethereal. It was utterly wrong, and yet he had never seen anything that could possibly be more *right*.

As the whole thing slowly pumped like a beating heart, strange energies floated in and out of it in spirals, vibrating in tandem with an alien tune. It was perfectly synchronous, though he had no idea why he believed so.

But what was it?

What was it?

WHAT WAS—

"Mortal."

He tore his gaze from the strange . . . object? The very action hurt, as if looking away from it was a grievous Sin, one that would take an eternity to repent for, if not longer.

Standing beside him was Inanna, her attire a flowing gown of emerald silk laced with veins of turquoise. A belt fashioned from braids of gold snaked its way around her waist, and her unbound jet-black hair fell past her hips. A creature of gentle curves and feminine loveliness, she was perfection given form. The barest of smiles graced her lips.

Lukas's sudden delirium about the object rapidly vanished now that he was no longer gazing at it. In fact, what was it he saw again? Any attempts to remember only left him with a blank.

"What was that?!"

"*That* is the Origin."

"The origin?" Lukas asked, perplexed. "Origin of what?"

"**Everything. Elohim. The Provenance. The Infinite Dream. The Cosmic Demiurge. It has as many names as there are civilizations, as many titles as there are ways to die. Every language in existence has tried to describe it in its own limited way, but nothing can truly capture its brilliance. This is the Womb of Creation. The source of everything that is Potential.**"

"The Origin," Lukas repeated blankly. "If there's no way of describing it, then how did I, you know, see it just a second ago?" The temptation to steal a glance out of the corner of his eye steadily grew, as did the unreal fear of what would follow should he succumb to his desire.

But I already did it once. What's the worst that could happen?

"**What you have seen is a reflection.**" She wrapped her lips around the words, drawing them out with a little tremor that dripped with wicked, secret laughter.

It seemed that scouring his thoughts and memories allowed her to steal modern vocabulary as well. The benefits of mind-sharing just kept on giving.

"Is it a reflection of the real thing?"

Inanna sighed wistfully. "**Of a memory.**"

"Yours?"

Surprisingly, she shook her head. "**Aeons ago, someone showed me her memory of the Origin. I am told it took her several levels of simplification before I could witness it without tempting insanity.**"

"And what I'm seeing is . . ."

"**I had to simplify my own understanding of it by several orders of magnitude. Just for you.**"

He tried very hard not to dwell on that fact. The goddess smiled, as if to say *you have no idea.* It promised to show him things that you just didn't talk about with other people. Things that could inspire dreams you only wished you could remember in the morning.

"**It is a good thing,**" Inanna declared, "**that mortal perception is bound by the illusion of linear existence. Beings of apocalyptic strength have gone mad trying to comprehend the Origin.**"

And wasn't that just ominous? Hearing her refer to the apocalypse reminded him of the one that had apparently destroyed his planet. He opened his mouth to—

"**Everything has its time, mortal. A little patience will not suffer you.**"

His jaws shut with an audible snap.

"**Now . . . look.**"

Lukas gazed ahead. The Origin was there, only this time it was more. He didn't understand how or why, but he could now see lands. He saw mountains, oceans, flowing rivers, arid deserts, and lush forests. It was like gazing at a flat

Earth. And there were several of them, floating and turning in all directions as they moved in non-Euclidean shapes around the Origin.

"Each is a fully formed world. A realm, the greatest form of worlds born of the Origin. Independent existences fixed in their own time-space. There are *always* a hundred and eight of them. Always have been."

"Why?"

"The number strongly resonates with Creation itself. Every mortal with a physical shell has a hundred and eight points from which lifeforce exudes out. For those who harvest the World's energy to craft mana, there are a hundred and eight channels to do just that."

Lukas could appreciate the symmetry present, especially how things at the micro level mirrored the macro. Unable to resist, he glanced at the Origin once more, only to find that it had rotated, revealing one large opening—or was it several narrow ones? Thousands of entrances—a single gateway—leading to everything and nothing. It was like looking into an ever-changing nebula of alien matter. It was both spectral and physical, dancing along the line that separated fantasy from reality.

Something that *was*, yet *was not*.

"Maddening, is it not?"

The scene in front of him enlarged further. Tiny orbs of energy pulsated with blinding light in a constant state of metamorphosis. They were all coming out of that single—thousands of—a giant opening—several small openings—

The constant superimposition of images made his head throb. "What are those?"

"Worlds in their infancy. Each is a concept of Creation given form, crafted out of crystallized information and Potential. An omphalos."

"Omphalos?" he asked, twisting his neck so fast toward the resident goddess that he nearly gave himself whiplash. "You mean like the one in my schema? The thing that gives me the Scan and other functions?"

"Yes. Think of it as a doorway, through which the Origin manifests its own essence into the cosmos."

"And these omphaloses . . . omphaloi? I'll be honest, I don't know the plural for omphalos."

Inanna threw her head back and laughed. It was a beautiful thing, rich and cultured and wholly mesmerizing. A sound so pure, so free, that he couldn't help but grin back. Then, realizing that he'd been staring at her for too long, he cleared his throat.

"Um, so, what kind of information are we talking about here?"

Inanna seemed inordinately pleased with the question for some reason. **"History."**

Lukas frowned. "Again, of what?"

"Of everything that is. And is not." Lukas wondered whether beings of her level were simply incapable of saying things simply, especially when it concerned cosmic matters. *The limitations of language,* she had called it. That, or she was being cryptic for the sake of being cryptic.

Either way, the important question was something different. And far more troubling.

If omphaloi are concepts of Creation, then what the fuck is one of them doing inside me?

"That is something you do not need to bother with at the moment."

"Oh, I do. If it's in me, then I need to know what it is and what it does."

Her eyes glinted. She looked like someone who had heard what she expected to hear. **"Very well. Once an omphalos materializes in the physical world, it creates a boundary layer around itself, transforming everything within its periphery to actualize the new World based on the information contained within it. Such a world is called an anomaly."**

"Like the one we're in," Lukas replied. "So the monsters—"

"Protections. Creations. Tools actualized to gain information. To consume *prey.*"

And then, as if seen through a kaleidoscope that had suddenly come into focus, everything began to make sense. A rift in reality created by an omphalos, granting the anomaly functional abilities in exchange for consuming prey. No way the similarities between him and these *anomalies* were just a coincidence. But he wasn't an anomaly. He wasn't a world, or even an environment. He was just a—

Base Host.

That was what the Screen had called him. What did it even mean?

Default consciousness.

He narrowed his eyes. *Of what?*

Anomaly.

He stared at it stupidly for a second. His Soulscape had omphalos attributes and omphalos functions listed in it. But so what? That didn't make him an anomaly. Right? Anomalies were worlds, not people.

A sudden, sinking feeling engulfed him. Inanna had told him that Earth's Cosmic Consciousness had latched onto him. *Consciousness,* not Potential—no, he couldn't make another juvenile mistake. Not again. The goddess had described it as consciousness but never implied that it was all that had merged with him. What were the chances that the planet's consciousness and the omphalos were two different entities?

. . .

"You're telling me that the Earth's omphalos fused with me, and I'm its new host?"

"Correct," she said. **"You are its Base Host."**

Lukas swallowed nervously. Everything he'd learned pointed toward him being an anomaly, but the cynic within vehemently argued against it, calling it a fantasy created by a delusional mind. Almost every mythology he'd come across painted the planet as a major-level deity, greater than most of the divinities listed in their respective pantheons. In Greek mythos, only Chaos preceded Gaia, the Goddess of Life and Mother Earth. In Hindu mythos, it was Prithvi, the "Vast One." In the Hopi Kokyangwuti, it was Spider Grandmother, who, with the sun god Tawa, created Earth and its creatures.

If gods and goddesses were real . . . If Inanna wasn't a figment of his imagination . . . Did that mean that Earth, the world he had come from, was now *within* him?

"I can't believe I'm seriously considering this," Lukas muttered, before nodding to himself. "What will it take for you to tell me everything about the omphalos in me and how it will affect me? I have a few theories I want to validate, and maybe I'll think of some more in the near future—"

"They are all focused on this topic."

" . . . Yes."

Inanna's green, glacial eyes were trained on his face, unblinking. **"You remain insouciant despite knowing what I am. You wear your independence with pride knowing that genuflecting in my presence can make your life easier. And now, you choose to bargain with me, after all that we have spoken of, merely to deepen your understanding of yourself?"**

"Is that a problem?"

"No. But it speaks a great deal about you." She sauntered toward him, her grace as deadly as it was beautiful, and cupped his chin. **"Your pride is a source of endless fascination for me. I would like to see it broken, just once. Bow down before me, mortal. Accept me as your salvation and your goddess. There is much I can teach you. All the answers you seek would be yours. My vaunted Kinetomancy yours to wield. You will know power and pleasure that few mortals have tasted."**

Listening to her voice was like being dosed on narcotics. It was easy, *too easy*, to justify why accepting it was a brilliant idea. This was a strange new world, where monsters were real and out to kill him. A world where might made right, where strength was all that mattered. No sense of morality, no government, and no law was going to help him if some creature wanted to make him into its evening meal.

Accepting the offer would make that fear go away. Deep within him, Lukas relished in the tiniest bit of power that the fractional fragment of Kinetomancy had given him. Being able to alter motion itself and shoot kinetic blasts out of his hands was downright magical, yet nothing compared to what Inanna was promising.

All it would cost him was his independence. He'd be in service to her. He'd defer to her. Every single one of his actions would be dictated by her whims. He'd be unstoppable.

But he would remain a servant.

"Forget it." He shook his head. "No deal. Is there anything else?"

She arched an eyebrow. **"Intriguing. Your independence weighs more in your eyes than power. If not that, then perhaps a request? A spell of my own choice."**

Lukas was flummoxed. "You want me to perform a spell? Like a magical spell? I don't even know how."

"No, mortal. I shall perform it. I merely require being in possession of your body. I want your word that you shall not try to inhibit me when I perform it."

He narrowed his eyes. "Why do you even need my permission at all?"

It was odd. Weird even. Inanna had already demonstrated that she could control the lifeforce within him. She had literally switched it off. And back then with that khorkhoi, he'd certainly had no clue that she was going to use Kinetomancy. All he had known was—

He stilled.

"Is . . . is it true?"

"Be more specific."

"You can cast anything—Kinetomancy, Alleviation, and who knows what else—when in control of my body. You can even affect my lifeforce. But you need my permission to enact a spell of your choice?"

Inanna stayed quiet.

"Is that why we had to make a bargain before you helped me earlier? We agreed that you'll help me get out of this place, and inhibiting my lifeforce falls under that request. Is that it? Do you need formal permission from me, the Host, to go about doing anything?"

"Stars," Inanna murmured. **"You are adorable."**

Lukas clenched his jaw. "That's not an answer."

"You truly expect me to tell you?"

"You're evading the question," he growled. "Why is this bargain necessary? Is it because of the omphalos?"

"Perhaps. Perhaps not. What is the answer worth to you?"

A dry chuckle escaped him. "Oh no, I'm not playing that game again. I'm not paying you with a bargain just so you can pull me into another."

"What an unpleasant mortal you are," she playfully chided. **"I suppose this information will forever stay out of your reach, then. Let us return to the previous bargain. One spell of my own choice, unhindered."**

Lukas pursed his lips and tried to cudgel his brain into working. Had he missed anything she'd use against him? Definitely. This was Inanna. Her offer seemed too simple, but then again, why not take the direct route?

"Fine. One spell, and one spell alone. So long as it doesn't harm me, or enslave me, or mind-fuck me into becoming your worshipper—"

"Faith cannot be enforced so crudely, mortal. And you *will* worship me. Someday. For now, you have my word that the spell will do nothing to you. Physically, mentally or spiritually."

"And you'll keep your word?"

Something utterly terrifying flickered in her eyes. **"Remember this, because I shall not repeat it again. My word is bond, even if the earth shakes and the sky falls on it. Are we in agreement?"**

Sighing, Lukas nodded. " . . . Yes. We are."

"Wonderful. I have a feeling our future bargains will be most fortuitous."

"Never. This is the last one. I won't bargain with you ever again."

"Yes. You will."

Her predatory smile did not make him feel any better. Not in the least.

PART II

Saints and Sinners

CHAPTER 8

A BANQUET OF SINNERS

The Black Moon shone in the sky.

Tanya watched silently as dark, smoky beams descended upon the ever-illuminated town of Haviskali, consuming the Eternal Light wherever they fell. It was a blatant disrespect to the power of the Great Goddess, yet they did it so leisurely. Carelessly, even.

The sight made her envious. She wished she could be like those beams. An existence without thought, capable of simply being. Not caring, thinking, or hurting. Then maybe she too could be free.

She stood in the inner courtyard of the Banksi estate, breathing in the aroma of jasmine flowers. Knowing what she did about nobles, she had expected to see flamboyant displays of wealth and power. However, she'd been welcomed at the gates by a middle-aged rōnin and a lone maid. For someone of Zuken Banksi's affluence, it was a painfully frugal way of living.

This was the house of someone who was comfortable living alone. She could empathize with him perfectly well. After all, when you were alone, no one could betray you.

Tanya heard shuffling a short distance away and suppressed the urge to flood her wristbands with mana. She turned around and saw the door slide open, revealing a compact, clean-cut man in his late twenties. He had precise features and a lot of very soft black hair. A mask of tranquility adorned his face, but there was a hint of wariness in those thoughtful brown eyes. He stepped through the entry, adorned in a white shirt overlaid by a deep green vest with engraved gold buttons. The black suit on top was long, and his dark brown wristbands, engraved with the Banksi insignia, signified his status as a ter-ramancer. Light glinted off of the rings on each finger, no doubt fortified with numerous protective enchantments.

Zuken Banksi. A member of one of the Sacred Eight Clans in the Asukan Empire.

Her eyes flickered white.

Mana	2200
Lifeforce	1960

Strong, but not overwhelmingly so.

"Miss Tanya," Zuken offered, a coy smile accompanying his words. "Welcome to my home. Though, I distinctly remember asking Hiroto to show you to the guest room."

The rōnin had certainly tried to. In fact, he'd looked a hairsbreadth away from whipping out his katana and forcing her to walk there at swordpoint. It might've been preferable. She could deal with people trying to kill her. But someone inviting her in and treating her with basic courtesy? Those were uncharted waters.

"I like it out here," Tanya brusquely replied. The courtyard gave her a clear view of the estate, and it was easier to escape should things . . . escalate.

"I see." A ghost of a frown flitted across his face. "Even so, the others are expecting you inside. Do not fret. I wouldn't dream of tarnishing my clan name by offering poor hospitality to a welcomed guest."

She supposed that was the best she could get. Nobles were all too obsessed with maintaining spotless images, to the point where swearing in the name of their clan was akin to an unbreakable vow. Of course, that didn't guarantee that Zuken Banksi wouldn't betray her.

After all, his clan's name would only be stained if she lived to tell the tale.

"Miss Tanya, I'm aware the Cobalt Army is looking for you. However, handing you over is not my intention. In fact, so long as you are here, you are immune to their reach. Should our meeting today prove fruitful, we're going to be professional peers, after all."

Tanya narrowed her eyes. *So long*, he had said. What about after that?

"Fine," she stiffly replied. "But if anyone inside attacks me—"

"Then I will consider it an attack on my person and react appropriately. That, I assure you, is a promise."

Tanya slowly nodded. "Okay. Let's go."

The door opened into a long hallway, just wide enough to let them walk through without feeling claustrophobic. The interior walls were decorated with graffiti while the air smelled like dewy wet grass. Almost every inch of the floor was elevated slightly above ground level, and knowing the Banksi Clan's reputation with earth shaping, she wondered whether she was entering a mansion or a garrison.

It begged the question of why a man so resourceful needed her, of all people.

There were two sides to the Haviskali Underground. The first was the taverns, where thieves and miscreants and government spies either sold or exchanged information. The second was people like Zuken Banksi, who owned entire organizations dedicated to under-the-table services—imposters, assassins, forgers, whores, and anyone else incredibly skilled and dedicated to their crafts.

But *her*? She was just some runaway.

Albeit a runaway who had committed a heinous crime in the past, but a runaway nonetheless.

"Charming place," she said as she walked alongside him. "A bit too spacious, I must say."

Zuken laughed. "I like to breathe in fresh air while I attend to my duties. Earthen philosophy is more than just layering defenses and gaining ground. It's about stability and foundations."

Tanya found his affability disconcerting. Even if it was for a job that required her skillset, he was being awfully accommodating. "Your letter mentioned a job . . ."

He raised a hand. "The others are waiting inside. I'd rather not repeat myself."

The end of the hallway led into a flight of stairs. She walked a step behind Zuken at all times, a wind blade just a twitch of her fingers away. The stairs led to a wide chamber, almost as large as the Seron Market, and filled with plush chairs, couches, tables, and a massive writing board around fifty feet long.

"Welcome to my conference room. I apologize if it seems a little cluttered."

Tanya followed Zuken inside and tensed. Nothing came screaming at her from the walls or the floor. Nobody had started firing at her either.

"Oooh, paranoid, aren't you?" someone commented. It was a thin, bubbly voice filled with amusement. Turning slightly, Tanya found herself facing a girl, tall and buxom, with dark brown tresses and an aura about her. She was dressed in a tight bodycon with her hands folded in front of her. Tanya noted her slender ears. *A ljósálfar? No, she seems less luminous. A changeling, then?*

Her eyes flickered again.

Mana	—
Lifeforce	**1100**

Definitely a changeling. A ljósálfar would have switched lifeforce for mana, and a dökkálfar's lifeforce reserves would have made this look like pocket change. She looked older too—for a changeling, that was. *A failure, perhaps? Though Zuken doesn't seem like the type to take in strays . . .*

"Play nice!" complained another girl. This one looked like an ordinary bremetan with ginger hair, brown eyes, a plum-shaped face, and a rather plump pair of lips. With a nod, she gestured toward one of the chairs.

Mana	—
Lifeforce	5000

Tanya nearly wheezed. *5000?* That was practically a walking bomb waiting to explode. The girl's numbers really did not match her disposition. Unnerved, Tanya took the seat farthest from the walls, allowing her to see the entrance without having to move.

"Is this it, Zuken?" asked the changeling, giving her a once-over.

"Just one more. He's already within the premises. In fact, he'll be with us right about . . . now."

"Ahem," came a new voice. "Apologies for the delay. I was—YOU?!"

Tanya whirled around. The man who stood before her was tall, with the build of an experienced soldier. A loose, sleeveless shirt exposed well-sculpted arms and oceanic blue bands around his wrists. He had shoulder-length hair, a fierce face, and eyes that seemed to glitter with savage laughter.

It was a face to dominate or fight, never one to patronize or pity. All his movements were large and perfectly balanced, and when he appeared in a room like this, he was like a wild animal trapped in a cage too small.

Which, in hindsight, made a lot of sense. After all, she was in the same room as him.

"May I introduce Olfric Bergott . . ." Banksi trailed off. "And with that, we now have everyone here."

Olfric, heir to Clan Bergott. A well-reputed noble family, though not a part of the Sacred Eight. He was an aquamancer, and an absolute pain in the ass.

Mana	3000
Lifeforce	2740

Tanya's eyes widened. *Three thousand? He must have leveled up again.*

Her fingers twitched. She glanced toward Zuken, whose poker face was impeccable. The two girls looked between her and Olfric, the ginger-haired one all bright-eyed and interested while the brunette remained justifiably apprehensive.

"What's she doing here?" Olfric demanded.

"She is here on my invitation," her host replied nonchalantly.

"She's an outlaw!"

"Not if we don't tell the law."

Olfric was nearly frothing at the mouth.

"So long as she enjoys the hospitality of the Banksi estate, her presence will remain a secret," Zuken firmly said. "If you have an issue with this, I suggest you take it up with the overseer, who I seem to recall appointed you in the first place."

"The overseer never said anything about having to work with her."

Zuken smiled disarmingly.

"You've grown more aggressive, Olfric," the ginger-haired woman commented.

"Maude," Olfric grunted, before jerking a finger in Tanya's direction. "I thought I made it clear that the next time I saw you, it'd be your last."

"Empty words," Tanya bit out. The only reason Olfric could be so bold was because she wasn't the rising star among adventurers that she used to be. Had things played out differently . . .

She bit her lip, unwilling to lose control so easily. Especially with the Black Moon ascending.

"I knew this would be a problem," she told Zuken.

The man in question leveled Olfric with a look. "Whatever problem you have with her, you can settle it after we're done. As long as this job is on the table, she enjoys the same diplomatic immunity that I do. As such, I implore you to treat her as a professional peer and an ally."

Olfric sneered.

But Zuken wasn't finished. "If you fail to do so, I'll treat it as a failure on the overseer's part to grant me appropriate support. If word of her presence here gets out, I will consider it a failure on your part to adhere to the customs of Asukan nobility, which will affect your standing in the Empire. Not to mention, I will mark it as an obstruction to this time-sensitive job."

Tanya felt her jaw drop, feeling both impressed and wary at the same time. If she didn't have an incentive to take the job before, she certainly did now.

"Does anyone else have a problem with her?"

The ginger-haired girl, Maude, resolutely shook her head. The brunette's expression was distant, and her eyes focused on nothing particular. She gave a slight shrug of her shoulders.

"Fine," Olfric replied, looking like he had just bitten into a rotten egg. "But I'll say this now. That girl is a danger to us all. By the Goddess, I can't believe you're even allowing her to enter your premises."

"She's integral to my plans."

"She's a Sinner."

"Which is exactly why she is here. To Sin so our hands stay clean."

Something ugly flickered far back in Olfric's eyes, but he nodded and stepped back. Zuken's smile never wavered.

"Right," interrupted the brunette, who stood up, smiling brightly at her. "Hi! You don't know me, but I'm Elena. Welcome to the team."

Tanya glanced at the changeling. To her knowledge, most changelings had their shifts by the time they were thirteen. Elena, for all her sensuality and youth, looked far older than that.

"So you're the infamous Tanya," she went on. "Mana output in the low four thousands. *Very* impressive. Youngest aeromancer in the Llaisy Kingdom to hit expert rank. They say you're actually close to a master at aerokinetic combat, but you tone down your performance to stick to plain average."

Tanya sent a glance in Olfric's direction. "Some also say I'm a demented wacko who kills babies for kicks."

"I choose which 'they' to listen to very carefully," Elena replied. Her voice went down to a whisper. "Did you know half the clans think you're actually the Baramunz princess, Taenis, in disguise?"

Tanya choked on her spit.

"Anyway," Elena chirped, "I'm a changeling. My occupation is whatever Zuken dictates. Oh, and I'm partial to peaches."

Tanya blinked again. Changelings were supposedly good at charming. She wondered what this girl's particular talents lay in. A man like Zuken wouldn't have had her attend this meeting otherwise.

"I'm Maude," the ginger shyly introduced herself. "I'm a naturopath."

A northern medic, Tanya translated. Someone who could draw out power from the earth and use it to pour lifeforce into others, accelerating their self-healing. She wondered if Maude had a vanir up in her lineage.

"By Eir's mercy," Maude went on, "I've never had anyone die in my presence."

And modest, too.

All four of Zuken's party were looking at her pointedly. Tanya realized they were waiting for her to introduce herself. She pushed the golden curls falling over her face behind her ear. "I'm Tanya. A nomad. I'm an aeromancer, and—"

"A nobody," Olfric interrupted. "Outlaws aren't listed on the adventurer rankings."

Tanya narrowed her icy blue eyes. "I'm going to say this one time. Back off before you get hurt."

The room became quiet and tense as Tanya stared down Olfric. Hard. Daring him to challenge her. To meet her on equal grounds and demonstrate how superior he really was.

"Easy," Elena soothed. "We're all professionals here, right? Take it easy."

Tanya tipped her head. "I apologize."

The changeling was right. It was obvious Zuken Banksi had called them there to discuss something important and beneficial for all of them. Getting irritated by Bergott and spoiling the mood wouldn't help. A calmness rose within her like a gentle tide, and her heartbeat slowed. Yes, she was here on a purpose and should just focus on—

She paused, her lips slightly open. Wait, why was she—

"Elena," Zuken chided, "no charming the crowd."

Tanya whirled toward the changeling, who was smiling like a cherub.

Had she just charmed her? Tanya was no expert at mental shielding, but she was no slouch either. That line of thought was clearly foreign, but she hadn't felt even the slightest breaching of her mental defenses.

Just what kind of crazy charmer was this girl?

She considered the group. A terramancer, aquamancer, and an aeromancer. A naturopath to heal wounds and apply fortifying magic, and a charmer to deal with scenarios when confrontation wouldn't do.

"There's something I don't understand," Olfric asserted. "The overseer told me this was a State-sponsored mission. But all State-sponsored work is to be postponed until the Black Moon wanes. Instead, we're having this meeting, and there's a Sinner on board. At least tell me you've a group of onmyōji in the other rooms praying to the Great Goddess right now?"

Not that she'd ever admit it, but she mentally sent the aquamancer her thanks. Something similar had crossed her mind several times in the last several minutes, but she had ignored it and focused on the people around her.

Zuken laughed. It was loud and boisterous. A bit too much. "By the Great Goddess, no. If anything, I told them to take the day off."

"But the Black Moon—"

"My good man," Zuken replied, "I went out of my way to arrange this meeting under the Black Moon. No doubt you're a devout bremetan. Tell me, are you aware of the effects of the Black Moon?"

"The Moon God falls to the curse of darkness," Olfric recited, "and ascends to the Central Sky, heralding the return of the Mists. The Hour of Evil Spirits."

Oumagatoki, Tanya didn't say. Even public mention of the term could evoke tensions. Not to mention the word originally had a far more deleterious meaning.

The Hour of Great Calamity. The End of the World.

Zuken nodded slowly. "And the other effect?"

Sweat beaded on the aquamancer's brow. Tanya didn't need to hire a scholar to know how deeply religious Olfric was. Even thinking such things was likely sacrilege to him.

"During the Black Moon . . ." Olfric's voice trembled sightly. "The All-Seeing Eye of the Goddess is blinded."

"I figured he'd react like this," Elena commented.

Zuken smiled. "Olfric Bergott, I arranged this meeting under such unholy conditions, because what I'm about to suggest can be construed as an act of high treason."

The table was quiet as the group finished their meals. Despite Olfric's protests, the terramancer had clammed up on the subject completely, suggesting they have their meals before they could get down to business. He had claimed that it would be a long meeting and he really didn't want them to sit through it with an empty stomach.

Finally, the maid-servant had placed several large glasses of whiskey on the table before bowing out.

"If I may," Tanya spoke up hesitantly, "what is this really about? You said something about having to Sin and—"

"You're already a Sinner?" Olfric offered. "Trust me, you don't have to broadcast your great accomplishment here. We all know it."

Tanya scowled but said nothing.

"Personally," Maude interjected, her tone neither warm nor cold, "I don't have any problems with her."

"Me neither," Elena chirped.

Don't look at me, I invited her," Zuken replied with a laugh.

"Well, I do," Olfric added darkly.

"So." Tanya steepled her hands in front of her. "can we get started?"

"Right!" Zuken stood up, clearing his throat. "Ladies and gentlemen, now that we've finally settled down and everything, we can move forward to the topic at hand. Some of you have been informed about a job offer. One with good pay, for both the job as well as your discretion."

A dirty job, then. High stakes, high pay, high chances of getting horribly murdered. It was right up her alley.

"Not to beat around the bush," Tanya spoke up again, "but is this an assassination mission? An enemy? Someone in the higher-ups, given the entire treason business?" She looked at Olfric and smirked. "A High Priest perhaps?"

"You—" Olfric got up, growling.

Zuken chuckled lightly. "No. Enemies are a waste of time. They're a distraction for those unwilling or incapable of dealing with such annoyances. *I*, on the other hand, prefer having friends. People I interact with frequently. Acquaintances to speak to on occasion. Then there is bremetan society beyond that. And at the end of the spectrum, there are targets. Never enemies."

The terramancer said it without any melodrama, the way most people talked about taking out the trash.

Elena continued to sip at her whiskey.

"As for the mission, I can't speak of any details until I am convinced you're all committed to it."

"And how will you know that?" Maude questioned.

Elena pulled out a stack of folders from the drawer under the table and slid one toward each of them.

"An Eztli contract," Zuken explained. "It's an unbreakable pact that is agreed upon, supported, and enforced by both parties in the name of the Great Goddess. Should you break the pact, it would trigger a lethal blood curse. Of course, the contract only covers an Oath of Silence. You are free to accept or reject the mission regardless."

Impossible, Tanya thought, eyeing the folder like it was about to sprout fangs. Zuken had to be bluffing. An Oath of Silence was a complete joke. Anyone with a creative enough mind would find a way to get the information out without triggering its curse. No, he probably had assassins ready just in case one of them decided to walk away from this offer.

She needed to act carefully. And soon. Or she might not make it out alive.

"Right . . ." she drawled, pushing the folder away. "I get it now."

"Oh?"

"I'm an outlaw, on the run from the Army, and then you summon me here, with him in tow"—she sent a withering glare in Olfric's direction—"asking, no, *coercing* me into committing a Sin so that you people can enjoy the benefits."

"She's pretty spot-on so far." Elena giggled.

Everyone stared at her.

" . . . what?"

"You said I'm immune as long as I'm here," Tanya said. "So if I say no, I'll be forced out, probably right into the Army's hands. But if I accept this mission, I'll be committing yet another Sin. And I can't even talk about it because of the contract." She stood up abruptly. "So why don't you just call the Army and end this charade?"

"Can we?" Olfric eagerly asked. "Call the Army?"

Zuken stared at her for a long, intense period of silence. "That's not how I operate."

Tanya leaned forward despite herself. "Then what is this about?"

"Something that will start making sense when you open the folder in front of you."

Curiosity finally winning her over, Tanya tore through the seal and opened it. The first document was, as he mentioned, a formal Oath of Silence detailing the stipulations. The second was a dictum from the office of the Shogun, the greatest authority in the entire Llaisy Kingdom, of which Haviskali was a part, stating—

"A complete pardon?" Tanya asked incredulously. She searched Zuken's face for any shred of falsehood. Anything that would tell her that this was all a fabrication. A ploy to take advantage of her. A twisted scheme that she would come to regret.

"Hey, wait a second!" Olfric yelled. "Pardon? You're *pardoning* her? That's it, I'm out of this—"

"Feel free," Zuken replied sternly. "Be advised, however, that apart from the Shogun himself and the overseer, the only people who know about this pardon are sitting here in this room. If word of this goes out, I'm sure the Shogun will be deeply interested in meeting you."

Olfric swallowed.

"The overseer promised me he'd send me some useful help. So far, all I'm seeing are obstructions. Perhaps I should talk to him tomorrow."

All traces of confidence faded from Olfric's face as he quietly sat down in his chair.

"So . . . is this true?" Tanya whispered softly, tenderly holding the document in her hands as carefully as one would cradle a child.

"I assure you, it is completely legal. If you join us on this job and we succeed, that becomes your new reality. Of course, the pardon only applies to crimes that fall under the jurisdiction of the Llaisy Kingdom. If you have outstanding charges in other areas, you will have to deal with them yourself."

"How do I know you aren't lying?" she demanded, slamming her hands on the table.

"Sign the contract, then walk to the overseer's office with me tomorrow. Verify it for yourself," he replied simply, shrugging. "And yes, you will be pardoned for both Sins."

"Just what is this damn job about?"

"Once again, nothing I can disclose without you signing that contract."

Tanya carefully considered her options. Never in her wildest dreams had she imagined something like this falling into her lap. A chance to start over? To clear her past history? She could establish herself as an adventurer and climb the ranks, rather than taking asylum in exchange for favors.

"What if I fail the job? Then all of this is for nothing."

"If you fail, then we all die."

Tanya slowly retreated into the comfort of her chair. More and more, she was realizing just how dangerous this mission was. But if everything Zuken had promised was true, then it was more than worth it.

One after another, all three of them signed it. Elena collected the folders and tucked them away.

"Now then," Zuken said, resting his chin on his hands, "let's discuss remuneration. Aside from the pardon granted to Tanya, you shall be paid fifty thousand mezals. Each. Twenty thousand up front, and the remainder after completing the mission."

Tanya's breath stopped for a second. Fifty thousand mezals? The freedom from the pardon would go a long way, but there were always bills to be paid. For someone who made eight thousand mezals in her best year, the sum was unimaginable.

"In addition, there will be other profitable avenues. It goes without saying, everything we find will be divided equally among ourselves."

"Just asking out of curiosity, how much would these 'extra avenues' be worth?" she asked.

"Enough to double your current remuneration."

Tanya nearly choked. The amount had gone from high to surreal to downright ridiculous. A hundred thousand was so much money, it had practically no real meaning to her.

"What is it you're after?" she asked.

"We've detected the presence of a Class-3 anomaly in the Namzuuhuu Desert," Zuken replied.

"An anomaly?" Olfric asked.

"Class-3?" Maude arched an eyebrow.

"In *the* desert?" Olfric finished.

Tanya stayed silent. An anomaly was good news. They were treasure troves of resources that included metal deposits, organic extracts, gemstones, and most importantly, work for the common people. By Wind, entire *towns* were constructed around an anomaly, especially if it was a Class-3 as Zuken proclaimed.

Anomaly-exploration missions were big news. She could visualize the Haviskali Shrine hosting a large event, inviting adventurers—local and foreign, to be part of the exploration missions. Depending upon the results, they'd sent a horde of metalcrafters, terramancers and miners to get the resources out. Something so grand was supposed to be the talk of the town, not be discussed in whispers enforced by an Oath of Silence.

What was she missing?

"The desert is out of bounds for all bremetans," Olfric asserted. "And even if you did go there, you'd be caught by the Army's scanners. Not to mention it is an accursed place."

"Oh, it's accursed all right," Zuken replied. "But that does not make this any less true. The mission is to sneak past the Army, get into the desert, and locate the anomaly. And once we've gotten what we want—"

The gears in Tanya's mind were already turning. So that was why she was brought here. This was the Sin Zuken had alluded to, the Sin he wanted her to commit.

"You want me to destroy the anomaly," she replied in a very small voice, ignoring the looks of surprise from the others. She had eyes only for Zuken, as if willing him to disagree.

"Yes," he said unflappably.

"WHAT?" Olfric sprang up, his legs knocking his chair backward. The shock in his face was too real to be faked. "Are you out of your mind? I knew our mission involved Sin, but an anomaly is a grand blessing from the World. To kill one is—"

"A very grave Sin," Tanya finished. "Something I've committed in the past."

"You destroyed a freaking *anomaly*?!" Maude exclaimed.

"Along with all her comrades," Olfric growled.

"Clearly not all of them," Tanya shot back. "You survived, after all."

The aquamancer went beet red. "No thanks to you."

"I tried my best."

The anomaly incident during her last mission was what had gotten her life screwed up. Olfric Bergott had been her staunchest adversary from the start, and had been loudest at accusing her for the deaths of the rest of the team members. It was what led to her being shamed and removed from the ranks.

"What I don't get is why we're even talking about destroying it in the first place," Maude said, "especially when she's being hunted for a similar offense."

Tanya could only snort derisively. The hypocrisies of the Empire no longer were a surprise to her.

"That is not your concern," Zuken replied airily. "The point is, the Black Moon will wane in forty-eight days. During this period, the All-Seeing Eye of the Goddess shall remain blind. We need to complete the anomaly exploration mission, figure out what's causing the spike, collect our loot and destroy the place on our way out. All within that time limit. And . . . take care of any witnesses we may find there."

Translation—kill everyone.

"Witnesses . . ." Tanya trailed off. "Do you mean other adventurers?"

"It is possible that the scanners in Cyffnar might have taken note of this and acted."

Of course they had. Cyffnar was situated on the other side of the desert. A city in the Eaborid Kingdom that didn't share friendly ties with Haviskali.

Zuken looked at everyone earnestly. "Do we have any quitters?"

No one said anything. Tanya glanced at Olfric and found him looking downward, fists clenched.

"In that case . . ." Zuken cleared his throat authoritatively. "Let's retire for now. I'm sure this is a lot to take in, and I'd advise you to sleep on it. Rooms have been prepared for you to rest in the mansion. Tomorrow, we will plan and prepare for the mission. We will leave as early as possible."

With that, he stood up from his chair and walked out with Elena in tow. Olfric followed soon after. Maude hovered around for a while before she stepped out of the room and called for the maid-servant to show her the sleeping quarters, leaving Tanya all by herself.

Alone.

Thinking.

Forty-eight days. Even assuming they managed to get started for the mission in around a week, they'd have to sneak past the Army, travel through the desert, and suffer its curse. Finding an anomaly there would be ludicrously difficult, not to mention the problems they were gonna face. And even if they managed to get to the anomaly and get the loot, there was no saying what could happen after.

Zuken had claimed to be willing to distribute the loot equally among all five of them.

Tanya had almost stood up and called him a liar to his face. Adventurers killing adventurers after uncovering loot wasn't unheard of. Money had a tendency to bring out the worst in people, and she doubted Zuken Banksi was any sort of holier-than-thou exception. The long-term wealth an anomaly could generate was enough to support the rise of kingdoms.

But he had given her an offer she couldn't refuse. And she could trust he would keep her alive to hold the burden of the Sin.

And once the anomaly was destroyed . . .

She warily eyed the now-empty room.

Everything was up in the air.

CHAPTER 9

STIRRING SHADOWS

Tanya awoke to a quiet room, red morning sunlight peeking through cracks in the shutters. She lay in bed for a moment, unsettled. Something felt wrong. It wasn't that she was waking up in an unfamiliar place. Traveling from one kingdom to the next for years had accustomed her to a nomadic lifestyle.

The room was empty. And large. And uncrowded. And . . .

Comfortable.

Yes, that was it. It was comfortable.

Her nice, circular bed was the size of her old room back at the Meewich Gate, draped in smooth, silky sheets with curtains of pure white drifting on gentle currents of cool air around her. The temperature was cold enough that her breath condensed when she exhaled, but she was still warm beneath the covers. She never really had an issue with the cold. Quite the opposite, in fact.

Tanya sat up with a frown. It felt weird having a room all to herself. Even at the Meewich Gate, she had to share her chambers with others, and finding privacy was an ongoing struggle. This, on the other hand, reminded her of a life she had chosen to forget. A different life that could have been hers, if not for—

Her knuckles turned white. Why did those days come to haunt her again and again?

Knock knock.

It took Tanya a second to realize they were expecting a response. "Come in." The door to her right opened to reveal a woman in traditional maid's attire, carrying a tray with an ornate porcelain cup and several containers of liquids, each of which looked more expensive than the last.

"Master Banksi has been informed that you have woken up," the maid stated, not at all surprised by her being awake. "The container with flowers has a beverage with several unique herbs mixed in for nutrition. The one without is a solution often drunk after a healing procedure."

"Healing?" she asked warily.

"My apologies, miss." The maid bowed politely. "My master arranged for Miss Maude to perform restoration magic upon you while you were asleep. The last meal you were served contained particular herbs to guarantee unbroken sleep for long hours for the procedure to be completed."

With a shriek, Tanya leaped out of bed. She knew she shouldn't have trusted him. Of *course* he had tried something. By the Great Goddess, if she was cursed or entrapped or had her kami taken away from her . . .

She paused. Her right shoulder . . . It wasn't painful anymore. The same went for those bruises she had above her left calf, on her ankles, and below the sternum. A quick glance at the mirror in the corner showed that even the darkened spots beneath her eyes were gone for good.

Tanya looked down at herself. Her usual clothes were gone, replaced by a ridiculous toga-like bedroom attire that extended to her thighs. Her body felt fresh and clean, something she hadn't felt in a long time. The svartalfar could arrange for cold water, but showers and foamy baths were more than a little odd to creatures that traveled through the very earth itself.

"Maude did all of this in one night?"

"You have been asleep for an entire day and then some, miss. It is close to the noontide now." The maid patiently put the tray down on the bedside table. "The door to your left contains a bathroom with a shower. My master took the discretion to purchase adventurer robes fitted to your size, along with anything else you might require for the mission. He and the rest of your team are in the conference room, expecting you in one hour. Please use this time to make yourself presentable. I suggest you hold any questions you have for him unless there is something else you would like to inquire of me."

Tanya opened and closed her mouth several times as she tried to get her stunned mind working again. "Wha—what's your name?"

"Fuyume," the maid replied. "I am one of the few fortunate enough to be in Master Banksi's service. My role in this household is to look after those who frequent the estate, such as yourself."

After the maid left through the same door she had come through, Tanya spent the next hour relaxing in bed, standing under the lukewarm spray of the shower, and fitting herself with the clothes Zuken had purchased for her. Eerily enough, the size was a perfect fit. She desperately hoped it was the maid who knew her so intimately. When she was ready, she walked out of her room and toward the conference room.

As she walked through the Banksi mansion, she could not help but think *wealthy* at every turn and corner. There were miniature forests of oak and birch planted with roads in between them, giving off the appearance of being outside in the wild while staying within the premises. With how many intricate carvings were etched into the architecture, the estate would have required the minds of several dozen terramancers and onmyōji to complete. And this was without considering the dozens of wards interspersed with one another like an elaborate spiderweb.

All in all, it was a poetic reflection of the man who lived there.

As she approached the conference room, she could hear voices from the open door. One could ward off sound using enchantments, but Zuken seemed to not care for the subtlety. That, or he simply wanted to make a point about his confidence and control of his household. It was both incredibly daring and impressive at the same time.

Her fingers twitched, and a thin blade of wind formed between her fingers. It felt colder than usual, with slower currents than she expected—worrisome, but not alarmingly so. Her powers had begun acting out a bit the last time there was a Black Moon in the sky too.

Tanya gritted her teeth. It would be safest for everyone if she just hid away under some rock until the Black Moon waned. But if she did that, she would lose her one chance at freedom.

She peeked in from around the corner of the door. A hearth burned at the side, adding some warmth to the otherwise chilly temperature. Winters in Haviskali were a biting cold, or so everyone said. Zuken Banksi stood with one elbow resting upon the hearth, a glass of expensive-looking wine in the other hand. Maude shared one of the couches with Olfric while Elena was sprawled across the other.

"Miss Tanya," Zuken greeted with a smile, noticing her standing outside. "Do come in."

"Just Tanya is fine," she replied, feeling somewhat self-conscious. Living life the way she had, she'd always found comfort in obscurity. Even when she worked as a sanctioned adventurer, she was always the silent member of the group, opting to do her job as instructed and staying out of others' way. Some, like Olfric, took it as standoffishness. His insecurity over her greater mana output and performance hadn't helped matters.

"Tanya, then. In the interests of a synergistic partnership, please call me Zuken."

Olfric scoffed derisively.

Tanya scanned the room and found two empty chairs, one next to the open window while the other was beside the changeling. Deciding not to trust the changeling's presence, she let out a resigned sigh and moved toward the window.

"I hope you like the attire," Zuken offered.

Tanya nodded slowly. The new wristbands were extremely supple and comfortable to wear. When she had tried channeling mana through them, she found the process far smoother than she was normally used to. She could really get used to this.

"Well, that's all of us," Maude said. "Can we get started on the specifics now?"

"Specifics?" Tanya asked.

"Not all of us are experienced on the subject of anomalies. I've worked with adventurer teams before, but never on an anomaly mission. Zuken and Elena have never needed to. Only you and Olfric are full-time adventurers, and . . . " She trailed off, looking a bit peaky. "You're the only one here who can say they've destroyed one."

Olfric rolled his eyes. "Excuse me for not wanting to drench my hands with Sin."

Zuken gave Tanya a wink. "Alright, let's talk. We've got something of a task ahead of ourselves, and the sooner we begin outlining a plan, the better."

"I assumed you'd already have a plan by now."

Zuken shrugged. "You were asleep."

"And all of you sat around doing *nothing* yesterday?" Tanya asked, flustered, before realizing that she might have come off as a little aggressive. "Sorry. That came out harsher than I thought it would."

But he waved her off. "We're peers now. There's no need to bring in additional complications. Feel free to treat me as a fellow team member."

A team member that controls my freedom, my career, and possibly my life.

"Plus, it's not all that bad," he continued. "I have people ready to provide for the rations and other amenities we might need for this mission. I'm hoping today's meeting will get me a list of everything we need to get going."

"What he means"—Elena smirked—"is that *I* talked to those people. Maude spent the day treating you while Zuken played shogi with Olfric."

Despite Zuken's insistence on everyone using his given name, there was something even more familiar in the manner the changeling addressed her employer. Clearly, there was more to their relationship than what met the eye.

"My dear," Zuken drawled, "if I have to do work, then I'm not doing my job."

Olfric snorted.

Zuken laughed. It was warm and unassuming. "I know what needs to happen and I have a few ideas on how to do it, but you don't just gather a group like this and tell them what to do. We can work this out together, starting with a list of problems we need to deal with."

"It sounds simple enough," Olfric said, raising a finger with each point he made. "We leave for Namzuuhuu Desert, walk in blind for anything that might strike at us there, try to find an anomaly that could be anywhere within the desert, find an entrance, kill everything that moves, collect hypothetical loot, and have our resident Sinner deal the final blow." He looked at everyone. "Have I missed anything? I'm running out of fingers."

"The part where we escape with our lives?" Maude helpfully supplied.

"Well, that's still up in the air, isn't it? It's entirely possible we get killed in the last step. The outlaw has already done it once before, but twice is better, right?"

Tanya reared up to give him a piece of her mind, but Maude interjected again before it could devolve into a shouting match. "I think our main problem is the lack of information about the desert. We can't hope to deal with the anomaly if we're obstructed by the desert itself," she said.

Zuken walked over to the blackboard and began writing.

Study the desert's curse and its possible counters.

He looked back at the team. "I've already acquired reports on the history of the desert. Elena has read them. She can describe them in brief for you afterward."

Tanya tried very hard not to look at anyone. The last thing she wanted was for the others to know that she had crossed that very desert in the past, or that she had firsthand information about the nature of its curse. It would accelerate their plans by a magnitude, but it could also end with her head on a spike.

"What else?" Zuken asked, tapping the piece of chalk against the board.

"We need a way to locate the anomaly without having to scour the whole desert," Olfric offered.

"Mentioning the anomaly brings up another point. How can we make sure we destroy it in time and get back?" Elena pitched in. "I doubt its vulnerable parts will be easily accessible."

Narrow down the anomaly's location went up on the board. As did *Study the structure, layouts and protections of anomalies.*

"I'm also going to add infiltration to the list," Zuken said. "It might turn out that Cyffnar has known about this anomaly for a while and has anointed soldiers to guard the entrances. We need to make sure we move unseen, while getting both in and out. And we also need somehow to get away with our loot. It'd be terrible if we had to leave everything behind and escape after going through all the effort."

"With Cyffnarians shooting at us from behind," Elena replied with a shudder.

"Anything else?" Zuken asked.

"Well," Tanya said dryly, "if we're listing all our problems, maybe add the fact that we're all unhinged and functionally insane for even considering doing this."

Zuken wrote down *Tanya's cynicism* right after *infiltration, recon, and evasion tactics.*

"Is that a bad thing?" Maude smirked. "I happen to think cynics are playful and cute."

Everyone laughed, except for Tanya, who frowned at the board, trying to decide whether this whole thing was a joke or not. The list on the board wasn't just daunting; it was outright disturbing. Finding a counter to the desert's curse? The same curse that kept the Great Goddess's power at bay for millennia? With the Black Moon present, all sorts of wraiths and spirits would be free to tear them to shreds.

"I can't believe you," she murmured. "Do you really think this will be easy?"

"You did it before," Olfric pointed out, and for once, the ever-present sneer on his face was missing.

"By luck," she countered. "And that was a Class-2. This is a *three*. It will be larger, more complex, with far superior monsters and who knows what kind of traps. And that's without considering its real defenses and its guardian. Plus, there's the desert to consider. How many of you have experience traversing it? How many of you can last in that place until we find an entrance into the anomaly?"

That shut everyone up.

"I hate myself for saying this," Olfric muttered, "but she has a point. Making a bulleted list is one thing, but the reality of it is different."

"The reality of it is exactly why we are in this conference room making a list, Bergott," Zuken answered softly. "To break down an immense problem into simpler steps until it no longer appears daunting. It might not give us a solution, but it does offer the opportunity to consider more angles than otherwise."

Tanya pursed her lips and decided to move ahead without adding anything else. The less attention she drew to herself, the better. "Fine," she grunted. "Let's get started. I suppose you have something on the origins of the desert's curse?"

"We do." Zuken chuckled. "And it made for very interesting reading too. Elena has painstakingly compiled narratives of the origins behind the desert's curse."

"Narratives? Plural?" Maude murmured. "I wasn't sure that writings of the Time Before existed, much less were available. Where did you get it?"

"Some of it is from my own library," Zuken replied, a hint of pride lining his words. "As one of the Sacred Eight, my Clan predates the current calendar. The rest is from the Graken Mountains up north. There are tribes there who follow the Old Folk. The residents remember what it was like before the days of the Great Goddess's ascension."

Before the Jade Empress ascended to the throne as the Great Goddess and let her Eternal Light scour the world and rid it of the darkness, Tanya surmised. She had studied the tales of the World Shaper and her war with Amaterasu, but she wasn't going to mention any of it here.

"It's unfortunate, actually," he went on, "that there's so little information about things older than the Asukan Empire. But that only makes the information we have worth more. I had to pay a good amount of mezals to acquire it." He pointed at the folder in Elena's hand. "That there contains the entire story of the yokai kingdom and the days before the Great War. The ascension of Amaterasu as the Great Goddess, the rise of the Asukan Empire, and most importantly, how the once-fertile lands of Namzuuhuu became an arid desert that kills everything within its borders."

"I don't know about everyone else," Maude said, "but I, for one, would love to read it. Knowing the curse's history may be instrumental in figuring out a way past it."

Elena got up from her position and fetched five more folders and passed them along.

"Happy reading!" She beamed.

Tanya's discomfort ballooned. Did these people not realize that the curse had held strong for millennia for a reason? Even more disturbing was how matter-of-factly they handled the issues. The group regarded their list of problems with grim yet mirthful determination, as if they understood they had a better chance of making the sun rise at night than they did of overthrowing the curse, yet would still try nonetheless.

Worse still, their pointless optimism was almost contagious enough to make her believe in it.

"I'm not sure why we need these alternative narratives," Olfric muttered, flapping across the pages from his folder. "The official translation alone should have done the job."

"Yeah! That way we'd all share a singularly biased way of looking at it." Maude laughed.

"Excuse me?" Olfric snapped, drawing himself up.

Tanya nearly formed a wind blade. Situations tended to escalate whenever Olfric was involved. Doubly so when his infamous Asukan pride was hurt.

"You heard me right," Maude replied, her voice steady. "I've read texts on our ancient history, about the war. How the empress transcended into the Great Goddess to exterminate an accursed civilization out of the annals of history."

"And?" Olfric demanded. "We all know that's the truth."

"No. We're *told* that that's the truth."

I should have seen this coming. Tanya grimaced. Maude wasn't a bremetan. She was a vanir, or at least half vanir. By the Great Goddess, she even used the Nordic gods to exclaim and curse. If anyone would take offense at a biased telling of history, it would be her.

Life in the Asukan Empire was difficult if you weren't bremetan. Other races had to register with the Cobalt Army first, at which point they were given a choice between worshiping the Great Goddess's pantheon and relocating to the fringe territories. Asukan Law was clear: if you weren't a worshiper of the Asukan pantheon, there was no place in the land of Eternal Light for you.

Although . . .

Tanya narrowed her eyes.

She makes no secret of her worship of the Aesir, and she's still here as part of the team. But unlike me, Bergott is on good terms with her. What's the catch?

Meanwhile, Elena looked utterly indifferent to the conflict. The changeling was another outlier. Sooner or later, every changeling morphed into a ljósálfar or a dökkálfar. The former, also known as light elves, were treated kindly in the Empire. It fit the Asukan narrative of light being holy and dark being evil. The other side of her heritage, the elves of shadow and darkness, were treated with absolute disdain and barely seen in the Empire. The official story was that when the dökkálfar had taken control of Alfheim and threw the ljósálfar out, the Asukan Empire gladly invited the luminous beings to become one of their own.

Yet, Elena seemed so utterly indifferent to it. Was it because she was destined to become a ljósálfar? Or had she simply developed a good poker face?

"You're overgeneralizing it, Maude," Olfric proclaimed.

"That's just what an Asukan noble would say!"

Tanya shared a glance with Zuken, who also seemed utterly unbothered by the sudden antagonism between team members. In fact, he was watching the developments with interest, as if he were studying them.

"Rather hypocritical of you, Maude. You're assured work by the nobility, regardless of how happily you ignore our faith, choosing to believe in gods that perished long ago."

A cold silence permeated across the room.

Maude slammed her palms on the table. "You're right, *Heir Bergott*. I work for the nobility despite not believing in your Great Goddess of the Light. Do you know why? Because it is my faith in Eir that allows me to perform naturopathy, the same art that has saved countless *Asukan* lives in the years I have served the Empire. The same Eir that *your* Empire doesn't care enough to recognize!"

She ruefully shook her head. "I never should have agreed to this plan. We—we will be defiling the world by destroying something as innately precious as an anomaly, a seed that would eventually give rise to new races, all because of politics. And I have to be a part of this process because that is what the great Asukan nobility demands of me."

Maude launched herself out of her chair and stormed toward the window. She stared out at the sky, where the Black Moon reigned. Tanya waited for someone to say something, anything. The abrupt silence was beginning to get to her.

"Unfortunately, Maude is correct," Zuken grimly said. "No one is perfect, not even the Empire. It's led by people, and people have agendas. But right or wrong, the Empire has shaped our beliefs for over a millennium. We don't have to speak up against it, but we can accept when someone calls out a wrong."

Silently, Tanya began perusing the document she had been handed. There were writings by famous scholars of the past, several of them being members of the Banksi Clan. There were theories on what had happened at the end of the war, and speculations on the reasoning behind the Ascension of the Empress Amaterasu into the Great Goddess they worshiped. But as she read through more and more pages, she began to realize something vital was off.

The texts were blatantly ignoring a fact that could spell disaster on every member of the team. If they kept operating like this, they wouldn't last in the desert. They would all die.

Hesitantly, she raised her hand.

"Yes?"

"There is something you must know," she began, feeling all the eyes in the room fall on her. "I'm a vagrant. You understand what that means?"

"A wanderer, traveling from place to place," Zuken replied. "Most freelancers and mercenaries fall under that category."

"And before coming to Haviskali, I wound up in Cyffnar for a time." She paused. "Then I came here. Through the desert."

Olfric shot up from his chair and slapped his arms against the table, his eyes scouring her face like an eagle eyeing its prey. "You've traveled through the desert? I knew there was something wrong about you when I first met you. No wonder you've Sin—"

"Enough!" Zuken snapped. This was the first time Tanya had seen him look annoyed. She wondered how much of that was because of Olfric and how much from her own admission. Zuken was, after all said and done, a member of the Sacred Eight. He might have a reputation for skirting the lines every now and then, but there were some lines he'd never cross.

Lines like the ones drawn by the Cobalt Army.

"Go on," he replied. "Tell us. Clearly you have something to say about it."

Tanya weighed her options. She had already opened that door and stepped inside. There was no going out.

"The official text says that the curse impairs the Eternal Light there, which is why it's declared a forbidden zone. The truth is, there in the desert, there is no Eternal Light at all."

An uncomfortable silence dragged on for several seconds. And the worst part of it, she couldn't blame them.

The Eternal Light was a manifestation of the Great Goddess Amaterasu herself, an illumination that bathed the Asukan Empire. Its radiance had no physical source, but it brightened every nook and corner, be it inside or outside, day or night, deep underground or in the middle of the street. It cast no shadow and exuded no heat. It was simply light. Pure, warm, holy light.

And it was absent in the desert.

"No Eternal Light?" Maude exclaimed. "Then at night—"

"There is no light. Only pure darkness, and all kinds of creatures that come out to hunt."

"*Evil* creatures," Olfric growled.

Tanya ignored him. For all his boasts, he had very little experience of the real world outside of the theatrics of nobility and adventuring. By Wind, he'd probably have a heart attack just by spending a day with a jotunn, much less a dökkálfar.

"You said you've crossed the desert," Elena chimed in. "What's that like?"

"The desert . . ." Tanya trailed off. "It hates you. It hates life. There's no food, no water, nothing but a never-ending ocean of bone-dry sand. During the day, it's like standing before a fiery wyrm, and at night, frost coats your skin. It feels as if death's hungry maw eyes you from everywhere. From the sands, the rocks, the decaying bodies of animals, and then . . ."

"Then?" Olfric gulped.

A dark part of her rejoiced at their pinched expressions. "And then there is this."

Tanya opened the very last page of the document and grabbed one of the pens from the table. After a moment of consideration, she began drawing a rough image of a man on it. It wasn't artistic by any means, but enough to get the point across. Finally, she drew a circle with rays emanating out of it on the upper left corner of the page and scratched the portion around the "man's" feet in black. A twisted reflection, tapering at the edges and larger than the man itself, only the reflection was on the floor and not in some mirror.

"This is called a shadow," she explained. "In absence of the Eternal Light, these . . . *things* form underneath your feet."

"Shadow?" Maude asked.

"Evil!" Olfric repeated.

Tanya snorted inwardly. The Eternal Light provided an all-pervading illumination from every direction. But there in the desert, the only source of light was the sun overhead. And that light cast a shadow beneath her.

"Call it whatever you want," she replied. "The Curse of the Desert, evil incarnate, monsters hiding in the dark—they're all the same. Shadows. If you're to travel through the desert, you've got to come to terms with it. Else we might as well just disband right now."

Zuken looked at her with unabashed curiosity. "Tell me more."

She continued in a harsh whisper. "Your shadow falls beneath you. Sometimes it extends ahead, blackening the path in front as if you were descending into madness with every step. Other times, it draws behind, like a dagger ready to pierce you from behind, something you will never see coming. And then it can coalesce right beneath you, making you stand in a pit of blackness of your own making."

Olfric staggered, pointing a finger at her shakily. "You lie! Nothing so sinister can exist under the All-Seeing Eye."

"But the All-Seeing Eye can't penetrate the desert's curse," Tanya replied, her voice soft and mysterious. "It's a land corrupted in all forms. A taboo upon the world, so vile and wrong that all mentions of it are erased from Asukan texts." She met the aquamancer's eyes. The conflicted expression on his face was a delight.

"The heat is cancerous. It blinds you, suffocates you, makes you *want* to seek a shadow. The cold is haunting. Everything there is either wicked and warped or blasted and burned. During the day you have cruel birds of prey circling you from above, spelling death and disease on you. In the night, an infinite void of blackness surrounds you. Wyrms and bats and hideous insects entrap you while you sleep. It's a vast pan of emptiness where everything sentient resents anything else alive. They want to rip into you, splinter your bones, and feast on your flesh. Everything has poison, paw, or claw. Or sorcery so malignant that even the demonic yokai couldn't have survived."

Elena began to hyperventilate. Olfric had gone deathly pale, like he'd seen a wraith. Maude shot worried looks between the both of them. And even Zuken no longer looked unflappable—his face was taut, like a stretched bow, as his sharp eyes followed her every movement.

"What?" Tanya asked, trying to keep the dark amusement from seeping into her tone.

"You . . . you're not making this all up, are you?" Zuken asked.

"You're Zuken Banksi. How difficult is it for you to confirm my words?"

"But—but—" Maude spluttered. "You crossed it, right? I mean, what you're describing is—"

"Impossible? Hardly!" Tanya challenged condescendingly. "The world is more vast than you can possibly imagine. Lots of things exist that do not fit the idyllic Asukan dream."

"If it's as bad as you say, how did you survive?" Olfric demanded.

Tanya bared her teeth. "I guess being a vagrant has given me a stronger appetite against the ugly."

Olfric scowled but said nothing.

"Then how did you do it?" Maude asked. "Cross the desert, I mean."

"The desert is a lover of the dead and hates anything alive. If you want to survive it, you have to become the dead."

"Become *what?*"

"Put simply, imitate the qualities of the dead. They're cold; they lie motionless beneath the earth and rest in the shadows. During the day, I lived in caves and underneath the rocks. When nothing was around, I covered myself with sand and placed my bags over my head, hiding from the sun. And when the light was gone and darkness covered the land, I came out and traveled."

"In the darkness?" Olfric asked in disbelief.

"In the darkness," Tanya confirmed. "When the other predators came out."

"But what if they attack you?" Elena asked, biting her nails.

Tanya arched an eyebrow but said nothing. If nothing else, her episode with the desert seemed to have shaken everyone, especially Olfric. Still, the respect seemed to be a double-edged knife. While it made her seem valuable, it also painted her in a darker tone. She could picture Olfric somehow citing her journey through the desert as the corruptive influence that led her to destroy the anomaly.

And the worst part? He'd be right. Partially.

"How is something as blessed as an anomaly even born in such an environment?" Maude asked.

Tanya shrugged. "Potential blooms in the unlikeliest of places. But yes, an anomaly blooming in the desert would probably be the weirdest anomaly we'd ever encounter. An anomaly seeks growth, and the curse eliminating all of its creations would be detrimental to that. The monsters are likely somehow immune to the desert's curse or are simply good at dealing with it."

"There's a third possibility," Zuken said. "The anomaly's creations survive the desert's curse by ignoring it. It could be underground."

Tanya looked at him with surprise. "Underground?"

"You said it yourself. To survive the desert, one needs to imitate the dead. The anomaly might well be sprawled across the desert, only below the surface."

And suddenly, Tanya knew what they were looking for.

"A cavern," she began, and everyone turned toward her. "One with tons of empty spaces allowing monsters within to locomote from one place to another. Probably a vast network of tunnels beneath the desert, deep enough to avoid the heat overhead, but close enough to the surface to allow for proper aeration, water resources, and, most importantly, entrances for prey to wander in."

"I imagine most of the monsters would be based on creatures that live underground." Olfric suggested, "Insects, spiders, snakes, worms—twisted into fiendish monstrosities."

Tanya grinned at him and then realized who she was grinning at. Quickly, she looked away.

"The way you describe it," Elena replied, still looking absolutely sick and pale, "it's like we're entering some kind of crypt."

Tanya nodded. "We just might be. A crypt of worms."

CHAPTER 10

BEHIND THE MASKS

Tanya stirred awake. It was an unusually slow process for her, whose dreams were constantly haunted and to whom awakening represented a respite from the nightmares.

Not the last few nights, though. She wasn't sure if it was the healing or simply a lack of her usual emotional drains, but she had been getting slumber so deep that she couldn't believe it. There were no dreams of any sort. Just a peaceful, lulling darkness that was free of thoughts. For the first time in a long while, she wasn't on the run, whether from the Army or her past. The crew wouldn't meet for another few hours, and until then, she had nothing to do.

It was a strange feeling.

Slipping out of bed, Tanya changed into her clothes, ready to step out of the room and into a bright, new day, filled with promises and—

She frowned.

That was probably a bit much, even with her newfound levity. She wasn't a naive little girl. The world was still as ugly as ever. She had just found a temporary respite against it, at least until she left for the mission and the ugliness returned with full force into her life. Yes, cynicism suited her much better. She felt more comfortable with taking things with a grain of salt. It spared her many bitter disappointments, and she had experienced enough of those to last a lifetime or two.

But still, she had never once thought that the day would come when someone would know about her past, some of it anyway, and not spit in her face or try to get her arrested. Her reverie was broken by the sound of footsteps approaching. Her instincts flaring, Tanya crouched beside the floor, trying to determine if the person was just walking out or approaching her room. The hallway fell silent, and eventually she breathed a quiet sigh of relief.

A knock sounded on the door just inches from her head.

Her start of surprise nearly knocked her to the ground.

Quickly ruffling her hair and rubbing her eyes, Tanya waited for just enough time to make it look like she had just gotten out of bed. She untucked her shirt and waited until the knock came again, before pulling the door open.

Maude lounged against the doorframe, a small garment bag dropped at her feet. She raised an eyebrow at Tanya's disheveled state.

"Yes?" Tanya asked, trying to sound drowsy.

"Did I wake you up?"

"Uh, yes."

"Sorry," Maude apologized. "I should have known you'd not be awake this early. I should've just asked Zuken."

"Zuken isn't here. After last night's meeting, he left to meet some people. Something about transportation facilities."

"And he didn't come back?"

Tanya shook her head. There was no need to tell Maude that she had conjured a tiny wind spell in front of everyone's rooms to warn her if they were inside or outside. And another spell on the floors to warn her if someone was coming downstairs.

Maude's lips twitched. "Anyway, Elena told me to give you this." She pointed at the bag on the floor.

"What's there?" Tanya asked.

"More accouterments, I think. Adventurer stuff."

Hesitantly, she reached out and stripped the bag open. If it contained something dangerous, then both she and Maude would bear the brunt of it. But she needn't have bothered with the thought. The insides contained a pair of traveling cloaks that looked to be enchanted to resist the elements and physical force—within limits. There were also several pouches made of tanuki skin, enchanted to have greater space on the inside than the outside, and a pair of thin blades.

Finally, her eyes landed on something that looked like lead shells, roughly spherical in shape and small enough for her to hold three of them in her fist. She looked up at Maude, almost expecting a hint of deception or malice. Instead, she found excitement.

Gingerly, she took one of them in her fingers and observed it. The shell was heavy for its size, enough to throw thirty to forty feet, but light enough to carry around. There was the all-familiar sigil of the Great Goddess on one side, and the Empire's emblem on the other.

"Flash grenades," Maude explained, seeing her bewildered look, "with Eternal Light bottled inside it. Olfric has been busy preparing these for our mission."

Tanya blinked.

"It's not as complicated as it looks. Just a simple infusion of Eternal Light on lead."

"But lead can't be—"

"Infused with Eternal Light, no. Here we aren't trying to sanctify the lead. Instead, the power gets trapped within, and explodes with a bright flash."

"Wow."

Maude grinned. "Cool, isn't it? Zuken constructed these shells and Olfric did the rest. I think you might have made our resident aquamancer way paranoid with your stories about the desert."

Tanya inspected the shells up close. The overall construction felt a little crude. Clearly, the two had been focusing on efficiency rather than decoration. She approved.

"It's terrible that this has no market in the Empire. Eir knows, the fringes would have gobbled these up."

Her eyes snapped open. "How do you—"

"Know that?" Maude smiled impishly. "You're not the only one hounded by the Cobalt Army."

"Wha—how? Why?"

"I have vanir heritage. My father is an onmyōji for the Empire."

"You're . . . a deviant."

That certainly explained it. The Asukan Empire did not look favorably upon bremetans breeding with other species—sad aftermath of the Great War. It was, of course, perfectly acceptable for nobles to dally with other species for an evening of fun or more, provided they . . . cleaned up their messes.

"I spent my childhood hiding in the fringes with others of my kind," Maude confided. "But like with everyone else, the Cobalt Army ended up getting to me. I was tried, then given to the nobility to allow them better use of my . . . unique skills."

"How bad was it?" Tanya couldn't help but ask. "I mean, even Bergott gives you an acceptable berth."

"I am a servant of the Empire. A useful tool for the nobility to use, but a tool nonetheless, regardless of how well I am treated. Given my unique talents, nobles are often in need of my aid. It's just good business to keep good relations with someone you'd hire to save your own life."

"I see."

Maude gave her a knowing smile. "I imagine you're not so different. A bremetan without any connections to nobility, yet bearing a wind spirit that can put most accomplished adventurers to shame? I think half the reason the Cobalt Army wants you so badly is probably because they think you have a lineage similar to mine."

Tanya suppressed the urge to sneer. "A deviant."

"Are you?"

She decided not to dignify that question with an answer. "What about Elena? She's a changeling, but changelings are an exception to deviancy."

Maude shrugged. "All I know is that she used to be a thief and a rather successful one at that. Then someone offered her a job to steal something from Zuken, and she got caught."

Tanya narrowed her eyes, instantly assuming the worst. "What happened?"

Maude laughed. "Rumor has it he was so impressed with her that he ended up hiring her. She's been working for him ever since." She laughed again, this time with palpable joy. "What a team we make! A Sinner, a thief, and an ex-fugitive, all outlaws working for a noble who deals with the worst of the lot."

Tanya couldn't help it. She chortled as well.

"So all of this . . ." She gestured at the bag. "Is this really everything?"

"Hardly," Maude snorted. "I saw barrels of ration being transported along with water. There's a lot of dry food. Should be enough to last us for four weeks. Post that, we're on our own."

How interesting! Zuken Banksi seemed to stop at nothing to maintain his *faithful associate* image, and she presumed it would stay that way until he could safely screw everyone over. Aside from him and Olfric, every team member was an outlaw to some degree—people who could just disappear and not have any investigation done about their absence. Given the nature of their job, it would be all too convenient to lay the blame at the feet of outlaws trying to undermine the Asukan hierarchy.

Something else came to mind.

"How are we going to travel all the way to the anomaly anyway? I think I scared them about the desert a little too much."

Maude grumbled good-naturedly. "You did, but not as much as you think. Besides, we already have a plan thanks to you. Instead of traveling through the desert, we're going to fly above it!"

"We're going to *fly*?"

"Fly."

"How?"

"Shkroi hawks," Maude replied, looking entirely amused by the exchange.

"As in, bloodthirsty, meat-loving birds about yay high?" Tanya asked, raising her hand up as far as she could. "A species with a terrifying history of killing their masters and eating them? Those shkroi hawks?"

"Yep."

Tanya felt like ripping her hair out. They were going to die before they even reached the anomaly. *"Why?!"*

"We were discussing the logistics of the hawks and how to get them the other day. Zuken doesn't want to waste time trying to pay his way through the Army channels. That reminds me, how did you travel through the desert without the Army catching on?"

And now Maude expected her to reveal her secrets. Was this why she had shared her sad little "origin" story? To get Tanya to open up and reveal potentially incriminating information? Tanya felt a little insulted about the lack of professional respect her actions implied.

"Let's just stick to talking about Zuken's plan."

Maude harrumphed, reddish hair slightly swaying as she shrugged her shoulders. "Fine. Zuken mentioned he knows a guy who knows a guy who runs shkroi hawk flights."

"And they won't get caught?"

"Anti-scanner tech, probably," Maude speculated. "Very skilled at avoiding the Army's detection panels. Good for smuggling goods and fugitives across borders."

"That's great and all," Tanya slowly replied, "if we can ride them without getting mauled?"

"Leave that to Elena. Apparently, she's great at taming monsters."

"Charming?"

"No idea."

Tanya bit her lip in thought. A changeling past her morphing age, with an expertise in charming, a history as a skilled thief, and now, a monster-taming skill. Elena was proving to be quite the character.

"Zuken and Olfric estimate it should take us three days to get there. After that, it's on us to find the entrance as quickly as possible."

Three days. Even in the worst-case scenario, we still have forty days to get into the anomaly and get out.

"Can I ask you something, Tanya?"

Tanya blinked. "Go ahead."

"What are the odds this mission will actually work out? Do you think we'll survive it?" Before Tanya could interject, Maude spoke up again. "I know there's a lot more to you than meets the eye. Your mana levels are off the charts, and I've seen you conjure wind blades in under a second. I haven't met anyone with this much skill in windcrafting."

Tanya looked at her in a new light. She fit into the classic rebel stereotype seamlessly, yet Olfric gave her a wide berth despite her brutish demeanor. She called herself a former fugitive and a tool for the nobility, yet here she was, establishing rapport with a Sinner.

Was the interaction genuine? Or was it simply a tool trying to extract information? Had Zuken put her up to this? It would be just like him, creating groups within groups, hiding plans within plans.

The worst part was, she was starting to enjoy it. The paranoia, the thrill, the not knowing everything. The chance of being betrayed and seeking potential avenues of betraying others. Digging into everyone's secrets, securing alliances, increasing her worth to the team, all while focusing on their main goal: the destruction of the anomaly and the benefits that would come out of it.

Tanya smiled. She'd worked with shadier people before, and she could work with Zuken Banksi too. If nothing else, this success would get her out of Haviskali and out of the Army's reach, if only for a brief time.

"Well?" Maude demanded uneasily.

Blue eyes met brown. "It takes a few decades for a Class-1 anomaly to evolve, and centuries for it to evolve into a Class-3. This thing has grown large enough for its radiation to escape the desert and register on the scanners. Who knows how long it's been alive?"

"That means—"

"The monsters inside have survived the desert's curse for centuries. Centuries of survival means centuries of accumulated experience." Tanya leveled her with a harsh look. "If you want to reap the benefits of this mission, you have to do more than survive it. You will need to kill whatever the anomaly throws at you, before it does the same to you."

"But I'm a healer!"

"Remember to tell that to the monsters before they tear your head clean off."

Maude's face turned ashen. "Oh. Right. I'll, uh, I'll go pack my battlestaff."

CHAPTER 11

HITTING HARD

An aeromancer for the past eight years, Tanya was no stranger to being airborne. It was fundamental to her identity, both her sword and shield. The ability to soar into the sky, leaving rock-crusted terrain behind with winds ruffling her cloak, was the closest she'd ever felt to the concept of true freedom. Yet somehow, sitting on the shkroi hawk, barely sixty feet above ground, was enough to make her sick.

This is a nightmare.

"How far are we?" she croaked, suppressing the urge to puke. Flying on a shkroi hawk was hardly the most comfortable mode of travel, given the speeds at which they soared across the skies. The putrid, congesting atmosphere of the desert didn't help either.

It was only thanks to Maude's skills that their group was still functional.

"Five," said the rider, a lanky, awkward-looking man dressed in gray. He'd given them the name Aered, no doubt made up. Smugglers were hardly famous for their professional integrity, but Zuken seemed perfectly content to hire them to help find the entrance to the anomaly, as well as act as spotters for any Cyffnarian soldier camps posted in the area.

Five meant five miles. They were most likely within the anomaly's radius already.

Tanya glanced down at the never-ending ocean of yellow beneath her. There was sand, more sand, and nothing else but sand. Great dunes shifted around like the waves of the Sea of Mone. The day prior, she and her group had witnessed a vicious sandstorm, an orgy of wanton violence that meandered through the Namzuuhuu Desert, leaving nothing but destruction in its wake. Compared to that, the dreary weather was rather tame.

"Me men have camp away cave." Aered's thick Maluscian accent was audible even through the dense, hot winds slapping Tanya about. "Force in the around the cave of."

Translation: There were Cyffnarian troops stationed near the entrance of the caves. His men set up camps out of their reach.

Which meant Zuken's suspicions were right. Cyffnar Scanners had definitely caught on to the energy spikes.

It made no sense. All bureaucratic work was supposed to shut down during the Black Moon Rising. And the desert was a forbidden zone. So what was Cyffnar up to, sending soldiers into the desert to capture this anomaly? And why did Zuken want it destroyed?

It was like for every answer she got, it raised five more questions in return.

"How far is that from the caves?"

Aered raised a single, sand-eaten finger.

"Alright." She nodded. "Take us to the camp. We'll set up our things there. What about getting us back to Haviskali after the mission is over?"

"Us wait."

Right. And she was the freaking emperor of this land. These smugglers would escape the moment they set foot into the caverns. No bremetan would choose to stay behind in the desert for a second longer than absolutely necessary, greed and professionalism be damned.

As Aered turned the massive hawk due west, the other birds quickly followed suit. The sky was clear, with no sandstorms on the horizon. She would need to start creating a cover for them before they trespassed into Cyffnarian troop territory.

No point complaining when you've a job to do, Tanya told herself, calling upon her lifeforce. Warmth exuded from every inch of her body, enhancing her muscles and augmenting all her physical capabilities. Her sense of balance and awareness sharpened, and the nausea dissipated into thin air.

With practiced ease, she shaped the wind with her fingers and sent a slash of pure energy down, raising a gale of sand into the air. While her right hand channeled enough wind to maintain a constant upward flux, her left moved in a graceful, horizontal semicircle, commanding them around her to follow through.

The key to successful windcrafting was finding the path of maximum flexibility and minimum resistance. But here in the desert, it was the opposite. Unless she exerted ironclad control over the element, it was all too easy for it to devolve into a powerful sandstorm, one that would hurt more than it would help.

Tanya waited with bated breath until the other flyers were safely within the eye of the sandstorm, before closing the circle. Cyffnarian troops or not, it would take a very brave soul to peek out of their rock-tents when there was a storm brewing.

"You won't have trouble seeing, right?"

Aered shook his head. "Us know flying sands."

Tanya nodded. Given their flying speed, they would be reaching their destination any moment now. As soon as she felt a sudden lurch of the hawk descending, she clenched her fists and bent the wind to follow her commands more closely.

Just a little more.

The elevated noise of the shifting sands drowned out Aered's voice as he tried to say something.

"Repeat yourself," she commanded.

"Problem!"

"What's—" Tanya began, but the smuggler raised a hand and pointed straight ahead. She squinted her eyes and poured some lifeforce into them, enhancing her vision. Even from her vantage point, she could now spot a gray, wispy thread climbing into the sky from blackened spots on the sandy terrain.

It took a second for her to register what she was seeing, and another to understand its implications.

"Isn't that your camp?" she gasped.

The gray thread couldn't be anything other than smoke. And smugglers were not stupid enough to light a fire within spitting distance from enemy troops—discretion was a part of the job description. Her anxiety weighed her down like bands of iron across her back and shoulders, and her head pounded from the tension combined with the glare of the sun above. Had something already gone wrong?

There are enough demons out there, Tanya, she calmly told herself. *No need to invent phantoms.*

Upon Aered's command, the hawk swooped downward, flapping its majestic wings as it neared the ground. Tanya barely had a moment before the bird shook violently, bucking her off and headfirst into the bright, hot sands. She spat out some sand and muttered a curse, and when she turned around, the shkroi hawk was glaring balefully at her.

It was enough to freeze her in her tracks.

Aered grabbed the reins and slapped his mount next to its beak, making it shake its head in confusion. When it looked back at her again, the rage was missing from its eyes.

That's weird.

"What's the matter?" she heard Olfric ask. "Are we already there?"

She ignored him with practiced ease and slowed the winds down. It was a taxing job—if she fuddled it up, the currents would smash into each other and create an explosion, but if she let it go, it would turn into a real sandstorm.

"We leave," Aered said, grabbing his reins. The other riders did the same. "Cover!"

"But—"

"Cover! NOW!"

Tanya did as asked without further protest. She watched as the four hawks, three with riders and one without, rose into the sky under the cover of a receding sandstorm, leaving them behind on top of a massive dune, overlooking the smuggler camp nearby.

The same camp from which fumes of smoke danced into the sky.

"I don't suppose they're having a picnic down there," Maude dryly said.

"We were too late!" Olfric muttered with disgust. "Cyffnar troops got to them first."

"What if it's all gone?!" Elena exclaimed.

"What if *what's* all gone?" Tanya asked, turning toward her.

"Those men over there were supposed to stock our rations for us!" Elena continued.

"We need to get those rations back," Olfric began, "before—"

He paused as an inky blackness loomed in front of him. It arose from his feet and spanned several feet ahead, forming a passing semblance to a bremetan outline. He took a step back. And the shadow followed.

"Be—before things get worse," he finished.

"Be practical, Olfric," Zuken replied. "We don't know the exact situation in the camp. We don't know how many enemy troops there are now, or how much the curse of the desert will interfere with our manacrafting. And none of us can operate in the . . ." His voice wavered. "In the *darkness*."

Tanya did not need to turn around to realize that everyone was staring at her. "Don't look at me," she mumbled. "My head's still throbbing from holding up the sandstorm."

"Like I said," Zuken said after a moment, "we'll wait this out and then attack in the morning."

"DAMN IT!" Olfric screamed, angrily kicking up some sand. "DAMN IT! DAMN IT! DAMN IT!"

"Olfric—"

"Don't you *Olfric* me! I don't know if you're being intentionally oblivious or not, but we're standing in the fucking Namzuuhuu Desert with these evil shadows already attached to our feet. This is our only chance to attack and capture the camp and our supplies, and—" His voice cracked as the dark shapes lengthened.

Tanya stepped forward. "Sunset is approaching. The shadows will keep lengthening until it goes completely dark. We don't have to worry. Nothing is out of place."

Olfric sneered and looked away.

She sighed. As crazy as he was acting, it wasn't without due reason. Sunset wasn't just about the sun moving across the horizon; it was a shift in supernatural energy. She could feel sunlight still gliding down to be trapped in the overcast, its presence and warmth fading, the concurrent stirring of magical forces as it did.

Soon, it would be night, the time of darkness. Of wild, unpredictable energies. Of forces of the spirit world that hunted when the sun went beyond the fringes of the Empire.

Dark things came out at night.

"It's not nothing! It's a shadow! Evil incarnate! And now we're stuck out in the middle of a non-warded location, in the desert, under the Black Moon!

"And you're throwing a fit!" Elena replied cheerily. "Hey, don't look at me like that! I thought we were just describing everything around us."

Olfric growled slightly. His face was pudgy and reddening with anger, or fear, or maybe both. Tanya didn't know for certain. All she knew was that he was one step away from doing something that would probably come back to haunt him later.

He's looking for someone to punish, she finally realized. It was the same as before, when they had met after the unfortunate mission and he'd condemned her in front of everyone, accusing her of murdering the team.

He raised his arm, his expression darkening dangerously as he took another step toward Elena—

Tanya's fingers twitched.

—and then he paused. Sighing, he turned away quietly and lowered his hand.

Tanya watched with surprise, and admittedly some concern, as the aquamancer waddled away to stare at the camp on the other side. She subtly glanced toward Elena, wondering if she had somehow allayed him into complying with Zuken's decision. Or was it something else?

The emotional shift was too quick to be natural, and it seemed Olfric had no inkling of what had just happened.

Was this why Zuken brought Elena along on the mission? To ensure that emotions didn't get in the way?

She exhaled, allowing the wind blade in her hand to dissipate. Judging from the knowing look in Maude's eyes, she wasn't as subtle as she had believed. Meanwhile, Olfric was still staring at the rising fumes.

"You know, I've often heard about how no plan survives enemy contact," Zuken said. "I suppose this is an example. Not that I'm surprised."

Tanya frowned. "What do you mean?"

He grinned. "You see, the most important part of a plan is to plan on things not going according to said plan. Which is why . . ." He began unzipping his bag. "I had some extra warded tents made for us, just in case of—"

"*Olfric!*" Elena yelled.

Tanya whirled around, took stock of where Elena was pointing, and then looked toward Olfric. The scene clicked in her mind all at once. Olfric Bergott had lost it and was madly rushing down the side of the dune in a downhill dash.

"—of such situations," Zuken lamely finished.

"What the hell?" Maude demanded. "He isn't planning a direct frontal assault, is he?"

Tanya just sighed.

And then they all started running downhill toward the camp, with Olfric leading the charge. The hysterical man was somehow sliding through the sand as if he were skiing through it, making it difficult for them to catch up with him. But she didn't have the time to play catch up. They were on the verge of losing their camp. If they lost Olfric as well, then they would lose their only source of water too.

Extending her awareness, she grabbed the wind right before the speeding aquamancer and yanked it backward, hitting Olfric right in the face and onto his ass. By the time he fought through the shock of the surprise attack, they had caught up.

"You *impossible* imbecile!" she snarled. "Did you think a frontal assault was a good idea?"

"When the other option is fighting in the dark? Then yes, I'll take my chances! Are you in, or are you not?"

"Zuken has a tent prepared for us as a contingency!"

"Yeah, and that camp has our rations for the entire mission!" Olfric countered. "I don't know about you, but I'm not going to risk letting them take it away. If we take shelter now, we risk starving to death in the safety of your contingency."

Tanya considered his words. The sun was going down and the wards would be up in a few minutes, which meant they either had to do something now, or sit tight and wait until morning.

"We have the advantage of surprise. We can hit them hard," Olfric suggested.

Elena squeaked. "Is that really necessary?"

"Well, do *you* have a better idea?" Tanya demanded.

"Actually I do," the changeling pompously declared. "I can go in and talk to them. You know, charm them."

"I considered it. I just decided it was too brainless and predictable."

"It's simpler to just talk to them! If it doesn't work, you can always kill them then."

"That is *simpler*. But once you set foot in that camp, whoever is in charge can *simply* raise the wards. The rest of us will *simply* have to put a lot of effort into breaking down the wards, and even if we *simply* recapture the camp, it won't stop the desert monsters from coming because the wards are *simply* not there anymore!"

Zuken hummed thoughtfully. "Then what do you suggest, Tanya?"

She squinted down at the camp below. "I hate to admit it, but if we're attacking, a direct blitz is the best bet. Can you use Terramancy to hold the wards down until I clear up everything inside?"

He nodded.

"What about me?" Olfric demanded.

Tanya gave him a condescending look. "You can get me some cool water to drink after I win the camp back."

Maude cheered and let out a soft whistle.

"Ambitious," Zuken muttered. "Dangerous too. They might have spiritists of their own, and they'll definitely be on the lookout for monster attacks."

"That's why we don't give them the chance," Olfric replied. "We go in, end them for good, and take everything."

Tanya was taken aback, not expecting the aquamancer to support her on anything publicly. "Alright then." She nodded to everyone. "Let's do this."

Standing five feet in the air, levitated by the power of wind circulating beneath her feet to counter gravity, Tanya drifted through the camp while the others stayed behind. There was no mistaking the coppery stench that assaulted her nostrils.

Blood.

If she had any remaining shred of doubt about what happened inside, it was firmly extinguished.

Focusing her power, Tanya aimed at one of the seven tents. If there were people inside, they'd either be killed or grievously injured. And if there weren't, at least they would scurry out of wherever they were hiding like rats. There were very few things in life more disorienting than a sudden explosion.

Skillfully, she wove her wind around and around, over and over, spinning at speeds high enough to draw in large amounts of sand and dust had she not maintained a tight closure on all ends. The pressure grew as her creation spun faster, and she took careful aim at the center of the tent.

Tanya had always maintained ironclad control over her powers, employing only the minimum violence necessary. But here in the desert, that control looked for every opportunity to slip.

This wasn't the time to play it smart. The more overwhelming she appeared, the more her teammates would respect her strength and accept her.

A wild grin crossed her lips and she let loose.

The spinning ball of wind leaped from her hands like a living thing and streaked through the air, traveling so fast that it appeared to be little more than a blue blur. In a single instance, it crossed half the distance to the target. A moment later, the tent imploded from pure force, and the camp erupted into activity.

There were soldiers, and . . . parts of the smuggling team? She didn't know what was happening. Had the team betrayed them and joined hands with the enemy? Or was there something more sinister going on that not even Zuken saw coming?

It didn't matter. She didn't need the smugglers anymore.

Conjuring a pair of wind blades in either hand, Tanya leaped into the fray. She landed on the sand and rolled over, hurling both blades successively to her left before gracefully spinning around to avoid a sharp dagger and sending yet another blade in the attacker's direction.

The three attackers were dead before they hit the floor.

Out of the corner of her eye, she spotted Olfric slashing an enormous watery tentacle at two soldiers, cutting off one of their arms. Another, wrapped around someone's chest, smashed them against the rock wall surrounding the compound. Several boulders of pure sand smashed into the troops coming from the tent farthest from her, leaving nothing but bones and blood in their wake.

Three anxiety-filled seconds later, there was no movement.

"Okay!" Olfric yelled frantically. "Okay! Now bring the wards down! Light the Eternal Light shells!"

Zuken, Maude, and Elena quickly made their way into the premises. Still sensing no movement, Tanya relaxed her stance and reviewed her work. The camp was now theirs, as were the food supplies. She walked toward the largest tent, the one on the right with bands of metal running around the surfaces. If she were a betting woman, she'd wager this was where the food supplies were being kept.

"That was one powerful spell." Zuken waved his hand casually, gathering the surrounding desert to bury the dead bodies together into one large sand coffin.

"Doesn't surprise me one bit," Olfric added out of nowhere. "Everyone in our original team thought she was hoarding a powerful kami. At least a century old."

Silence fell.

"What?" Tanya demanded, flustered from the odd gazes she was receiving from her team.

"Well, is that true?" Zuken probed.

Tanya sighed. "It was my father's. I got it from him moments after he died."

"I'm sorry to hear that," Maude offered. "Was he an adventurer too?"

Tanya looked away, a bit of shame on her face. "Not really. I suppose you could call him a vagrant, like myself. Nowhere to go, no one to call his own. Except, well, me."

"A mercenary then." Zuken peered at her. "Are you sure you don't have nobility in your ancestry?"

"No," she deadpanned.

Everyone chuckled at that.

"Anyway," Zuken continued, clearing his throat. "I guess what I wanted to say is that you're good. Really good. A real asset to any team, especially this one."

"Gush later," Tanya said, as dryly as the sand beneath her feet. "We still have some work to do. The sun's about to go down."

"What work?" Olfric asked. "We have the camp. There are no more troops around. What's the worst that can happen?"

Tanya didn't know whether to groan or punch the man in the face. Olfric Bergott was a noble, but he was also an idiot. Intelligent people knew better than to tempt the universe like that.

Turning away, she regarded the vast desert around her.

I wonder, would you be proud of me, Father?

CHAPTER 12

MASSACRE

Tanya's mouth was agape as she took in the impossible sight before her.

According to their information, Cyffnar had appointed a troop of soldiers to patrol the anomaly caves and keep invaders away. She had estimated a small camp—maybe twenty or so soldiers—close to the cavernous openings, banking on the desert's curse to keep the count low. After the previous night's skirmish, she had optimistically considered the majority of their "Cyffnar" problem to be taken care of.

Clearly, that wasn't the case.

"This isn't a camp!" Maude exclaimed from behind her. "It's a freaking city!"

It was an overstatement, but only just so. An enormous square of stakewall was built around the soldiers' encampments and stores, with two gates leading in and out of the base camp. Tents of blackened fabric, too many to count, were laid out row after row, and smaller barrels and equipment were strewn around, like flies buzzing around a sleeping beast.

Tanya's gaze landed on the five interspersed cavernous openings in the middle of the fortified complex. Entire cohorts of men were in formation practicing combat and maneuvers while being drilled by officers riding atop bicorns. Terramancers were working on additional openings to get mineral deposits out of the anomaly, while aquamancers filled a central lagoon of water for people and animals to drink from. All the while, beast tamers patrolled the periphery.

"This is one of the times I wish I wasn't right," Zuken sighed. "Cyffnar plans to drain this anomaly dry before the Black Moon wanes."

"You expected this to happen?" Tanya asked.

"Not to this level, but . . . I always bet on people being greedy." He grimaced.

Tanya licked her lips and peered at the garrison. "If we want to get into the caverns, we have to go through them. It seems like a terrible idea no matter which way you slice it."

Olfric snorted. "Scared already?"

Tanya raised an eyebrow at him, and then glanced at his feet.

Olfric followed her line of sight and staggered back.

The shadow followed.

"Why doesn't it just—" he began, stomping on the sand, hoping to distort the shadow and make it vanish.

She rolled her eyes. Out of her entire team, the shadows seemed to affect Olfric the most. It was amusing, but not unexpected. Maude was a half vanir that held no reservations about her lack of faith in the Asukan gods. Elena was a changeling, plain and simple; a few ljósálfars held only minor positions in the Asukan pantheon. Olfric, however, was a devout Asukan to the core, so his fear of the shadows was a no-brainer.

But it was Zuken's reaction that truly surprised her.

Zuken Banksi displayed himself as a man of personal strength and mental fortitude. His prowess in Terramancy bolstered his nerves to extraordinary levels, allowing him to maintain his composure in even the most stressful situations. Even so, his apparent nonchalance about the presence of shadows beneath his feet raised all sorts of red flags in Tanya's mind.

Pay attention, but don't point it out, she told herself. She was there to do her job and gain her freedom, not pry into secrets that had nothing to do with her.

"For the Goddess's sake, Bergott, it's a fucking shadow," she snapped. "I get that it's difficult to swallow for someone who's lived his entire life in the Eternal Light, but your reactions are ridiculous. Get it through your overinflated noble head. When light falls on an object, it generates a shadow. Not because it's a curse or darkspawn, but because the object is obstructing the light's path."

Olfric stood quietly, frowning as he tried to imagine such a thing.

"I've traveled to the other side of the Graken Mountains," Tanya said. "The lands there are still blessed with the Eternal Light, but only weakly. Sooner or later, you'll find yourself in a corner stained with shadows. I spent an entire year in that place and I turned out just fine."

"What were you doing there all by yourself?" Elena asked.

"This and that."

Elena gave her the stink eye, which Tanya promptly ignored.

"What are we, you know . . ." Maude trailed off, gesturing toward the Cyffnarians. "Going to do about this?"

"This isn't some regular border patrol," Zuken said, carefully observing the soldiers. "They're professional military. Cyffnar is spending serious coin to make sure their operation goes smoothly."

"We could report this anonymously to the shogun," Olfric suggested. "He can demand answers from Lord Straff."

Tanya grimaced. Lord Straff was the shogun of the Eaborid Kingdom, of which Cyffnar was only a mere part. She had encountered the man only once in her life, and he'd made a terrible first impression.

"And what will that accomplish?" Zuken drawled. "All bureaucratic work is down until the moon wanes. I'd bet my life these people are privately funded to squeeze the anomaly dry and clean everything up before the Waning. Even if our government accuses them of something fishy, they can always deny it." He looked away. "No doubt the men would kill us immediately if they spot us, and no one would know any better. Besides, don't forget why we are here."

"We could always fight them," Tanya offered.

But Zuken shook his head. "The three of us might be able to put up a strong resistance. But someone still needs to protect Elena and Maude, and we can't do that if we're busy defending ourselves."

"I can protect myself!" Maude began.

Tanya observed that Elena made no attempt to counter Zuken's opinion of her.

"What about digging our way through?" Tanya offered. At everyone's blank looks, she explained. "The anomaly is beneath us, right? And we have a proficient terramancer on our team. Why don't we dig ourselves there?"

"We can't dig anywhere within scanning distance from their camp," Zuken explained. "Plus, if we dig during the day, the heat will strike us down. And digging at night will be . . ." He left the rest unsaid.

"We could dig from our own camp!" Maude exclaimed. "It's not like anything's coming after us there, even at night."

"Maybe, but there's also the time factor," Olfric chimed in. "I doubt an underground anomaly will be near the surface. For all we know, it could be half a mile deep. Digging that far with such time constraints would set us back by several days. And that's assuming the anomaly even goes beneath our camp."

Tanya looked at Zuken, and he glanced back at her, his face troubled. She could see the reflection of her own thoughts and fears in his eyes. A lot was dependent on the success of this mission, and they were already being pushed back by several steps at the starting line itself.

They needed a game changer—something to win this unwinnable situation. An unstoppable force that could blitz through the garrison like it meant nothing. And conveniently enough, she had one. But revealing it might cause problems for her down the road.

But Zuken and the others aren't here to commit Sin. They wouldn't mind. Though . . .

Trying to restrain it was difficult on the best of days. Here, there was no Eternal Light, and add in the fact that they were in the middle of a cursed desert . . .

But why restrain? a dark part of her pointed out. *Look at all those spiritists. Will they be restrained when they attack you?*

But—

This is your last chance to gain everything you want. Money. Freedom. Your purpose on this team is to Sin. What does a little more or less matter in the face of that?

Tanya remained silent.

You cannot hide it forever.

She wanted to deny it. To tell herself that she could. That she could lock that part of herself away forever, and pretend like it didn't exist.

But it would be a lie.

"Tanya?" Zuken inquired. "You've been awfully quiet. What's on your mind?"

Tanya came to a decision. "You were right earlier," she said. "About my kami. It's strong. Very strong. Strong enough that most of my power is spent in restraining its power rather than using it. I can take them down if I go all out."

She carefully regarded her teammates' reactions. Elena was curious. Zuken was cautious. Olfric was skeptical. And Maude . . . Maude had a shadow of a knowing smile on her face. By the winds, just what impression did the vanir have of her, and why?

"How many?"

"All of them."

Olfric laughed aloud. "I know the desert will amplify your wind attacks, but you're still far too sure of yourself. I'll admit that *distraction* of yours earlier was interesting, but it's nowhere close to what we need to decimate them all. You're only going to get yourself killed."

"How touching!" Tanya smirked. "I didn't know you cared."

He bristled. "If we lose our Sinner, this mission is over."

Tanya looked at the sun overhead. The enchantments they had on to protect themselves from the searing heat would last another half hour at best. After that, they'd have to return to camp or take shelter amidst the sands. "Trust me. I know I can."

"How?" the aquamancer repeated.

"I can . . . manifest it in its bound state."

Silence fell upon the group.

" . . . what did you just say?" Olfric croaked.

Tanya chuckled at his gobsmacked expression. Not that she could blame him, really. The concept of kami binding was the core of being a spiritist. Using the Shikigami Ritual, one was able to bind a kami to their soul by sacrificing an appropriate portion of their Soul Capacity. By doing so, the spiritist could utilize the kami's skills, albeit in a far more diluted and controlled fashion. It was what allowed ordinary bremetans, who by nature should have been able to wield only lifeforce, to become terramancers, aeromancers, aquamancers, and so on.

Sacrificing potential to gain control over an element. That was the primary philosophy behind spiritism.

On the other hand, what she was suggesting was—

"That's just stupid!" Zuken replied, his tone carefully toeing the line between bewilderment and skepticism. "The Shikigami Ritual binds the kami to our souls. Manifesting them means shattering those restraints and undoing the ritual. There is no . . . keeping it bound once you've manifested it. You may as well kiss your kami goodbye."

Tanya shrugged. "I've said this before, and I'll say it again. It's a big world out there. One that doesn't always conform to Asukan beliefs." When Zuken said nothing else in protest, she glanced around, daring the others to contradict her. "I say we return to camp for now, gather everything we need, and prepare to attack this evening—"

"How would you do it?" Olfric asked out of nowhere. There was a surprising lack of hostility in his tone. "Is such a thing even possible?"

"You'll see," she replied mysteriously.

The group quickly rushed back to their own camp, the one they took over the previous day. They had gotten everything they needed packed up for the mission while ensuring they wouldn't be slowed down by the extra weight. That meant leaving behind a lion's share of the food and other resources. Olfric kept the majority of the grenades in his bag, much to everyone's amusement, while Zuken packed a bottle of oil and some cotton to avoid over-dependence on torches.

Maude and Elena washed the blood and dirt off the clothes of the dead soldiers from the camp, all except one. Maude was going to pretend to be wounded and hurt. The idea was to pretend to be Cyffnarian troops so they could get past the camp's gates without drawing unnecessary attention.

"Alright," Zuken began as they neared the Cyffnarian encampment once more. "I'll be going over the plan one last time. If you have any questions, ask them now." When nobody interrupted, he continued. "Between Elena's charming and Maude's wounds, we should be able to lower their suspicions. Once inside, Elena can rile up the bicorns inside and set them astray. While Tanya takes advantage of the distraction and wreaks havoc, the rest of us will grab bicorns and race toward the caverns."

Maude raised a hand. "Will it really be safe to ride them after they've gone crazy?"

Elena smiled at her. "Leave that to me."

"I'll ride with you then." The half vanir chuckled. "Wounded, remember?"

"Moving on," Zuken continued, "as we ride, most of the troops should be going toward Tanya because she's the most noticeable. I'll take the back guard to keep anyone from coming behind us, while Olfric takes the front. Maude says she can maintain a healing circle around us so long as we stay together."

The naturopath in question nodded. "Ten feet max. Any more and you're on your own."

Elena looked at Tanya. "Is there anything you want to tell us before we attack? Something to raise morale?"

Tanya blinked. "Uh, yeah, sure. This is going to suck and you should expect horrible things to happen to each of us. So don't let your guard down."

Elena crossed her arms and pouted. "I was looking for something *inspiring*."

"Inspiration leads to overconfidence," Olfric replied.

"Don't side with her!" she yelled.

"There's just one thing I can't place," Olfric continued, squinting. "The caverns are fairly far from the ward line. Even riding bicorns, it will take us at least fifteen minutes to cover the distance. How is she"—he glanced at Tanya—"going to fight while riding a bicorn?"

"I won't need one," Tanya promised.

"Then?"

Her smile became predatory. "You'll see."

Their plan went into motion fabulously. Between Elena's allaying powers, their Cyffnarian attire, and the wounds on Maude's body, they passed through the border patrol without any issues. It turned out that the soldiers who raided their camp were supposed to return after eliminating the smuggling crew. After that, everything else just fell into place; it was almost insulting how easy it was.

Then, it was time for the first distraction. Tanya wouldn't have believed it if she hadn't seen it firsthand.

One moment, Elena was conversing with the crowd, and in the next, several of the bicorns neighed furiously, rattling against their chains as if the end of the world was nigh. Some quick-and-dirty Terramancy on Zuken's part broke through their bindings, taking care of the rest.

And now, as her team hopped onto the two-horned equines, it was her turn to step up.

Rolling her neck, Tanya began to alter the air currents around her. Siphoning them backward allowed her to propel forward in whatever direction she wanted. Adding in a little gravity manipulation trick she'd learned back in Maluscion, and to any neutral observer, it would look like she was flying.

"*She can FLY?!*"

She smirked at Olfric's fading screech as he rode toward the caverns.

Of course, flying had its own share of issues. She could dodge if she saw the projectile coming at her, and she could even weave through attack patterns. But attacking while maintaining flight was still beyond her. Taking a single shot would mess up her balance and send her plummeting.

But that was fine. It was simply a method to get away from the others and attract attention. Before she *really* got started.

"Attack!" roared a Cyffnarian soldier, wielding one of the greatswords preferred by the Cobalt Army. Tanya landed on the ground and rushed toward the nearest soldier coming toward her. She aimed a hit at his elbow, reversed the hilt of his sword, and shoved it straight through his stomach.

He was dead before he hit the ground.

More steel glittered ahead of her. Tanya pulled the heavy sword out of the slain soldier's gut and sent it flying at the next attacker, a bit of Aeromancy doubling the sword's speed. Her opponent was skilled enough to deflect the sword's blow, but not fast enough to dodge the blade of wind hidden underneath that pierced through his neck.

Two gone. Tons more to go.

"AEROMANCER!" someone yelled, and before she knew it, the ground in front of her shot up into spikes that aimed for her face. Tanya leaped back with three somersaults and sent a concussive blast of wind at her opponents. But one of them raised a sand wall, proving himself to be yet another terramancer, while the other stepped out of the way, with only a cut on the cheek to show for it.

"Nimble, ain'tcha?" commented one of the swordsmen circling her like a predator. Between the two terramancers and two sword-wielding soldiers, she was effectively locked in place. Any wind attacks would be instantly blocked by walls, while the swordsmen carefully wove their way closer and closer to her.

Taking a deep breath, Tanya closed her eyes, before snapping them wide open. Alert. Focused. No more reservations, or holding back for the sake of holding back. The battle was hers to win, and she would guide it in whatever direction she saw fit.

Her show of confidence didn't faze them in the slightest. The first swordsman came at her from the side, her twin swords spinning like dazzling blurs while a terramancer charged from the back with a chunk of rock cloaking his fist. A second swordsman slid under her guard, aiming for a sweeping slash of her legs.

Three against one. A splendid tactic to take her down before she could react.

But, for all their coordination, it didn't change the fact that they were simply too slow.

Tanya blurred into motion. The twin-sword user's eyes widened and the blades twirling around her wrists abruptly *clanged* above her in a blocking cross.

A heartbeat later, a wind hammer smashed against the woman's hastily pre-pared guard. The swordsman strained, and she buckled when a slashing gesture tore through her legs.

Tanya backflipped and grabbed the terramancer by the wrist, redirecting his motion toward the ground as she flipped him over her shoulder. She spat a wind blade into the man's eyes at the same time as she grasped the hilt of the other swordsman's sword, snatching it out of his hands.

The man stared back at her, resignation written all over his face. " . . . This is going to hurt, isn't it?"

"A little," she admitted.

A second later, the soldier's decapitated head bounced along the sandy floor.

"FIRE!" came a shout, and a volley of flaming arrows sped toward Tanya. One second, she felt the stirring of wind around her, pressing against her in just the right ways, shaping her body into the proper angle, propelling herself into the air. The very next, she was high up in the air with a bird's-eye view of the large contingent gathered below her.

In the distance, Zuken and the others were being chased by a cavalry despite his and Olfric's attempts at keeping them away. A large group of spiritists were waiting for them midway, while archers stood at attention, ready to take them out from afar. Finally, there was—

Oh no! A pincer attack—

"AAGH FUCK!" Tanya cried, feeling a sharp surge of agony as a metal arrow stabbed through her calf. The sudden pain knocked her off-balance, making her vulnerable to gravity once more. She barely managed to pour wind under her feet in time to avoid getting a broken leg.

"Well, well, what do we have here?" came an ominous voice. Behind her, a strongly built man crossed his arms and looked down at her with a mix of condescension and pity. "A tiny, injured birdie. Where did you come from, little girl?"

Tanya ignored his words and focused on his wristbands. Crimson. Three layers. He was a pyromancer, and a damn good one at that. Two pairs of swordsmen took positions behind him, while another three scimitar-wielding warriors circled back around her. What was it with these Cyffnarians and try-ing to intimidate her with numbers?

"It looked like there was a party." She shrugged, standing back up with a grimace. "So I decided to join in on the fun. But frankly, it's been a little disappointing."

"Is that so?" The pyromancer grinned, his yellow teeth on full display. "Get her."

Tanya watched the approaching troop with detached interest. Her eyes hardened and became ice-cold, and she made a motion of rubbing errant dust off of her shoulders. She knew that she would have no trouble taking them down, because she knew something they didn't. A fundamental truth, of sorts.

Most people were not prepared to die.

They weren't prepared for the possibility that their final moment was approaching. One could not function if they constantly lived in fear of that demise. And so they chose to pretend that everything was fine. They rubbed shoulders and took solace in the collective lie that they told one another.

It was why this group of soldiers approached the lone injured aeromancer with gleeful grins, not stopping to consider that the same woman had slaughtered half a dozen of their men just moments ago.

Tanya smiled. She would teach them better.

She grabbed the neck of the nearest person, dragged his jaws open, and—*power flowed into her*—sent a blast of wind through his mouth. Quickly accelerating herself to the left, she circulated wind around her right arm and pierced straight through another's chest.

More power flowed in.

Her left hand played with force. Her right hand bent the wind. Her immediate vicinity was filled with a series of sickening cracks and groans as she systematically aimed for their essential bones with a mechanical precision.

Femurs. Knees. Elbows. Ankles. Ribs. Spine. Skull.

"MY ARM!"

—power—

"SH—*ARKK*!"

—more power—

"MONSTER!"

"Someone HEL—!"

—more, more, more—

Horrified, begging, gurgling screeches dripped out of their dying mouths as the soldiers fell to the ground—some on their knees, others face-first, but all of them broken by her actions. Tanya jerked her hand back and punched someone at the base of his spine, her fingers grabbing at something far more powerful and metaphysical than bone.

It surged into her—

—Tanya crushed the man's vertebrae, dropping him to the floor like a stringless puppet. She looked at the spiraling, contorting web of energy in her hand and felt it sink into her body.

Lifeforce Gained—3466

She had nearly forgotten the euphoric feeling. Every time she sank her fingers into someone, their lifeforce—their very lifeblood—became hers. Hers to tear out. Hers to use. Her to *consume*. But it didn't matter. It wasn't like these people—*FOOD*—would have used it properly anyway.

But . . .

"Should it be so easy to end a life?" she asked aloud, to no one in particular.

The large pyromancer from before coughed out a glob of blood onto the ground. "Now I see. You're no Asukan, are ya? You're something else, ain'tcha? A deviant fuckin' bastard."

"You're still here?" Tanya wondered. "I thought you'd have run away by now."

The man cackled, undeterred by her icy gaze. "Run? *Run?* Are you fuckin' serious? The kind of mezals I'm gonna get from the Cobalt Army when I send a deviant packing is—is—"

His mouth opened and closed, but no words came out.

His hands twitched, but they no longer moved.

His eyes widened as he screamed silently, in a voice that no one could hear. And then he died. Just like that.

. . .

Tanya snorted. "So much for that." She turned toward the caverns leading into the anomaly, where her teammates were waiting for her. It was going to be weird explaining what had happened to them, especially considering she hadn't unleashed her kami at all.

But the lifeforce tasted wonderful.

A satisfied sigh escaped her lips as Tanya stared up at the Black Moon. With no further ado, she began to walk toward her destination, uncaring of the piles of bodies that littered her path.

THE BEATEN PATH

I t happened twelve years ago.

Back then, she believed she knew what it meant to be the heiress of the Shimizu Clan, one of the Sacred Eight of the Asukan Empire. She had thought she understood.

Then one day, her father told her everything.

And Tanya realized how truly little she knew.

She remembered it like it was yesterday. A medley of emotions danced across Yanric Shimizu's face, twisting his features into something she couldn't recognize. Even in the illumination of the Eternal Light, it was like peering through a foggy window, despite them sitting right next to one another.

She had passed her apprenticeship from the Susanoo Shrine in Cyffnar, and her results had shown her to be a promising candidate for spiritist training. Her lifeforce was above average, and her Soul Capacity was head and shoulders above what most bremetans of her level could boast of. She had a solid grasp of holy theory and demonstrated a perfect execution of the Shikigami Ritual to her examiners.

Tanya was ready for more. Her teachers had trained her in a fighting style best suited to rapid, fluidic movements used to set up sharp lethal attacks. She had picked it up like a fish to water. There was no doubt that a water-type kami would complement her perfectly. She'd been elated about it. And as a Shimizu, it was now her birthright to be taken to the Shimizu Well and granted the opportunity to choose her familiar. Her *kami*.

But they did not go to the well.

Instead, her father brought her to a solitary room in the heart of the compound, with nothing but worn tatami mats beneath their feet and wards to protect them from prying eyes and ears.

And he had many secrets to share. Not one or two, but many. Dozens. Hundreds. In a room where no one else would ever learn of the words spoken between them, her father told her all the secrets of their clan.

Asukans were not good people.

Not honest. Not kind. Not fair. One did not get to the top of the food chain by having those virtues. One did that by ambition, ruthlessness, and betrayal, and the Shimizu Clan was no different. They had their own skeletons in their closet, both literal and metaphorical. An entire clan of Asukans that was centuries old, whose secrets could have filled a graveyard. And yet, they could not allow them to be forgotten.

As the daughter of the current Clan-Lord, that meant Tanya would one day carry the burden of all those secrets. Graduation from the Shrine was the perfect opportunity to be inducted into the dirtier aspects of becoming an heiress.

Yanric, her father, chose to begin with the most relevant of them all.

Kami.

Elements made manifest in an ethereal body, granted consciousness by the blessing of the Great Goddess. And it was only thanks to the Goddess that an Asukan learned to wield their powers. That was what she was taught at the Shrine.

Wrong, her father had said. Kami were apparitions, creatures of consciousness and perception that no Asukan would ever be able to comprehend. Creatures from the Ikai Realm—the World of the Other. A world that ran parallel to their own, a world where the *yokai* dwelt.

"But that can't be true," she had stressed. Vehemently so. "The yokai are all gone. No spirit can possibly enter the land of Eternal Light freely."

Her father had laughed.

"What do you think the well is?"

It was when he had told her the truth.

"The well is nothing more than a hole, a tear in reality itself that connects our territory with a place that's neither in this world, nor in the Other, yet seamlessly fits into both. A borderland."

"Borderland . . ."

"These are places where reality meets fantasy." Nostalgia shone from her father's eyes. "A place so saturated with mana that most bremetans would suffocate within an hour. It's where these kami are from. Their zone of power, their dominion."

"And . . . you've been there?"

Yanric laughed. "Every ambitious adventurer has tried to enter into borderlands at least once in their lifetime. The idea of catching a wild kami is a dream that's hard to ditch, even for the staunchest Asukan."

"Then the well—"

"It is a trap. Once the kami has your attention, you lure it out, through the well into the real world where the Eternal Light can weaken them, make them vulnerable, susceptible to their control."

"That feels like cheating!"

Yanric laughed at that answer. "My little princess! What would you have us do? Fight a kami inside its own dominion? No one but the kings can even think of making that attempt."

"But then—"Tanya had scrunched her face. "Why did they lie to me at the Shrine?"

Yanric had sighed at that. "Because the truth is a dangerous thing, daughter. Can you imagine what would happen if every bremetan out there tried to enter into wild borderlands in hopes of capturing kami?"

Tanya swallowed.

"It'd be a massacre. Doubly so if the kami came out and there was no one to bind it. That is why the kami binding is performed at the Shrines, under supervision. Or in private wells, like ours."

Tanya understood it that night. It had nothing to do with truth and deception. It was about control. And control was the lifeblood of the Empire. And what greater control than having a powerful kami under one's command?

"You will not be performing the Shikigami Ritual," Yanric told his distraught daughter, "because you are born for greatness. I can't have you wasting your Potential behind a newborn kami."

"But Father—"

"No, Tanya. You will achieve what I could not. What my father could not. Come with me."

Yanric stood up and folded one of the tatami mats, revealing a secret door beneath with stairs that went downward. Silently, Tanya descended behind her father until they were standing in front of a cubicle made of what appeared to be glass. And inside it was . . .

Something.

It seemed to have been crafted out of air, only thicker. Like someone had gathered all the air in the compound and forced it together. Gelatinous in appearance, the thing had blackened, metallic constructs placed upon it. Though, it was more apt to say that the thing was wearing those constructs like a soldier wore armor.

"This is Ezzeron," her father explained at her confused look.

"Who?"

He smiled indulgently. "Do you not remember your great-grandfather Wakamura?"

Tanya arched an eyebrow. "Really? You're asking if I don't remember the legendary Wind King? He's made our Clan what it is."

Yanric gestured back to the cube. "This is the source of his power. His kami, Ezzeron."

Tanya's eyes widened to saucers. She couldn't believe her father's words. She couldn't believe what she was seeing with her own eyes. This—this was the *Wind King's* kami?

"You—you can't be serious!" she exclaimed. "This is—this is just—"

"Unbelievable?" Yanric suggested. "I assure you. Ezzeron is very real."

"But it's—"

"After your grandfather's demise, the emperor allowed our Clan to retain the kami for ourselves. An incentive for Wakamura's descendants to rise up and meet the requirements to tame the untamable Ezzeron. Whoever did that would have a chance to become the next Wind King."

Tanya studied her father for several seconds, trying to appraise the man. She knew that there existed five titles in the Empire, and their holders were unparalleled in the manipulation of their respective elements. The positions of Wind King and Ether King were lying dormant, with the death of her great grandfather close to a century ago, and the Ether King's far before that—patiently waiting for the next claimant to take their place.

"What does that have to do with me?" she asked.

Yanric knelt down and placed his hands on her shoulders. "Neither I nor your grandfather were strong enough to come even close to taming Ezzeron. My father had been . . . devastated when he failed to take up his father's title. A burden that then fell upon me when I came of age. But I too, like my father, failed. You, on the other hand . . ."

Tanya stood still, waiting. She knew what was about to come.

"I know your potential. Every single elder of our Clan does. We know that someday, you will rise to become a Pathforger just like your great-grandfather. It is in your blood. It is in your soul."

"But Father—"

"Tanya!" her father asserted. "You are my greatest joy, and my greatest hope. The Shimizu Clan has failed to rise up to the challenge for two consecutive generations. If we fail a third, the Empire might not look at us favorably. The status of being one of the Sacred Eight is at stake, and only you can keep it from being taken away. You must tame Ezzeron."

Tanya flinched. Her father's blind faith in her was touching, but this was Ezzeron. It was at least several centuries old and had been in the family for at least three generations now. Shikigami Rituals were about domination. About balance. About being the immovable object against the overwhelming force that were kami. Trying to tame this nigh-invincible spirit was not just fool-hardy. It was madness.

"Obviously you cannot do that now," Yanric admitted. "But you will some-day. Until then, I wish for you to train yourself in lifeforce, make yourself indomitable in mind, body, and spirit until you can match Ezzeron's might. *That* is the destiny I see for you, my daughter. You will fulfill my wish, won't you? You will make sure we don't lose our pride?"

" . . . Undoubtedly," Tanya replied, an unmistakable tightness in her voice. She could feel her dreams of being an aquamancer go down the drain. Her fighting style, her perfected skills—all of them would no longer matter. She'd have to renew her training, develop a combat style in Aeromancy, no matter how difficult it might be.

Because that was what the Clan expected of her.

"I'll . . ." Her heart broke, even as her visage stayed firm. "I'll do my best."

Yanric hugged her gently. "I know you will, my child. I know you will."

He never noticed the small tear that trickled down her cheek.

PART III

Fork in the Road

CHAPTER 13

SUCKER PUNCH

SOULSCAPE	
NAME	Lukas Aguilar
Type	Base Host
Level	4
OMPHALOS ATTRIBUTES	
Energy Reservoir Capacity	∞
Current Energy Level	722,436,714 units
OMPHALOS FUNCTIONS	
Scan	Level 1
Analyze	Level 1

Damn," Lukas muttered, banging his head gently against the stone wall before him. "Damn, damn, *damn!*"

"I know you came to the realization a while ago. My words merely confirmed it," Inanna whispered in his ears. **"Then why this reaction now?"**

Glaring at someone was difficult when you couldn't see them, so he settled for angrily glaring at the wall instead. And when that wasn't satisfactory, he glared at the Screen, as if willing it to change from his intense gaze alone.

"I realized it, yeah, but it was only a theory. The more I think about it, the more real it's becoming. The Screen is more confirmation, and your words even more so."

"If you choose to believe in me, then yes."

"Would you cancel our bargain if I said I didn't?"

Inanna chuckled derisively.

"Yeah, I didn't think so," he grumbled. "The way I see it, I can either choose to believe you or just paw around in the dark. Maybe you're right, or maybe you're wrong and delusional. Maybe I'm an idiot for taking this at face value. And maybe you'll look at this moment in the near future and say *I told you so.* In the end, it comes down to a single thing."

"And what is that?"

"You're the one with the answers. And I'm not."

"A sound argument. One you would do well not to forget." She briefly paused. **"You appear quite distressed."**

"Shouldn't I be?" he bit out, gritting his teeth. "My planet's fucking omphalos is inside me. If that's here, then what's over there?"

He punched the wall. The act bruised his knuckles, but the pain didn't make his inner confusion go away.

"Your world is a lostbelt."

"What?"

"A lostbelt," Inanna repeated. **"There have been events in the past when a realm has its connection with the Origin hindered. It can escape into the blackness of the In-Between."**

"What happens to them?" Lukas asked curiously. "These lostbelts?"

"They become existences in their own right. Realms that depend upon their own reserves to grow until they run out of fuel. And when that happens . . ."

"They shatter," he murmured. "Is that what happened to Earth?"

"I cannot say for certain. This is the only time I have been in one. It is possible your lostbelt stopped supplying the creatures born upon it with Potential as a way to counter the shortage of its energy."

"But wouldn't that have stagnated its growth?"

"Survival at the expense of stagnation," the goddess speculated with disgust. **"Hardly an enviable choice. I can say with certainty that a shard of its omphalos has fused with you, making you an anomaly while keeping its memories."**

Memories? Lukas frowned. "I don't have any mem—"

"The omphalos in you has memories of the lostbelt. You, on the other hand, are merely its host, a consciousness that happens to reside within the body."

"It's *my* body."

"Not anymore," the goddess flippantly replied.

Lukas moved his arms and legs around as if to prove a point.

"Your attempt at levity will not alter the facts, mortal. I will be candid. This is the first time I have encountered something as novel as yourself."

"I don't know whether to be flattered or amused."

"Perhaps both. An omphalos will always choose to mutate matter around it, living or inanimate. The shard could have done nearly anything to you."

"Maybe it didn't have time?" he offered. "You did tell me you brought us here right after."

"**True,**" she agreed, "**but there are an endless number of things it could have done regardless. If nothing else, it could have used your body as its primary material and crafted a proper anomaly. Perhaps combining it with rocks and metals and such.**"

Lukas was mentally greeted by the image of his own mangled body, in some kind of weird rock-khorkhoi amalgamation.

He shuddered.

"**But it did not. Instead, the shard left you as you were and accepted your body as a fully functional anomaly. No more or less complete, but an anomaly nonetheless. A system that can grow, hunt down prey, and gain everything that it desires. I suppose the best way to describe you would be a . . . wildcard.**"

"Well, what does it want from me then?"

"**What do you think it wants?**"

Lukas hummed in thought. What did a place like this want? He looked at the dank caverns all around him—the tunnels, the caves, the mossy outgrowths, the monsters. Hell, there was even fresh water here. It was a perfect, isolated biosphere. Yet it was also a creature, one that created monsters.

But to do what?

Eliminate prey. The answer was violently obvious. He'd seen it glaring at him several times in his recent past.

What did the prey give it? Sustenance? He had seen the azolgs eat each other, though. Any physical sustenance would go to the predators themselves, not the anomaly that was the Crypt of Fiendish Worms.

He was an anomaly. What did he get when he eliminated prey?

Experience.

The Experience gathered over time, and then depending on his Experience Conversion Ratio, it would be converted to Soul Capacity when he leveled up. But that was just him. Inanna had said every organism had a schema like his, and so functioned similarly to him. It wasn't special to an anomaly.

He rubbed the bridge of his nose. Maybe he was looking at it from the wrong perspective. An anomaly was, very technically, a living thing. Only it employed monsters that it created to do its bidding. The more a creature fought, the more its skills grew, as his own did. If this anomaly was creating these creatures, it must've had genetic blueprints at hand. Add in the concept of Potential and leveling up . . .

"It's using prey to strengthen its creatures," Lukas muttered in awe. "It learns from the battles, and once they level up, it uses newer, modified blueprints to create stronger creatures."

"**Correct. But there is one more aspect to it that you are not seeing. Of**

course, I do not blame you. You cannot see it from your limited sensory perception, and thus remain ignorant of it."

Leave it to Inanna to make anything sound like an insult.

"Any creature that perishes inside an anomaly has its soul absorbed into it. It is later used to create new monsters based on this."

"So," Lukas mused. "That means if I die here—"

"Yes. The crypt will be able to create life-forms based on yourself."

Even scarier was the unsaid implication hanging ominously between her words. If an anomaly absorbed the souls of creatures that died in it, then the souls would go to the omphalos like data to a hard drive. A soul-storing hard drive.

"So, if Earth was this lostbelt you spoke of, then the millions of species on Earth, their souls, they're all there in its omphalos, right?"

"It is possible," Inanna said.

"But I don't see any. I'm just me, and if my body is the anomaly, then that makes this Screen an interface. Connecting my mind to this anomaly—yes—yes, that makes this—" He narrowed his eyes. "Show me the list of creatures whose souls are stored in the omphalos."

Access denied.

Lukas blinked. If nothing else, it proved her words to be correct. Thank God for small mercies.

"You are welcome."

He rolled his eyes, focusing his attention back onto the Screen. This interface was his only chance at obtaining information without having to bargain.

"Why am I denied access?"

Base Host not authorized for access to System Configuration in the current protocol.

"And what is the current Protocol?"

Babysitter Protocol

Inanna's peals of laughter rang in his ears.

"Funny," he deadpanned. "What does the protocol do?"

BABYSITTER PROTOCOL
A system set up to ensure the survival of amateur Host.

That made sense. In an annoying way.

"Well, good for you. But I'm skilled now. What's the next stage?"

Access denied.

Lukas mentally counted down from ten. If someone was trying to subtly teach him that he had a long way to go still, then they were succeeding at it. At teaching, that was. Certainly not at being subtle.

He tried another avenue. "What are omphalos functions?"

Operational faculties available to an anomaly for survival and growth.

That was good news. By that logic, since he also counted as an anomaly, he should technically have the same share of functions that most anomalies did. "What are the basic functions of anomalies?"

Insufficient data.

Lukas sighed. He supposed it was overly optimistic of him to think he'd get all the facts so easily. Luckily for him, he had an expert on the subject ready to answer his questions. Maybe the bargain wasn't such a bad deal after all.

He immediately hesitated at the thought, wary of the slippery slope he was treading. It was hard not to feel the occasional yearning for a taste of the power his resident goddess promised. He had no doubt she would keep her word in a bargain. Knowledge, power, companionship, and everything else he could possibly want would be at his fingertips.

But he would also be beholden to her. Never free.

Inanna chortled again.

"What are the functions that anomalies have in general?" he asked.

"You realize that anomalies are normally creations of earth and other elements, not walking, talking, frail mortal bodies of flesh and bone?"

"Well, yes, but if I know what the basic functions are, I can work out what they would translate into in my unique case since I probably have functions built for my fleshy environment."

"Very well. There are four: mutation, assimilation, rejuvenation, and creation."

His hand twitched as the sudden urge to find a notebook and jot things down overwhelmed him.

"Mutation. An anomaly mutates the terrain around it and reforms it in its own image. Assimilation. An anomaly assimilates the souls of prey it consumes. Rejuvenation. An anomaly rejuvenates any portion of itself deemed to be an injury to its body. Creation. An anomaly creates monsters and environmental adaptations to increase its defensive and offensive capabilities. These are the four fundamental functions of every anomaly. It may, however, develop more attributes to serve its purpose."

Lukas considered what he already had. His Scan and Analyze functions probably counted as information gathering of some sort. A scanner to identify new creatures, an analysis program to identify it—in case it turned out to be a new one; then he could proceed with incapacitation—elimination through combat, and finally assimilation. The last one, he was still a bit unclear about, mostly because he couldn't see it happening.

He went back to the four fundamentals. A mutation function, how would that work? Mutating his body? He doubted that would be the brightest thing to try. Assimilation mostly had to do with feeding his omphalos with new creatures; it was nothing of consequence to him or his survival, as far as he could tell.

Creation held some promise. It would've been nice to spontaneously create things as he needed them. Considering what he'd learned about skills, even the most rudimentary creation was probably a ways away for someone as inexperienced as him.

That left rejuvenation. Healing. Repair of body tissue. Protection from diseases and the like. It was something that every living body had by virtue of its nature, including his own. Only so far, he'd healed at the rate of natural human healing. Seeing Inanna's spell act upon him had been wonderful, but she had subtly implied that her Alleviation skill did not follow the natural order.

The natural order . . .

Lukas closed his eyes. He focused on the bruises in his right hand, on how it felt. The pain, the damaged skin, the oozing blood. He knew the human body's immune system acted as soon as receptors brought forth information about a potential injury. If his body was also an anomaly, then surely it would trigger something within the omphalos if he thought about it enough—

New OMPHALOS FUNCTION added!		
FUNCTION	**LEVEL**	**ENERGY COST**
Prophylaxis	**1**	**(Variable)**
DESCRIPTION		
A healing function that operates on one wound at a time until it heals. Limited to physical restoration.		

Something thick and viscous oozed out of his bleeding knuckles and covered the entire area of the bruise, turning it into a patchwork of dermal cells that spread across the entire area like a fungus. Before he knew it, the tips of his knuckles were back to what they had been. Even the scratches from earlier were now covered under fresh, blemish-free skin.

"Impressive. I daresay your chances at survival are no longer nearly as pathetic."

Coming from someone like Inanna, that was practically singing his praises. A part of him was exhilarated at the thought of acquiring a healing skill as an omphalos function, especially since it would cost him no Soul Capacity to obtain. And given the seemingly endless amount of energy he had at his command, he was confident he could heal himself over and over in the future.

Then there was the other part of him. The part that stared at his new skin, eyes wide in horror as its significance finally sank in. Inanna was right. His body wasn't his any longer. It was an anomaly.

He was an anomaly.

"There is something else you are ignoring," Inanna replied, sounding all too happy with herself. **"With this great success of yours, I have completed my end of our bargain."**

"That's not true," he blurted out. "I still have other questions I want to ask about—"

"Not this bargain. The other one."

Lukas froze. The other bargain. The one where he'd held himself hostage to force her to teach him how to heal himself.

"And now you have. You did not specify any particular details or premises. In fact, I explicitly stated you would gain no skills from this. I have fulfilled my end of the accord, and you will never again hold yourself hostage during a bargain with me."

This he had certainly not seen coming. In hindsight, he should've noticed something was odd when she'd offered him information so freely. But he had been too carried away in learning about the world and the universe at large to pay much attention.

The discourse on the Origin. Omphaloi and anomalies. He saw it for what it was now. It had all been a ploy aimed at his curiosity and fear so that he would seek her aid.

"You remain insouciant despite knowing what I am. You wear your independence with pride knowing that genuflecting in my presence can make your life easier. And now, you choose to bargain with me, after all that we have spoken of, merely to deepen your understanding of yourself . . . It speaks a great deal about you."

He'd been played like a sucker. Mutation was too dangerous. He had no need for assimilation. Creation was beyond him, at least without her aid. That left rejuvenation: the one thing he had forced her to teach him.

And teach him she did . . . while also extracting a promise from him.

"A spell of my own choice . . . I merely require being in possession of your body. I want your word that you shall not try to inhibit me when I perform it."

Inanna mockingly laughed. **"It was enjoyable squabbling with you, mortal. We should do it again."**

Lukas leaned against the wall and sighed. "In the spirit of good sportsmanship, would you at least tell me one final thing?"

"I may."

It was something that had bothered him for a long time. The biggest question that had plagued his mind over the time he had spent in her presence. The fact that he hadn't already asked her about it was weird by itself.

How did his world end? What caused it? What was it like?

Lukas opened his mouth to ask.

But no words came.

Instead, his attention was diverted by a sudden sensation. He looked down and, to his surprise, found his left arm shaking. Was something wrong with it? Maybe it had taken some injury and he was only now noticing the effects? Within seconds, the intensity of the vibrations grew to a point that he actually had to hold it within his right arm. That didn't help at all, and instead, the shaking was joined by a discordant hum that came from his head pounding against his ears. It slowly increased in volume, as if it were the herald of something terrible.

"Did you notice that?" Lukas demanded, looking around with rising panic. Every single hair from his neck to his ankles was standing up.

"Notice what?" came the goddess's serene answer.

"That!"

"You're just tired and seeing things," Inanna replied amiably. **"Several of your delusions have just been shredded apart. Perhaps you are having a panic attack?"**

Again? The last time he had one was—

"Breathe," she commanded. **"Stop thinking about these things, and just *focus on my voice!*"**

Lukas closed his eyes and quickly drew a deep, centering breath. A look of serenity began to form on his face. It was a lie. Deep beneath the apparent calm of his mind, there was a part of him that was frantic and terrified as it desperately tried to forget everything, and started counting multiples of thirteen at rapid frequency, focusing on the process as intently as he would while performing a Skill.

"One forty-three. One fifty-six. One sixty-nine," he muttered through clenched teeth. "One eighty-two. One ninety-five. Two hundred—"

And on and on he went.

CHAPTER 14

FREE LUNCH

Ever since he'd acquired the Prophylaxis function, Lukas had spent every waking moment practicing his skills and getting more used to using them. It was a strange feeling, being able to perform something so flawlessly yet not have the slightest familiarity with it. It was like he was drawing on someone else's experiences while his body acted out the movements.

"I told you. There is a difference between learning something and acquiring a skill. The former is familiarity drawn from your own limited experience. The latter is an ability etched into your very being. Just as you do not forget to breathe, you will not exercise a skill improperly."

"It just makes no sense," Lukas replied. "I'll never do it wrong?"

"Never."

Frowning, he placed his right hand over the surface of the still water. Once he'd found a groundwater pond, he took the opportunity to clean himself up and get rid of his horrid stench. Moss, as it turned out, was a perfectly good substitute for commercial scrub.

This entire experience was turning out to be a life changer for him. No contact with the outside world, no phones or computers or internet, no classes to attend, no social normal to entertain. All he had to contend with was a primal lifestyle that involved gaining strength, fighting monsters, and feeding to sate his hunger.

And the weirdest thing was . . .

He was starting to enjoy it.

Survival of the fittest. There was just something utterly beautiful about the simplicity of it—to stay in a world where danger lurked in every shadow, where even the weakest of things could kill you if caught off guard. He'd always been a light sleeper, but now his nap shattered from the slightest breeze. He'd travel all day, Scanning and Analyzing anything that caught his attention. He'd find prey worth his time, slice it in half, then roast it over a fire made by rubbing flint together.

It evoked a part of himself he never wanted to recognize. A part that did not concern itself with good and evil, or right and wrong. There was no morality, law, or culture down here. Merely the feeling of dominating another creature and seeing life slowly leave its eyes.

It was the feeling that came with being a hunter.

Focusing inward, Lukas felt lifeforce surge within him. A sudden warmth spread in his right hand—

Splash!

The still waters of the pond were disturbed by a massive upward spurt as a bar of pure kinetic motion escaped his arm and hit the water's surface, splashing it everywhere.

"Having fun?"

"Successful experiments always are," he replied with a satisfied grin. The more he studied his skills, the more he realized that they were far more than they appeared. The skill known as Momentum Manipulation allowed him to release lifeforce in the form of kinetic force outside his body. He may have acquired it mid-fight in a hopeless attempt to smack projectiles off of his hand, but now he could perform it anywhere.

More strangely, it was only one component of the skill. And because he'd unlocked it, it meant he could learn how to use the other components too. Provided he found them first.

It made no sense, but he supposed that was his life now.

"It took you less time to believe that your planet was gone and you were now carrying its consciousness within yourself. What does this say about you, I wonder."

"That I'm a sucker who hates change," Lukas grumbled, frustrated by his progress. He'd been testing his skills over and over, with different body parts each time. *Every* body part. It was only when he'd broken his nose and nearly fractured his ribs that he'd accepted her words at face value.

Although . . .

His fingers lightly twitched.

A little experimentation always squirreled its way into his daily activities.

"I don't get it." He let out a harsh breath. "I can shoot concussive blasts out of my freaking ass. Why is this simple trick so difficult? What am I missing here?"

"You are learning it from nothing," Inanna deigned to reply, **"rather than from the goddess who happens to speak to you from your mind."**

"But it's the—"

"It is not the same thing. You are attempting to convert your lifeforce from its raw form into something more finely attuned to your body's energy system."

"I'm *breathing*."

"Yes. While converting your lifeforce from its raw form into something more finely attuned to your body's energy system."

Lukas rolled his eyes. "Now you remind me of my teachers."

"Likely because you have the intelligence and wisdom of a child. Tell me, mortal, do you even realize what lifeforce is?"

"It's a form of energy produced by my body, and . . ." He trailed off. "Um, yeah. That's about it."

"I see." Inanna nodded. "It is astounding how every time my estimation of you rises by an inch, you manage to push it down by a foot."

His grin faltered. "Well, why don't you explain it then? Without making a bargain out of it," he quickly added.

"Unfortunately, it seems like the only way we will get around to doing something productive."

Lukas's eyes widened. Surely he had misheard? She hadn't just—?

"I am merely taking pity on your stupidity," she replied. "I already have two favors to collect from you. Might as well see them collected rather than watching you flounder about in this cavern for eternity."

"Thank you," he said, swallowing his inner wise-ass, despite how much he wanted to tell her what he really thought about her response.

"Lifeforce is, simply put, an energy of creation."

"*An* energy?" Lukas asked. "Are you implying that there are more? Like mana and stuff?"

As soon as he uttered the words, his surroundings shifted. Gone was the pool and the rocky floor and the cavern walls. He was now in one of his university classrooms, wearing a clean T-shirt and sweatpants.

And in front of him stood the kind of beauty that wars were started over.

Lukas's jaw hit the proverbial floor. Inanna wore a woman's suit of charcoal gray, its cut immaculate. The pencil skirt and high heels accentuated her legs, and she wore a bone-white V-neck beneath her jacket, its neckline deep enough to make him want to watch if she took a deep breath. Opals set in silver flashed on her ears and at her throat, glittering through an array of colors like a strobing rainbow. Her black tresses were tightly wound into a neat bun behind her head, and she stood behind the teacher's desk, staring at him knowingly.

Inanna hummed, observing herself with a scrutinizing eye. "How queer! This attire shows far less skin than my royal robes, yet it feels different somehow."

"It uh, looks good on you," he awkwardly said, thanking his lucky stars at being able to do something other than gawk at her like an imbecile.

"You should know this by now, mortal. Anything looks good on me."

And wasn't that the truth. Inanna was the sort of beauty that could rock a potato sack.

"Now then . . ." She sat atop the teacher's desk and crossed her legs. **"Let us continue."**

"Continue . . . what?"

Her smile widened.

"Right, lifeforce." His mind finished rebooting. "You were telling me about the energies."

"Indeed," she replied, resting her palms on either side. **"There are four Paths of Creation. The Physical Path. The Immaterial Path. The Divine Path. And finally, the Demonic Path. The Physical Path is manifested through lifeforce. The Immaterial, through mana. The Divine is sought by harnessing faith, while the Demonic employs Sin to do its bidding. You and every other creature that is physical and can draw breath and use lifeforce. With it, you may perform anything and everything, limited only by your own frail form."**

"What you just said makes no sense."

Inanna dangerously arched an eyebrow.

"Sorry." He winced. He needed to be more careful with his choice of words. "What I meant to say was, how can lifeforce do everything? Then there would be no reason for the other energies to exist."

"I understand your quandary. It is easy to see why your mortal mind would limit possibilities to those constraints."

"What are you, bigoted against mortals or something?"

Inanna laughed. The sound made him feel warm and fuzzy inside.

"I am not insulting you. You are limited to a linear comprehension of existence because of the illusions you believe in. But understand this. Creation is like mud. Its shape, size, charm, and worth all depend upon the whims of the creator. If you evoke the Paths of Creation, any of them, with the intention of nothing, then nothing is what you will create."

Lukas fell silent. So far, he'd seen lifeforce used to perform a wide variety of things, from augmenting his body to throwing out concussive energy blasts. If it really was a single energy source, then it was the most versatile one he'd ever known. In fact, the only thing remotely similar to it was—

"What about the omphalos energy reserves? The ones I use for my anomaly functions?"

The goddess smiled again. **"Anomalous energy. Very good. If there is a precursor to the four I mentioned, it would be that. The raw, wild power that** comes from the Origin itself. A power that can be real or ethereal, or both. A power that makes no distinction between demonic and divine."

Lukas narrowed his eyes. *Precursor, huh?* Did that imply that the four were derived from anomalous energy?

"Indeed," she answered, happily proving once again that she could hear his waking thoughts. **"The lifeforce within physical creations is synthesized from their essence, which is, at its core, a smidgen of anomalous energy. Immaterial creations lack an essence, but can churn anomalous energy into mana. Faith and Sin are slightly more complex and require an understanding of the divine and demonic manifestations associated with the World. Put simply, they too can be converted from anomalous energy all the same."**

Oh.

Oh.

So that was what all this was about.

"Professor Inanna." Lukas raised his hand. "I think I've figured you out."

Her eyes glittered. **"Oh?"**

"Yup. You see, I've been having a bit of a bad time lately, what with the apocalyptic end of my planet and me finding myself in this crypt of worms or whatever."

"I fail to see how that is relevant to our discussion."

Lukas went on. "Then you come in, frighten the hell out of me, and win yourself a bargain where I play Sherlock Holmes for you. You twist circumstances so that I fall deeper into bargains that I should've gotten for free anyway. And now you come sauntering in, offering free help while," he glanced over at her attire, "being ridiculously distracting. To be honest, I'm feeling too lucky."

"Fortune is finicky. Sometimes it smiles upon the desperate."

He shrugged. "Maybe it does. But I've been thinking that if something's too good to be true, then it probably is. It doesn't matter who's doing it."

Inanna's lips lifted in a silent snarl, and suddenly he wasn't able to move. He couldn't speak. He couldn't breathe. He couldn't do anything except clutch his head as his skull turned into a curtain of searing agony.

And then, it was over.

"Question my word again, and I will squash your head."

Lukas stared at her, half-dazed from the pain and deeply, sincerely, wisely frightened. "I—" He coughed, spewing some blood from his mouth. "I don't think you spoke anything but the truth! Just that it's not the entire picture." He felt her eyes zero in on him. "You unveiled the potential of the anomalous energy within me. Potential that I can't harness on my own. I remember."

He stood up—or at least tried to. On the fourth try, he finally steadied himself with the support of the bench. "I remember your offer, Goddess Inanna.

You wanted me to serve you. All of this wasn't to help. This show of power was just another attempt at manipulating me into a bargain."

As his vision grew steadier, his words found confidence.

"This was a way of showing me just how much I could gain. But I told you to look somewhere else. I don't want to serve you."

The angry, conceited look on Inanna's face drained away bit by bit, leaving behind a blank mask that was empty of all emotion, like a sheet of pressed metal. It was unsettling to see a face so lovely suddenly transform into something alien, as though something lurked behind her eyes that had little in common with him and simply wouldn't care to make the effort to understand.

Her features made his throat tighten, and he had to work not to tremble. But then she did something that made her look even more alien. More *frightening*.

She smiled. A slow smile, cruel and sharp, like broken glass. And when she spoke next, her voice sounded just as beautiful as it had before, but it was also empty and haunting. Each word made him want to lean closer to her, just so he could hear it more clearly.

"Liar," Inanna said quietly, studying his face with calm, heavy eyes. **"You crave it. You crave it so much that it pains you to deny your true nature. But your eyes cannot lie nearly as well as your tongue."**

"And what if I do?" he challenged. "Regardless, I won't accept your offer. You may have tricked me twice, but that's it. No more bargains between us."

"Not today, perhaps, but one day you will be down upon your knees, begging me to give you such an offer. So I have decreed, so mote it be."

The illusion wavered, and the feeling of being drenched in water returned as Lukas found himself back on the edge of the pond.

"So . . ." Lukas trailed off. "In the spirit of offering free tutelage, would you be willing to tell me what mana is? I mean, I've seen it used frequently in my world's literature, so I'd like to know any differences that exist."

A beat of silence passed before Inanna replied, her tone eerily calm. **"You truly expect me to aid you?"**

"I could always phrase it differently. In a way that fits our previous bargain."

"Then do so."

"You told me that anomalous energy is the precursor of lifeforce, mana, faith, and Sin, and that it's possible for the former to create the latter. If the world can do that using its own energy, then since I'm an anomaly, shouldn't I be able to do the same?"

"In theory."

Lukas grinned. That was good enough for him. "And how exactly does a world create or release mana into the environment? I imagine I have a similar capability within me."

"You aim too high, mortal," Inanna replied. "You are a physical creature, which is why lifeforce runs within you. With proper tutelage and a healthy amount of sheer blind luck, you may even discover how to convert anomalous energy into additional lifeforce. But to access the forge that would enable mana creation? You would need a mana skill."

"That sounds good to me. How do I get a mana skill?"

"By accessing a forge, and learning how to manipulate the mana created into performing a skill."

He blinked. "So, what you're telling me is I need a forge to get the skill. But I need the skill to access the forge in the first place? That's . . ."

"Poetic?"

"A fallacy. A really bizarre one, too."

"What you call mana is also known as elemental energy. Using a mana forge, a creature can transmute it into a manifestation of the elements. Fire. Air. Water. Earth. Ether."

Lukas couldn't help but think about the mythologies he was familiar with. Stories of Merlin wielding magic against Morgana and the Saxons, of devas and asuras clashing, of the animated versions of angels and demons throwing around ice and fire like they were toys to play with. He thought of the holy people of the Native American tribes, the Aztecs, of Zeus hurling thunderbolts and Poseidon raising the tides.

If gods and goddesses were real, if *mana* was now real . . .

Were all those stories real?

He thought of the Screen. *How do I use—no, how do I synthesize mana?*

By accessing the Ley Line Network.

Lukas blinked. *So . . . I have ley lines?*

No.

Can I have ley lines?

Yes.

How?

By developing mana skills.

And how do I develop a mana skill?

Performing an act of mana and etching it to the Soul.

How do I perform an act of mana?

> **By accessing the Ley Line Network.**

Lukas closed his eyes in resignation. He could practically feel Inanna's smugness emanating from her mental presence. "Yes, I get it. Mana is a closed loop for me because I'm not supposed to wield it. The only way to do that is to acquire the skill from someone else." He paused. "From you."

"I do not believe in charity, mortal."

"Shocker," came his deadpan answer. "But you're underestimating me. I haven't forgotten that I still need more Soul Capacity before I can even think of acquiring new skills, whether they're bargained for or developed from scratch. That means you can't make me make impulsive choices. You want me to play hardball? Fine, I'll do it. Skills or no skills, I can learn the hard way. I have a lifetime ahead of me to do it."

"I see. Then what will you do now?"

"Attempt to convert my lifeforce from its raw form into something more finely attuned to my body's energy."

"Ah. In my day we called that breathing."

CHAPTER 15

MYSTERY

The rats in the Crypt of Fiendish Worms were monstrous. With their razor-sharp teeth, claws that looked like they were stolen from a butcher's shop, two horn-like protrusions above their ears, and bright crimson eyes that glowed malevolently in the dim dungeon light, the two-foot-tall creatures gave off a ghoulish appearance.

But they were rats nonetheless. And that meant they fit into the category of monsters that Lukas was fond of: *best when cooked well.*

Unfortunately they also attacked in packs, which was why he was currently facing about a dozen of them, with more possibly lurking in the shadows, ready to pounce at a moment's notice.

CINDERFACE
Quadruped creature with sharp, metallic claws. The claws and fangs have poison. Expert diggers.

As if in acknowledgement, the closest cinderface unhinged its jaw, revealing two pairs of fangs that glinted in the darkness.

"My, what big teeth you have, Grandmother." Lukas chuckled, pumping lifeforce into a pulsing ball of energy in his right hand. He had, very recently, learned how to mold lifeforce into physical shapes, though the constructs only remained stable for a few seconds. But that suited him just fine.

The pest army squeaked and lunged toward him.

Lukas crouched, dodging an aerial attack as one of the cinderfaces soared over his head. He hurled the unstable sphere toward another cinderface, and the ball exploded upon contact with its belly, spraying purple blood over the cavern floor.

It was the first to die.

But Lukas was far from done. Exercising Kinetomancy, he grabbed the motion of the now-dead cinderface and pulled it back in a sharp twirl. The dead rat's body flew in a perfect arc and slammed two more into the ground. Another pulse of lifeforce quickly followed suit.

---

3 prey eliminated.
+17 Experience

"Wasteful," Inanna noted. **"You will soon tire if you keep that up."**

"Everyone's a critic," Lukas grumbled to himself. He kicked the closest monster with a wide sweep of his leg and threw up a wall of inertia that held three more in their place. The creatures snapped at him and tried to move, but it was all in vain; they were unable to break past his power. Lining his hands with lifeforce, he ran his palms through them.

---

3 prey eliminated.
+17 Experience

His right palm dripping with dense, purplish bodily fluids, Lukas wearily regarded the remaining assailants. There were two on the left and two more in front of him, but they were all roughly telegraphing their movements.

Lukas deeply inhaled. Lifeforce flooded his body, specifically his lungs—a simple, yet no less significant change. The results were instantaneous. As increased amounts of oxygen rushed to all his organs, most importantly his brain, he felt his senses sharpen and his vitality skyrocket. The haze of adrenaline that permeated his very being lessened just a smidge, and Lukas felt his calm focus return.

The two cinderfaces on the left leaped of their own accord, acting like individuals instead of two separate units of a pack. The first met with a thin layer of lifeforce that diagonally tore through its face. The second, however, was more agile. It leaped to the side and then lunged toward his face, claws extended and ready to rend. Lukas gasped at the sudden proximity and instinctively sidestepped in the nick of time, dodging the attack by millimeters. The creature snarled and leaped back at him for a second attempt but was greeted with a lifeforce-enhanced punch that marked its end.

Eight down. Three to go.

"None, actually. The rest are fleeing."

Inanna was right. The remaining monsters, including the ones he couldn't count hiding in the shadows, had turned tail and scurried out of sight. Was it because one of the slain creatures was the leader of their group? Even in a strange, new world, animal behavior was similar to what he was familiar with. Overthrow the leader, and the flunkies would flee.

Though, now that he thought about it, some humans behaved like that too.

"So," he tiredly panted, "did it work?"

"Better than the last few times. You must keep doing it until your body assimilates the process."

"And then?"

"Once you manage to enhance an organ function with lifeforce, it will unlock the skill. Be advised, mortal, that this will not help you augment the other organs by default. But you will not have to worry about employing lifeforce the wrong way."

Bottom line—it would still be an arduous job, but at least he'd get there faster.

"I'll take whatever victory I can get," Lukas replied, sucking in deeper breaths. His constant pumping of lifeforce into his lungs was his way of learning Body Augmentation, a component of Raw Lifeforce Manipulation that, according to Inanna, would open doors to countless future opportunities. Like augmenting existing processes in organs. Or increasing the efficiency of body tissues. Or, even better, creating cascading effects with multiple organs to generate new skills. The possibilities were endless.

Once he managed to acquire them, he would need to unlock more lifeforce production to level up his skills. But to get there, there was one more obstacle to face.

A threshold, rather.

SOULSCAPE	
NAME	Lukas Aguilar
Type	Base Host
Level	4
Experience	387
Current Threshold	640
Utilized Soul Capacity	1379/1379
ESSENCE	
Maximum Lifeforce Output	725
Replenishment Rate	180 / hour

SKILL ATTRIBUTES		
SKILL	**LEVEL**	**CONSUMED SOUL CAPACITY**
Raw Lifeforce Manipulation	1	50
Momentum Manipulation	1	50
Kinetomancy (FRAGMENTED)	APEX	1279

OMPHALOS ATTRIBUTES	
Energy Reservoir Capacity	∞
Current Energy Level	722,434,311 units
OMPHALOS FUNCTIONS	
Scan	Level 1
Analyze	Level 1

Still too far. Lukas cursed, slamming his right fist into the ground. *It's still not enough.*

"Whining does not a warrior make," the goddess sagely replied. **"You should feel lucky that you already have a healing function, courtesy of the omphalos within you. At least you can no longer bruise yourself to death."**

FUNCTION - Prophylaxis	Level - 1
TASK - Complete	Energy Cost - 73 units

Lukas supposed she was right, though he had learned that Prophylaxis was a finicky thing. The skill operated on one wound at a time, and if there were multiple of them, then it would heal one at random while the rest patiently waited for their turn. On the bright side, the healing was perfect. As good as new, really.

"You still have yet to fully master your skills at hand. Mastering the basics is essential to growth."

"I'm trying!" Lukas gritted out. Truth be told, he no longer had a burning need to level up so quickly. Earlier, he had a solid reason when he chose to keep the fragmented Kinetomancy skill and exhaust his Soul Capacity. There had also been a stark need for a healing skill, but now he had Prophylaxis.

He could afford to take it a little more slowly. If anything, he was pushing himself even harder than he was at the start.

"I—I'm having trouble sleeping."

As the words were spoken, Lukas felt a small weight lift from his shoulders. He had finally said it out loud. "All this fighting, hunting monsters, using lifeforce, feeling the adrenaline . . ." His hands clenched into fists. "It's like it *wants* me to go on. Every time a breeze touches my skin, my sleep breaks. Every time I hear a sound, lifeforce floods into my hands faster than I can process what happened. I guess I . . . I just want to feel something other than constant confusion and danger. At least if I level up, I'll feel like I . . . I don't know, I'll have accomplished something. Become *more*."

Inanna took a moment to answer. **"Monsters are forged through war and battle. Do you know how you rise to the top? You do not sleep. You do not eat. You do not rest. You live and breathe the art of combat. Every waking moment must be dedicated to training and improving yourself. And perhaps at the end of it, you may find yourself at the top. And I daresay you have taken the first step in this path."**

Lukas was taken aback. "I . . . Thanks, but I can't help but feel it's a bit undeserved. None of this would've been possible without the skills you gave me."

"Do not mistake my actions for charity. You obtained any such skills through a bargain. Likewise, you may bargain something else in exchange for a mana skill. Perhaps it will bring about a similar feeling of accomplishment."

"No thanks." He laughed, but there was no humor in his voice.

Truth be told, he hadn't been completely upfront with her. There was no surefire way to explain it, but he had still been suffering from anxiety attacks. There was just *something* there—a thought, a question, a memory—something constantly trying to push its ugly head out of the ground. A hideous terror that would send his heart racing like a frenzy and make him scream madly if he ever remembered what it was.

But as quickly as it came, it was gone again, as if it were never there at all.

"Is there anything else you wish to tell me?"

" . . . No. Nothing else."

Deciding he'd had enough of this conversation, Lukas proceeded deeper into the anomaly.

The Crypt of Fiendish Worms was an endless, stone-walled labyrinth. A dark, deadly place lit only by the luminescent moss lying around. It was a veritable stronghold, filled with vicious monsters that rose out of every shadow. But now, the stone walls slowly came to a close and led into a deep underground forest.

Lukas respected forests, aware of their contribution toward generating oxygen and providing a habitat for countless ecosystems and species on Earth.

After going on several expeditions with his grandfather, he also experienced the flip side—the feelings that came from wading through thick, dank jungles filled to the brim with insects and predators.

Forests were scary.

It was already dangerous walking through a dimly lit cavern, skills be damned. But to walk through an *underground* forest? It was something out of a nightmare.

He really couldn't see much, if at all. A plethora of sounds assaulted his ears, from the rustling of leaves and roots to the movement of animals somewhere inside this enormous fauna-filled area. Invisible things kept encroaching on his personal space, from the remnants of spiderwebs to fallen twigs, to simple leaves that fell from the branches.

The ground shifted every now and then. Sometimes, the elevation was low, and other times, it was high. Stones tripped his feet, and broken vines and thorns and branches obstructed him every step of the way. If something large and nasty were to come after him right now, he'd have no choice but to stumble around in the dark in a feeble attempt to escape.

Most likely, he'd immediately trip and fall over, with sharp thorns digging into his tender flesh. And that was him being optimistic.

"You ignore the fact that this allows you a perfect opportunity to train, mortal."

"It's always sunshine and daisies with you," Lukas groaned. The constant use of lifeforce to reinforce his respiratory system was still underway.

Inhale.

Exhale.

Breathing was the most natural instinct anyone could have. Easier than locomotion, more natural than feeding, and less tiring than mating. If repetition was the mother of learning, a vehicle through which the body could develop fixed patterns of employing lifeforce, then breathing was the best process with which to practice.

Every time Lukas inhaled, lifeforce flooded his lungs, enhancing the entire breathing process. A little bit more oxygen was carried in than usual. And every time he exhaled, a little bit more deoxygenated air left his lungs than was normal.

With every waking moment spent doing this one thing repeatedly, he was beginning to feel the effects. While the use of lifeforce generally left an adrenaline rush in its wake, reinforcing his respiration had a calming effect on him, reducing said rush. His mind felt sharper and clearer.

The irony that he was using lifeforce to counter another effect of lifeforce was not lost on him.

"How long will it take until I can do this subconsciously?" Lukas asked.

"You will know."

"When?"

"Once you gain the skill."

Inanna's penchant for vague responses was only matched by the prowess of her sarcasm.

Sighing, Lukas shifted gears. "Alright, fine. Then tell me about anomalies again."

"What is it you wish to know?"

"How do I get out of this anomaly?" he asked.

"I will hear your thoughts first, mortal."

"Well, since I haven't seen any sunlight since I stepped in, we might be inside a mountain, or maybe underground. I don't know which is more distressing," he said, lightly shivering. "Also, the air smells pretty fresh, meaning it isn't too deep beneath the surface if it's underground. And if it is in fact in a mountain . . . well, anomalies want prey to enter. That means entrances. Lots of entrances.

"Any other questions you would like to answer yourself?"

"Not at the moment, no," Lukas quipped, pausing to deeply inhale and exhale. "So theoretically, I can start looking for a way out of this hellhole." He considered the thought carefully. "Just imagine if I leave and find my way to civilization. New species, new places, new languages I won't have a clue about. Here's hoping they're friendly and don't want to dissect me immediately."

"I concur."

"But if I stay, I can level up and work on my skills and powers. In a worst-case scenario, I'd have a better chance at fighting if the people I eventually meet turn out to be antagonistic."

Lukas glanced down at himself, wondering if they would see him as some sort of savage. His shirt was mostly shredded through wear and tear, but he'd held onto it for sentimental purposes. His trousers weren't in the best form either, with the portions below his knees practically threadbare. A thick strip of monster hide was tied around his waist, doubling as both armor and belt.

In hindsight, he was lucky he had shaved the day before his world turned upside down. He really didn't want to imagine himself with a long, scraggly beard covering his face. It would look terribly—

Lukas's thoughts screeched to a halt. An unearthly chill came into being at the base of his spine, slowly slithering its way up his back and over his neck. Settling into a defensive stance, he looked around and Scanned for visible threats.

When he found nothing, he inhaled and began circulating lifeforce within him, keeping his senses as sharp as could be. But still, there was nothing.

Being in a world full of monsters has made you paranoid, Aguilar.

Lukas shook his head. If nothing else, he was well-rested, with enough lifeforce to handle things should they go south. But maybe he was just being too jumpy. Maybe it was just some monster squirrel looking around for flies, or another cinderface that had a bone to pick with him.

Suddenly, he heard a loud scratching noise from the ground. Even though it was outside his Scan Radius, it was obvious that the creature in question was crawling along the floor, with multiple bony appendages being dragged about. Either that, or it loved to incessantly scratch at walls for no good reason.

Knowing his luck, it was probably both.

"Mortal," Inanna's voice rang out. **"Look up."**

Lukas did as she asked. And stared. And kept on staring.

Hanging on the walls by invisible threads, smoldering balls of bluish flames lined the entire cave ahead of him, illuminating the way. Even in the thin, ghostly glow, Lukas could clearly make out the strange sigils and engraving etched upon the walls. The pathway seemed to flow into the endless depths of the anomaly itself. In the distance, on one of the walls, a rectangular cross-section appeared to protrude out slightly.

Lukas gawked with wide, open eyes as he realized what he was looking at.

"Is . . . is that a *door?*"

He made his way forward carefully, looking around with his awareness as well as his eyes in case his nigh-omniscient Scan Radius glitched and failed to classify a threat for what it was. The pathway was unsettling, with walls that looked too clean and too sharp to be natural. This was no natural forest cave. It was a corridor, and a well-frequented one at that. The squarish protrusions on the walls were definitely sliding doors of some kind, and the markings must have served some greater purpose than this world's variant of graffiti, especially considering how they shimmered in the azure glow of the levitating flames.

There was also a strangeness in the area, like a dissonance of energies. It tickled at a sixth sense that Lukas didn't even know he had.

"It is the omphalos within you reacting," Inanna chimed in. **"You are correct. This path is not natural. There is something here."**

The interest in the goddess's voice did not make him feel any better.

"Mortal, get a closer look at those markings."

Why?

"Because I told you to."

Not wanting to entertain the imminent argument, Lukas stepped forward and eyed the etchings on the wall. The strange markings bore a startling structural resemblance to East Asian languages. His grandfather had kept copies of some really old manuscripts that had letters similar to these.

Analyze.

Insufficient data.

"Languages are neither skills nor existences. I would be shocked if your schema could decipher them."

Lukas pursed his lips. "What about you, then? Do you know what they say?"

". . . I can sense that they are enchantments. The sigils are magical, and they are enacting something here."

"Like what?"

There was a long, uncertain pause before the goddess whispered again. **"I—I do not know what they are."**

He frowned, reasonably sure he hadn't imagined the uncertainty—or worse, *fear*—in her tone. But why seeing a new language was such a big issue for her, he wasn't sure. One couldn't know everything, after all. Not even a goddess.

"You do not understand. These are not languages, they are enchantments. Enchantments abide by the World's Rules. The same World that worships me as a goddess. Whatever the language may be, the Rules do not change. Yet these enchantments do not follow the Rules I remember."

Inanna was a goddess. There was very little she did not know, despite how scarcely she shared that knowledge freely. For her to say something like that about some engraving on rock did not feel odd. It felt *wrong*.

"Surely you have some idea about what they do?" Lukas probed.

"I can tell you that they are gathering negative energy. Dark desires, curses, leftovers, remnants of souls. The dissonance you are feeling is being exuded from these sigils. I cannot say why or how, but these enchantments are entrapping this energy."

There were hundreds, possibly thousands, of such sigils adorning the walls. And if the doors led to more of these corridors, then there was no saying what else he'd find there.

Still, a part of Lukas was actually looking forward to meeting whoever was behind those doors. Would they be people? Real, humanoid, people? Inanna was a goddess, and she looked completely human—at least appearance-wise. At the same time, however, there was no saying how dangerous it would be.

Do you think I should—

"Escape?" Inanna mused. **"The idea is not without its merits. However, should you stay, you may find out more. Perhaps even—"** She paused. **"Something approaches."**

As she said those words, the dissonance in the air grew, making him feel oddly nauseous.

Scan, he thought.

No prey within Scan Radius.

Lukas narrowed his eyes. Could it be that *Inanna* was wrong?
Even the eerie feeling from before was waning.
Maybe it was just . . . a breeze or something.

No prey within Scan Radius.

Then he felt it.

Lukas whirled around, right in time to see a . . . something. The thing was humanoid in shape, but lower, longer, and leaner. It was bipedal, but everything else was wrong. The head looked toad-like, if he was willing to ignore the long, tentacular protrusions coming out of its hundred-fanged maw. Two more flailing tentacles jutted out from its torso into hands, and its feet were that of a bird.

No face. No eyes. And it was floating toward him.

"More monsters," Lukas groaned. "Damned things!"

He slashed his arm at the creature, but the burst of lifeforce passed through it without hurting it in the slightest, merely sending it drifting backward a few steps. The sigils on the walls were also engraved on the creature's lower body, and they glowed sinisterly.

"What the hell is that?!"

Insufficient data.

Huh?

Whether it was earthly or alien, the Analyze function had always returned something, ever since he killed that strange bat on his first day in the crypt. First, the sigils had Inanna baffled, and now his schema wasn't able to help him? What the hell was going on?

"Behind you."

Two more of the blasted creatures were behind him, their tentacles undulating in the air as they let out weird, clicking noises. To Lukas's growing dread, another appeared through the wall and joined the pair. He turned back around, and the first one was now three. The walls became flimsier and more wavy, like a curtain.

When the creatures crouched simultaneously, the cluster of tentacles around their head quivered in unison, the motion becoming more and more energetic as time went on. Then suddenly, one of them flew forward, producing a sound so deep that Lukas could feel it more strongly than he could hear it.

Lukas did the only thing that came to mind. Using his left hand, he grabbed its motion in a way that still made little sense to him and guided it upward. With his right, he added an extra push. The creature was flung to the opposite side, where it crashed against two others of its kind.

I can't hurt them, but they can hurt each other.

Lukas gave the sprawled bodies a momentary glance, then turned around and did the only sensible thing anyone in his place could do.

He ran.

And the creatures followed. He wasn't sure how many were on his trail; it was more than half a dozen, but fewer than twenty. They made odd, light, creepy noises as they drifted toward him, passing through stone walls as one would through open doors. Some followed him from directly behind while others snuck up on him through the floor and ceiling.

Lukas jumped and flipped and ran down the long corridor, his lifeforce shutting down any fatigue as he made his way through the seemingly endless labyrinth.

"They are no longer close," Inanna said. **"But remain cautious."**

He slowed down his pace but continued to stay on the move. "Just what were those things? Definitely not part of the local crowd." If they were from the crypt, he had a feeling that the Analyze function would've worked.

"Ethereal beings."

"They certainly *felt* solid enough," he complained. "You saw it. I could grab their motion. Remember how one of them fell onto its friends? You can't be ethereal and do that at the same time. Can you?" he added at the end, remembering just who he was speaking to. These days, it seemed anything was possible.

"The physical bodies were not real. They were constructs. False creations. I could sense them absorbing energy from the world around them."

"Is that why they could phase through walls?"

"Simultaneous deconstruction and reconstruction of different areas of the physical construct. I imagine they are metamantic beings oriented toward such false body construction."

"In mortal-speak, please?"

The goddess let out a soul-suffering sigh. **"Do you recall our discussion on the nature of mana?"**

Lukas nodded even as he ran. "Five elements. Fire, water, wind, earth, ether. Manacrafters could harness them to use as weapons or augment themselves."

"Metamancy is the manipulation of the ether, the fabric of false creation. Temporary construction. Conjuration. Illusion."

Lukas hummed. "So blunt force attacks won't work on them."

Prey found you.

Cursing, Lukas frantically gathered energy and dashed ahead to avoid getting surrounded. For all their wackiness, if they couldn't catch up with him, then they couldn't hurt—

He staggered, suddenly feeling dizzy. Before he knew it, he planted facefirst into the ground and bruised his cheek and forehead. His heart beat violently and his entire body felt like a thoroughly shaken bottle of Pepsi. He turned back over, blinking his eyes owlishly.

What the hell was—

The thought shriveled and died as one of the creatures came charging toward him. Using Kinetomancy, Lukas grabbed its motion and shifted it by a few degrees. The monster was tossed against a stone wall but phased right through it.

"Damn it!" He got up drunkenly. "How the hell do I fight these things?"

"You cannot. Not as you are. However, I can provide you a way out," Innana offered with a smile. **"You need only ask for it."**

Lukas gritted his teeth. "Forget it."

Running would only exhaust him further. Whatever these creatures were, they had the home-field advantage. But as he scrutinized their movements, Lukas found that the creatures weren't really gliding toward him. They scuttled forward, as if they stopped and considered each burst of motion before committing to it. There was something unnervingly primitive about it. Reptilian. Insectile, even.

"You cannot defeat an ethereal construct using pure force," the goddess advised. **"You must use an element. I find that fire works best. Especially natural fires."**

What's the difference?

"Survive, and perhaps I will deign to teach you the difference between elemental conjuration and the natural operation of the universe."

Worriedly, he glanced at the creatures encircling him from all sides and came to a grim conclusion: he would not be able to fight them as he was now. He had to improvise.

Inanna suggested fire. But somehow, he doubted the creatures would wait until he'd managed to rub two pieces of flint together to create a spark. He needed a different solution. Something combustible.

Another monster glided toward him, its tentacles frothing at the ends. Lukas whirled it around and smashed it against the wall on the left. It slid straight through, but some moss shook from the remnants of his Kinetomancy and fell.

41 prey eliminated.

Lukas narrowed his eyes. And then it hit him.

Of course.

He slapped his palms together, as if in prayer. The irony of the action was not lost on him. Glancing at the nearest abomination, he gave it a Cheshire grin. "Come to Daddy."

As the monster shot into motion toward him, Lukas trusted his instincts and channeled as much kinetic energy as possible into both hands. He then slashed it against the creature's body, both hands rubbing against one another.

A brilliant wave of flames emerged.

The abomination screeched loudly, two deep scorch marks now prominently displayed on its body. It turned around to escape—

"Oh, no you don't." Lukas chuckled, grabbing it with Kinetomancy. "I didn't say you could leave."

What was fire if not excited particles exuding the extra energy? The more excitement, the more motion, and the more power he had over them. Invisible hands grabbed at the creature, and Lukas whirled it around him, over and over, spinning it in circles, fanning the flames with ever-increasing friction. He then grabbed the burning creature and launched it toward its brethren.

The screeching cries made by the monsters were like honey to his ears.

Burn, you greasy toad-faced bastards! Burn in hell!

Lukas stood amidst it all, grinning at the change in the tide of battle. Wielding the flames using Kinetomancy gave him a surreal feeling, like he was being *burned* from within, but not in a bad way. The flickers of flame spreading from one creature to the next reflected in his eyes, and a dark power within him sang, wanting to cause more destruction.

He grabbed another monster that tried to escape and did the same to it, igniting yet another group. Everything around him exploded into motion, shadows flashing through brightness, seeking escape, screaming.

But Lukas would not let it happen.

For he was—

"Stay in control," Inanna warned.

Fuck control! Lukas acerbically thought. He *wanted* this. He yearned to give into the impulses he'd always kept shackled, to unleash it all into obliterating everything around him. His mind felt like it was splitting at the seams, consumed by the deepest pits of hell itself as he let his instincts take control of his body.

"Die! Die! DIE! DIE! *DIE! DIE! DIE!* **DIE!DIE!DIE!DIE!DIE!DIE! DIE!!!!!!**"

The carnage was like ambrosia. The more the monster screeched, the more *something* inside of him luxuriated. A gleam of insanity shone in his eyes as he madly slashed at everything around him, using the dead bodies of the creatures and slamming them into each other even though they were deader than dead. He utterly fell prey to his ecstasy like a hedonist on a pleasure trip.

"Mortal. Stop this now."

He spat at the notion. What did she know?

Gathering power in his palms, he propelled it against the stone walls, causing more moss to fall. As they cracked and crumbled, a gale of dust brewed amidst the still burning bodies. It made him feel sick and hollow, but *strong*.

"Should you let it take control of you, you shall lose yourself forever."

"FUCK OFF!" he snarled.

"Very well. I shall not ask again."

Her words disturbed the purity of his lust for battle. How dare *she*, a mere reflection residing in jewelry that was forced to seek rent in his mind, ask *him* to stop when she herself had butchered thousands to craft her throne? He finally got to taste the pleasures of victory and domination, and now this *harlot* was trying to put an end to his enjoyment? How dare—

Without warning, Lukas's world became endless pain.

His power melted like ice in the afternoon sun. Every injury, every bruise, every splintered bone, every torn muscle, scratch and strain—it all crashed into him at once. As his limbs gave up, he staggered forward and bonelessly fell to the floor like dead weight.

And then, Lukas moved no more.

CHAPTER 16

ALONE WITH EVERYBODY

Lukas blearily opened his eyes.

Sunlight stabbed at his pupils as it snuck past his window curtains, faintly illuminating his room. His fingers twitched, feeling the tender weight of a fluffy white blanket pressing down on him. He felt toasty, but for some reason, it was still comfortable. Like he was wrapped in a cocoon of safety.

He took a deep breath, basking in the familiar scent of jasmine. Turning to the side, he wrinkled his nose as long, luxurious black hair tickled him relentlessly. Pushing it aside, his attention was quickly focused on the body next to him.

Emma quietly stirred in place, taking the time to sit up and stretch. The white blanket they'd been curled under glided down the gentle curves of her breasts. She blew the hair away from her face with a single huff, shooting him a languid, half-awake smile.

He suddenly felt like a heel, realizing his sudden movements must've woken her up.

"Hey, you . . ."

"Hey," Lukas softly responded in kind, his gaze not leaving her slightly pale, soft skin—from the top of her shoulders, flowing down across her slender arms until it dove behind the covers. The morning light did exquisite things to her naked flesh, and he'd be lying if he said he wasn't a fan.

"My, my. Looks like last night wasn't enough for someone." Emma winked, her salacious smile dripping with forbidden promises.

An abrupt sensation pulled at Lukas's core, as simple and unyielding as gravity. He felt the urge to grab her, to feel that slender waist between his hands as she writhed underneath him in ecstasy, looking up with half-lidded eyes. He inadvertently blushed, unable to fathom where the sudden dash of sexual attraction came from. This was Emma, after all. Someone he'd shared his room and life with for several years.

The feeling vanished almost as quickly as it came. Really, what was he thinking? He'd seen her naked before. Many times. Last night, even, from the looks of things.

Whatever. When in Rome . . .

Lukas leaned into her slender neck, breathing in the scent of her perfume once more.

"Mmm, someone's feeling pretty cozy today," she murmured, reaching for his lips. He wasted no time meeting her midway with his own. They felt soft. Comforting. Homey.

"Maybe a bit," he cheekily replied, before suddenly holding a palm to his throbbing forehead. His body ached from head to toe, and all his joints demanded that he stay in bed and recuperate. For weeks on end, if the intensity was any indication. He'd had pleasurable nights, but never like this. So why was his head pounding as if he'd just run a marathon and then some?

"I need some fucking aspirin," he muttered, pushing himself up.

"Oh?" Emma arched an eyebrow, her smile not ebbing in the slightest as she coiled against his left arm with effortless feline grace. "Was last night a little too much for you?"

Lukas rolled his eyes. Emma had no compunctions using her feminine wiles to boost her own ego and get what she wanted. It was funny and ironic, seeing as the girl somehow had no concept of what her sensuality could do to most men. Only him, for some reason.

Glancing at his desk, he ruffled his hair as he grabbed for his shirt.

Instead, his hands hit the glass of water on the table. It fell down to the ground and shattered.

"Damn it," he sighed. Biting back a groan, Lukas pushed the covers off of him and gently freed himself from a mewling Emma to bend down and look at the shattered glass pieces. His fingers barely grazed the surface of one of the shards when he felt something pale and grainy on the surface. The hairs on the back of his neck all suddenly stood to attention, and he felt his shoulders tighten—

Something cold and wet and crimson dripped onto his fingers.

Blood, his mind belatedly registered as he rubbed it between his fingertips. Had he cut himself somehow? No, that wouldn't explain how it came onto his hand. Curiously, he craned his neck upward, wondering why blood would be coming from his ceiling, and—

Found a gigantic chunk of plaster falling toward the bed.

"GET BACK!" Lukas screamed, shoving Emma off the other side of the bed. He instinctively raised his right hand up, a strange power thrumming through his body as he batted away the falling debris. Invisible arms grabbed the plaster and smashed it against the wall on the other side, shattering the chunk at the point of contact. The sheer momentum of the collision sent the broken pieces speeding in multiple directions. As if on autopilot, Lukas leaped backward, uncaring of his nudity as he vaulted over the bed and landed calmly on the other side of it, his right hand raised to conjure a—

. . . a what?

Lukas blinked.

The entire exchange took a second at most.

And yet, for him, it had felt like ten.

"How the hell did you do that?" Emma gaped, her tone tinged with shock and awe.

Lukas flickered his gaze between her bewildered face and the now-broken ceiling. He shifted his stare toward the large, broken pieces of plaster littering the floor, then toward his own unbruised right hand, wondering what in the hell had just happened.

"Luke!" Emma hissed, scrambling to her feet. "What was that?"

"I . . ." Lukas tried, but no words came to mind to describe it. "I don't know."

"You don't know?"

"I don't know," he repeated, feeling strangely hysterical and defensive about the weird phenomenon. "I guess I just—" He glanced back up at the ceiling, as if all the answers lay in the hole that was just created. "Look, are you—are you alright? I didn't push you too hard or anything, did I?"

"No," Emma breathed, examining him as if seeing him for the first time. "I'm fine. Clearly, going to the gym has done you wonders."

"Yeah, I suppose so." Lukas awkwardly chuckled, clenching and unclenching his fists.

If Emma recognized the uncertainty and puzzlement in his voice, she made no move to voice it. "Anyway, you should really call someone to repair it soon." She pointed at the debris. "We don't want another accident when we're in bed, now do we?" She punctuated the words with a wink.

"No." Lukas gulped, wary of the gleam in her eyes. "No, we don't."

For some reason, his attention kept returning to the glass shards on the floor, with the drop of blood still on its edges. He still wasn't sure where it came from either—was there some bird stuck in his ceiling? A strange, acute sense of anxiety constantly hammered away at his mind, and it took everything he had not to give into it.

Get over yourself, Aguilar, Lukas chided himself. *It was just a freak accident. Nobody's out to get you.*

He repeated the statement over and over in his mind. But the pit in his stomach never went away.

It took fifteen minutes for the two of them to get dressed and step out of his apartment. Oddly enough, Lukas felt a strange sensation of déjà vu as he descended the staircase. He felt like finding the window on the other side and jumping through it onto the backstreet. And the moment he was about to cross the threshold to the outside, he was overcome with an eerie feeling that made him halt.

The odd looks Emma lobbed toward him didn't help at all.

Emma drove a 2011-model Nissan, though it wasn't really as old as one would imagine. Both the doors had been refurbished recently, and the hood was replaced with a cheaper but newer substitute. Hopping into the driver's seat—as he always did—he revved the car.

The vehicle growled and grunted as Lukas took it out onto the main street, just a few blocks shy of Victoria Avenue. But for some reason, he kept shooting glances at the rearview mirror, as if expecting something to happen. A strange tension knotted up his muscles and had his mind in a tizzy, one he couldn't make heads or tails of.

Instinctively, he picked up speed.

"No need to hurry, y'know!" Emma broke in. "Just drop me at the office as usual. Unless you've got something else planned?"

Planned? No, he didn't have anything planned. He just wanted to drop her off and get the hell out of there. His gut kept telling him that something, or someone, was after him. That much was certain.

First the ceiling incident. And now this.

There was no need to drag Emma into his weird problems.

"—kas? Lukas!"

"Wha—no, nothing else." He took a quick left. "I'll just take the bus to the—" He paused. Bus? When was the last time he'd taken a bus to the university? It had always been—

"Luke!"

"Yeah?" he asked, turning toward her. "You know what, I think it's best if I—" He glanced at the mirror once more. "If I just took your car to uni. Would that be alright?"

"That's fine . . ." She trailed off. "But what's gotten into you? You've had this weird, distant look in your eyes since this morning."

"I'm—"

Emma gently cupped his chin. "Chill out, Luke. Don't get so freaked out over a bit of plaster. It's not that hard to fix a ceiling."

Lukas wasn't jumpy about some shoddy architecture, but he didn't feel like explaining that to her. Besides, what would he even say? That he felt odd about things he did on a daily basis? Walking out of his apartment building, driving her car, going to the university? That he'd felt a foreign energy flood through his arm and obliterate a chunk of plaster that should've knocked him out into debris?

What was next? Finding out he had superpowers and a dead uncle?

This was reality, not fiction.

And he was no superhero. Just a regular mortal.

Mortal.

Mortal.

Mortal. *Mortal. Mortal. MoRtAl. mOrTal. MOrtaL. m**ORTAL**. m**ORtal**. MorTal. **MORTAL—***

"LUKE!" He felt someone—Emma—grab onto the steering wheel and twist it to the left. The Nissan swerved off the road and screeched to a halt, missing the heavy truck in their path by mere inches. His fingers shaking, Lukas saw Emma step out of the car and slam the door. She marched over to his side, opened the door, and angrily grabbed his collar with both her hands.

"WHAT IN THE EVER-LOVING HELL IS *WRONG* WITH YOU?"

But Lukas paid her no mind. His mind raced on overdrive as he replayed the voice in his head. Or were those several voices? Or just him talking? Listening? Doing—undoing—redoing—***MORTAL—***

"—NEARLY KILLED US, YOU PRICK! WHAT THE FUCK WERE YOU—"

"STOP!" he screamed, covering his ears with both hands as he slammed his right foot—

CRASH!

Lukas looked down at the car's floorboard. Or what used to be the floorboard. His leg had gone clean through the case of the vehicle, the metal cracked and bent and torn apart at the point of impact.

And yet, his feet didn't feel a sting.

Emma stared at him, her eyes as wide as saucers as she began to slowly back away. "Did—did you just—"

"I'm—I'm so sorry," Lukas shakily replied, confused about whether to laugh or cry. Pulling the car door shut, he revved the engine again as he threw one last glance at his girlfriend. "About this. About all of today, really."

"Lukas," Emma breathed, her countenance softening. It was obvious she wanted to say more, but the words didn't make it past her lips.

"I'll be fine." He tossed her a lopsided grin. The car sprung to life as he pushed the pedal to the metal—or what remained of it. And without a backward glance, Lukas drove away.

With everything that was happening, he decided that keeping off the main roads was a good idea. Instead, he took a right onto Adams Street and drove past the tall buildings until he reached Lincoln Avenue, the place with the buildings he'd visited with a friend to get a mortgage loan. Digby LLC was right around the corner, a place he used to visit for a summer internship back in his freshman year. The speedometer dial swung to the right as the car sped up, and with it grew his unnatural anxiety.

Something was telling him that he'd picked up a tail.

The question was—who was it? What was it? Why were they following him?

He took a few extra turns purely out of paranoia, even though he couldn't spot any vehicles behind him. After all, that wasn't very conclusive. Just because he couldn't see them coming for him, didn't mean they weren't there.

They were probably just beyond the reach of his Scan Radius, especially if the hair-raising sensation was—

He blinked.

Scan Radius? What the hell is a—

SPLAT!

Something small and wide and covered in blood slammed against his windshield. With an incredibly unmanly yelp, Lukas floored the brakes and jumped out of the car to look at what had hit him like a mini kamikaze missile. It was a large creature, with wings and a round tummy that was split open and oozing blood all over his windshield.

"Is that a . . . bat?

Netopyr.

"Netopyr bat," he corrected himself, before freezing. Where had he learned that name? For him to recognize it so readily . . . Was it a species he'd come across before?

Lukas looked at the bloodied corpse again but found it to be completely unrecognizable.

"This is so fucking weird," he muttered, holding his palms to his temples. He switched on the wipers, and while most of the gore was knocked off the car, the blood was sticky enough not to budge. Here, in the middle of some random street, and especially with his sudden, uncontrollable paranoia, the last thing he wanted was to be stuck explaining to some random idiot why he was cleaning blood off of his car.

It really couldn't get worse from here.

Naturally, as soon as the thought had flitted past his mind, the ground began to tremble.

"An earthquake?" Lukas asked in disbelief. "Now of all times?"

But as he looked around at his surroundings, something told him this was no normal earthquake. For a brief moment, the skyscrapers and roads and shrubbery all flickered, as if it was just some sort of illusion. Instead, he could see slender filaments of light and stone walls, and hear songs of metal striking against metal and droplets of water dripping from great stalactites hanging down from cavernous ceilings. And fire—blazing, black fire, with blue lightning and crimson tongues tearing through the buildings like they weren't even solid structures, as if the million people who lived here were suddenly replaced by countless strands of energy, painting the world in a garish, monochromatic light.

Don't do it. Don't do it. Don't do it—

Lukas couldn't help it. His eyes met the rearview mirror.

And time itself felt frozen.

What he saw was a stomach-churning, nightmare-inducing mass of horribly sharp scales, all twisting and turning and crisscrossing onto itself with thousands of long tubules merging into each other to create a twisted caricature of a monster that no sane individual would ever conjure, even in their wildest nightmares. A stale, rotting stench assaulted his nose as a maw boasting hundreds of thousands of fangs erupted out of the earth's crust, followed by tails—two, three, four—ten—twenty—*ohMyGOdIamGoingToDiE*—thirty tails that destroyed and crushed and obliterated everything around it into smithereens. Looking at this creature was like trying to peer into raw sewage, as the utter wrongness it exuded far outstripped any fear he felt.

Lukas gulped. That strange feeling, the one he'd had roiling inside of him since this morning, told him that this monster was here for him.

Someone screamed, and Lukas dimly noted that the base of his throat felt itchy. Of course, the two things were *obviously* unrelated. A *Wham! Wham!* emanated from the other side of the car, and he instinctively crouched to avoid whatever was assaulting Emma's favorite mode of transportation. Instead, he turned around, intent on sprinting far, far away from this horrible hell-raiser turned real.

Car horns blared all at once like an impatient symphony. But as quickly as it all appeared, it disappeared, followed by a brief cacophony of destruction. A subtle glance was enough for him to understand that the offending cars had all been picked up and tossed away by the creature like yesterday's garbage.

What a fucking nightmare!

He could feel something damp on his cheeks—maybe he was crying—maybe it was more blood dripping onto him—maybe it was—

There's no time for that, Lukas screamed in his mind as he saw a car fly over his head and land in front of him, now a crumpled heap of metal, leather, and plastic. And steadily leaking gasoline.

BOOM!

He needed to focus. First escape from the hungry, ravaging monster-beast, then sit and break down the happenings of today's events afterward. He didn't have time for thought and analysis when Death was trailing his ass—what on God's green earth was that thing anyway?

Even remotely thinking back to the monster he saw froze his mind like a block of ice. His legs kept up the motions of running, but there was a sense of detachment from his mortal form. For a few seconds, his mental instructions had no bearing on his bodily functions.

Alright. No more monster thoughts.

He quickly came across a gas station, one with a parked police car in the nearby lot. Maybe the police were carrying some big guns that could bring down this thing?

CRASH!

Another car landed in a heap of steel, and this time it was right on top of said police car. Clearly, if there was any hope of being saved from this thing, it wasn't going to come from local law enforcement—

"It will pounce from the left."

Lukas didn't question the sudden whisper in his head. For once, it felt natural. Like a missing piece of him returned to complete the puzzle. Throwing all caution to the wind, he threw himself toward the right and onto the ground, landing on his hands to reduce the impact. A large, monstrous tail slammed into where he had been just a moment ago, creating a chasm of empty space where there had been a pavement.

Clearly, he was right to trust the mystery voice.

Jumping back onto his feet, he sprinted in a different direction this time without looking back. But the more he ran, the more déjà vu he felt swirling within him. It was like he'd been through this exact situation before—running away from this creature in abject terror, diving to the ground, doing everything in his power to survive . . .

Except, he hadn't.

And yet, he had.

The lines between fact and fiction began to blur.

But Lukas chose not to question it. With his body quivering and tears trailing down his cheeks, he continued to run. His legs kept pushing on and on, as if the concept of fatigue did not apply to them. Around him, buildings and cars and broken rocks and upturned pavements fell out of the sky like an Armageddon.

He forced himself to run even faster. If he were any less scared, he'd have questioned how he was able to sweep through close dives, pivot quickly without slipping, and leap across large boulders of rubble like they were playground structures.

But self-preservation was higher on his to-do list. So he didn't.

"Turn right."

He was past caring now. The voice in his head was distinctly feminine—not Emma, but who else could it be? It wasn't like there were that many women in his life. He had no clue, but it didn't matter. Voice or no voice, he needed a miracle to save his life.

"A miracle."

Was that amusement he sensed from her tone? For that matter, how was he able to sense some random person's emotio—

"It is not impossible for you to be saved. But miracles come at a price."

"WHAT PRICE?!" he bellowed, swerving yet another heavy blow. He nearly managed to avoid it, but a single protruding scale slashed against his abdomen, and warm, red blood oozed out from underneath his skin.

Meanwhile, other abominations started to form around him. A creature that looked like someone had taken a snail, painted it neon-green, and enlarged it to the size of a small elephant was spraying something bright and corrosive in his direction. Rats larger than most household cats ran across the street in strange patterns.

Lukas kept running.

"What price?" he repeated, hoping against all hope that the voice would have a plan—something, anything that would save his sorry ass from this demonic monstrosity. "Come on, what's the fucking *PRICE?!*"

An eerie laugh emanated from the darkness.

"This is indeed different from the first time around. I wonder what changed." She laughed some more. *"Tell me, if I grant you the power to exterminate this vermin, will you fulfill a wish of mine?"*

"What wish?" Lukas warily asked. Deal or no deal, he was a lawyer-in-training first and foremost. He'd always hear the conditions first.

"To fulfill what you once promised, but chose to forget."

"Huh?" He narrowly dodged another hit, and kicked one of the rats—*cinderfaces,* his brain offered—before running again. Where were the fucking police already? EMTs? SWAT teams? The National Guard? Had no one realized that a Jurassic-level monster was obliterating the city? "I don't—I don't understand. Just please, help!"

A swipe from one of the creature's several tails flung him away by several feet. He fell onto his back, groaning in pain as he pushed himself to his feet once more.

Unfortunately, it was ill-timed—

"Then we have an accord."

—as another tail was headed straight for him. Barely ten feet away.

A spike of raw emotions slammed into Lukas like a physical blow, and his mind couldn't recognize a distinct one among them. Hate, fear, agony, stubbornness, anxiety, failure—it was all a vast mélange, a cocktail so dense it nearly drove him to his knees.

He was tired. He was struggling, running, and dodging. But to what end? There was no escaping this nightmare. No amount of resilience would save him from this twisted demon from hell. No matter how much he tried to tread water in this ocean of madness incarnate, he would eventually drown in endless paranoia.

In just a moment, everything would be over.

"It is time for you to . . . "

"To do what?" he begged, his heart palpitating frantically. To die? To become a splattered smudge of red on the ground? That was going to happen anyway. He raised his right arm, hoping that his earlier superhuman feat would repeat itself and save his sorry ass a second time. Logic and reason dictated that his hand would be squashed like a grape, and his face and body were to follow.

But nothing about this screamed logic and reason anymore.

The tail approached, now less than a foot away.

"To remember."

As the tail slammed against his arm, memories rammed into him like a freight train.

A massive earthquake—diving under the floor—opening up into a giant chasm—blood—pendant—pain. His mind threatened to tear itself apart as memories kept pouring in. His pupils flickered left and right erratically as information, far more than he could assimilate, kept entering. Another memory—finding himself in the *anomaly*—the bat, azolgs, khorkhoi, cinderfaces—fighting, learning, falling in pain—ethereal creatures that phased through the walls—*INANNA*—

It all came back to him like waves crashing against a sandy coast, tides that ebbed but once again flowed. He was seeing things that made little sense, of a world that couldn't possibly have been real. But the endless swirls of memories didn't let up, and with each new one, his grasp on reality became thinner.

He was becoming *more*, and Lukas Aguilar was becoming *less*.

He had no head, yet it shook in denial.

He had no eyes, yet they stared back in defiance.

He would break, yet he would not bend. Not to this.

His heart throbbed violently, the dull thrum increasing in volume as his unease became mounting dread. Clenching his eyes shut, Lukas tried to ignore the feeling, but every hair on his body was raised. He could tell that something deeply unnatural was approaching. A new frightening uncertainty that was alien and taboo and, above all, far beyond his own understanding.

"Get out!"

It drew nearer.

"Get out!" he desperately repeated. Where was it? Outside him? Around him? Inside him? The thrum deepened in intensity, and his head was pounding in sync with his heart.

"GET OUT!"

His vision was inundated with burning, dazzling, white light. Uncountable memories tore through his mind, flowing in without pause or reprieve. They simply would not stop. And with the memories came power, surety, and confidence all rushing back to him. An ever-boiling ocean of lifeforce stirred within him, taking back what was once its domain.

But it didn't end there.

Dense, liquid, white power flowed through him. Power that was alien. Power that could not belong to any human, only to a world. Creation. Rejuvenation. Mutation. Assimilation.

Lifeforce.

Mana.

Anomalous energy.

Omphalos.

Information he couldn't make heads or tails of flooded his mind. The data could not be comprehended by a meager existence such as himself, and the whole process was excruciatingly painful and dangerous to his very existence. It wasn't something he was keen on repeating. Ever. Not if he could help it.

. . .

But in the end, he survived. For he was Lukas Aguilar.

No, he was an anomaly.

He was ███████ ██████, and he would not be defeated.

Liquid lightning rippled through his skin, crackling and radiating power as space shattered around him, like the flickering wisps of a blazing inferno. The force of the tail slamming into him created a shockwave that sent several cars hurling away. It felt as if the very Earth shook.

Lukas's lips twisted into a maniacal grin as his arm held steady against the blow. Everything was clear to him now. These khorkhoi, cinderfaces, monsters . . . none of them were real. It was all a twisted illusion trying to mimic reality by transforming his mindscape.

And behind all that transformation was—

His lips moved.

"Analyze."

YUREI

Spiritual Parasite. Energy core constitutes mana forge for Ether. Capable of creating false constructs using Metamancy.

As the realization gripped his conscious mind, everything around him twisted into strange shapes. Manifestations of the parasite's alien mind.

"Yurei," Lukas growled. "You tried to fuck with my mind. That was a mistake." He clenched his fists, gathering power within him. "And I'll show you why!"

He blurred into motion. Faster than the human eye could track, the khorkhoi's tail swiped toward him, aiming to shatter his face into blood and tissue. He grabbed the motion around the tail and yanked it, pulling the massive creature toward himself. Raising his other hand like an executioner's blade, Lukas brought it down on the tail segment and severed it from the middle. The amputated limb flailed uselessly before returning to motes of thin purple mist.

Meanwhile, the remaining army of monsters attacked Lukas.

Not that it mattered. This was *his* mind. This was where he was at his strongest.

Extending both hands outwards, lifeforce emerged from them in the shape of blades nearly as long as he was tall. Lukas spun around, drawing on Kinetomancy to increase his momentum, and struck the incoming barrage with extreme prejudice. Netopyr bats, large and small, came at him like missiles, but he killed them as easily as one would wipe sweat off his brow.

The thousand-fanged monster roared and dove underground, sending tectonic waves all across the terrain.

Lukas chuckled. This fake creature could try all he might, but it wouldn't be able to take him by surprise.

Scan.

Prey found you.

No, he mused darkly, *I found prey.*

The lifeforce blades merged to become one large greatsword as Lukas raised his hands and brought it down, just in time, as the creature dug out from below his feet.

Blinding light ensued.

And Lukas Aguilar, eyes wide open, let out a soul-wrenching scream.

CHAPTER 17

ASSIMILATION

Darkness.

The STATE of the anomaly was damaged. Multiple issues were detected, but nothing that PROPHYLAXIS could not deal with. Discharge of copious amounts of LIFEFORCE was a bad idea since discharge points appeared to be blocked. Foreign bindings on HOST BODY were keeping it from breaking out.

It was almost enough to register as a PROBLEM.

The sudden influx of a foreign SOUL into HOST BODY triggered the reaction. The omphalos observed it, running equations about the relative value of utilizing the new SOUL PROTOTYPE as an acceptable substitute for BASE HOST.

Silently, it ran the numbers.

SOUL PROTOTYPE ANALYZED	
RACE	**Yurei**
TYPE	**Spiritual Parasite**
ENERGY CORE	**Ether Mana**
Match with HOST BODY	**9%**

If the omphalos had lips, it would have pouted. 9%? That was practically nothing. Anything less than a 95% match was not worth considering. Normally, it would have left BASE HOST at the helm, but the unwanted attribute RATIONALITY was a recurring problem.

It was an added attribute that came with its own share of benefits and concerns. The omphalos could work with a LIVING BIOLOGICAL

ENVIRONMENT, but the extra baggage of BASE HOST MIND and its unwanted attributes were a problem.

Especially with MENTAL STATE maintained at a default HUMAN setting.

How . . . [human adjective] *tedious*.

The omphalos reached deeper. Vital statistics showed the situation was bordering on [human adjective] *irksome*. Any further decrease in MENTAL STATE to unacceptable levels of shock carried the potential to push the matter to [human adjective] *aggravating*.

Unacceptable.

The omphalos acted.

Activating Intensive Repair . . . CANCEL! Path Reset.

Activate Auto-Scan, Auto-Analyze

A spherical wave burst from HOST BODY, invisible to all but omphalos-kind. The omphalos sensed the GREATER ANOMALY outside HOST BODY.

GREATER ANOMALY IDENTIFIED	
CRYPT OF FIENDISH WORMS	
Size	**Class-3**
Potential	**Sub-Singularity**
Estimated Monster Count	**2381**
Estimated Energy Reserves	**917,277,532 Units**

Odd. It seemed like CRYPT OF FIENDISH WORMS was larger in size, but younger. It had an immense number of MONSTER HOSTS, but a majority were PRIMITIVE beings. It was spread out over a larger geographical area but equipped with rudimentary functions at best.

A confusing confusion.

Recommended: Deactivation of BASE HOST MIND until better Alternatives are present

---

Tempting. But deactivation of BASE HOST MIND would allow the PARASITE SOUL to take over and ALTER the HOST BODY.

Not an option.

The omphalos came to a decision. It was likely too early for this, but even HOST MIND needed to start somewhere.

Balance Reality Foundation—Counterbalance
Equalizing . . .

Base Focus Medium Chosen
Host Identified

Enacting LEGACY PROTOCOL

That was it. There was no turning back now.

New OMPHALOS FUNCTION Added!		
FUNCTION	**LEVEL**	**ENERGY COST**
Soul Siphon	N/A	20
DESCRIPTION Consumption of Soul Prototypes post the death of the organism and their storage in the Monster Prototype Array.		

New OMPHALOS FUNCTION Added!		
FUNCTION	**LEVEL**	**ENERGY COST**
Alpha Condition	1	Variable
DESCRIPTION Allows for Allowed Possession of Host Body by Monster Prototypes and eventual release of Host Body upon completion. Passive resistance against mental intrusion.		

Yes. This would do. Wait—

ALIEN TRUTH from PRESENCE

POTENTIALLY UNAVAILABLE in absence of BASE HOST

The omphalos did not curse its inability to frown. It did not have time nor inclination for such things. Instead, it simply ran the numbers once more.

The GODDESS had a BOND with BASE HOST. Quite naturally SHE had recognized the ACTIVE ROLE the omphalos was taking in molding HOST BODY to suit its purposes better. This must have been the GODDESS's attempt to balance the scales.

Still, there was a TRUTH attached to this GODDESS.

Not a bad augmentation. Allowed.
   . . . for now.
BASE HOST activated. HOST BODY responded. Eyes opened.

HOST MIND AUTO-ACTIVATE.

PROCESS CALCULATED. INTERCEPT ROUTINES.

ENACT.

PART IV

AMONG THE OTHER

CHAPTER 18

IMPRISONED

Lukas came to his senses in complete darkness, feeling cold, dry rock beneath him. There was a sharp pain in his head and his heart pounded uncontrollably. He pushed himself off of his back and looked around, drinking in every inch of his surroundings with growing hysteria.

A particularly cold draft of wind made him realize he was stark naked. His clothes were gone, and the large belt of monster hide that had been wound around his waist was gone too. Granted, his shirt hadn't been much, and his trousers had been only about the length of his boxers and had gaping holes in them.

His wrists chafed and his shoulders ached, and he tugged at the bindings around his arms and feet. It hurt. It hurt a lot.

Why hadn't the healing function set in yet?

Prophylaxis, he thought to himself.

FUNCTION - Prophylaxis	Level - 1
TASK - Ongoing	Estimated Energy Cost - 2,378 units

The estimated energy cost was a large figure, as far as Prophylaxis was concerned. Lukas poured lifeforce into his limbs and winced as his muscles screamed in protest.

A moment later, the pain was gone, as was the lifeforce, leaving Lukas feeling like he'd just run a marathon. He readied himself once more, attempting to form a sphere of raw lifeforce like he'd gotten accustomed to.

"I would advise against that."

"Inanna!" Lukas exclaimed elatedly. Even though he was trapped in darkness without his lifeforce, at least she was still there.

Inanna laughed at his response. **"It pleases me to know you value my presence so much, mortal."**

He managed to roll his eyes in spite of the pain. "What's going on?"

"Something unanticipated. The parasite possessed you. You lost control of yourself and gave in to the creature's instincts."

Slowly, he began to remember. He had used Kinetomancy to generate friction and create flames to burn those monsters. And then—

"I shut off your lifeforce and forced you into your subconsciousness."

"The parasite thing created some kind of false reality. In my own mind." Lukas frowned. "I remember it now. The plaster. The glass shattering. The earthquake—"

"That was your mind trying to break you out."

"And you helped me."

"I am owed favors, mortal. I intend to collect."

He snorted. Of course she did. "Still . . . Thank you for the help."

An uncomfortable silence acknowledged his gratitude. **"You should look into your Soulscape. Being possessed has had its effects on you."**

Lukas opened his Soulscape immediately.

SOULSCAPE	
NAME	**Lukas Aguilar**
Type	**Base Host**
Level	**4**
Experience	**417**
Current Threshold	**640**
Utilized Soul Capacity	**1479/2379**
ESSENCE	
Maximum Lifeforce Output	**725**
Replenishment Rate	**180 / hour**

SKILL ATTRIBUTES		
SKILL	**LEVEL**	**CONSUMED SOUL CAPACITY**
Raw Lifeforce Manipulation	1	50

Momentum Manipulation	1	50
Friction Modulation	1	50
Pressure Modulation	1	50
Kinetomancy (FRAGMENTED)	APEX	1279

OMPHALOS ATTRIBUTES	
Energy Reservoir Capacity	∞
Current Energy Level	722,429,743 units
OMPHALOS FUNCTIONS	
Scan	Level 2 [Upgraded]
Analyze	Level 2 [Upgraded]
Prophylaxis	Level 2 [Upgraded]
Soul Siphon	N/A [New]
Alpha Condition	Level 1 [New]

"**Congratulations are in order,**" the goddess praised. "**It seems you have accomplished something.**"

"Wha—but—" he spluttered. "How did it happen? I mean, I didn't level up yet." He glanced through the list. A thousand-point increase in Soul Capacity? Upgrades on his omphalos functions? New skills?

He checked the Experience section. 417. That was a minor improvement at best. He had estimated a jump of at least fifty or so points.

"**It seems your omphalos took matters into its own hands.** Lukas glanced back at his Soulscape. *Soul Siphon. Alpha Condition. What are these things?*

FUNCTION	LEVEL	ENERGY COST
Soul Siphon	N/A	20
DESCRIPTION		
Consumption of Soul Prototypes post the death of the organism and their storage in the Monster Prototype Array.		

FUNCTION	LEVEL	ENERGY COST
Alpha Condition	1	Variable
DESCRIPTION		
Allows for Allowed Possession of Host Body by Monster Prototypes and eventual release of Host Body upon completion. Passive resistance against mental intrusion.		

"You've gotta be kidding me," Lukas muttered, running his fingers through his hair, trying to digest the sudden series of surprises. *Consumption* of soul prototypes? Had he consumed that wraith? Was it now inside his body?

MONSTER PROTOTYPE ARRAY	
RACE	**SOUL SIZE**
Yurei	1050

Define it.

MONSTER PROTOTYPE: YUREI		
DESCRIPTION		
Spiritual Parasite. Energy Core constitutes mana forge for Ether. Capable of creating False Constructs using Metamancy. Enhances the lifeforce production of the victim at the expense of rationality.		
SKILLS	**LEVEL**	**SOUL CAPACITY CONSUMED**
Possession	2	500
Conjuration	2	500
Disintegration	1	50

Right, thank you, Lukas shuddered. The monster soul was now stored within him. *Show me my skills.*

SKILL ATTRIBUTES		
SKILL	**LEVEL**	**SOUL CAPACITY CONSUMED**
Raw Lifeforce Manipulation	1	50

Momentum Manipulation	1	50
Friction Modulation	1	50
Pressure Modulation	1	50
Kinetomancy (FRAGMENTED)	APEX	1279

SKILL	LEVEL	SOUL CAPACITY CONSUMED
Friction Modulation	1	50
DESCRIPTION		
Allows for manipulation of frictional forces. Sub-abilities include Deceleration, Resistance Modulation, Heat Manipulation, and Motion Negation.		

Lukas blinked in shock. That was far more comprehensive of a description than he'd seen before. Not one to look a gift horse in its mouth, he checked the rest.

SKILL	LEVEL	SOUL CAPACITY CONSUMED
Pressure Modulation	1	50
DESCRIPTION		
Allows for manipulation of pressure. Sub-abilities include Expansion, Compression, and Vacuum Creation.		

SKILL	LEVEL	SOUL CAPACITY CONSUMED
Raw Lifeforce Manipulation	1	50
DESCRIPTION		
Allows for manipulation of raw lifeforce within the body. Sub-abilities include Body Augmentation, Lifeforce Absorption and Neural Suppression.		

SKILL	LEVEL	SOUL CAPACITY CONSUMED
Momentum Manipulation	1	50
DESCRIPTION		
Allows for manipulation of lifeforce within the body. Sub-abilities include Acceleration, Force Generation, Manipulation & Transference.		

SKILL	LEVEL	SOUL CAPACITY CONSUMED
Kinetomancy [Fragmented]	APEX	1279
DESCRIPTION		
Allows for Motion Negation, Deflection, Telekinetic Maneuvers and ███ ███ ███ ███		

"That's weird," Lukas said curiously. This was the first time he'd ever seen redacted text in his Screen. Futilely he raised his hand, straining to produce lifeforce in his palm, and sighed at the failure. It was torturous, having so many new skills yet lacking the ability to try them out.

"A little patience would do you good, mortal. The bindings on your person are blocking your lifeforce. If you attempt to force some out, it will pool at the source and cause lifeforce poisoning."

Lukas tried to get loose by working his limbs methodically and testing the ropes, but it was hard to tell whether he was making any progress. After a few minutes, he turned over and lay face-first, too tired to struggle as his bound limbs screamed out in protest. The pendant was squeezed between his chest and the floor. Lukas idly wondered why his kidnapper had left it on him. **"They are incapable of sensing it."**

What do you mean?

"I cast a Veil of Ignorance on the pendant when I first took control over your frail form. No one who does not know about the pendant may sense it."

So . . . it's invisible.

Inanna sniffed imperiously at the description. **"To all mortal senses, yes."**

Except for mine. Lukas cursed, wincing at the discomfort he was feeling against his rib cage.

"Do not overexert yourself. Let the healing do its job."

Right. The healing. For some reason, whatever stopped him from accessing his lifeforce hadn't affected the omphalos or the reserves within him.

Prey found you.

The door opened, and a sudden light stabbed at his pupils. Two people came through with a pair of floating torches lighting the way.

Whatever joy and surprise he'd hoped to feel from meeting another person was extinguished by the knowledge that they'd bound and imprisoned him.

"Let me out of here!"

The two figures didn't so much as look at him. The larger, masculine one took a place closer to the wall on the opposite side, while the other took a few steps in his direction. She stepped up close and lifted off the hood covering her face, revealing a twenty-something girl with jet-black locks that fell on both sides of her face and matching eyes. She had a little Cupid's bow of a mouth, framed by small dimples on either side that contrasted her squared-off chin and stopped an eyelash shy of masculine. Her dark eyes flashed with amusement as her lustrous hair came free of its hood. But perhaps the most striking thing about her was the strength in her expression, and the confidence in her gaze.

"Nhueut fer yakho ah e nhueat fer yakho djoo'lin layhte?"

" . . . I don't understand," Lukas replied.

The girl edged closer to him. "Yakho djoo'lin layhte?"

He wildly shook his face, trying to get rid of his binds. Seriously, who were these people? "I've got no clue what you're saying."

That made her pause. She barked some orders to the man in the shadows, who grunted back. She then turned back to face him.

"Nhueut fer yakho ah e nhueat fer yakho djoo'lin layhte?"

Lukas didn't know what she'd done, but there was something in her words this time around. A most primal desire to reply to her question arose within him. He opened his mouth and said, "I really, *really* don't understand what you are saying."

" . . . "

Can you understand her? Lukas thought clearly.

"I may."

May?

"I am weighing the pros and cons of doing so."

What's that supposed to mean—

His mental diatribe was cut short as the girl grabbed his face and pushed him back in a most unorthodox fashion. Lukas felt his muscles strain as he was pushed back onto his knees.

Analyze?

Unable to analyze verbal languages.

The girl barked something to the man in the shadows a second time. Within seconds, a third person entered the room. He was a soldier, or at least appeared to be one based on his attire. Brown bangs for hair, a sort of forgettable face, metal-plated chest armor, and a metallic skirt on the waist to protect his valuables. All he needed was a Corinthian helmet, and he'd be perfect for an extra in a medieval fantasy movie.

"Rhoussewudz leyht!" she barked.

"Leyht?" the man asked, visibly surprised by the sudden demand.

Lukas had a suspicion that he was not going to like what followed. "Look," he tried, futilely trying to move his hands, "can we just talk about this? I really mean you no—"

The soldier toppled over onto the floor with a resounding thud.

" . . . harm."

Lukas's eyes widened, and a bead of sweat trickled down the side of his face. Did that—did the soldier just . . . *die?* Was this some kind of interrogation technique? A threat? As every second passed, he felt more and more nervous. Were they going to kill him next? Were—

"Cease your mental drivel and *look*," the goddess chided.

Lukas paused. And looked. And kept on looking, his eyes widening with growing horror, as motes of light began to arise out of the fallen man, coalescing together to form a—

OhMyGodwhatthehellisthat—

An eight-legged canine took shape, with three pairs of eyes, a maw too sharp for his liking, and one of those sigils engraved between its eyes. The creature let out an unearthly growl.

"Let's not do anything hasty," he said in a panic, slipping in his haste at trying to escape. "No no NO DON'T—"

It dove at him.

. . .

. . .

. . .

When he woke up next, Lukas found himself facedown on the floor, with his legs aching to no end. Merely breathing felt like a motion that stretched at sore muscles. He felt ravenously thirsty and hungry, and considering the complaints from his bladder, he'd been out for quite a while.

He looked around. The prison was still there, only this time, his arms were no longer bound behind his back. But they weren't free either. Strange metallic bracelets were wrapped against his wrists, ankles, and abdomen. Startled, he looked at his own body, checking himself. That hound-like wraith thing had dived into his body, hadn't it? What had it done to him? Another possession?

Lukas pushed himself up and looked around. There was no one in the room.

He rubbed his face with his palms and leaned against the wall. His body felt healed, though he still couldn't feel any lifeforce flooding into his body. These bracelets, whatever they did, were keeping it sealed away.

Show me the Monster Prototype Array.

MONSTER PROTOTYPE ARRAY		
RACE	**ENERGY CORE**	**SOUL SIZE**
Yurei	Mana (Ether)	1050
Reiki	Mana (Ether)	1550

Holy— Another one?

MONSTER PROTOTYPE: REIKI		
DESCRIPTION		
Wraith-like parasitic creature. Capable of Altering the physiological structure of its host to a minor extent. Enhances lifeforce production of Host at the expense of rationality.		
SKILLS	**LEVEL**	**SOUL CAPACITY CONSUMED**
Possession	1	50
Conjuration	2	500
Disintegration	2	500
Raw Lifeforce Manipulation	2	500

What is this, some kind of "Possess Lukas" day?

"**Cease your whining, mortal,**" Inanna said irritably. "**If anything, you are the one who stands to profit. The Soul Siphon function is quite reliable that way.**"

"Until the one time it isn't, and then I'd be too dead to complain about it," he muttered. "Not to mention I can't understand a damn thing these people—"

"**Be silent. Someone approaches.**"

Prey found you.

The familiar, black-haired girl stepped through the door, followed by the man who had originally stood in the shadows. This time, the lighting was a little better, so he could see his face. Clean-shaved, with strange cracks across his skull that looked too large to be just left open like that, the man looked to be in his fifties. Just who were these peo—*creatures?* More reiki? Or, perhaps, yurei?

Analyze.

Insufficient data.

Neither then. Great.

"Listen," Lukas began heatedly, "you don't just try to possess people because they entered some—"

"Yhell mehd, khaan yakho . . . duunhd'and nhueat ah'd . . . saying, can you?"

"Come again?"

"I asked," she testily repeated, "who are you?"

He frowned. Why was he suddenly able to understand her? Was it because of the Soul Siphon? Had he magically understood their language because he had absorbed it?

Language Identified—Ualbesh
Replicating . . .

It took him everything not to react to the sudden notification.

Ualbesh? Never heard of that one.

"Listen, I began—"

"So," the stranger drawled, her eyebrows slightly raised, "you *are* capable of speaking it."

Lukas narrowed his eyes. What language did she think he was speaking in?

She tilted her head slightly as she observed him. "Interesting. You speak it fluently, and I think you understand it too. Do you believe you are speaking in your own native tongue?"

"I am . . . not?"

The girl took a step back. "Tell me, what language do you think we are speaking?"

Lukas frowned. "English?"

"In-lis?"

Something inside of him died. Lukas knew he was being hopelessly optimistic, but he really wanted her to recognize that term. It was official—this was not Earth. These people might look human, but they weren't from his planet. This was . . . somewhere else.

"**Rejoice!**" Inanna said bitingly. "**Now you have more** *proof.*"

How am I doing this? Because of the Soul—

"**No. The translation and replication of languages are two of the pendant's many functions. I merely allowed you access to it.**"

What languages?

"**Any.**"

. . . Any?

"**Every language that has existed, exists, and will exist.**"

I hate to be the one to point this out, but what you say makes zero sense.

"**How utterly devastating.**"

I'm serious, Lukas mentally replied, trying to avoid looking at the black-haired girl's eyes. *There can't exist a universal translator without knowledge of all languages first. I can understand mana turning into elements, but how do you translate a language that does not yet exist?*

"**You simply need to look beyond your illusions of linear existence.**"

"I wonder," his interrogator spoke again. "Do you know what language you are actually speaking?"

Slowly, carefully, Lukas shook his head. "What am I speaking? It sounds like English."

"Ualbesh. It's a common language around here. Does that sound familiar to you?"

Lukas shook his head again.

"Interesting." She turned to the other man. "Qwe Fyt tha—do you think, Nihil?"

Language Identified—Felleisen
Replicate?

No, Lukas thought hard. *Just keep translating.*

"He does look bremetan, Solana," the strange man—or man-like creature—said. He had a gravelly voice and spoke in slow, gathered sentences. "Few bremetans can resist possession, let alone twice. But it doesn't seem that he has become an obake, or . . . an oni."

Oni? As a diligent student of mythology, it was a rather familiar term. From Japanese folklore, oni were large, scary creatures, some taller than even trees. They were mostly depicted with horns, red or blue skin, and fang-like tusks, and were said to bring disaster, disease, and punish the damned in hell.

Lukas found himself mildly offended. He certainly was not an oni.

"Do you understand me now?" the girl—*Solana*—spoke up again.

Still Felleisen.

"Uh . . . what? I can't understand you. Is this still . . . What did you call it? Woolways?"

The slight irritation that flickered across Solana's face made his inner child happy. "Ualbesh," she corrected. "And no. We were speaking in Felleisen."

Language Identified—Ualbesh

"Ah," Lukas replied. "Yes. I can understand you now. No clue why. What . . ." He donned a look of intense wariness. "What have you done to me?"

Solana ignored his question entirely. "Who are you? How did you arrive here?"

"I'm not from around here. I was caught in an accident—"

"What kind of accident?"

"A spell gone wrong," he lied. "The next thing I knew, I found myself inside this cave."

"Where are you from?" she demanded.

"Earth." He felt a pang in his heart at the lack of familiarity in her expression. "I'm from the US. Surely you've heard of it?"

"He's bluffing," the man—Nihil—said in Felleisen. "He's making it all up."

"And the language?" Solana threw back in the same tongue. "Did he make that up as well? How does someone who speaks Ualbesh and is immune to possession drop into the desert out of nowhere?"

Lukas filed the information away. Was he in a desert? An anomaly cavern inside a desert?

"What race are you?" she asked. "Bremetan?"

There was that term again. *Bremetan.* What did it mean? "I'm a human."

"Hue-mane?"

"Human," Lukas corrected.

"Human. From Yu-Es? Is it a kingdom in your lands?"

Lukas made an elaborate show of gulping. "I guess . . . I guess my fears were right. This isn't Earth. I'm in a different world, aren't I? A different realm?"

Nihil made a strangled choking noise. Solana, on the other hand, maintained her calm, dispassionate expression, her ice-cold eyes observing his every movement.

"Is it?" he demanded again, adding some hysteria into his voice.

Solana gave a slight shrug of her shoulders. "That is a tall assumption. I assume you have a name?"

"Lukas. Lukas Aguilar."

"Not a bremetan name, Aguilar. It's not a clan name, is it?"

"It's my surname."

Her lips curled. "I see. What do you think, Nihil?"

Language Identified—Faecani
Replicate?

No, Lukas thought with a mental frown. *Just keep translating until I say so.*

The man walked up closer, looking oddly disturbed. "I . . . do not know what to say," he continued in fluent Faecani. "If what he says is the truth, then . . . do you think—"

Solana sighed. "No, this is not the time for that nonsense."

"But the reiki is gone. It's clear it hasn't possessed him. It was definitely killed during the attempt," Nihil exclaimed.

Solana hummed thoughtfully. "I will admit, I have never heard of anyone killing a reiki, let alone a yurei, in that particular way. Resist possession, perhaps. But *kill?* No. He is speaking Ualbesh, so I thought he might have absorbed the reiki. But the reiki could speak Faecani too, yet he does not seem to understand it."

Solana peered at him with narrowed eyes and continued to speak in fluent Faecani. "Is his soul naturally immune to possession, or is it a matter of high resistance? The reiki was a weakling. The yurei guards, on the other hand . . ."

"What are you suggesting?" Nihil croaked. "Surely—"

"We have to know what is going on with this Outsider! If he even *is* an Outsider." Her dark eyes narrowed. "Bring in Quonnan. Arrange a trial by combat."

Lukas felt a cold shiver drawl down his spine. "What are you saying?" he tried. "Please, just let me go. We can forget any of this ever happened."

Her mirthless smile vanished at his question, and she switched back to Ualbesh again. "I wish to know what happened to that reiki that attempted to possess you. You are going to face one of my fighters. Quonnan. She is a kasha. Do you know what that is?"

He shook his head.

"Always an uphill climb," Solana murmured. "We wish to see how you perform against her. Or rather, if there is any bit of my soldier left within you."

This is my chance. Now or never.

Lukas raised his arms. "I can't use lifeforce because of these bands. You want me to fight? Fine. But at least free me first."

"Fear not. You will be freed of those shackles before the trial. Give us a good fight, or it may very well be your last." With those ominous words, Solana stood up and walked away with Nihil following suit, leaving a thoughtful Lukas behind.

CHAPTER 19

FIGHT TO LIVE

Learn to fight naked and you can never be disarmed.

It was a line from Sun Tzu's *The Art of War*, and a perfectly good philosophy to follow. Unfortunately, it didn't translate to being comfortable while walking naked into battle, with easily a hundred or more alien spectators, some humanoid and others not so much, surrounding him on all sides. It took serious effort to convince himself that they were leering at him and not his bits.

"You can always cover yourself with your hands rather than fight," Inanna suggested.

Lukas did not deign to reply. Instead, he looked around at everything but the jeering spectators. He was standing outside a large circle that had been marked with the same sigils he'd seen painted on the walls.

"Step inside," Nihil said in fluent Ualbesh from behind him.

"I can't fight unless these are removed." Lukas lifted his arms to show the bracelets on his wrists.

"Step. Inside." The man's voice rumbled like shifting tectonic plates.

Not wanting to enrage the man any further, Lukas calmly walked forward. The moment he stepped into the circle, power saturated the air around him. It was potent, almost unbearably so. His hair stood on end, and an instinctive awareness from the omphalos within was telling him to get out as quickly as he could.

Without warning, the bracelets opened with a harsh click and fell off.

It felt as if a lightning bolt hit his chest, an agonizing ribbon of power that nearly brought him to his knees. His lifeforce, no longer restrained, ripped through his body with reckless abandon.

The rush drove the shame away. The rush made him confident. The rush felt *good*.

Lukas was ready to fight. To tear his opponent to shreds.

Amidst a howling cry of cheers and shouts, a tall, lean female stepped into the ring. He felt the word "female" was more apt than "woman" because she was far from human. And if the humans in this world were called "bremetans," then this creature wouldn't classify as bremetan either.

She had bright red hair that extended into a mane all the way down her back and continued out into a long, muscular tail with a sharp metallic spear end as a tip. She had two pairs of purple eyeballs, one set above the other, constantly registering his every move. Her lips opened to reveal long, thin fangs and her hands brandished nails—or rather, *claws*—that were jagged and easily the size of her fingers.

"QUON—NAN! QUON—NAN!" the crowd chanted.

Quonnan. Solana had referred to her as a kasha earlier. When Lukas checked the Screen for more information, he ended up finding nothing. Then again, he didn't think he had come across that particular term before. And that was assuming tales of this creature even existed back on Earth.

Solana chose that moment to grace everyone with her presence. The cacophony of cheers made him wonder if she was some kind of hotshot among the local hierarchy. The mysterious woman moved with a feline grace that complemented her looks as she casually sauntered along the periphery of the circle. Lukas noted that the crowds dutifully stepped back to allow her space.

"This is a trial by combat." Solana spoke in clear Ualbesh. Every single entity fell silent as soon as she began to speak. "Our fighter Quonnan will fight Lukas Aguilar, who, by his own admission, is an *Outsider.*"

And just like that, the whispers began. Angry, furious whispers. The gazes shifted. Leers turned into looks of speculation. Those that were jeering now sported calculating eyes, with several bearing caution in their expressions. Hell, even Quonnan's gaze had shifted from being predatory to outright calculative. Just what was it about being an Outsider that was so special?

"The rules are thus." Her voice pierced the silence. "Everything goes. Life-force. Mana. Possession. Any other tricks the Outsider might have up his sleeve. The battle is only over when one of the two fighters is dead."

Lukas narrowed his eyes. Somehow, he doubted Solana was setting up one of her own fighters to die. No, it was more like she didn't believe he was capable of killing the kasha, should it attempt a similar possession.

The idea he had implanted in her mind had borne fruit.

She didn't want him dead. She wanted him *possessed*, then to observe the results for herself. She wanted to see if he, the Outsider, was actually immune or had something unique about him that could be of potential use for her. And she had no qualms about sacrificing one of her own warriors for her little experiment.

"A woman after my own heart." Inanna chuckled.

"Second," Solana continued, "all attacks must be concentrated within this circle. If either one of you tries to break this circle open, I will kill you myself. Third, it is customary for participants to speak their last wishes before the trial commences."

Quonnan was the first to speak, her tone curt. "Who cares about last wishes? I want to kill him, and then, I want that body." She pointed at Lukas with a clawed finger, all the while slowly, playfully, licking her lips. "It looks *juicy*."

A flash of sudden displeasure appeared on Solana's face, before it was covered up with careful neutrality.

Lukas tipped his head forward imperceptibly, before refocusing on the task at hand. A last wish was granted to a person before his execution. Unless the rules were vastly different here, it meant he was allowed to ask for anything within reasonable limits.

But what could he ask for? Clothes would help preserve his modesty—whatever was left of it. He could ask for food or water, or maybe even weapons to fight against Quonnan. All of them were sensible wishes, but none of them would contribute to the upcoming fight in a meaningful capacity.

The odds here were long. He was alone, surrounded by monsters that only looked human. Given the kasha's confidence, Lukas had to trust that she was going to be tough as nails. But even if he managed to kill this one, there was no way he could take them all down by himself.

He needed some kind of edge. A game changer.

In fact . . .

A game changer was exactly what he needed.

He narrowed his eyes and reflected on what he had known about these creatures.

One. They were ethereal and capable of manipulating the elements. At the very least, the ether element, if the yurei and the reiki were any indication.

Two. They *loved* to possess others and got really excited when they found something they couldn't possess.

Three. Solana could have just killed him in that prison, but she didn't. Instead, she arranged this spectacle. Somehow, giving him a messy, public execution didn't seem like her style.

Four. The same black-haired beauty had mentioned his status as an Outsider to the crowd, but nothing about his supposed immunity against possession.

Five. It was clear that Quonnan had nothing to gain from this twisted caricature of Make-A-Wish. Chances were that it was another opportunity that could be twisted in his favor.

Six. No one here knew about his Soul Siphon ability, or his true nature as an anomaly.

"Why don't we make it interesting?" Lukas finally said out loud. "Let's make a bit of a game out of this trial?"

The chamber became intense all at once, as if a hundred throats all inhaled at the same time. Lukas could practically feel the air around him saturate with sharpened interest.

"You are supposed to make your last wish," Solana informed him drolly.

"And I am stating it. My last wish is to make a game out of this trial."

Solana cocked her head, studying him. "This trial is already a game, Outsider."

"Then surely you wouldn't mind changing the stakes. What if you could get more out of it?"

Quonnan narrowed her eyes. "What more could you lose than your life?"

Lukas gave her his meanest version of a patronizing smile before casually ignoring her and turning toward Solana. "I'll tell you how I did it."

"Did what?"

"Stupidity doesn't suit you."

Her stare intensified.

" . . . And if you win?"

"I go free. Unharmed, physically and spiritually."

Solana threw her head back and laughed. "You amuse me, Outsider. But I'm not letting you go just because you somehow managed to defeat her."

"Not very confident in your fighter, are you?" Lukas jerked his head in Quonnan's direction. "What was it? Nobody volunteered, so you chose the only one you could bribe with candy?"

"Leader . . . " Quonnan growled, gathering herself into a crouch, ready to pounce. She flexed her hands. It sounded like a popcorn popper. He tried very hard not to think about how her claws could tear him to shreds with a single slash.

"Tell me, Outsider." Solana's expression bore as much resemblance to a smile as a shark did to a dolphin. "What stops me from torturing you until you simply spill your secrets?"

"Because if you wanted to do it, you'd have done it. And also, it's boring."

"You are suicidal," Inanna proclaimed with amusement.

"I still will not agree to it, Outsider," Solana said, shaking her head.

"Chicken!"

"Must you antagonize her so?"

Solana looked like she'd like nothing better than to wring his neck with her bare hands. Meanwhile, he stared at her with a wolfish smile on his face, enjoying every second of her reaction. It was clear she hadn't been talked to like this in a long time, if ever.

Then her expression shifted. Lukas watched with growing dread as *things* moved beneath her face, shifting and rolling where nothing should have existed that could shift and roll. As easy as it was to think of them as humans with special abilities, they were something far more terrifying than he could comprehend.

"Very well," she said at last. "I won't kill you or restrain you. But you will be under my employment."

Lukas felt his jaw hit the floor. Just what was it with these extraterrestrial and supernatural women wanting to have him under their employment? First Inanna—

"Take a moment to think before you finish that sentence."

He banished the thought immediately. "Employment?" he began angrily.

"Enough chatter!" growled the kasha, who looked like she was going to evaporate out of sheer anger. "Now get ready to die!"

" . . . Right," Lukas said, observing the kasha in front of him. "Duel time."

"You are a fool if you think this will be easily settled."

Are you offering your help?

Inanna sniffed. **"You should know by now, mortal. I am always offering. It is your reticence that keeps you from accepting. In a fight such as this, my power could be the difference between crushing defeat and overwhelming victory. With my aid, what monster can hope to touch you?"**

Drop it. I'm no one's puppet.

A little cold spot formed in the pit of his stomach, but before he could act upon it, the horn blew.

"Let the trial begin!" Solana announced.

Lukas took a deep breath, the very act bringing him a level of clarity that would've been impossible otherwise. And for the better too, as Quonnan moved in for the kill right then, her claws piercing through the air, reaching for his throat, ready to decapitate him with a single blow.

He threw himself back as the claws tore through the space his neck had occupied just a moment ago, the tip of the claw skimming so close to his throat that he could feel it on his skin as it passed. His dodge had left him momentarily off-balance and in the short amount of time it took him to regain his footing, Quonnan was already on him.

Using the momentum of her missed strike to fuel her motion, she spun around in a full circle, her hair trailing behind her like a cape, and slammed her left leg into his abdomen. Lukas was caught between bending like a bow, distraught under the absolute agony, and being flung into the ground like a rag doll. His back was severely bruised by the rocky terrain, and he could feel something wet and sticky on his back.

He coughed up blood. He must have clipped his head at some point because stars were swirling in his vision.

By the time he had managed to sit upright, the panic had already set in. That could have been a critical blow. Already he could feel one of his ribs cracked and, given the pain that was trying to take over his sanity, he was sure that he would soon lose consciousness if he didn't do something. Had she managed to hit him a little higher or lower . . .

He'd be dead. Or at least broken, bleeding, and utterly at the mercy of this creature that wanted to take over his body and claim it for her own. A creature that was currently looking at him like a hungry wolf as she prepared her next blow.

He had to get up. Fighting back wasn't an option because if he didn't manage to get up any time soon, he wouldn't live long enough to have a chance.

And the worst part was, he hadn't even been able to follow her attack. Quonnan had been simply too fast for his eyes, and her reflexes were too quick for him to counter with Kinetomancy.

So he breathed. And focused. And poured more lifeforce into his system. The raw power moved into his bones and muscles, bringing with it a strength that his body did not possess. His sense of pain dulled and the adrenaline reached a new high.

Get up! he chided himself. He'd faced quite a number of monsters inside the Crypt of Fiendish Worms. The formless ghol trapping him to the wall, the massive khorkhoi that had caught his trail, the numerous monsters he had taken head-on. And he had survived all of them.

So he could survive this too.

Quonnan walked toward him slowly, like a predator closing in on her wounded prey. "How disappointing!" she replied in Felleisen. "I thought you would be different. But you are all the same. You are all *prey*."

The cold feeling in his chest returned, and Lukas knew, right that moment, that if nothing changed, then he was going to die. The realization galvanized him. Quonnan screeched out a vicious war cry and lunged at him, ready to tear him down like useless meat.

Lukas raised both arms at her. Raw kinetic force exploded out of him, smashing into her chest like a sledgehammer. He could see Quonnan's eyes widen for a split second, and her fork-like tongue escaped her mouth as she was flung twenty feet back and slammed against something invisible. Her body bent in half as it bounced off the circle's invisible barrier and dropped to the floor.

Only, he had other plans.

Grabbing her falling motion, Lukas shoved her to the right, smashing against the invisible barrier there. The kasha's battered form bounced off and crumpled to the floor again like a dishrag. Even with his disoriented vision, he could see a mesh of skin, blood, and something that looked awfully like bones sticking out of the portion where the chest was supposed to be.

The kasha wasn't moving, yet her eyes seemed to glare at him hatefully.

Lukas pushed himself up, wincing at the sudden jolts of pain that arose from his stomach. Prophylaxis was working, but there was only so much it could do mid-battle. He pumped in even more lifeforce, which eased the pain, if only by a little bit.

"Get up!" he taunted, staring daggers at the fallen kasha. "I didn't even hit you that hard!"

Conjuring a single, pulsating orb of lifeforce in his right hand, he launched it in her direction. It ended up hitting the ground easily two inches away from her body, ripping out chunks of rock from the floor and sending it flying.

Lukas wobbled. His coordination had gone wonky, but there was no way one could survive getting their chest blown up. Right?

His hopes were dashed when the kasha raised her left hand and pulled out the bone sticking out of her chest before discarding it. She punched herself right below the heart region, twisting her body in ways that shouldn't have been possible. Then she got up and cracked her neck, as if nothing had happened.

"Interesting trick," she replied in Ualbesh.

"My next trick involves bunnies, I swear," he replied, his body still shaking. "Just stand there and give me a moment. Or ten."

Quonnan did not rise to the taunt. Instead, a hot wind blew inside the circle, making the hairs on Lukas's back stand on end. A flash of sensation flickered over him as the kasha drew in power.

A *lot* of power.

He took a defensive stance, utterly clueless about what the kasha was going to do to him next.

If she decided to launch a melee attack, he'd be a goner. Maybe if he was lucky, he could stop her using Kinetomancy and try to blast her head off—body-possessing parasite or not, there was only so much one could go after getting one's head blown off.

"And you believe she will grant you the chance?" Inanna questioned. **"That creature is your better in skills, experience, and ruthlessness."**

Always the shining ball of optimism, aren't you?

Meanwhile, Quonnan's clothes dissolved into smoke, forming a clinging, almost crimson mist that drifted around her in spiraling tendrils. He watched with surreal fascination and growing horror as the mist became sullen, glowing flames.

Is she—

A cry of pure fury tore through the air.

Quonnan turned her palms up, and searing points of violent light appeared at the center—her skin blistering and dissolving and opening the way for something else as waves of heat shimmered around her body.

The kasha howled and hurled a sphere of liquid flame, easily the size of a basketball, at him.

Lukas sidestepped like a nervous horse, but it hadn't been enough. The fireball missed him, but the residual heat left a lasting impression on his left arm, below the elbow. The skin blistered, but he ignored it. Blistered skin was the least of his troubles right now.

I guess we now know what element she uses.

"Fire," Inanna replied wistfully. **"My favorite among the elements. Note that the parasite is the user, not the physical shell."**

And wasn't that the truth? Little by little, Quonnan's body was dissolving. He could see the skin singeing and charring, as more and more heat exuded from her body. What had the kasha said? She'd possess his body and make it her own? That meant her own was disposable.

Though, why she'd want to risk burning her future body was beyond him.

"Look."

The kasha's body slowly healed, reforming in a twisted sort of way. The tissues were forced back into place while more of them were being formed, filling in any gaps. The burnt skin was being knit, and charred flesh and bone were being put back into place.

> ## ETHER CONSTRUCTS
> ### False Construction of Biological tissue through Metamancy.

"Ether constructs? It looks exactly like human tissue."

Quonnan was reforming the outer structure. Not exactly healing, but rather creating a shell to keep the structure in place. If the shell was anything like the ones the yurei had crafted earlier, a solid physical blow should do the trick. That and fire—

Lukas narrowed his eyes. Why would a creature of fire use an ability that made her specifically vulnerable to her own element? Unless she was immune to it—no, that wasn't it. Regardless, one thing was certain—possessed bodies or false constructs, they all followed laws. If it was a human body, or even remotely human, it was fragile.

It could be broken. It could bleed. It could burn.

And after a certain point, no amount of bullshitting could get it back into working order.

He just needed to ensure that he survived until Quonnan burned herself to bits. And then—

"You burned the ones back there. It did not stop them from possessing you."

I know. Nothing stopping her from attempting that right now. But I know she won't.

"Oh? How so?"

Her ego. I'm just hoping she'd immolate herself before that happens.

"Can you guarantee your win?"

Well, I can't keep living in fear.

"Give up!" Quonann spat. "I'd rather not destroy your body."

"I'm trying to let you down gently, you ugly freak!"

An orb of searing white heat came hurling in his direction. Raising his right hand, Lukas grabbed the motion of the incoming fireball and tugged it slightly toward the left. A second ball shot toward his groin, and Lukas managed to deflect that too, hastily raising a shield of pure force. The kasha had apparently decided to take him seriously, and the smell of charring flesh saturated the arena as she kept shooting fireballs relentlessly in his direction.

Just a bit more, Lukas thought, hiding behind a shimmering wall of force. Kinetomancy, he was finding out, was a rather versatile tool. The sheer number of applications of Momentum Manipulation was mind-boggling. The tenth sphere smashed against his makeshift shield and exploded upon contact into a cloud of flame that expanded along the length of the entire shield.

Quonnan let out a cry of frustration. Her thought process had been obvious. If she could keep pouring fire at him, she'd eventually burn through it, or exhaust his ability to hold it up. Lukas had been cheating, slowing down the momentum of the fireballs right before they slammed against his force shield, and once it became too hot for him to handle, he dissipated it and created a new one to take its place.

Unfortunately, it was a stalemate that couldn't last forever.

He had to do something.

"DIE!" Quonnan howled. Lukas barely managed to look past his shield and found a small inferno where Quonnan had been standing. Her body was aflame, and the smell of sulfur inundated the air. She planted her feet and inhaled—

"Oh crap!"

—before opening her mouth and unleashing a torrent of flames at him.

Fire, in general, was difficult to argue with. Especially when it was coming at you like a great, angry, monstrous serpent ready to swallow you whole. Trying to punch it with lifeforce was a stupid idea, as was trying to punch lifeforce bullets into it. The former would burn him alive, while the latter would explode upon contact . . . and then burn him alive.

Trying to raise a wall wouldn't work either. The sheer momentum of such a massive attack would not just smash past his shields, but also send him flying. Even in the best-case scenario where he managed to stop it, it'd leave him completely drained. It would be like trying to stop a truck head-on.

He'd be paste on the floor. Burnt paste. So instead, Lukas redirected it.

Kinetomancy was about more than catching objects midair and sending them flying in different directions. It was about manipulating the vectors of objects—their weight, their motion, and most importantly, their direction. He had seen Inanna stop the khorkhoi's tail midway as it was about to descend.

But in reality, she hadn't stopped it. No, she had simply snatched away its momentum, bringing it from motion to rest in the blink of an eye.

And then, she'd returned the motion and altered its direction.

Inertia Negation and *Motion Reversal*, she had called it. And that was just a broken fragment of what true Kinetomancy was capable of. Lukas couldn't replicate that. He didn't have the skill or the power reserves to pull it off. But what he could do was redirect an existing motion into a convenient direction as long as it wasn't facing much natural resistance.

And so, he did.

His stance widened, almost instinctively, and his right hand moved up, while his left stayed at the bottom, palms wide open as if holding something and guiding it upward along a slanted axis. The torrent of flames crashed against him and was guided upward through the invisible convex surface, its own momentum propelling it along the path. The motion carried the devastating power of those flames up against the roof of the cavern, exploding out like some volcanic geyser.

Lukas would have described it as beautiful if he weren't too busy trying to keep himself from getting scalded.

Quonnan screeched out something. Lukas was too preoccupied to hear what it was. Instead, he slowly pushed his right arm downward, slanting his imaginary convex surface further, bending it in a misshapen U. The last thing he could see was her widened eyes of dismay and understanding as she realized the consequences of what had just happened.

The torrent of flames smashed into her in one massive explosion, enough to push him back by several steps. The noise was terrible. The destruction was appalling. Almost every inch of the floor caught in the blast radius had been blasted apart if not melted into slag. And yet, the magic circle stayed as it was. Unwavering.

Which was good, he supposed.

He fell to one knee, exhausted, his nigh-transparent force shield disappearing the very next second. He had never moved something of that much momentum before, and it had been incredibly taxing. Gods, if he hadn't been prepared for that blow . . .

Lukas exhaled. He really didn't want to think about it. Not when—

There was a sudden sound of a rushing wind.

"Oh come on!" he yelled. "Give me a fucking break!"

"*OUTSIDER!*" Quonnan—the *true* Quonnan—rose out of the smoldering ashes of the fallen form. The wraith, if she could be called that, did not look human at all. She bore a lizard-like countenance and clawed arms, and her legs had morphed into an ethereal tail. Her hair was replaced by thousands of bright red filaments that sprouted from her nape to the tip of her tail like the violent embers of a bonfire.

This was the kasha. A body-possessing parasitic species, capable of generating fire.

And since the Screen had not awarded him any Experience, Lukas held no doubt that destroying the body amounted to little more than nothing as far as killing her was concerned.

"*I. WILL. HAVE. YOU!*" the kasha roared.

"YOU'RE NOT MY TYPE!" Lukas yelled back, bracing himself as the kasha dove at him.

CHAPTER 20

SOUL SIPHON

This is odd.

Quonnan couldn't help but feel distinctly uncomfortable as she grabbed the Outsider's consciousness and pushed it down, gaining an upper hand over the body's facilities. It was good. Strong. With a healthy amount of lifeforce flooding from the Essence. She could sense the Outsider's stubbornness and put up a resistance, but she hadn't reached where she was by playing nice. Grabbing the metaphorical reins of the physical body, Quonnan gathered power from the surroundings to morph it into—

There was power already? How? Physical creatures had lifeforce rushing through them. The oni were capable of performing both—often at the expense of mutilating their physical forms. But having raw, World Energy within the body? No, this was *wrong*. This couldn't be. Or—or perhaps it had something to do with it being an Outsider's body?

No matter. It only made things too easy for her.

She absorbed the World Energy and rushed it through her mana forge to produce flames, and sent the flame-mana rushing through the body. Once it was out, she coalesced them into spherical balls of congealed flame, pulsating, burning, ready to incinerate anything that fell into its grasp.

Quonnan smirked. It would be so exhilarating to see the Outsider's consciousness scream as his insides boiled.

So color her surprised when a piece of random information from the Outsider's schema distracted her from her enjoyment.

You have used Mana for the first time!

Adding Mana Attributes to Soulscape
Modifying Host Stats to enable configuration by Mana Skills
Body Alteration delayed until Level Up

New SKILL Added!		
SKILL	**LEVEL**	**SOUL CAPACITY CONSUMED**
Fire Creation	1	50
DESCRIPTION		
Direct creation of flames through forging fire-mana from the World's Energy.		

New SKILL Added!		
SKILL	**LEVEL**	**SOUL CAPACITY CONSUMED**
Fire Manipulation	1	50
DESCRIPTION		
Allows for modulating the external shape and size of flames.		

Quonnan blinked. Mana skills? And *two* of them? Impossible.

She blinked again.

Yes. Definitely impossible. She moved *her* hands. The body moved accordingly.

She still had complete control over the body. But this was a physical form. This did not have a mana forge. As such, the fire-mana should have burned it. Charred it. Something like this could NEVER register a Mana skill, and yet—

Activating Prophylaxis

Initiate Intense-repair.
Initiate Self-Scan Self-Analyze

Reporting for flawed functional development
Canceling existing processes!

And the flames in *her* hands were put out.

Just like that.

. . . What was going on?

More information came in.

SOUL PROTOTYPE ANALYZED	
RACE	Kasha
TYPE	Spiritual Parasite
ENERGY CORE	Mana (89% inclination to FIRE and 37% inclination to ETHER)
Match with HOST BODY	3%

Quonnan lost her temper. She had lost her host body to this Outsider. She'd not be kept away from claiming this one as her own.

Not by this stupid Screen.

She poured in more Fire-mana.

As much as she could.

Enormous, shining orbs of pure white heat appeared in the body's hands. She'd show this—this—

New SKILL Added!		
SKILL	LEVEL	SOUL CAPACITY CONSUMED
Temperature Modulation	1	50
DESCRIPTION Allows for altering flame temperature.		

And it didn't just end there.

Adequate Mana Skill identified
Initiating LEY LINE NETWORK
Ley Line Network Accessed
Initiate Addition to LEGACY PROTOCOL

Quonnan was beginning to think that something fishy was going on.

New OMPHALOS FUNCTION Added!

FUNCTION	LEVEL	ENERGY COST
Evocation	1	Variable

DESCRIPTION
Allows BASE HOST access to Ley Line Network for Mana Synthesis and Manipulation. Mana Synthesis to be done from Anomalous Energy Reserves.

Compatibility with Host Body—3% Foreign Soul Prototype REJECTED for BASE HOST MIND consideration Initiating SOUL SIPHON

But it was too late. For her.

An alien, burning sensation began to form within her. It was terribly uncomfortable, as Quonnan felt as if she was being . . . churned from the inside, from the outside, from—from inside to outside. Like she was being inverted, twisted, turned inward, and flattened out at the same time. For an ethereal creature to feel such physical sensations was utterly, utterly confusing.

And absolutely terrifying.

I have to leave! I have to escape! I have to—

Quonnan rose out to get out of this strange, alien form—

Only for something like tendrils to grab her back.

Pull her.

Drain her.

Make her *less.*

NO! Quonnan thought. This wouldn't end like this. This couldn't end like this. For she was—

She was—

The body was gone. Away from her. And she—

Who was she?

She—

She was—

Was—

Gone.

SOUL SIPHON Success! Absorbed Monster Prototype KASHA

One moment, Lukas was being possessed by the kasha with flames rising out of him. The next, he was down on his knees, and his entire body felt like someone had replaced his bones with thick weights of lead. His vision was limited to barely a foot above the ground, with the smoking, charred remains of the kasha strewn on the ground before him.

Forcing more and more lifeforce into his body, he allowed himself to be carried away by the rush, letting it dull his sense of pain. It was an incredibly bad idea, but desperate times called for desperate measures.

Especially when he was surrounded by a group of aliens that were eyeing him like a piece of steak.

"I—I won," he replied almost drunkenly. It hurt to speak, but by now, Lukas was the master of pain. He ignored the jolts of agony spreading through his chest every time he said a word, and instead pushed himself up on his left hand.

"I *won!*"

The right hand came to support him next. Breathing felt a little easier now. More bearable.

He bared his teeth at Solana.

"I WON!"

"Congratulations," the black-haired beauty said dispassionately. "Guards, restrain him."

"What?" Lukas spluttered. "We had a deal!"

Solana stared at him, her expression as bleak and remote as a far mountain. "Did we now?"

"You gave me your word!"

Her lips twisted into a cruel smile. "A predator does not bargain with her prey. You have served your purpose, so I shall keep you around until I have a need for you again. That, or I will simply kill you."

"I told you this duel will solve nothing," he heard Inanna whisper conspiratorially in his head. **"However, you still have a chance. Take my offer and burn these heathens to ash."**

Lukas's mouth worked up and down, but no words came out. How could they? Words couldn't possibly contain the frustration, the rage, the fear that consumed him. It cut through his weariness, sharp as thorns and barbed wire. It wasn't fair. He had done everything he could. He had risked everything. And he had lost.

Around him were more than a hundred creatures, all of which might look human, but were hideous beings that wore that skin like a mask. Even with Kinetomancy, he couldn't fight them alone. And if they put those manacles back on him, he'd lose his ability to wield lifeforce as well.

He was hurt. He was alone. And if he didn't do something soon, it would all be over.

Desperation like that could do things to a person. The fear, the rage, the self-loathing arising out of that powerlessness could drive a person to do things. Some would probably snap out of anger and go into a suicidal rage. Others would probably try to run away and try to escape, despite knowing the futility of their attempt. And some would break from inside like glass.

But for Lukas, desperation set him on fire.

Fire in his thoughts. Fire in his heart. Fire in his eyes. He burned, burned, and *burned* so deep in his gut that even the kasha's strongest flames were but a flickering spark to his inferno.

Lukas didn't know how he did it. He remembered reaching for it, consumed with the idea that even if he'd go down, he would take them with him. He wouldn't be captured. He would burn these backstabbing, soulless, body-possessing parasites down. He would show them the powers that Lukas Aguilar—no, that **[LOSTBELT EARTH]** had at its command.

The next thing he knew, he was standing up and all the aches vanished from his body.

His mouth moved once more, but this time, a single word was snarled out. *"BURN!"*

Fire answered.

The entire periphery of the barrier circle exploded into blazes of crimson light, with angry, vengeful flames climbing up its invisible walls to tear apart its resistance and swallow the world outside. Fire leaped up into the air—ten feet, twenty feet, thirty feet—until it touched the very ceiling.

Lukas stood amidst his dome of fiery power, his dark emotions brilliantly lit by the flames. He could feel the power rise within him, but unlike how the kasha had done it, this belonged to him. It wasn't being drawn from the world, but synthesized inside. It didn't burn his tissues as it struggled for an escape. Instead, it utilized the Ley Line Network that brilliantly allowed it as many outlets as it desired.

He could see the creatures slither away, the white heat from the flames hurting their frail flesh masks. Lukas reveled in that sight, gleefully watching as they whimpered. The barrier began to glow like a spotlight, reaching its limit, and in the middle of it all stood Solana, unmoving, her dark eyes watching him with something like . . . *satisfaction?*

"Mortal, calm yourself."

The fury in him grew. It swelled and swelled as the flames reached higher. He'd shatter this shield, and he'd burn them all alive. He'd—

"Mortal." Inanna's voice rumbled like thunder. **"You are wasting precious power. You have made your move. Had your victory. Proved your worth. Now allow her to make hers."**

You're asking me to trust her? After she's already betrayed our agreement?

"Do not be a fool!" Each of her words slammed into him. **"I am not asking you to trust her. I am asking you to put faith in *my* judgment."**

That brought him to a pause.

Lukas felt his heart clench, felt his knees sway, felt the roaring wave of power slow down to a trickle. The barrage of flames began to die down, replaced by smoke and the smoldering remains of molten rock on the floor. He saw Solana whip her hand sidewards as the barrier around him cracked and vanished, leaving him at the mercy of those that surrounded him.

If I die here, Lukas thought, *I'm blaming you.*

He didn't have to. Because no one was attacking him. Instead, they were down on their knees. Their eyes stared up at him—not with fear, anger, or a misplaced sense of vengeance.

But with wonder. With awe. With *hope*.

"Everyone! Laugh! Make merry! Rejoice! Our unending wait has finally borne fruit! The Key has arrived!"

Lukas felt his knees give away. But before he hit the floor, he felt hands underneath him, supporting him as he slowly descended into a restful pose. His vision blurred with every passing second, but he could make out the blurry figure of Solana walking toward him.

"Rest for now, Outsider. You have faced your challenge and come out victorious. When you wake, there is a lot we need to discuss."

"Can't . . . wait . . ." he slurred.

And then, everything became a merciful black.

CHAPTER 21

QUID PRO QUO

The darkness that swallowed Lukas kept him for a long time. There was nothing but silence where he drifted, nothing but endless night. He wasn't cold. He wasn't warm. He wasn't anything. No thought, no dreams . . . nothing. It was too good to last, as he slowly awoke.

The pain of the burns came first. He felt the scars on his left arm and elbow, and the feel of fresh, frail tissue forming over them. The injuries were mostly healed, but they throbbed with a dull persistence that robbed him of peace. All the other assorted scrapes and bruises and cuts came back to him as well. Lukas felt like a collection of complaints and malfunctions. He ached everywhere.

His memory came next. The fight. The kasha. Quonnan. Kinetomancy. Burning her alive. Being possessed. Solana ordering for his capture. The *FIRE*—

Lukas sat up with a start.

Groaning, he rubbed his coarse, gummy eyes. Something told him he was supposed to feel pain while he moved his arms and legs, but the sensation was oddly absent.

At least his chest didn't feel like it was being sat on by a small elephant. It still hurt to breathe, but he was getting used to it. His body was just as naked as he remembered, but at least these parasites had given him a bed this time, which was far better than their prior attempt at hospitality.

Taking a deep breath, he glanced around at the room. It boasted spartan features, with a bed crafted out of pure rock and several layers of thick monster hide on top. There was an earthen jug with water splattered around it, and a door to his south. The walls were stone, with bioluminescent moss growing on them acting as a natural light source.

"Where am I?"

"Your abductors placed you in this room to rest," Inanna said.

"Without any restraints?"

"Obviously," the goddess drawled. **"Though . . . I cannot sense anyone close. It is possible this room is just warded against detection."**

"Do you think . . ." He trailed off, pushing his legs off of the bed. "Maybe I could—"

"Escape? Why bother? Staying costs you nothing, and may fetch us relevant information about this world."

"Don't you ever sleep?" he mumbled.

"Sleep is for the weak, and mortals that have a tendency to exhaust themselves needlessly."

Lukas mockingly flinched back and touched his chest. "So caustic. What's gotten into you?"

"Merely bewildered at your luck. It is honestly . . . surprising. One would almost call it a minor miracle."

"What are you talking about?"

Inanna's voice turned darker. **"Do you not remember what you did?"**

"I . . . I used fire, didn't I?"

"A crude way of presenting it, but you are an ignorant mortal so it is to be expected."

Lukas rolled his eyes. "I remember. When the kasha used it. I think it was—"

Soulscape.

SOULSCAPE	
NAME	Lukas Aguilar
Type	Base Host
Level	4
Experience	417
Current Threshold	640
Utilized Soul Capacity	1629/2379
ESSENCE	
Maximum Lifeforce Output	725
Replenishment Rate	180 / hour
LEY LINE NETWORK	
Maximum Mana Output	400
Synthesis Rate	80 / hour

SKILL ATTRIBUTES		
SKILL	**LEVEL**	**CONSUMED SOUL CAPACITY**
Raw Lifeforce Manipulation	1	50
Momentum Manipulation	1	50
Friction Modulation	1	50
Pressure Modulation	1	50
Kinetomancy (FRAGMENTED)	APEX	1279
Fire Creation	1	50
Fire Manipulation	1	50
Temperature Modulation	1	50

OMPHALOS ATTRIBUTES	
Energy Reservoir Capacity	∞
Current Energy Level	722,428,138 units
OMPHALOS FUNCTIONS	
Scan	Level 2
Analyze	Level 2
Prophylaxis	Level 2
Soul Siphon	NA
Alpha Condition	Level 1
Evocation	Level 1

Still no rise in Experience. It seemed souls absorbed via Soul Siphon did not add to his Experience. Lukas didn't know what to think about that. However, he could easily spot the newest additions to the schema. The first was, of course, the Ley Line Network's activation, with appropriate attributes related to mana synthesis and its capacity. The other was the latest omphalos function sitting snugly at the bottom of it.

FUNCTION	LEVEL	ENERGY COST
Evocation	**1**	**Variable**
DESCRIPTION		
Allows BASE HOST access to Ley Line Network for Mana Synthesis and Manipulation. Mana Synthesis to be done from Anomalous Energy Reserves.		

Lukas briefly recalled something about an omphalos function popping up when Quonnan had taken over and tried to exert her dominance over his body by creating fireballs in either hand.

In hindsight, that was what had led to her being consumed in the first place.

"Something to keep in mind," Inanna advised. **"It was not you that kept her from taking over. It was her own ego that did it."**

And wasn't that a humbling thought? The idea had been to use the Alpha Condition function to assert his own dominance, but Lukas had been too weak to even be in any position to exert it. The very moment Quonnan had dived into him, she had wrested control over his body. The only reason he was back in control and she was trapped away as a monster prototype was because she wasn't a good match for the body.

But if she had been?

A cold pit began to form inside his stomach. He had been lucky this time. But his luck was destined to run out sooner or later. Yes, the reiki had been a weakling, and it had activated the Soul Siphon function, which was also probably why the omphalos system had been so quick to employ it. Imagine if Quonnan had been the first to do this . . .

Would he—would there even be a "he" left?

Lukas Aguilar would be gone. Deleted. Vanished. With something else in command. An alien entity that saw the world through his eyes.

All because he had been too weak.

Too insignificant.

Too—

"You can always strike a bargain," Inanna offered.

"Lead me not into temptation," Lukas sighed. "I'm already facing a property dispute over my own body with my planet's omphalos. Trying to one-up that by selling my soul away to become your hatchetman gets me further into this mess, not out of it."

"But you would have nothing to fear. Under my tutelage and blessing, your power shall be great."

"Yes, yes, I'd have power too great and terrible. And you'd have a greater, more terrible hold over me."

"Your derision will not unmake the truth. Already you have faced the beings that reside in this world, and already you have suffered their whims. Tell me, mortal, are your morals worth your suffering?"

Lukas sighed again. "You know . . . just the night before the earthquake, Emma promised to treat me out at a bar. I had been worrying about my exams that were round the corner." He let out a mirthless chuckle. "Worrying? Hah! More like scared. Trying to balance my editing job while studying for my exams. And then this happened."

He balled his hands into fists. "I lost everything. My life, dreams, career . . . friends. I literally have nothing left. My life is gone. My world is gone. Instead, I am in a hellhole with monsters out to eat me. These parasites want to possess me one moment and laud me the next. I don't know if my body will be my own by the week's end."

He let out a harsh breath. "You ask if my morals are worth my suffering. No. They aren't. I'm not some idealist who'd die to uphold his views. Hell, even *I* know that it's barely an excuse, one that keeps getting thinner with every passing day. Maybe it's just my way of trying to distract myself. To let myself think that the same rules apply. But that's all that I have left. When I use lifeforce, I become a predator. When I unleashed all that fire, I wanted to destroy everything. These . . . morals are probably what remains of the true Lukas Aguilar. I accept your offer, and I lose them. I'm . . . just not sure if I'll survive that."

Inanna was silent for a few moments.

"Your fears are not unfounded, mortal. The world is not black and white. Parasite or not, you have already absorbed three of them. By the time you are done with this place, countless more will die by your hands."

Lukas grimaced. "I did that to protect myself. If I start to give in, what difference would there be between me and them?"

"One would be alive, and the other dead."

"Then let's hope my luck doesn't run out any time soon, and that I can train myself to be strong enough."

". . . Fascinating."

Lukas could feel her smile at him. It wasn't just a smile. He could literally *feel* it. Like watching the first rays of the morning sun caress his cheek, Inanna's emotions coursed through his body. It made him want to walk and run and laugh around without a care for anything in the world.

"Tell me, would you like to know what your bargain entails? About the object I wish for you to find?"

And just like that, the happiness drained out of him, replaced with an acute wariness. Nothing good ever came out of Inanna offering to provide him with information without a price. There was always a catch. *Especially* when she mentioned anything related to the nature of the task.

Still, as they say, curiosity killed the cat.

" . . . Yes. I would."

And the world changed.

. . .

. . .

. . .

"She'll pay."

The realm itself was trauma incarnate. Sins and desires, the ugly basal instincts that tainted the hearts of men, were the very texture of its environment. Those that hid in the darkness lay in wait, ready to jump and kill and feast upon anything that was even remotely alive. To be in such a place was to be in a lucid dream, one fraught with drunkenness and acute despair.

Upon one of the large, monolithic walls that adorned this realm was a corpse.

The form of a woman.

Naked.

Defiled.

Hacked open.

Insects and worms of the most heinous sort formed hives inside her organs. Pests feasted upon her flesh as parasites fed on the marrow in her bones and lapped up the blood that flowed through her veins. The corpse had already lost track of how long it had been hanging there. For no matter how much time had passed, her body remained eternally fresh, just as it was when it was hung there. Blood would continue to drip from the carcass onto the floor as the body healed itself with extraordinary lifeforce.

The power of a goddess kept her alive.

The power of a goddess prolonged her suffering.

The power of a goddess kept her sane as her mind and soul were constantly violated.

Such was her misfortune.

Such was her curse.

And yet . . .

"She'll pay."

Her spirit remained unbroken.

"She'll pay."

That single thought kept her from giving up, from giving in to the torture. Because deep inside, she knew that the realm would not hold her forever. She would break out, and when she did . . .

Inanna would have her vengeance.

And it would be glorious.

. . .

. . .

. . .

Lukas's eyes snapped open.

A cold sweat soaked his entire naked form. His body quivered as he felt hundreds of tiny insects gnawing into his stomach, feeding upon his innards, laying their eggs. It was almost like someone had pushed him in front of a speeding train, only to pull him back when he felt the cold metal of its coach on the tip of his nose.

The unspeakable pain and horror of constantly being eaten alive while trapped inside that purgatory were—

Lukas couldn't help it. He threw up.

"Weak," Inanna scoffed.

"What—*what the fuck* was that?" he asked, his throat burning as he felt another hot feeling rise up in his chest. He'd thought he'd faced suffering before, but that was a daydream compared to this. To be robbed of one's identity and stuck in a body more dead than alive, bearing the eternal agony of having *all those little worms and insects nibbling on his*—

Lukas clenched his eyes shut.

"A speck of my past. My present. And until you fulfill your part of the bargain, my future. It is my last true memory as the Supreme Queen of An and Ki. Therein Ereshkigal's domain, trapped within the Seven Gates, is my true form. My authorities buried, my powers trapped within my form, my divinity acting as a curse that keeps my body alive. Suffering in eternal torment."

"But . . . why?"

"My sister Ereshkigal, Empress of the Dead, betrayed me. What you felt is the outcome."

Lukas frowned. "I don't get it. If that's your last true memory, and you call it your present and future, then who are *you?*"

"A reflection. Starlight that left its origin aeons ago. A speck of myself, sheltered in a relic of my own making. A shrine in a distant realm that was cut off to become a lostbelt. One who would find her way back to my true form."

"You're a copy," he concluded.

"I am as much a copy of the true Inanna as you are of the Lukas Aguilar that lived on Earth. Just as you wish to find a way back home, I too desire to be one with my true self. To rise once again and sentence the vermin who betrayed me to eternal torment. You, my dear mortal, will ensure that vengeance is mine in the end."

Lukas swallowed. "I . . ."

"This is what I wish for you to recover, mortal. My true form. You will trespass into Irkalla, the realm of the dead, and shatter the Gates that keep me from my freedom."

"That sounds like a suicide mission."

"As you are now, dying will be the least of your worries."

Lukas wholeheartedly agreed. What Inanna was asking him to do was hilariously stupid. A bad joke. Sure, he'd been able to survive some monsters. Sure, he had unlocked some cool abilities. But a *goddess?* Lukas had seen what Inanna could do with a casual demonstration of the weakest of her skills. She may as well have asked him to outfight her at the peak of her power and survive.

"An apt comparison," the goddess replied, answering his thoughts. **"In all this time, her power will have grown greatly. But I am not asking you to fight."** Her tone grew sharper. **"I am asking you to steal. And I shall aid you every step of the way."**

"And let me guess," Lukas sighed. "Agreeing to your offer is part of the process?"

"Certainly. You cannot acquire the blessings of a goddess without worshiping her any more than you can feel sunlight on your skin without standing in the sun."

"You can if you're using something to reflect it toward you."

"How very apt," the goddess replied, amused, **"for I am a reflection of my true form in many ways."**

He didn't have a response to that. But there was one question still buzzing around his head.

"Why show me this? Why now? You'd have been better off keeping me in the dark about it. It's impossible. Absolutely, hilariously impossible. It'd be way easier to get me to agree to a bargain if I hadn't seen this."

"Inanna is many things. But a woman of bad faith she is not. You do not wish to accept my offer, and I can assure you that you cannot accomplish the task otherwise. I showed you what awaits you at the end so you may make an informed decision about it."

"And it didn't occur to you that I could just renege on my word?"

"Would you?" she asked. **"I would not stop you if you did."**

Silence fell.

"Why not?" Lukas asked quietly.

"You need my blessings to reach the zenith I've seen for you, and faith cannot be forced."

" . . . this is why you keep offering me bargains, don't you? To ensure that I bind myself into following you."

"Indeed," said the goddess. **"I will not force your faith, but your**

independence is another thing entirely. However, I have since realized that it will work with you. And as such—"

"As such you're—you're—"

"Yes," she said simply, and suddenly Lukas was overcome with the sensation of a trap closing around him. **"I have no need for an unwilling vessel. The task I want you to complete is already a fool's errand. If I do not have your loyalty or your devotion to this task, I will be setting myself up for abysmal failure. I would rather use a far superior tactic."**

"Which is . . ."

"The truth," Inanna said. **"I have shown you what I asked you to acquire for me. I have also told you of the tools you would have to assist you on your quest. But I do not wish for you to tread this path out of coercion."** She paused for a second. **"If, and I do mean if, you accept this quest, you will do it because you wish to honor the agreement."**

"Not out of coercion."

"No. No more tricks. No more deception. This simply is."

Lukas stared at the floor blankly. Just closing his eyes was enough to send him back to that image of Inanna—hanging on the wall, with maggots feasting on her flesh while her body shook in endless torment. He remembered running from the khorkhoi, making a deal with the goddess, and trying to get the best deal out of her. He remembered how he had been inches from losing himself forever because he had been simply too weak to stop the yurei from claiming him.

Inanna had been the one to help him then.

"To fulfill what you've once promised, but chosen to forget."

That was what she had said. She could have bartered something new in return, but she hadn't. She could twist things in her favor and play him like a fiddle if she wanted. But she hadn't. Instead, she had chosen to honor their agreement.

And now . . .

And now—

She was doing it again. It was like she had once told him—

"You remain insouciant despite knowing what I am. You wear your independence with pride knowing that genuflecting in my presence can make your life easier. And now, you choose to bargain with me, after all that we have spoken of, merely to deepen your understanding of yourself?"

And just like that, Lukas *understood.* He knew what Inanna was doing. Why she had done what she had done just now.

Inanna had shown him her true situation to make perfectly clear what choice he was about to make. Certainly, it might influence his decision, but when a stark-naked truth stares you in the face . . . shouldn't it?

He had never known that it was possible to manipulate someone with candor and truth until now.

She was right. Every time he rejected a deal, it told her a little about him. Every single time he made a choice, it shed light on the core tenets of his personality. Inanna had spent her days observing the deepest nature of her Host—*him*, and only after she had been confident about it all had she come up with this . . .

This . . .

What did one even call this?

His fists clenched. There was always a chance of him dying at the hands of some monster inside this anomaly. There was always the chance of the omphalos finding a better alternative for a Base Host than himself. He could grow and learn and maybe even make himself capable enough to survive, but what did that mean in a world that he didn't even belong to?

Especially when he'd be spending his days and nights with a pendant hanging around his neck and a goddess in his head. When every single second of her presence would remind him that he had made a bargain and he had ditched it out of fear. Somehow, the moral high ground for not accepting her offer suddenly didn't feel so high anymore.

And just like that, Inanna had him.

For all her claims to the contrary, Lukas didn't believe for a second that she was truly willing to let him go. Inanna wasn't the sort of person who'd take a no for an answer. All her talk about not putting him under coercion was simply that—talk. In her mind, it was less about giving him a choice or showing him the truth, and more about saying the things she thought he needed to hear to make him do what she wanted.

That was how people manipulated other people, by telling them what they wanted to hear instead of what they needed.

"I . . ." he replied, his tone slow and controlled. "I want you to know that I utterly, utterly, *despise you* for doing this to me."

A throaty laugh escaped her. It made him hate her even more. But the decision had been made. The die had been cast. He knew it. Inanna knew it. And she knew that he knew it.

"But I won't give away my independence. My will is still my own. I may have yielded to your task, but only because of my morals and my humanity. I don't see a reason to lose that now. If I did, I wouldn't be what you need."

"What are you trying to say?"

He felt a tinge of pleasure at the annoyance in her tone. "I meant it. I'll help you in your quest. Not out of coercion, but because my own ideals, my own sense of right and wrong bids me do so. You want me to grow stronger. You want me to trespass into places that should not be entered and shatter things that probably can't be shattered. I'll do those things, but I'll do it my way. If I want your help, I will ask for it. You will not try to force it upon me."

"You dare command me, mortal?"

"No. I'm just telling you what I'm gonna do. I'm willing to honor our agreement. But I'll do it in my own way."

"You expect me to have faith in a mortal not to break his word."

Lukas smiled. It was genuine. "I suppose I do."

"Trust breeds betrayal. I have seen it as a child. I have seen it in Ereshkigal. Your words will not shake me."

"Probably not," Lukas replied, still smiling. "But that's all I have to offer. Do we have an accord?"

The silence that followed his proclamation was too beautiful to ignore.

CHAPTER 22

REVELATIONS

Lukas was not disturbed for the next several hours.

With the resident goddess effectively tongue-tied with his standing offer, there had been precious little for him to do within that little room. Sleep would not come to him no matter what, and the door on the side had remained shut. Hell, not a single entity had encroached upon his Scan Radius—a whopping twenty feet in all directions ever since the upgrade.

It was as surprising as it was confusing.

Naturally, he had turned toward studying his schema, getting as much information as possible about it. If his math was correct, his lifeforce and mana levels were already at the brim, and the Prophylaxis function had already healed every single wound that needed attention. That meant that if he were to be attacked right now, he'd be fighting in peak form.

Prey found you.

Lukas looked up as the door opened and a young woman came into the room. She had long, sleep-tousled dark hair, dark eyes, and a face a little too lean to be conventionally pretty. She wore a kimono of red silk belted loosely enough that gaps appeared as she moved. Evidently, she wore nothing underneath.

She was followed by another male soldier—armor-clad, brown bangs, with a long metallic spear resting upon his right shoulder. He had a trolley covered with a sheet of cloth that he was dragging behind him as he followed into the room with her.

Lukas gave the second newcomer a closer look. Even in the dim light, he could spot the strangeness of the man's expression. It was an odd contrast between happiness and downright hysteria. The muscles on his face kept twisting, even as he stood as if he were trying to say something and keep his mouth shut at the same time. The constant state of tension seemed obvious in the way his fists remained clenched, even though the man stood in complete silence.

Another one of those possessions? Reiki?

He scanned the soldier.

BREMETAN

Bipedal, lifeforce-producing organisms. 99.9% similarity with the HUMAN species.

That was both good and bad news. Good because it had confirmed that there existed a race that was identical to humanity as he knew it. Though unlike humans, bremetans were perfectly capable of using lifeforce—then again, he could too. The bad news was that he was currently being held captive by a predatory species that switched bremetan bodies left and right.

Then there was the fact that the Screen had not sensed any reiki. The Scan and Analyze functions operated at the soul level. They registered the presence of a soul within the established radius and identified it through cross-checking. The identity of this "database" was beyond him, but he was certain the answer would be mind-boggling.

If the Screen hadn't registered the reiki, it came down to two options.

Either the Screen was incapable of spotting a possessed spirit, which made no sense since the possessor's spirit didn't merge with the victim—something he could confirm from his rather recent firsthand experience. Or . . .

Lukas carefully considered the girl.

REIKI

Soul Architecture shows 100% similarity to REIKI from Monster Prototype Array.

BREMETAN

Bipedal, lifeforce-producing organisms. 99.9% similarity with the HUMAN species.

Soul Architecture damaged. Extreme signs of possession.

Well, wasn't that just *alarming?*

Possession didn't just override one's hold over his body but also caused significant injury to the victimized soul itself. It was clear that the armored man wasn't possessed any more. But what happened to him to make him like that? Were these the aftereffects of being possessed for significant periods of time?

His fingers twitched, and an overwhelming desire to *crush* this girl—more precisely, the reiki that possessed her—rose to the forefront of his mind. To trap her. To consume her. *To add her to his ever-growing collection of*—

Lukas blinked, wondering what had just happened.

"Greetings." The girl spoke in a strange, accented Felleisen, yawning and stretching cattily. "I be called Mizo. Food and water I brought for you, and . . . " Her eyes traveled all over his body. "Attire to cover form."

The mention of food made him feel painfully, desperately hungry. He glanced at the cloth-covered trolley and then met the girl's dark eyes again and spoke in Ualbesh. "I don't speak Felleisen."

The edges of her lips twitched. "Silly game you play, Outsider. Mizo be told that Outsider says this. Leader says 'Outsider *understands* but pretends not.'"

His fingers twitched again.

Mizo continued in Felleisen. "Leader be waiting until Outsider feasted." She turned around and walked away with the soldier in tow, until she was out of the room, and shut the door.

Lukas felt her leaving his Scan Radius and sighed. So much for deception.

Still, it wasn't like Solana had him completely pegged. Maybe she'd been telling the truth about the reiki being capable of speaking in Felleisen. She was probably thinking that he had *absorbed* the reiki, yurei, and the kasha for that matter, and gained the ability to comprehend and speak the languages they knew in return. It was bullshit as far as reasons went, but what else was she supposed to think?

His eyes scanned the trolley again. Pushing himself off the bed, he tore off its cover. Inside were several china cups, steak, something that looked like mashed potatoes, and some kind of soup. The aroma was exotic and made his stomach gurgle.

Hunger is the real enemy, he thought as he grabbed the cup closest to him.

After heartily finishing his meal, Lukas slipped into the attire that was provided. It consisted of a sleeveless tunic crafted out of a fabric that could have been mistaken for cotton for how soft it was and a pair of thick trousers crafted out of monster hide, given the thick and scaly exterior on the outer side. There was a leather belt to tie it in place, and two slots that likely went for pockets in this world and would serve as a snug fit for a knife-sized weapon. There was also a pair of strapped shoes, which Lukas would have ditched for his own shoes had that been an option. He looked like a slave merchant from the Roman Empire.

Inanna was right, Lukas thought as he followed Mizo to Solana's office. He wasn't being treated like a pig for slaughter. This was . . . something else. They wanted something from him. But what?

Well, I'm suited up for my meeting. Do you intend to drag the silence on for the rest of the day?

"Does it not strike you that I simply do not wish to constantly commune in your thoughts?"

Knowing a lost cause when he saw one, he let it go. *Let's go see what Solana wants from me this time.*

"Already so familiar with your captor. I wonder if I should have forced you to bend right from the start."

Guess we'll never know.

"A pity."

Lukas walked toward the end of what seemed like a very long corridor. They had already crossed two sets of stairs, and he could've sworn that he could see squarish rooms arranged in horizontal stacks going on for at least a mile. It made him wonder just how *massive* the Crypt of Fiendish Worms must have been if these people were occupying a mere portion of the entire thing.

Mizo went through the door first, and Lukas followed, mentally preparing himself for combat should things head south. But nothing came screaming at him from the shadows. None of those lifeforce-restraining manacles either.

Like the one he had just left, this room too was mostly spartan. Like every other surface in this damn place, it had sigils engraved on its surface, except for the portions covered with moss graffiti. Several of those floating flames hung along the walls like light bulbs, illuminating the room more brightly than any others he had seen so far. On the far end, he could see Solana sitting on a rocking chair. A few feet away from her sat a large, sprawling table with a *dog* laid spread-eagled on top, unmoving.

The sight gave him pause.

A waft of intense cold breeze blew across the room, chilling him to the bone. The air smelled like mildew and felt like a very cold, very old, death.

"Charming place," he said in Ualbesh.

Solana smiled pleasantly, beckoning him to the sole remaining chair on the other side of the table.

Lukas looked around and found Mizo standing stiff at a corner in the room, alongside several of those soldiers. He tried to meet the girl's eyes but found her avoiding his gaze.

"So, what's with the security?"

"They will leave as soon as you take a seat."

"I prefer to stand."

Her dark eyes glinted. "Perhaps you didn't understand me earlier. I said *sit.*"

A powerful, invisible force grabbed him by his shoulders and physically pressed him down. Despite his struggles, he was forced to bend his knees as something flat with sharp edges rose up to meet him. Before he knew it, he was sitting on a chair that hadn't been there a moment ago.

"Such prowess in Terramancy," Inanna murmured with approval. **"Gugalanna would have been envious."**

Why? What did Solana do?

"Terramancy. On a symbolic level, it represents the manipulation of terrain, stability, strength, force, and resistance. The creature disintegrated the chair and simultaneously reconstructed it behind you while maintaining absolute control of the room, and perhaps farther beyond."

Lukas sat wide-eyed, his fingers scratching against the smooth surface of the chair. "Uh, five words or less?"

"She is stronger than you."

The statement left the coppery taste of blood on his tongue. It carried with itself the cold affirmation that Soul Siphon or not, he wasn't immune to these creatures, especially the one sitting in front of him. He had used his fear of these unknown beings to keep himself ready on his feet. He had used his anger to put steel into his spine and push his resolve into taking action.

But Solana had just snatched those two emotions out of him, leaving him naked and vulnerable.

His exterior facade was calm, but inside, he felt hollow.

"You listen, but you do not understand," Inanna chastised. **"She is employing Terramancy upon you. So long as you stay within her territory, you remain calm and resilient. Prone to logical thought instead of remaining your usual self."**

Just how is she . . . Analyze.

Insufficient data.

This was getting worse. Absorbing the souls of the reiki and kasha had done nothing to help him Scan her, and he had no idea why. Was he missing something about the way the Analyze function worked or was Solana somehow shielding herself from his discerning gaze?

"Are you done?" Solana asked.

" . . . Done what?"

"Discerning things, I imagine," she replied casually, her lips twisting slightly at the slight widening of his eyes. "I have good eyes, Aguilar. I know you do more than merely *see* who stands before you before interacting with them. I am curious, though. Is that trait particular to you or is it common amongst your people? Just what is it that you can see?"

Lukas closed his eyes. If Solana wanted him *stable*, then she'd have to reap the consequences of that. "I don't know what to tell you . . . but it's a wide universe out there. Though you're right; people from where I'm from do tend to register a while when something unfamiliar hits them in the face."

Solana snorted. "Levity. Good, you'll need it."

He glanced at the unmoving dog corpse on the table. "Always do. But what am I doing here?"

"To the point then," she replied, crossing her fingers and placing her chin on top. "Tell me, Outsider, how well are you acquainted with the Asukan Empire?"

Lukas relaxed into the chair. "Never heard of it."

"Never?"

"What part of *finding myself inside the cavern because of a mishap* was unclear before? I told you, I don't know anything about this world. Hell, I couldn't even understand your language before I—"

"Was possessed by my troops."

"The yurei, yes." Lukas cocked his head to the right. "I'll admit, I did pretend to not understand Felleisen earlier."

"And Faecani?"

"What about it?"

"Do you understand what I'm saying?" She spoke in perfect Faecani.

Lukas didn't have an instant answer for that, so rather than lie, he decided to say nothing at all. In the end, it seemed enough for Solana to draw her own conclusions.

"I see . . ." She sighed, sounding almost fond as she did, her lips twitching into a small smile. "I suppose we all are entitled to keeping our secrets. In the end, it does not matter."

Her eyes met his, and Lukas did not look away. He knew it couldn't have been more than seconds, but it felt like hours. The more he gazed at her, the more he thought he could see something beyond those dark depths. A flicker of movement. A shadow that hid behind shades of black. And though he couldn't discern what it was he was, he was almost certain it was *staring back at him and*—

Solana was the first to break her gaze.

Lukas let out a breath he hadn't known he was holding. Slumping back into his chair, he stared at his own hands as if he had never seen them before. They were open, and there were two pulsating balls of pure lifeforce, the largest he'd ever created, surrounded by a cloak of crimson flames in the center of both of his palms. He could feel the lifeforce that had already saturated his hands, as if—

It hit him like icy water. He had been ready to attack her. To *attack* Solana, while sitting in her room, from the chair she had casually constructed for him with no effort.

"That," Solana said at last, "was a surprise. I have never had a reaction like that before."

Lukas decided he must've gotten a few screws loose from that alien experience because, for a fleeting moment, he thought he heard something like *sadness* in her voice.

"Tell me, Outsider, do you know what I am?"

Lukas shook his head. "I'll admit that these bremetans—" He turned around, only to find the room empty. "They look very similar to my kind. Maybe we're the same race, only living in different worlds."

"I assure you," Solana replied, her tone bitingly sharp, "I have never encountered a bremetan immune to possession."

"Maybe we evolved?" he suggested casually. "I mean, leveling up is a thing in this world, isn't it?"

"What you describe is a path of progress. To augment what exists and become a better version. But that's all it is. Copper cannot evolve to gold. You cannot alter the soul to such a degree without losing your original identity."

"You'd know, given how you twist bremetan souls while possessing—" Lukas paused, suddenly realizing he had given away more information than he'd intended. And now it was too late.

Solana had noticed it too, as the edges of her lips quirked up. "Twisting bremetan souls . . . interesting choice of words. It makes me wonder if you can actually *see* it."

Lukas wisely kept quiet.

"No," she affirmed, "you are not bremetan. No bremetan could do what you can. Not even their so-called *Pathforgers*. But let us return to the original question. Do you know what I am?"

"Dominatrix with a penchant for flashy displays?"

He heard Inanna sigh and mutter something along the lines of *doomed*.

And then Solana did something surprising. She threw her head back and laughed. It was warm, genuine, with a lot of belly in it. "You wear your lack of concern like an armor. I admire that."

"And now you flatter me," Lukas replied.

"I'm not exactly sure what it is that you are. I know you—or rather, some of your kind—are parasitic and possess bremetans. I know your possession damages their soul architecture to the point that they become little more than living corpses. I know that some among you, like that kasha Quonnan, are capable of manacrafting, and the yurei can create false constructs. Have I missed anything?"

"You have us all figured out," Solana replied dryly, her expression almost amused. "Except for one thing. We are not parasites."

"So Quonnan was trying to give me a spiritual cuddle?"

Solana snorted. "What I mean is, we are spiritual predators not because we choose to be, but rather because the Empire has left us with no choice."

Yes, and wolves kill sheep because they are backed against the wall. Lukas was about to say it, but a mental kick from the resident goddess stopped him before he could open his mouth. It was enough to make him sigh.

Stuck between two powerful women. One was currently in his mind, and the other looked like she wanted to possess his body for herself. One had him in a bargain he couldn't get out of because of his principles, and the other had him effectively caged inside her place of power.

"You look like you have something to say," Solana said.

"Not really. I'm fine with just *thinking* about it," he replied.

"Be that as it may, I was not speaking untruth. The Eternal Light outside weakens us. That is why we have sought shelter for centuries in the desert."

"And the soldiers?"

"Greed drives people to do all sorts of things. Greed for the resources of this underground anomaly has prompted the bremetans from the edges of the desert to encroach upon our lands."

"So you possess them."

"We have to look out for ourselves," she huffed. "The Eternal Light does not affect us when possessing bremetans as it does in our spiritual forms."

"And what *is* your spiritual form?" Lukas asked. "That soldier had been a reiki. Quonnan was a kasha. That jolly Mizo you sent earlier, another reiki. What about you?"

"Oh?" Solana imperiously arched an eyebrow. "What an interesting question. One I will entertain. I am what is called a yosuzume. A *skinwalker*. Does that sound familiar to you?

Oh, it did. It certainly did. Not the yosu thing, but he knew what *skinwalkers* were. Granted, the name was reserved for the mystical theriomorphs in Native American myths, whereas the other terms—kasha, yurei and reiki— sounded a little too eastern to fall on the same side of the world.

Lukas schooled his features. "No. I've never heard of any of you, or of spiritual predators for that matter. Unless we're talking about ghosts." He hesitated, before pushing forward. "What are you all, really?"

Solana sat up straight, her back stiff as she spoke in a voice colder and harder than frozen stone.

"Who are . . . *we?*"

As she said those words, Lukas felt an immense pressure fall upon his senses. Like he was trying to breathe underwater. Like he had just died and come back.

"The bremetans called us Outlanders. Strangers. Walkers from the Other. We came from a distant world, one very unlike this one, our fates mingling with bremetans. We came from the skies. We settled upon these lands. We created our kingdoms. These bremetans . . . worshiped us. Feared us. Welcomed us. Embraced us. But deep down, they resented us."

Something terrible flickered across her features.

"And then, they betrayed us."

An icy feeling spread across Lukas's chest as her words invoked all sorts of dangerous thoughts.

"The . . . Other?" he asked, the term feeling strangely familiar, like he had heard it before. Somewhere. "What is the Other?"

Solana stared at him with wide, open eyes, her alien face void of expression.

"The Other is of the ethereal, Outsider," she said, her voice softer and far more terrible than a moment ago. Her eyes grew colder. *"What is visible is Sight. That which is beyond Sight is the Other. That which can be heard is Sound. That which is beyond Sound is the Other."*

Lukas felt his whole body shudder. Like a guitar's string quivering when the proper note is played near it. Every single word seemed to pull at his consciousness. About an ethereal world that seemingly existed parallel to the real. A world that did not follow any rules applicable to the real, and yet, consisted of several species that mingled with humans to such an extent that they became an accepted part of the real world.

"That which pumps lifeblood is the force. That which is beyond it is the Other."

Solana's inhuman eyes raked at his face, gleaming in a deathly glow. A feeling of emptiness surrounded him like a thick blanket, as if wanting to conceal him away from the world.

"We are of the Other, Outsider," she whispered. "We are . . . *yokai!*"

CHAPTER 23

SKIN IN THE GAME

Japanese myths spoke of a third race apart from the demonic and the divine. A race of creatures that couldn't be revered as gods, nor feared as demons. They were neither good nor bad. They were something different. No one knew where they came from or how they existed, but they permeated the world on a much deeper level than humans could begin to comprehend.

Perhaps they had always been there. Maybe even before humanity moved from cave walls to pen and paper.

Walking among them like specters, they permeated everything. The air, the earth, the lush green grasses, these beings of spirit blended seamlessly into the World, becoming part of everything living and inanimate. Their world ran parallel to the human world, and it was between these borders that these beings kept traveling in and out as one would through open doors.

They were strange. They were ethereal. They were the yokai, and they didn't *exist*.

Yet, Lukas Aguilar was currently sitting in a room with one of them. Staring at her.

How had his life turned upside down like this again?

"It is fascinating how facts keep getting twisted by the passage of time," Inanna whispered. **"You must tell me someday what your myths say about me."**

. . . I'm not sure that's such a great idea, Lukas thought back. Seriously, what was he going to say? The macabre sight he had seen through Inanna's eyes had been very different from what his grandfather's texts said. *Maybe when this is over.*

"I will hold you to that."

Roger that. He felt her confusion rise. *Uh . . . I mean, I promise.*

"Yokai," he mumbled out loud, his voice coming out a lot hoarser than expected. After spending all this time digesting the fact that he had a real goddess living in his head, Lukas thought he'd have been more accepting of the existence of entities from other mythologies.

"You're . . . yokai."

As it turned out, he may have overestimated himself.

Solana's eyes brightened. "So, you recognize the name. *Interesting*. I presume your kind has heard of us."

Lukas gave her a slow, silent nod.

"Not surprising," she said. "Since our arrival in this World, we have interacted with a great many civilizations and pantheons. The jotunn, the vanir, the svartalfars."

He did his best to keep his jaw from dropping to the floor as he cudgeled his brain to make sense of what she was saying. Jotunn? Vanir? The Aesir? There was no doubt whom she was describing. If they existed, then Alfheim, Vanaheim, Svartalfheim . . . The branches of the Yggdrasil, the great ash tree that transcended the World. They were real, and the world around him had interacted with them on—

"Focus."

The mental slap from the resident goddess brought him back to the present.

"Interesting," Solana murmured, crossing her arms. He could see calculation and thought in her dark eyes, faster than he could follow. "You recognize them. Whether by firsthand experience or hearsay tales, it doesn't matter. You know what they are, and what they are capable of." Her teeth gleamed. "And it terrifies you."

Lukas clenched his fists. *Is she a psychic?*

"No. Your face is simply as open as a book. And the term is psion, not psychic."

What's a psion—

"*Focus!*"

"I've heard of them," Lukas said after a moment of consideration, "just like I've heard of the yokai. That said, this is the first time I've encountered either."

Or came to know they're real, for that matter.

"Indeed? Then your realm must be among the ones that revolve around this World. Or perhaps you come from the other side of the Boundless Sea. Our ancestors forbade us from ever crossing it, so we know very little about the other side. Are you certain you've never heard of the Empire?"

The Asukan Empire?

"Can you tell me about the gods worshiped in the Empire?"

Solana's eyes darkened. "Even the mere mention of their name is forbidden in our lands, but in the interest of our discussion, I reluctantly shall. The Asukan pantheon is large, varying, and ever-growing. It has a multitude of deities, several of which are originally from other pantheons but had to settle for a lower berth."

"And they agreed to that?"

The yokai commander shrugged. "It was either that or extinction."

Divine politics, he thought to himself. *Why am I not surprised?*

"The highest echelons of the Divine Council only have room for the Big Three. The children of the Primordials themselves."

Lukas swallowed.

"The God of Storms, Susanoo. The Moon God, Tsukuyomi. And finally the Goddess of Eternal Light—"

"Amaterasu," Lukas murmured, registering the dark look that flickered over Solana's face for a fraction of a second. "Right?"

Her mouth turned faintly up at the corners. "You know of our kind, but do not recognize us. You know about the Yggdrasil but have never encountered it. You are terrified of the gods of different pantheons that have ruled this World for eons, but know not of the Asukan Empire. Quite the confounding creature you are, Outsider."

"One of my talents. It makes my Outsider powers grow when others give me these confused, blank looks."

Solana gave him a dry stare.

"Well, this has certainly been an illuminating conversation, but I believe you wish to know why you're here."

"The thought did cross my mind," Lukas replied, "but I didn't want to steal your moment."

Solana turned her face up toward the ceiling and barked out a laugh of genuine amusement.

"I have a few guesses," he continued, "and I think they're good ones. The food and lack of restraints were a tip-off. That and your words right before the fight, proclaiming my status as an *Outsider.* Something tells me that the term means something to you as more than just someone who intrudes into your property. Then there was that odd behavior from your people after I decided to give them a show."

The wispiest shade of a smile line graced the corners of her eyes. "Ah. You have a certain amount of perception, then."

"I used to think so," Lukas said. "But the more I experience life, the more I realize how clueless I am. Because honestly, I can't think of a way I can help you apart from being a lab rat for possession immunity."

Her eyes wrinkled at the corners. "You are right. It means something. Tell me, do you believe in prophecies?"

Lukas leaned back, flummoxed. "I . . . haven't dealt with prophecies before, but I think . . . *I hate them?* They're all cryptic warnings whose only true meaning can be figured out after the event is over. All it does is make people believe in its nonsense and act upon it in certain ways that trigger events to happen exactly in the order as defined in the prophecy. It's the worst kind of self-fulfilling crap."

People made new choices in every moment of their lives. The idea that somehow, the outcome of all those choices, those infinite futures, could all somehow have a common confluence that could be divined with the help of obscure tools was simply too fantastical to be true.

As were gods and goddesses and yokai. But here he was.

"A rather cynical viewpoint," Solana murmured. "But one I can appreciate, for once. You are full of surprises, Aguilar."

"It's hard not to be an overachiever."

Solana let out a long-suffering sigh. "In the interests of efficiency, let us return to the point. Around a millennium ago, the yokai kingdom faced the might of the Asukan Empire in an all-out war. We . . . we lost everything. Our lands, destroyed. Our people thinned to small pockets scattered across the world. Our relics were taken away and stored in the Empire's treasury. Our gods . . . killed. Even our own realm, Ikai, once a bright star of Potential, now stands fragmented and splattered across Asukan lands, infiltrated by their filthy hands as Asukans continue to pollute and exploit our resources."

"Asukans," Lukas noted, "not bremetans."

"Hardly a difference," Solana sniffed. "Any bremetan that follows the Asukan religion and worships Amaterasu's might calls oneself an Asukan."

Which implied that there were those that didn't. What gods did they worship? Aesir? Vanir? Yokai?

What do you think? Lukas mentally asked.

"She spins a fine yarn, but all I hear are words." Inanna scoffed.

It's rather odd. Solana strikes me as someone confident in her own power. To beg someone else and portray herself as weak—

"Makes you think that this ruse is real?" Inanna snorted. **"Often the greatest lies are ones that hold a sliver of falsehood in an ocean of truth."**

. . . Point taken.

"I see," Lukas replied to Solana, rubbing his eyes.

Solana nodded. "Our legends speak of an event. The emergence of a certain individual . . . one that would unleash something tremendous. A power that can undo everything that has happened to us. It will bring about the Hour of the Great Calamity. *Oumagatoki.*"

"Night of a Hundred Demons." It was a concept that had grown popular with the rising attraction for Japanese mythos and culture in mainstream media. Lukas had always thought it to be an imitation of the Proto-Germanic

"Wild Hunt," given their thematic similarities and shared emphasis on carnage brought about by mystical beings.

But if the Nordic gods were real . . . and the yokai were real . . .

Perhaps the Night of a Hundred Demons was real too?

Maybe, just maybe Oumagatoki and the Wild Hunt were the same thing, seen through the lens of two different mythologies, kind of like how multiple myths referenced the Great Flood in one way or another.

"I get it," Lukas replied, shaking his head slightly, "but why are you telling me this?

"Because"—Solana spoke with that same unnerving intensity—"I—or rather, *we* have a strong suspicion that this individual might be you."

Lukas couldn't help himself. He rose from the chair. "Seriously? I'm your prophesied Outsider? That's why you've gotten me here and given me the prisoner version of five-star treatment? I'm just from a different world, like the nine worlds of Yggdrasil. I'm not your fabled hero of legend, woman. Give me a break!"

"Sit."

"Next thing you're gonna tell me is—"

"*Sit.*"

Lukas sat down. Or rather, his body did without his permission.

"Neither your disbelief nor your attempt at levity will alter the course of events." Solana spoke in a low, tense, whisper. "You are no Hero. I do not think you even *can* be one. The prophesied one isn't the bringer of Change. He's simply the—"

"Key," Lukas finished. "That's what you called me the other day."

"Yes, and we have strong reasons to believe it is you. So you see, there are two ways we can do this."

"Oh yeah?" Lukas asked. Truly, a master of repartee, he was.

"Indeed. Either you listen to what I have to say and we will decide how that shapes our plans . . ." She placed her hands upon the table, palms downward. "Or I will slice your throat open and see if your unique talents help you survive. Either way, the debacle will end in this very room."

She said it in a scary way, without any melodrama to it at all. It was the way most people would say that they needed to take out the trash.

And Lukas believed her. There was no doubt in his mind that Solana would kill him. She'd do everything in her power to guarantee his demise. He doubted even his *soul* would ever be allowed to escape this place without being malformed in some way.

In the spirit of academic interest . . . Lukas thought.

"No," Inanna replied. **"Accepting my power has its perks. But in this form, my power is limited. Even if I were to use everything, the sudden**

influx of my Truth would alter you horribly. You would become your worst nightmare.”

Lukas believed her too. Stuck between the devil and the deep blue sea . . . and both had their ultimatums thrown at him. He exhaled and met Solana's eyes, speaking as calmly as humanly possible. “Join up or die. Not the best opening for a business deal.”

“I don't do business with cattle. I *eat* them.”

“Eating me will give you indigestion.”

“I'm willing to risk that.” Solana laughed. “Are you? I'd rather you hear our side of things before you die needlessly.”

Lukas doubted that Solana's version of *need* matched his own.

“Fine,” he sighed. “Tell me about this legend.”

Solana closed her eyes, as if searching her mind for the legend in question. He watched with growing confusion as she concentrated hard. It was like someone had fudged her mind and she was having difficulty trying to remember . . .

Whatever it was she was trying to remember.

Lukas wondered what could possibly do something like that to *her*.

“I presume it is similar in function to my Veil of Ignorance. The information is sealed away, even from her conscious thoughts. A rather useful tool. Mortal, should you agree to their proposition, ensure that you learn this art. I demand it.”

In exchange for what?

The goddess's surprise lasted an entire second. **“A tool like this would be invariably useful in preserving your secrets. Gain it or not, it is your choice.”**

Damn. Lukas frowned. Still, having a skill like that would be wonderful. That was when he noticed the painful expression on Solana's face.

“Um, do you need to use the bathroom . . .” he began.

“Wait . . .” she breathed. “I have it. I have it. Yes . . .” A spark lit up her eyes. “I will not entrust the entire prophecy to you, so I shall share a small part of it. There are two—forgive me, *three* signs that our ancestors left for us to help identify that individual when it—when *he*—comes. He'd be neither Asukan nor yokai but would hold power over both. He'd unleash the power that would cause Oumagatoki. And he'd have the power to end the world.”

Lukas went through her words in his head. “That . . . is a very vague set of statements.”

Even if he were to assume it applied to him, that meant he had some power that allowed him to dominate both races. He doubted it'd be something as simple as channeling fire-mana without being possessed, or the pendant's ability with language translation. No, the only thing that stood out was—

"My immunity against possession," he murmured. "That's the power you think I hold over your kind."

"Can you deny it?" Solana demanded. "Spiritual predation has always been our choice of weapon against bremetans. But somehow, you are not only *immune* to it, but can also seamlessly *consume* your predator's soul. I imagine this is how you acquired your command of fire."

Lukas nodded.

"It could also be your nature as an anomaly, or your future as someone under my vassalage," Inanna suggested. **"Both of those avenues grant significant power against these beings."**

He considered that for a moment, before a different question troubled him. Why was *Inanna* so interested in all this? He had half expected the goddess to try to bring him into a new bargain while getting him to fight his way out of this place.

"On the contrary, I am exhilarated by this opportunity. You are merely too simpleminded to see it."

What do you—?

He shook his head. He could get into long-drawn arguments with the goddess later. Right now, he needed to focus on this. He pushed himself off the chair and walked toward the wall on his right. Walking always had a way of clearing his mind and helping him focus better.

"Let's assume you're right," he began, his eyes boring into the wall. "Even then that's only one side of the coin. I have never encountered an Asukan before, assuming the ones standing outside are quintessential specimens of the race."

Solana cackled. "Hardly. But this much, I can tell you. To be an Asukan is to be a *tamer*. A collector. One who grabs what is not theirs, and binds them into servitude. Sometimes it is a monster, and others, a spirit. Even lesser creatures of our own kind are bound to follow their whims."

Inanna chortled.

. . . *What?* Lukas mentally asked, dumbfounded by her reaction. That seemed to make her laugh even harder.

"Do not trouble yourself," the goddess replied mirthfully. **"Just know that you have *much* to hold over those pesky creatures. And if you play your cards well, you stand much to gain from them as well."**

If you say so.

"I do."

You realize these yokai won't really let me go, right? Even if this legend is true, and even if it really applies to me, all I see is one giant trap. I don't care for these people or their wars. All of this is just to keep me on their side and use me to accomplish something. Worse comes to worst, they kill me before the other side can get their hands on me.

"Well elucidated," the goddess replied. **"Naturally, I expect better, superior treachery on your part. I want you to squeeze everything you can get out of them before leaving them out to dry."**

Lukas almost snorted. Why did he expect anything different? This was Inanna. If there was anyone who could spot a profit in a hopeless situation, it'd be her.

Let me guess . . . You want me to double-cross them before they double-cross me? While sticking to following their instructions and gaining everything that I can gain?

"Is it not quite the game?" Inanna asked, chuckling. **"I'd have enjoyed such a thing had it happened to me."**

This time he really snorted. Out loud.

Solana arched an eyebrow.

"Sorry," Lukas replied. "Just reflecting on how things turned out for me. And before you even get the idea, I *don't* have any sort of world-ending power."

"Not now, perhaps"—Solana grinned—"but in time."

"Why?" Lukas demanded. "You have literal *gods* on both sides. Why would an Outsider even matter? Surely you don't think that I'm powerful enough to . . ." Lukas froze, realizing the irony of what he was about to say. "Challenge a god?"

"Because no *god* can end the world. It goes against their very existence. Even ending part of the world is a Sin grave enough to *obliterate* entire pantheons. Trust me, *I'd know.*"

"She speaks the truth," Inanna interjected. **"Gods are terribly powerful existences. But with their terrible power also comes certain stringent limitations."**

"Which is where you come in," Solana went on. "A god cannot end the world, but—"

"With the Key, one might," Lukas murmured.

An icy shiver ran down his spine. Even if the Empire was half as bad as Solana was painting it out to be, and even if she had relayed to him the truest version of events, Lukas couldn't help but be reminded that he had been drawn into a war between those that looked and felt human, and the monsters of the night.

And he was standing on the monsters' side.

And the ironic part of it? It made him feel like he was defending a criminal in court.

Still think it's a golden opportunity?

"Very much so," Inanna whispered. **"As long as you do not do anything monumentally stupid."**

You say the sweetest things, Lukas thought back, and then considered the situation again. Trying to weasel out was not an option. Nor was getting angry and fighting his way out. Ignoring everything else, Lukas focused on what he had just learned.

He thought about what he'd received from Solana so far. The manner in which he was given these things. What they meant to someone that was definitely an alien, and didn't necessarily operate from the human "common sense" he was used to dealing with. He thought about what "equivalent exchange" meant to her, and to himself. What he represented. Who he was. What he wanted. What Solana wanted. The means of transaction for their deal. What was on the table? What wasn't? What could be safely removed? Factoring in pride—both his and her own.

"Let's hypothetically agree that I am indeed this . . . Outsider, as you make me out to be. That perhaps I *do* have some apocalyptic power that even I might not know of. What does that mean for me? I'm assuming you have something more to offer than the 'join me or die' approach you tried earlier."

Solana steepled her hands together on the table and rested her chin upon her fingers. "Some would say your continued existence is incentive enough."

"Ridiculous!" Lukas retorted dryly, turning his back against the wall. "Pay me in something I'd naturally need to even be of any help to you? Not exactly how business should be done."

"This feels nostalgic."

You did say that she's a woman after your own heart.

"I see," Solana murmured after a long period of silence. "And what do you expect in return?"

"Equivalent exchange." Lukas crossed his arms. "I'm not dumb enough to reject you to your face and try to walk away. And I don't think *you're* foolish enough to think you can scare me into being loyal. What about a compromise? You spoke of employment earlier. Certain tasks, perhaps, in exchange for favors?"

"And what would these favors be?"

Lukas slowly sauntered back to his chair and sat down, his eyes never once leaving hers. Eye contact was very important in negotiation. His lips quirked up at the edges. "Surprise me. You said I'd stand to gain a lot if I sided with you. Is it too much to ask for a sampling of goods before we shake on it?"

Solana stared down at him for several seconds. "You don't even *know* what your task is."

"Does it matter?" Lukas shrugged. "We've established that I don't have any lost love for you or your kind. Now either you can force me into following your orders—which could *probably* work, but only because you'd *force me to do it*. I'd have the initiative of a statue. Or, you could show me what I stand to gain by staying on your side. That way you know that I won't screw you over."

She hummed thoughtfully. "You speak a lot for someone with less-than-stellar skills, from what I've seen during that battle."

Lukas smirked. "Then get me an opportunity to elevate them. You seem to have quite a following. Perhaps they'd be interested in helping their *Key* fare better against the big, bad Empire?"

"I didn't peg you for the greedy kind."

"There's a saying back in my world," he replied with a sly grin. "Greed . . . is *good*."

Solana eyed him thoroughly. "Very well," she said, finally standing up. "Follow me."

As the two slowly walked to their destination, the surrounding space soon became washed with mist, damp and foggy, covering the terrain as far as the eye could see. The pale, dirty-white shade made it impossible to peer through it. There was no up or down, no left or right. Nothing but an endless void of shadowy mist.

Lukas squinted. Still nothing. He hadn't learned how to augment his senses using lifeforce yet, but a little attempt couldn't hurt. All he needed to do was pump a little lifeforce into his system and—

His words escaped him midway, as he stared at . . . the thing in front of him.

What was initially a layer of shadows interspersed with each other was now a shade of bright neon pink. Confused, he looked to his right at a particularly dark shade of chocolate that gave a curtain-like appearance to the entire area. He returned to look at the original place and found it now changed into a light shade of teal. He had barely managed to turn his head toward his left when a metallic-blue line shot out of nowhere straight toward him. He stepped back, but instead of finding ground, his left foot dug deeper.

Into water.

Or something that felt like water.

But how? Was he standing in a pool? His right leg didn't feel wet, yet his left—

Something rippled beneath his feet.

I—I'm not standing in a pool. I'm standing—he looked down, but found nothing but a greenish mist—*I'm standing on water. Walking on it. But . . . how?*

Lukas frowned. *Analyze.*

Insufficient data.

Scan.

Pre-registered prey within Scan Radius.

Lukas knew what it was talking about. Or rather, *who*.

"Welcome, Outsider," Solana murmured as she stood beside him, her posture one of complete nonchalance, "to the Haze. A shredded reality that was once part of our true World—Ikai."

"**The Haze . . .**" Inanna murmured inside his head. "**An apt description. A world with broken laws, broken rules, and broken Truths. A relic that would have fared better by constricting back into itself, or . . .**"

Or?

Inanna's voice felt uncertain. "**Or it could have fused with a singular creature and become something new.**"

Like me.

"**Precisely. This is sprawled out, tearing through a different world like the roots of a tree that no longer breathes. Existing for the sake of existence and nothing more.**"

Lukas blinked. *So . . . it's useless?* The thought felt odd. Why would Solana show this to him if it was? Was she banking on his unfamiliarity with this world? If so, she was in for a rough awakening.

"**Nothing is truly useless. Especially in my capable hands. But this all-pervading mist is indeed a remnant of the past and nothing more.**"

Huh, Lukas noted. "Well, I suppose Haze is an apt description," he said aloud. "I don't see anything except random colors. And phantom water. Not exactly my first choice for a first date."

Solana shot him a very mildly suffering look. "You realize I can kill you on a whim, right?"

"You've repeated that point too many times in the past hour to forget."

"And yet, perhaps not enough."

"I've been called thick-headed before."

She clucked reprovingly and took a step forward. Eerily enough, even though there was no real light in this place, he could see her. Her face, her eyes, even the little buttons on her overcoat. It was as if the multicolored mists only cared about occluding him from the rest of the environment.

"Why am I here?" he finally demanded. "I thought you wanted to show me something?"

"This *is* that something. An ever-expanding reticulum that gnaws through reality itself. The rules of space do not exist here. If you know how to, you may use the Haze as a spatial shortcut. You could travel from my base in the desert to the Graken Mountains for breakfast, make it to the heart of the Empire for lunch, and be back by supper. Political boundaries, geography—the Haze cares nothing for them."

A spatial shortcut? An intra-world wormhole that could be used to travel around in this world with impunity? With this, he could be anywhere. Accomplish nearly anything. The fact that such a thing even existed was just so—so—

Unreal.

"You expect me to believe that such a facility exists, yet this *Empire* somehow has you cornered?"

"The Haze is of the Other, and only those of the Other can access it," the yokai commander replied without the slightest inflection in her tone. "It is what has kept us from being hunted to extinction by the Empire's Cobalt Army."

The mysteries continued to deepen. His world didn't have Potential, yet it seemed like it was frequented by visitors from other realms. Could that have been what led to the surprisingly high quality of architecture and scientific progress that showed up from time to time in the past? The pyramids of Egypt? The Philosopher's Stone of ancient India? Was he going to find that the real Atlantis was lying around here somewhere?

Questions. So many questions. And every time he got close to an answer, all he found were more questions.

"If this Haze is only accessible to your kind, it's worth nothing to me."

"True." Solana nodded sagely. "But you are different. You are the *Key*. One who has successfully absorbed three of my kind and gained parts of their powers. It is possible that with practice, you might be able to access it." She looked almost wistful. "Perhaps you could even rise out of your mortal shell and transcend into spiritual form, traveling across the Haze without care or consideration."

"I'd very much advise against it, mortal," Inanna warned. **"Remember, your body—"**

Belongs to the omphalos, Lukas thought, his lips twisting in disgust. *I know.*

"Something displeases you?" Solana asked.

" . . . It's nothing," he replied. "But I still don't see what I stand to gain from all this. I mean, I haven't even seen the world. Rising out of my body could be a cool trick, but I happen to like staying physical."

"Suit yourself. But for now . . ." She lifted her right hand and extended it out to him. "Give me your hand."

"Uh, I need my hand. Both of them."

Solana shot him another look.

Lukas gave his surroundings a sidelong glance before putting his palm on top of hers. She grasped it, and a tidal wave of disorientation, dizzying but not unpleasantly so, scrambled his sense of direction. He felt a breeze on his face, a sense of movement, but he couldn't tell whether he was falling or rising or moving forward.

The movement stopped, and the whirling sensations passed. Thunder rumbled again, very loudly, and the surface he stood on shook with it. Light played against his closed eyelids.

"Open your eyes."

Lukas opened his eyes. And staggered.

A sudden rush of impressions stormed into his mind. It tore at his perceptions, flooding them with random images and smells and sensations. It was like standing in a sandstorm, only instead of inflicting pain, every random grain forced you through an experience, a memory, so disjointed and intense and rapid that there was nothing to hold onto. Overflowing lava burnt his skin while the coldness of the frigid tundra settled on his fingertips. The earth shook as hills and plateaus rose out of it while tides of a hungry ocean wanted to sweep him away and tear him into nothingness. Lightning streaked across the skies while a calming breeze carried the scent of flowers to his nostrils. The images doubled, redoubled, multiplied into thousands of separate impressions all coming at once.

They hammered against his mind as Lukas tried to keep his own identity from being sandblasted away by these foreign sensations.

And then—

And then they were gone.

He was back in the shadowy mists.

Lukas gulped, then glanced at the poisonously lovely, black-haired yokai that was looking down at him. *Down*, because he was currently on his knees, his heart pounding like it wanted to complete a lifetime's worth of beats in the next hour.

"What," he panted, "the *hell* was that?"

It made Solana smile. "Those were what we call *kami*, Aguilar. Manifestations of the elements themselves. Parasitic beings that cannot evolve without a Host, and are tremendously attuned to the elements themselves. You already have an element within you. Should you be able to finish your first task, I shall grant you access to a kami of your choice and allow you to devour it. Provided you can."

"You'd have one of your own devoured just to keep me on your side?" Lukas cringed, as his voice came out unsteady and quieter than he'd have liked.

"I would."

"Why?"

"Does that matter?"

"The reason *always* matters."

The yosuzume's gaze stayed on him, unblinking. "Kami are blessed with tremendous elemental affinity, but that comes at the expense of their nature. Or rather, their incompleteness. You cannot stop a kami from trying to possess a Host in hopes to steal its Soul Capacity any more than you can keep a fire from burning things. Asukans take advantage of this."

That got him interested. "How?"

"There exists a way. A . . . ritual, harnessing the powers of Amaterasu's Eternal Light. It allows them to lure kami out, and trap them. Force them into becoming their *pet beasts*." Solana's eyes glittered, anger showing for a moment, cool and far away. "They pervert our kind and use them to fight against us."

"How is my devouring them any different?" Lukas challenged.

"Simple. You will use their powers for *our* benefit. Not the Asukans."

"I could grow to like this girl," Inanna crowed.

Why don't you two marry each other?

The goddess laughed at his complaints. **"The poor dear. Thinks she can have my vessel for herself. Mortal, make sure you don't kill this creature by mistake. I want to do it myself and relish every moment of it."**

. . . You're pretty weird.

"And you are a mortal."

Lukas chuckled inwardly. Still, he couldn't help but wonder just what it was that Solana wanted him to accomplish as his *first task*. She could paint it to be trivial, but he knew that the yokai considered him as a potential weapon, a priceless asset against this Empire. And one did not waste a potential asset on trivialities.

"Just what *is* this task you want me to accomplish?"

Solana's features shifted subtly. They became paler, more like marble and less like something that belonged to a living human person. "What I have in mind is straightforward. I wish for you to seek the core of this anomaly and destroy it."

Lukas blinked. Destroy the core? The omphalos? Was that even possible?

"Crafty." Inanna applauded. **"Very crafty. Destroying an omphalos of something this large is an act of grave Sin. The moment you do it, you are a Sinner in the eyes of every god out there. Had this been in Akkad, you'd have been exiled from the Empire. I imagine things have not changed much in this regard since then."**

This is the second time you've mentioned that. Sin. Faith I get, but Sin?

"What of it?"

You said the demonic employed Sin to do its bidding, right? Unless you're telling me that killing an omphalos turns the killer into some kind of demon—

"It does not turn you into a demon, but it is as good a start as any. A demon is the opposite of a god. Both shed their mortal origins to become an embodiment of the powers they manifest. Whereas a god is supported by the world, sustained by the faith of their worshippers, demons are reviled. They seek shelter in the Great Dirge. They are Those-That-Wait-in-Darkness, growing stronger each time a mortal cries out in fear in their sleep. Every moment of dread, every bit of Sin, it beckons them. Calls for them to come. To ravage and undo everything until the World has returned to the black, empty void that predates Creation."

Everything fell in place. The moment Lukas performed an act of Sin, the Empire would no longer be an option for him. Solana and the yokai would accept him with open arms. Even hand him a kami to devour. They'd help him grow strong, while slowly feeding him with negative ideologies about the Empire until he'd be able to consider them as an enemy. And just like that, the Outsider would be theirs.

But can I even—

"**Yes,**" Inanna cut him off. "**Now listen. This is what I want you to do.**"

He did. She told him.

"Well?" Solana demanded, when it became clear that he wasn't going to reply. "Are we at a consensus?"

"Yeah . . ." Lukas trailed off, digging into his left ear with his pinky. "I'm not so sure about that. I don't know about you, but the monsters I've fought so far have been crazy fast and strong. If you want me to go toe-to-toe with the strongest monsters in this anomaly, I'll need more than that. I need skills. Proper skills. Fusing with that kasha gave me this fire-casting ability. I want you to get me someone to help hone it."

She held up her hand. "I do not make a habit of paying for things before they are done."

"You're telling me to risk my life because you decided this overgrown anomaly is an annoyance to you, yet you can't even be bothered to prepare me for it?" Lukas countered. "All this Haze and kami stuff means nothing if I end up getting killed. You wouldn't want your Outsider pawn to die so soon, would you?"

"It seems I have misjudged you, Aguilar," Solana replied coldly. "You seem to have the Asukan talent of *haggling* over things that do not belong to you."

"I'm shacking up with soul-twisting parasites," Lukas replied with a shrug. "I can't live in fear."

Solana's eyes darkened by several shades, and her lips twisted into something that was almost but not quite a smile. "Well then . . . I seem to have my work cut out for me, don't I? It's time we leave."

"Where are we going?" Lukas asked.

"Back."

As she said those words, the world around him faded and Lukas found himself back in the same room where he had been sitting with her a while ago. Only he was sitting on the chair, all alone, with no one else in the room. Solana had left to arrange matters for him.

Lukas exhaled with relief. The black-haired yokai's plan had been a good one. She was betting on his lack of knowledge about the world to trick him into becoming a Sinner. Had it been someone else in his position, the plan would probably have even worked.

He was new to this, yes, but he wasn't ignorant. There existed an entity in the deep recesses of his mind that far exceeded Solana in experience, power, and knowledge. A reflection of a goddess that had her plans in motion and would not allow Solana to ruin things for her.

Plus, he was an anomaly. An exception to the rules. Where any other creature would have committed a grave Sin, him consuming the crypt's omphalos would be a case of anomaly eating anomaly. Cannibalism, as Inanna put it, would not incur any Sin.

But Solana didn't know any of that, which was why she'd probably agree on letting him gain some skills before he left for his mission. After all, it wasn't like he'd have anywhere else to return to.

Wrong.

Lukas closed his eyes, his face morphing into a serene expression. Solana was partially right. He wouldn't be using those powers for the Empire. But he wouldn't use them for the yokai either. He'd use them for *himself.* It seemed fitting, and almost poetic since the legend didn't call him a yokai savior.

It called him an—

"Outsider." Solana walked in, with a male creature in tow. "This is Ryu. You will be under his tutelage until he deems you at an acceptable level for your task."

Oh, to be back in grad school again, Lukas thought to himself as he eyed his new helper.

It was a kasha—not the lean, feline female he had fought earlier, but a kasha nonetheless. It was a man in his fifties, medium build, just shy of six feet tall. He wore an outfit similar to Lukas's own, minus the shirt. Droplets of dark reddish brown stained one side of his face. Just like Quonnan, he had thick hair running down to the bottom of his spine, but the color had dulled to brown.

As he approached closer, Lukas was able to glean more details.

The kasha had a brand on his throat. One of his eyebrows was missing, and almost the entirety of his tail looked like it was crafted of metal. He approached Solana and bowed before her.

"What are my orders?" Ryu asked.

"He is our Outsider," Solana replied, her voice almost gentle. "He has demonstrated an affinity for Quonnan's powers. Your job is to help him recover her skills, and have him combat-ready before he starts on his task."

"To what degree am I permitted to act?"

Solana's sharp white teeth gleamed. "You may indulge yourself."

The man's mouth twisted into a wide, dangerous smile of its own, and he bowed his head toward his leader.

"And now"—Solana turned back to face Lukas—"Ryu will make sure you are not so easily captured like you were by my yurei earlier."

Lukas swallowed but did not say anything. Instead—

Accessing Monster Prototype Array	
RACE	**ENERGY CORE**
Yurei	Mana (Ether)
Reiki	Mana (Ether)
Kasha	Mana (Fire)

"I see," Lukas replied, the memory of being overwhelmed by those monsters resurfacing in his mind. His throat felt altogether too dry to get any more words out. "What did you mean by recovering *all* her skills?"

"Quonnan was a boisterous nuisance, but she was skilled. If you have devoured her, then I want those skills to reappear in you. Anything else would be a waste." She gave him a solemn stare. "I have now completed my end of the bargain, Outsider. I only hope that you will fulfill yours. Ryu is a veteran, and Quonnan was no slouch. You have the chance to learn from the former and have inherited the latter's skills. See to it that this opportunity is not wasted."

Lukas lazily saluted. "You got it."

And then Solana was gone. Just *gone*. Vanishing into thin air like she hadn't existed in the first place.

"I watched your fight, Outsider," Ryu grunted, the lines of his face stretching and becoming more prominent as he spoke. "You relied too much on your lifeforce, not unlike bremetans whose skin I wear. You deflected Quonnan's flames using invisible shields and used it against her."

Invisible shields. He supposed one could describe motion bending in those terms, at least from an observer's point of view.

"But if you want to truly shape fire, then turn off your tricks and use only fire. If you want to learn, you must face someone far more skilled than you," he said coolly. "You have to become one with the flames you wield until they are but an extension of yourself. Until you manage to do that"—Ryu's lips twisted into a bloodthirsty grin—"be ready to *burn*."

Lukas realized he may have made a mistake in demanding this training so eagerly. And when Ryu suddenly vanished from his sight and practically *teleported* behind him, blasting him away with a burst of superheated air, he knew his worst fears had come true.

"This new vermin is correct," Inanna chimed in. **"You cannot depend upon your luck every time. Do you not wish to survive against entities hilariously above you in strength, skill, and power? Then you must learn by blood."**

"Prepare yourself," Ryu said as he stepped forward menacingly. The already superheated air in the room went up a notch higher.

Lukas scrambled to his feet and shifted into a defensive posture, wincing as he stretched his scorched back.

I'm definitely going to regret this.

CHAPTER 24

TRAINING

Everything smelled of sulfur.

The terrain around them exploded as Ryu slammed his massive, fiery broadsword upon the floor. It wasn't made of metal, but a conjuration of pure flame willed into shape, capable of scorching anything with but a touch. Ryu's raw strength was only matched by his superlative technique and instinct. The veteran warrior certainly lived up to Solana's initial description, and no matter what he did, Lukas wasn't able to force him into a defensive position.

"Aguilar!" the kasha snapped, wiping a smidgen of blood from his lips. "You are mimicking my style well, but that's all. Even after all this time spent getting cut, pounded to the ground, muscles pulled, and bones broken . . . you *still* do not understand what I am trying to teach you."

"Well, I did smash my fist against your chin a second ago," Lukas retorted. It was really difficult to know how much time had passed, but if he had to wager a guess, he'd say a week. Every day, he received *instruction* from the veteran combatant and after it was over, dragged himself back to his quarters and let Prophylaxis fix him up. Every day, Ryu found new and inventive ways to torture him.

And all Inanna would do was laugh.

"Do you not know by now, mortal? It is my nature to find bliss in others' sufferings. Especially when said suffering is brought about by their own actions."

Not helping! Lukas snapped.

"That was a fluke," Ryu growled. "You will not get that chance again."

"Then I'll come up with a new way to kick your ass each time," Lukas hollered back, raising his right hand and propelling a sphere of blazing hellfire. At the same time, his left hand leveled a single finger at Ryu's chest.

Psychologically, it could be described as a manipulation of long-term memory—especially procedural memory—to create "false" memories that allowed for unconscious, reflexive behaviors. For Lukas, all that meant was that he was using Quonnan's skill at Fire Manipulation, now his own, to shoot fire bullets out of his fingers.

A single loud crack erupted from the other side of the battlefield as red blood spurted out of Ryu's chest. A small, dark stain formed on his chest, while he casually flicked away the fireball from earlier.

Ryu shot Lukas an annoyed look.

" . . . What?" Lukas defended. "You're the veteran warrior. I need to improvise or get my ass kicked."

"That was not improvising. That was dirty fighting!"

"Right, because using tactics *you* taught me is clearly the best way to beat you."

Ryu snickered. "You've been learning fire shaping for a week, and you think you already stand a chance against me?" A dark smile formed on his face. "Allow me to correct your misconception."

The kasha blurred into motion, and an instant later, Lukas found himself fending off a furious assault that bordered on lethal. His combat instincts had matured to a level that let him see a faint, preemptive shadow of the next attack an instant before it was executed. It was great, since he needed all the advantage it provided when he fought Ryu.

Lukas conjured a barrier between his arms, just in time to avoid being decapitated by the greatsword that Ryu swung from above. The second it hit the barrier, every speck of its momentum was drained away, leaving behind just the heat for Lukas to deal with.

It bought him a fraction of a second of respite at best.

Ryu didn't push ahead with the attack, having had enough experience with Lukas's barriers over the last week of grilling training. Instead, he simply raised the sword back and came slashing from the left. Then the right. Then left, right, up, up, right, down—constant hammering against invisible barriers in lightning-fast jabs, sounding like a lunatic woodchipper, with Lukas barely able to keep up with the barrage of attacks against him.

"*FIGHT!*" snarled Ryu, slamming his sword against his defenses. "FIGHT LIKE YOUR LIFE DEPENDS ON IT! BEING DEFENSIVE WILL NOT SAVE YOU, *BOY!*"

"Easy for you to say," Lukas yelled back, pushing a little lifeforce into his legs as he leaped back out of Ryu's reach.

Or so he thought.

Before he knew it, the kasha had already closed the gap. Lukas barely managed to halt the sword's motion, but even his senses failed to register the crushing knee that Ryu had delivered to his abdomen. Tears ran unbidden down his face at the beating he had taken, before another superheated blow from Ryu's open palm sent him flying, half of his face charred from the heat.

Ryu walked up to him. "Every single time you fail in countering me, but *why?* You can perceive my movements when you pay attention. Your barriers can drain the momentum of my blows away, regardless of how hard I try. Your healing abilities are way more profound than any Metamancy I could conjure. If only I had the option of possessing your body and your skills, I could have matched Leader in combat."

Lukas wasn't sure whether to be surprised at Ryu's wistful tone or alarmed by what he had just said. Even by kasha standards, Ryu was a monster, and that guy thought that he needed Kinetomancy and Prophylaxis to match Solana in combat.

It was a humbling realization that made Lukas realize that, anomaly or not, his immunity against possession or not, he was hopelessly, hilariously outgunned by the beings around him.

"Good," Inanna commented. **"That is the approach you must follow if you wish to achieve your goals. The key to victory is climbing uphill while also realizing that there is always someone that outshines you in strength, dexterity, and skill."**

That's great and all, but it tells me nothing about keeping up with this monster. I can't win if I cannot perceive his movements.

"Like always, you listen but you do not understand. It is possible to uplift one's mental perception by magnitudes through lifeforce, far greater than what you can do. But given your proficiency in making things difficult for yourself, your mind would collapse in the process."

Then teach me.

"And what do you offer in return?"

You aren't getting my undying loyalty, but it'll make my job easier. As you said, I'm sure to fry my brain rather than achieve this . . . whatever it is.

Inanna laughed. **"Is that your attempt at persuading me?"**

Is it working?

That made her laugh even harder. **"I suppose there is no harm in adding an incentive once in a while. Even in Akkad, it was the policy to award slaves with delicacies after a good day's work."**

I'm not your pack mule!

"You are what I make of you," the goddess replied. **"But I will not break my own rules, mortal. If you want something, you must be willing to give something in exchange."**

Not again—

"Surely it wouldn't harm you to listen to my offer?"

Lukas sighed.

"This is what I propose. I shall endeavor to impart the mind arts to you. It will allow you to elevate your thought, your perception, and your clarity in battle."

And in return?

"In return, you must channel the power you gain after harvesting the omphalos of this crypt to the pendant."

Isn't that a tall order? I don't even know if I can get to the core in the first place.

"Well then," the goddess replied, amused, "it is in my best interests to ensure you are sufficiently prepared. Do we have an accord?"

As far as deals went, it was as good as it could get. He was already bound to attempt destroying or assimilating the core. The amount of energy he'd acquire could be substantially high, maybe even greater than the reserves he currently boasted, but did he *really* need it? Even with his expanding skill set, there was enough power to last him an entire lifetime.

The opportunity of being taught something new by the goddess herself was also too rare to miss out on.

We have an accord.

"Good. Now focus. You have a battle to win."

"If you're this impaired from just one blow, you are even weaker than I thought," Ryu scoffed. "You cannot even scratch me without your tricks."

Lukas squinted his eyes and gave his opponent a glance-over. He staggered a bit and tried to regain his balance. "Not even a scratch, you say. Let's see if I can make one then."

Ryu reshaped his broadsword to extend its tip outward on either side, forming a battle ax.

Show-off. Lukas focused inward. This would be the first time he'd attempt this, but it was now or never. One did not throw away an opportunity for learning something from Inanna. No matter the risk, the rewards would always be greater.

He knew that from experience.

Activate Alpha Condition.

ALPHA CONDITION Activated Accessing Monster Prototype Array		
RACE	**ENERGY CORE**	**SOUL SIZE**
Yurei	Mana (Ether)	1050
Reiki	Mana (Ether)	1550
Kasha	Mana (Fire)	2100

He took a deep breath.

Activate Kasha.

MONSTER PROTOTYPE: KASHA		
SKILLS	**LEVEL**	**SOUL CAPACITY CONSUMED**
Possession	2	500
Conjuration	2	500
Fire Creation	2	500
Fire Manipulation	2	500
Temperature Modulation	1	50

Activating Monster Prototype Kasha . . .
Initiating Consciousness Shift . . .
Enact.

Space splits.

Or is it his senses? They feel everywhere. He senses himself. His body. Human. Mortal. Hu–mortal? Mor–human? Or is it Lostbelt Earth? Omphalos?

Memories. Events. Impressions. Inanna. Memories of a goddess. Memories of a human. Memories of a lostbelt. Anomaly. Singularity. Realm. Lostbelt. Orig—

Cracks appear. Cracks diffuse. Cracks get larger. Brighter. Cracks converge. Diverge. Shatter. Reform.

His mind devolves.

Instinct arises. Instincts of a human. Instincts of anomaly. Instincts from skills. Instincts from monster prototypes. Instincts from—

There is no pain. The cognition of pain no longer matters. He is swallowed by injury. By his senses. By information. By Anomaly. By Power. By Mind. By—

He falls into a swirling maelstrom of pain.

He doesn't know where he is.

He doesn't know who he is.

He doesn't know what it means.

It doesn't matter.

He sees it now. Like a large integrated circuit. What is a circuit? How does it integrate? What is seeing? Information? Information assimilation? Where would that be? Why would that be? What does—

The complexities increase. They twist. They bend. They form shapes that shouldn't exist. Shapes he knows have always existed. Three-dimensional. Ten-dimensional. Matrices. Lattices.

His vision narrows. What is vision?

The world expands.

He concentrates on random, arbitrary thoughts. Why? He knows he will split in half otherwise. How does he know?

Unnecessary.

The world is too big for this small body. The monster prototypes are too large for this soul. The Spiritual Presence is too grand to be hidden within this shell.

Yet the world fits. Yet the prototypes exist in segregation. Yet the Presence stays hidden. Bound. Forged. Fused.

He is being repelled. He can't be repelled.

He is reaching it. He can't reach it.

He shouldn't reach it. Not reaching it will be unforgivable.

He is reaching out.

He is reaching out.

He is REACHING OUT.

His eyes burn. His brain burns. He extends his arms and they extend and extend and extend—

GRHRAAAAA—

GET THERE—

GET THERE—

GET THERE RIGHT NOW—

"*Ha—agh—gag!*"

His eyes are focused now. They are dripping blood.

Right and wrong. Black and white. Colorful and grayscale.

He is opening his eyes. He is human. He is monster. Not human. Monster. His perceptions blur. Dim and bright. Pitch-black darkness and bloodred.

His tail extends. A second pair of eyes open. His claws retract and extend. Raw power flares within his body. His ears block all reception. He has no extra eyes. He has no tail. He has no claws. He is no spirit.

He is.

He isn't.

He is and he isn't. And yet, he manifests his— ██████████ *—and uses it with great efficiency.*

He is awake. He is fire. Fire that never surrenders. If it cannot burn, it will burn everything around it. Block its path and it will ignite the air, and begin its blaze along a newer path. Fire will find a way.

It always does.

He always does.

Power cloaks him. Unbridled. Chaos in flesh and blood. Rage without restraint. Force without balance.

He sees it. The kasha. He understands it. He has become it. Human is monster. Monster is human. Lukas is kasha and—
An unholy roar emerges from his throat.
—Kasha is Lukas.

Fire lashed out from Lukas's left hand—not a gout of flame like he could normally call up, but a slender *whip* of fire so bright that it hurt the eyes to see. With a proficiency he did not possess, Lukas slashed it against Ryu, who had but a moment to register the sudden shift in the battle and leap backward, using the ax to deflect the attack from slicing him into half, while throwing a burst of flames in Lukas's direction.

Lukas let the whip vanish and caught the incoming blast of flames in a grip of invisible power and hurled it around him in a perfect circle before sending it back at Ryu. He was a creature of *fire*. This opponent, another kasha or not, would not get the better of him using flames.

He leaped forward and slammed a punch of pure, smoldering heat at him. But in a manner that Lukas could not comprehend, Ryu grabbed the heat from his punches and dissipated it out into the air, while grabbing Lukas's fist within his own and twisting it. Suppressing the urge to let out a furious howl, he twisted his body and sent a blast of pure force at Ryu's face before turning around and kicking him in the temples with his knee, now enveloped with flames. Ryu was sent staggering back. Taking advantage of his loss of balance, Lukas coated his palm with fire and stabbed the veteran head-on.

Right through the stomach.

He then spun around, giving himself a momentum boost to pound a hammer-heavy blow of pure force at Ryu's head. A lance of pure fire formed in his other palm, and he swung it down, streaking it through the air, ready to decapitate the kasha and—

Stopped.

Just like that.

Lukas tried to push farther, but invisible hands held him back. He would *not be denied his prey. He would decapitate this thing and burn its body to shreds until there was—*

"Enough."

Lukas hadn't even begun to register who or what said it when a force of a hundred anvils smashed against him from all sides. The flames disintegrated into motes of crimson dust as he gasped like a landed fish, struggling to move, but he couldn't so much as lift a single finger. He poured in lifeforce, with the idea of deflecting some of whatever force was being thrown at him, but it was to no avail.

He could no more escape its grip or force it away than could an insect stop a shoe from descending.

In the instant that realization came upon him, the force vanished, evaporating the bloodlust with it as if it had never been there in the first place. And with that came a sudden and surprising sensation that Lukas hadn't been able to feel before.

He could sense *it*.

He didn't quite understand the details, but he knew intuitively that the kasha was the reason behind this sudden bloodlust. It was the thing that was enabling him to think and perceive the world in a vastly alien format that would otherwise be incomputable to his human mind. And now, Lukas realized he had wanted to kill Ryu. To give in to homicidal rage and cut this creature down in cold blood.

He knew that if it had succeeded, *it* would win. And he would be lost to a fate he didn't understand except that it was somehow *worse* than death.

He forced himself to calm down. From somewhere deep within himself, he could almost hear a howl of impotent fury as *it* receded into the lowest, most primal depths of his mind to hide once more.

Monster Prototype Kasha Deactivated
Reverting Consciousness Shift to Base Host
Enact

And just like that, it was over.

Lukas took repeated breaths, uncaring of Solana's calculating gaze upon his person. He was now down upon his knees, barely a foot away from Ryu, who was down on his knees too, exhaling softly as the tissues around the wound began to self-cauterize and bind together.

Metamancy at work.

"Your potential as an anomaly is limitless, mortal," Inanna chided him, **"but it will turn you into a mindless beast should you let it control you."**

You pulled me out.

It wasn't an accusation. Just a confirmation of a fact.

"Who else would it be?"

Lukas couldn't help himself. He grinned.

Suddenly, notifications started popping up.

URGENT!!!			
REGISTERED SKILL	**UPGRADE**	**SOUL CAPACITY**	**ISSUE**

Fire Manipulation	LEVEL 2	+450	Requires confirmation for assimilation.
Host Body requires calibration!			

Show me my Soul Capacity.

Soul Capacity Consumed	1629/2379

Lukas frowned. A part of him did not want to spend yet another large chunk of whatever Soul Capacity he had, since it would once again limit him from gaining other skills he might just come across. Another part of him pointed out the sheer irony that here he was, choosing *not* to assimilate a skill when he had the capacity for it, while just some weeks ago, he would have bent backward to gain a single one.

"The ability to siphon souls has spoiled you for choices," Inanna replied fondly. **"Most people would jump to acquire the skill regardless of all else."**

Her words had merit. Both Solana and Ryu had seen him operate on a far superior level than he had presented for the entire duration of his training montage with the latter. Returning to a subpar level would raise unnecessary questions he didn't want to entertain at the moment.

Besides, he reasoned wistfully, *the whip and fire lance were kind of cool.*

He came to a decision.

Assimilate it.

Skill Assimilation Successful		
Utilized Soul Capacity		2079/2379
SKILL ATTRIBUTES		
SKILL	LEVEL	CONSUMED SOUL CAPACITY
Raw Lifeforce Manipulation	1	50
Momentum Manipulation	1	50
Friction Modulation	1	50
Pressure Modulation	1	50

Kinetomancy (FRAGMENTED)	APEX	1279
Fire Creation	1	50
Fire Manipulation	2	500
Temperature Modulation	1	50

Lukas glanced at Ryu, who was, surprisingly enough, grinning at him like a loon. Solana, on the other hand—

Shit!

"That stance . . ." the leader of the yokai mused. "That was all Quonnan. You were drawing from her memories."

Technically, she was only half right. It wasn't her memories he was drawing from, but her skills. Her instincts. And being a creature of fire whose very nature embodied the element she represented, just using her skills drew on her instincts without consciously trying.

It was both an enlightening and frightening prospect that could have terrible repercussions if he didn't pay attention.

Solana took a step forward. "You absorbed Quonnan's soul, but she is still there in memory, uncorrupted. Not only that, but you also knew when the change would happen. Perhaps I would even be correct in saying you *engineered* said change yourself."

Lukas schooled his features. Solana was getting dangerously close to the truth. "Right . . . well, keep up the guesswork," he replied. "Now, can we take a break? Fighting so hard can be taxing for Outsiders like me."

Solana eyed him hungrily. For a moment, he thought she would attack him.

"Sure." She shrugged. "I don't think Ryu will be able to train you any more today."

Lukas gave her a serious nod, and turned away, just in time for—

"I do not understand you, Outsider. But one thing is certain . . . we are never letting you go."

> **Language Identified—Eusmian**
> **Replicate?**

Lukas didn't pause, not in the slightest. He took another step forward, then another, one foot in front of the other, and kept on walking. It was only after he reached his room and slammed the door shut behind him that he allowed himself to take a deep, relieved breath.

Every time he spoke to Solana, it was like she peeled layers off of him like an onion, tearing his secrets out of him one at a time and figuring out precisely how he ticked. The longer he was among the yokai, the more he could feel the heat of the magnifying glass looming above him.

Huffing, Lukas shook his head. Now wasn't the time to worry about that.

Inanna had been willing to teach him for once, and he was *excited*.

Sitting cross-legged in the middle of his room, he slowly let himself go. Entering the mindscape was no longer the utterly alien experience it used to be. Now, it was just three steps.

The first was ensuring his body was safe. Despite his misgivings about being among the yokai, he was relatively safe in his room since the yokai were ordered to maintain a distance from him by Solana.

The second was taking long, deep breaths, allowing the increased oxygen to stimulate his brain.

But the third step was still tricky.

The moment he stepped in, the outer world was shed like a second skin. All physical sensations were left at the door, leaving him at the mercy of the world around him. There may not have been any monsters around at the moment, but if some ill-intentioned yokai attacked him, he wouldn't realize it until it was too late. Luckily, he had just the thing to help prevent that.

The Screen.

Each time he stepped into his mind, Scan and Analyze activated by themselves, remaining in play until he was back in the physical world. The moment something came near, the Screen triggered a message and Inanna sent him rushing "back" to deal with the problem.

So far, it had happened a grand total of two times. And rapidly being flung out of his mind felt like a rollercoaster ride.

Exhilarating, but absolutely nauseating.

"Welcome to your first class on how to become a monster."

"Hilarious," Lukas sarcastically retorted, looking toward where the voice came from and—

Whoa . . .

Inanna wore white like a second skin. The silken robe flowed from just above her bountiful breasts all the way to her knees, emphasizing her generous assets quite beautifully. She was mere inches shorter than him, but with her semi-transparent heels and her figure, she looked a tad taller. Her shining skin and glossy black hair falling down to her waist only added to her beauty, unmarred by the casually arrogant expression on her face.

This was no person.

This was—she was—

It was at this point that Lukas realized he was openly staring, and he tried to look away.

. . .

He found the task a monumental effort.

"There is no Sin in appreciating beauty, mortal. Even if it is far beyond one's reach."

No wisecracks came out of his mouth this time around.

Inanna's lips twisted into a beaming smile.

"Shall we continue?"

"About that 'speeding up my mind' thing?"

Inanna frowned at him, or perhaps, at his crude description. Or maybe both. It was difficult to tell with her.

"The mind arts are an intricate and dangerous field of study. The mortal mind is body-bound. That in itself limits what you can think, feel and act. But the moment you delve into psionics, you irrevocably shatter those limitations."

"And . . . that's a bad thing?"

"Imagine waking up as your five-year-old self. Would that be comfortable for you?"

Lukas shook his head, understanding her point. When he had first leveled up, he'd suffered from a lack of coordination with his body. It took him a while to get used to his improved anatomy and not fall flat on his face with every step he took.

For something as complex as the mind, the problem would be exponentially greater.

"I guess I'd better use it correctly then. Is it . . . Do you think it's within my abilities to learn it?"

"One cannot be sure unless they have tried. Though, given your past performances, I may as well talk about ascension to a pebble."

He had a slight suspicion that he had annoyed her recently. She seemed to take more potshots at him than usual. And that was saying something.

"—start from the basics or the basics of the basics. Shouldn't be harder than teaching a rodent."

Lukas snorted. He could almost picture her holding a book with a title like that: *The Many Similarities in Training Rats and Mortals.*

A moment later, said book sat inconspicuously on the chair beside him, its bright orange cover too glaring to be missed by human eyes.

"Perhaps you will show promise after a month, but that requires an unrealistic level of optimism."

"Alright, alright, too many low blows at once." He coughed.

"This is not a jest, mortal. Psionics is a difficult art, even for the most

brilliant of minds. *You* are far from that. Your progress will be slow, terribly in fact, in the beginning. Only the most fortuitous progress beyond the very basics without severely damaging their mind."

"No pressure then."

The goddess smirked.

Never one to shy away from hard work, Lukas returned her a brief nod. "So . . . what does this skill entail?"

Inanna cocked her head slightly backward. **"Psionics isn't a singular skill, mortal, but a cluster of closely related skill sets, the most infamous of which is the enthrallment of another. It is important you understand, because the creature you call Solana is rather proficient in that art."**

Lukas wiped his hand across his face as he sought to process this. He remembered his interactions with Solana, about how she had all but *forced* him to speak in Ualbesh—an unsuccessful attempt since he couldn't until Inanna had activated the pendant's function.

Solana was the most dangerous creature in this anomaly thus far. Lukas knew it by heart and soul. And yet, he had been strangely at ease around her, while being on edge near every other yokai in this place.

A nasty thought entered his mind.

" . . . Do you think she's controlling me?"

"Impossible. Your Alpha Condition function grants you some degree of resistance, which is also the underlying reason behind your relative immunity against possession. And even if she could bypass it, the creature's paltry abilities cannot bypass one such as myself."

It was at times like this that Lukas could appreciate her self-confidence.

"That being said, possessing your *body* and affecting your mind are entirely different, at least from the omphalos's perspective."

Lukas physically winced at her words. The omphalos considered his body to be its anomaly. His human mind was simply an added attribute that suited the circumstances better than anything else. An attack on the body would be repelled with extreme prejudice, which was why the omphalos had reacted so heavily to possession. The fact that the yokai were so little attuned to his body only exacerbated the reaction.

But his mind? His mind was his own. And he had always acted out as he wished. Even if Solana could subliminally influence him, would the omphalos register that as a threat?

At the same time, a part of him couldn't help but point out that Inanna was only mentioning this because being under Solana's influence would mean resistance to her own plans. Even when she was helping him, she was using him.

Still, he needed to learn. He needed to grow. The activation of the new omphalos functions would accelerate his growth, and his strength and finesse would rise with experience.

"What are you going to teach me first then?"

A chair appeared behind her as Inanna sat down, legs crossed, and stared back at him. **"In my era, it was tradition to learn how to dilute one's subjective awareness to the flow of time. It allowed you to study your surroundings more thoroughly and make better decisions."** She paused for a second. **"I shall endeavor to impart the same lesson onto you."**

Lukas could almost visualize it as the goddess described it to him.

"With little effort, one could perceive a speeding arrow as if it were dragging through the air. A sword's trajectory could be calculated mid-swing. In your case, it would allow you greater leeway to fall into your many mental tangents mid-battle."

That got a laugh out of him.

Seemingly pleased with herself, Inanna continued. **"This skill is called Shensivueh. Nine out of ten aspirants perish in their attempts to master this technique. But take heed, mortal, it bears its own share of troubles. If you maintain this altered mental state for more than what your heart can keep up with, you risk a complete breakdown of your brain functions. I believe the human word for it is . . . aneurysm."**

"Wait a second," Lukas blurted out. "I know what that is."

A sudden increase in one's perception of time, marked by an increased heart rate and sometimes followed by cardiac arrest or brain aneurysm. He'd heard of this phenomenon. He'd studied it. This wasn't some fancy technique—it was a psychological condition that resulted in an extremely high dilation of perception. This 'sensivu' or whatever you call it, I've seen happen. Back on Earth, we call it—"

An image of a drug-addicted athlete capable of supernatural feats came to mind. He had first come across the concept back in college. The phenomenon was generally known as—

"Tachypsychia!"

" . . . "

CHAPTER 25

TO BE A MONSTER

Given how everything had happened in his life since waking up in this crypt, it was pretty on-brand for Inanna's training regimen to be filled with pain.

Ever since he and the goddess had come to an accord, things had changed between them. Inanna had seemingly given up on trying to throw him into more bargains and instead seemed to be working in favor of the stipulations Lukas had set forth.

To a neutral observer, Lukas would spend hours in backbreaking training, resting only when he passed out from exhaustion. But in reality, he was meeting the goddess in his mindscape and discussing his current situation. Inanna listened to his opinions about the yokai, their society, powers, and agendas. In return, the goddess shared her own experience with ethereal creatures she had interacted with back in her time.

That, and they worked on their own mindscape training.

Meanwhile, Prophylaxis would act upon his battered and bruised body to make him ready for the next day.

Lots of pain.

Every time he took a breath, a searing burst of agony radiated from his chest. He staved off his next breath for as long as he could, but eventually, his lungs gave up, and he winced as a burning fire took root once more. The cycle repeated every few moments, as his entire reality was consumed by the simple struggle to breathe and try avoiding the torment. The pain didn't exactly lessen, but over time, it became a little more bearable.

He idly wondered if he was becoming a masochist.

"Good, mortal." Inanna's melodious voice felt like a rasp to his tired ears. **"Very good."**

Lukas managed to push himself over and onto his back. His arms and legs felt like someone had replaced his bones with lead, and his muscles and tendons simply couldn't overcome the inertia to make a single movement.

He tried opening his mouth, but it just ended in a fit of coughs and pain surging down his spine.

It hurt, but at least it meant he was alive.

"Get up!" the unrepentantly vicious goddess ordered. **"This is your mind. The only pain you shall feel is what you allow yourself to. Pain, injury, fatigue—they are nothing but sensory information fed to your mind. Refuse to let any of it in. Reject it."**

Lukas just groaned from where he lay. It was easier said than done, but he supposed she didn't get to where she was by stopping to think about things.

Inanna had been teaching him Neural Suppression—a skill that was pretty much an on and off switch for his pain receptors. It was a technique that would allow him to function even with grave injuries. Unlike force bursts or tachypsychia, the concept of leveling up did not apply to this skill.

She had patiently and painstakingly tried the mental route at first, but his ability with psionics hadn't progressed enough to let him modulate his receptors so freely.

So here he was. *Sparring.* Or, as Lukas liked to call it, getting beaten up until he looked like one giant bruise so he could practice willing the pain to go away.

And so far, the results were nonexistent.

"On the bright side," Inanna said brightly, **"you are gaining experience fighting an opponent hilariously beyond your own proficiency in combat."**

And as much as he hated it, her words were true. Over the past two weeks, Lukas had suffered through nineteen such sessions. Inanna had come up with all sorts of cruel, inventive, and pragmatic ways of breaking him down. Sometimes, she'd push him through an exhausting number of tasks. Singularly, each task was benign, but in tandem, the experience made him curse his own existence.

Other times, she'd give him an extraordinarily simple task to perform, but under impossibly ridiculous conditions.

Exhibit A—picking fresh leaves and roots from thick underbrush while maintaining his tachypsychia.

Before today, never had he imagined how terrifying it was to watch oneself perform a mindlessly effortless task with extreme slowness. Not only did he have to keep cardiac failure at bay from the exertion, but his patience was stretched so thin that Lukas felt like he'd snap at any moment.

But that was the tip of the iceberg.

There were sessions where she'd conjure an ax, of all things, and rush toward him, making him dodge, jump, leap, and perform all sorts of acrobatics to avoid being torn to shreds. It might've all been an illusion—something happening within his mind—but the pain of having the blade go through him was overwhelming. He wouldn't put it past her to manipulate his pain receptors to crank them into overdrive.

What was worse, he wasn't allowed to use Kinetomancy to create defenses, instead forced to rely on his developing psionic skills to appraise the incoming blow's trajectory and get out of the way.

In another, he'd found himself inside a large glass box filled with spiders, worms, and snakes of all shapes and sizes and colors. According to her, it was an exercise in controlling tension and responding to sudden spikes in fear and stress. It had taken him several sessions of suffering through spider bites and snake venom before he'd gotten the hang of maintaining his cool, even under such duress.

Pain, as the saying went, was an excellent motivator.

"You should feel privileged. Healing bones in real life would have been far more excruciating and slow."

"You're a true giver," he groused. If nothing else, it was perfectly clear that this wasn't training.

It was refinement. Refinement through the furnace known as pain.

"As it should be." The goddess smiled facetiously. **"Teaching is the part of planting a seed and nurturing it. I have seen your memories, seen how you mortals prattle over the feeding of useless information in exchange for currency. Real education is the art of inculcating skills into the future generation—true abilities that will help with evolution. In front of such a reward, pain is no true cost."**

What was he thinking, asking her of all people to train him?

"This isn't working!" he yelled back. "All you're doing is torturing me at this point!"

Inanna crouched down beside his fallen form, arching a single elegant eyebrow toward him. **"A pity,"** she drawled. **"And to think you once showed a glimmer of potential."**

A very familiar ax materialized right in front of her, and her fingers easily found their way around the handle into a firm grip within seconds. **"Fear not, mortal. We shall not stop until we find it once more."**

With a graceful, gravity-defying swing, Inanna hefted the ax until it was well above her head and brought it straight down onto him.

It was almost surreal. No matter how many times he performed it, each time was different. His awareness of time screeched to an incredibly slow pace, dragging out what should have been the blink of an eye to several seconds.

Everything around him became a twisted fusion of reality and a stationary image as the world descended into a strange, crawling mess.

And in the middle of all that, his perception expanded.

Thump!

Once a blur to the naked eye, the falling blade of the ax was no longer as fast as it used to be. It practically crawled toward his chest. He could feel the naked sharpness of the edge, thinner and sharper than anything his mind could conjure.

Thump! Thump!

His body blurred into action. To an observer, it would have been immensely quick, but to his own perception, he was moving at a snail's pace. His right leg moved forward, then his hip moved in coordination with it. His left hand slowly shifted upward and to the side, just enough to get out of the way as the rest of his body dragged and dragged and *dragged*—

Thummmppp!

The dichotomy was nothing short of terrifying. He could see the ax slowly pass downward, feel it touch the skin from his left arm, and—

No! I won't let it end like this!

His body screamed as raw force exploded from his arm, pushing him just enough to escape being *sliceeedddd*—

Lukas let it go. He was already slamming his leg against the weapon's handle. Somewhere along the line, his brain caught up with the act and strongly pointed out to him how the handle hadn't fractured despite multiple lifeforce-enhanced punches in the past.

His knee couldn't possibly fare any better.

Before his instinct could catch back up, his leg was already in motion, smashing into the bar with enough force that, by all means, should be impossible even in his best state. When he first noticed the hairline fracture slowly spreading through the handle's surface, he realized he was still maintaining his elevated perception as well.

His leg moved a little farther.

And something cracked. Whether it was his bone or something else, he didn't know.

Another thin fracture appeared.

Followed by another crack.

And then, it exploded with the force of a small bomb. The handle imploded in its center, blasting out small pieces of incomprehensibly hard metal as his leg passed through the area where the handle had been. The dangerous metallic head of the ax, meanwhile, remained stuck to the ground.

Completing his sweeping motion, Lukas flipped back and pulled himself up into a cautious position—half-crouched, hands up and ready to deflect anything that approached.

Inanna let out a delighted, silvery laugh as she clapped her hands. **"Beautiful,"** she intoned. **"Brutal. Vicious. Beautiful."**

But Lukas was far less amused. "Next time you try something like that," he snarled, "I won't stop at the ax."

Before he knew it, her body was spinning, her right leg swerving in a clean sweep toward his head. Tachypsychia or not, there was absolutely nothing he could do to stop her.

THUMP!

He crouched lower. Her leg was still sweeping across the air. There was simply not enough time to evade such a hit.

THUMP! THUMP!

His left hand moved up to block. But it wouldn't matter. Surviving a hit from Inanna at such close proximity was a pipe dream. At best, he'd be left with a broken arm.

No, the real issue was what would happen after she broke his arm.

He recognized her posture. Her leg was arriving in a single sweep as her other foot remained perfectly perched on the floor. Completely still. Unmoving. Functioning as a fulcrum, one that maintained her balance during the attack. And in a perfectly stable position to pull off a second, consecutive hit to his head as soon as this foot touched the ground.

THUMP!

His left hand was now right in front of his left ear. A hit this close would literally kill him. Dreamland or not, he didn't want to take any chances. The arm would shatter—that much was a given by now. What he needed to do now was ignore the pain, which, ironically enough, was the purpose of this session in the first place.

Lifeforce surged through him, and his body reacted out of pure instinct.

The leg met his arm.

His ulna shattered.

But Lukas was well past thinking about the pain.

THUMP! THUMP!

Her foot touched the ground.

And her other foot was already in motion.

Had Kinetomancy been on the table, he'd have used the opportunity to push it backward, tossing her off. But it wasn't, so he did the only thing he had available to him.

He threw force at her.

Of course, an attack like that wouldn't do jack shit to the goddess. Nothing that he was capable of would even come close to fazing her. But luckily for him, that wasn't what he intended to do.

In a battle of force versus unyielding strength, the solution you looked for need not be to overpower it. There was a third possibility—to escape her reach.

Just because the force of his hit wasn't strong enough to push the goddess's leg away, it didn't mean it wasn't strong enough to push himself out of reach.

And that's exactly what he did, allowing the push to send him skidding across the floor—completely out of her reach.

Inanna planted both feet firmly on the ground with perfect poise. **"Care to repeat your statement, mortal?"**

There was no mirth in her demand. If he didn't answer appropriately this time, this could very well be his end. But fortunately for Lukas, he was an incredibly reasonable and rational individual.

Except for when he wasn't.

"I said, I'm not willing to roll over and be fucked on a whim. You might be a reflection of a goddess, but that doesn't guarantee my obedience."

Inanna's inhuman eyes practically shimmered. **"I expected no less of you. Were you not strong enough to cast such defiance into my teeth, you would be useless to my purpose."** Her smile widened. **"To *our* purpose."**

He clenched his fists.

"Look at you," the goddess purred, as if the raw, murderous desire he was exuding was nothing out of the ordinary. **"It seems even weaklings can bite if you push them far enough. How fun."**

Once the grueling training session was finally over, Lukas quickly found himself sitting in Solana's office room. Despite all of Inanna's taunts, despite her thrashing him about, despite his pain and broken bones, he had to admit . . .

SOULSCAPE	
NAME	Lukas Aguilar
Type	**Base Host**
Level	**4**
Experience	**417**
Current Threshold	**640**
Utilized Soul Capacity	**2129/2379**
ESSENCE	
Maximum Lifeforce Output	**725**
Replenishment Rate	**180 / hour**
LEY LINE NETWORK	
Maximum Mana Output	**400**
Synthesis Rate	**80 / hour**

SKILL ATTRIBUTES		
SKILL	LEVEL	CONSUMED SOUL CAPACITY
Raw Lifeforce Manipulation	1	50
Momentum Manipulation	1	50
Friction Modulation	1	50
Pressure Modulation	1	50
Kinetomancy (FRAGMENTED)	APEX	1279
Fire Creation	1	50
Fire Manipulation	2	500
Temperature Modulation	1	50
Perception Manipulation	1	50

OMPHALOS ATTRIBUTES	
Energy Reservoir Capacity	∞
Current Energy Level	722,415,138 units
OMPHALOS FUNCTIONS	
Scan	Level 2
Analyze	Level 2
Prophylaxis	Level 2
Soul Siphon	NA
Alpha Condition	Level 1
Evocation	Level 1

His progress felt good. *He* felt good.

Between facing off against Ryu in mortal combat using fire as his primary weapon, and pushing his mind to the extreme edge to master the psionic cluster under Inanna's tutelage, he could see the changes within himself. Every time he broke through his own limits, he felt a little different, as if he were discovering a new himself, a growing divide between the Lukas Aguilar he used to be and what he was now.

The process of becoming a monster wasn't indulgence in the temptation of Sin. Nor was it about taking a darker road or losing himself in a single moment of despair.

It was about conscious choice. The act of entering the grinder willingly. Throwing one's soul into the furnace over and over, being hammered and reforged, blow after blow, until you couldn't even recognize what came out of it. That was what was happening to him.

And now, he was ready. Both within and without.

"I have kept my word, Outsider," Solana replied, regarding him with luminous, unblinking eyes. "I have allowed you enough opportunity to harness Quonnan's power that lay shimmering inside you. While there is much that you need to learn about pyrokinetic combat, no longer is it necessary for someone to hold your hand and teach it to you."

He glanced at her wearily.

"Therefore," Solana murmured, "it is time you start fulfilling your end of the bargain. You will traverse out of my territory and find the core of this anomaly. And when you do it, you shall destroy it."

"Destroy it?"

Solana waved a hand, utterly nonchalant about the whole ordeal. "I have seen enough to know that you hide several skills. It matters not what you do with the anomaly, as long as its consciousness is gone. But yes, doing so will garner the attention of the beasts that guard the core. To that effect, I will loan you the services of two of my soldiers, to aid you in this quest. My personal servant, Mizo, with whom you are well-acquainted; and Malon, one of the yurei you fought in the beginning. Both of them are skilled at taking out monsters, but will not be able to aid against the guardians."

"Guardians? As in, more than one?"

"The anomaly around us had ample time to study us. It has crafted a metal that hurts our kind, in whose presence our control grows weaker. It is possible that your Pyromancy might weaken in its presence."

"Amateur," Inanna scoffed with disgust. **"Her efforts at trying to maintain control are deplorable."**

Even Lukas had to agree with that statement. Sending a reiki and a yurei? That was hardly a random selection. He had assimilated both of those races earlier but had yet to display any of their skills in public. Perhaps Solana was assuming he lacked affinity for ether manipulation? Or was it because she didn't want to hand over yet another element to him just in case he decided to escape?

Either way, a poor play.

"I see." Lukas cocked his head. "So your aid is useless when it counts."

"Had my soldiers been able to exterminate the anomaly, they would have already done so."

"That alone proves that their presence is superficial."

"They are there to *help*," she insisted.

"Bullshit!" he threw back. "You're sending them to make sure that I don't double-cross you and leave when I get the chance. And to keep an eye out for any hidden powers that I have yet to demonstrate."

"Do you?" Solana's lips spread into a wide, dangerous smile. "Have hidden powers, I mean."

Lukas answered with his most condescending smile. "This isn't a power play. It's a mockery of one. You and I have an accord, so let me do things my way. You send your people behind my back, and I make no guarantees about what might happen to them."

Solana's tone gained an icy edge. "Your reaction does nothing to showcase your trustworthiness, Outsider."

Because giving someone a choice between death and servitude was such a great way to ensure a trusting relationship, Lukas didn't say. Instead, he lowered his voice to a bare growl. "Trust isn't a one-way street. You want me to finish this task? Then quit making things difficult for me!"

Solana threw her head back and let out a . . . sound. It was a weird mix of a witch's cackle, and someone being strangled at the same time. Whatever it was, he refused to believe it was a laugh.

"Yes," Solana replied, a wild light around her eyes, her head swaying slightly. "Oh yes, you will do. Fine, do it your way. You will face no obstruction from me."

"She will still send troops behind your back."

I'm counting on it.

"However . . ." Solana's eyes twinkled madly. "I will give you one last piece of advice. Take it as you will." Her voice went down to a whisper. "The world around this anomaly is a vast, nigh-endless desert that hates all things living. Even should you entertain the idea of escaping, you will not go far. I will catch you. And when I do, I will kill you."

He smiled. There wasn't an ounce of mirth in it. "I guess it's beneficial for both of us to stick to our word then."

"It is," Solana whispered. "Find the core of the anomaly. Destroy it."

"And when you do," Inanna viciously promised, **"the real game will begin."**

CHAPTER 26

RULE BREAKER

I *look like a train wreck.*

That was the first thought that went through Lukas's mind as he stared at his reflection in the shining waters of the pond. His messy black hair had grown into thick bangs, hiding most of his gaunt face, yet also accentuating his sharp features. His face now looked more elongated, making his cheeks look sucked in. His stubble hadn't grown very much, but it was beginning to feel as sharp as the edge of a business card. His eyes looked bloodshot, and he could see veins tight against his skin.

If this continues, I'll end up looking like a vampire in no time.

"What is a vampire?"

A creature that sucks blood.

"Such as a bat?"

Like a bat, only human. Well, actually it's dead, and can turn into a bat . . . I think.

He rubbed circles on his temples. Thinking hurt, and he was done feeling pain. Then again, it was all he felt nowadays. Between suffering through Inanna's brutal training when asleep, and fighting monsters when awake, his brain was being taxed like never before. Pain always dissipated when he woke up, but the mental exertion left a lasting mark.

"A dead human that turns into a bat? That sounds like an oxymoron." She hummed for a moment. **"Oxymoron. What a curious term. We did not have such peculiar terms in Akkad."**

Lukas had initially presumed that because the goddess was communicating with him directly through thought, the process bypassed lingual barriers. But now it seemed that not only was she *speaking* English, she was also drawing on his vocabulary.

It's nice to see the modern tongue appreciated by a goddess. Lukas wryly grinned. *Also, why's that an oxymoron?*

"Those of the dead belong within the Underworld. It is not their place to cross the veil and enter the mortal plane."

Is that so? Lukas mused. Filing the information away for later, he reached for the cool water and splashed it over his face. Calculating the passage of time inside an anomaly was difficult on the best of days. It wasn't as if sleep cycles were all about precision. Still, he wagered it'd been three, maybe four days since he had stepped out of the yokai territory with the intention to slay the core of this anomaly, something that Inanna had proclaimed to be within his powers. How? He had no idea.

"You are an anomaly. This cavern is an anomaly. In a battle to devour the other, the stronger will win."

"It's definitely not plain and simple," Lukas retorted. "I'm just . . . me. That khorkhoi back then would have killed me if it weren't for you. And there might be an endless number of beasts around. Even with my skills, there is only so much I can . . ."

He trailed off as a realization hit him.

If he wanted to beat the system, loopholes would have to be his focus. For whatever reason, the schema mirrored video game mechanics to a tee. To accomplish the daunting task ahead of him, he needed to stop perceiving the world around him as if the challenges were insurmountable and instead think of it as a complex game where his job was to defeat the main boss—in this case, the omphalos of this anomaly.

Typically, the way to finish a game in the fastest time possible was to meticulously study the exploits, bugs, and features that existed in the game system and identify potential shortcuts to reach there. And he had already unlocked, so to speak, one of the biggest cheats that could allow him to maximize his growth in the shortest time possible.

Soul Siphon was an irrationally broken ability that allowed him to simply grab another's skills and paste them onto himself. The only problem was . . . he needed to figure out how to gain more Soul Capacity.

Soulscape.

SOULSCAPE	
NAME	Lukas Aguilar
Type	**Base Host**
Level	**4**
Experience	**529**

Current Threshold	640
Utilized Soul Capacity	2129/2379

529 Experience. He needed just a little more before he'd hit 640 and then—
Lukas froze. Could—could it be that simple? Had he really not noticed it
before?

"Screen," he called out, "show me everything you've got on Experience."

> **Experience**
> **PREDATOR acquires Experience upon killing PREY. The quantity
> of Experience gained is proportional to the Soul Size of the fallen prey.
> Experience can be harvested into Soul Capacity depending upon the
> PREDATOR's Experience Conversion Ratio.**

That explained why he'd gained so much Experience after killing the
khorkhoi, even though it had been Inanna who'd accomplished the feat. In a
similar vein, it also explained why he had to eliminate 130 pieces of moss just
to gain a *single* Experience point. If he were to go kill creatures that held Soul
Capacity greater than him, his feat would be greater. Thus, more Experience.
Thus, more Soul Capacity.

But how would he do it? How did one identify greater monsters from lesser
ones?

. . .

. . .

He palmed his face.

> **Scan [LEVEL 2]**

"I feel like an idiot."

"About time."

"Wait! Do you mean to say that you were just waiting for me to figure it
out all this while?"

A mental scoff was his answer. **"I will not babysit you, mortal. If you cannot even figure out the basics on your own, you are of little use to me."**

"There's just one issue. Stronger monsters will mean a greater life risk for me."

"You expect to gain strength without working for it?"

"Honestly, yeah," he responded. He was a young man from the twenty-first
century. The era of smart computing. He was now in a world where beings
could routinely ignore the laws of nature he had come to accept as absolutes.
And his job was to figure out the shortest path to power.

" . . . Explain yourself."

Translation: she didn't understand. That was alright. He didn't expect her to either.

"You and I . . . belong to different worlds. More than the difference between mortal and divine. You have potential. We have ingenuity. You have evolution and the ability to ignore the laws of nature to transcend into becoming more. We have the determination and capacity to use the immutable laws of reality and twist them in our favor. We cannot transcend, but we can be strong."

"By being a parasite?"

"By being smart. And by *building* things to do my work for me. That's what machines are for. Soul Siphon has already granted me a way to gain skills that I would probably never have gained in the first place. All I need to do is search for the monsters that have the skills most optimal for my needs. And as for the latter . . ."

MONSTER PROTOTYPE: YUREI		
SKILLS	**LEVEL**	**SOUL CAPACITY CONSUMED**
Possession	1	50
Conjuration	2	500
Disintegration	2	500

"I know just the thing I need."

Conjuration—or, as he preferred to call it, false construction—was an absurdly broken skill. The ability let him craft mana, or more particularly, ether, into a solid structure. It would be a temporary creation and would dissipate as soon as the task was complete.

To a creator, it was a fake. A cheat. An insult to the forging process.

But to a hunter? It was the ultimate arsenal.

All he needed to do was level up that particular skill to the maximum.

"For someone so caring about the sanctity of life and the soul, your approach renders other creatures as nothing but a set of skills for you to grab."

Lukas ferally grinned. "What can I say? I'm an anomaly, right? This is what anomalies do. They *devour.*"

He took a deep breath, then smirked. "Activate Alpha Condition."

And everything changed.

Space splits.

Cracks appear. Cracks diffuse. Cracks get larger. Brighter. Cracks converge. Diverge. Shatter. Reform.

His mind devolves.

Human instincts dull. Yurei instincts arise.

His perceptions are different. Not human, but colorful. They are not gray-scale. He is a spirit. He is unseen. He is unfelt. Nothing can impact him for he is ██████████

Yet he exists.

Yet he shapes the world.

Through creation. One just as ████████ *as him.*

He wants to build.

He wants to possess.

The energies within him contort as he raises them with a ██████████ —

"So, how does it feel?" Inanna asked.

Feel? Feeling? What was that? Sensations were physical. They belonged to the tangible world. He, on the other hand, had—

Body? Arms? Legs? Face? Skin?

He was . . . solid?

The dichotomy could not have been graver had he tried. No matter what he did, he could feel *nothing*. Not the absence of sensation, but truly *nothing*. There was no connection, no feeling, no hopes, no dreams, no desires. Just a cold, numbing, empty void that made the world around him seem smaller with every pointless, mechanical movement. Unlike the kasha, whose instincts wanted to burn the world down, to ignite everything and set it ablaze, the yurei made him feel hollow.

Every single moment he spent as the yurei . . . it was like he became *less*.

But that was just the beginning.

A strange sound exuded from his throat, and then Lukas realized he had lips.

"I—I feel—"

Power rose within him. It was dark and empty and reminded him of the stillness between heartbeats, of the silence that accompanied the death of a loved one, and of the nightmare that made one wake up in the middle of the night. Cold power, like frosted metal held to the neck, a fraction of an inch away from spilling warm blood.

"I feel . . . strong."

He did not have hands, but they rose up. Power surged through him, but he had no guide for this kind of spell. No focus, no target, and certainly not the kind of power he was used to working with. He shoved his senses down, blanked out everything, and just focused on the strange power humming through him.

And then, he *understood*.

"Okay," he breathed out. "I'm ready."

"**Go ahead,**" Inanna replied. Her voice was soft. Soothing. "**Imagine what you wish to create. Push the ether into it. Give your imagination form.**"

Lukas focused on the most basic of implements. One that served as the first milestone between human and animal. One of the very first *tools* that allowed mankind to progress from lurking in caves to becoming hunters, food gatherers, and farmers.

Ether erupted out of his hand, filling the entirety of his half-clenched fist, and elongated on both sides until it was easily taller than him. He pushed more mana, and the object gained more attributes. The first prototype felt granular, almost like sand.

Sand? No, sand would not do.

He needed something harder, with far greater strength.

He focused on the feel of the rock-hard terrain beneath his feet. He thought of the strength that a crystal lattice added to an object's physical structure. The ether element was in itself incapable of materializing by its own power. And yet in a twist of irony, its domains were along the lines of composition, dissolution, modification, separation, unification, and alteration of shapeless bodies materialized into physical form. And the clearer and more precise the knowledge, the better he could see it in his mind. Density. Mineral constituents. Lattice. Tensile strength. Weight. Sharp edges.

He opened his eyes. And stared.

And kept on staring.

"I—"

He opened his mouth, but no words came to him. The surprise overwhelmed the alien mindset he was operating with and pushed back those instincts with extreme prejudice, leaving—

"I—I created—"

"**Congratulations are in order, mortal.**" Inanna's voice was rich, and . . . was that pride he sensed in her tone? "**You have created your first implement.**"

New SKILL Registered!		
SKILL	**LEVEL**	**SOUL CAPACITY CONSUMED**
Conjuration	1	50
DESCRIPTION		
Creation of temporary solid constructs using Ether.		

He had done it. In his hand was a slim rod, with a diameter that fitted perfectly within his palm, and a length just enough to serve as a ranged weapon. One edge was curved, while the other protruded like a naked blade.

A spear.

Lukas closed his eyes and *thought*.

The spear dissipated into motes of silvery powder.

New SKILL Registered!		
SKILL	**LEVEL**	**SOUL CAPACITY CONSUMED**
Disintegration	1	50
DESCRIPTION **Reverting Conjured Constructs into Ether.**		

He opened his eyes, staring at his now empty hand. There was just so much he wanted to say about it. A hundred thoughts swam in his mind, but only one managed to escape out of his lips.

"Deactivate Alpha Condition."

Monster Prototype Yurei Deactivated   **Reverting Consciousness Shift to Base Host**   **Enact**

With a sudden jolt, Lukas found himself standing, spear in hand. His entire body was shaking, and his heart was beating at least twice as fast. Yet he could only focus on the feeling of accomplishment.

URGENT!!!			
REGISTERED SKILL	**LEVEL**	**SOUL CAPACITY**	**ISSUE**
Conjuration	LEVEL 1	+50	**Requires confirmation for assimilation.**
Disintegration	LEVEL 1	+50	**Requires confirmation for assimilation.**
Host Body requires calibration!			

There was no conflict in his voice this time around.

Assimilate them.

"What next?" the goddess inquired.

"Next, I start hunting down monsters. Let's see what this crypt's got."

It didn't take long for him to find his first challenge. The thoggua was a strange creature, easily the size of a hippopotamus, with three long and slimy tails, each of which ended in a sharp, metallic blade capable of carving through the ground if the constant etching noises were any indication.

No face. No eyes. Just a singular oral opening lined with endless fangs. And most importantly, it sensed the world through vibrations on the ground, and once it found a target, the metallic tails would instantly lock on its position and stab it with perfect precision.

Joy.

"And full of flesh on the inside."

Flesh was good. Tasty. It meant roasted meat over a fire and a filled stomach. Leagues better than that gruel Solana's folks had fed him. Then again, what did ethereal beings care for something so material as *flavor?* The only reason they ate food was to keep their flesh masks active.

Ugh, I really need to stop thinking with my stomach.

"Are you sure?" the goddess jested. **"It is more consistent than your brain. No useless tangents either."**

Lukas rolled his eyes, before refocusing on the creature in front of him. The monster was around ten feet away, slowly gobbling up a pair of azolg it had sliced apart with its vicious tails.

That thing has got to weigh at least three thousand pounds.

He'd read the parable about David and Goliath. Who hadn't? The famous story about an underdog managing to win despite overwhelming odds. Hollywood had shamelessly adopted it to showcase how large and powerful monsters could be defeated by seemingly tiny, weak, yet unafraid heroes who played to their own strengths and cunning to persevere through overwhelming odds.

But that's all it was. A story.

In reality, if your enemy weighed twenty times more than you, it meant you left the realm of real combat and were now in a Tom and Jerry cartoon. And in real life, Jerry always had the short end of the stick.

He'd once had a pet cat, and not once had it ever come home with mouse-afflicted injuries.

Lukas brought his hands closer, touching at the base of the palm, and aimed it in the direction of the thoggua as an unholy crimson power flooded through him.

"Burn!"

CHAPTER 27

TOE TO TOE

Being choked unconscious hurt. A lot.

It was difficult to describe with precision, but it was almost like this horrible, crushing pain along your neck, followed by an immense internal pressure that made you feel like your head was going to burst into a thousand tiny pieces. Blood was pounding away, throbbing through your veins with every heartbeat, right alongside the jolts of pain it carried with it.

Of course, if one was sloppy about it, it could cause even more pain than that.

The neothelid that was currently entwined all around him, its thick, muscular, tubular body contracting powerfully from every direction, was no expert on the subject. Instead, it just pressed all around him uniformly.

Inanna could have gotten out of this chokehold with effortless grace. But Lukas was no Inanna. He lacked her grace. He lacked her strength. Her power. Her experience.

And he was about as subtle as a sledgehammer.

But sometimes, a sledgehammer to the head was a sledgehammer to the head.

His eyes squinted, and hot crimson mana flooded through his veins. The power of ether sang along its side, carefully giving shape to the form in his mind. Fire was a good weapon. But a thick, viciously sharp blade of fire? Even better.

And then the neothelid began to *scream*.

SOULSCAPE	
NAME	Lukas Aguilar
Type	**Base Host**

Level	6
Experience	122
Current Threshold	1440
Utilized Soul Capacity	2829 / 3494
ESSENCE	
Maximum Lifeforce Output	2250
Replenishment Rate	400 / hour
LEY LINE NETWORK	
Maximum Mana Output	1925
Synthesis Rate	200 / hour

SKILL ATTRIBUTES		
SKILL	LEVEL	CONSUMED SOUL CAPACITY
Raw Lifeforce Manipulation	1	50
Momentum Manipulation	2	500
Friction Modulation	1	50
Pressure Modulation	1	50
Kinetomancy (FRAGMENTED)	APEX	1279
Fire Creation	1	50
Fire Manipulation	2	500
Temperature Modulation	1	50
Perception Manipulation	1	50
Conjuration	1	50
Disintegration	1	50

Seismic Sensing	1	50
Shatterpoint Intuition	1	50
Psychomancy	1	50

OMPHALOS ATTRIBUTES	
Energy Reservoir Capacity	∞
Current Energy Level	722,401,138 units
OMPHALOS FUNCTIONS	
Scan	Level 2
Analyze	Level 2
Prophylaxis	Level 2
Soul Siphon	NA
Alpha Condition	Level 1
Evocation	Level 1

Lukas stood up from the floor and wiped the dust off his clothes. Solana had been gracious enough to grant him a fresh pair in addition to the one he had been wearing before he left, though the armor had only been a singular copy.

Not that it mattered. If he really wanted some armor, he could create a temporary attire out of air. Metamancy was useful like that. No more would he ever find himself forced into a situation without his pants on.

He shuddered at the memory.

"You have been constantly pitting yourself against stronger and more lethal opponents every waking moment, and *that* is what gives you nightmares?"

I don't see you posing naked during our training sessions.

"Do you really believe you can survive that, mortal?"

Lukas was about to call her out on her ego but thought better of it. Some women had a quality about them, something intangible and indefinable. Emma had it. Solana, as much as he hated to admit it, had it in spades. And Inanna . . . well, she put them both to shame.

He was always extremely aware of her, and Inanna knew precisely what sort of effect she had on him. Merely standing in front of her inside his mindscape kicked his libido into overdrive. The fact that the new Level Ups had gotten an increase in lifeforce flooding his system didn't help matters either.

Lifeforce was more than physical strength and agility. It was the spiritual home of all things primal and primitive. It wanted him to be a hunter, to tear something's spine off and see the light leave its eyes. There were times when the lunacy rose to degrees that made it damn near impossible to control.

"If only there was a way to leech psionic skills without hard work."

Lukas rolled his eyes. For all her power and divinity, Inanna was old school, believing in the concept of equivalent exchange between risk and reward. She applauded his decision to choose his battles but scoffed at *farming* monsters to gain particular skills rather than elevating what he had.

A *leech's mindset,* she called it.

"I have an advantage. Tell me why I shouldn't use it."

"You would forever stay a weakling if not for your ability to leech others."

Something about her words stirred something within him. A desire to be proven right, to make her back off, and *know her place.* He gnashed his teeth, rage and displeasure rising at the callous way she determined his progress as *inconsequential.* Like he was *nothing.* He, who had survived countless eons in which paltry gods and goddesses did their best to instill faith in creatures he'd given birth to, was being treated like a—

" . . . "

And just like that, that line of thought was gone.

Vanished. As if it had never existed in the first place.

"It seems," Inanna replied, her voice surprisingly thoughtful, **"that perhaps a reevaluation of your abilities might be in order."**

His lips moved by their own accord. "Bring it on!"

An instant later, the two were in his mindscape, battling it out. A thin stream of lifeforce burst out from behind Lukas, adding a small jolt of acceleration as he minimized the distance between himself and his opponent. His right foot jammed itself into the ground as he twisted his torso, bringing his left leg in a complete sweep against her.

Inanna effortlessly blocked the kick with one arm, grabbing at his toes with another. Lukas allowed himself a single moment to be distracted by the utter feline grace with which she'd outmaneuvered him. Her touch was featherlight, yet strong enough a grip that he couldn't pull his leg back without losing his own balance.

"Uncomfortable, is it not?" the goddess asked, a smile on her face. **"To be victorious, one must first learn how to be comfortable with the state of being uncomfortable."**

Lukas pushed a burst of lifeforce from his leg, but Inanna dropped it right at that moment. Before he could get enough footing, she softly pushed his knee with an open palm. His leg bent to the left, the lifeforce burst driving it farther and destroying his coordination. Lukas dropped to the floor like a stringless puppet on his left arm. Pain spiked from the strain, but Neural Suppression dumbed it down to acceptable levels. Inanna casually kicked against his elbow, dropping him farther, and rested her heel upon his face.

"**Inadequate.**" She sighed. "**You must come at me with the intent to kill. Anything less will net you no results.**"

Lukas hurled a fireball from his right hand, but Inanna twirled around, effortlessly dodging it and bringing her heel straight toward his heart. And it was *fast*. Fast enough to obliterate his heart before he could even begin to conjure a—

THUMP!

Perceptual dilation, or tachypsychia as he called it, came into effect. With it came seismic sense. The former drastically drew out his perception. The latter allowed him to sense the blow's trajectory. There was no time to conjure a shield, or fireball, or any protection Metamancy could conjure.

His right arm moved, Shatterpoint Intuition guiding its trajectory. The skill allowed him to direct his attacks with absolute accuracy and lent itself to determining the exact position to move his body to get his task accomplished. The arm was barely able to—

THUMP!

—reach his chest as the lethal blow from the heel drew nearer and nearer.

"URGKK!"

The force of the blow bent him in half and sent him flying, limp and broken, across the floor before he skidded to a harsh halt. The shock of the blow had dislocated his shoulder and tore his biceps. And this was after his body had already been reinforced to the max with lifeforce.

This is temporary, Lukas told himself amidst the pain. *My real body won't have these wounds.*

"**Pathetic!**" Inanna rasped. "**At this rate, aeons will pass before you can even *stand* in Ereshkigal's presence. What a worm I have chosen as my Host. Perhaps it was fate that you fell in this worm-pit, amongst your own kind.**"

Lukas pushed himself up. With a well-aimed hit with his palm, he snapped his shoulder into place and prepared himself for another attempt.

During the entire time he had trained with Inanna, the goddess had limited herself to simple combat techniques—grappling, chokes, takedowns, joint locks—nothing that an ordinary person on Earth couldn't perform. Lukas had come down upon her with his ever-increasing arsenal of skills, used every single permutation and combination he could think of mid-fight, but had still ended up with his ass kicked.

It was times like this that reminded him that no matter how *human* Inanna looked, she wasn't one.

She was a goddess. Reflection or otherwise.

He settled himself into a fighting stance, one of the few she had taught him.

Inanna smiled, gesturing toward him with a beckoning finger.

"Come."

"With pleasure."

Tachypsychia activated at full throttle, slowing down her movements to his discerning eye. And then, Inanna went even *faster.*

POW!

"Fuck!"

He swerved his fist but found Inanna's foot inches away from connecting with his cheek.

BAM!

"Oww!"

Lukas knew he was fighting Inanna, a literal goddess by her own right. No amount of training, however intense, would be able to get the better of her.

But that wasn't all.

He'd learned something fundamental. After constant exposure to the goddess's thought process and constantly applying his ingrained skills against all the predators that lurked in this crypt, he was beginning to understand crucial aspects about fighting predators. Things he never noticed as a part of civilized society.

Predators always went after the weak. The wounded. The unaware.

The notion went double for solitary predators like the thoggua, or worse, monsters like the neothelid. Solitary predators, more often than not, attacked when they had the element of surprise on their side. Or when they had every single advantage stacked in their favor. Hell, even the larger and more powerful monsters abided by that rule.

Predators never picked a fair fight. Such a notion ran counter to their nature and robbed them of their inherent advantage.

And Inanna? She was very much a predator.

Unknowingly or not, Inanna never let an opportunity slip by when she could instead increase the advantages she held over him. Whether it was showing off her magical abilities, enhancing her supernatural charm, or something as simple as exposing more of her marble-white skin, the goddess always went out of her way to ensure he held nothing short of awe for her very presence.

"Another round?" he asked, readying himself.

The goddess tilted her head to the left. Very slightly.

"Try as you might, you will never be a match for me. My fighting prowess is something I developed from scratch. No pretender, no matter how many skills one might have leeched, can reach this level."

"Give me another chance," he replied, taking deep breaths. "I'm sure I can make a scratch."

"Scratching and pawing like vermin," she taunted. **"You are showing your true nature."**

"Talk is cheap!" he shot back.

The goddess laughed. **"Very well. Howev—"**

Lukas didn't wait for her to finish. He flooded key areas of his body with power—his calves, glutes, hip flexors, hamstrings—instantly pushing them to maximum efficiency. His quadriceps worked in conjunction with his hamstrings and pushed even *further*.

In a burst of speed, Lukas vanished, before sharply reappearing in front of the goddess, his fingers clenched into a fire-cloaked fist hurtling toward her face. Inanna sank down, her legs extending outwards like a ballerina doing the splits, grabbed his wrist with her left hand and pushed it upward—

Just as he unleashed the fire and forced it out like a modified flamethrower.

Dammit, Lukas cursed. If only he'd been a fraction of a second faster, the attack would have hit her face and—

The rest of his thoughts evaporated as something terrifying caught his attention. His wrist was still within her grip and she—

Was.

Smiling.

At him.

Oh, fu—

THUMMMP!!!

Her left leg shot up, tearing through the air. It met with his lower jaw, shattering half of his teeth, and sending his back in recoil. Her leg moved farther upward, while her solid grip upon his wrist yanked him closer, bending him down upon his knees—

THUMMMP! THUMP!

Shatterpoint Intuition activated. Lukas knew this would make it or break it.

THUMPPPP!

The leg came down like the scythe of the grim reaper and hacked right into his pectoral girdle, *obliterating* it. Lukas's eyes widened, and a silent scream exuded out of his throat, before Neural Suppression stepped in.

His left arm moved closer, using the momentum from her leg's strike into propelling himself forward, his intuition skill guiding the way.

And slammed his open palm against her right knee.

Lukas had once read that an average person was actually three times stronger than what they believed. And yet, most people never used that strength except under absolutely dire circumstances when their mind entered a tunnel vision. It was this inhibition that kept them from destroying themselves while fighting.

Luckily for him, fighting without inhibitions was precisely what Neural Suppression was all about.

The concept behind Shatterpoint Intuition was to lock on a precise location and guide an attack there with full force. A perfect analogy would be to use a knife to shatter a wall by employing maximum kinetic pressure at a single point.

Either the structure would shatter, or the knife would break.

Add in lifeforce and a timely application of Kinetomancy into the mix, and you got an explosive amount of strength.

That was essentially what happened.

Inanna's knee popped like a balloon from the force of his strike, dislocating the ball from its socket as the goddess let out something that, if he didn't know any better, sounded like a muffled whimper.

And then she *looked* at him.

Before he knew it, she had slammed her fist into his stomach.

"GAHHH!"

Air rushed out of his lungs, followed by saliva, stomach acid, and what felt like half of his internal organs.

Several of his ribs snapped right then and there. Neural Suppression was active, but there was only so much you could ignore. In the back of his mind, he genuinely wondered if he had been split in half, as the pain traversed through his body and emerged out the back. By the time his pain-addled brain had registered what was happening, he was skidding across the floor, hitting, *bouncing*, sliding, like a broken ragdoll.

"KUH!"

Lukas blearily opened his eyes and found himself lying on the floor, right next to the burning campfire. He coughed out some soot that managed to get in his nose but flinched as every single breath sent a jolt of immense pain through him. Despite the fact that they were phantom pains at best and illusions at worst, his mind seemed to have trouble keeping the two apart.

Nothing—neither the monsters he had faced nor Ryu's fast-paced blows—had been remotely close to replicating the agony he'd felt from that single punch thrown by Inanna. It was probably a good thing the training happened in his mindscape.

Yet, despite all that, a maniacal grin burst from his lips. "Did . . . did I win?"

"In a manner of speaking," Inanna softly spoke. **"To lose control for something so petty is unworthy of me."**

That, Lukas decided, was the closest he'd come to getting an apology out of her.

"A mountain has no business apologizing to an insect, mortal," the goddess coldly retorted. **"I am merely reflecting upon my own momentary loss of control."**

"No harm done," he cheekily replied. "Frankly, I'm still surprised it worked at all."

"Do you know why it did?" Inanna's voice sounded distant.

"What do you mean? Are you going to tell me you weren't ready or something—"

"How do you defeat an opponent who has proven to be stronger than you, faster than you, and cannot be snuck up on?"

"Trick him. Or bide your time until he underestimates you."

Inanna shook her head. **"I shall rephrase. In a battle between equals, who will win?"**

"Well . . ." Lukas paused as he thought carefully. "If they're equally skilled, then the one with the greater luck."

"Wrong. It is the one willing to pay the greater price."

"Price?"

"What you did in our fight . . . I have done something similar myself. In one of my earliest battles, I found myself . . . outmatched." The word sounded like it was painful to get out. **"My opponent was stronger, faster, and had greater reach. Death was a near certainty."**

Lukas found himself riveted by the tale. It wasn't often that Inanna willingly spoke of her past. "So how did you manage to win?"

"I let his blow cleave through my arm. And in return, I lopped off his head."

" . . . "

"Men of power . . . mages of strength . . . countless warriors have fallen for a simple reason. They could not handle the pain. A mere gash stripped them of their rationality, and their self-preservation prevented them from winning the battle at the cost of a wound." She stared down at him, her gaze as unyielding as a mountain. **"Your strength is limited by your will. If you truly want to become strong, there is a single lesson that you must learn."**

"Which is?" he asked, the trepidation rising in his heart.

"How to take a blow." She smiled. **"At least you do not shy away from pain. A praiseworthy attribute for someone who thinks like a leech."**

Despite the way it ended, that might have been the most sincere praise he'd ever received from her.

Unfortunately he didn't have time to enjoy it. Instead, he broke out into coughs. He had the oddest feeling that there should've been blood, but all that came out was spit. His entire body felt like a living, breathing dichotomy—one that could tell every single body part was in functioning order yet still feel completely wounded and paralyzed for the foreseeable future.

Phantom pains, he reminded himself. *They're not real.*

With conscious effort, he closed his eyes and began breathing rhythmically. It hurt the first few times, but as lifeforce circulated through his body, the feeling of intense agony began to slowly dissipate. Neural Suppression was working.

"You should allow your body and mind to rest for a while. Agony so severe leaves a lasting impression on the mind, phantom or otherwise. Once you are healed, you may continue your perverse preoccupation of . . ." Her lips curled in distaste. ***"farming* monsters for their skills."**

"You dislike it that much?"

"I abhor it," she spat, **"but it cannot be helped. Everyone is born with unique strengths and weaknesses. As someone who rose from nothing to a divine queen with nothing save my own hard-earned strength and skill, I take offense at seeing such things *stolen* so easily."**

Lukas was briefly reminded that his unique circumstances had also allowed him to *steal* an APEX-rank skill for himself, simply because he was at the right place at the right time. A skill that, by all rights, belonged to a goddess.

And that was before he had gained access to Soul Siphon.

"However," Inanna continued, **"I have contemplated the situation further while you were unconscious. You are an anomaly, and it is in your nature to devour foreign species and take their skills for yourself. Ordinarily, these would be inserted in monsters, but you are adding them to your schema to make them your own. A twist, given your unusual powers, but *yours* nonetheless. Leeching or otherwise, it would not have been possible for you to grow as much as you have without diligent training in your gifts."**

"Thanks," Lukas said, dipping his head to no one in particular. "I know my way of gaining skills is unusual, but I won't use them as a crutch. I'll hone every single skill I acquire."

"Make sure you do so," the goddess said. **"Be it a monster or goddess, it takes time and effort to develop a skill. And starting now, I intend to exact a price every time the chance presents itself,"** she said with a gentle smile.

It was a thing of beauty, really.

So why did he feel like he was about to be mauled by a ravenous lion?

CHAPTER 28

A STITCH IN MEMORY

Flames encompassed everything.

They razed and consumed the land, darkening the sky as if cursing it for its distance yet longing for its peacefulness. Screams of pain and anguish and despair filled the air like smoke as scorched bodies lay strewn across burnt ground, a testament to the merciless fury of fire. Malice saturated the atmosphere like a thick blanket as a malevolent red light poured out like liquid fire. Scarlet tongues of flame flickered, caressing and striking at one another like snakes wanting to devour everything, even themselves, as the massive inferno threatened to devour everything.

And it was there, in the wafting odor of sulfur and brimstone, that she stood.

"Are you sure this will work?"

"Not really," her companion muttered. The other person—a child, based on voice and size—wore a dark hooded robe covering her entire form. "But for someone with your aspirations, this is the only way forward."

"Someone of my aspirations . . ." she muttered, her emerald eyes reflecting the crimson embers around as she peered into the flames. "You failed to mention that it involves walking through Vikahl itself."

"You wish to stand in defiance of the God of Fire, and yet here you are, trembling before this?" the child mocked.

To be looked down upon as inconsequential . . . To be treated like vermin . . .

The very notion made her insides boil.

"What must I do?"

The renewed strength in her tone gave the child pause.

"Only a fire may devour another. Asshur burns brightly in the sky. Fire that gives life, provides warmth, brings hope in even the direst of situations. That is the nemesis you have claimed for yourself. One might even consider it an impossible task."

She exhaled, biting back a retort. Appearing to be a child or not, she knew who the figure beneath the robes truly was. Or at least, what she had once been. It would not do to burn the one bridge she could latch onto at the moment.

Not until she managed to defeat Asshur.

A mortal defeating a god. The very thought brought a smile to her lips.

"To do so," the child continued, "you must be the flames that burn in darkness. The jaws that consume life. The fire that pollutes, purges, and destroys. The Vikahl Ashlands are merely a stepping-stone in fulfilling that dream."

Dream.

Oh how she loathed having her ambitions reduced to merely a "dream." As if they were merely figments of her imagination and would remain as such.

She would not stand for this.

Silently, she disrobed. Her manacles went first. Then her vest. The cloth around her neck fell next. And finally, her waistguard. These were all earthly possessions that would be consumed and turned to ash in the flames.

"What happens if the flames are stronger?" she asked the child.

"You will learn to overpower them."

The answer was cryptic, but was she really expecting anything else?

So be it, she told herself, staring into the flames once more.

Contending with fire was a fool's errand, which was precisely what made it such a dangerous weapon. She had always used Kinetomancy to wield it, but here, in the heart of fire, she wondered if it would save her from becoming scattered ashes.

A small, nervous smile flickered on her face as her hands lightly twitched with a few nervous little gestures. Then, clenching her jaw, she gathered her courage and strode through the passage, her body completely unclothed and unprotected.

Great walls of flame rose to meet her, as if they had an awareness all their own, crashing upon her like waves on a shore. Motion writhed around her, deflecting the incoming barrage and recoiling into a web all around her as miniature typhoons of flame rose to consume her whole. She grunted as the primordial force crashed against her own might. For this was not just fire—it was consumption given form. She could save herself from the searing flames, but the mental pressure of the situation was almost enough to shatter her will to pieces.

No matter how much she poured out, the flames devoured it all.

No matter how much she deflected, there was always more.

No matter how much she struggled, there was no path forward.

But such was the precise line of thought that would ensure her failure. She needed to save herself, and to do so, she needed to survive. To survive, she needed power. And for power, she needed to step forward.

And so she did.

The flames continued to lash around like the tentacles of a ravenous beast. It was *all too terrifying, as every single emotion within begged her to escape. To save herself and run away from the inferno before it consumed her.*

But escape was no longer an option. To continue forward, she needed to stop feeling. And so she did.

When she became too scared to move, she stopped feeling her fear. When the burns became too great a challenge, she stopped feeling pain. When she was unable to push back against the force, she stopped her very own thoughts.

With every new step, she left a piece of herself behind. With every step, she became less than she was before.

With every step, the flames coalesced around her. Purging her, unmaking her, adding to her, breaking her, strengthening her.

And when it was all over, the pain vanished.

The pressure faded.

And bright emerald eyes sprang open in the darkness.

Lukas's eyes snapped open, as he struggled to gather his wits through a familiar pounding headache, piecing together fragments of memories and perceptions he had just seen, waiting for the dizzying rush of clarity to return. It was almost customary at this point—visiting Inanna's memories ended with him feeling his head had gained twice its weight.

His heart started to thud hard into his chest, as the sheer fear from the dream made his limbs feel cold.

"That—"

"Another facet of my life," the goddess murmured, **"one predating my rise as the Supreme Queen. A quest to achieve power enough to eclipse a god's own, seized by a mortal."**

"Mortal?"

"I too was mortal once," Inanna said wistfully. **"Every god that exists once was.**

Lukas frowned, pushing himself up. "I don't get it. If you—if gods are immortal, then how did you kill them?"

"I said immortal, not eternal," she corrected. **"Power of a certain variety, in the right hands, is capable of ending *everyone*, even myself."**

"Like the flames in the . . . Ashlands?"

"The Vikahl Ashlands are truly ancient, even for divinity. A power that only exists to purge others. A power that was the antithesis of Asshur's Truth. I embraced it. For a time. For a price."

Price. Lukas shuddered at the thought. He had seen—no, he had *been* Inanna in that dream. The feeling of slowly throwing away pieces of his humanity at every step he made into the flaming valley wasn't something he was going to forget any time soon.

"Is that why you always refer to me as 'mortal'? To remind yourself that you aren't?"

"A bit of advice, *mortal*. Do not speak so much. That way, you sound less ignorant."

"Funny," Lukas scoffed good-naturedly, still wondering how Inanna was able to use those flames. Not as a goddess, but a mortal. One would think that he finally had some answers. But in reality, he had only crossed a small hill and found a mountain behind it.

Sighing to himself, Lukas checked his schema. He had been sauntering through the tunnels for quite some time now, fighting monsters and, should they have a useful skill, trying to assimilate them into his Array. So far his successes on that front had been few, though each and every one of them had ended up granting him some pretty unique skills. Whatever benefits Solana would have gotten by the destruction of this crypt, sending him to do the job was only amplifying his power and growth by a mile a day.

He wondered how she would react upon finding that out.

Speaking of which—

"There's this . . . thing that's kind of bugging me. Soul Siphon. It's not killing these monsters. It's stealing them. *I'm* stealing them. I'm just surprised this crypt hasn't taken it personally. I know I'd have."

"Does the concept of strategy evade you?"

"They're *monsters*," he drawled, as if that explained everything. Strategy was a human element, or at the very least, reserved for beings with greater sapience. Not that animals were incapable of strategizing, but the monsters he had faced so far attacked him out of territorial instinct, not in a drawn-out manner to test his strengths and weaken him.

"That is because you're mistaking the trees for the forest."

Lukas froze. Had he? He was an anomaly, and he had access to some prototypes. But while he'd use them for his benefit, he didn't care for them individually. He was only interested in *his* own growth.

If he applied the same concept to this crypt—

"You're telling me that monsters are nothing but lab rats."

Confusion ebbed from her.

"Lab rats. Guinea pigs. It's a human thing. We run our tests and experiments first on verm—on rats, to check if a product is working and safe before releasing it for people."

"Is that not the role every lesser being is born to play?"

No, Lukas wanted to say. But he'd only showcase his own hypocrisy at that. One didn't think of a cockroach's feelings before spraying pesticide at it. One didn't ponder a cow's feelings when feasting on grilled steak. They were lesser species, and thus, they didn't count.

Really, what did it mean to be human?

Why was it that humans placed importance on themselves above all things? Societal reasons? Religious? Was it simply a facet of evolution and survival across the ages? Or was it the developed concepts of morality? Humans didn't want to hurt others because they didn't want to be hurt in turn.

It was simple.

Except in this world, that was where problems began to emerge. Inanna was a goddess, an entity so far beyond human reach that in her eyes, a human was little more than a cockroach that could speak. Hell, even he himself couldn't be considered human anymore. It was like comparing a saber-toothed tiger to a tabby cat.

An unfair comparison, some would argue, but the results spoke for themselves. With the power of lifeforce flooding his veins, he could smash his way through a modern-day infantry. His top speed, coupled with Shatterpoint Intuition, could evade suppressive bullet fire. He could launch fire with the same efficacy as a modern-day flamethrower. And he healed at levels that were downright miraculous.

Considering everything, he may as well be compared to a god amongst humanity.

"Your world was an isolated system. A puddle of water separated from the endless ocean. For all your claims about morality, systems, and values, the truth is that your pathetic kind was the most powerful, so you took the world and shaped it in your image."

"That's not—"

"Is it not?" Her surprised, innocent tone reeked of mockery. **"Do enlighten me. Did these . . . guinea pigs** *choose* **to be ruled by you and yours?"**

Silence was the only thing he could offer.

The goddess laughed at his face. **"Did you believe your kind ruled the world because of** *mortal superiority***?"**

"No," he mumbled. "It's survival of the fittest."

"Precisely. A dragon does not concern itself with the opinion of lizards. It steps on them. Being ruled is the natural state of the weak. Subjugation is the *prerogative* **of the strong."**

"No," Lukas staunchly protested. "Even the weak are living beings. Even they have rights."

"Rights?" The word rolled off her tongue as if completely foreign to her. **"What are rights?"**

"A product of civilization. A group of fundamental tenets we recognize all living beings to possess."

"I see. And who guarantees these *rights***?"**

"The government."

"**Your masters, you mean to say.**"

"Elected officials," he argued, "not masters we blindly serve. We elect them by exercising our rights—"

Inanna's peals of laughter silenced him. "**Not only do you obey your masters, but you also exercise your** *freedom* **to unequivocally choose a master to obey?**" Her burgeoning laughter reverberated throughout his mind. "**Man, woman, or monster, nobody has rights. No one. Nowhere. It is nothing more than a fantasy.**"

Lukas vehemently shook his head. No matter what his argument was, Inanna was hell-bent on twisting his words to serve her own outdated views instead of seeing sense.

"**I assure you, I am not,**" she argued. "**Tell me, do these** *guinea pigs* **have rights?** **The same rights that you enjoy?**"

Silence.

"**You live in a world where entire** *species* **exist that are to you what your humanity once was to guinea pigs. No longer are you at the apex of the food chain. There will be time for** *morality* **once you reach it.**"

Lukas gritted his teeth and tried to summon a salvo of snark. It wouldn't come. Inanna had hit the right buttons—and with good reason to back it up.

"**Your attitude is disappointing. Did you learn** *nothing* **from my memory of the Vikahl Ashlands?**"

"No, but I did get a nice headache out of it." He frowned. "Speaking of which, I think there's actually something wrong with my mind. I used to think it was a fluke, but—it's like every time I think about a—"

Gooseflesh erupted all over his body. Palpitation rose. Lukas looked around wildly, his sensation of unease blossoming into mounting dread and fear despite his best efforts to ignore it.

His heart throbbed faster and faster, even worse than it did when using tachypsychia. Every passing second, he was reminded with frightening certainty that *something was coming* in response to his thoughts.

"**About what?**"

Lukas kept his lips sealed. He couldn't say it. He *couldn't* say it. If he did, something *alien* and *taboo* and *wrong* would come. Something utterly, utterly beyond his understanding. With controlled breaths, he focused on prime numbers. Then multiples of fourteen. Then fifteen, sixteen, seventeen and so on.

"**Mortal?**" Inanna stressed.

One thirty-six. One fifty-three. "It's something that I have to actively *not* think of." *One seventy.* "Or I feel like I'll die of a heart attack or an aneurysm or something," he said frustratedly. *One eighty-seven.*

"**I see,**" Inanna replied very quietly. "**You should have told me this before.**"

" . . . What?"

"Tell me, mortal, do you ever wonder about . . . how your world ended?"

That did it.

Lukas felt a sharp pain in his hand. Then on his knee. Then his waist. Shoulders. Wrist. Ankles—it kept increasing, both in location and intensity. But he persevered.

"I did. I do, but whenever I—I—"

He became aware of a familiar, intense humming that grew louder and louder with each passing second—

"Back when you asked me about anomalies, there was something else you—"

But Lukas wasn't listening. His knees gave away. Convulsing, he fell down to the floor, putting a hand on each side of his head as something *horrifying* began to ERUPT OUT OF THE FRACTURES IN EVERYTHING AND—

The last thing he remembered was hearing the goddess mutter something, and then the world shifted.

He was standing there in the cavern. Not where he currently stood, but someplace absolutely familiar. Maybe he had seen this place in the past? As in, this was a memory, right? Then—but why was he seeing a memory?

Wait. Whose memory was this?

Inanna's mocking laughter resounded in his ears. **"It was enjoyable squabbling with you, mortal. We should do it again."**

That was it. That was why this place had seemed so familiar. He had been here. He had walked this path. It was just after he had unlocked Prophylaxis for the first time, and Inanna had proved what a trickster she was.

But why did her voice sound so . . . distant?

"Somehow, I knew you had something planned."

Lukas stilled. Because those words—his words—had not come out of his mouth. It had come from—

He looked to his right. At himself. At a different Lukas Aguilar.

Was this his own memory? It must have been. He was still wearing the tattered shirt and pants, before he'd been captured by the yokai and made to fight the kasha buck naked. Before he had unlocked Soul Siphon. That Lukas was scary in his ignorance, in his confidence and willingness to believe that he would return to his planet someday, and all this would go away as a demented dream.

The Other-Lukas leaned against the wall. "In the spirit of good sportsmanship, would you at least tell me one final thing?"

"I may."

But why was he revisiting this memory? He knew what was about to happen.

"How did my world end?"

. . .

. . .

Wait. That was wrong. This wasn't supposed to happen. This hadn't happened. He tried to ask about—something, but he'd have a panic attack—and then—

"**Keep watching,**" came Inanna's voice, this time from his own ears. Lukas staggered in surprise. "**Do not panic. It is only me.**"

"But—but this—"

"**Keep watching.**"

Other-Inanna's distant chuckle became a quiet, rolling laugh. "**Stars,**" *Other-Inanna replied,* "**You're adorable.**"

"Just answer the question."

"**No.**"

"Why?" Other-Lukas demanded. "You're oath-bound to answer any question related to my existence as an anomaly."

"**Not quite,**" *Other-Inanna replied.* "**I am only oath-bound to tell you about the effects the omphalos can have upon you, and validate your theories about its nature. Nothing more. Nothing less.**"

"Knowing about how this came to be would only help me theorize better."

"**Then you should have worded your bargain differently. Do not blame me for your own shortcomings. Besides, even if you did, I'd advise you not to ask that of me.**"

"And why is that?"

"**Because you are only mortal. Perceiving an event spawning across dimensions greater than you can comprehend will break you. It will shatter your mind.**"

"Or it wouldn't. You don't know for sure. Maybe things will work differently and I'll get to know what happened."

"**You will not. It is enough that you are alive. Knowing the fate of your world will bring you neither happiness nor satisfaction. It would damage you in ways you cannot comprehend.**"

"Maybe you're right, but you're not the one that's pulled away from their world. I think I deserve to know, and if stuff happens because of that, I fully deserve what happens to me. We can make a bargain out of it if we must."

Lukas jerked back in shock. He—the other him—was he really desperate enough to invoke another bargain? He'd already acted hastily once, demanding information about the omphalos within him in return for a spell of Inanna's choice. That this Other-Lukas was anxious enough to force a second bargain was downright alarming.

"What is this?" he couldn't help but ask. "This didn't happen to me. I didn't make any new deals. Hell. We never had this conversation. Then—how?"

"**Keep watching.**"

The Other-Inanna's voice reverberated all around him. "**A bargain is made when both sides have something to gain. Handing someone a piece of misfortune**" *willingly is hustling, but a bargain. Fine, this is on your head. If you must witness the End of your World, then so be it."*

Then he felt it.

There was a sudden, horrible pressure, a whole-body agony. The force of her memory pressing against his own was like trying to hold off the weight of a tide. But the sea had tried to wash his mind away before now, and he knew the secret of facing the power of incomprehensible sensations. He might be nothing but a grain of sand on the shore of that ocean. But while the ocean could pound it across shores over and over, after the tide was gone and the waters receded, the grain of sand would remain.

So he took the pressure. His head felt like someone was trying to squeeze it through his nose and ears, but he kept his will focused on trying to survive it. Alpha Condition rose to his aid. His training with psionics raised mental barriers but the force came in anyway.

Lukas saw light.

Darkness.

Wind.

Lightning.

Shadows.

Fire. Water. Ground. Living, non-living, trees, animals, insects—a hundred thousand impressions sandblasted against him. It was like someone had taken a bag of sand and smashed against his face repeatedly. He could smell the mud and the fish and animals and trees and—and Life.

He felt Life. Ferocious wind and cloudy storms tore across the sky. Vicious magma erupted out of the crust, cloaking the world with smoke and inky blackness. Wet drops of rain fell upon his cheeks, while searing heat threatened to charr his skin to ashes.

The roar of power came next. Wild, crimson and golden light emanated from one direction, followed by choking, searing heat that threatened to overwhelm his entire existence. Cold, horrible, deathly powers followed suit—winter and frost made manifest—soaring up at full strength to meet their nemeses, colliding in the middle. No matter what Lukas tried, he couldn't make heaven or hell out of these abstract senses as they thrashed his entire existence around. One force pulled at his emotions, making him weep and cry in happiness and despair, while another made him want to rage and annihilate everything in his path. He was like an ant in between two brawling elephants, with the jungle itself suffering the wrath of the behemoths. It was the kind of power that cowed mortals and made them believe in the demonic and the divine. Powers too great for their feeble minds to even begin to comprehend, lest they be driven insane just by being in their very presence.

His mouth fell open, his eyes gazing starkly at the sight. He hadn't even known when his knees had given away—when he had fallen down to the ground, curling into himself like a newborn and weeping tears of joy and sadness, of hatred and remorse. Every word he tried to express came out as gibberish. Every thought he conjured shattered like a raindrop hitting the earth from above.

He screamed.

And in the middle of it all was the Earth itself. Not the beautiful and familiar world he knew all too well, but the real Earth—a wellspring of potential now swamped with corruption and death, slowly sinking into the inky blackness of its own creations. Dark emotions—greed, lust, hatred and rage—hung over it like a thick shroud, covering it, engulfing it, distorting it. Every single inch of space was filled with extreme malevolence and a burning tar-like substance that threatened to suck in light and life and leave cataclysms in its wake. Ghosts, wraiths and restless spirits soared everywhere, and skulls of all shapes formed entire mountains as far as the eye could see. It was a ghastly sight, the likes of which he could never have imagined in his worst nightmares.

His eyes burned like coals as his taut muscles strained even further, silent screams escaping his throat. His mind recoiled at the horrors he was witnessing, and they never stopped.

This was Death. Solid, tangible, real death draped atop the world around him. Death by fire, death by penalty, death by betrayal, death by murder, death by burning and death and death and death and—

SNAP!

A powerful, radiant orb of power manifested before him. It took him a couple of seconds to realize that he was down on his knees, blood crawling out of his eyes and nostrils, while Inanna—the real deal—stood in front of him, golden motes of power exuding from her form. Even in such a despicable state, he couldn't help but feel how *grand* she was.

Like watching a snow-capped mountain from afar.

Or a volcano during an eruption.

The goddess lifted her hand, the gesture elegant, and pointed forward at the orb with one finger.

It exploded with light that tore at his eyes and sound that clawed at his ears, a nauseating ripple in the air caused by so much energy being unleashed before him, and a clap of thunder.

And then it was gone.

Just like that.

"What was that?" Lukas gasped.

Inanna turned to face him. **"I warned you. Perception of that magnitude would shatter your mind. And it did. I was forced to step in and seal the memory, but the damage was done. The panic and trauma you suffer are the scars that remain."**

"But . . . I just saw the memory."

"What you saw is a mere *reflection* of your original experience. And look at what it did to you."

"Then why show it?"

"You were losing control. The restraints on the memory were buckling because of your constant curiosity. This was the only way forward. Be warned, if you unseal the memory, you *will* die."

"R—right," Lukas stammered. "Good to know."

THE LEGEND OF THE FOX

Records from the Banksi Library
    Title: The Legend of the Fox
Record Date: Unknown
Archivist: Unknown
Accuracy: Unknown

In the beginning, there was no world. No earth. No heaven. There was only the Endless.

And in that Endless, two Primordials made their home. Their names were Izanagi and Izanami. Man and woman. Heaven and Earth. Potential and substratum. Physical and ethereal. Manifestations of the duality of the universe. Together, they made the World. They made the sky, the land, the oceans, the forests, the volcanoes. They conceived lightning before it streaked across the sky. They imbued within the barren matrix life with Potential.

They named it Onogoro.

Aeons passed. The World they created grew, became more. It gave birth to newer worlds. Different, sophisticated, each with their own creations, living and inanimate, yet they all revolved around the World they sprang from like children vying for their mother's attention.

A multitude of species spawned in time in the different worlds. Svartalfar, ljósálfar, dökkálfar, vanir, jotunns, and many more. They developed their own rules, their own realities, and even minor gods to believe in. The Primordials did not care, for they had eyes for only their personal creation.

Onogoro.

Or, as the infant realms called it, Midgard.

The land of the bremetans. The land where people knew about their true origins, about the Primordials. The world that was ruled by Izanagi and Izanami's daughter: the Empress Amaterasu.

But then, a calamity descended upon Onogoro. A vile wyrm of cosmic proportions that called itself the World Serpent. A draconian creature the empress named Ryujin, the beast of the ocean floors. A being of endless regeneration and venom that could destroy even the divine. A monster that held ironclad control over the dark depths of the oceans. A darkness so deep that even Amaterasu's Eternal Light could not penetrate it without losing itself to its madness.

To defeat it, they needed something more. Something that could change the Rules. A true exception to the World System was needed. Thus, the Primordials created a being capable of warping reality itself. A creature that would henceforth serve as guardian and protector of the empress.

With nine lustrous tails, each holding its own mystery, the creature was not a bremetan. It was not a monster. It was not a demon. And it was not a god. It was something that did not fit into the World, like a puzzle piece that belonged to a different set, yet somehow managed to blend in. It straddled the line between reality and fantasy, inhabiting both Heaven and Onogoro at once, wandering from one existence to another as easily as walking through a door.

It was the Nine-Tailed Fox.

The fearsome fox clashed with the deadly Ryujin, and after a long-drawn-out war, emerged victorious, banishing the serpent into the endless depths of the ocean. Its job accomplished, it was ordered to return to the Primordials to continue its duty.

But the fox denied the command.

Boastful of its victory and proud of its skill, the fox decided it wanted more. Serving as guardian of the Primordials would not quench its desires any longer. That which could bend any reality, now wanted to forge its own destiny.

And so it did.

Using powers vested upon it by the Primordials themselves, it crafted an entire world, one that was just as twisted as itself. The bremetans called it Ikai—the Other World. A realm that both did and did not exist. This world gave birth to creatures that were twisted caricatures of true life. Because the fox was an aberration, so too were the species its world gave birth to.

Creatures that could not stand the Eternal Light took shelter in the dark.

Creatures denied the blessings of the Primordials and existed in a perpetual wraith-like state.

Creatures that were cursed to become the strange apparitions of the night.

They were the yokai.

The yokai were demons. By bremetan logic, they were not alive, nor were they dead; they floated between the physical and the ethereal. Their powers, derived from the fox's corruptive influence, allowed them to bastardize the World's energy around them and mutate it, mimicking the elements. Such perversity allowed them to gain power, and with power came greed. Came insanity. Came violence.

In an attempt to outshine the brilliance of the empress, they formed their own empire, centered around Namzuuhuu, a fertile valley along the coast of the great ocean, the very place where the Nine-Tailed Fox won its first victory against the vicious serpent. An empire of leftovers and has-beens. Of svartalfar that had nowhere to go after the destruction of the Nine Realms. Of vanir, and dökkálfar, and jotunns, and countless other beasts. Agglomerations of lower life-forms that did not wish to submit before the might of the empress.

But Amaterasu, in her eternal benevolence, let them thrive.

Until they committed a corruption most vile.

Until they created . . . oni.

There are no words to describe the atrocity they commited. A vile corruption that was inconceivable to the bremetan mind. A flood of madness and horror followed by a twisted insanity, caused by a fusion of yokai and bremetan—corrupting the very essence of the bremetan soul to become something horrifying.

A mindless predator. A wicked demon with nigh-impossible levels of lifeforce at its command.

And they were being created in the dozens, hundreds and thousands.

Thus came the war.

Amaterasu and siblings Tsukuyomi and Susanoo, both gods in their own right, declared war upon the yokai lands. Tsukuyomi, the beloved Moon God, engaged the Nine-Tailed Fox in a battle of illusions, a battle that led to the curse known to all as the Black Moon.

What happened next is unclear. The only thing that scholars agree on is that a Taboo was cast upon the land—an act so ominous that even its mention must be held in contempt. It is unclear what precisely happened, but it ripped all Potential from Namzuuhuu, converting the once fertile lands into a deadly desert that rejects the living. An act of ultimate defilement that not even the World could forgive.

The Nine-Tailed Fox, in a desperate last stand, tried to engulf our World with the Ikai, letting the deadly mists engulf our prosperous civilization and end everything. Neither Tsukuyomi nor Susanoo, for all their might, could stand against that.

It is what happened then that marked the birth of the tale of the Great Goddess.

Amaterasu, who had forever sworn to uphold the duties of the empress, realized how much the World needed her. She embraced godhood, bathing the World with her Eternal Light. In its glorious presence, the mists receded, taking back the shadows with them. Since the day of her ascension, the apparitions of the night could not stand to be in the presence of the light.

And since then, they have never entered the great and mighty Asukan Empire.

PART V

HEART OF ICE

CHAPTER 29

TROUBLE

I never thought anomalies would be this big!" said Elena.

Normally, such a statement would be accompanied by animated hand gestures and facial expressions. Tanya had come to expect that and more from the quirky changeling, but Elena was too tired to care. Instead, she scrunched up her face into an expression of disgust.

"UGH!" she cried in distaste. "I smell like a gutter!"

Zuken moved closer and sniffed behind her ear. "Close, but you're not quite there yet."

She scowled and shoved him lightly. Their group leader took it with a good-natured chuckle.

Tanya watched the proceedings with a soft smile. Finally, after two whole weeks of searching the desert high and low, their group found the anomaly a few dozen miles away from the Cyffnar-occupied base camp. After packing a handful of supplies, they made their descent.

And Elena wasn't wrong. Day after day, the subterranean chamber around them kept going, farther than the eye could see, with more tunnels and forks than she could be bothered to count. It was surprisingly well-lit by the green moss on the walls, with thick roots burrowing through every stone wall in sight.

But that wasn't all.

The smile faded from her lips, replaced by grim resignation. She didn't know if the others felt it or not—maybe it was her sensitivity with changes in the wind or a manifestation of the desert's curse—but she could feel leashed violence in the air. A strange dissonance of energies that swayed from tunnel to tunnel like a watchful warden, keeping an eye on them closely.

"Can you *not* be so chipper?" Maude sighed in annoyance. "I just want to go home and take a long, hot bath!"

"Talk about vanity," Elena muttered.

Tanya silently inspected her own fingernails. They were dirty, with smudges of black around the corners. Once this was over, she was going to spend a week at Bombshells. It was the best spa in all of Haviskali, but too expensive for her.

Until now, anyway. With forty thousand mezals . . .

She'd be damned if she didn't get herself a week there. That, *and* a wardrobe. She needed a complete set—maybe two. And boots. And some adventurer attire. And napkins. One could never have enough napkins. Throw in some cosmetic jewelry and maybe a visit or two at the Zwaray Keep for some fancy svartalfar trinkets and—

"Oh, just shut up!" Maude exclaimed, chasing away Tanya's daydreams. "I'm a naturopath. Cleanliness comes naturally to me. Instead, I'm stuck in this subterranean cave for Eir knows how long!"

Tanya felt like banging her head against a wall. Maude and Elena's . . . bitch-fest—Olfric's words, not her own—had been going on for an hour, and as much as she wanted to pretend otherwise, this wasn't the first time it was happening. Frankly, she'd expected an argument to break out between herself and Olfric, given their mutual antagonism. Elena and Maude even seemed like fast friends when she'd met them for the first time.

Now, though . . .

She glanced at Olfric, who was currently doing some push-ups, his baggage dropped beside him. A lifelong fitness freak, Olfric Bergott never gave up the chance to get some physical exercise done or show off his muscles. It was a pity she liked men who were lean and sturdy instead of overly muscular. Not that the aquamancer would ever demonstrate an interest in her.

Though, the way he'd look at her sometimes . . .

Tanya crushed the thought midway, and instead considered the other two women in the group. Maude, despite her strange relationship with Olfric, was too free-spirited and different to consider dating a staunch Asukan. Elena, on the other hand, was clearly involved with Zuken, though it was hard to decipher the exact nature of their relationship. There was no doubt the changeling warmed the Banksi's bed, but the casual interaction between the two indicated something far deeper.

It was at this point Tanya realized that being inside a subterranean anomaly was likely having some side effects on her. Why else would she be mentally classifying the *relationship statuses* of her comrades instead of doing something productive?

"How long do you think these tunnels go?" Olfric suddenly asked her.

Tanya gave him a side-eyed glance. The aquamancer had been behaving oddly ever since . . . well, ever since she'd sided with him and agreed to attack the camp.

"Shouldn't that be a question for our terramancer?" Tanya replied.

"I did ask him," Olfric admitted, getting up and putting on his shirt. "He said that it went as far as he could sense, and possibly even farther. Something this long . . . maybe it's penetrated Haviskali itself."

Tanya snorted. "If it goes really deep, I wonder how long it will be before the air turns unbreathable."

"In that case, we just have to collapse the anomaly from above and walk out."

"Which would probably help as much as Elena's attempt to charm monsters in here."

"HEY!"

Both of them ignored the changeling's shout.

"We don't know how far this thing goes," Tanya continued. "Like you said, it's possible it's close to Haviskali. It's also equally possible it's penetrated Cyffnar already. Collapsing one portion won't help if you don't destroy the core."

She expected the aquamancer to respond with something. Instead, he sighed in resignation. "There goes my chance of getting away from this god-forsaken place."

"You chose this, and we're already deep inside the anomaly."

"Besides," Zuken replied, smiling, "there might be a little bit more in it for us . . ."

Tanya perked up at that.

"Featherglass," the terramancer said. "I've been sensing the presence of featherglass in this pit. If we can find its location—"

"We can take it for ourselves," Olfric replied, all traces of disagreement now evaporated from his face.

Tanya cocked up her head. Featherglass was an incredibly rare metal used to craft artifacts and weapons of immeasurable value. The wristbands she wore contained a thin sliver of featherglass, and they cost a pretty penny.

Maude was smiling. "Well now," she said slowly, "that's a big enough prize to be tempting."

"Isn't it a good thing that we get to divide it equally?" Zuken quipped.

Olfric snorted. "Nice try, but I already know you're going to make way more than the rest of us."

"Huh?" Maude exclaimed. "How's that?"

"The Ruling House of Asuka has an ironclad hold on the featherglass supply," Olfric explained. "It only sells the metal out in fixed amounts, charging outrageous sums in return. You'd need someone with deep pockets and connections to get any of it sold."

"Someone like him." Tanya pointed at Zuken, who laughed.

"Don't give me that look." The terramancer grinned. "I promised to share the loot equally, not offer free brokerage services."

"What happens if one of us goes rogue and blows the whistle? Selling featherglass illegally will get you capital punishment, lord or no lord," Olfric argued.

"And who's gonna go rogue, Olfric? You?" Zuken asked. There was a strange glint in his eyes that Tanya couldn't place. Something that reminded her that as affable as Zuken Banksi was to her and everyone else, there was a reason he was the loudest voice in the Haviskali Underground. "We're already in the middle of an illegal mission. If the Empire got the slightest whiff of this, we'd all hang. Make no mistake, we are in this together. And contrary to what some might think, I'm *not* in the habit of assassinating my fellow partners out of paranoia. It simply isn't good for business."

Impossible, Tanya thought. He was clearly bluffing to keep up the crew's morale. Nobody was that trusting. After all, Zuken already hired a Maluscian smuggling crew for transportation. There was no telling if there were now mercenaries following them at this very moment, waiting on a signal to slit their collective throats.

"No arguments there," Olfric grunted. "But I do have a question. For Tanya." He glanced toward her. "If she can answer it without snapping back, that is."

"Alright." She shrugged. "What do you want to know?"

"How did you destroy the anomaly back then?"

That got her undivided attention. "Why, *Heir* Bergott?" she drawled, a smirk on her face. "Why would an Asukan noble show interest in such heresy?"

Olfric rolled his eyes. "Don't worry, I'm not trying to take your job. If you tell me . . . *us*, how you did it, we can think of ways to get it done faster. Five minds are better than one, right?"

"They are," Tanya slowly agreed, eyeing the aquamancer, trying to read past his expression. Just what was he fishing for? Something to pin against her when things went south?

Ultimately, she folded her arms. "But I got chased across the kingdom by the Cobalt Army for this. I think I'm entitled to some secrecy."

"Fair enough," he agreed. "But tell me this. Will it affect your skills?"

"I'll manage," she replied coolly. "Unless you doubt my ability—"

"No one's doubting anything," he replied, perhaps a touch too quickly. "Especially after what I saw you do out there in the desert."

Right. Her *performance* at the enemy camp. No wonder Olfric was giving her a wide berth. The man was an Asukan to the core, and if there was one thing that impressed Asukans, it was power. But there was something else, something in his tone that she couldn't quite put a finger on.

"Then there should be no cause for concern," Tanya said.

Olfric drew himself up, but she was not impressed. People like him liked having power over others and controlled everyone else through fear. Whether this domination was exerted by social hierarchy, political acumen, and connections, or the old-fashioned power differences, it didn't matter.

"All I'm saying is, you were in your element in the desert. Here, on the other hand . . ." Olfric trailed off.

Oh.

Oh.

Compared to the desert outside, wind was practically non-existent inside the cavern. Their group had encountered a multitude of monsters, but Tanya had fought each of them with Qi-empowered skills and nothing more. However, there was more to Aeromancy than simply channeling the power of the wind into a hammer blow. It was about manipulating density, pressure, and vacuums. It was about taking the gaseous state of matter and playing god with it.

The abundance of wind out there had actually halved her arsenal.

But in here . . .

Tanya suppressed a smile. "Don't worry about me. I'll manage just fine."

Olfric sniffed imperiously. "Whatever. I'm just looking out for my team."

"How adorable. Who knew *the* Olfric Bergott had a—"

The rest of Tanya's words died in her throat as every single hair on her neck rose. Gooseflesh erupted over her entire body at once, and a primal wave of utter terror flickered through her brain, utterly dislodging every rational thought in her head.

For a spiritist, that was bad. Control over one's emotions was something every aspirant learned during their years at the Shrine. Otherwise, all kinds of horrible things could happen. It was only too easy for a spiritist's emotions to go haywire upon using the kami's mana beyond a certain limit—a common situation in a battlefield.

Quickly, she wrestled her emotions back under control.

That was when she saw *it*.

The thing that slithered into existence was the size of an average bremetan. Humanoid and bipedal, with the legs more or less right, but longer and leaner. But that was where the similarities ended.

Its head was bumpy and covered in warts, and tentacles slithered out of hundreds of fangs in the center of its body. Hands branched out somewhere in the middle into two flailing tentacles, while its feet gave the appearance of an eagle's talons. It had no face. It had no eyes. And its feet didn't touch the floor.

The creature had a strange slipperiness to it, as if the memory of its outer structure would slip away from her mind if she didn't spend conscious effort behind it.

And as if that wasn't discomfiting enough, there were *five* of them.

"Tentacles," Maude muttered from behind her. "Disgusting, slimy things."

Tentacles were the least of their problems if that psychic disruption was any clue. Tanya focused on the familiar feeling of a wind blade forming within her palms. The coalescing currents shook slightly as they contorted and—

Wait. *Shook?*

Tanya looked down at her own palms. They were *shaking*. As were her arms. And her legs. And—

Dizziness hit her like a sledgehammer. She stumbled forward before a pair of steady hands caught her from behind. It took a moment to click before Tanya became acutely aware that she was pressed against Olfric.

She hurriedly took a step forward.

"They—they aren't monsters!" Elena squeaked, quaking in her boots. "Those things are not monsters!"

Not monsters? Tanya focused on the creatures before her.

Mana	—
Lifeforce	—

It was impossible. No lifeforce and no mana? The creatures were unnatural and capable of psychic disruption. Not to mention that malevolent aura . . . No creature could pull that off without a minimum level of Qi or mana in their bodies. Then . . . how were they doing it?

Only one way to find out, Tanya thought to herself.

Holding a wind blade in a reverse grip, she hurled it toward the closest monster. The blade dove into its body and vanished. Before she could get past the initial moment of shock, the creature lunged in her direction, its tentacular arms morphing into vicious claw-endings.

Tanya flinched. It nearly cost her her life. The razor-sharp claw came closer, now barely inches away, and—

Was promptly captured in a blob of pure water, while Olfric sent a wave of raw force with his other hand at the creature's face. It pushed it back by no more than a foot.

"My turn," Zuken said, and before she knew it, she was witnessing a barrage of rocks, each no larger than a bremetan's fist, their tail-ends sharpened, shooting from behind and piercing them. Head, abdomen, shoulders, tentacles, maw—there wasn't a place that wasn't perforated by the rock onslaught. The monster let out a mechanical, grating scream and was slammed against the wall, turning into something amorphous.

As Tanya slowly came to the realization that there was no blood from the monster's wounds, a faint sound emanated from the other side. The rest of the creatures, all of them larger and more well-muscled than the first, drifted toward them. Tanya raised her hand without thinking and unleashed her power.

A twister of biting-cold wind exploded out of her palm and smashed into the nearest monster. The creature was instantly frozen, before the accompanying force blasted it into smithereens.

Dozens of frozen monster bits fell down on the floor.

Maude whistled.

Zuken had gotten two more with his rock bullets, while Olfric hacked one of them apart with a water whip.

"Not dead! Not *DEAD*!" Elena kept yelling. "They'll come from the bottom!"

As if on cue, something shot out of the ground below Tanya's feet, hitting her in the chin and flinging her against the wall. She used the wind to break her momentum and land on her feet, shaken but otherwise fine.

None of their attacks mattered. It didn't matter that four of them had their bodies torn apart, and a fifth utterly disintegrated to the bone. They were there, as if time itself had been unwound for them, returning them to their base state.

The five creatures bared their fanged maws and—

A small, cylindrical canister tumbled across the floor. Tanya watched as the small sigil engraved on its surface began to emit a preternatural glow.

And then, the world was lost in white.

Eternal Light shone onto the creatures from all directions, tearing pieces of them away like bits of rotten meat peeled off a carcass by a sandblaster. The creatures screamed, and their strange slippery bodies sloughed like a snake's scales before dissipating into motes of gray. By the time the light faded, the creatures were gone. Disintegrated to dust.

"As I suspected," Maude said, an uncharacteristically manic grin on her face. "Those bodies weren't physical. And Eternal Light burns all spiritual beasts, those monsters that possess living beings and transform them into ghoulish monstrosities."

"I—I don't understand," Tanya exclaimed.

"Don't you?" a tense, shivering Elena asked. "It means the Black Moon has finally ascended to the Central Sky. The Night Parade of a Hundred Demons has begun!"

The Night Parade was a concept that had its roots deep in pre-Asukan mysticism. It was said that when the Black Moon ascended to the Central Sky, and the Eternal Light was at its weakest, a cataclysm would rise, a portent that heralded the rise of shadows and specters—wraiths flying in the sky, ghosts and vengeful spirits of the dead coming out of their graves, and a cavalcade of specters plundering the Asukan lands as omens of the dark days prophesied to return. They would ride across the land in hopes of finding their lost deity, the Nine-Tailed Fox, ravaging the Empire until nothing but madness, fire, and darkness remained.

The only problem was . . . they were in the middle of the desert, where there was *no* Eternal Light. There was no saying whether the Night Parade sensed their presence in the anomaly, or something far more sinister was at play.

"Elena, you're supposed to be good with monsters, right?" Tanya asked grumpily. "Can't you just, I don't know, make these things do our bidding? Or at least keep them away from us?"

"Those weren't monsters!" Maude reiterated. "They were yokai!"

Olfric snorted. "Really now! Yokai? After all this time?"

The changeling, on the other hand, looked like she'd been slapped. "It's not working! Something about this place is weird. None of the monsters are responding to my charms like they're supposed to."

"Maybe it's the desert's curse?" Maude offered.

"It's just a stupid curse," Tanya fired back. "It's not the reason for every unexplainable thing."

"Do you have a better idea?"

She didn't. But she wasn't going to admit that out loud.

"I think it's because of her."

It took Tanya an entire second to recognize that Olfric had been pointing at her, and two more to realize what he meant. Whirling around, she put her hands on her waist and angrily stared him down.

"Care to repeat that?" she asked, tapping her foot.

"I *said*," the aquamancer repeated, "that it's probably because of you. Am I the only one who's noticed that the monsters are weirdly focused on her? I've visited my share of anomalies in the past, and what's happening here is downright freaky."

Tanya stilled. It was true that they were being hounded by monsters. Like, *a lot*. And even she had noticed how they'd single her out and attack her with utmost prejudice, like they were out for her from the start. She had tried to rationalize that it was because she was the most dangerous fighter in the group, but when Olfric put it like that—

"That's a singularly biased way of looking at it," Zuken defended her. "She's the one who's been killing them most. It's animal nature to seek out the dangerous threat and address it first."

"Yeah, but these aren't animals. They're *monsters*. Born from an anomaly. And she—"

"You think because I've sinned in the past," Tanya mumbled, "the monsters—"

"Are attacking us," the aquamancer finished with a leer. "You being here with us is a danger in itself."

"And what would you have us do, Olfric?" Zuken demanded. The undercurrent of steel in his voice did not go unheard. "Throw her out of the group?

Let her wander about by herself to attract monsters so that we can relax around?"

Olfric's face broke into an open sneer.

"I didn't know you were that willing to give up your life for some Sinning, murderous—"

Tanya had heard enough. Mission or no mission, she wasn't obligated to just stand there and listen to this bastard spill his vitriol. A wind blade began to form within her right palm, but before she could so much as launch it, someone else acted.

There was a *smack-thud* of impact as an invisible fist smacked the living daylights out of Olfric Bergott, sending him back against the wall. The aquamancer gasped, blood leaking out of his lower lip.

Maude stepped forward, her battlestaff held firmly in her right hand.

"Maude!" Olfric snapped. "What in the nine hells do you think you're doing?!"

"Sorry," Maude replied in a polite tone that fooled no one. "I meant to say 'Stop,' but I punched you instead!"

"I didn't see a punch!" Elena interjected.

"You didn't, huh?" the naturopath asked with a smile. "I wonder why."

Olfric's face split into an ugly leer, repulsive in just how hateful it was. "This will—"

Maude slammed her battlestaff down onto the floor, shutting him off. "Now you listen to me," she asserted. "Last I checked, Tanya created the sandstorm. Tanya got us to our camp. Tanya destroyed the Cyffnarian base. Zuken here has funded everything and arranged for everything. Elena's ensured things don't fall apart, and I've done the job I was brought in for. You, on the other hand, have been a *glorified laundry boy!*"

Something furious hit his eyes, and Tanya prepared herself for a direct confrontation. Olfric Bergott was a bully who cried unfair whenever the universe refused to bow down to his whims, and took out his frustrations on whoever he damn well pleased. And currently, he was unhappy with her.

"Alright, that's enough!" Zuken chastised, stepping between them all. "That comment was way out of line, Olfric. I suggest you apologize."

Neither of them missed the steel lining his voice.

"Make me!" Olfric sneered.

"*That won't be necessary,*" Elena replied, a beaming smile on her face. "Come on guys, we have this job because only we have what it takes. We're *extraordinarily* good at what we do. We can do the undoable and fool the unfoolable. We know how to take an incredibly large task and break it down to manageable pieces, then deal with each of those pieces. We know how to get what we want, and *that* is why we can get this job done. Together."

The sudden shift in Olfric's demeanor was as beautiful as it was frighten-ing. One moment, disdain colored his features, and in the next, a thin veneer of civility was all that was present. The changeling was either good, or lucky, or both. All Tanya had felt was a soft, featherlike touch against her mental defenses, but that was only because she knew what to look for. It was *that* subtle.

The Bergott heir crossed his arms. "The Goddess knows, I've never shied away from a challenge. But"—his expression drew dark—"this Sinful task, in this evil environment . . . It's getting to me. I—I just can't help it."

"We're all in a difficult situation, Olfric," Maude replied softly. "We're in the Namzuuhuu Desert, a land with no Eternal Light, with the Black Moon overhead, committing a task that goes directly against both your and my beliefs. But that's no reason to lash out at our team members."

Olfric wiped his lip and waddled away in a different direction.

"Where are you going?" Zuken called out.

"Taking a walk," the aquamancer mumbled as he lumbered off. "I need some time alone to clear my head."

Maude sighed. "Don't worry, I'll go after him."

"Is that really a good idea?" Tanya worriedly asked.

"Yes, it is," Elena said, surprising everyone present.

Tanya reluctantly glanced at Maude and mumbled her thanks.

The naturopath rolled her eyes and winked back, before following in Olfric's direction.

CHAPTER 30

WHEELS WITHIN WHEELS

The Black Moon shone overhead.

Olfric Bergott ignored the ever-constant drain on his lifeforce as he walked down the road. The hood over his face kept the heat at bay, along with the inquisitive looks that he'd have gotten from the surrounding masses who had nothing better to do than to gossip about their betters. All businesses were closed, all bureaucratic tasks suspended until the Waning, yet here he was, promenading across the starkly empty streets toward the overseer's office.

He crossed the threshold of the property and walked up the steps. The entire edifice felt empty. Olfric trudged up the stairs until he was standing in front of the office door. He raised a finger to knock—

"Come in."

Olfric wasn't uncouth enough to say anything aloud, but privately, he thought it was rude of the overseer to always invite people in before they actually knocked. It was the wily bureaucrat's way of asserting dominance over visitors before they even made it into his office. No doubt a proximity ward and a scrying zone were set up somewhere around the door.

Exhaling, he walked inside.

The overseer was not alone. Seated on a lavish chair on the other side of the table, a glass of wine in his hand, was a man Olfric recognized instantly. Everyone in Haviskali knew him. An heir to the famed Banksi clan of terramancers, one of the Sacred Eight in the Asukan Empire. Ruling both legal and illegal markets with an iron fist, the man's casual attitude served as a dagger he used to strike at others' backs. He was infamously known as the Dark Hand of the Shogun.

"Olfric Bergott," said the overseer, standing up, "meet Zuken Banksi. He has a very interesting proposal, mandated by Shogun Naowa himself, and he wants to hire you for it."

Zuken stood up and inclined his head. "Good afternoon. Thanks for attending this summon at such short notice."

Olfric shrugged. "It was a call from the Overseer's office." He made a rough jerk with his own head. "He hasn't been very forthcoming about the nature of the job, but he guarantees I'll have to play my cards pretty close to my chest."

"An inch below your heart, just to be sure."

Olfric blinked at the odd joke.

Zuken set his wine glass down and pulled out a large envelope, which he then offered to him.

Olfric regarded it carefully. "What is it?"

"One of the reasons I wish to hire you for this mission."

If nothing else, the man knew how to bait others. Fine. He'd bite. Inside it was a photograph. A girl with striking blonde hair and beautiful features. Her blue eyes looked sharp as ever. It was a face he'd recognize anywhere.

Olfric's face hardened. "What has she done now? Last I heard, the Army was on the watch for her. Are you telling me she's done something even worse?"

"On the contrary, if you agree to my offer, then she's going to be your teammate."

"Impossible!" Olfric exclaimed.

Zuken smiled. "Had it been an easy task, I wouldn't have asked Overseer Kinosu to personally ask for you. I have seen your records. You're one of the very best, and have a lot of personal history with her."

"We hate each other. Is that good enough history for you?"

Banksi smiled. "That's exactly what I need."

"And you think . . . you can make her do . . . whatever this is about?"

"Yes."

Olfric considered it for a moment. "She's a loose cannon. You're being stupid if you're resting the fate of the mission on her professional integrity." He then realized where he was and who he was talking to. ". . . Sir."

"I'm not asking you to trust her integrity," Zuken laughed. "I'm asking you to trust mine."

The overseer pushed a glass of expensive wine in Olfric's direction. "Olfric, you know I wouldn't have asked for this if it wasn't necessary. It's a direct order from the Shogun himself."

". . . Very well."

"I'm glad."

Olfric exhaled. "Overseer Kinosu tells me that it is top secret, and that I'd have to be part of some pretty diabolical things. Makes me wonder if I'm signing my own death warrant, Heir Banksi."

"We all live in interesting times, Olfric Bergott. Also, since we're going to be working together, call me Zuken."

* * *

It was like being stuck inside a fishbowl.

Was he annoyed at being in the anomaly, realizing he was part of a team whose purpose was a grave Sin, or the desert's curse just messing with his mind? Or was it guilt from the knowledge that he was carrying out an entirely different mission under the guise of this anomaly mission?

Olfric didn't know, and truthfully, he was getting mad about it. He was an aquamancer who'd risen through the ranks with nothing save his sheer diligence and competence. His nobility was a symbol of his allegiance to the Asukan Empire and a reminder of his faith in the Great Goddess.

But above all, it was the symbol of the Bergott Clan. A clan he wanted to take over as its lord someday. It was why despite his personal beliefs . . . despite knowing that destroying an anomaly was an act of grave Sin and treason against the Empire . . . he'd agreed to the mission.

When it succeeded, the support of the overseer and Zuken Banksi would get him a stronger hold on the state of affairs of his clan inside the Llaisy Kingdom.

The mission was simple enough when it started. Tanya was a Sinner. She should've been behind bars. She should've had her kami extracted and herself sentenced to a lifetime of imprisonment for what she did during their previous mission. But both the Cobalt Army and the overseer were very interested in her for reasons they were not willing to divulge. And somehow, Zuken Banksi was involved in this mess.

But now, after spending so much time in her presence, Olfric was starting to have second thoughts.

Tanya was . . . different.

She refrained from getting noticed, even if it was as casual as raising a question. The only times she did so were when she realized things were going in the wrong direction, more often than not triggered by her own experience in similar situations. How a girl who wasn't even in her mid-twenties managed to possess so much power and experience was beyond him.

And *maybe* she was a little attractive too.

Olfric looked up at the ceiling and sighed loudly. The quarrel with Tanya had gotten out of hand, but he was certain the monsters were after the blonde aeromancer, which was why it was safer if she didn't travel with them. Zuken claimed Olfric was being a selfish bastard who wanted to throw her to the monsters to save his own life, but Olfric knew that Zuken knew better.

This wasn't about saving his life.

This was about saving *hers*.

Olfric wasn't the smartest tool in the shed. The thing was, when you knew you weren't the smartest, you learned to pay attention. Every person had their own quirks and habits. You could learn a lot by watching how a person moved and what they looked out for during a fight. It painted a far more concrete picture of them than their stats or accomplishments ever would.

Olfric had seen Tanya hurl wind and force at close range. He had witnessed her fight monsters in tandem with a crowd, and at times, while running or escaping. He had seen her shoot down opponents one after the other, and also seen her blitz through an entire army like an avenging angel.

If he were to sum it up in a single word, it would be . . .

Inconsistent.

As part of a group, her contribution was at the level of an average team player. But when she was alone against an entire horde of enemies, a different side of her came out. This Tanya was more analytical. There was logic behind her every step and a patient understanding of the predicament they'd found themselves in. There was an underlying sense of caution and a calculated perception of consequences. With that analytical mindset came a predatory vibe that made him want to find the nearest rock and hide under it.

It was almost like watching two different people who just so happened to reside in the same body.

That, or she went out of her way to hide her abilities except for when she was alone and unhindered.

Olfric didn't know why she did that. He had, in his own style, tried to fish for information from her. Tanya had instantly gotten defensive about it. He had seen the giddy expression in her eyes when she truly got to fight, unhindered. It was like seeing a natural predator in action. A warmonger that was best at what she did.

But the moment she was fighting as part of their team, that brightness was gone, replaced by a dull sliver of concentration. If Olfric had to guess, he'd have said that Tanya was actually fighting *herself.*

It was probably for the best that she left the group and traveled alone. But before he could've gotten to the heart of the matter and made his thoughts known, things had escalated in an entirely different direction.

Maude didn't know what was going on. It was obvious she'd react the way she did.

Olfric suddenly paused and glanced behind him. He turned down random tunnels to be certain. There was someone following him, moving relatively quietly. Even in the damp greenish hue, the best he could see was a dark shadow—*ugh*—from time to time.

Rounding a sharp corner, he grabbed a stalactite from overhead with a watery tentacle and lifted himself off the ground soundlessly. Turnabout was fair play, after all.

Olfric didn't have to wait long. A few moments later, he heard the sound of footsteps. Surging forward, he dispersed the water and flung out his other arm to create another tendril, wrapping the figure around where the neck was. There was a distinct *thud!* as the rocky shard fell on its head, and then a yelp.

"LET ME GO!"

It took him half a moment to register the voice.

"Maude!" Olfric exclaimed incredulously, releasing her. "What in the nine hells do you think you're doing?"

The naturopath staggered forward, her hands holding her neck, before turning to stare, wide-eyed, at him. "Wotan's Eye!" she exclaimed. "Are you quite mad?"

"Hey! You had the bright idea to follow me!"

Maude flushed at the statement, unable to deny the accusation. "I just wanted to know where you went. How did you know I was following you?"

"I pay attention. That's how!" he rebuked. "Now what are you doing here?"

"I—I just thought I should get you back before—"

"I do something rash in anger?"

"I just wanted to make sure there weren't any hard feelings," Maude said, leaning back against the wall.

"Hard feelings?"

"About what happened earlier. I didn't want to complicate things between you and Zuken, after all."

Me and Zuken? Olfric frowned, staring at her as he tried to construe possible subtexts of her words. Just how much did she know?

"You're adorable when you're thinking like that," the vanir replied, her eyes sparkling. "I can almost hear the cogs going around and around."

Olfric glowered at her. "I don't know what you're talking about."

Her face threatened to tear itself apart with amusement. "Sure you don't. Perhaps a little reminder is in order? Maybe when you met Zuken for the first time, *before* our meeting at his mansion?"

"You know about that?!"

Maude nodded, looking all too pleased with herself. "We all don masks. Mine fits like a velvet glove, so soft that it almost feels natural. But your mask is hard and brittle, screwed so tight that it probably hurts every time you so much as smile."

"That's an . . . evocative way of putting it, I suppose," he remarked, "but what's that got to do with this? Why are you here whispering about secrets and following me around instead of wiping that Sinner's tears?"

Maude shrugged. "Tanya's a big girl. She can manage. Besides, I helped you out enough."

That gave Olfric pause. Sometimes, it was easy to forget that Maude was more than just a medic. She had vanir heritage. Vanir were deeply perceptive creatures with powers of observation second only to their ability with the arts.

He recalled everything that had happened, putting it under this new lens. And his jaw fell open.

"You interfered in the quarrel, attracting Tanya's attention to the people around her. You reacted so she wouldn't have to, helping her restrain herself from attacking me. Your response wasn't anger. It was damage control!"

"Was it now?"

Olfric snorted. "I thought Zuken brought the changeling for that. But to think you had a similar role . . ."

It was just like Zuken Banksi, he supposed. Wheels within wheels. Groups within groups. Secrets within secrets. Was there any doubt left in his mind why this mission was so damn annoying?

"Elena is maintaining a constant featherlight touch on Tanya's emotions. It was essential that she felt part of the group at all times. It's what keeps her restrained. We don't want a repeat of what happened in the desert in here, do we? Among ourselves?"

Olfric shivered. "Has Zuken figured her out yet?"

Maude shrugged again. "You'll have to talk to him about it later. But we know she isn't a spy, and we know she doesn't have any nefarious intentions. She's capable of sustained flight, so she could have escaped whenever she wanted to in the desert."

"But she hasn't."

"She hasn't. Instead, she's been forthcoming about her aid, even at the risk of revealing her past to us."

"Wasn't that the plan? To figure out *how* she did it?"

"Don't ignore the forest for the trees, Olfric. We need her help to complete this mission. You driving her away from the group, regardless of your reason, isn't helping."

"But that *is* my role. The overly large, noisy, antagonistic distraction that keeps her focused and alert."

"And you've done it fine, but a degree of restraint is necessary. Going over the top can potentially destroy everything that we've all been working on."

Olfric bit his lip. He hadn't thought of that. Something between playing his role and being part of the team again had made him unconsciously treat Tanya as one of his teammates. And Olfric Bergott took his team's security very seriously.

"And after the mission's over? What then?"

Maude slightly tensed. "If things stay the same, Zuken is thinking of employing her, as he promised. But personally, I think he's found some dirt on her. Something—" But Maude didn't finish the rest. Instead, she grabbed his arms and pulled him flush against the wall with her, then pressed her palm against his mouth.

"*Shh*," she whispered, darting her eyes to the right.

Dressed in Cyffnarian attire was a black-haired soldier. He had a thin face, sharp eyes, and cheeks tapering down into a sharp chin. A thin lance of liquid blue light rose out of one of his fists.

A Cyffnarian pyromancer? He must have been inside when Tanya killed the rest.

For whatever reason, the man's eyes were shut and his other hand was folded behind his back while he went through a series of . . . *motions*. Olfric had never seen such a strange sword style before. There were no sweeping hits or stabs or slashes. Instead, he seemed utterly content to practice piercing and thrusting motions in the air with the fiery lance.

Arguing with fire was difficult. It was why it was the favored weapon of the early ages. The heat, the power, the light—fire boasted an unmatched intensity. It was also the natural representation of the very concept of a predator. It could burn you, scald you, and scorch you to ashes, yet it also provided light against the darkness and all the things that went bump in it.

However, fire was also a difficult element to control. Seeing the lance left no doubt in Olfric's mind about its wielder's skill in shape and temperature manipulation. Blue was one of the hottest kinds of flames you could reach in mortal limits.

"Odds are he's not alone," Maude whispered into his ear. Her words carried a tone of wearily familiar annoyance. "We can probably escape if we try."

Olfric kept his gaze trained on the Cyffnarian, as his kami generated as much mana as it could in the meantime. "Odds are we might get spotted even if we try to escape. Finding our way back in the dark is hard enough. Having a pyromancer on our heels is just madness."

"Not if we can distract him and escape."

"If we mess up, our sloppy exit will make us targets."

"Then what do we do?"

Olfric smirked. "We take the opportunity and go offensive right off the bat."

"I'm not going anywhere near that lance."

"Good for you. Neither am I."

"Then?" Maude asked.

"Wait and watch."

Olfric, standing with his feet firm against the ground in a familiar pose, extended his arms out, drawing on his kami's power to create a helical blade of pure water in front of him. Then came the next part.

Duplication.

The spell instilled within the helical water blade actualized, creating two—four—eight—sixteen—twenty copies all at once. This was the first time he was launching an attack with this much mana within it, but it was justified. Unlike a certain aeromancer he could name, Olfric was not interested in gauging his opponent's strength with controlled, weaker attacks.

The only good opponent was a dead one, his father often said. It was a mantra Olfric had internalized.

"Let's see him dodge this."

All twenty blades flew in spiral, uneven, non-intersecting trajectories that all aimed at the pyromancer in the middle. It didn't matter if the man was fast or had extreme reflexes, because that was where the second property of the blades came into effect.

By applying the chief characteristics of water, ebb and flow, Olfric could create untraceable paths for all copies of his helix blade and make them converge at the pyromancer.

The Cyffnarian, as expected, reacted. However, he could not dodge.

The first hit was a large gash against the man's right arm, severing the tendons. The second lacerated his lower abdomen, tearing through skin and muscles like a hot knife through butter. The final one slashed against his knee, breaking it. The Cyffnarian looked at him with shock and confusion, and his fiery lance exploded as a fourth blade hit him in the knuckles.

"Apologies," Olfric replied, tightly smiling. "It was nothing personal. You were simply at the wrong place at the wrong time." With those words, he turned away as the rest of his helix blades converged onto the pyromancer, throwing up a mist of red in the air.

Maude stared at the scene, slack jawed. "That—that was—"

"A MIS-TA-KE!"

Olfric whirled around, fists clenched, as he locked eyes with the source of the new voice. To his left stood a young girl of slender build, wrapped in what could loosely be called a kimono. She was pale-skinned and had long, flowing brown hair that fell all the way to her waist. Her voice had been less bremetan and more like someone dragging metal across glass.

But her strangest feature was the glowing sigil at the center of her forehead.

Olfric narrowed his eyes. Was she another Cyffnarian? Her attire did not give away such insignia. Perhaps she was part of the hired military, working with the pyromancer as a mercenary?

"Who are you?"

The mysterious girl glared daggers at him. "Asukan hurt him. Mizo hurt Asukan." A wave of power began to roll off her.

"I told you we should've run!" Maude hissed.

"Relax!" Olfric scoffed. He grabbed the water on the floor and yanked it in the girl's direction, reforging the water into thin needles midair. They pierced the girl in several vital areas—chest, neck, abdomen, knees, arms—and blood spurted out from each injury before the girl could even register what had just happened.

"As I said," Olfric replied, smiling. "I got this."

"NO!" the strange girl bellowed, a deathly aura exuding from her. "DEATH. GOT. YOU!"

Olfric's amusement quickly faded as the girl changed from bremetan to full-on demon. The first to appear were two ashen wings made entirely out of sharp bone, bursting out of her back. Her body grew from five feet to a towering seven, and her small arms bulked and darkened in color, appearing along with a set of thick, jagged claws. Her legs and chest expanded and rippled with powerful energies, while a thick, bone-plated tail jutted out from her back.

The bremetan-demon doubled down, going from a two-limbed rush to an animalistic four.

The mouth became a snout. Teeth became sharp canines. Nostrils became slits. Hair became a mane. And finally, her eyes gleamed a luminous silver, while the glowing sigil above her head began to display a sinister crimson sheen.

When Olfric took in the sight of several hundred pounds of angry-looking monster charging straight toward him, he did the only thing any reasonable person would have done.

He turned around and ran like hell.

With Maude right on his tail.

The demonic, transforming girl bellowed out a vicious, spitting growl and leaped in their direction, and all Olfric could feel was a growing sense of fear, disbelief, and desperation.

"I can't believe it!" Maude yelled. "A reiki? A fucking *reiki*?"

Olfric shakily bobbed his head, even as he ran. He'd heard stories about the monsters that roamed the Black Moon nights. Some believed them to be the vengeful spirits of the dead, intent on haunting their murderers into insanity, while others thought they were acolytes of dead gods possessing beasts to take revenge on the victors. The more superstitious lot referred to them as demons, ghosts, and even demon-ghosts, if such an inexplicable existence made sense.

It was why people stayed home during the Black Moon Rising, trusting the spiritual barriers empowered by their faith to hold up against the demons of the Mist.

"I knew we forgot something!" Maude gasped as she ran. "We're in the desert! During Black Moon Rising! Of *course* there would be reiki. Why didn't we plan for it?"

"Because they're supposed to be myths!"

"Reiki are yokai. Spiritual predators. Here in the desert, they're effectively immortal." She looked over her shoulder, and her eyes widened. "Does that still look like a *myth* to you?"

"Not anymo—MOVE!" Olfric yelled, throwing himself over Maude and covering them with a cocoon of water. The reiki soared over them and landed at the mouth of the tunnel, a good twenty feet ahead.

"Come on!" Olfric yelled. "We've got to move!"

Spiritual predators, he thought to himself as they ran in the other direction, the demon right behind them in pursuit. It meant the reiki had decades, or even centuries, of time to practice their skills. Even modest talents could grow fearsome teeth by then, never mind their practical experience. Even discounting their powers of possession, that thing would be a force to be reckoned with.

"Any ideas?" Olfric snarled. "That thing isn't slowing down at all!"

"It isn't a physical being," Maude quickly explained. "It won't tire or slow down! We've got to destroy its shell in one hit, then try to escape while it's reforming."

It was easier said than done. He was an aquamancer. Cutting, striking and taking physical damage were his strengths. Hammer blows weren't exactly his forté, and facing it head-on in combat would get him killed faster than he could say "unfair."

But that didn't mean he was helpless either. Far from it, in fact.

Olfric whirled around and faced the yokai. With a sweep of his palm, a thin jet of water shot forward like an arrow, puncturing through its right eye and tearing a nasty hole. Caught between shock, agony, and impairment of sight, the reiki faltered and crashed like a weathered metal can against the floor.

"Good, now let's escape!" Maude exclaimed, tugging on his sleeve as the reiki howled with rage.

"Not yet," he muttered, pulling out a small vial from his robes. It was filled with a fluorescent violet liquid. Taking the stopper off, Olfric conjured a sphere of water in his left palm and poured a single drop of the liquid into it. He watched with a grim smile as the whole orb of water turned a sickly purple shade, before corking the vial and stowing it away.

"What is that?" the naturopath asked hesitantly.

"Watch."

The orb shot forward at the demonic creature and splattered all over its form, seeping into its pores.

Then, the screams began.

"Poison. From the one-horned toad," Olfric eagerly explained. "A single drop can kill a mammoth."

"No . . ." Maude breathed out. "No that won't—"

The demon turned a hateful, murderous, one-eyed gaze onto him. Olfric watched with dawning horror as the wound from the punctured eye reformed, the mutilated tissues reknitting in place. Soon enough, a new eyeball was in its place, as if nothing ever happened. The hateful gaze doubled in intensity.

"Okay, that is just bullshit!" he snapped.

"It's a spiritual thing," she hissed fearfully. "It's using Metamancy. False construction. I told you, nothing but destroying its shell can do anything to it. We need to—*URKKK!*"

Maude lurched forward, bending at the waist as her legs remained frozen. Shock and disbelief overtook her as her jaw fell open, rivulets of drool falling from her lips. Thin cuts appeared over her face, crisscrossing each other to make illegible sigils that glowed crimson with her leaking blood. Two were on her cheeks next to her ears, two right beneath each eye, and one lay in the center of her forehead. All of them glowed eerily.

Then, the vanir sigils that adorned her shoulders, her waist, all the way up to her ankles . . .

They too began to glow.

"Maude . . ." Olfric started, reaching out a trembling hand. "Are you . . ."

"Like my friend said," Maude replied, her voice similar, yet *so* different. "Death. Got. *You.*"

A cold pit formed in his stomach. "Maude! Remember your gods! Shield yourself in faith! Fight it!"

"Fight?" Maude asked with sick amusement. "Why, I've never felt better in all my life!"

"No, that's what it wants you to think!"

Suddenly, the demonic reiki came slashing at him, and it was only his instincts and nimbleness that let him fling his body to the side. He was in a tight spot. Physically, he had no chance of seriously harming the creature, and he'd left his stash of Eternal Light torches in his bag with the others.

He rushed toward Maude, who glared back hungrily. Conjuring a pair of water whips, he cuffed her arms together, but she shattered through them like they were made of paper. A third watery tendril grabbed her by the ankles and tripped her, and Maude fell back, just in time for him to envelope her head with a sphere of water.

Olfric smirked, then turned to face the reiki. "Right, Tiny. It's your turn now."

And then, he let loose.

His kami, Shahxith, was what was called a marid. In simple terms, it embodied the elements of water and ether. The combination of both allowed Shahxith to exercise solidity in the otherwise fluid water element, allowing the creation of whips and constructs—solid enough to act as weapons, but fluid enough to flow and disintegrate at a thought.

Additionally, the ether element lent itself heavily to conjuration, letting Olfric gather tremendous amounts of water at will.

The floor shimmered brilliantly, right before an immense shower of water submerged it from above, creating a makeshift pool inside the chamber. The effort winded Olfric and dropped him to his knees. Casting a spell like that, with the desert outside, had been incredibly taxing on his reserves.

But it was worth it. For he was in a watery environment now. The rules had changed. He wouldn't need any more conjuration, not when he could get as much water as he wanted from the large pool. Besides, being exposed to water would increase his inner rejuvenation.

Circular logic? Perhaps. But circles were exactly what water was all about. Ebb and flow.

Olfric blitzed forward through the water as if he was sliding on it, then sent a quick succession of water bullets aimed for the creature's groin, then its eyes. The reiki slipped and fell, then tried to stand up, but it was all too easy to make it crash down on its own weight.

He laughed, before raising dozens of sharp watery blades into its face from the pool.

"That's a lesson for you," he casually remarked. "Don't take on an aquamancer in his element."

A wave of unseen force smashed into his back, sending him tumbling into the water face-first. His nose smashed against the rocky floor and began to seep red. Olfric tried to flip over, but it felt like someone had inserted a hot, metallic rod into his spine.

Damn! Must have fractured.

Gritting his teeth, he turned around carefully, and there was Maude, walking toward him with a lazy, confident sway in her hips. "Did you miss me?"

He could only groan. "I should have known that little bubble wouldn't hold you."

Maude laughed melodiously. It was a sound he'd never heard from her before. "Oh, Olfric . . . It was painfully clear you didn't want to kill me. Just enough to keep me distracted for a while. Once I stopped breathing and *I* took over, it was no problem at all."

Olfric twitched at her words. Just who was this entity? Maude or the—the other thing?

"If you're in there, Maude, then you won't want to hurt me. Fight it! We'll take you back to the Empire and you can be healed. You'll be free!"

"Healed?" the naturopath asked incredulously. "My whole life, I've desired freedom, and I spent every bit of it as someone's lap dog. Trestan Banksi, the emperor, and then . . . " She trailed off, her eyes shining with malice. "But things are *so much* different now! This—" Her face contorted, and then a spark of recognition made itself known. "This yurei is different. It has no goals, only instinct. Just a monster that wants to hunt down everything that enters its lair, and it wants *me* to do it. And I can do it however I want. Its Metamancy is mine to wield, and my own oaths hold me back no more. And you know what's the best part? *There is no ETERNAL LIGHT to trap me this time around!"*

She edged closer to him. "For the first time in my life, *I'm free!"*

With a roar of pure joy and bloodlust, she charged at him.

CHAPTER 31

BLOOD IN THE WATER

Tanya observed as Zuken Banksi poured whiskey into three paper cups, and she was a little sad that this wasn't the most surreal thing she'd seen all day.

"Don't worry," Zuken said reassuringly. "Maude will bring him back."

"Last I checked, Elena's the charmer in our group," Tanya countered.

And yet, despite the changeling's best efforts, the monsters in the anomaly were strangely fixated on her and wouldn't relent. As much as she hated to admit it, Olfric had a point. Even the shkroi hawks they'd used to travel seemed to hold a grudge against her. She didn't know if it was her past Sin or not that made these creatures behave strangely, but there had to be some connection. Something to do with her.

Zuken handed her a cup, then Elena one as well. "Not everything requires charming, Tanya. There is such a thing as reason and logic," he said, sipping at his whiskey as he eyed her carefully. "And so you know, I do agree with Olfric. Do you know why the monsters have taken a liking to you?"

Liking was not the word she would have used.

Tanya took a long drink, suppressing the urge to cough as the whiskey burned its way down her throat and gut. "Do we have to go through this again? Just throw me out of the group. I can manage."

"I know you can. Our little episode with reclaiming the camp is proof enough of that."

"Is that why you all keep staring at me when you think I'm not looking?"

Zuken silently sipped at his whiskey again.

Tanya shook her head. "I wasn't born yesterday. I've noticed the glances everyone sends my way. You, Elena, Maude. It's like you all think I'll turn into some bloodthirsty killing machine and slaughter you all the moment you're not looking." She drained her cup in one go. "But I don't blame you, I guess. You've read Olfric's testimony on how I butchered my old teammates."

"I did read it," Zuken confirmed casually, "and I found it quite illuminating, actually. Especially in light of more recent events."

Slowly, cautiously, she extended her senses out. She needed to know if he was laying a trap. "What is this about? You're having a change of plans? Have I become a liability now?"

The question brought a twinkle of amusement to his eyes. "Why would I do that? Employees of your caliber are difficult to come by. If anything, this mission should serve as a test for your future missions."

"Forgive me for not taking you at your word."

Zuken laughed. "A sensible precaution. But in the spirit of the conversation, can I ask you something?"

Tanya nodded.

"Why didn't you run?"

She regarded him blankly.

"You had ample time to escape when we were in the desert," he explained. "I'm a firsthand witness of your speed. You could have left us any moment, so why didn't you?"

Good question. Why hadn't she? It would've been nice to not have to deal with Olfric's temper tantrums. She wouldn't have to Sin yet again. She could travel through the desert and into the Eaborid Kingdom easily.

But she didn't.

"I guess . . . I just don't want to prove Olfric right. I'm not a betrayer."

"Admirable," Zuken praised. "There's just . . . one more thing I don't get."

She eyed him warily. "What is it now?"

"Was there really no better option than the life of a nomad, Tanya *Shimizu*?"

Tanya stilled. She did not panic. Panic was what got you killed. Endless options ran through her head—playing diplomacy with Zuken, killing him quickly with a wind blade, decapitating Elena and dumping their mutilated bodies for monsters to feed.

Tanya's face revealed nothing, but a part of her remained vigilant, ready to produce freshly materialized wind blades should the need arise. Another part of her calmly observed how Elena was watching her like a hawk. No doubt tapping into her surface emotions.

This meeting, this conversation over whiskey—it was a setup. Knowing Zuken, he had planned the entire thing from the start. Had he even planned on getting Olfric out the picture, with Maude following behind? Engineering a situation like this was exactly someone like Zuken's forte.

The question was—*why?*

With monumental effort, Tanya forced herself to relax, and exhaled slowly.

Zuken's expression turned to one of relief. "Good. I calculated a rather high chance of being immediately attacked. This makes things easier."

This time, Tanya actually growled. Here she was, ready to commit a grave Sin for these people, going out of her way to keep them out of danger, and this man was dangling the knowledge of her past in front of her.

"Where did you learn that name?" she asked.

"You're not going to deny it?"

She massaged the bridge of her nose. "Would it help?"

"No. Your reaction confirmed it."

Meanwhile, Elena sat straighter, her eyes drilling into her.

"And what do you want in exchange for keeping this a secret?" The words came out like the grunts of a chained animal. "Are you going to use this to blackmail me and make me commit even more Sins?"

Zuken's eyes studied her face. "I didn't lie to you about the employment offer. But I have questions. Lots of them. Chiefly, why are you living like this? Like a nomad, taking missions under the table, running from the Army? You realize what your heritage can give you, right?"

A small jerk of her head was all she was willing to give.

"I won't force you to reveal your intentions, but if we're to have any future business together, you're going to have to come clean with me."

"Why are *you* so interested in this?" Tanya demanded. "The Shim—that line is *dead*. Gone, and its heritage and future with it."

Someone screamed, interrupting the conversation. Tanya was almost grateful. She couldn't tell if it was a man or a woman, but it was high-pitched and desperate. Then there was the sound of something crashing against a wall, a frantic scream of something too harsh and too brassy to be bremetan, followed by a long, drawn-out howl.

Her eyes landed on Elena, who was staring in the direction where Olfric and Maude had walked out with barely concealed horror. Grabbing her waist bag, Tanya quickly sprinted into the tunnel, Zuken and Elena following swiftly behind.

Then she finally recognized the screaming.

It was Maude.

"Right! Elena yelled from behind. Tanya changed tracks and took the next turn.

Every instinct in her body urged her forward as a predatory territoriality arose within her. And with that came a distinct need for violence. To defend her territory, to defend those that were part of her team.

"There!" Zuken pointed out. Tanya took in the sight that lay before them.

The entire chamber was in ruins. One of the walls had crashed completely, and the floor was submerged in water. She spotted Olfric in one corner—fallen and bleeding, but otherwise defiant—while a creature pulled straight out of nightmares growled at him.

And there was Maude, in the middle of it all, coalescing power at her fingertips as her entire body glowed with strange, crimson sigils. And she was walking toward Olfric.

Tanya didn't stop to think. A wall of wind shimmered between Olfric and Maude, before rushing in Maude's direction and throwing her back. Two wide arcs of wind sliced the demon into three pieces, leaving behind a black-ish miasma that spread around the floor.

Two shafts of rock arose on either side of Maude, courtesy of Zuken, trapping both her wrists in them. The same quickly happened with her waist and ankles, holding her in place.

"What the hell is going on here?" Tanya demanded. Olfric's face drooped, and his body was unmoving.

"*Tanya*," Maude eerily whispered. "You always keep all the fun to yourself, don't you?" With an annoyed grunt, she shook the earthly bindings off of herself, like they were nothing but sand. The crimson sigils on her glowed ominously, and she was raised up, like invisible hands were pushing her from beneath.

"Maude . . ." Tanya staggered back. "What happened to you?"

The vanir barked out a laugh. "Me? It's simple. I was . . . *unleashed.*"

Maude charged forward, and Tanya met her lunge in earnest, her wind blades bearing the brunt of her lifeforce-enhanced arms. The force from the collision was enough to raise a gale around them. Tanya gritted her teeth, digging her feet in and releasing a burst of wind behind her for support. Swatting her arms aside, she stepped into Maude's guard, who swept back in at an angle Tanya hadn't anticipated and threw a closed fist at her chest.

Tanya grabbed it with one hand and conjured a wind blade in another, ready to impale through—

"NO! DON'T KILL HER!"

Elena's sudden shriek caught her by surprise. That proved to be her undoing as a haze of red filled the air.

It hadn't come from Maude.

One of Maude's fingers, now extended into a long, jagged, bony claw, had pierced through Tanya's chest.

"Hesitation will cost you." Maude let out a bone-chilling laugh as she kicked Tanya in the abdomen, sending her falling on her back. Her head was spinning, but this wasn't the time to lose focus. She could hear sounds of yelling and things smashing into each other. Gritting her teeth, she managed to open

a single eye and saw Zuken summoning rocks from the walls and hurling them toward Maude.

The vanir punched every single one of them to dust.

"Why are you doing this?" Zuken demanded, his wristbands glowing as he raised dozens of rocky slabs from different sides, sharpening them into spears midair, and launching them at the vanir. Maude crouched and swept her left leg in a semicircular arc, raising a wall of force to meet his projectiles.

What is happening? Tanya wondered. *Why is she—?*

Panic began to set in, and with it came lightheadedness and a rising thirst of lifeforce. If only—if only she had a little lifeforce to drink—

Her sight flickered to grayscale for a passing moment.

No! Tanya thought, her heart throbbing valiantly. She couldn't! She wouldn't give up, not when she had managed to keep it down for so long!

"Elena!" Zuken cried. "I'll keep her busy and join you later. Get Olfric and Tanya out of here!"

"Actually, I think I'll keep you here!"

And with that insolent, casual boast, *Olfric Bergott* stood up.

" . . . Impossible!" Tanya heard Zuken mutter.

"Olfric . . ." Elena whispered. "You . . . what?"

Olfric—if he was still Olfric—didn't exactly walk. In fact, he didn't appear to have moved at all. If anything, it was the blackened water that raised him up. Thin cuts formed on Olfric's handsome face, forming sigils similar to Maude's. Blood trickled through the cuts, emanating a malevolent, crimson glow.

"What . . . What am I looking at?" Zuken murmured.

"Zuken, we should retreat now!" Elena yelled.

"But you'll miss out on all the fun!" Olfric sang. Raising a hand, he directed the blackened water to smash through Zuken's trap, freeing Maude completely.

The vanir climbed out of it, spitting out sand from her mouth. "That—" she coughed, "was terrible!"

Tanya would have replied, had she not suddenly felt Olfric's gaze on her, as if nobody else in the world existed anymore. His manic smile only widened.

"They're possessed!" Elena whispered, her eyes frantically shifting from Maude to Olfric and back. "Olfric—Maude—they must be resisting it! We need to set them free! If you can hold them for some time, I can—I think I can—"

"You think?" Tanya bit out.

Elena glared at her. "Do you have a better idea?"

Tanya sighed. "Fine! But if we die, I'm blaming you."

"If you end up dying," Elena chirped, "I give you full permission to hate me."

Tanya chuckled and turned to face Olfric. "You couldn't defeat me even if I was blindfolded. Do you really think being possessed increases your chances?"

Olfric wiped the blood from his lips. *"Doesn't it? The 'me' of now is very different from the 'me' you terrified earlier, Tanya. Let's see how you fare!"*

Tanya smirked, dropping into a ready stance. "Come on then. Care to find out who the better killer is?"

Olfric pulled his greatsword from his back and charged at her.

Tanya slashed against his blow, sparks leaping from the clash of weapons and a tiny cut opening on her cheek despite her block, but she had little chance to do anything about it. Olfric's blade had already retreated and thrust again by the time she'd even registered she'd been wounded, then again, and again. The strikes kept coming so fast that they were nearly simultaneous. Only her keen battle instincts, compounded with her ability to sense the shifts in the air, kept her from being skewered.

Still, Tanya was trapped outside her effective range, forced onto the defensive, and being chipped down by dozens—maybe hundreds—of tiny cuts. Blood flowed down her legs, kept from pooling in her boots by her constantly moving feet. Each block took slightly more effort than the one before it.

She was losing. The smell of blood, of lifeforce, of *life*, was creating a distraction that was getting harder and harder to ignore.

She couldn't win. Not as she was.

But if she loosened her restraint just a little . . .

The wind blade in her hand became suddenly visible, now coated with dense hoarfrost, as a sliver of winter flooded her veins. A power as primal as the universe sang within her, a contained typhoon that could bring about the annihilation of everything, should it be let out. Tanya allowed it to gain a small opening, compressing the flow to the barest trickle.

It was little. Too little. A mockery of what she could have been.

But it was enough.

"Come." Tanya smiled.

Olfric yelled out a battle cry and struck her head on. His sword wedged itself into the flesh of her naked shoulder, as if she were a thick block of ice. Tanya contemptuously grabbed Olfric by his neck, snapping the hand that held the weapon. Olfric struggled, and his sigils glowed a sinister sheen, but the damage was done.

Lifeforce consumed—622

Two things happened right then.

The first was that Olfric threw his head back and opened his mouth to scream. His vocal chords tensed and his entire body convulsed like it was being electrocuted, but not a single sound came out of his lips.

The second, and more important, was the bright, bluish sheen that erupted out of his back. The ethereal creature merged with the water below. Before she knew it, a strange turbulence erupted amidst the water in the shape of a four-legged creature and dashed out of the chamber.

Olfric sagged down to the ground, senseless.

Silence rang in the entire chamber.

It was then that she realized that everyone—Zuken, Elena, and even Maude—was staring at her. Especially Maude. She looked like she'd seen a ghost. It wasn't *fear* that flickered all across her face, but a strange familiarity mixed with disbelief. For a moment, Tanya had this feeling that Maude wanted to *tell* her something, but Zuken broke the silence right then.

" . . . Tanya?" he ventured. "You . . . you're okay, right?"

Of course she was okay. She'd just fed on lifeforce. Now she could heal her wounds back. What could possibly be wrong with her?

"I'm fine!" she replied, pulling Olfric up from the ground and dragging his nigh unconscious form across the wet floor. She grabbed him by his chin and made him face Elena.

"It won't work!" Maude replied, her maniacal personality now absent. "*We* cannot be undone! We are what we are! Already his kami has deserted him and escaped! There is nothing you can do. *Leave* this place," she said, her voice almost soft. "If you want to live, leave and don't come back."

"That was a quick change in tone," Zuken threw back. "What happened? Don't like your odds anymore?"

"You want to try your luck? Then do so. But he's *gone*. You can't get him back. Not now. Not ever!"

Tanya glanced at Elena, who didn't look the slightest bit intimidated.

"We'll take our chances!" the changeling bellowed.

Maude began to coalesce power around her. Zuken did the same. "Do what you have to do," he said. "I'll hold her off."

Elena nodded and crossed her arms across her chest, her fingers paused in a particular hand gesture, as if symbolizing something. Then, she slowly uncrossed them, both hands parallel to each other. Despite the simplicity behind the gesture, Tanya felt a weird sensation of a lock opening. Whatever the changeling was trying to do, it was clear she was channeling a power she kept leashed away from the world.

A spiritual beast?

"*Shokan!*" Elena snapped, and something small and pulsating manifested in front of her. It was fairly anthropoidal with a squid-like head and a face ending with a mass of feelers. The thing, with its bright eyes, emanated a sudden, strange, utterly *alien* malignancy that made her shiver.

But she didn't stop staring.

And staring.

And staring.

—A blur of images, both strange and nauseating, sandblasted against her psyche. She felt her limbs go numb as she leaned back and floated across an endless ocean. She could sense other creatures, writhing in obscene embraces on the ocean floor, amid broken columns and ancient statues of things that somehow seemed to bend themselves into more than three dimensions. Sensations flared through her thoughts, so absolutely alien to anything bremetan that it may as well have been pure agony—

She thought she saw something dark and gray erupt out of Olfric's form.

But she kept on staring.

And staring—

—would be there when the world would stop moving. When the frigid tundra would howl and howl and nothing save the meanest glimmer of potential would be left behind, only to be gobbled by—

Tanya heard a shrill noise. Her throat vibrated. It took a minute to put two and two together.

She was screaming. She couldn't stop.

She couldn't stop.

She COULDN'T STOP! SHE COULDN'T STOP! SHE COULDN'T—

Her arms moved by their own accord. Elena, Zuken, Olfric—all three of them were lifted by a gale of rushing wind and swept out of the chamber, before a second wave struck, caving the ceiling between them.

Leaving her all alone with the yokai.

"Tanya . . ." Maude murmured. "You're—"

"It's been quite some time since I've had a good feast," Tanya replied, slowly standing up from the floor. "I'd hate for you to disappoint me, Maude."

And then, her eyes shifted to a glacial white.

CHAPTER 32

WINTER IN MY BLOOD

Nausea, vertigo, and an unbearable feeling of intrusion stirred her from her slumber.

"Ah, she's waking up!"

"About damn time," came another unfamiliar voice. "Just look at her. We hit it big, alright. She's gon' be worth a ton!"

"We're not selling her!" the first voice cracked across the room like a whip. "We had a deal."

Thirteen-year-old Tanya blearily opened her eyes, the ominous words piercing through the haze of fatigue that fogged her mind, only to be replaced by an even more horrifying realization. She didn't know where she was. She didn't know who she was with. She couldn't see anything.

What was going on?

She tried to move but only chafed her own wrists in the process. Forcefully calming herself, Tanya reanalyzed her situation. She was immobilized by chains, and blindfolded to take away her most precious sense.

Despite all her training, it took all her might simply to not break down into sobs. Tales of thugs kidnapping nobles only to do heinous things to them flitted through her mind, each scenario more gruesome than the last. While Tanya had been warned of the cruelty of the outside world, she had never expected something like this to happen to her.

Her manacles clinked.

Still, she wasn't completely helpless. They had taken her sight and limited her touch, but Tanya was more than that.

She was the Shimizu heir. She was the future wielder of the mighty Ezzeron.

She had lifeforce. Far more than any of these thugs could ever imagine in their miserable lives.

Composing herself, she dug deep into the power she'd been born with, and the familiar feeling flooded through her veins. She did not have a kami. Not because she was weak, but because she didn't need one.

Lifeforce flowed through her like a tide—

And then . . . died.

The manacles clinked.

Tanya tried again, only to suffer the same results. Then again, and again, and again and again and again. Every time she tried using lifeforce, something snatched away her control and returned the wave of power to the well from where it came. It was almost as if—

"Look 'ere, lads! The lass seems like she's figured it out!"

"What have you done to me?" Tanya asked, unable to mask her anxiety, if the wobble in her voice was any indication.

"It won't work," the first voice interrupted amusedly. "Those manacles are specially made. They won't let you use lifeforce, little Shimizu princess. But don't just take my word for it."

Furious and filled with disbelief, Tanya focused even harder and tried again—

But nothing answered her call. Just like the man had said.

"Silly little girl." The man cruelly laughed. "Did you really think we weren't prepared for something so simple? Even if you had a kami to summon, it still wouldn't work."

"Just—" She grunted, struggling against her binds. "Let me go!"

"No can do, lass," the second voice replied. "Yer a princess. Ye'll fetch us a good deal when I send ye all wrapped up to our customers. Those desert-dwellers know their shit, I suppose—"

Tanya stilled. Desert-dwellers? No one lived in the desert. You couldn't. It was anathema, and the source of endless horror tales.

"Shut your mouth!" the first cried out in alarm, attracting her attention. "You'll rat us out!"

"Bah!" the second sneered. "As if this li'l lass can do anything 'cept cry!"

Tanya gritted her teeth, her helplessness only amplified by the man's callous words. She tried ripping the chains apart again, but to no avail. What was happening? Why couldn't she just tear through the bindings?

She made a third attempt, but still nothing. It was like her connection to her own lifeforce had been muted. But how? The growing pit of despair in her stomach lurched as cold, heartless laughter reverberated throughout the chamber.

"What? Ya done already? Don'tcha have some fight left in ya? Man, givin' up so easy . . . what're they even feedin' nobles these days?"

"Please," Tanya finally sobbed. "Just let me go."

It hurt. Shimizu didn't beg—her father had taught her that. And yet here she was, a proud princess begging her captors. Begging these vile dogs for mercy. To be simply left alone.

The sound of footsteps grew louder, followed by another vile laugh. Tanya moved back instinctively, as much as her bonds would allow. "Don't—don't touch me!"

"Are ya scared, li'l lass? Frightened?"

A cold, sticky palm caressed her face, before a sudden burst of light caused her to blink rapidly. A moment later, the blurry face of a middle-aged man swam into focus, a thin black strip of cloth held in his right hand.

"That's the best part, ya know." He grinned cruelly. "The fear, I mean."

Tears began to track down her cheeks as she cried. Loudly.

"Oi, Tauren! Make her shut up!"

The man in front of her—Tauren—snickered. Gripping her arm tightly, he pulled her up until she was at eye-level and—

SLAP!

Tanya was sent tumbling to the floor, reeling in pain as warm, sticky blood filled her mouth.

"Not so great, are ya now, huh? Ya nobles think yer so fuckin' great? That e'ryone else exists to be yer fuckin' dogs? Do ya even see us as people?"

Tanya felt a sharp pain in her stomach as the man casually rammed his boot into it.

"Well, do ya?" he asked, raising his voice. "Answer me!"

But she didn't answer. Overcome by fear and pain, all she could do was curl up into a ball and cry harder. The man continued kicking her—not hard enough to cause permanent damage, but enough to cause pain and, more importantly, humiliation.

But then, something deep within her stirred.

The pain began to fade. Sensation began to fade. And something cold began to rise.

With that cold came the numbness. The fear, the anxiety, the anger . . . it all simply vanished. All that remained was ice-cold logic. The absolute knowledge that the garbage in front of her was nothing more than—

Food.

"Oi, what in the hell's happenin'? Her mana levels, her eyes! I thought ye sealed—"

CRUNCH!

A long, jagged spear of ice tore through his body like wet paper. Tanya watched in fascination as the ice slowly covered his body, the glimmer in his eyes slowly transitioning from surprise to fear to resignation, to nothing.

Killing him had been . . . surprisingly easy.

Distantly, she could make out the sound of something metallic shattering.

But Tanya didn't care. Rubbing her arms, she turned toward the rest of the men as their remaining companions all rushed into the room at once.

"You—you killed him!"

Her lips spread into a gentle smile.

"Yes. I did."

She raised her hand and called it forth. It needed no training, nor any additional knowledge on how to be used. The ice responded to her like a memory, like something she had always known how to use, simply waiting to be called upon once more.

Before the men in front of her could so much as twitch, ice spears tore through their stomachs and out their backs. But she was more careful this time. Instead of freezing them all at once, she held herself back. This time, it would be slower . . . more painful . . .

"No—wait—you don't—"

"Shhhh . . . " Tanya softly chuckled, her palm caressing the closest man's cheek. A moment later, he became immobilized as frost danced across her palm and onto his face. He was unable to do anything but suffer from torturous cold as his very life essence was drained to feed her hunger.

Feed her Frost.

"M—monster," another gasped, drawing her attention.

Once more, she gently smiled.

"Yes. I am."

Alluring white eyes snapped open in the darkness. The cold soon followed.

Tanya did not try to force it. She might as well try forcing a river into submission. No, she had to surrender to its current and use its inherent motion to one's advantage.

Plus, it wasn't just *any* power. It was Frost. A bitter chill so frigid, so *cold* that it would trickle away all life that came under its domain. It was the embodiment of the absence of heat. This was her power, and she had used it time and time before. It had answered when nothing else had.

But this time, it was different.

Before, she'd kept it suppressed to the best of her ability in the depths of her mind, ignoring its cries of impotent fury. The presence of Eternal Light kept it weak, which was why she had never deserted the Empire despite her utter contempt for the Asukan gods and society.

But not anymore.

For the Eternal Light was not present in the Namzuuhuu Desert.

And in the skies above, the Black Moon rose, ascending to the Central Sky.

"Oh, I've missed *this!*" Tanya exclaimed, stretching her hands and body. "Life feels best in the flesh!"

She shrugged off the jacket and undid the top button of her sleeveless shirt, tossing the former away. Stretching and yawning, she felt her limbs. Felt her own supple skin. Felt the bones and the muscles stretching as she twisted her body in near-impossible ways.

Power filled her mind, and her inhibitions slowly washed away. It was a power she hated using, yet paradoxically, she loved the loss of control it brought forth.

How could she have ever hated something that felt *so* good?

The grayish spirit from before had merged with the water below to forge a temporary physical shell. Beside her, the vanir crouched low as she prepared for attack.

"Oh right! The possessed *vanir*. I nearly forgot about you." Tanya chuckled mirthfully, completely indifferent to the creatures in her presence. "Let's see now . . . Yes, I think I remember. Honestly, being stuck in that uppity regular mindset is so boring. Why do I even do that?"

A furious voice filled the air, shaking the cavern walls as the spirit thrust a watery arm, thick as a trunk, right at her face and—

The arm froze.

Into frost.

And fell down to the floor. Shattering into a thousand fragments.

"Naughty! Naughty!" Tanya wiggled a finger at it.

The vanir dashed toward her in a burst of power, throwing a lifeforce-enhanced punch at her face. It had enough power to destroy half a dozen walls. But Tanya simply caught it with her palms, and her fingers gripped it tightly. "Try something *other* than lifeforce when you strike me," she said, her eyes glinting.

And then, she drained the lifeforce from her arm.

Lifeforce Absorbed: 729

"That won't do!" She frowned. "I need more. *More*. Real food. What was I thinking? Staying without *real food* for all this time?" She cupped her chin with her hand. "No matter. Surely in this vast anomaly there must be—*QUIT SQUIRMING FOR A MOMENT! I'M THINKING HERE!*"

With a casual twist, she broke the vanir's wrist before letting it go. The soft sound of the bones fracturing sounded like music to her ears. Whimpering, the vanir retracted her steps until she was standing behind the kami.

"Who—*what* are you?" she asked.

"You don't recognize me?" Tanya asked back, feigning hurt. "I'm *Tanya*, of course. Who else would I be?"

"Tanya is not—not this—"

That made her smile. "So . . . you do know me, don't you? Is that you, Maude? I'd have thought it was the other. How very interesting!"

The vanir took a step back.

"You feel it, don't you? The power? The *cold*? Does your vanir instinct tell you to flee? What is that little parasite whispering in your ears? But don't you worry!" Tanya waved it off. "It wouldn't matter. We're in an anomaly! Away from the accursed Light! And I can sense the Black Moon too. Plus, so much food. What a *wonderful* time to be liberated!"

Her hands moved up. Inviting. Welcoming. The dark feeling inundated her, permeating her with its very presence. Every bit of ice, every bit of chill, every shard of it was an extension of herself.

Her lips quivered, and words came out.

"Ice is my soul."

The floor beneath her feet suddenly turned white as jagged lines began to appear, giving the appearance that all the world was made of glass that had suddenly shattered. The lines didn't stop, and instead raced away from her stationary form in every direction, spreading up and around the intersection itself in three dimensions. The air around her grew thick, replacing dust with icy mist.

"Everfrost."

Frost erupted from the floor, morphing from mere white lines to sheets of ice. It extended, stretching between each of the previous lines and thickening, coating everything in nearly inch-thick sheets of frozen shelling. The ice erupted in spots, forming enormous stalagmites and stalactites, teeth-like daggers of the element swelling and erupting with violent force. It only lasted a handful of moments, but in those seconds the world changed from the dusty confines of an underground cavern to a scene straight out of an ice age.

The walls of the cavern shook violently, and a thin fracture began to develop on the walls from three sides. Tanya tilted her head, casually watching as the walls moved apart, allowing monsters, dozens of them, to spill forth. Spiders, rats, giant lizards, serpentine creatures that could gobble a human whole, sludge-like goo slowly trickling down the walls—

They were coming.

They were coming for her.

"How flattering!" Tanya squealed. "Now that's what I call a good feast!"

She flicked both wrists, and twin swords of frost erupted out of the floor, snugly fitting into her hands.

She looked back ahead but found the little kami missing. As was the vanir. Tanya reminded herself that she had to *catch* the little water-type. Not for herself though. It held power, but it wasn't compatible. Besides . . . Ezzeron would mind.

But she had promised the others. She'd find it. And maybe, if she was in the mood, save the vanir and not kill it.

But only after she had had some quality food. Wiggling two fingers, she gestured toward the horde of monsters surrounding her.

"Come."

And *everything* attacked.

The skirmishes happened as rapidly as they ended. With a swoosh here and a splat there, tentacles continued to fall off. Heads began to roll. Body organs were pierced. A foot-thick endoskeleton fared no better than formless ghol as her frost blades hacked into the enemy, cutting through everything with nigh-impossible ease.

"HAAA!" Tanya yelled as her blades cut deep, slashing one of the creatures' abdomens in half. Another blade dug into its spine. Thick shafts of jagged ice erupted from the floor, impaling half a dozen monsters from the bottom.

It was a rain of falling limbs.

A shower of blood.

Tanya did not care. She simply exhaled and moved to her next prey.

Pinpoint precision. Hammer blows. Frost that tore through metal and muscle with equal dexterity. Wind that decapitated creatures before they knew it.

+3670 Experience Gathered
You have reached Level 18

Useless, Tanya thought. As if such *paltry* things were worth her time.

Lifeforce Absorbed: 6277

That brought her to a pause.

Not bad, she mused. *Not bad at all.*

A cold, hungry laugh escaped her throat as every remaining monster in her vicinity hesitated.

That was when she felt . . . *it.*

A presence. Not her own. But powerful. Intriguing. Stalking its way through this nest full of prey. Something that she wanted to subdue and claim for herself. The cold rhythm of battle logic clamped down on any wayward hint of emotion as all thoughts unrelated to combat were shunted aside.

Compartmentalization was key.

And the decision was made. She'd get through his pointless rabble first. She'd kill them all. Then she'd find this new presence. She'd make it *hers.*

The rabble charged altogether in some blind hope. As if they could even dream of overpowering her.

She flipped her golden curls.

The massacre continued.

INTERLUDE III

TWISTED SOUL

It scraped across the wooden floor like the clawed feet of mice scrambling across boards—though far larger than any mouse had a right to be—as it disturbed the peaceful silence of night. Moonlight slipped through the blinds, throwing bands of light across an otherwise darkened room, illuminating the various articles of clothing littering the floor. In one corner, across from the bedroom closet, sat the large bed Tanya had all to herself.

Her room. Her bed. Hers.

But tonight, it all felt alien.

Ever since her kidnapping by the hands of those thugs, Tanya hadn't gotten an ounce of sound sleep. Every time the fifteen-year-old closed her eyes, something dark and unseen crept its way into the depths of her dreams.

And tonight was no exception.

Scuttle

"Hello?" she whispered, her voice laden with fear.

Nothing answered, but the moonlight continued to make odd shadows dance across her room.

Scuttle

"Is—is anyone there?" she whispered again, mustering a little more courage into her weakened voice. She didn't know what made her feel so . . . insecure and afraid. She was the Shimizu heir, a prodigy, and a talented user of lifeforce. Even without a kami, she was perfectly able to fend for herself.

But the kidnapping had struck a severe blow to her confidence.

And there was also that . . . thing.

Scrape

"There's no use hiding. I can hear you. I know you're there." She tried to sound brave, but the nervous quiver in her voice betrayed her. "Come out now, and I won't *be mad." Her eyes cast another glance around the room, as if trying to pierce through the darkness. "I promise."*

Once again, Tanya was met with nothing but palpable silence.

She warily watched the edge of her bed, ready for anything to appear, but when nothing happened, she knew she was the one who had to make the first move. Swallowing nervously, she crawled on her hands and knees, making her way forward. She had barely lowered her head enough to look into the pitch-black darkness beneath—

"I am not under the bed, young one."

The voice came as a thin whisper, right next to her ear. Tanya could feel something cold breathing down her neck, and she shrieked loudly, before losing her balance and falling headfirst onto the cold wooden floor. Lifeforce flooded into her arms and legs and her instincts kicked in.

"Who—whoever you are, don't come near me!" Tanya warbled. "I'll—I'll kill—"

"Of course you will, youngling. That is what you're born to be."

Scuttle

Managing to limit her reaction to the barest of flinches, Tanya flooded her palm with lifeforce. It glowed with a familiar blue light, one of the easiest tricks her father had taught her with the esoteric power.

What wasn't familiar to her, however, was the eerie coldness that accompanied it. She couldn't help but shiver as the strange voice laughed in the darkness.

What was happening?

"Stop laughing!" Tanya yelled, no longer holding back her tears. "Who—whoever you are, stop playing your dirty tricks with me."

"Oh, but I am not, youngling."

She had long ago learned about the spirits that roamed the lands during the Black Moon Rising. Things that the wards of their homes kept them safe from. Wraiths, spirits, monsters of the vilest kind that made people's skins crawl by mere mention of their name.

"Listen," she intoned, putting on a brave face despite the wetness of her cheeks. "My father is very strong. He'll kill you no matter what you are. So if you want to live, come out and face me!"

A brief silence followed the declaration, before it was broken.

"If you insist."

Nothing happened.

". . . Where are you?"

She felt a strange pressure on her skin from her left. Tanya turned but found nothing except the ornate mirror on the edge of the bed.

"Come closer."

She didn't know why, but she crawled across the bed. Until she was right in front of the mirror.

That was when Tanya saw it.

Frost.

Spikes of ice jutted out from "her" right hand, coating the bed with sheets of dense hoarfrost. Tanya squealed and looked at her own hand, and found nothing. She looked back into the mirror. The frost was slowly climbing up her reflection's entire right arm, like rings of thorns coiled around the stem of a rose, contorted in random meandering patterns. Jagged barbs, their chilling surfaces serrated like the edge of a knife, sat in rows across her skin. First her breasts, then her abdomen, her left shoulder and left hand, until her reflection appeared to be encrusted in frost.

"This is—this is—an illusion," Tanya screamed, pushing herself back, touching her own skin. Everything felt normal. She glanced at the mirror again.

Glacial white eyes met oceanic blue.

"An illusion. That's what this is," she repeated. "YOU HEAR ME? I'M NOT AFRAID OF YOUR ILLUSION. I'M NOT AFRAID—"

Hoarfrost erupted out of her fingernails, coating them in white.

"LOOK AT ME!"

The command in that voice was so overwhelming that Tanya couldn't fight it. Her entire body was shaking, her heart beating a million times a minute. Every bit of her instincts screamed at her to run away. To her father. To the elders. Someone. Anyone. They'd take care of this frost. Of this—of this—

Slowly, cautiously, she trudged toward the mirror.

She'd face it.

Face her distorted reflection.

Face her—

Wait. Where did she go?

The mirror was empty. There was no reflection. Nothing. It was as if she wasn't standing in front of the mirror at all. It was like—

"Looking for me?"

Tanya whirled around and looked up.

The creature in front of her looked absolutely fiendish, with two bulbous, blue eyes staring right at her. Tanya felt like she was sitting in the nude with the way its gaze stared right through her, as if it looked beyond her outer skin and flesh right at her soul.

A pair of sharp, ivory fangs showed themselves next.

Its arms were too large for its misshapen body.

Its hands were too large for its gargantuan arms.

It was . . . this was . . . a nightmare made manifest.

It was Frost.

And it had come for her.

"You—" Tanya pointed an erratically shaking finger toward it. "You're a monster."

"Yes," the monster replied. "And you are me."

PART VI

BATTLEGROUND

CHAPTER 33

NATURE OF THE BEAST

The first time Lukas opened his eyes, he was blinded. Everything felt too white. It felt quite jarring to his senses and he closed his eyes. He spent a few minutes feeling his body for any injuries before opening his eyes again. This time he found the familiar darkness awaiting him, with the green bioluminescence upon the walls—a sight he had gotten used to seeing.

"Back to the world of living, I guess . . ." he murmured. For better or worse, his pain seemed to lessen. There was an ever-constant throbbing on the left side of his head, right above the ear, but nothing he couldn't deal with. His fingers slowly traced along his stomach, trying to feel the wounds that should have been there.

They weren't.

He tried to move his right leg, inwardly preparing himself to feel jolts of pain from broken bones. He felt his chest, and around his neck. His fingers quested out and touched the pendant there, just as solid and unbreakable as he remembered. There was no laceration in his arm either.

Everything seemed fine. It was as if he hadn't been hurt at all.

"It is not complicated, mortal," Inanna murmured in his ear. **"I saved your life."**

Lukas blinked. Something was wrong with that statement. "You—" It hurt to speak. "You saved my life?"

"Yes."

" . . . Why?"

Genuine amusement flooded through him. **"Is that how you humans react upon being saved? Questioning your savior?"**

"But you don't do anything for free."

"It was not, as you said, for *free,*" Inanna chided. **"Do you not remember your last words?"**

Prey found you.

Lukas was barely able to open his eyes when—
PAIN!

It came from three different strikes, all at once, and lashed against his body. The first slashed at his right arm, severing his biceps in half. The second came at his abdomen, tearing through the skin and muscles like a hot knife through butter. The final one slashed against his knee. It was probably his luck that it hit his knee, fracturing it. Had it hit muscle, he would have been devoid of a leg.

Three strikes in one go. There was no time to react. There was no rage, no question, nothing, just pain, pain, and endless pain. A reddish shade engulfed his mind, much like the blood spurting out of his body, and Lukas let out an agonized whimper . . .

"Help . . . me . . . "

The only thing he could see through the reddish hue was the tall, hawk-faced man with dark brown hair.

"I asked you to save me?"

"You did."

Her words took the wind out of his sails. Lukas pushed himself up straight, stretching tiredly. If this went on, he might as well just give up in his attempts to secure his independence and accept her offer.

"It would certainly do away with having to keep track of every favor you owe me."

And wasn't that true? Apart from the hilariously suicidal task of finding Ereshkigal's domain, sneaking into it and acquiring Inanna's trapped form—a job that would likely cost him the remainder of his life—he was also obligated to allow her to perform a spell, of her choice, at a time of her choice. And last but not least, he was obligated to channel the power of the core of this Crypt of Fiendish Worms into the pendant.

Assuming he managed to do that in the first place.

Yeah, he was right in not wasting time on a five-year plan.

"How did you do it this time though?" he asked, pushing himself up. "Alleviation again?"

Inanna said nothing. After all, why use words when silence would suffice?

His mind went back to that lethal experience—the pain assaulting his nerves, the mental breakdown from all that agony all at once. He remembered that image—the brown-haired man with a hawk-like face. And finally that attack . . .

He shivered.

Just who the hell *was* that guy? And why had he attacked him out of nowhere?

"There is something you would find interesting," the goddess remarked. **"You were attacked with *water*. More specifically, helical blades crafted out of it, moving in random trajectories and converging upon you. Given the level of damage, the pressure had to be significant."**

Lukas scowled. He knew where this was going. He could use a *fire whip*, but that involved Fire Manipulation and Temperature Modulation. Fire was a dangerous thing on its own without needing to involve the pressure component in its equation. And while he did mold lifeforce into specific shapes during combat, just Raw Lifeforce Manipulation skill had been more than enough for that.

But water was different. Water required *pressure*, not temperature. Though if he could apply the Temperature Modulation skill to water to make it scalding hot, the effect would be twice as dangerous. That, or perhaps cool it to *ice?* Water was a fluid medium and most susceptible to changing forms.

His fists clenched. "Think it was a yokai that attacked me?"

"Unlikely, considering how your protectors attacked this individual."

That took him by surprise.

" . . . Protectors?"

"The ether crafter from before. And the creature that brought you meals."

Malon and Mizo, Lukas remembered. The ones Solana had offered to send with him. No wonder the two of them had maintained their distance from him. But that would mean—

"They observed you battling the monsters. Gaining skills. Becoming . . . more."

"Huh," he said, cleaning his left ear with his pinky. "Well, can't say I didn't see that coming. At least they can't see my Soulscape. Or you, for that matter."

"But they can hear you talk. To yourself. A lot."

"Considering the alternative, being thought of as crazy is the least of my issues."

He had the sneakiest suspicion that the goddess wanted to tell him something, to point out a flaw in his otherwise impeccable logic, but had decided otherwise.

"Who do you think that guy was?" he asked. If he wasn't a yokai, then perhaps one of those Asukans? Bremetans? Whatever. Perhaps one of those with a *kami?*

It was definitely within the realms of possibility. The yokai captured bremetan soldiers that came close to their territory. It was not impossible to believe that these kami-wielders were also present inside this anomaly. Though why anyone from that crowd would want to attack him was beyond him at the moment. Still, it was a phenomenal offensive technique, one that could be his if he could chance upon a water-type kami.

"You are allowing your greed to take over again, mortal," the goddess chided. **"If anything, this experience alone should tell you what you truly need."**

And wasn't that true? His skills had rapidly expanded in a multitude of directions, and while it had brought versatility and unpredictability to his arsenal, he had attained it through sacrifice of potential mastery of selective skills.

"I did not reach the zenith of Kinetomancy by grabbing at everything I could. I took *one* path and walked."

Her words had merit. Specialization was always the key to growth, even in terms of humanity. Lawyers, doctors, scientists, bankers—none of them reached the zenith of their profession by reaching out to everything, but chose a way and focused on it forward.

But that doesn't apply to me, Lukas found himself thinking. *I'm not an individual, but a World. The greater the variety, the greater I'll be. Adding souls to my unlimited array of prototypes, all of them part of the greater whole that is me. I will give rise to an endless number of species. I'll see them grow, see them populate and reach new zeniths of potential. With their rise, I shall ascend into the brightest star, no matter what some chisel-jawed pretty goddess was going to—*

He closed his eyes out of frustration. Hunger, growth, expansion—none of that was him. That was the omphalos talking through him.

"Sorry," he muttered sullenly.

To his luck, Inanna hadn't reacted in any way, to his thoughts, or his anger, or his apology. She just studied him. **"I wish to impart advice to you. I am not trying to make you do anything, but you need to hear it."**

" . . . I'm listening."

"I am a predator, as are you. We prey on the weak, and those that are stronger prey on you. No one is free from this cycle. Not gods, not demons, not beasts, no one. It is the nature of life. The stronger you get, the more specialized you get, the lesser the chances of you being preyed upon."

"I understand."

"Anomalies, on the other hand, are *worlds*. Creators. Givers. Makers. They hold the Mud of Creation and give birth to it. No one, god or not, can compare even to the smallest anomaly, when it comes to the aspect of Creation. The better it gets at creating greater and more complex life-forms, the quicker it ascends."

Lukas frowned. "I already know this."

"Do you? Because you've certainly not noticed what you're becoming."

"What do you mean?"

"You are Lukas Aguilar. An individual. A predator. You are also an anomaly of Lostbelt Earth. A creator. A maker. What you do not recognize

is that somewhere along your journey to become *more*, you are embodying aspects of both, and not necessarily in a positive way."

His blood ran cold. "I'm not."

"You *are*. You strive for growth, but by *usurping* from others. You want to create, but want to *grab* useful skills first to create better prototypes. Not to become a master of creation, but to create a better, well-equipped arsenal that would aid you to usurp more. An *invader*."

Lukas didn't want her words to be true.

"Going into denial isn't going to help. I have seen how you justify things. You look at it as an anomaly when it serves your benefit, and revert to the human approach when it doesn't."

"You think I'll turn into some mindless beast that will keep killing and consuming everything in my sight?"

"Yes," she said unrepentantly. **"If you do not recognize what motivates you and control it, you will. Perhaps not today, perhaps not tomorrow. But eventually. If you ignore your instincts, they will catch you off guard. And when they do . . ."**

Lukas silently frowned at the floor. "I've . . . been messing things up, haven't I?"

"That is the nature of the beast," Inanna softly replied. **"We all create our own demons. I became a butcher of gods and demigods and entire pantheons. It is possible it was because, somewhere along the line, I gave in to my instincts. The core concept that drives me."**

"Which is?"

"*Desire*."

Desire? "A desire for what?"

Her voice lowered to an icy whisper. **"*Everything*. The good, the bad. Power and prejudice. To rule over the heavens, yet commit the worst sins. Desire. Lust. Depredation."**

Lukas could relate to that. While not as broad as her vision, he had often felt something similar on an anomaly level. To have an *unlimited array of monsters* . . . to create them, breed them, *manufacture* newer and deadlier and more sophisticated creatures and *expand* outward until the entire *realm was his own and—*

He bit his tongue. The sudden jolt of pain broke him from the line of thought.

"You feel it, do you not? You relish the concept of owning everything. Of invading. Bringing everything unto yourself. This nature of yours is what makes me believe how well you would serve under me. My nature resonates with yours. My goal aligns with your ambition. Together, we could be *unstoppable*. All you need to do is . . ."

"Accept your offer."

She nodded. **"Give up this foolish stubbornness. Preserve your life. Your rationality. Taste power like none you've ever known."** Her voice was a narcotic promise. **"There is much I can teach you."**

There was no retort this time around. No jesting or pop-culture reference to show how useless her sales tactic was. Instead, there was this little voice inside him that wanted to throw the rules away, stop trying to be responsible, and just *take* what he wanted.

For a passing moment, he wondered what it might feel like to accept her offer.

Inanna was a goddess. She had access to skills that would take a lifetime to acquire, provided he managed to live that long. He already owed her a considerable number of debts, and given how things were progressing, it would only increase with time. But if he gave in and accepted her offer, he wouldn't have to worry about it any longer. She would teach him *everything* he needed. She'd make him strong. She'd—

Be out of my reach.

Somewhere at the very bottom of his heart, there was this mad desire to *have* her. She was the most sensual thing he had ever chanced upon, and their daily interactions had only *doubled* that primal need. He had kept his urges down, but if he accepted it, if he *accepted* her employment, he'd be subservient to her. He'd—

He'd—

No. A primal fury rose through his heart. That would not do. Why would he want to be subservient? He was a World. She was a goddess. A pinnacle of Potential. She belonged to him, not the other—

"My, my." Inanna let out a low, throaty laugh. **"What a greedy one you are."**

Lukas struggled to control the flow of his thoughts. "I—"

"I will not make you apologize," said the goddess. **"Let this be another portent of what you are becoming. Not long ago, you stood on this very ground, skeptical about my very existence. Now you not only accept me, but also want to make me *yours*."**

"You also told me to open my eyes and evolve, and now I have to constrict myself to a singular path?"

"For your own benefit."

"As an individual, not an anomaly," Lukas fired back. "I might not be the sharpest tool in the shed, but even *I* can see this. You can dominate over me, as a *person*. But as an anomaly? A World? Not so much. That's why you need my word to enact things. That's why you commit these *bargains*."

"You would choose to put your trust in a mindless schema over me?" Inanna probed.

"It's not about trust. No matter which way you slice it, you're using me, as is this omphalos inside me. The only difference is, you can manipulate one aspect of me, while the omphalos chooses the other. And I have to live with both. I can't throw the omphalos in me out, just as my heart won't allow me to betray my given word to you."

"Is that your excuse?"

"It is a fact." Lukas sighed, feeling decades older all of a sudden. "I didn't choose to put this omphalos in me, or to bring myself to this world. I didn't choose to be presented with certain death on one side and a bargain with a goddess on the other. You did all those things at your own leisure without my knowing. I've simply been trying to stay afloat and survive."

"I see." Inanna's voice became stiff. **"It seems I have misjudged you yet again."**

"Probably," Lukas replied, more calmly than he felt. "It's easy to make false assumptions based on your personal standards. But . . ." He trailed off. "You've healed me, and I'm thankful for that. Now I owe you another favor. What do you want in return?"

"What do I want?" the goddess replied wistfully. **"Nothing you can provide for now. Willingly, at least. A favor, then? One to be repaid in the future?"**

Lukas shrugged. "A favor for a favor. Seems legit. And it isn't like—"

The rest of his words were drowned in chaos as the air was split with the screams and battle cries of monsters—hissing noises of neothelids, strangled moans of bouda, wild ululations of formless ghol, and even chittering sounds of cinderfaces. But even those noises fell into a thin spectrum compared to the tremendous *roar* that followed behind them.

Whatever it was, it was big. And loud.

And they were all coming toward him.

Lukas glanced at his surroundings. Running through the narrow passage when something was chasing you was generally a terrible idea. The larger the passage, the greater the chances of it opening up into newer ones rather than a dead end. Unfortunately, the moss-covered walls around him were rather slippery, and trying to hang on to them would only get him killed faster. Fighting the monsters with fire would probably kill some, but it would enrage the rest. It would paint a bright neon sign on his back.

No, the only real option was to fight in a way that held the maximum chances of survival and potential gain.

And right now, he could only think of one.

Lukas grabbed two of the metal tail-ends he had amputated from the thoggua. He was no metallurgical expert, but he knew for sure that the metal was stronger and sharper than anything else he had seen in his life. It was incredibly light, yet sharp enough to cut through rocks like they were soggy paper.

A lifeforce-enhanced slash of his hand could hack into flesh, but a casual flick from this thing could splinter bone.

Vatuatil. That was what the Screen called it. An unfamiliar name, but he'd not be surprised if it held special powers. Something this sharp and hard had no business being so featherlight, but who was he to judge?

A surge of adrenaline spiked through him as the creatures began to get closer and closer. This was the very first time he was going to face so many of them, in such variety, in melee combat. The feeling was both foreign and welcome at the same time.

"Activate Alpha Condition. Select Thoggua."

MONSTER PROTOTYPE: THOGGUA		
SKILLS	**LEVEL**	**SOUL CAPACITY CONSUMED**
Seismic Sensing	2	500
Raw Lifeforce Manipulation	1	50
Shatterpoint Intuition	2	500

Activating Monster Prototype Thoggua **Initiating Consciousness Shift** **Enact**

Space splits.

Cracks appear. Cracks diffuse. Cracks get larger. Brighter. Cracks converge. Diverge. Shatter. Reform.

His mind devolves.

Human instincts dull. Thoggua instincts arise.

Perceptions clash. He is not human. He has no body. No eyes. No hands. No legs. No structure.

He is slime. He is formless. Yet he rises. Yet he falls.

There is no sight. There is no sound. There is only . . .

VIBRATION.

Fire is a vibration. As is light. As is pressure. As is pain.

He has tails. Hands that feel like tails. Not very stretchable, but he can work with it. The metal ends feel familiar.

Power rushes through them.

Yes.

He will hunt.
He will kill.
He will kill them all.

He'd remember the next few moments the same way a man would remember being caught in a raging storm.

Surrounded from all sides, assaulted from every angle, his human brain had shut down and switched to a simplistic, primal and yet wildly alien level of perception. Details were lost amid a swirl of imagery. Solid information was washed over by a sea of blurred pictures. His eyes closed, sinking him into an ocean of blackness, and yet, he could sense the world's contours on a level that was beyond imagination.

Strings everywhere. Vibrations.

From the slightest shift of his feet, to the sliding of dust, to the sudden impact of a monster's feet within his sensory range, he could sense them all. Everything came down to two basic things. To sense their precise location, and then to apply Shatterpoint Intuition to guide his *tails* at the exact spot. To muscle memory that was not his. To reflexes and reaction times that were strained far beyond mortal breaking point. The surroundings became an afterthought. The environment, a lazy blur. Everything became indistinct, muddled, and that included those he fought against.

He parried blows from a thick, bony paw before slashing through its neck. He deflected claw strikes from a quadruped. Projectiles showered at him from every direction—energies, sonic waves, poison, acid. Craters were blasted upon the ground near his vicinity and electrical discharges narrowly missed him. Instinctively he knew what they were, what caused them, and how they would affect him if they made contact, but his mind was too dimmed to care.

All that mattered was killing. Standing his ground. It was about guiding his *tails,* and slashing into prey with the pointed ends. He gave as good as he got. His actions became mechanical in nature, his limbs—*limbs?*—moving as automatic extensions of will onto his body. His opponents were strong. Tough. Powerful even. But they were not the best. Not even close.

A tremendous roar shook the cavern. The mighty force crashed against the stone walls, reverberating to such an extent that he was effectively blinded as the resonating sound smashed against his hypersensitive ears. The blades dropped from his hands, and his tails—hands—hands with fingers in them— moved up and covered his . . . ear? His Eyes . . . ? Visual receptors activated and suddenly everything was lost. Everything was a mess. Everything was—

He did not have lips. He did not have vocal cords. Yet, he yelled—

"DEACTIVATE!"

> **Monster Prototype Thoggua Deactivated**
> **Reverting Consciousness Shift to Base Host**
> **Enact**

Lukas opened his eyes.

Surrounding him were body parts. Dead body parts. Heads. Claws. Forelimbs. Hindlimbs. Tails. Slime creations shredded to large globules. Serpentine monsters, sliced in six pieces but somehow joined together by a thin layer of tissue.

> **+1514 Experience gained**
> **Level Up?**

That was good news compared to the sudden attack on his senses. Leveling up meant more Soul Capacity. More Soul Capacity meant more accumulation of skills. It would mean—

A second wave of resonant noise crashed.

That was when he noticed.

Water.

Water was everywhere.

Water was flooding inside the chamber. And it was coming from the—

" . . . Fuck me!"

A *tsunami* smashed through the walls of the cavern, shattering through stone as an enormous watery arm pushed its way through it, inundating half the chamber with blue-green water.

"WHAT THE HELL IS THAT?"

> **?**
> **78% Spiritual Similarity with Yokai Species. Lack of physical body.**
> **Energy Core employs Water Mana.**

The aquatic monster raised one of its giant, watery arms, its girth comparable to a thick tree trunk, and smashed it in his direction. Lukas leaped out of the attack radius and prepped himself up. Winning against this thing would be far more difficult than the kasha, against whom he had both the advantage of unpredictability and surprise. Besides, the kasha had been humanoid, not this gargantuan water titan. Trying to deflect that much motion would get him killed faster than he could say "Oops!"

"Look!" he exclaimed, altering his speech to Feacani, the language Solana had used to speak to the other yokai privately. "Whatever you think I did—"

The monster faltered, if only for a moment, before lunging at him again.

A swirling shaft of water, rotating at incredible speed and pressure, came rushing at him. And no, he wasn't stupid enough to stop it. Too much energy and momentum. If Quonnan's final blow had been a five out of ten, this would probably classify as an eight.

Lukas focused on the nature of the beast. Fluidity was an essential attribute of water. Much more than fire. "If this works and I don't get myself killed, I'm gonna look really awesome while doing it."

The blades went back into his belt. His fists unclenched. His fingers relaxed. Lukas raised both hands at shoulder level and readjusted his posture to create the path of least resistance.

The water torrent came, but he didn't resist it.

Instead, he welcomed it. Embraced it. Guided it.

Closing his eyes, he felt the motion of the water gushing at him. The force, the power, the momentum—there was something absolutely beautiful and lethal about it. He felt himself meld with the motion of the spinning water currents. Felt himself connecting to the pressure driving the jet forward.

Closing his eyes, he mimicked the graceful spin that Inanna often employed during their spars. He weaved a layer of pure motion around him, siphoning the water currents into it. Lukas spun around. And around and around until he was completely surrounded by a cylinder of water, enclosing him from all sides. The sheer volume of water was getting more and more difficult to maintain with every passing second, but he needed to keep going.

Just a bit more, he told himself.

He could see the kami swooshing and wailing around as the pressure kept decreasing. Quite natural, because one couldn't endlessly produce water. And if he had understood it right, trying to conjure water inside this anomaly in the middle of a desert was doubly difficult. The fact that this creature—kami, Lukas guessed—was capable of this much water creation was testament to its capabilities.

With a final spin, Lukas let out a roar and sent the swirling currents, now amplified by his own momentum, toward the kami. Suddenly, there was a large, obdurate, and extremely solid wall of water rushing at the kami like an oncoming freight train, shedding a trail of water in its wake.

The creature recognized the danger a second too late. Call it surprise or the lack of experience of fighting a kinetomancer, even one as amateurish as he was—the kami wasn't ready for it. It had focused entirely on offense, not on protecting itself as well, and couldn't come up with a counter in time.

The wall of water hit it with the same force as an oncoming garbage truck and blew it right into the wall farther ahead. Water splashed against water to become one large, wet explosion, and suddenly the entire place looked like a massive flood zone. There were no voices, no scratches or movements whatsoever. It was as if whatever sentience the water possessed had entirely vanished, leaving nothing but a pool in its wake.

Boy, was he wrong.

Something yanked at his feet, dropping him down headfirst into the ground. It was only his instincts that allowed him to instantly slow down his perception, shifting his body to land on his arm instead of his head. But the moment of distraction cost him from seeing the greater picture.

A wave of water engulfed him, and *something* plunged into him.

CHAPTER 34

NO QUARTER

You'd think that after siphoning not one, but multiple creatures—physical and ethereal, of different sizes, temperaments, and skills—Lukas would have reached a state when he'd have understood the underlying concepts behind Soul Siphon. Every siphoned creature would boast a certain amount of Soul Capacity, all of which would be filled with its own plethora of skills. The same skills that Lukas could later assimilate into his own schema by sacrificing appropriate Soul Capacity.

So it was quite natural that after the well-timed Level Up, he was looking forward to assimilating some of the skills from this aquatic monster that had tried to possess him and unwittingly ended up being siphoned.

Instead, he got this.

MONSTER PROTOTYPE: MARID		
Spiritual Parasite. Subspecies of KAMI monster prototype. Energy Core constitutes mana forge for Water. Capable of water creation and manipulation.		
APTITUDE	**LEVEL**	**SOUL CAPACITY REQUIRED**
Possession	1	50
Water Creation	2	500
Water Manipulation	3	5000
Pressure Modulation	2	500

Aptitudes. A new curve ball that the universe had decided to throw at him.

Lukas grimaced. If what he understood was correct, this new classification was akin to disks containing compressed information on skills. A backup of sorts. Using Alpha Condition to use the marid's skill wouldn't work, because he needed the skills engraved on his soul first to use them.

In short, Alpha Condition was useless as far as kami were concerned.

"I swear it's like the universe goes out of its way to fuck with me!" he snapped, kicking a pebble that had been innocently sitting on the floor.

"Do not be so arrogant, mortal," Inanna chimed in. **"You are not significant enough for it to register your existence. That said, this creature reminds me of the Ugallu. Ereshkigal's familiars. They manifested as negative aspects of the World—drought, plague, flood, earthquakes, and the like."**

"Whatever," Lukas growled. "Either way, I don't have the available Soul Capacity to use right now. I'll just leave it on the backburner until I can."

"An appropriate resolution. Perhaps there is hope for you yet."

"Very funny." The expression quickly fell off his face. "Something about this bugs me though. All those monsters . . . It's unlikely they were just coming at me to attack. This marid must have been attacking them, but that strange guy from earlier also used water attacks. What are the chances that—"

"There are two powerful water shapers in the vicinity?" the goddess mused. **"Unlikely."**

"We don't know much about the Empire," Lukas defended. "It's possible there are more of these . . . adventurers around. Maybe having a marid might be more common than we think."

"Anything is possible."

"But there was that guy earlier. And now a kami. Maybe . . ." A strange inflection hit his tone. "Maybe there are more of them around?"

"Mortal, restrain yourself from doing anything monumentally insane."

"Give me a break!" Lukas scoffed. "I'm not going to go look for them or anything. But you know . . . there's always the chance that others might not be as trigger-happy as that guy."

"Your optimism feels strange. The parasites have offered you home and hearth. They trained you in skills and gave you knowledge, yet you would not think twice before trying to escape their clutches. On the contrary, the first _human_like creature has tried to deal a lethal blow upon your person. Yet, you would give them a second chance simply because they _look_ a certain way?"

"I'm not—" Lukas began hotly.

"You are," the goddess replied reprovingly. **"Your excitement is proof in itself. Why is it that appearance alone counts so much in your eyes?"**

What bullshit! Lukas thought. Appearance was no guarantee of character or competence. One couldn't be a good lawyer if one made one's assumptions based on looks alone. Saying that he was being too trusting and optimistic just because they *looked human* was—

His lips parted, but the words did not come out of his mouth.

It couldn't be, could it? Just because someone looked human didn't make the person trustworthy, but if the choice was between someone that appeared human and an animal, who would he trust? After everything was said and done, he was a human and would always instinctively favor his own species. Looking at a dog being run over by a car might elicit sympathy out of one, but it was momentary at best. But even the most law-abiding citizen would falter if asked to kill someone, even if the victim were guilty of committing heinous crimes. At a fundamental level, humans were humans, and animals were animals.

Inanna was the shadow of a goddess that existed in his mind. Still, she appeared human. Felt like one. Interacted like one. Reasoned like one. Even with all her quirks, Lukas had no problems choosing to trust *her* over all else. It was probably also why he was so comfortable with Solana, despite knowing that she was the most dangerous creature in the entire yokai territory. Quonnan was weaker than her, as was Ryu. As was that Nihil fellow and the reiki called Mizo. And yet, Solana was the only one that looked human.

More than the others, anyway.

"I—" he began, but stopped, noticing the sudden stir in the water all around him. The ripples were unsteady and were growing with time. He glanced toward the wall on the other end, from which the ripples seemingly originated.

Had he misunderstood something? Surely there was nothing there after he had—

"Beware, mortal," Inanna interrupted. Her voice resonated with something he couldn't quite place. **"A greater power approaches. You must—"**

BOOOM!

Before Lukas knew it, several tons of frosted rock came blasting out of the wall. The noise that accompanied it was terrible. The destruction, appalling. Frost-covered stones were skidding in random directions, with several of them shooting in his direction. Water splashed everywhere. Lukas fell down to one knee, bent forward at the waist, and hastily drew a force shield over him. The entire arena had been engulfed in a strange fog of dust and . . . coldness.

Then he saw her.

She was lean and tall, closer to his own height. Blonde curls fell on both sides of her head, shining as if flecks of ice were embedded in them. Thin, piercing eyes held a most alien smile while her right hand held a disembodied spider-like monster by the head, before flinging it to the other side. She wore a pale sleeveless shirt with trousers that felt similar to his own and looked entirely too pleased to see him there.

Lukas gawked at her. Brown eyes met glacial white.

And then, the Screen popped up with a most unexpected notification.

Predator found you.

Predator?!

It was one of those moments that would have had dramatic music if his life were a movie, but instead he got the constant pitter-patter of water dripping to the floor from the rocks above.

But just in case, he drew up on his power, which covered him like a cloak, ready to defend, to attack, to protect or to destroy. He didn't know what this girl wanted, but he did want her to know that if she had come looking for a fight, he'd be willing to oblige her.

Analyze.

BREMETAN
Bipedal, lifeforce-producing organisms. 99.9% similarity with the HUMAN species

---

?

78% Spiritual Similarity with Yokai Species.
92% Spiritual Similarity with Monster Prototype MARID.
Lack of physical body. Energy Core employs Wind Mana.

?

34% Similarity to Earthly Frost. Lack of Physical Body. Lack of Spiritual Body.
Energy Core employs ???

"Can I help you?" he offered in fluent Ualbesh.

The girl met his eyes. "Give it to me."

"That's . . . very forward of you," he replied, rubbing the back of his head.

"I sense a pattern, mortal. First myself, then Solana, and now her. Perhaps you are a masochist deep within?"

For the love of all that's holy, I really hope that ain't the truth.

"You're rather uppity. For food, that is." The young woman tilted her head slightly. "Now, give the kami back to me."

"Kami?" Lukas asked, feigning curiosity. "What kami are you talking about?"

The blonde seemed amused. "The water shifter. The marid. I can sense it within you."

"The marid?" he repeated, recognizing the term. "Why didn't you say so? That thing nearly killed me."

He called upon fire, manifesting it as a tiny fireball at the tip of his finger.

"Fortunately, I happen to have a counter for it."

That seemed to give her pause.

Lukas smiled inwardly. Part of his learning program with Ryu had been about gaining a good understanding of the world around them, especially the politically divided zones in the Asukan Empire. He had crafted a proper back-story for himself, with enough random titbits thrown in to pass as an adventurer. Lukas had argued about the possibility of encountering other Asukans during his voyage to the core of the anomaly, and it would be a terrible thing if they realized that he was an Outsider.

Solana had not been amused.

From what she had told him, the number of Asukans wielding more than one kami could be counted on one hand. In that light, him performing a nifty fire trick was easy and legitimate proof of him *not* having the water-type kami.

"A Cyffnarian pyromancer." The girl licked her lips. "How interesting. Very well, perhaps my senses had me fooled."

Lukas shrugged. "Happens to everyone. Now if you don't mind, I'd really like to be on my—"

SHINK!

A jagged shard of ice slammed into the floor, inches away from his feet, impaling the rock. Lukas took a moment to see the hit and one more to register that it had indeed been *ice* that had cut through the rocky floor. He slowly turned around to look at her.

Ice. There are ice-types as well? But that explosion couldn't be from ice. So . . . what was that from?

The girl gave him an impish smile. "No one is going anywhere."

She took a step forward.

"Bite me," Lukas shot back.

"Oh, I will."

Lukas weaved an immaterial wall of lifeforce around him. He solidified his hold on his own power and stomped on the ground. The cracking sound of it echoed back and forth across the half-destroyed chamber.

"Walk away," he growled. "I'm not kidding."

"I want to see what is so special about this power exuding from you. It beckoned me from so far away. I must have it."

"Mortal," Inanna whispered. **"Kill it."**

Out of nowhere, a spinning projectile of jagged ice came shooting toward him, straight for his heart.

During the course of his training, Lukas had traded blows with several individuals. There was Quonnan, fast and furious with a proclivity for throwing overpowered bursts of fire to overwhelm her opponent. There had been Ryu, whose speed allowed him to blitz through the opponent's attack without even resorting to using fire. And finally there was the thoggua, whose skill at vibration sensing and precision allowed it to slay dozens of creatures without moving from its position.

This blonde girl made all of them look *slow*.

The shard of hoarfrost clashed against the layer of lifeforce he had conjured around himself, lighting it up like a floodlight. Despite doing all he could to divert the energy, the blow hit him like a professional linebacker. If it wasn't for the lifeforce shield taking the blow evenly across its surface, Lukas was sure the icicle would have pierced through his body. Instead, he was thrown against the floor and somehow managed to turn the momentum into a roll.

He must have clipped his head at some point, because stars were swirling in his vision. But that wasn't all that happened. His shield hadn't borne the brunt of the attack, nor had it shattered.

No, it had been dispersed. Absorbed. As if imploding into itself or—

He glanced at the piece of hoarfrost, now several times larger than he remembered from a second ago, and his eyes widened with horror.

Did that thing just—

Before he could finish the thought, a raw, invisible wind came rushing toward him. Lukas was lifted up and thrown against the wall. By the time he managed to push himself upright, he was beyond scared. The girl was powerful, fast and capable of using ice, force, and probably *wind* unless he had made a mistake. Her speed was absolutely nothing to scoff at, and if he didn't up his game, he'd be deader than dead. Lukas forced all thoughts and doubts from his mind and readied himself for a second time.

"Disappointing," said the girl, walking toward him again. "I had hoped you'd put up a better show than this."

A flash of sensation flickered over him as the girl drew in power. A *lot* of power.

There would be no stopping this attack. This girl was on a different level with force manipulation, and her style favored mid-range combat. If he wanted to make a difference, he'd need to change that first.

Pumping lifeforce into his legs, Lukas dashed forward. With a sudden sprint, he appeared right in front of the girl, a blade firmly grasped in his right hand.

The girl snarled and extended her own hand.

Lukas expected a blast of wind, maybe accompanied by force or something similar. What he got was a bolt of pure, crushing force that blasted forth from her palm. The air screamed and the chamber shook as the terrible attack impacted against his shield. Lukas's eyes shone, and his teeth clattered in his skull as he caught the bolt of destructive force on his shield. He had a feeling it was actually *penetrating* his defense.

"You must redirect it!" shouted the goddess. **"Release it with a counter evocation, or you will feel the impact of the hit. Use the reflection technique!"**

That's too—

"NOW!" commanded Inanna, and Lukas obeyed, his whole body trembling with effort to contain the tremendous force. Pushing his hands in the girl's direction, he poured fire to join the spell he had caught, feeling the shield grow hotter by the second.

"Enough. Now reflect it," the goddess intoned.

His right hand balancing the shield in place, Lukas moved his left hand in a graceful lateral arc, extending the shield around him. The destructive force was guided through the shield, the rotation guided by its own inertia as it traveled in a perfect circle—

"MY TURN!" he shouted. Mixed with his flames, the girl's attack was now a spiraling typhoon of crimson flame that shot back toward her. She realized what had happened a tad too late and hastily surrounded herself with a wall of pure ice.

It barely made a difference, as the blonde was bodily picked up and thrown back, only to be promptly buried under the rubble of the destructive force.

"That," Lukas panted amidst heavy breaths, "was one crazy move!"

"You spent too much energy redirecting the attack," Inanna told him thoughtfully. **"Now, kill it while you still have the chance!"**

"What's the hurr—OH CRAP!"

He had but a moment's warning. The entire wall facing him exploded with a deafening sound, as huge sections of it came crashing down. Within a single instant, the entire chamber was reduced to nothing but a land of rubble and floating dust.

And in the middle of that, bruised and charred, stood the blonde. Her face was red with pain and fury, but the sinister smile upon her face promised retribution of the worst sort.

"Impressive," she said, something dangerous in her eyes. "I have not been hit with such force in years."

"What do you *want?*" Lukas snapped. "You know I don't have the kami you mentioned. So why the hell are you attacking me?"

A blue blur came out of her hand, hissing like a striking snake, and stabbed outward toward Lukas, who sidestepped the blow.

"A frost whip. How droll. You need more imagination," Lukas chided.

"An excellent suggestion," she replied, and sharp icicles protruded out of the whip as she snapped it back to her. A long, jagged, frosted dagger appeared in her left hand. From her posture alone, he could infer that she was skilled in using that particular weapon pair.

That was fine. He had something ready for her this time around.

Holding a dagger in reverse grip in each palm, he beckoned her forward. *"Come."*

A single clash of weapons. Then they separated.

Three seconds later, another clash. Another disengagement.

Two seconds.

One second.

Half.

One. Half. Two. Half. Half. One.

The rapid skirmishes began as quickly as they ended. Traveling all across the chamber. Back and forth. Scattering sparks along the floor like small geysers of fireflies in the night.

"HAAA!"

Lifeforce-enhanced metal blades met an unholy frosted chain, cutting through with impossible ease. It was more like the frost momentarily expanded when it touched the metal and became brittle, shattering and allowing the blade to pass through. The remains scraped against the flats of the victorious weapon as they passed.

The wielder of the butchered chain moved a bare centimeter out of the way of the edge of the tool that destroyed her weapon and subsequently contorted out of the path of its matching partner. The maneuver prevented her from accurately lashing out with a kick that would have crushed the skull of her opponent.

The fighters passed one another, another failed attempt at the other's life. But it was far from the last.

Both kept moving, turning with the momentum they gathered. Power was gathered. Tools were repaired. Bodies were reinforced. Eyes narrowed.

This was how Lukas fought with the girl. A never-ending series of single passes that had them gambling with death every single time. It was a battle between two forces that did not possess the ability to stop the other without severely risking themselves.

The blonde's speed was leagues above what any human could ever achieve naturally, and the strength of her blows could easily destroy bones and bodies with seemingly little effort. Her lean physique might be defensively weak, but the speed it offered more than made up for it.

And that was without considering the frost and wind.

Weapons crashed. Bodies moved.

Lukas's lungs were on fire, desperate to supply oxygen to his body tissues as he pushed himself farther than should have been possible. His limbs shouldn't have been able to move under the combined stress of his exhaustion and her overwhelming blows.

The surging lifeforce kept him focused and hyper-aware, but the slowly developing exhaustion was slowing him down. His body was still in pain from the wounds he had gotten from her, but Prophylaxis was perpetually healing him. Shatterpoint Intuition allowed him to intuitively determine the best place to ensure a killing blow.

But the two *still* weren't enough.

"My apologies," the blonde replied, "I really am trying to make this painless for you. But your constant attempts at deflection are irritating me. Hold still, please."

Lukas spat out a tooth and rose to his feet again, gripping his blades in bloodied hands. He hacked away at the frost chain, but it shattered again. He didn't care. He'd stopped keeping the count after the first thirty times it happened. Honestly, Lukas wasn't sure how he was keeping up.

The spar with Ryu felt like it was an eternity ago. He remembered the moment when Quonnan's instincts had taken over him, and quadrupled his speed by going all out on his lifeforce. He had practically vanished from one point and reappeared at another in the blink of an eye. There had been a similar moment when he was sparring with Inanna but even then, it was his max. Half of that was far below what he was at now, and yet here he was moving at only double speed, courtesy of accelerating his body with lifeforce and using tachypsychia in healthy doses.

He shouldn't have been able to improve his performance by this degree in so short a time.

But it didn't matter.

Just a little faster, he thought drunkenly as he matched weapons with her, *and I'll be able to keep up.*

The lifeforce-enhanced blades were a horrifically overpowered tool for this fight. Something about the frost made it go brittle the moment it touched them. Though incidentally, the very act also dissipated the lifeforce from the blades, as if the frost was *consuming* it. But that made no sense.

Ice simply didn't work that way. Did it?

The girl already had her fair share of bruises and weeping cuts on her body from when she had underestimated him early on. She had not made the same mistake twice.

Lukas reinforced his body far beyond what he had normally thought possible. Every single muscle fiber and every bone fragment was oversaturated with it.

Raw Lifeforce Manipulation wasn't a skill he had managed to progress beyond Level 1, but he wondered if it was still out of his reach given his current prowess.

Momentum Manipulation doubled the acceleration and power behind his blows. Shatterpoint Intuition guided them through paths of least resistance.

Every time they passed, the girl would reconstruct her broken whip.

Faster.

Every time they passed, she had to abandon her attempt to destroy his body with a single blow in order to avoid a counterattack with his blade, lest she be impaled through the heart or the neck.

Faster.

Every time they passed, the girl's features became just a hair more monstrous. Her glacial eyes became sharper and glassy, and an arctic mist cloaked her form little by little.

It was a game of low-risk, high-reward tactics. Exposing themselves like that wasn't in either's best interests, even though the fight had devolved into a never-ending series of skirmishes. Small bouts that compounded into a battle of attrition—something that played against both of them.

Every time they passed, Lukas would pour a little more lifeforce into the blades.

Faster.

Every time they passed, he lost himself more and more to primal instincts that were not him.

Faster.

Every time they passed, Prophylaxis healed him a little more.

Faster!

Just a little more and he'd cleave her head off.

Faster!

Just a little more and his body would fail.

FASTER!

"You cannot keep going on like this," the goddess warned. **"You must end this fight."**

Easy to say, Lukas thought, swaying his blade in a lateral swing and bringing it inches close to the girl's neck, even as the chain came inches from striking his own heart.

Both spun around and dodged each other's blow.

"You've done it before. Do what you did in our last spar."

Had he been able to spare unnecessary energy in facial muscular constructions, he'd have rolled his eyes. Do what he had done during his last spar? It had gotten him kicked in a way that had jerked him out of sleep, and he had felt the pain for a lasting number of days. And all he had accomplished was a single hit on her knee, and that after taking a . . .

"Take a blow," Inanna finished. "Find an opportunity to take a calculated hit. Use it to deliver a final strike."

He had done something similar back then, albeit subconsciously, and he wasn't even intending to achieve that. But the goal of that spar hadn't been to win, but rather to land a blow on her, regardless of the cost. On top of that, he had been operating from the mindset that it was all in his mind, allowing him to be significantly more relaxed with his self-preservation instincts.

But to apply such to a *real* fight? One with his life on the line?

His muscles clenched painfully as he forcefully turned, and just for a moment, he stalled.

The girl recognized the opening instantly and moved in to exploit it.

THUMMMP!

The steady beat of his heart came into focus and the world slowed around him as his perceptual dilation set in.

THUMP! THUMP!

Her left hand shot out, the frosted dagger piercing through Lukas's right palm, right through the middle. Every bit of protection from the conjured metamantic layer dissipated as the dagger drove through body tissue, carving a bloodied hole as it tore out from the other side. Her knee moved in simultaneously and slammed right into his abdomen.

He let it.

THUMP! THUMP!

It hurt. He wouldn't be surprised if she'd shattered through several vertebrae and *actually* split him in half. It was still nowhere compared to that one mind-shattering blow the goddess had let him taste in a sudden loss of control.

His injured right hand flexed like a viper's maw, grabbing at the girl's very momentum. Shatterpoint Intuition guided him to the most optimal path to pull on the velocity guiding the girl's neck and *yank* her forward.

And then he stabbed her with a lance of pure, blue flame.

At the same time, an obdurate wall of wild wind crashed against his chest. Even if there was the slightest chance that his rib cage had gotten through the ordeal with some light chafing, this blow powdered them to bits. Lukas widened his eyes as he heard several *snaps* from his chest. Blood erupted out from his mouth.

WARNING!
Extreme physiological damage to Host Body. Lifeforce Drainage below Critical Limit.
Shutting down offensive functions until Prophylaxis Recovery is complete!

That, Lukas drunkenly agreed, as his head smashed against a particularly sharp rock, was all kinds of bad.

The girl staggered back, the blue flame now having left an open gash, starting from the neat hole through her chest, all the way through her left shoulder and a very thin scratch on her chin. The flesh was completely charred black, with blood oozing out of it, a horrible mix of red and black ichor. Given how she was stumbling around, there was no doubt the blow had been fatal, or at least near fatal.

Not that it mattered. At this rate, he would be dead soon.

He coughed out a wad of blood and forced his lungs to breathe. He tried to make his nerves ignore the signals of his destroyed rib cage by passing lifeforce. He needed air more than he needed the warning that he had been hurt.

It didn't work. Maybe he'd need to pour in a little more—

Blood drained from his face. His stomach suddenly felt bottomless as the surging lifeforce was squirreled away toward his right palm. He could feel his heart beating slower and slower. Had he subconsciously activated tachypsychia? Not that he could tell. His vision became increasingly hazy by the second.

And yet, he couldn't help but stare at the deceivingly inconspicuous thing that was on his body.

The shard of ice that had penetrated through his flesh.

It was now twice—thrice—no, several times more than that.

And it was expanding. Already he could see jagged lines of thin ice crawling out of the completely frozen and ice-clad appendage that used to be his right palm.

That was what was draining his lifeforce. Not his battered body. Not his injuries. Not the system.

He had seen it before. The frost had gobbled up the lifeforce from his shield, lost its momentum, and dropped down to the floor. Was it the same whenever the frost whip crashed against his lifeforce-enhanced blades? The frost gobbled up the lifeforce and expanded, becoming brittle.

At least, Lukas thought with growing delirium, *I killed her with that hit.*

"You might want to check again."

The blonde was down on all fours, crawling like a wounded spider as she held herself up with her hands. The burned area was sort of seething, with some kind of thick mist or steam, as her body tried to fight the injury he had inflicted upon her.

It took him another second to register what it was he was seeing.

It wasn't steam. Wasn't mist either.

It was *frost*.

Growing on the surface of her body. Cooling it. Freezing it.

Lukas had no clue if having a kami with powers of ice manipulation could do that to the wielder, but he sure wanted to find out. Ice that absorbed life-force? Ice that healed? What kind of fucked-up world had he ended up falling into?

Her eyes locked on him as she pushed herself to her feet. "Taking the hit on your arm like that," she cackled. "That was a mistake." At his glare, she cackled even louder. "If you're frustrated, I understand. You feel overwhelmed. You fear you're going to die, so you're lashing out. You want to *hurt* something. It's not your fault. But disfiguring my face like that is an unforgivable crime—"

Disfiguring? Lukas stared at her in disbelief. It was barely a scratch.

"—And I'm afraid I'll have to take it very, *very seriously!*"

A shaft of ice tore out of the cave floor, piercing through his left leg, just above the ankle. Before the pain could even register, two more rose up, piercing through his other leg and left hand. Lukas found himself completely spreadea-gled, trapped and bleeding, with only one foreseeable conclusion ahead.

One that he wouldn't be able to escape out of unless—

"*Tell me, mortal, are your morals worth your suffering?*"

Inanna had once asked him that. Back then, he was completely healed and in possession of new powers and alternatives. His morals were what was left of the true Lukas Aguilar, that was what he had said. But when faced with immi-nent death, was it really an excuse he wanted to hide behind?

Three times, she had offered him the chance to serve her. Three times, he denied her. The first, while offering information about his own nature as an anomaly. The second, after he'd faced Quonnan and survived. The third, right after he'd woken up and found himself healed.

There hadn't been a fourth time. And if he didn't do anything, there *wouldn't* be.

"Tell me this before you die." The blonde trudged forward, the lines of white around her becoming more and more distinct. "Who *are* you?"

Lukas coughed again, spitting out blood. "Someone who'll kick your ass next time if given the chance."

"Answer me, and I will grant you a swift death."

His answering grin was bloody. "*That's* your attempt at negotiation? Don't quit your day job."

Prophylaxis: 11% Complete

It was too slow. His body was battered and broken, and he was over-whelmed with bone-crushing weariness. Mana generation would be unavail-able until Prophylaxis was over. If he didn't pull off a miracle, it would be Game Over before he knew it.

He looked at the blonde again. That dimpled smile, the perfect surety in her manner and expression, was something more than rampant ego or fanatic conviction. He had studied similar characteristics as part of his study program on human psychology.

It was pure madness. Whatever else this blonde was, she was calmly and horribly insane.

You're enjoying this, aren't you? he asked the goddess.

There was no answer.

You told me you'd have me beg at your feet for power. Well, I'm not gonna do that. But in the spirit of survival and . . . and to fulfill the promise I made you earlier, I'm willing to agree to a bargain—

"Denied."

Lukas gasped in surprise. Inanna had never been one to reject a chance to settle on a bargain. She had gone out of her way to orchestrate things that would arrange for more bargains. To deny such an open offer was completely contradictory to her behavior.

Meanwhile, the blonde edged closer.

Lukas panicked. *Look, the circumstances are crazy, and I want to survive. So if you don't get off your royal ass and jump on it, I'm walking!*

"What you can offer, I have no need for. And what I need, you decline to offer. As such, I have no reason to bargain."

So you'd blackmail me into working for you?

"The only thing I have done is refuse an offer. A notion you are rather familiar with."

Bullshit, Lukas snarled, panic rising up his throat. *You're bullying me into accepting the job—*

"You have made it very clear to me that you will not willingly accept my offer," Inanna reasoned. **"And having you as a puppet will render you useless to me. I must therefore see to it that circumstances force you to accept my offer."**

How is that any better?! This—this isn't fair!

"Life is hardly *fair*, mortal, as you well know."

Why would you do this? We were developing something nice here. A partnership. Why now of all times?

"Because it is necessary," Inanna intoned. **"Perhaps to protect you from destroying yourself, or perhaps . . . because I simply *can*. In the end, it does not matter. All that matters is what is. You know what I want. I know what you want. The ball, as you mortals say, is in your court."**

Lukas clenched his teeth, inhaling and exhaling a few times, if only to keep the desperation from leaking through to his voice. A part of him pointed out that maybe this was Inanna *asking politely,* because she could have always made him into a puppet. He was already learning from her, and they had long since determined that sooner or later, he'd have to accept the deal. Rejecting it now was only delaying the inevitable, not solving a problem. He already had too many problems. What was the need to create more?

There was a curious expression on the blonde's visage as she peered down at him. "The power that exudes from you is *odd*, stranger. You wield flames, but there is no stench of a kami. None of their spectrum. Tell me what you are, or I will make you."

"Bullshit. If you could do that, you'd have done it by now, instead of standing there looking stupid."

She took another step toward him, now inches away from where he lay. "I prefer to attempt reason before I destroy a mind. It's a taxing activity." She frowned. "That damned changeling makes it look easy. Are you sure you wouldn't rather cooperate?"

Lukas gulped. She was talking about psionics. His training with Inanna had given him more than a little introduction to the subject, but mental resistance wasn't something he had forayed into so far. Alpha Condition was usually good enough to tackle the invading instincts of his siphoned soul prototypes. But a direct psychomantic attack, on the other hand—

"Stay away from me," he warned.

It didn't deter her. There was a slow, sinuous enjoyment to her stride. She bent forward, her arctic fingers grabbing his chin as she made him face her.

Inanna had warned him how plenty of things could affect him if he was caught aware in a direct gaze between them. The glacial eyes kept gazing at him, as Lukas tried his best to keep looking in all possible directions except at her.

"Stop. *Avoiding.* Me," she snarled, and dug a frosted finger into his chest. The sudden jolt of pain startled him, and suddenly, he was losing himself in her eyes. Literally. There was no sudden vacuum, pouring his thoughts out. There was no sudden feeling of intrusion, no pain or agony. Instead, all he felt was—

Exhaustion.

Here he was fighting monsters, in a place he didn't want to be, for a goddess he couldn't even *trust*. He had survived extensive trials, but after each one was yet another ordeal to take care of. Another monster to fight and bury, with the only alternative being death.

His shoulders helplessly drooped as a horrible weight settled onto his heart.

Hadn't he been through enough? More than enough? Hadn't his life handed him enough misery and grief and pain and loneliness these past few months? First, he'd lost the life he knew and found himself inside this hellhole. Then he'd been constantly forced to fight to survive. The yokai were yet another nail in the coffin crafted by a goddess that constantly pulled him into her eternal servitude through bargains.

It was always something else, something new and scary galumphing toward him by the legion. What was the point? No matter what he did, no matter how much stronger or smarter he got, no matter what monster prototypes he collected, the bad guys would only become bigger and stronger. All of that suffering, in a hopeless attempt to return to a home that may not even exist anymore?

Was he an idiot?

His hands shook and knees weakened, slowly losing their ability to stand firm. No, it would be far simpler to just give up. Let someone else suffer her whims. He'd earned his rest.

The blonde goddess that stood before him offered sweet rest. Freedom from his suffering. Eternal silence. All he needed to do was—it was—

No.

He was forgetting something. Something he could do. Something that could help him fight against this. Lukas knew if he could just focus on that for a second, he could get things back on track. Something—something—

Psionics. He remembered.

Skill Inactive.

The murkiness around his thoughts darkened.

He tried to move his head, his hands, his eyes.

He remembered something else this time. Alpha—Alpha Alpha—Alpha what? Condition. Yes. Alpha Condition—

Alpha Condition Inactive.

"Get out!" Lukas yelled, bashing his head against the floor. "Get out! Get out! *GET OUT!*"

"Give up!" said a voice of utmost serenity. "Give up and become mine. I will devour your soul and digest that *potential* brimming within you. All your pain will end. Just . . . give in . . . to me."

That was when something clicked within him, and Lukas *understood.* Understood what the girl had just admitted. What it meant to him. What it meant to the entity residing within him. Add in the discussion that had just happened—

Lukas couldn't help it. He barked out a laugh.

The look of confusion on her face only made him laugh harder. It didn't matter if the action sent flares of agony down his spine and made his insides burn. The irony of the entire situation was simply too funny to ignore.

"She—she was right. I really do have the most bizarre luck."

The blonde arched a pale eyebrow at him.

Lukas laughed again. "You'll find it troubling to devour my soul."

"And why is that?"

"Because," he coughed out, "if you try that, it'll throw a wrench in her plans. Take my word for it. She will take it *very personally.*"

"Oh?" said the soothing voice, though an undercurrent of incredulity was vivid in it. "And who is *she*?"

An amused smile graced his lips as the first stirrings of a primal flame kindled within him. There was that all-too-familiar feeling of weightlessness. The sudden splash of liquid chill entered his mind. A most familiar sensation of power—power too great, too bright, and too devastating for him to even comprehend—emanating out of him, seeking a way out, begging for release. Lukas let it flow through him, the thin smile now spreading across his face.

In that brilliant light, even the murkiness of the blonde's Psychomancy began to dissipate like morning mist.

And from deep within that primordial power came something else. Lukas's lips opened, and his vocal cords constricted, speaking words that were not his own.

"That . . . would be me."

CHAPTER 35

PRESTIGE

Weaving through a psychic mindscape was an arduous affair.

Not because it was difficult, since any idiot with a smudge of psionic potential could throw psionic power at someone's mind like a battering ram. But more often than not, it would induce extreme reactions, often resulting in a mind-melting pot of agony for the victim and causing all psychic structures within the mind to go haywire.

The trick was to pass undetected and guide the victim's mind into thinking in specific directions without leaving behind obvious signs of manipulation. The inception of ideas was always a difficult thing since the bremetan mind was always quick to identify which thought was conceived by itself versus foreign stimuli. Most minds quickly recognized intrusions and sent out flares to their consciousness, causing the victims to scream in agony, once again, destabilizing the psychic structure.

One might as well find a thorn in a haystack after that.

Tanya had picked up some handy psionic skills during her travels, but she'd always lacked the finesse required for the job. Subtlety was the name of the game, and between her ability as an aeromancer and the frost, Tanya's approach was far better suited to be a sledgehammer. Direct intrusion, psionic bursts, enthrallment—those were her thing. Navigating through psychic matrices like the changeling? That was way above her paygrade.

Still, the mind of this pyromancer was . . . strange. Not because he had powerful defenses or budding psionic skills, but because of how exceedingly easy it was. If she didn't know any better, she'd say she was entering the mind of someone with a broken psychic architecture.

Not for the first time, she wished the changeling was there. It was ironic. Now that her inhibitions were suppressed, she was actively recognizing the changeling's prowess, when she had gone out of her way to avoid it in the past.

Tanya slowly felt the sensation of having a body come back, despite knowing such feelings were purely illusory. Closing her eyes for a moment, she allowed her other senses to come to the fore. Satisfied there were no hazards nearby, she looked around and—

Blinked in surprise.

The land in front of her was . . . impossible. She could see stars with such clarity that was impossible in the Asukan lands. She watched as a different time, a different place, a different era began to superimpose with the present. Lightning flashed across the horizon, with meteors flying across the heavens. And there, upon a floor that seemed levitated in endless space, in a hall that would have caused the Asukan gods to go green in envy, was a royal throne, and upon it, sat someone Tanya had never seen.

Her hair was blacker than the darkest of nights, with skin as white as the finest marble. Her lips were the color of frozen mulberries, fitting perfectly onto a smooth, lovely face that had the most beautiful eyes she had ever seen. And yet, no matter how much she tried, how perfect each one of her facial features was individually, Tanya couldn't behold her perfection in its entirety.

All around her were hundreds of entities—real and phantasmal, human and not, creatures of myth and history—all genuflecting in reverence.

This wasn't just *any* entity. Who she was, and what she was doing in the stranger's mind, Tanya had no idea.

The entity raised a finger, and smiled cruelly at her.

"Scum!"

The force of will that condensed on her in that single word was so dense that Tanya thought it was going to break something. Like maybe the entire World. She was thrown out of the mindscape and found herself on the floor, gasping like a landed fish. She struggled to push herself up, but couldn't move so much as a finger. She brought her will into focus, the power of Frost singing in her veins, with the idea of using it to deflect some of that force away from her and—

—and suddenly, sharply, felt her will directly in contention with another. The power that held her down was no ordinary force or Terramancy. It was no gravity or pressure modulation pushed to bizarre extremes. It was the simple, raw, brute application of the will of this being that held her pinned down upon the floor, and she could no more escape from it than an insect could stop a shoe from descending.

Tanya fought against that psychic pressure with all her might, and after expending every single bit of lifeforce she could muster, she was only able to raise her head up and—

And stared at the impossibility before her.

The stranger was free, standing upright, no longer broken and bound. The shards of Everfrost on his limbs, on the other hand, had been shattered to bits, with his entire body healed as if it had never been hurt in the first place.

It was impossible. In all her time traveling across the Empire, there had been *nothing* she couldn't overpower with the Frost. Even Ezzeron had bowed before it, and the kami was one of the strongest in the entire Asukan Empire. The ice that would feed on life and destroy to its content until *the universe itself was wholly submerged into eternal darkness. She was the Claws, the Teeth, the horror that made bremetans seek shelter within their homes at night. She was—*

She was—

She was ███████████████

"Shard of an emperor." The stranger smiled maliciously, the female's words coming from his lips. **"Did you think I would not recognize that vile stench? Not even a god, and you dare lay your hands on what is mine?"**

The stranger lowered her pointing finger.

"Know your place!"

Energy rippled across the stranger's skin like liquid lightning, exploding out in a radial wave with a huge, crackling roar. Space itself warped and shattered around him like the flickering wisps of an inferno. For a split second, gravity vanished around the young man's body, making every single slab of shattered rock rise up, as if caught in an invisible force. Then that enormous power slammed everything and everyone straight down, as if crushed by a single, gigantic, invisible anvil.

Tanya could feel her own bones straining under that enormous pressure. Despite her anger and her defiance, she knew for a fact that had this pressure been directed solely at her, it would have compressed her mind into something too dense and too inert to function, like a tiny diamond formed out of crushed coal.

This cannot be real, she tried to reason. *This is an illusion. It has to be. It has to—*

"I know of your ilk," the stranger replied. **"Vestiges of a power lost to time. Clinging to life by staining the souls of your descendants."**

Control didn't feel so easy now; the gentle whispers of the Frost at the back of her mind had now become a chorus calling for blood, *now, before everything was ruined—*

"I know of your kind. Castoffs that forever live in the delusion of getting it all back. Becoming a whole that you never were."

Tanya screamed, rage and bitterness bubbling up against her will like poison from a wound, so intense and cold that it made the Frost itself feel warm in comparison. She did not lash out; her *pain* did it for her without any conscious effort, as a *thousand* spears of frigid tundra erupted out of her body in a storm of death.

Each one was stopped in midair by invisible hands.

The stranger hadn't so much as lifted his finger.

And the point had been made.

"I know of you."

The stranger spread his hands out invitingly.

"But do you know of me?"

She felt Ezzeron throw his impossible might to propel the spears ahead, but they would. Not. Move. The anger rising within her could have scorched the entire chamber. Her frustration and contempt could freeze everything within sight into an arctic tundra. But some part of her, a part that felt utterly alien even to herself, *recognized* this power. This was a ████████ ████████—

A . . . what? Not one of the divinities. No Asukan god or goddess would enter the zone where Amaterasu's Light held no sway. None of them would ever suffer the ignominy of possessing a mortal mind like a parasite. Not an emperor either, so that only left—

Tanya's eyes widened.

The stranger's teeth showed.

"Then why are you not kneeling?"

Kneel? Tanya may have had the short end of the stick. She may pale in front of this individual's power. But she could *absolutely* defy anyone. Even this stranger.

The fight would certainly be lopsided, but not hopeless. And by Wind and Thunder, she was not going to allow *anyone's* will to stretch her out on the floor like a lamb for slaughter. She stopped pressing at her bindings with her limbs and started using her mind instead. She didn't try to push them away, or break them, or slip free of them. Instead, she allowed Frost to take over. She allowed the primal impulses that she had always kept restrained to overwhelm her, and focused on *that* reality, where the power of Everfrost would freeze those bindings and shatter them to dust.

As it happened, Tanya reached into the part of her soul where one of the primal forces of the universe existed. Coldness. Hunger. Death. A flood of madness and horror and pain and raw, shrieking loneliness so intense that it chilled her to her soul, all running rampant through her brain without her consent or any response to her attempts to fight it off. During all this time, the Frost had only lowered her inhibitions and projected its own common sense upon herself, but this was the first time she was reaching for it, allowing it to not just assault her physical form, but also lay waste to the territory of her soul, the most hideous indignity imaginable. As the Asukan part of her screamed in utter horror at this invasion and defilement by this obscene, twisted insanity, she had something of an epiphany.

Such coldness. Such hate. Such hunger.

And *power.* Power like nothing she had ever felt. Not even when she'd faced Ezzeron at his mightiest.

Even as the tide of darkness battered against her mind, Tanya studied it, analyzed the composition, learned and adapted, and the thing engulfed her and she began to *truly* understand it.

This wasn't just Frost. This wasn't just a lifeforce-leeching twisted creation. This was ███ bu██████ r.

Tanya had no idea how it would interact with Ezzeron's powers, but at this point, she barely had anything to lose. She gathered up the Frost within her, used it to infuse herself while allowing Ezzeron to flood her with every bit of his energy, and cast the resulting compound against her bonds. She was casting *everything* she had done, everything she believed in, everything she had chosen—everything *she was*—against the will of a likely ancient being of terror and malice, a fundamental power of the World.

The result of that wasn't an explosion. Not really. There was no light, or sound, or force. Rather, it was a mad outpouring of power that tore through her entire form. Part of it condensed into hoarfrost and crawled all over her left side, with icicles protruding out at random places. It covered her face, her neck, her breasts, all the way to her shoes, making her look like a crystal mannequin. A long, thin tendril erupted out of her left palm, forming a familiar frost whip. The rest of the energy expanded outward, forming wind that spun around her right half, forming an identical whip, only crafted purely out of wind.

And suddenly, the stranger's will could not hold her.

"You don't get it, do you?" she whispered, slowly pushing herself to stand up straight. "This power that flows through me devours energy. You may be stronger than me, and you may pin me down. But I can feed and feed on you until you are nothing. And that makes me your predator."

Her face became a thundercloud, her lips twisting into a snarl of pure hate. "You want me to kneel, do you? This is what I'll do. For bringing me such quality food, I will make your demise quick."

The stranger threw his head back and laughed. Scorn ran in that laughter, with genuine amusement—the cold, alien amusement of a spider. It made her want to clutch her head. He stood there, hands hanging free, completely disregarding her threat, in a manner akin to the primal dictator that shone in the Asukan skies.

"I won't."

CHAPTER 36

———

JUGGERNAUT

Less.

He was always Less.

No matter what the omphalos came up with, Lukas Aguilar was always less compared to the information the system was trying to write into him. It was happening over and over, tens and hundreds and thousands of times, and he was constantly being rebuilt in another's image, only to be found lacking and deconstructed for the process to begin anew.

And again.

And again.

The loop went on and on, and throughout it all, there was always this constant attempt to match the construction with a certain set of attributes. Skills. Nature. Powers. Aptitudes. It was similar to the process of Alpha Condition, only instead of the monster prototypes being raised to the forefront and having their instincts overwhelm his own, the opposite was happening. His own existence was being made to adapt to Skills, Power, Instinct, and Experience that belonged to someone so hilariously above his pay grade that even the omphalos system was having trouble trying to set things up without crashing. One might as well try to run a space station from a kid's laptop.

His body was no longer his own. His thoughts, his memories, his desires and habits—it was like someone had taken every single component that was Lukas Aguilar and shoved it aside, leaving him nothing but a naked consciousness that had no choice but to speculate, unable to dictate the flow of his body. Floating in a web of raw energy, Lukas gazed through his own eyes, and at the same time, *stared* at himself, from a different vantage point. His eyes had lost their natural brown hue, replaced by an *electric green* that pulsed with familiar power and authority far greater than his own. Power that could burn, destroy, and annihilate everything that stood before it.

It was like watching a movie where the lead character was someone that looked exactly like him, and yet there was the knowledge, the absolute certainty, that *he* was not *him*.

And yet at the same time, he was.

Quite naturally, the Screen went crazy.

BREACH DETECTED!
INVASION OF FOREIGN SOUL PROTOTYPE
SOUL SIPHON ATTEMPTED . . .
FAILED!
ATTEMPTING BASE HOST AUGMENTATION—
SOUL SIPHON ATTEMPTED . . .
FAILED!
SOUL SIPHON ATTEMPTED . . .
FAILED!
SOUL SIPHON ATTEMPTED . . .

It went on and on as the omphalos relentlessly kept trying to assimilate this power—Inanna's power—into itself. He could understand why it was happening, but there was nothing to be done. The last time Inanna had possessed his body, he hadn't yet unlocked many of the abilities he had now.

And now, with available Soul Capacity, the omphalos would not be denied.

Initiating Parallel Matrices

Safety Off! Overclock Set!
Intercepting Routines

Enact

SKILL UPGRADE Registered!		
SKILL	**LEVEL**	**SOUL CAPACITY REQUIRED**
Kinetomancy (FRAGMENTED)	**APEX**	**177764**
DESCRIPTION		
Absolute Manipulation of magnitude and direction of Momentum Vectors.		

SKILL UPGRADE Registered!		
SKILL	**LEVEL**	**SOUL CAPACITY REQUIRED**
Momentum Manipulation	4	50000
DESCRIPTION Alteration of momentum of any force and objects within an established radius.		

New SKILL Registered!		
SKILL	**LEVEL**	**SOUL CAPACITY REQUIRED**
Alleviation	3	5000
DESCRIPTION Removal of any and all unreasonableness of the Body to return it to its calculated original format.		

The blonde transformed into a half-frosted, half-human thing, with a mini blizzard swirling around her like a protective cocoon. Two whips, one entirely of frost and the other entirely of wind, were in either hand. For someone that had felt a wide range of different powers ever since his arrival upon this world, Lukas had a sneaking suspicion that this girl's power was unnatural.

Solana's power was dominating. Inanna's power was all-encompassing, as if the entire world was soaked in it. Ryu and Quonnan had been the flashy, destructive type. Every single time any of the powerful entities had slung major mojo around them, the elements would charge up the immediate environment and soak it up with raw mana residue. If the caster was strong, the mana would shroud around them like a cloud of violent power, manifesting according to one's emotional spectrum.

This was different.

The blonde's power didn't fill up the place. Instead, it emptied it in a way that most people wouldn't probably comprehend. Utter stillness spread out of her. Not peace, but something horrible and hungry and wrong, something that drew its power from being *not*. It was made from the emptiness at the loss of a loved one, the silence between heart beats and the inevitability of death.

And it was strong.

For the first time, Lukas truly began to comprehend why she was listed by the Screen as a *predator* and not *prey*.

It was when he noticed it.

The blonde was not moving.

Neither was his body—Inanna, that is.

Despite being ethereal, Lukas kind of drifted forward and watched himself, and then the girl. It was then that he realized that the quality of the light around him had changed, and had frozen. Chips of stone that were fluttering were stuck midair, and even the Wind around the blonde appeared to be little more than a sedentary congealed mass of something viscous and translucent.

The hairs at the back of his spiritual neck didn't go up so much as they let out tiny, hirsute whimpers and started trembling violently as the rest of him.

"Incredible," came Inanna's voice in a basso rumble from behind him. **"Your luck knows no bounds."**

Slowly, Lukas turned. Behind him stood Inanna, just as spiritual as he was, with motes with crimson light exuding out of her form. Lukas gawked at her, and then at his own body that was still under her control, and then back to her again. He felt his stomach twist, and suddenly had to fight not to throw up. Or fall down. Or weep.

"Wh—" he stammered, "bu—are—how?!"

Her stare made him forget what he was about to say. She looked at him for a breath, her eyes unreadable. Then she looked searchingly up at him, and spoke in a slow, quiet, ever so slightly *jealous* tone. **"Somehow, despite your repeated denial of my offer, events turned out in such a manner that allows you access to skills you've done nothing to deserve. *Again*. I find this most vexing."**

"I'm sorry?" Lukas tried.

"Perhaps this is for the best. You shall now see something the world has not seen in aeons."

"What's that?"

"The goddess Inanna at war." She glanced at his body. **"The creature that stands before you is a shard of something just as ancient as myself. A pity it is in such a sad state. It'd have been a worthy prey at the peak of its strength."**

That, Lukas decided, said all one needed to know about the Supreme Queen of An and Ki.

"But now, it is feeble. Grounded. Trying to crawl its way into this world. Nothing to be threatened about, but something that could harm a god if given the chance."

"Even you?"

"I am immortal, not eternal. This is power that belongs to the ancient world. A fundamental force of the universe. If left alone, the things it could unleash would be . . . unsettling."

Lukas tried to think of the kind of situation that would unsettle *Inanna.* The sigils came to mind.

"The sigils. The legends. Your own puzzling existence. And now ... this. I know not what the future holds, but it is shaping up to be rather intriguing."

"What are you going to do?" Lukas asked.

Inanna's face blossomed into a carnivorous grin. **"This creature is one of instinct. Ugly. Hateful. Unruly. It needs a firm hand to teach it balance. I intend to be that hand."**

An image of Inanna *spanking* the blonde came to mind. Lukas shook his head, discarding it as quickly as it came. He already had enough nightmares to deal with. So he looked back at the frozen view and returned to meet the goddess's eyes.

"Time is relative. Do not be concerned with its passage. It currently passes very, very slowly in the real world, compared to here."

"Right," he said. "That's . . . good." He wanted to ask what "here" meant but decided not to annoy her with more frivolity. Instead, he settled on accepting it as a fact. "Is there anything you want me to do?"

"Pardon?"

"You said she's dangerous and of the ancient world. Plus, she has a wind kami. And you've said before that my body is frail and you can only use the minimum of your power. So . . ."

The Supreme Monarch of An and Ki cast back her head, her eyes going wild, her smile widening to inhuman proportions. **"The numbers stand at one Inanna to none. That advantage shall be sufficient. I confess, it has been aeons since I have taken the field in earnest, mortal."** Her teeth gleamed. **"I shall enjoy it."**

"Enjoy?"

Inanna turned in a wave of silken black hair and starlight and strode toward where his real body now stood, before merging with it. And just like that, time unfroze.

And the fight began.

The blonde was like a swift wind. Even when Lukas had faced her at maximum acceleration, her speed had been nothing short of absurdly unfair. Now? She was even faster.

Lukas watched wide-eyed as she brought down her whips from above at Inanna, aiming for her shoulders. The whips slammed home with such force that the floor beneath her feet cracked. By all logic, his body should have been bereft of arms.

Instead, the goddess gave her a shark-like grin and twisted her body, looping her left hand in an overhead chop, shattering both whips and hurling a spinning boomerang of pure force at her. The ice-eyed girl spun a shield of wind to deflect the thrust, projecting a wind blade at Inanna's knees even as she knocked the kinetic boomerang skyward. Inanna mirrored her movement, using the momentum of the now-deflected blow to shatter the wind blade, while bringing a new slashing wave wheeling around to decapitate the blonde's head.

The girl hastily raised a rime-covered hand to deflect the blow and was sent skidding across the floor by a hammer blow in the face.

Inanna stared down at the blonde, her expression one of confused annoyance. **"So stubborn for one so frail."**

"Don't tell me I wounded your pride, *False God.*"

"Far from it," Inanna said, **"In fact, I am actually starting to enjoy this. It has been quite some time since I have been so entertained."**

The windcrafter vanished, leaving a furious roar of wind in her wake. She appeared right before Inanna, stabbing a wind blade at her chest. Right, left, up, down, sidewards, backward—the blonde kept up a relentless stream of attacks, every strike carrying within itself an unspeakable ferocity that made Ryu seem like a small sardine in an ocean. Hoarfrost coated her limbs in thin sheets, a frigid tundra air moving around her like a dark, firm, undeniable outline.

Lukas watched her pierce Inanna with half a dozen icicle shards, while conjuring a cylinder of vacuum around the goddess's body, causing the air around them to slam into her from all directions with all the might of a sledgehammer, all the while hurling more than a dozen arcs of pure energy toward her.

The space around Inanna exploded.

"Tch!" The blonde grimaced. "That was easier than expected—"

"Was it?"

Lukas witnessed the gale of dust scatter off, revealing Inanna, standing there, completely unruffled. None of her—*his* body parts were missing. Even his clothes looked unruffled.

"How are you doing that? I felt my shards pierce you. The vacuum should've obliterated you. All of my attacks hit. I know they did!"

Inanna smiled playfully. **"To put it simply. You missed me."**

"NO! I DIDN'T!"

"What a stubborn one you are. You did. Not that I expect you to perceive it. You *are* rather weak, after all."

The blonde responded to her questions with techniques that could only come from decades of bone-breaking practice. The grace, the power, the efficiency—it made Lukas wonder how he had even survived against her earlier.

The girl quickly became a blur of images, each one acting out its own chaotic dance that was also somehow graceful. It was awe-inspiring to see potential, possible realities overlapping while the girl fought to predict the future, adjusting and counter-adjusting her actions based on what she could perceive.

It didn't even touch his body.

"It feels so *good* to be back after so long," Inanna exclaimed, casually grabbing the blonde's right arm and throwing her into a wall. **"Surely you can put in a little more power when you strike me?"**

The blonde gritted her teeth and raised her arms, conjuring dozens—no, hundreds—*thousands* of ice shards. With a wail of pure rage, she converged all of them toward Inanna.

Every single one of them was stopped by invisible hands.

Without Inanna even lifting a finger.

Balance Reality Foundation—Counterbalance

Equalizing . . .

Ingrain supplementary protocols.
Establishing . . .

The skills Inanna had been commanding were powerful, requiring Soul Capacity well beyond what the omphalos was comfortable with unleashing. Reflection or not, this was a *goddess*, and her skills weren't something that could be taken by any ordinary Soul Siphon.

Something different was required.

Something that could accomplish the most while maintaining the base state unchanged.

Initiating . . .

Maximizing Free Soul Capacity Allocation.
Soul Capacity: +10000

URGENT!!!			
REGISTERED SKILL	**LEVEL**	**SOUL CAPACITY**	**ISSUE**
Kinetomancy (FRAGMENTED)	**APEX**	**177764**	**Insufficient Soul Capacity**
Alleviation	**3**	**5000**	**Requires Confirmation before Assimilation**

Momentum Manipulation	4	50000	Insufficient Soul Capacity
Host Body requires calibration!			

Lukas wanted to laugh at the sheer irony of it. A gift of *ten thousand* Soul Capacity from the omphalos as a last-ditch effort to balance the scales, and it still made no difference whatsoever.

He glanced back at the ongoing fight and found the blonde lunging at Inanna, blades in each hand.

Inanna did not move, the girl slowing down as she approached her, the very motion that propelled her draining from her body. The goddess gazed at her contemptuously. Then she raised her hand slowly—

And slapped her across the face.

"I must say, this body took to my skills rather well," Inanna commented. Blood and spit escaped the blonde's nose and mouth as Inanna casually grabbed her by her neck and smashed her against the floor. **"It instinctively channels Kinetomancy without the slightest resistance."** Then, she looked down at the fallen blonde in abject disappointment. **"You're not finished already, are you?"**

Lukas swallowed.

CHAPTER 37

JUDGEMENT

This is bad.

There was no other way to explain it, to explain how utterly horrible the situation was. Her belly and chest were on fire. Blood from her mouth had trickled back into her left eye and had crusted her eyelashes together so that she couldn't open it again. She tried to look around but couldn't get her right eye to move properly. All of those things were horrible by themselves, and yet, somehow, they all paled in comparison to the *real* thing.

She felt the stranger's foot upon her right cheek, his toes massaging against the wound, sending jolts of agony into her face. It was nothing compared to the others, and the stranger knew that. This wasn't torture. This was—

Humiliation.

She was being humiliated.

Toyed with. Played with.

Enraged, she tried to move her hands but they felt like frozen steel, slender and immovable. Her vision went from red to black. Her sensations were slowly beginning to recede. She could feel the Frost crawl upon her form, coating her in more rime.

The Frost was a thing of hunger. It could hack, tear, and rip things apart. It could drink another dry of their lifeforce, and it could add it to her. But healing? That was totally dependent upon her own skills.

Unfortunately for her, the Frost hadn't been able to devour any lifeforce, no matter how many strikes she had made at this entity. And she had been doing quite a lot of striking.

Tanya knew that the entity was toying with her. She—he—did it even matter? This entity wasn't even pretending to do otherwise anymore. It had all but broken her in half with that single blow, and could have easily torn her apart but was instead content to watch her struggle.

Meanwhile, the static behind her eyes grew more intense.

She had the power. She could feel it rushing through her veins, empowering each and every attack she threw at the stranger. She could have made a thousand shards of Frost without running low on power, but that wasn't what mattered. Every time she drew on its power, it made the ice within her burn. Her healing skills dulled the pain, let her keep going, but she could feel something behind it, breaking her down from within. Her vision was so coated in static she could barely see. She was frosting from within, her own weapon killing her from the inside, one cell at a time.

Was that what this entity wanted? To give her a frustrating death? See her slowly drain away her life in a pathetic attempt to strike her down?

No, she decided, slowly raising her right hand. Her right eye peered open, her expression locked in a snarl of hate. If Frost wouldn't work, then perhaps Ezzeron would. Yes, Ezzeron was her last hope.

"Wind Shie—"

The stranger grabbed her wrist.

And all hope was extinguished.

How? Tanya wanted to yell. Dissipating the energy out of a spell mid-creation? This wasn't lifeforce at work. Wasn't mana either. Wasn't absorption. Wasn't metamorphosis. Wasn't Alteration or Corruption. It hadn't been from within. It hadn't been from the outside. One moment the spell was building up within her palm, and the next moment it was—

"Do not look so surprised. It is almost embarrassing. That spell would have accomplished nothing anyway."

Gone. Unraveled. Dissipated. One moment the energy was taking form. Becoming more. The next moment, it was dissipating. Breaking away. Energy just didn't *function* like that.

Either she was missing something or someone was ignoring the Rules.

"Such a doll you are," the stranger replied. **"Almost as interesting as my mortal. You know, originally I was annoyed at having to share power without getting anything in return."** The stranger threw his head back and laughed. **"Do you see it, mortal? *This* is the power you resist. This is the power that you refused to keep your pesky morality."**

Mortal? Resist? Tanya's mind was running on overdrive. Had she— Was she facing the ire of a *god?*

Her belly went cold.

"You're afraid. Not of death, but of this helplessness. You're afraid of being beneath me. Afraid of what is to come. You're so afraid that I can almost *taste it*. It's ecstatic."

The stranger lifted her chin. Tanya shivered. Something about his touch was just raw and suggestive. Carnal feelings that she had always suppressed rose to the forefront of her mind. Desires began to ebb at his supernatural, animal attraction.

For a moment, Tanya wondered how his lips would taste.

The stranger's eyes met hers and gave her a slow, slow smile. Tanya felt her entire body thrum in response to him, to his presence, his proximity, his . . . everything. That smile contained something within it, something that conveyed to her in a flashing instant—an image of herself looking up at him in ecstasy, him above her, looking down at her with that expression as she *screamed* over and over in mindless pleasure. And with that image came a thousand others, each of them a single captured moment, the kind of moments that are the only ones to survive a frenzied dream, frozen and layered atop one another, each of them a promise, a prediction, and every one of them aimed right at the most base, most primitive parts of her brain. It wasn't limited to visual imagery. Each layer of flash had its own round of sensual memory, every one of them only partial but intense—touch, taste, sound, scent, and vision—dozens and dozens of dreams and fantasies compressed into that single instant of dark inspiration.

A surprising sensation of dampness brought her out of that haze.

Shame, indignation, and a burning sense of disbelief rushed through her, the strength to stop him no longer present.

"Your power and existence fascinates me. This frost of yours, it's raw, unhoned, a monster run by instincts. Like a sword, it cares not where it falls, only that it's swung. Such a sword needs proper hands to wield it, guide it, give it direction. I will be that hand."

Tanya felt the stranger's face get closer to hers.

Glacial white met electric green.

"You see, neither you nor my mortal here truly understands what *Power* really is. So I'll use it. To show you exactly what real Power is."

"No! Stop!" Tanya struggled feebly against the stranger's strength, her fingers scrabbling for purchase against the ground as she tried in vain to drag herself away from his alluring eyes.

The stranger's eyes shifted ever so slightly. **"I think it might be wise for you to indulge me."**

Another multisensory slideshow hit her head, and every single image was something that she should have known better than to find intriguing, but that she could not bring herself to entirely ignore. Tanya felt her head light up with lunatic pleasure-maybes, dizzying, electrifying, and she felt as if she were about to tear her way out of her clothes.

A final image passed through her mind, accompanied by an intense emotion—herself, looking up at the stranger as she lay at his feet. He stretched out his hand and lightly touched her head, an absently fond gesture. An over-whelming sense of well-being flooded into her like shining, liquid light, filling every empty place within her, calming every anger, every pain, every bit of suffering. She almost wept in relief, at the abrupt release from all worries. Her body trembled.

So easy. It would be so easy. To bow down before him. He could care for her, teach her, comfort her. Her place would be there, at the warmth of his feet—

Tanya's head snapped up for a second.

Enthrallment. She was being enthralled. No, that wasn't it. There had been absolutely no attacks upon her mental defenses. There was no emotional manipulation either. Either this person was the kind of psionicist that made Elena look like a rookie—

Or he was something else.

She had to fight. She had to get away. Or else—

Or else she'd die. That or she would no longer be herself.

The knowledge of what was about to happen had galvanized her from within.

And Everfrost answered.

Ice erupted out of the floor, no more limited to hoarfrost but thick sheets of it. Jagged stalagmites that arose out of the floor like coffins out of a graveyard, teeth-like daggers of the element swelling and erupting with violent force. It only lasted for a handful of moments, but in those seconds, it brought with itself a scene of an ice age.

And it was *still* not enough.

"Quite a show!" said the stranger, utterly uncaring about it all. Tanya watched, her eyes now bulging out, fear paling her face, realizing that none of the ice shards had gotten even remotely close to the stranger, and instead, had grown *around* him.

Just—just what was he—what was—

"You!" Tanya snarled, "I won't! *I will KILL YOU! I WILL—I WILL KILL—*"

"Your defiance is disappointing. The Supreme Queen permitted your existence, for she is unmatched in magnanimity. She *mandated* that your future shall be at her feet. Yet, you try to rise above that position? Though I showed you supreme mercy, you still seek to end my reign? You who sought to enthrall my Host, *vermin, you dared touch what is mine?*"

The stranger's words rang across the entire chamber. Even in her state, Tanya could feel that power encompassed everything, feeling it slowly engulf her like a cocoon. A crimson shade of power began to emanate out of his body and intensify. A flame so brilliant that one might as well be looking at the sun.

"Did you believe you could just extinguish the flame I rekindled? I, who ruled over Heaven and Earth? Nothing has the right to be born without my permission.

Nothing has the right to die without my permission. I have declared that this vessel shall manifest my wishes into reality and anyone that will question my resolve will—"

"Burn!!!"

The world around her cracked. All across the frigid zone encompassing the chamber, a brilliant crimson light began to exude. The ice shattered upon the slightest contact with the crimson hue, as flames spread out, burning brighter, larger, growing and connecting, passing far out of sight in every direction as the stranger stood in the center of it like an eternal juggernaut.

Even though she knew that it wouldn't end well for her, Tanya couldn't help but realize that this was a defining moment in their world.

The Frost within her echoed through the burning light, incoherently howling and sobbing with rage and sadness so deep that even she felt sorry for it. There were no words, but roars of defiance so honest and brutal that it spoke all on its own. It didn't *want* to be suppressed. Not again. It would face death but not bow down to anyone's will. It would reign supreme and would bring about the █o███yp█ █a█ █████o█ A ██—

"My will is unquestioned. My desire consumes All. Shine now, the power of Depredation. Birth a new reality in which this vermin may abide in subjugation forevermore. A penalty that lasts until the end of time."

It was an uncaring judge looking down at the sobbing defendant from high. A swirling vortex of power flared up to touch the burning heavens, and within the black chasm of nothingness came down a shaft of pure power and then—

Darkness.

CHAPTER 38

BOY MEETS GIRL

Well . . . Lukas surmised, *that happened.*

"Your ability to state the obvious is astounding."

The battle between the strange blonde girl and Inanna had come to an end after Inanna had cast judgment upon her. The exact mechanics were still unclear to him, especially the entire power of Depredation thing, but he assumed it had something to do with her power as a goddess.

He glanced toward the blonde, still fallen upon the ground, the hoarfrost on her person now completely undone, leaving behind unblemished human skin. How? He had no clue. Her clothes were tattered, and she wore a belt-bag around her waist. After spending a couple of moments uselessly debating between decency and moral obligation, he decided to unzip it and pull out a cloak to put over her.

There had also been some canned food inside her bag. Lukas stole it without hesitation. The food felt exotic to his tongue, but anything was better than roasted meat after this long. She had been the one to assault him out of nowhere. The least she could do was share her food.

On a side note, it felt great to be back in control. Watching the goddess kick ass was awesome and, not that he wanted to admit it, arousing, but he liked his bodily freedom too much to complain.

Her words, not his.

Maybe if things were different, he'd have questioned her about the switch back. Knowing her, she'd probably scoff and say something disparaging about his mortality, followed by how she despised inhabiting a lower life-form for a second longer than was absolutely necessary.

"It is refreshing to see someone aware of their position on the food chain. But no, that is not it."

Then?

"You forget that this form of mine is inevitably restricted by the pendant you bear on your person. Possessing your frail body and exerting my Truth took a toll on it."

Truth?

"The core conceptualization behind my Ascension. My mark on the Origin, if you will. It is what makes me a goddess. But I digress. It is clear to me that this realm is not my own. As such, I shall need to scry for it."

A tide of frustration swept over him. If it weren't for Alpha Condition, he'd have drowned in it.

"Unfortunately, the power to accomplish that is far beyond what this pendant can procure. It is . . . vexing."

"You need more power? You could always use some from my omphalos reserves."

The goddess eyed him strangely, then shook her head. **"You must think thrice before making such an offer. Such naivety is beneath one who bears my torch. To answer your question, the omphalos in you will not allow for that."**

Lukas was baffled by the thought. A single spell enough to run his reserves dry? The same omphalos reserves that would last him ten lifetimes?

His mind replayed the bargain he and Inanna had struck back in yokai territory. The goddess had demanded he channel the power he'd gain by harvesting the crypt's omphalos to her. In a previous bargain, she had extracted a promise out of him to be allowed to perform a single spell of her choice.

Nigh-unlimited power, and a spell that could be anything.

And now, she wanted to scry for her realm.

There was this strange gnawing at the back of his mind that told him he was missing something. Something that was looking him in the face, yet he was ignoring it.

But what?

He glanced down at the girl. She looked . . . vulnerable in her sleep. It was almost impossible to believe she had nearly killed him several times, and had enough skill to stand against Inanna, no matter how short a while.

A power just as ancient as herself, Inanna had described her frost powers. Powers she had bent before her will by applying her—

Lukas stilled. "I see now," he finally said. "It's not about finding your realm at all. You could do that anyway after I kill this crypt. Besides, you yourself said that I had a long, long way to go before I could even imagine trying to enter Ereshkigal's domain. The reason for your frustration is something else."

He pointed at the sleeping girl.

"It's her, isn't it? You used your divine powers to crush her. But you're a reflection of the original. A starlight housed in a pendant, in a lostbelt with no gods and . . . no faith. What little you had, you used it to subdue her." His lips widened into a smile. "You want to scry for your realm so you can acquire more faith."

Inanna was silent for a moment. Then, she sighed. **"The problem is, you just do not *sound* that bright, mortal. Perhaps it is skewing my expectations."**

"But that's what it is," he stressed. "Isn't it?"

She slowly nodded. **"If the girl is any indication, there will be entities that cannot be suppressed through sheer power alone."**

He knew it. He didn't like it, and certainly didn't want to accept it, but he knew it to be true. He was going to be stranded in this world for some time. But that was okay. He'd come to terms with that. Earth wasn't there anymore, so he needed to shack up somewhere either way. Why not here?

Speaking of which . . .

"Soulscape."

SOULSCAPE	
NAME	Lukas Aguilar
Type	**Base Host**
Level	**7**
Experience	**161**
Current Threshold	**1960**
Utilized Soul Capacity	**13629 / 14473**
ESSENCE	
Maximum Lifeforce Output	**3475**
Replenishment Rate	**540 / hour**
LEY LINE NETWORK	
Maximum Mana Output	**3150**
Synthesis Rate	**340 / hour**

SKILL ATTRIBUTES		
SKILL	**LEVEL**	**CONSUMED SOUL CAPACITY**
Raw Lifeforce Manipulation	**3**	**5000**

Momentum Manipulation	3	5000
Friction Modulation	2	500
Pressure Modulation	2	500
Kinetomancy (FRAGMENTED)	APEX	1279
Fire Creation	1	50
Fire Manipulation	2	500
Temperature Modulation	1	50
Perception Manipulation	1	50
Conjuration	1	50
Disintegration	1	50
Seismic Sensing	1	50
Shatterpoint Intuition	2	500
Psychomancy	1	50

OMPHALOS ATTRIBUTES	
Energy Reservoir Capacity	∞
Current Energy Level	722,386,138 units
OMPHALOS FUNCTIONS	
Scan	Level 2
Analyze	Level 2
Prophylaxis	Level 2
Soul Siphon	NA
Alpha Condition	Level 1
Evocation	Level 1

No matter how many times he saw it, it was unreal to his eyes. He already had Soul Capacity to begin with *and* had been gifted with ten thousand more. And yet—

Inanna's scornful laughter rang in his ears. **"Did you think it would be so easy to steal my skill once again? Even if you had multitudes more of available Soul Capacity, you would still be playing with its basic skills before you can make *any* foray into Kinetomancy."**

"But I still have Soul Capacity left!" he seethed. The last time it had taken up everything he could afford. But this time, it was left untouched.

"Kinetomancy is the culmination of several lifeforce skills. Raw Lifeforce Manipulation, Momentum Manipulation, Regokinesis, Molecular Acceleration, Friction Modulation, and many more. What you have is merely a taste of it. Unless you develop the related skills, you will not progress any further."

"But why?"

"Without synchronizing your body to the other skills, it will tear itself apart. Physics is the manipulation of the nature of reality. It is not a toy. It is the weapon that allowed me to butcher gods and beasts alike."

Lukas chewed his bottom lip. "I suppose there's no free lunch."

"No free lunch?" Inanna sneered. **"I do not wish to hear such a thing from *you*. You just acquired the third level in not one, but *two* skills. Freely. That alone would have taken you *years* of training."**

That sounded a bit too unreal. *Years?* He had gained a significant number of Level Ones lately, though he supposed he had Soul Siphon to thank for that. Assimilation of monster prototypes and allowing them to take over while himself holding the reins thanks to Alpha Condition had greatly speeded his growth. The generous bonuses the omphalos threw at him from time to time helped as well.

But still . . . *Years?*

He returned to the Screen for information.

"Show me information on skills."

SKILLS
Skills are abilities performed using Natural or derivative energy sources, engraved upon the Soul at the expense of Soul Capacity.

That much he already knew.

"Tell me about skill levels."

SKILL LEVELS

When initially engraved to the Soul, Skills are at Level 1, a state of minimum power requirements and minimum results. With exception of Immutables, all Skills can be leveled up to Level 5, each Level increasing power requirements and results exponentially.

SKILL LEVEL	SOUL CAPACITY CONSUMED
1	50
2	500
3	5000
4	50000
5	500000

Lukas gulped. 500,000? For a single skill? He had seen a somewhat smaller number listed next to the broken skill, but she was a goddess, so it was obvious that her powers would be way above mortal pay grade. But if a Level 5 required *500,000* Soul Capacity then—

"What registered on your schema was a broken fragment of my true skill."

"I might regret asking, but what is the actual cost of your Kinetomancy?"

Inanna proceeded to rattle off an obscenely large number.

Lukas's mind went blank as he processed the weight of the value he'd just heard.

"If it helps, the only time I used my divine powers was at the end, and those . . . aren't really registered through Soul Capacity."

"Then—"

"Check for arcane skills."

He did.

ARCANE SKILLS

Skills that are gained through BLESSINGS of Divinities, and have specific Faith requirements to be engraved on the Soul. Once engraved, Arcane Skills can be fueled by natural or derivative energy sources.

And suddenly, it all made sense.

"You said you could teach me things beyond my comprehension if I accepted your offer. Power beyond measure. You were talking about arcane skills."

Ah." She grinned. **"Your understanding has finally arrived."**

Lukas snorted, glancing down at the blonde. "Her frost. It was unnatural. Was that another arcane skill?"

"I doubt it. Its origins are closer to my own nature."

Slowly, hesitantly, he extended his hand out. There she was, lying on the floor, covered in her cloak. It was so easy to imagine her as asleep.

"Mortal."

His hand stiffened.

"I made an investment in the girl. I will be most displeased if it yields nothing."

All investments carried a risk, Lukas wanted to say, but decided otherwise. The girl was powerful. Unreasonably so. Having her on his side would make things easier.

Making up his mind, he slowly touched her shoulder.

The girl's eyes snapped open. She glanced at his hand, then at him and then back at herself. He could see calculations running in her mind and—

The girl spun around, getting up faster than humanly possible, and threw him onto the floor. Before he knew it, she was perched on top of him, two wind blades scratching at the soft flesh of his neck.

" . . . Ow," he said lamely.

"Who are you?" she demanded, pressing the blades tighter. A little more, and she'd draw blood.

"Seriously," he asked, frowning. "You break through a wall, accuse me of a theft I didn't commit, and then try to kill me. Multiple times. And now you're asking me who I am? That's rich!"

He felt something wet on his neck, but didn't bother attacking. It would be hilariously easy to snap her neck at such close proximity if he wanted. The blonde he had fought earlier was an aggressive attacker. But the girl before him? He could clearly see the hesitation, confusion, and fear in her eyes.

What did you do to her? Why doesn't she recognize me?

"I removed her memories of the fight. The important ones, at least. She has not done anything deserving to have a memory of me."

That's . . . one way of putting it, I suppose.

"Don't you remember anything?" Lukas asked the blonde. "Anything at all?"

The gentle question made her hesitate. Her frown deepened, and she peered at him in mute disbelief. Lukas could almost see the cogs running inside her head. This close, he couldn't help but study her profile. She was built like a well-proportioned statue, and at the same time, looked like a starved thing, twitching at every sound and motion like a feral cat. Her eyes were alert, trying to watch the whole world at once, and she was coiled like a spring ready to go off at a moment's notice.

"My name is Lukas," he finally said in Ualbesh. "It's nice to meet you."

The blonde glared at him, teeth gritted, unsure how to deal with the sudden politeness. She pulled the blades away, but only enough to not hurt him anymore.

" . . . Tanya," she replied, her voice barely above a whisper. "I'm Tanya."

"Tanya." A common name back on Earth. "Can you please remove that blade from my neck? I like being alive."

She didn't budge.

"Look," he tried, "why don't you tell me how you came here? Or . . . what's the last thing you remember?"

"I—" she began. Lukas watched as her expression blossomed into confusion. "I . . . can't seem to remember what happened. I think we . . . fought?"

"You called me food, then attacked me out of nowhere with ice and wind of all things. A pretty interesting combination, honestly."

Tanya stiffened at that. "You . . . you fought me when I was using the Frost?"

"Drove a spear of it right through my hand, actually," he replied, enjoying her growing trepidation more than he should have. "And my left arm. And the legs, too."

Tanya seized his chin with one hand and brought the wind blade closer again. Lukas could feel the wind current flaring against his beard.

"You're *lying!*" she snarled. "No one can survive after being impaled by Frost."

"Then how do you explain this?" He shifted his head toward one of his blades, lying on the floor near him. Layered upon it was a thin sliver of rime. "A souvenir from our battle. You came in, demanding me to give back a kami. A marid, a shape-shifting water demon. I denied having it, and you attacked me."

Tanya winced, holding her head with her fingers lightly. "You—you're a pyromancer?"

"Ah," Lukas drawled, "finally."

"I—I think I remember now." She took another step back, her stance openly antagonistic. "You're Cyffnarian, aren't you?"

"Look, I get that you're confused and just acting out—"

Half a dozen wind blades materialized in the air, all aimed toward him.

"—which is perfectly natural," he finished, slowly raising his arms in surrender. "But I assure you, I'm worth one decent conversation without resorting to blows."

The wind blades doubled.

Lukas sighed. "Look, if you're going to take offense at every word that comes out of my mouth, we really can't have a conversation. So why don't you send those blades away, and I don't have to—"

"Kill me?"

" . . . Fight you," Lukas corrected. "Again, I might add. But that works too. I mean, you did try to kill me earlier."

"I—I remember hurting. And you, standing above me. Your foot on my cheek."

"Of all the things— Look! I'm sure we can agree that all of this was just a rotten first impression. Now I'm *not* from this Cyffnar place, and clearly you're not the murder-happy psychopath I remember, so why don't we just . . . you know"—he slowly got up—"sit down, and talk about it. *Just* talk."

She wiped a hand over her eyes, then mirrored his posture slowly, a bit too slowly for his taste. "I swear, if this is some kind of—"

"Not a trap. It's a discussion," Lukas interrupted her. "Civilized people tend to have one from time to time. You know, instead of throwing blades at each other's faces."

She rolled her eyes. "Fine. If you're not Cyffnarian, where are you from?"

"Maluscion."

Tanya quirked an eyebrow at him. "Where in Maluscion?"

"Ravenside," Lukas replied easily. He'd selected Maluscion for three reasons—it was densely populated, it had an alarmingly large number of nomadic adventurers, and most importantly, it was part of the fringes. Just enough to call itself a part of the Empire, yet distant enough to avoid a full-fledged investigation. While Ualbesh was generally spoken around those regions, one needed to have a passing familiarity with Felleisen as well.

That wasn't a problem for him.

One of the possessed soldiers at the yokai base had had a freelancing adventurer from Ravenside, the main port city of Maluscion. Given the kind of damage soul possession did to the victims, getting him to speak had been child's play.

The memory brought a grimace to his lips.

"And how did a Maluscion adventurer get here?" Tanya asked warily.

"You wouldn't believe me if I told you."

Her eyes narrowed in challenge. "Try me."

He looked her dead in the eye. "Fine. Would you believe me if I said that I suffered a spell mishap, then found myself in this anomaly with nothing but the clothes on my back?"

Tanya frowned. "Of course not."

"Well, I suffered a spell accident, then found myself in this anomaly with nothing but the clothes on my back."

CHAPTER 39

CONVERGING PATHS

Tanya had experienced her fair share of weird.

She'd come far from that scared little girl trembling in her bed, listening to an alien force of nature as it told her how she was a monster. She had grown older, stronger, and far more in control of herself and the Frost since then.

Apparently, it meant nothing where it really counted.

She had lingering memories of the fight against the strange spiritual creatures. Maude completely under their possession, her tremendous reserves of lifeforce that she used for healing others now desecrated and used to create massively overpowered explosions to kill everything around her. She remembered lacerating the wild boar into half a dozen pieces, only for it to possess Olfric and then Elena released that *THING* and—

She let out a hiss. Even trying to remember what happened after that was painful. There was this muddled image of fighting a watery—watery creature—*Olfric's kami,* she realized—and then—

She had given in to the Frost.

Against this man, who claimed to have suddenly woken up in the middle of the anomaly because of a *spell mishap.*

"Do you think I'm an idiot or something?"

" . . . I'm not sure if you want me to answer that," he replied cheekily.

It made her bristle. His mannerisms reminded her of Banksi during one of their discussions. The terramancer had the nasty habit of leading others on by their own words.

"Prove you're what you say you are!" she yelled.

"You're a deeply distrusting person, aren't you?"

Tanya hissed.

"Which I can understand," he backpedaled, much to her surprise. "But I don't believe I warrant this much suspicion. Despite your attempts to kill me, I laid you down and covered you with your cloak."

She narrowed her eyes. "What do you mean by covered me—"

It took her an entire second to realize her current state, another to process it, and yet another to actually react. Flushing a vivid red, she acted out of instinct and threw her hands up at Lukas, erecting a wall of—

" . . . Frost?"

Tanya looked at her own hand, as if seeing it for the first time. "This is—I can—"

Narrowing her eyes, she flicked her right hand again and raised a wall of ice, this one perpendicular to the first one. It wasn't that using Frost was a difficult thing for her. Rather, it was the easiest thing for her to summon. It didn't deplete her lifeforce, or her mana pool. It was always there, manifesting upon this world from an ever-abundant source.

All she needed to do was give in to the *hunger*. Lose herself and become a predator.

But now? There was nothing. No feeling of coldness arose within her. No spike in her emotions either.

There was simply . . . nothing.

And somehow, Frost still answered her.

What was going on?

Lukas cleared his throat, a frown marring his face. "Well, I'm not sure what *that* was for, but I hope you're satisfied now."

Tanya looked up, tongue-tied, suddenly realizing she had unwittingly attacked the man. Murmuring a soft apology, she looked for her bag and grabbed it. Luckily, there was another set of clothes in it, which she quickly changed into after raising two more walls of ice to create a private space. Given the kind of thoughts her blurry memories had generated, added with the burning arousal below her navel, finding herself dressed so skimpily in front of *him* felt absolutely mortifying. Her face burned so deeply that she wondered if she might have gotten a fever. Much to her relief—and simultaneous disappointment—the frozen walls kept him from watching her.

She tried to beat the feeling down, but she was having a harder time than usual. The idea of her writhing in ecstasy under him was now burned into her mind.

Just *what* did this stranger do to her?

Breathing normally was getting harder by the minute, and Tanya grabbed the frozen walls for support. The sudden feeling of arctic cold on her bare palms served as a good distraction.

"Are you fine?" asked the stranger.

"I—" She fumbled over what to say. "I'll be done in a moment."

"Good. Then we can sit down and speak like civilized people."

Silently, she finished putting on her new clothes before shattering the walls to smithereens with a simple touch. The self-proclaimed Maluscian pyromancer was stripped down to his waist and seated on the ground. Tanya was intrigued by the scars on his chest. They made intriguing patterns where they crisscrossed.

"You don't run from much, do you?" she asked out of nowhere, noticing the lack of scarring on his back as she walked over to him.

"I try not to. Not unless it's absolutely necessary. If you let yourself get attacked from behind, you don't get scars. You get a hole in the ground."

Considering he'd fought against her and survived, Tanya couldn't begin to imagine what kind of situation could force this man to desert a fight. He was a pyromancer, and a strong one at that. Adventurers of such skill didn't just appear out of thin air. It was more likely that he was hired as part of the militant force they'd encountered outside the cave. His Cyffnarian clothes only helped support that narrative.

But at the same time, this *Lukas* wasn't treating her like a threat. It wasn't that he was looking down on her, but instead, it felt like he was detached from the situation, as if the chance of another skirmish had nothing to do with him. He didn't think she could kill him. Hurt him, maybe, but not kill. It made sense he wasn't afraid of her. If he was to be believed, he had faced her with her Frost and came out unscathed.

"You . . . really believe you're in no danger, don't you?"

"Yes, I do," he replied with what sounded like complete honesty. "If you want to walk away, feel free. But"—his voice lowered to a cold, hard whisper— "remember the state of my back before you think about driving one of your wind blades through it. I'll fucking *bury* you."

That tone . . . Tanya had heard it before.

She had *been* that tone before.

She recalled the many assassins she'd buried to their necks in the earth, and the savage satisfaction that filled her when it was over. They had come for her, wronged her, and paid the price. There was something bright about that pure, righteous anger.

By Wind, she knew how he felt. She knew how that fire in his chest burned. Dare she say, she even respected him for it.

"Why does a Maluscian adventurer wear Cyffnarian battle attire?" Tanya asked, changing the subject.

His expression did not falter in the least. Interesting. Was he truly not an enemy?

"This little thing?" he asked, looking down. "I encountered some kind of foot soldier wandering around. We had a little disagreement. He left his armor behind as an apology."

Tanya was smart enough not to ask what that meant. "And those blades?"

"Custom made from a greedy bastard in Galvore."

"Where were you employed last?"

"Why is that important?"

"Because it is."

"Is that so?" he grunted, arms crossed against his chest. "Well then, my secrets are mine to keep, just like yours."

Tanya furrowed her brows. His story was perfect, and he knew enough to pass for a Maluscian adventurer. Add in his confidence and his skill level, and it made for a striking picture. And she had no conclusive evidence to prove he was part of the Cyffnarian camp, seeing as how he didn't seem to want to fight her.

Her eyes flickered white for an instant.

Mana	3000
Lifeforce	3500

. . . Three thousand?

That's impossible.

She tried again.

Mana	3000
Lifeforce	3500

For once, she was genuinely short on words. The upper three thousands was a respectable place to be—not overwhelming, but nothing to scoff at either. Lukas was stronger than both Zuken and Olfric in lifeforce and manacrafting, but her allies had the elemental advantage. As did she.

Even so, he somehow kicked her ass.

Mana	3000
Lifeforce	3500

This couldn't be the entire picture. There *had* to be something else. Something that had allowed him to triumph over her own skills amplified by Ezzeron and the Frost.

Unless he's like me? Having something that could get him killed if others knew about it?

A part of her wanted to give up on this man and run away. Between her own dexterity and Ezzeron's powers, she could vanish faster than he could blink. But every time she considered doing just that, an overwhelming sense of *wrongness pervaded her*. She considered killing him, but then *shot down each of those ideas with extreme prejudice*. Instead, she was stuck here with an *irresistible* need to speak to him.

Tanya supposed it wasn't all that bad. She was *defeated and alone* in this anomaly, surrounded by monsters baying for her blood. Staying near a *powerful* warrior who wasn't antagonistic toward her *and was also easy on the eyes* wasn't a bad trade-off.

The burning feelings of desire wanted him close, preferably using a rather indecent, primitive approach to get him there. And he wasn't using any spell-craft upon her. Her mental defenses would've warned her of the slightest attempts at Psychomancy.

It had to be from using so much Frost all at once.

"Well," Lukas started, pushing himself up off the floor, "I'm done resting. It's time for me to move on."

"To where?"

He grinned. "To the heart of this anomaly."

"Are you serious?"

"Perfectly," he replied as he started walking. Tanya quickly followed.

"But *why?*"

"Because I want to."

"That's not an answer!"

"Yes. It is."

She didn't miss the undercurrent of sternness in his tone, all but demanding she let the matter drop.

"I'm an adventurer just like you. It's safe to assume our interests either coincide or clash, and I won't reveal anything else until I receive confirmation of which it is."

"Then maybe you should've thought of that before being so nice to me," she replied.

A slow smile spread across his lips. "All I've told you is where I'm going. What you do with the information will decide the rest."

"What do you mean?"

"You're wound up tighter than a coiled spring. You're nervous and scared and angry, and you'd kill for a little breathing space. You came in demanding the water kami earlier, and you have a wind-type kami. That means it belongs to someone else. Someone you know. Meaning, you have friends. Coworkers. Associates. And yet, despite that, you're walking with me instead of trying to go find them."

"You don't know that!" she snapped. "It's all just conjecture!"

"Maybe, but not without its merits," he easily replied. "It makes me wonder why an aeromancer as skilled as yourself doesn't want to find her associates. I'm pretty sure you have ways to find them, yet you haven't. The other possibility? They're all dead."

Her insides clenched. She didn't let it show. There was no doubt that an extremely sharp mind lurked behind his flippant attitude. Just like a certain Banksi she knew. Adventurers were supposed to be the cold, uncaring, and ruthless types. Doubly so during missions. Instead, Lukas was being . . . *nice.* Creepily so.

Why does he keep doing that? What is he . . . Why is he smiling? she thought with growing desperation. Her strangely active libido didn't help matters either.

As if sensing her discomfort, she felt Ezzeron's questioning in her mind. Not a thought, as he wasn't really able to do that. What came through their connection was more like an impulse, one that could easily be put into words.

Kill?

Never let it be said that Ezzeron needed speech to get his point across. Although she hadn't released her kami, she could picture him just fine. An elephantine avian, with wings as black as the nights in the desert. With just one word from her, Ezzeron could materialize in the physical world and slaughter anyone, destroying anything she commanded him to do. It was all he could do, and he did it well.

No, she responded. *Not yet.*

The kami within her tensed, like a taut bow, ready to pounce upon the young man. That in itself was all kinds of bad. Ezzeron, by his very nature, had the tendency to ignore nearly everything around him, classifying them as *weak.*

But not Lukas.

"You're right. I have associates," Tanya confirmed. "But we got attacked by monsters and separated."

And then she turned into a far more vicious monster and tore everything apart, until she ran into him.

"Oh? There's more of you?" His eyes brightened. "Where are they? Speaking of which, where are you from?"

"The Llaisy Kingdom."

She noted the spark of recognition in his eyes.

"That means you must have come in through, uh, Haviskali, right?"

And there it was again. His casual familiarity with the place. For someone who claimed to have been spatially displaced by several thousand miles, he was awfully knowledgeable about the desert and its surrounding regions. Someone like that, randomly walking through the tunnels, searching for something . . .

He couldn't have been looking for Experience. Or treasure. That left—

Tanya froze. Lukas was going deeper into the anomaly. Deeper. Toward the core. Her hands tightened to the point that she almost drew blood, before forcing herself to relax again. "So that's how it is."

"Hm?"

" . . . Nothing. I'm just thinking out loud."

Tanya had underestimated the situation. Underestimated *him*. The clues had always been there. He had never quite been shy about it. The casual demeanor. The cocky attitude. The unwavering confidence that he would prevail should a fight happen. The strange impulses she got about him. The Frost's anomalous behavior. Him *defeating* her. Ezzeron's wariness. Him walking to the center of the anomaly.

"That look there on your face tells me you've come to some kind of conclusion," Lukas said, matching her stare with his own. To her shame, she was the first to look away. "For your sake, I hope you don't do anything foolish about it."

She bit her lip. If she played her cards right, this could turn into a favorable situation for her.

"I believe you," she finally said, leaning back against the wall, crossing her legs and pushing her chest subtly forward. Distracted people gave away more than they intended, and she was rather good at distracting. "You're not Cyffnarian. And you're right. Neither of us are obligated to answer the other's questions. Nonetheless, I think . . . I think I understand what you're after."

His smile turned predatory. "Do you now?"

"I think you want to destroy the anomaly core."

A flicker of amusement crossed his face. "And what makes you think that?"

"Beside the point, since there's no evidence of the fact," she quickly replied. "But let's say, hypothetically, that you were aware of someone in this very anomaly capable of . . . destroying the core. Hypothetically, if someone wanted to acquire this person's services, how would they go about doing it?"

The amusement slid off his face like butter, replaced by surprise. "*You* want to destroy the anomaly's core?"

"Well, uh, hypothetically—"

"And you'd *pay* for this service?"

"I mean—"

"How much?"

"Fine! Yes!" Tanya threw her hands up in the air and gave up all pretenses of the act. "For reasons I can't reveal, I have to destroy the core of this anomaly." She saw him open his mouth and barreled on. "Yes, I know. It's a Sin, and I have no option to commit it. It won't be a problem for me, or so I'm told."

He frowned thoughtfully. "Is that why you don't want to find your associates? Because they're forcing you to do this?"

She shook her head. "I'm doing it of my own accord. It's . . . Let's just say it's an offer I can't refuse."

Lukas's expression had lost all traces of humor. It was replaced by something

. . . else. His eyes bore into hers for several long seconds, as if searching for any lies in her statements. Finally, he nodded tersely. "I'll deal with it."

Tanya shrugged off the inexplicable fear that had risen in her at his sudden shift. "You didn't answer my question. What would you want in return?"

"As I said, I'll take care of it."

"And what do you want in return?" she repeated.

Lukas sighed. "There's . . . a chance that things might not work out the way I want them to. Should that happen, I may need a place to stay for the considerable future."

Her eyes widened in surprise. "Why not go back to Maluscion? I'm certain travel arrangements can be made if you need—"

"I want a fresh start. New identity. New documents. A place to live."

"Are you running from the Cobalt Army?" she asked quietly, after a long pause.

"Not . . . exactly," Lukas said. "Circumstances prohibit me from using my current identity. You asked me what I wanted? I need a new one. Can you and your associates provide it?"

It was an easy question.

"Yes. I can promise to talk to my associates about this deal. But I can't promise they'd agree to it."

"And why's that?"

"The Sin."

"Oh, that." The look of puzzlement on his face dissipated. "That won't be a problem."

"Excuse me?" she exclaimed.

"I'm able to destroy the core without Sinning," he said, as if he hadn't just uttered the most ridiculous thing she had ever heard in her life.

"That makes no sense!"

"I'm devastated by that."

"Stop fucking around!" Tanya replied hotly, the words coming out with more hostility than she intended. "I've Sinned before. I know how it works. You do know what an anomaly core is, don't you?"

The pyromancer rolled his eyes. "Let's just say I'm capable of doing it without amassing any Sin, and leave it at that. The 'how' doesn't matter."

"The 'how' *always* matters."

Lukas eyed her strangely, before a slow smile laden with secrets made itself known. It was like a joke only he was privy to, no one else. The kind that he laughed at alone, while everyone looked on with bemusement.

Not that he would tell her if she asked. They were strangers, after all.

"Sure," she sighed. "Fine, I guess it doesn't matter. Just know that while my Frost is useful against an anomaly core, your Pyromancy really isn't. You'll have trouble if you use it."

"Well then"—he grinned—"I suppose it's a good thing I won't be using fire."

. . .

Tanya was *this* close to losing her sanity completely and utterly.

"Can you at least tell me *why* you want to destroy it in the first place?" she asked, making certain her tone carried urgency without sounding like a demand. "We have our reasons. What about you?"

"Why do you want to know?"

"It's common sense, isn't it? If you're going to be my ally, then I need to know more so I can trust you."

"Ally, huh?" He chuckled. "Don't worry. You can trust that I know what I'm doing."

"Then what are you after, at least?"

"Power."

Tanya was taken aback by how matter-of-factly he said it.

"The spell mishap that brought me here. I want to perform it," he said. "Successfully, this time. And to do that, I'll need lots of power."

"You want to take it from the core," Tanya said.

It wasn't a question or suggestion—it was a fact. An omphalos was a thing of pure power. Power beyond the use of any bremetan. However, the energy from an omphalos was incredibly lethal to a bremetan upon direct exposure. It was why she had to use her powers of Frost to leech it away. The Frost would feast upon it and freeze the entire place by the time it was over.

"How would you do it? Anomalous energy is harmful to bremetans."

"I have my ways."

"And you're certain your ways would work?"

She could see the frustration rising within him. Just a little more and he'd crack like an egg. That or he'd attack her and they'd fight. Again. Either way, it would lead to something. Standing here at such close proximity was doing *odd things to her*. She wasn't sure how long she could take the tension.

Seduction by talking someone to death. That had to be a first.

"I'm reliably certain I can use it. Again, why does any of this matter? I take care of the anomaly core without amassing Sin, and you and your folks get me a fresh identity. It's that simple, isn't it?"

" . . . I suppose."

"Well then." He grinned brightly, and she couldn't help but match it. "We have an accord!" Then, all of a sudden, his hand shot out toward her navel. Tanya stepped back instantly, a wind blade in her palm.

"What was that?!"

Lukas staggered back, not out of fear, but surprise. "I, uh, I was just about to shake hands with you."

"Shake . . . hands?"

She watched worriedly as something akin to distress flickered across his face, before disappearing, as if it were never there at all. "Forgive me. It is a gesture among my people. Shaking hands."

He thrust his arm out again, slower this time. It stayed at the navel level, but didn't move any farther down. What was she supposed to do? Hold it? Was that what this was about? Holding hands? *Not that she'd complain.*

Hesitantly, she grabbed it with her own.

"Is this right?"

"Sort of."

So he *did* want to hold her hand. And then shake it up and down for some reason.

That was fine. It felt nice.

PART VII

LIVE AND LET DIE

CHAPTER 40

25TH HOUR

Darkness.

Its STATE was damaged beyond repair. Multiple wreckages of constructed terrain were consuming large quantities of Anomalous Energy. Sudden spike in Monster Soul Prototype influx was alarming. Whatever intruder had invaded past its defenses, the Crypt of Fiendish Worms was finding it difficult to put it down.

This could be a MAJOR PROBLEM.

Invaders were a non-issue. NORMAL Invader Activity was essential to constant survival. Information from the Watchers indicated the presence of a He-Who-Consumes-Within. Conflicting observation, since no foreign Anomalous Energy was traced.

The Crypt of Fiendish Worms extended its awareness outwards. EXTERNAL ALTERATIONS negative, as usual. The land was soaked in ANTI-LIFE concepts.

Not consumable. Rejected.

It turned its gaze inward. Vital statistics showed the INNER LAYER bordering on NEARLY DESTROYED.

Intruder He-Who-Consumes-Within REMOVED Monster Prototype THOGGUA from SOUL CRYPT.

Intruder He-Who-Consumes-Within REMOVED Monster Prototype OROCORAN from SOUL CRYPT.

Intruder He-Who-Consumes-Within REMOVED Monster Prototype SEUGATHI from SOUL CRYPT.

Intruder He-Who-Consumes-Within REMOVED Monster Prototype NEOTHELID from SOUL CRYPT.

. . .

. . .

The list went on and on. This was OUTRAGEOUS.

He-Who-Consumes-Within was CONSUMING Monster Prototypes from ITSELF, and the Crypt of Fiendish Worms was doing NULL. It could do NULL about it.

Unacceptable.

Unacceptable.

A wave of Anomalous Energy expanded outward from ITSELF, radiating from the crystals of the SOUL CRYPT.

Anomalous Energy Reflected

Anomalous Energy Absorbed

Neonate Anomaly Detected within Expansion Radius
PREDATOR Detected within Expansion Radius
Probability of Destruction of SOUL CRYPT = 47%

Unacceptable.

Utterly Unacceptable.

He-Who-Consumes-Within is a CONTRADICTION
PREDATOR is an AGGRAVATION
RECOMMENDATION
Instant-Termination of both Species.

Tempting recommendation. But Instant-Termination would require a forceful trigger of FAILSAFE.

Not recommended.

But . . . necessary.

Soul Crypt contraction was underway. Monster count had been drastically reduced. All Anomalous Expansions were on hold.

It was time for Instant-Termination.

Safety Off!
Initiate Extermination

CHAPTER 41

SOMETHING WICKED THIS WAY COMES

It was like being caught flat-footed in the gaze of a serpent.

Lukas and Tanya had traveled a long way, but there was no telling how much farther he'd have to go. His instincts told him it was the right way, but there were fewer and fewer monsters on their path.

And then the Screen went crazy.

Prey found you.

He turned around, glancing at the path they had just traveled from.

Prey found you.

Right. Left. Up. Down.
All the same.

Prey found you.

Analyze.

INCOMPLETE **INCOMPLETE Parts that are INCOMPLETE without** **AGGREGATION.**

" . . . what are you doing?" Tanya demanded.

"There's . . . something around us," he quickly responded, the urgency in his tone conveyed with steel-like composure. The Scan function was going haywire, and he could feel something dark and hungry coiling around him. It was eerily similar to the time he'd encountered the khorkhoi. Something stirred against the moss-covered walls, slowly extending inward from all directions. The bioluminescence from the moss did little against its inky blackness.

"What is it?" Tanya hissed, falling into a familiar fighting stance.

"Don't worry, it's not going to attack us. Yet."

"What's not going to attack us? I don't see anything," she said, looking around. "I've been gauging the lifeforce around us. It's just moss."

She's got a method for discerning strength?

"What do I register on your gauging scale?" Lukas tried to sound casual.

"In the upper three thousands. Why do you ask?"

. . . Shit.

He hadn't considered the fact that other people, or creatures for that matter, could sense his strength. Sense how much lifeforce flooded through his veins. Sensed how much mana he could use. Maybe even more than mere specifics.

Was this why Solana was so cool when dealing with him? Because she could gauge his strength and knew he was little more than an amoeba in front of her? Sure, an amoeba with interesting skills, but an amoeba nonetheless. Had she known that he'd be able to fight Quonnan and survive? And if so, what else had she known?

Suddenly, his control over his yokai situation didn't feel as concrete.

"About time you learned that lesson yourself."

Solana had perfectly known his power levels, but his personal confidence and his ability to Soul Siphon must have sold the idea that there was more, a lot more about him that she couldn't read.

"Is something wrong?" Tanya asked.

"No. Everything's alright," he replied. "It's just, whatever spell you're using isn't giving you the full picture."

"Excuse me?"

Lukas attempted to find the right words. "The best way to describe this thing is 'incomplete.'"

"That doesn't make any sense. You mean it's dead?"

No, it definitely wasn't dead. But he half expected it not to make sense. It was just one of those quirks that came with being an anomaly. He instinctively knew how certain things worked, but the reasons behind them were blurry at best. A plus B was C, but why that was true was beyond him.

"I'm . . . not particularly knowledgeable in this branch of analysis," he began explaining, careful not to use any words that could give away his own nature. "The thing around us is part of a set. An extremely defined set. Somehow, this has been, for lack of a better term, *emphasized* exponentially, to the point where it's almost a rule in itself. The *set* is somehow more important to this thing than *being*, if that makes any sense."

If Tanya's deadpan expression was anything to go off of, she was far from enlightened.

Lukas nervously rubbed the back of his neck. "How do I explain this? The thing—or things, whatever they are—exist. That means the rest of it must surely be around." He glanced at the walls before continuing. "It's a basic concept being pushed to the extreme, but I can't tell how it's being implemented. The things around us are part of the greater whole, and it's this greater whole that gives it its identity. Without the whole, they may as well be pebbles on the ground."

" . . . Right." She frowned. By the looks of it, she was having a hard time following his bizarre, circular logic. "So where exactly is this *greater whole* you're talking about?"

"Somewhere around us. It's assimilating, I suppose," Lukas said, his voice slightly hollow. "That's why I think these things won't attack us."

"I don't follow."

"Whatever these things are, they're effectively inert until the greater whole comes into the picture. But it's already surrounded us from all sides." There was no escaping this place. Lukas could feel something nagging at the back of his mind, telling him that the greater whole would be incredibly dangerous. What this creature was, it was stronger than anything else he had ever faced before.

"I am impressed, mortal," Inanna praised from within his mind. **"Attempting to explain an alien mindset is no minor feat."**

Sighing, he plopped down onto the rocky floor. Glancing toward Tanya, he patted the spot on the floor beside him. "Come sit. There's hardly anything we can do until the fight begins."

Tanya just stared at him, mouth slightly ajar.

"Yeah, I know," he murmured, eyeing her with amusement. "Sucks to be me."

With nothing else but time on their hands, Lukas and Tanya sat down and ate the last of their food. Spelunking through underground caverns was much easier when you could ignite fire with just a snap of your fingers. Years of living with his grandfather had made him self-sufficient at cooking. He was no Thomas Keller, but he could do a decent grilled lamb. Tanya had requested a sauteed meat dish, but since he was the cook, he'd sternly informed her that this was no democracy, and that they would gratefully eat grilled steak.

When the monster finally formed, it was strangely calm, much to Lukas's disappointment.

No sudden explosion of power. No massive tentacles erupting from the floor. No glowing eyes forming in the air radiating destructive, unadulterated malevolence. Instead, there was this weird power twisting and writhing into something *else*—that in itself was grounds for running for the hills, if there were any.

And that wasn't all.

The power was flowing inward. Alien world or not, Lukas wanted to believe that the law of conservation of energy still held true. If the things around him were sucking in energy, then it had come from somewhere else. Considering that this monster—if he could even call it that—was everywhere, the chances of finding its source of power were practically zero. Already, rocks and debris started to fall around. Cracks formed on the walls. They were thin, jagged lines so far, but still enough cause for caution.

"I don't believe it!" Tanya murmured. The girl was practically quaking in her boots. "Its power—"

"How much?" Lukas interrupted. The fact that she could sense the amount of energy in something else while he, an anomaly, could not, felt like a slap to his face. Maybe he would unlock this capability with future upgrades on the Analyze function, but until then, he reserved the right to be grumpy about it.

"Twenty-six thousand."

Lukas whistled. "Must be an eat-all-you-want buffet for you then."

Tanya turned away. "It's not that simple."

"Your frost consumes life—lifeforce," Lukas replied nonchalantly. "This thing has a lot of lifeforce. Doesn't get any simpler than that."

She shook her head. "It's true that my Frost can consume lifeforce. But it—" She frowned. "How do I put it? The frost simply channels the lifeforce into me, and replenishes my reserves."

He goggled at her in total disbelief. "You're telling me you can just absorb lifeforce from others and use it to fuel your attacks? That means you're capable of fighting endlessly!"

" . . . Theoretically. But sooner or later, the muscles fatigue. The lungs, the heart—they can only run on overdrive for so long. After a certain point, they accumulate damage. No lifeforce can heal that."

Lukas thought back to Inanna's Alleviation technique: a skill that literally returned the host body to a backup of itself. "Yeah . . . that's true," he lied.

"Also, too much lifeforce flowing through your veins can have . . . side effects."

Lukas looked at her, or rather, the faint color in her cheeks.

Oh.

Oh.

" . . . Yeah, I get that," he replied, feeling a little uncomfortable.

Tanya rummaged through her waist bag and pulled out a pair of thin, cylindrical canisters. She tossed one of them at him. Looking at it up close, he could see strange sigils etched on its surface. Sigils that looked no different than the ones he had seen at the yokai territory.

"**Not true,**" replied the goddess. "**This one represents illumination. Light that brightens. Light that disperses the shadow. And nothing else.**"

He faltered. Nothing as in—

"**No heat. No destruction. No growth. No purity. Only illumination.**"

"Eternal Light torches," Tanya said, as if the statement was self-explanatory. "I only have two left."

So this is Eternal Light. Lukas absentmindedly rolled the canister around. Eternal Light, an illumination that yokai feared to tread into. The magical flashlights of this world.

"Best not to use both at once," Tanya said, her attention focused on the miasma rolling on the walls. And then she switched on her light.

There was no radiant beam shooting out of it. Instead, something white exploded around them, inundating the area with light. It was like daytime, only there was no sun overhead. No sense of heat either. Only an eerie illumination that somehow made the cavern feel colder.

This—this wasn't what light was supposed to feel like. This was a twisted facsimile of the real thing, a terrible parody crafted by someone playing God. Just being in its presence made him want to throw up.

Alien TRUTH from PRESENCE registered.
Initiating Activation of LIVING ANOMALY state . . .

New OMPHALOS FUNCTION Added!		
FUNCTION	**LEVEL**	**ENERGY COST**
Living Anomaly	N/A	Variable
DESCRIPTION		
The User is a Living Anomaly, an enigmatic being that exists within a System while escaping its Rules.		
VOLUNTARY	**Currently Set to OFF**	
Set STATE to ON?		

"**Keep it off,**" Inanna advised. "**You do not want to stand out so soon by ignoring the Truths of the divinities of this World.**"

Lukas did so, and looked back at Tanya, finding her staring at the walls, transfixed. He followed her line of sight to the walls. Every inch was now covered by . . . *it.*

Someone screamed, he dimly noted. His eyes were transfixed to it. Flesh, dead and dried. Flesh, alive and writhing. The languid, arrhythmic pulsing of corpses filled with maggots. Claws and nails on a chalkboard. Bone. Flesh. Slime. Metal. The Analyze function threw him a set of contradictions that he couldn't make heads or tails of, except that the stomach-churning, nightmare-inducing *wrongness* was now all around him. Seeing it in the illumination only made it appear more grotesque. It took everything he had not to just throw up on the spot.

Instead he watched as the thing became more.

Gathering. Twisting. Churning.

Then, *they* began to form.

Utterly pitch black, it was a monstrosity made of ropy tentacles, each easily three times his size, standing on stumpy, hoofed legs. Another mass of tentacles, their surfaces shining with a metallic luster, protruded out of their necks, spiraling upward before combining into puckered maws, dripping silvery-green goo that covered their flanks. The ghastly caricature resembled trees in silhouette, with the trunks being short legs and the tops of the trees representing ropy, branching bodies. The macabre things twisted and trudged around on legs too short to carry them, shaking the very floor with every step.

"S-six," he heard her stutter, as she carefully bent over to pick up her flashlight. "There are six of them."

"For now," he replied, cracking his neck as the screen flashed with new information.

DRANZITHL
Chimeric Miasma brought to life. Extremely thick dermal layer with regenerative miasmatic tissue underneath. Compound 360-degree sensory awareness. Capable of DECAY synthesis.

Probable progeny of [INCOMPLETE]

Decay? That was new. And potentially dangerous. The Screen rarely warned him about skills.

"Congratulations. You have awoken the guardian. The greatest defense an anomaly can have. Its failsafe."

"Yomi has well and truly opened up on us," Tanya cursed. Frost began to coat her arms. "These creatures are made of flesh. I think I can freeze them."

Lukas watched her discreetly from a corner of his eye. This was the first time he was going to work in tandem with someone. Facing her had given him a good idea of what she was capable of. All that remained was to see how much Inanna's spell would affect her performance.

"I suppose we shall find out."

The things in front of him roared. Not the cry of an animal, but the howling of a hurricane ready to make landfall. It shook the cavern, deepening the darkness within. Even Lukas felt the cold against his skin. Not the sudden frosting that Tanya was capable of, but actual lowering of temperature all around him.

It took him a second to register what exactly was happening.

"A monster so antithetical to life that merely being in its proximity triggers such a reaction? What is a gem like this doing in this decrepit pit?"

. . . No. He wasn't going to dignify that with a comment.

"I do not jest, mortal. You would do well to assimilate this creature into your arsenal. The applications of Decay are nearly limitless."

Decay, huh?

DECAY EFFECT
Lifeforce condensed to 87% potency and above. Upon direct exposure to living tissues, it causes instant weakening, followed by withering, rotting, and eventual death.

This anomaly was a gift that just kept on giving. Fighting a slime was like fighting a hydra, where every head that was lopped off would be replaced by two more. Add in bone, flesh and metal, the power to Decay, and access to far more lifeforce than he could use in a week, and you got one crazy creature.

Kinetomancy would be near useless against this one. As would his general combat style.

He needed an alternative.

SKILL ATTRIBUTES		
SKILL	**LEVEL**	**CONSUMED SOUL CAPACITY**
Raw Lifeforce Manipulation	3	5000
Momentum Manipulation	3	5000
Friction Modulation	2	500
Pressure Modulation	2	500
Kinetomancy (FRAGMENTED)	APEX	1279
Fire Creation	1	50
Fire Manipulation	2	500

Temperature Modulation	1	50
Perception Manipulation	1	50
Conjuration	1	50
Disintegration	1	50
Seismic Sensing	1	50
Shatterpoint Intuition	2	500
Psychomancy	1	50

Fire was always an option. But this wasn't just some regular, singular thing. It was a conglomeration that covered the entire chamber—the floor, the walls, the ceiling. Given his luck, the creature would probably just explode in one go, taking him and Tanya with it.

He needed a safer option.

Tanya's frost could drag lifeforce out of it. But that alone wouldn't work. It was a perfect knife, one that could be used to segregate. He needed a hammer. One that would allow him to constantly fight this thing without being exposed to the Decay.

Lukas Aguilar wasn't an entity suited to fighting against monsters. Instead, it would be more apt to say that he was designed to fight against their powers, skills, and weapons. Countering strengths and exploiting weaknesses, rather than taking on the ones that possessed them.

The more he knew about his enemy, the easier it was to strip them of what made them strong and strike at their core with the least resistance possible. Literally. That meant finding yet another new set of skills to add to his list of options for combat. A new way to fight. A new way to win.

> **Accessing Monster Prototype Array . . .**

The kasha was a bad idea for obvious reasons. The yurei was out as well. The reiki needed him to possess something else and focused extensively on high-powered lifeforce attacks. The neothelid was admittedly a good start, as its passive powers would provide him a resistance against the Decay. He wasn't sure what channeling electricity would do to his nervous system, but he didn't want to try that mid-battle.

The marid might work too. With its ability to manipulate water, and possibly other liquids, Lukas was certain he could use it in conjunction with Tanya's frost to freeze the thing to death. However, doing that would raise all kinds of questions about how he was able to use both fire and water.

He needed something else. A skillset of pure offense, one that didn't require tremendous quantities of lifeforce or access to any of the elements. Yet something that could destroy this enemy without leaving any lasting repercussions on himself.

It was an utterly selfish, unrealistic thing to demand when backed into a corner.

And it was sitting right there, in his Monster Prototype Array, waiting to be used.

Something that fought, not as a human, but a slime.

Activating Monster Prototype Thoggua . . .
Initiating Consciousness Shift . . .
Enact.

CHAPTER 42

HURRICANE

Tanya wasn't entirely sure what she should've been doing.

There were six of those hideous things—she refused to call them monsters, even in her mind. Miasma crawled and twisted all around them. But the only thing she had eyes for was Lukas himself. The pyromancer stood in the center, blade in each hand. Both of his legs were cemented to the floor, unmoving.

But the rest of his body was a blur.

Lukas fought three of them at once. Like a lunatic woodchipper, his blades met flesh. Tentacles fell one after another, unable to survive his onslaught despite layers of thick endoskeleton and slime. Tanya knew those daggers were sharp, but this was the first time she realized how horrifically powerful they were in close combat.

"HAAA!" he yelled, as his blades cut off one of their legs in a clean sweep, carving through muscle and bone as thick as a tree trunk without slowing down in the slightest.

One of its many mouths spit corrosive acid at his face, only for the droplets to freeze midair. Lukas swept his blades through the floating acid and drove it straight into a second one's head.

Her eyes widened as the monster's arm, composed of a great many tentacles to form an incredibly dense limb, exploded in a shower of gore. She didn't know what the pyromancer had done, but his single punch had obliterated the entire tentacle-arm. *And he wasn't even using fire.*

A second later, several pairs of tentacles, two legs, and a crushed head dropped to the floor, unmoving.

Lukas didn't seem to care. He just went on to his next target.

Tanya reflexively swallowed. She was capable of some high-speed swordcraft herself, but this was something else. It was hideous. The empty cleaving of a butcher, without regard to skill or artistry. It was fast, and strong, and every single attack struck with unerring precision and the sound of metal hacking into flesh.

The miasma hissed as it rose from the floor, before converging into pieces of bodily tissue that slithered about, before combining again and coming back to life.

"Oh, no," Tanya snarled. "No one said you could do that!"

Everfrost pierced through its leg, and almost immediately, hoarfrost covered the surface and began to drink the miasma's power. Crystals of growing, putrid ice, black and twisted from the corrupted lifeforce, began to rise all around the fallen body tissue.

But then a writhing tendril of shadows slammed against it, shattering the outgrowth into pieces.

Tanya grimaced. This grotesque thing even used lifeforce differently. She was no expert, but she knew lifeforce to be a useful tool for creation, rejuvenation, and fortification. But tonight, she was witnessing a fourth use of it. One not very prevalent in bremetan society.

Decay.

WAAANNNNNCCHHHHH!

The sound was less like noise and more like getting dunked into a vat of sewage. Tanya staggered back, no longer able to breathe. There was a building pressure against her skin, and her ears burned with pain. She dropped to one knee and clutched her ears as her entire body shook, leaving her dizzy and disoriented. A sound of something swooping made her raise her head, and she instantly froze as a contorted tentacle-limb plunged toward her. Before she could so much as think about moving, a blade came tearing through the air, pinning it down to the ground.

And then it was yanked back into Lukas's hand.

"Tanya?" she heard Lukas ask, his entire form spattered with monster blood. "Are you alright?"

"No," she said, anger and humiliation choking her voice. "No, I'm really, really not."

And then Lukas was gone again, lost to the raging storm of battle. He parried blows from a gigantic limb as it swooped down to impale his heart, but sidestepped and chopped at it from the middle, slicing it in half. It didn't matter that he was surrounded by the miasma, or that the creatures around him were just as quick to regenerate as he was at incapacitating them.

Tanya slowly realized that Lukas simply did not care.

"Now!" came his voice. Tanya jolted, then immediately sent a fresh torrent of arctic frost at the monsters. Hoarfrost spread across their bodies, coating them with dark, corrupted rime once more. Lukas made a motion with his hand, and a moment later, the ice shattered into pieces.

"Yeah, this miasma definitely classifies as a failsafe for the anomaly," he chuckled, eyeing the hulking deformities around them. "Dumpy here was a lot faster than he looked."

"He?" Tanya asked.

"Hmm? Do you think it's a she?" He cocked his head, watching as the miasma slowly coalesced, giving birth to more monsters. Freezing them was a stop-gap measure at best as long as the miasma existed. He had to know that. So why did he keep trying the same strategy?

"This regen is such bullshit. Formless ghol have nothing on them." He snickered, as if it was a joke only he understood. "Although . . . you!" he yelled at one of the remaining creatures, before speeding forward and hacking at its leg, dropping it to the floor. He reared back his fist and let it fly, and a moment later, there was no more monster.

Until its tendrils reformed and it began regenerating. Again.

A foreboding feeling overwhelmed Tanya as she saw the amused expression on Lukas's face.

"So weird," he dryly replied. "No matter where you cut it, it just keeps coming back." He cupped his chin, as if deep in thought. "I wonder what'll make it stay dead."

"Are you . . . are you *enjoying* this?" she asked, a hint of fear in her voice despite herself.

Lukas blinked owlishly, before staring at her incredulously. "Are you *not?*"

"Of course not!" she snapped at him. "Use your fucking fire attacks already. Killing them is obviously child's play to you, so why not just finish it already?"

He flashed her a mad grin. "First of all, it wouldn't be any fun if I did that. Second, using fire has its demerits. And third, I genuinely can't kill them. At least not as they are now." His brows furrowed as he paused to consider his words. "Come to think of it, that last one should've been the first reason."

"But—" Tanya tried.

"I've had enough time to analyze this creature," the pyromancer explained, almost like he was giving her a lecture. "Unless you can freeze the entirety of this miasma all at once, it won't die. But since you can't do that, I'll just have to keep on killing it. Until it gives up on me, or the anomaly gives up on the monster. One second, please excuse me—"

Lukas suddenly spun around, slashing at the next unfortunate thing that came hurtling his way.

"What the hell, man!" He glared at the creatures, waving his hands angrily. "Can't you see I'm in the middle of a conversation here?"

Tanya staggered back. She couldn't tell who she was more afraid of.

Lukas's good mood was gone, as he glared down at the quivering mass of shadows and miasma like it was the root of all the world's problems. "I swear no matter how many times I kill this thing, it just won't die." He looked up and stared at Tanya imploringly. "You agree with me, right? This is *wrong!* People die when they're killed. This thing should too!"

"I . . . yes. It should."

He wolfishly grinned. "See? There's gotta be laws about this stuff. If you're killed, you die. You move on. Allow the next monster to do its shit. Die and let die, you know?"

She took another step back.

"Well," Lukas said, clearly lost in his own world, "I can't say I'm terribly upset about any of this. Ever since, well, recently, I've been itching for a good battle. You know how itches can be. Absolutely maddening, I tell you."

"Yeah," she murmured, wondering if she would even contribute to this fight at all. "I can see that."

"Thought so," Lukas continued, oblivious to her expression. "Hey, can your friend also get me set up as an adventurer in Haviskali?"

Tanya knew she had one of the fastest growths as an adventurer in Haviskali's recent history, but her situation was unique. This lunatic, on the other hand? She wouldn't be surprised if he was sitting on the top of the Haviskali Guild food chain by the end of the week. And that was just considering everything he could do with lifeforce alone.

She paused, an idea forming in her mind.

Maybe—just *maybe*—if she played her cards right, she could use this to her advantage. Between the two of them, they'd make one hell of a team, especially now that she could use her ice powers without losing herself in the process.

Another thing I'm thankful for.

Tanya glanced toward him. Whether he was slightly unhinged or not, she was glad things turned out the way they did. And that was without considering the constant itch she felt for him because of whatever he'd done to her, with the added effect of the Frost whispering to her.

She looked back at the walls as the miasma slid down to the floor. For a moment, Tanya feared an all-out strike. But as anxious seconds passed without tentacular monsters showing up, a different realization came to pass.

They weren't going to attack.

"Is it . . ." she hesitantly asked. "Are they not coming back?"

Lukas didn't answer.

"Lukas?" she asked again.

"Shhh . . . hang on. Something is happening."

That didn't inspire hope in her. Forming a wind blade in her palm, she glared nervously at the black sludge lying motionless near their feet. The pyromancer seemed almost frozen, staring at the sludge with an intense look, as if trying to decipher a complex problem only he could see. Finally, after a series of excruciating seconds, he exhaled and looked back up at her.

"Never mind. It's dead."

Tanya arched an eyebrow. "You sound almost disappointed."

"Maybe I am." He chuckled. "All this fighting, and then the anomaly just cuts off its power supply. That's what killed it. Not our efforts. Feels anticlimactic if you ask me."

She rolled her eyes. "What a pity. But take heart. I don't think it's quite dead yet."

"And why d'you say that?"

"Well for one thing, I haven't gained any Experience from it. Have you?"

She didn't miss the sudden stiffening in his posture. "Trust me. It's dead," he replied.

Her belly tightened. It was obvious there was something going on, and she wasn't privy to the full picture. Whatever had happened with the black sludge, it was clear Lukas knew more than she did. Just like their fight. A fight where she remembered kicking his ass, and at the same time, remembered being played with by the same individual. Two opposite realities, both superimposed into a single, muddy memory.

It was driving her insane.

"Something the matter?" he asked.

Tanya's expression bled off her face. "No. Nothing. Nothing at all."

"Didn't seem like—*urgh!*"

The rest of his words died in his throat as Lukas lurched backward, his eyes as wide as dinner plates. The blades fell from his shaking fingers and onto the floor with a loud *clang!* His entire body trembled as if he'd been hit by a hundred of those kinetic waves he threw around without a care. Before Tanya could take stock of the situation, he'd fallen to his knees, gasping in anguish. Rich, crimson blood oozed out of his ears and nose, and even his fingernails.

"What—"

The word came out as a mix between a scream and a croak. His vocal cords visibly contorted, causing him to choke on blood as it dripped from the corners of his mouth. His eyes bulged out, as if they were trying to tear their way out of his face. His nails angrily scratched the floor in a frenzy as copious amounts of lifeforce emanated from him in thick, overwhelming waves.

"Wha"—*screech!*—"what is happe—*nnninnggg!*"

The grating sound that emanated from his throat was like dragging rusted iron against glass. Crackling and squelching noises came from his twitching body, as if he were being zapped by lightning.

It was a gruesome sight.

Tanya slowly reached out to touch him, but couldn't. For all her curiosity, there was just something utterly repulsive about him. Her instincts screamed at her to go away, to escape while there was still time and ample opportunity.

But she didn't. Instead, she stood there, hands raised, paralyzed with indecision.

Lukas snapped his neck in her direction, his eyes rolled back enough that she could only see the whites of his eyeballs. His teeth gnashed together, and reddish drool flowed from his lips like a waterfall.

"Ru—*nghaaah!*"

Blood splattered across the floor.

"*Rghunnnnnnnnh!*" he yelled, his voice louder, larger, *thrumming* with power.

Tanya stilled.

"*RUNNNNNGHHHHHHNNNN!*" he roared, raising his right hand as he punched—

Space itself was distorted in its wake. The entire floor was drowned by the sound of a howling wind as the air between his punch and the stone floor rippled, sending a shockwave of invisible force hurling forward, smashing against the wind barrier she had hastily raised.

It was all that saved her life. Her windshield lit up like a floodlight, and if she hadn't been able to smooth it out and take it evenly across the whole front of her body, it might have broken her nose or ribs or collarbone, depending on where the energy bled through. Instead it felt like she had been hit with one of those clubs the jotunn of the Far North used for battles.

Meanwhile, the deafening sound met the cavernous walls of stone around them and—

Stone gave out first.

The mighty walls buckled as a spider web of fractures twisted their way through the slabs, expanding at an alarming rate. Crevices the size of roads emerged on the floor's surface, starting from where he stood and spreading in all directions. It was as if the entire floor was a touch away from shattering like glass.

And in the middle of it all, stood Lukas.

Only . . . he was different now. So much *more.*

An aura descended upon the cavern, an all-consuming feeling of rage and bloodlust backed by a power as implacable and unyielding as a mountain. It was far beyond any mere matter of strength, but rather a sensation both primal and terrible that flooded into her consciousness. It was the feeling of a rabbit that had been cornered by a wolf, helpless and terrified in the wake of its fate.

Tanya found herself unable to move, her pain momentarily forgotten. Gone were the wolfish grin and the casual demeanor her companion had portrayed. His eyes were now pale red, pulsing with rage as Decay, dark and twisted and oh so potent, spiraled out of him like ribbons. The mindless, impossible power he exuded rooted her to the spot. It was worse than her blackest nightmares, like staring at an incoming hurricane, frozen in fear and awe alike by the unimaginable destructive potential and the prospect of certain death.

And in that moment, she came to an understanding.

This was no warrior.

Lukas was something more. A destroyer. A being wholly dedicated to the obliteration of life. He had no purpose but to attack. Attacking with relentless fury and unstoppable force until his target was nothing but wet meat on the ground. And then he would choose another target, then another, then another until he was surrounded by nothing but dust and blood.

That very same Lukas turned to her with bloodshot eyes. And again, he repeated the same command.

"Run."

CHAPTER 43

Retaliation

Extermination Protocol was underway.

Such protocols were always in a state of CONSTANT UPGRADE, altered according to Experience and information gathered from INVASION DATA and Analysis of Invader Soul Architecture.

Even so, the current version of Extermination was taking longer than usual. This could become a potential PROBLEM.

The Omphalos of the Crypt of Fiendish Worms recoiled, analyzing the effects of the Protocol. Extermination was always an action performed under Extreme Duress, and was almost immediately altered post the encounter with INVASION.

Information rose before the Omphalos's own meta-consciousness.

Extermination 3.0

Version 3.0.

The Omphalos reared back, aggressively rechecking historical data. As a creature of growth and evolution, Historical Data was mostly rendered obsolete after every one million oscillations. Even so, reports of Extermination Protocols were retained, owing to the constant presence of CURSE on the exterior side of the Anomaly.

Extermination Protocol 1.0
Launched against Wraith Invasion

Attacks from the desert above. The very first danger against the Crypt of Fiendish Worms.

More information flooded in.

> **POST-EXTERMINATION ANALYSIS**
> **Heteromorphic Monsters survived with minimum damage against Mental Erosion**
> **Croisium found effective against Spiritual existences**

It quickly checked the results.

> **Non-heteromorphic monster proliferation suspended.**
> **Heteromorphic Monster proliferation heightened to maximum capacity.**
> **Active Synthesis of Croisium**
> **Mental Erosion analyzed, replicated, and added to SOUL CRYPT**

More information was required.
The Omphalos looked deeper.

> **Extermination Protocol 2.0**
> **Launched against Yokai Invasion**

> **INVADER ANALYSIS**
> **Mental Erosion Wraiths**
> **Elemental Wraiths**
> **Creatures with natural mana-synthesis facilities**
> **Creatures capable of POSSESSION and CONTORTION of possessed body tissues**

> **POST EXTERMINATION ANALYSIS**
> **Heteromorphic Monsters unable to deal with Mana Synthesis**
> **Croisium found effective against Spiritual existences**
> **Innate slowness of heteromorphs found lacking**

> **INFERENCE REPORT**
> **Continued Synthesis of Croisium in the Heart of SOUL CRYPT.**
> **Freezing of MANA-SYNTHESIZERS owing to lack of substantial replicative information.**
> **Postponed production of Monsters with MANA-SYNTHESIS capabilities. Stored in SOUL CRYPT.**
> **Addition of VATUATIL metal to heteromorphic monster prototypes.**
> **Assimilation of cartilaginous tissue and metal endo- and exo-skeletons to heteromorphic hybrids.**
> **Facilitated production of heteromorphic hybrids.**

It knew the rest. The Failsafe had been manufactured as per the Inference Report. An alloy of Croisium and Vatuatil were used to construct its structure, the former in minute proportions owing to its inability to fuse with organic flesh. Extreme regeneration was added, keeping true to the reports from the first Invasion Inference Report, and an appropriate skill structure had been perfected.

That brought it to the current problem.

Anomaly Health less than Threshold
Shutting down auxiliary operations

And that was it.

Extreme Regeneration required a healthy amount of Anomalous Energy to be converted into lifeforce. Vatuatil had a very low Energy to Lifeforce Conversion Ratio, causing an even greater waste of anomalous energy. Plus, DECAY required a 97.6% Lifeforce potency, causing even greater drain.

But it could still deal with that. What it couldn't deal with was—

PREDATOR draining Failsafe

He-Who-Consumes-Within was causing the Failsafe to regenerate endlessly. Predator, on the other hand, was draining the lifeforce and diluting its potency. This was causing ESSENTIAL OPERATIONS to be rendered temporarily dormant while all power was directed toward Failsafe, allowing it to function independently and with complete autonomy until Extermination was achieved.

And yet—

Anomaly Disintegration Rate - 7%
Shutting Down all Regenerative Processes

Auxiliary Power Sources Absent
Anomaly Lattice Disintegration Active

WARNING!
Power Drainage by FAILSAFE exceeded Threshold Limit

The rift was deepening.

Something drastic needed to be done.

DENIAL!
Shut down Failsafe?

. . . No.

Intentional suppression of Failsafe was not going to aid against INVA-SION. Alternate countermeasures needed to be deployed. Alternate Failsafes required to be created.

The Crypt of Fiendish Worms expanded its awareness, looking for resources.

Alternative Countermeasures absent

This was bad.

Perhaps an alternate method could be used?

If Failsafe could not be interrupted, could it be accelerated?

Auxiliary Power Sources absent

Anomaly Disintegration Rate - 11%
Anomaly Lattice Disintegration Active

Power Drainage by FAILSAFE exceeded Critical Value
Shut down Failsafe?

Yes.

No.

Yes.

No.

This was confusing.

It was confused.

It did not like being confused.

Shut Down Failsafe?

. . . Yes.

Shutting Down Failsafe!
Activating Recovery Operations

Initiate Scanning for alternative Failsafe Operations
DENIAL of new outgrowths
DENIAL OF ▮▮ ▮ ▮▮▮ ▮▮

. . . ?

This was odd, and unexpected.

And frightening.
More information arrived.

**Ongoing Removal of FAILSAFE PROTOTYPE from SOUL CRYPT
Initiate Retrieval?**

Yes.

There was no other option but yes.

Yet the Omphalos of the Crypt of Fiendish Worms stayed its hand.

This was not the first time that He-Who-Consumes-Within had devoured a Monster Prototype from its Soul Crypt, and given how this was the FAIL-SAFE Prototype, chances of its selection for Assimilation were greater than 91%. It could initiate a retrieval, or the fifty-one alternative options it had set up for such contingencies. However . . . this wasn't just an ordinary Monster Prototype.

This was the FAILSAFE.

Something that was integrated with the Crypt in a far, deeper way. A Bond that went beyond Soul Architecture and Evolution. A door that allowed the FAILSAFE access to resources that no other monster was allowed access to.

And doors opened on both sides.

He-Who-Consumes-Within was a Neonate at best. The FAILSAFE was engineered for a far superior Anomaly Design. That, along with the backdoor into the FAILSAFE spiritual lattice, allowed the Omphalos to enact all kinds of interesting things.

Initiate Soul Contortion.

Yes, the Omphalos decided.

All kinds of interesting things indeed.

CHAPTER 44

PREDATOR – PREY

*S*pace *splits.*

Or is it his senses? They feel everywhere. He senses himself. His body. Human. Mortal. Or is it Lostbelt Earth? Omphalos? **Crypt** ███ ██████ ██████*—?*

Memories. Events. Impressions. Self and foreign. A human. A lostbelt. Anomaly. Singularity. Realm. Lostbelt. **Underground. Aboveground. Desert—**

Cracks appear. Cracks diffuse. Cracks get larger. Brighter. Cracks converge. Diverge. Shatter. Reform.

His mind devolves.

Instinct arises. Instincts of a human. Instincts of anomaly. Instincts from skills. Instincts from monster prototypes. Instincts from—███*S*██*E of the Cr*██*f* ██*di*███ *wo*██

There is no pain. The cognition of pain no longer matters. He is swallowed by injury. By his senses. By information. By Anomaly. By Power. By Mind. By—

He falls into a swirling maelstrom of pain.

He doesn't know where he is.

He doesn't know who he is.

He doesn't know what it means.

It doesn't matter.

He sees it now. Like a large integrated circuit. What is a circuit? How does it integrate? What is seeing? Information? Information assimilation? Where would that be? Why would that be? What does—

The complexities increase. They twist. They bend. They form shapes that shouldn't exist. Shapes he knows have always existed. Three-dimensional. Ten-dimensional. Matrices. Lattices.

His vision narrows. What is vision?

The world expands.

He concentrates on the needless. Why? He knows he will split in half otherwise. How does he know?

Unnecessary.

The world is too big for this small body. The monster prototypes are too large for this soul. The Spiritual Presence is too grand to be hidden within this shell.

Yet the world fits. Yet the prototypes exist in segregation. Yet the Presence stays hidden. Bound. Forged. Fused.

He is being repelled. He can't be repelled.

He is reaching it. He can't reach it.

He shouldn't reach it. Not reaching it will be unforgivable.

He is reaching out.

He is reaching out.

He is REACHING OUT.

His eyes burn. His brain burns. He extends his arms and they extend and extend and exten—

SCCRREEECHHHHH!

GET THERE—

GET THERE—

GET THERE RIGHT NOW—

"Ha—agh—gag!"

His eyes are focused now. They are also dripping blood.

Right and wrong. Black and white. Colorful and grayscale.

He is opening his eyes. He is human. He is monster. Not human. Monster. His perceptions blur. Dim and bright. Pitch-black darkness and bloodred.

His tendrils elongate. He opens his mouth. His extensions move. Raw power enters his body. Power from Ley Lines. Power from Self. Power from—██████

His ears block all reception. He has no eyes. He has no ears. And yet he does. He raises his—████████ ████████*—and uses it with great efficiency.*

He is awake. He is hungry. He is always hungry after awakening. He is large, slimy, filled with—██████ ██████*—he'd rise and he'd not starve. Not like—*████████████ ███*—and he would howl—*████ ████████ *and—*█████ ██████*—as the cycle continues forever.*

Power cloaks him. Unbridled. Chaos in flesh and blood. Rage without restraint. Force without balance.

He sees it. He understands it. He has become it. Human is monster. Monster is human. Lukas is the ████████ *and—*

An unholy roar emerges from his throat.

—████████████ *is Lukas.*

There were few things in life as primal as hunger.

No questions about right or wrong. No quibbles. No compunctions. No liabilities. No alternative motivations. No doubts. The very feeling serene in its throb. The lingering pain of starvation burned away everything inconsequential. Made it all seem simple.

Really, why hadn't he thought about it this way before?

His senses felt different. His perception felt heightened in certain places and dulled to the point of non-existence in others. And with it came a whole new approach to being . . . *him*. He looked around at the carnage, at the quivering miasma all around him.

It felt right. He was no weakling. He was a killer, and he had no other purpose. He could protect in a way, he supposed, by killing everything that stood in the way of that which he shielded. But why would he do such a thing?

Killing indiscriminately was easier. Killing was better. Killing was joyful.

He *hungered* to kill.

He noticed the familiar glint on the floor. His blades, useless pieces of trash. Sharp, but useless. For what use was a tool when he possessed this much power at his fingertips? Vestiges of his powerless self, perhaps? Souvenirs at best. He was above them. He was—

SYSTEM OVERRIDDEN!
New Auxiliary Power Sources from ███████████ Added!
███████ ██████████ Protocol Initiated!
Base Host is under the effect of ██████ █ ██████ ██████

FOREIGN OMPHALOS FUNCTION Added!		
FUNCTION	**LEVEL**	**ENERGY COST**
Capacitance	NA	NA
DESCRIPTION		
Absorption of Energy from the World to bolster Omphalos Energy Reserves		
VOLUNTARY	**Currently Set to ON**	

MONSTER PROTOTYPE: ██████████		
SKILLS	**LEVEL**	**SOUL CAPACITY CONSUMED**
Raw Lifeforce Manipulation	3	5000
Regeneration	3	5000

███████████	3	500
██████ ████	2	500

Monster Prototype ███████████ Activated
Consciousness Shift Active

LIVING ANOMALY Activated!
Enact Reverse Shift?

Reverse? Why would he—

"...Lukas?"

He looked up. The world was still grayscale.

And in it stood PREDATOR. Alone. Confused. Angry.

Afraid.

She flinched as his gaze fell upon her.

His lips twitched.

PREDATOR took a single step back. He could sense power building within her. Blue. Elemental Wind Mana. White. Elemental Frost. Gold. Life-force surge.

Was that a challenge he sensed?

His lips twisted in feral anticipation.

She raised her right hand.

A spinning ball of wind erupted out of it like a living thing and streaked through the space between them, crossing the distance in a fraction of a second.

His chest exploded. Ribs shattered. Lungs punctured. Blood erupted out of his mouth and eyes. His muscles tore. His left arm shattered, leaving a stump attached to the shoulder.

And then, they weren't.

REGENERATION Activated!

Ribs reformed. Muscles sewed back. Organs reknit. Bones pushed back into place. Power whirled around him like a hurricane, and he was the eye of the storm. This power—it was his. He would use it. He would embrace it. With this he would kill the AGGRAVATION, kill this PREDATOR. He was He-Who-Consumes-Within and now he would become the new ███████████ of this Crypt of Fiendish Worms.

"MORE!!" he bellowed. **"GIVE ME MOOREE!"**

He put a single foot forward.

PREDATOR turned and ran.

He let out a whoop of joy, the ravenous hunter to kill roaring inside him, batting away rationality like a tidal wave. This . . . this was so much simpler than the alternative. There was no need for thought, for calculation, for speaking, for friends, for goals—for anything.

Right now, he was the hunter.

PREDATOR was now PREY.

She made funny little gasps and whimpers as she fled. She slipped and bruised herself over a sharp rock. Bled a little. Cursing, she continued to run. She was terrified, and not without good reason.

After all, out of all the monsters in this cavern, the most dangerous one was on her tail.

She was lithe. Curved in the right places, with an athletic, lean build. But she was human. Or bremetan. In any case, one thing was certain—she was afraid. And fearful people made mistakes. Errors in judgment. Anxiety prevailed over instinct.

And that was her disadvantage. Which made it his advantage.

Slipping past a small turn up ahead, she faced him for a moment, her countenance shining with fear and hysteria in equal amounts. Her right arm moved up, and power stirred within.

It only made him smile.

He slowed down to a walk, letting her have the chance. The look of confusion on her face was only to be expected. After all, she had expected him to come faster. To cross the gap between them and prevent her from going through with it. It was only natural.

Ironic, really, that even in such moments, the human mind tried to enforce rationality.

Bremetan mind, he corrected himself. *Not human. Bremetan.*

"Lukas!" He could hear the pleading in her tone. "Remember who you are! Remember! We're in this together!"

Pleading. Request. Did she think it would work on him? No. No, it wouldn't. That last attack was strong. Destructive. Possibly one of her strongest. It hadn't worked. That was why she was pleading.

Classic prey tactics.

He'd teach her better. He was a predator, and she was prey. They were in it together, actors on the oldest stage of the sapient world.

The hunting grounds.

Another burst of wind hit him. A lance, this time.

It disintegrated to shreds before it managed to get a foot within his vicinity.

PREDATOR shrieked. Anger. Frustration. Anxiety. Fear. All rolled into one. Nice. Exquisite. Then, the little idiot raised both arms.

Again.

"FUCK!" she yelled, and thrust out both hands. A howling lance of glacier-blue, coherent, observable, utter *cold* flooded into the cavern. The very air around him screamed in protest at the sudden, wild shift in temperature, with steam and mist boiling off everything in a cloud. That beam struck at him, forming a wall of crystalline ice, easily ten feet tall and doubly thick, and curving forward like a breaking wave.

It did not reach him.

Howling in reply, Lukas slew the oncoming attack with pure Decay, colliding it with the frost wave with all the power and momentum of a freight train. There was an enormous roar, a series of impacts, and cracks exploded through the clear ice in a spiderweb of crazed lines.

The wall held.

The still-standing wall of ice filled him with rage, boiling black, all-consuming and all-encompassing. Like a rabid dog whose chain had been severed, he lashed out, reaching to the very depths of the titanic reserves his body now had access to. His pain receptors were silenced, rendered vestigial, and a violent red mist warded off anything remotely resembling sanity.

And then, he struck.

There was a low quiver in the floor beneath his feet, a hideous pressure in the air, and then, a column of red-white energy, pure power, erupted out of his right hand—which exploded right away—and hammered into the frost wall. It shattered like a toy.

Lukas looked down at his destroyed arm. Regeneration activated. Bones expanded. Muscles reknit. Blood oozed out, just a little. Again, as good as new.

But PREDATOR was nowhere to be seen. She had taken advantage of the barrier and ran for her life.

How pathetic! She was supposed to be strong! She was the PREDATOR, not this weakling! Just for this disappointment, he'd find her. And when he did, he'd kill her. He'd bleed the life out of her.

And then—

He'd assimilate her.

Make her *his*.

The Crypt of Fiendish Worms would have her ████████████—

No. He was an anomaly. A creation of Lostbelt Earth. Only that should get access to the Truth that was ██████████, NOT this PALTRY cavern—NOT—YES—NOT—

He shook his head. He was wasting time. He needed to find her. But trying to find her in this endless labyrinth was an exercise in futility. She was lithe and quick on her feet, and that wind spirit made her faster than he was.

Lukas Aguilar might have needed to run after her. But the ████████████ of this Crypt of Fiendish Worms didn't. Not when he was empowered by the crypt itself. Every nook, every cranny, every single stone wall through which the ley lines ran, empowering the anomaly to expand in all directions, was his to wield. Raw, unadulterated power that could be used to create, to mutate, to expand. Power that made his own reserves look like pocket change. And that wasn't the only thing he had gotten through this connection.

A small grin formed on his lips.

"You can run!" he whispered, a savage grin twisting his features. *"But you can't hide!"*

CHAPTER 45

ESCAPE

*W*onderful.

That single word, saturated with all the sarcasm Tanya could muster, summarized the entire situation.

Lukas, her prey-turned-ally-turned-hunter, was currently after her, a wolf chasing a rabbit. The fact that she, even after everything she had been through, had been pushed into the *rabbit* category spoke volumes about just how far everything had devolved. Thankfully, that ice wall had given her enough of a head start.

It was surreal, it was nasty, and it made no sense. Worse yet, she couldn't bring herself to throw anything lethal at him. Maybe it was whatever he did to her. Or maybe it was so she could savor the sensation of being in control of her Frost without giving in.

The rational part of her argued that her *Wind Shear* would have classified as lethal enough for almost everyone else she had faced in the past. It had been the same technique that had allowed her to single-handedly massacre her way through the Cyffnarian battalion and capture their camp in one go.

But against Lukas?

Ribs exploded. Lungs punctured. His entire front had been blown to bits. She could see splintered bits and ends of bone and cartilage hanging out. Blood was splattered everywhere. Lukas—Lukas had died.

And then—

His lips moved. His body reknit. His muscles were sewn back. Bones reforged. Organs shaped back into place.

* * *

That wasn't healing. That was . . . that was something else. Something impossible. It was almost like turning back time, if such a thing was possible. That level of rejuvenation wasn't bremetan. And yet—

It wasn't the most shocking thing about him.

Tanya had looked down. At his feet.

More specifically, at the shadow forming at his feet.

It was impossible. Shadows formed in the desert because the Eternal Light didn't penetrate within. But their torches were imbued with the Great Goddess's blessings. A smidgen of Eternal Light, enough to illuminate everything within a certain radius of the canister.

Even so, Lukas cast a shadow. It was utterly impossible.

Then, the power of Decay? It was the skill of the monster they were fighting. It was impossible that Lukas just so *happened* to share that particular skill with that monster and yet never used it. It couldn't be some cosmic coincidence. There had to be a connection. He'd proclaimed the monster was dead, despite her not gaining any Experience.

Had Lukas, by some unfathomable sorcery, stolen the monster's skill for himself?

No way, Tanya told herself as she ran. *No way he's just an adventurer. He beat me down during an Everfrost frenzy. He can steal skills. By Wind, even Ezzeron is wary of him. And that agility . . . None of that is normal. And he has a damn shadow! What is he? WHAT IS—*

Every hair on her nape suddenly stood on end. Gooseflesh erupted over her body all at once, and a primeval wave of terror flickered through her brain, dislodging every rational thought in her mind.

Tanya didn't fight those instincts. Instead, she weaved the strongest obdurate bubble of wind around her.

The world gasped and went scarlet as blue-white light flooded through the wall on her left, vaporizing everything it came in contact with and leaving a sea of flames in its wake. The force of the resulting explosion was so powerful that a wall of air buffeted her shield of wind and shattered it, pushing her back by several feet. As the gale of rising dust subsided, she found the wall on the other end splintered from the shock waves. All that remained of the floor was one large crater of melting rock.

Lukas stepped through the newly created hole in the wall, a sphere of liquid light pulsing in his right hand, completely uncaring about the gale of dust and hot wind blowing all around him.

Pyromancy? *Pyromancy?* What a joke! That wasn't fire. That was liquid death floating above the center of his palm. Frost or no frost, nothing in her arsenal would be able to kill him. She had seen him regenerate *organs* in a matter of seconds. Unless she managed to obliterate him entirely in a single strike, there was nothing she could do to stop him from killing her.

This wasn't a task she could do by herself. She needed help. Elemental help.

Wind would be useless against such intense flames. Frost could be a useful counter, but it would stalemate him at best. And that was ignoring his powers of decay, though maybe she could use Frost to dilute the lifeforce in it and neutralize its power. The only thing remotely useful in her arsenal was Pressure-based. Olfric's kami wouldn't work either, which only left—

Zuken. Surrounded by his element all around, the Banksi's Terramancy would be at his peak. With his help and a well-timed Pressure spell, she could—

Her heart fluttered with hope, and something uglier.

—she could kill him.

But do I want to do that? After all, he's—

Tanya shook her head. "Why are you attacking me?" she demanded of him.

A malevolent grin formed on Lukas's lips.

He hissed something under his breath, and hurled the sphere toward her. Giving in to her instincts, Tanya slashed her right hand and sent a lance of pure frost right at it. The air shimmered as fire and frost met each other in a swirling mass of steam.

Tanya didn't bother to wait. Conjuring a pressure spell, she hurled it into the mist, turned around, and ran, the sounds of the exploding walls and Lukas's malevolent laughter reverberating in her ears.

She needed to find Zuken. She needed to escape this place.

Before it was too late.

With Ezzeron's power amplifying her speed, Tanya sprinted into the tunnel, scurrying away for dear life.

CHAPTER 46

REUNION

Olfric had lost. He'd failed them all.

He should have stayed. He should have held his temper. He should have listened to Maude when he had the chance. Instead, here he was, running, fighting, struggling to resist and defy the nightmares that threatened to kill him in this never-ending horror of an anomaly. A darkness born of the cursed sands, of faith corrupted into insanity, of chaos that had become eternal.

"To your left!" he heard a distant voice say. Zuken, maybe. Or Elena. He didn't know. It didn't matter.

What did he have left anyway? Shahxith was gone. His kami, the one passed down in his clan—first wielded by his great-granduncle, then his elder cousin, and now him—was lost forever. Unbound and free to escape inside this anomaly, and it was all his fault. What would his Clan think of him? He shamed them all.

"Olfric! Get back! The stingers!"

He had been fighting monsters using his sword since then. He could use his lifeforce, but every time he did, it felt like a facsimile of the real thing. That creature—it had unlocked so much power, and then—it was all gone. That power was gone. His Shahxith was gone. And now, he was—

Nothing.

The hands that held his sword were nothing.

Weak.

"Don't get closer! You can't possibly—"

A *clang!* was heard as metal met carapace.

The horde of monsters were twisted hybrids, somewhere between a praying mantis and a spider, crafted out of a meshwork of carapace and metal, layered with ligamentous tissue holding everything together. Long, thick tails with sharp stingers protruded out from the end, with two pairs of eyes on either side of the head. They painted a twisted caricature that could be considered anathema to anything that enjoyed living.

Calling the fight unfair was an understatement because fights weren't supposed to last this long. Especially not fights between a lifeforce slinger and terrors like these.

"These things keep on coming!" Olfric snarled. "I can't keep this up for long!" Without Shahxith's power, he was limited to his blademastery. It wasn't anything to scoff at, but still barely in the Adept stage.

In response, Zuken lashed out with his fist, shouting something that sounded vaguely Felleisen, and the earth rippled up in a wave that flew out radially. Olfric had never fought against terramancers before, but he knew enough to not want to be in the way when attacks got near him. Holding the sword in reverse grip, he avoided the large boulder coming his way and let it smash against the monster he was fighting.

The terramancer wasn't done. A heavy stomp of his foot sent a ripple through the ground, the unseen force dropping monsters down like bowling pins. Another twist of his wrist drew grasping waves of rock and earth up to clamp down on them. He closed his fist, and the earth tightened, drawing back down into the ground, cutting and tearing its way through monster flesh and carapace.

In less than five seconds, Zuken Banksi had taken down fourteen monsters.

Olfric barely had the time to nod in acknowledgment, when more screeches attracted his attention. Monsters came swarming out of the woodwork in droves. Olfric decapitated a particularly ugly-looking thing with a swing of his sword, while Zuken hammered the ground with unseen force. He then lashed out with some kind of dense, blackish spell Olfric had never seen before, and the monsters closest to him simply fell apart into what looked like grains of sand.

Olfric whistled.

"Disintegration spell." The terramancer laughed. "It's been ages since I got the chance to use it."

"And you only thought of using them now?" Olfric shook his head. "You know what? Never mind. We've gotta get out of here!"

"No way," Elena yelled. "I'm not leaving the others behind."

BOOM!

Another explosion shook the anomaly around them. Just as Zuken claimed, the walls around them held. But that didn't mean it was the same everywhere else. Floors were collapsing, the tunnels caved inward, and the stalactites fell like projectiles, fully capable of killing those that fought beneath. Any more damage and the anomaly wouldn't just collapse; it would take everyone with it.

"For all we know, Tanya's *causing* these explosions!" Olfric snarled.

"Don't be ridiculous! She's an aeromancer!"

"When has that ever stopped her from destroying things?!"

" . . . That's a fair point," Elena conceded. "But she went after the thing that possessed Maude, right? That means your kami's there too. If we find her—"

"The anomaly is about to collapse! Maude is gone! Tanya is probably out by now! We're the only ones left!"

"I don't believe that!" the changeling replied with surprising ferocity. "Tanya is still here, and we're not leaving her behind. We're going to save her! We're going to save them both!" Tears cascaded down her cheeks. "I don't know how, but we're going to do it. We're not giving up until we find them!"

"And how do you—"

Olfric's words were cut short, as he grabbed Elena's arm and jumped away, just in time to avoid another bombardment of falling debris. Conversing with the changeling, fighting alongside her, saving her life—all of those were great ways to stay angry. Being angry meant he was too busy to be scared.

And in their situation, that was a good thing. Because being scared was a step away from being dead.

"Elena, can you sense her?" Zuken asked.

"I can try," she quickly replied.

"Be quick. We'll take care of the monsters."

As if on cue, more monsters rushed toward them. Zuken sat down on the floor, cross legged, and two columns of rock shot out of the floor on either side, forming concentric semi-circles to create a barrier between the inside and the outside. As far as the monsters outside were concerned, they may as well be crawling their way through a pulp grinder.

That left the ones within.

With a yell, Olfric charged at the first creature he could find and thrust his blade into its skull. It let out a vicious, pain-filled screech, but before its partners could retaliate, the earthen floor disintegrated in thin sand, entrapping most of the monster herd within. He took advantage and pushed his blade deeper.

"Come on!" he hissed. "Just a bit more and you'll die. Stop moving around so much!"

The monster continued to scratch and claw at him in furious agony despite his words.

"Stop it!"

Olfric stopped short. He glanced back toward Elena, who had decided in a feat of bravery and even greater stupidity to walk up to the monsters.

"Don't attack us!" she yelled. As if the monsters would simply listen to her. "Go away! Eat something else!" And to his utter surprise, the monsters paused.

Even the one under his blade had stopped screeching and stared at the girl like she'd grown a second head.

"Did you not hear me?" the changeling snapped, her voice stern like a scolding mother. "I said *go away!*"

Olfric was having trouble trusting his sight. In that moment, it looked like the monsters were actually considering her suggestion.

Maybe she was onto something with that monster taming of hers.

"Elena—" Banksi hissed from his vantage point.

"No, Zuken," Elena yelled back. "I'm—I'm getting tired of this trip. So *you*"—she glared at a random duo of monsters—"are going to walk away from here and leave us alone." She took another step forward, within arm's reach of the monster Olfric was trying so hard to kill. "You don't have to hurt us and we won't kill you," she said, her voice now tender. "*Run away. Everything will be fine.*"

The monster in front of them stared at her blankly, its two pairs of beady eyes glowing, yet empty. It took a measured step backward, and Olfric carefully pulled his only weapon out from its head.

. . .

The monster swerved its forelimb in a large sweep, straight toward the girl's exposed, fleshy neck.

Given the surprised look on her face, it was clear she didn't really think the monster was going to kill her. Olfric would have called it naïveté if it wasn't for the confidence in her gait.

Halfway through the swing, the appendage was intercepted by a rock slab that sprung out of the ground like a coffin. Capitalizing on the chance, he picked up Elena like a sack of potatoes and scurried away.

"Wha—what was that?" the changeling squeaked, too startled to make out an eloquent reply.

"Why the fuck did you think that would work?!" Olfric shouted at her.

"I was trying to be heroic!" she babbled. "I—I've never had problems with it before!"

"Everyone! Focus!" came Zuken's voice. "I can't do this all day," he coughed out. Olfric didn't miss the flecks of red suddenly dotting the ground in front of the terramancer.

That wasn't a good sign.

"DUCK!" Elena shrieked.

Digging his legs into the ground, Olfric fell forward, with Elena still over his shoulder. Zuken was still doing an admirable job in throwing timely obstructions against the spider-like creatures. But if the blood were any clue, he had used too much mana in a short while, throwing his elemental balance into complete disarray. In other words, mana poisoning.

A spiritist with a kami could do a great many things. But use too much of it, and it could easily kill you.

Olfric looked toward the changeling again, who looked borderline catatonic. "Hey you, changeling!"

"My name is Elena!" she threw back, snapping out of her trance.

"Whatever!" he scoffed. "Tell me, can you really control these monsters? Back there, I saw them pause for a split second, like they were fighting against your will."

"I can! It works for most monsters, but these ones are *hungry,* so it's not that easy."

"What the hell do you mean by hung—"

BOOM!

He hurriedly turned toward the changeling. "Look, I don't care how you do it. Can you actually do it right this time?"

Elena scowled at him. "I don't like you."

Did she really think he cared what she thought? "Nice to see you're so spirited. It's adorable. Now get going, and don't get killed until the monsters are taken care of."

"We don't need to do that. I think I'm sensing someone. It's nearby and— BEHIND YOU!"

Without the slightest warning or change of expression, Olfric dropped her and plunged his blade into the monster behind him. There were three more remaining. Growling, he readied himself. He'd trained himself in a fighting style that suited aquamancers to a tee, which was why he used a long blade capable of making wide, graceful swathes. He might not be able to call on water anymore, but he was still an aquamancer.

Zuken was strong and stable, like the element he wielded. Tanya was like the wind—free, confounding, stormy, uncontrollable. Water, however, could be both strong like earth and fluid like air. Nothing was softer, and there was nothing it couldn't crush under its strength.

Offering a quick prayer to Susanoo, Olfric readied himself for his greatest technique.

He closed his eyes and felt a rush of lifeforce through his arms. It was so easy to imagine that it was water flowing through his skin instead. Keeping the illusion intact in his mind, he pushed himself forward. Right, up, right, up, then left, followed by a wide clockwise swing of his blade.

The unfortunate monster before him was chopped into dozens of pieces.

Olfric felt an intense pain in his ribs. What had he been thinking? Trying to perform it without the protection of his element was beyond foolhardy.

Clearly, his time spent among these idiots was getting to him.

There were still more monsters to deal with, and he had already fractured several of his ribs. The changeling was less than useful, and Zuken was busy keeping as many of the monsters away as he could. At this point, they needed a miracle if they wanted to see another day.

And then, a miracle happened.

From the opposite direction, something was moving so fast it looked like it had phased straight through Zuken's protective barrier. The figure, a humanoid shape, slowed to a stop, her blonde hair swaying from the resulting shockwave of wind.

"TANYA!" Zuken and Elena both yelled in surprise.

"Guess she didn't run away after all," Olfric snorted.

"Whatever you do, don't let your guard down!" Tanya yelled frantically. "Hit him with everything you've got!"

Him? Who was she talking about?

The answer came in the form of their newest arrival. Standing on the other side of Zuken's revolving barrier, with a cocky grin on his face and a fiery blue blade in each hand, was a black-haired bremetan. He had sharp eyes, a chiseled jaw, and wore half-damaged Cyffnarian battle armor—

Olfric narrowed his eyes.

Brown eyes. Black hair. Those sharp features. Armor. It couldn't—

His jaw fell.

This couldn't be happening. He had seen the water blades tear through this man—heart, limbs, abdomen—and then his lance had exploded in his face. Skilled or not, no pyromancer could have survived that.

"That's impossible!" he breathed. "There's no way anyone could have survived that attack!"

The stranger's dark eyes rose to focus on him, and a terrible, frightening rage overtook his features. *"You."* His voice was deadly quiet. The blades in his hand dispersed into sparks of flame, and his voice rose to a wrathful roar as the ground began to tremble.

"YOU!"

The scream threatened to deafen him by sheer volume, but it was far, far more painful than that. Olfric could feel it press against the vaults of his mind, an emotion so violent and intense that it would tear his sanity apart if he let even a portion of that into his head.

And then, a whirlwind of power erupted out of the stranger. Stone shattered to dust. Raw energy exploded upward through the ceiling, maybe even through the floors above that. Pure heat surged out with it in a wave of such breadth and power that five minutes ago, Olfric would have considered it impossible.

The stranger raised a hand in their direction. Zuken's barrier was no longer there.

There was nothing between them.

Oh shit.

The stranger conjured a sphere of liquid fire and launched it in their direction, while twisting his body backward, dodging Zuken's sudden attack. The fireball was intercepted by a raised slab of rock that instantly shattered to pieces.

But that wasn't all. The sudden movement cost the bremetan his body coordination.

Olfric took advantage of that, leaping to the side before bringing his sword over the man's head at an angle, aiming to separate his neck from the rest of his body. The sword hit his shoulder at breakneck speeds, piercing through bone and cartilage, but got stuck. Before he could pull his blade away, he was sent flying by a powerful burst of energy.

Tanya stepped into the fight. She rushed forward with blades of wind but had to alter the course of her moves mid-leap to prevent a ricocheted chunk of rock from taking her left arm. As for her own attack, her blade struck the stranger in the chest, just below the neck. A perfect stroke.

It dissipated before it managed to pierce the skin.

Zuken, who was already weak from too much mana usage, gathered more power and sent a dozen rocks at him from all directions. The stranger punched the incoming projectiles head-on with a strange, animalistic enthusiasm, which only seemed to worsen as the terramancer poured more mana into the move. Rocks became boulders. Boulders became shrapnel. Shrapnel became blades and spears and maces that kept flying at the pyromancer and turning into dust by his blows.

Olfric had had enough.

Rather than take shelter, he slipped into the man's vicinity and thrust his blade forward, aiming for his heart.

The stranger swatted him aside. Blood fountained from Olfric's mouth, and his sword shattered just from the impact of the powerful bremetan's fist. Olfric staggered back, but before the stranger could go after him, Tanya came to his aid, slapping him aside with a wall of air.

The stranger threw his head back and laughed. "IS THIS ALL YOU CAN DO?"

Zuken spat out some more blood—

"Yes."

—and yanked his hand upward, raising the fallen dust and debris. Right into the bremetan's eyes.

The ground beneath his feet instantly turned to sand and yanked him down feet-first, entrapping him up to the waist. The pyromancer madly tried to escape from the sand prison, but Zuken clenched his hand into a fist and yanked downward. A stalactite fell down from the ceiling, right onto the man's head.

And that was it. He finally stopped moving.

"Well, that was easy," Zuken said, panting heavily, rivulets of blood dripping down his chin. "You're saying this guy was giving you trouble, Tanya?"

The aeromancer rolled her eyes. "Just wait and see," she muttered, her gaze affixed to the gash on the stranger's shoulder. Olfric, curious as to what she meant, stared at the wound he'd given the stranger earlier. The strike had cleaved through his right collarbone but missed anything vital. Had he struck a few inches lower, he'd have nicked an artery or even a lung.

Ah, well. Beggars couldn't be choosers—

Olfric narrowed his eyes. The wound . . . it was already beginning to close, and rapidly too. Left alone, it would be as good as new in under a minute. The bleeding was stemming, and skin began to knit itself back.

Judging from the looks the others were giving him, they had caught it too.

"That's some healing there," Zuken said, peering at the wound with thinly veiled interest. "I thought Maude was good, but that . . . " He paused, halting mid-word. Then, his expression twisted into a frown. "Tanya, is there a reason he's attacking you?"

"Yeah," she said, without looking any of them in the eye. "There is."

"And I suppose negotiations aren't on the table?"

"Enough of this!" Olfric snapped. "What are we waiting around for? Let's kill him while we have the chance!"

"No," Tanya denied, stepping forward. "We need him alive."

"For what?"

"For . . . reasons I can't state until it's clear we're on the same page."

"Well, I'm all ears."

Tanya looked at him in annoyance. "I have a contract with Zuken and the rest of you regarding the mission, and I've gone way out of my way to hold up my end of the bargain."

"No doubt about that," Zuken agreed.

"At the same time, I have a verbal contract with this guy." She pointed at the unconscious, weirdly powerful, bremetan. "And I need him alive to fulfill it. Rather, we need him alive."

"Are you out of your damn mind?" Olfric demanded. "This nutjob was trying to kill us!"

"Actually, he was trying to kill me, and only because the anomaly's guardian did . . . things to him."

"Things," Elena repeated.

"Things," Tanya confirmed.

"Stop saying *things* and explain properly!" Olfric snapped. He'd had it with this damn group and their easygoing attitudes. His kami was gone, Maude was gone, and they nearly died! Was he the only one who realized that?

"This guy helped me kill the anomaly's guardian." Tanya paused. "Well, actually, he killed the guardian all by himself while I just stood there. If it wasn't for him, we'd probably all be at the—" She paused again.

"At where?" Zuken probed.

Tanya suppressed a wince. "Look, it'll take some time to explain, and it's been a long day. Can you just keep him trapped until I get a second to breathe?" Her stomach rumbled. "And maybe something to eat?"

Elena laughed and reached for her bag.

Olfric threw his broken hilt at the wall.

CHAPTER 47

———

EXPANSION

Lukas Aguilar was gone.

No, it would be more accurate to say that the *information* representing Lukas Aguilar was overwritten. Something strange and alien had infected him from within, corrupting his soul, his very existence, and marred it beyond recognition. There was no agony or wound. Rather, it was an intimate violation of his very conscience.

In that moment, Lukas felt like he had been rebuilt in another's image, only to be found lacking, and deconstructed and reconstructed to build something that was like him, yet anathema to his existence. When his mind tried to call forth any information related to "Lukas Aguilar," all that answered were the sick, unusable, contorted caricatures created to serve as his substitute.

I am nothing.

Masses of cold power, of Decay, as if even that information was scrapped and melted down.

And then nothing at all.

Leaving behind nothing but a blank void, until all that remained was a cold, marble floor, an empty ceiling of eternal blackness, and dazzling white walls. A prison of white, under a void of black.

Within is nothing but an abyss that devours the world.

His body was no longer his own. His thoughts scattered in the endless void. He was naked. Alone. Vulnerable. A consciousness that was nothing. Would be nothing.

An empty placeholder for an endless array of ███████

███████ ——

Without is nothing but a killing machine.

And he was cold.

His eyes were open, but he couldn't see.

His ears were intact, but he couldn't hear.

He felt no pain, no fear, nothing but a pervasive numbing chill that filled his body and locked his muscles in place. Beyond the chill, it was not unpleasant. Everything was blank, frozen in a block of black ice, simply waiting for his consciousness to disperse because the host was not dead.

And yet, he couldn't let go. As tempting as it was to surrender to blackness, some niggling feeling continued to poke and prod at him, like a tune he could not quite remember.

"Mortal."

The word appeared in his mind, bypassing his useless ears, burning itself into the core of his consciousness. And with it came something like perspective.

A goddess clad in regal attire. A dimly lit cavern. An oceanic blue pendant. An offer. A vision. A bargain. A goal.

The words filled him with worry, and a connection to something outside his own mind brought more sensation to his reawakening mind. The goddess—*Inanna*—was connected to him. Somewhere. Somehow. And something had happened. Nothing good, given what he saw and felt, but what it was, he could not say.

"Lukas."

Another vision, blurry and vague, but . . . a different girl. Golden hair. Blue. Frost.

A companion. A fighter. Predator. Prey.

Then there was the power. So much of it. Power that could make his omphalos reserves feel inadequate. Power and awareness. Power and—

AwAReNesS

Yes. He could remember it. He could see it. He could sense it.

He was Lukas Aguilar.

He was also the anomaly of [LOSTBELT EARTH].

Activating Intense Repair . . .
Correcting Soul Contortion . . .

Path Reset!
Activate Auto-Scan Auto-Analyze.

Set.

He could see it now. The [CRYPT OF FIENDISH WORMS] had tried to corrupt him from within.

He had stolen monster prototypes from the crypt. The crypt had used his own mechanisms to hack into his system when he had siphoned the FAILSAFE.

Balance Reality Foundation—Counterbalance Equalizing . . .

**Base Focus Medium Chosen
Host Identified**

The cavern. The tunnels. Moss lining the walls. Bryophytes. Ferns. Lichens. Monsters—reptilian, slime, insectoid. Creatures of various skills, various attributes, each occupying a finite amount of Soul Capacity from the nigh endless reserves held inside the center. The source of the crypt's existence.

Suddenly, everything began to make sense, as the crypt's memories flooded his mind.

He could see it. He could sense it. From the lowest fern to the greatest monstrosity, everything was part of the crypt. It always was. The unnatural curse that existed above the ground, the replication of the curse crafted to create DECAY and engraving it into the FAILSAFE . . . He could see everything. The crystal cave, the metal deposits, the churning chamber where ████████████ was being manufactured. ████████ had a strong advantage against spiritual beings. He could win back the territory claimed by the spiritual predators. Access to the spiritual soul prototypes in the Soul Crypt was beyond him, but with access to new prototypes, he could craft Creation Protocols to synthesize new prototypes of a spiritual variety.

The awareness extended, accessing his memories of a world that was a blur of color and energy—the Haze—

Accessing information from Soul Prototype MARID—

Accessing information from Soul Prototype YUREI—

Accessing information from Soul Prototype KASHA—

Yes. There was a lot of information. He could access the HAZE through the acclaimed territory. He could corrupt the ████████████ and access the HAZE and within it the other prototypes. All for itself. Everything for itself—

Everything would be itself—

Everything would be HIS—

Accessing information from BASE HOST—

Accessing information from CRYPT OF FIENDISH WORMS—

TRANSLATING—

Yes. The numbers were positive. The synthesis of ████████████ would gain HIM advantage against spiritual predators. New spiritual prototypes would give advantage against physical predators. Access to the HAZE would grant him access to the reticulum spread across the entire WORLD SYSTEM and then—

He could see it very clearly.

Spreading through the tunnels of the Crypt of Fiendish Worms. Gaining control. Expanding into the Haze. Corrupting it. New information. New Truths. New horizons. New prototypes. Infect the reticulum, infect the World System, corrupt the creatures outside.

Kill, Expand, Kill, Expand, Kill, Expand, Expand and Expand.

Until he was everywhere.

Until he was EVERYTHING.

Enact Warmonger Protocol.

Lukas's eyes snapped open.

He didn't wake up, per se. It was more like he cobbled together some kind of awareness, the same way a carpenter built a table. The reality he awoke to was a cold marble floor, with dazzling white walls on four sides and a pitch-black sky.

Then he saw something else.

Someone's toes. In front of his face.

Lukas frowned. He was certain they hadn't been there a second before. But now, there they were. There *she* was. Seated on a chair, one leg crossed over the other, was Inanna. And as always, she looked breathtakingly beautiful.

She wore a sparkling white gown, tinted here and there with streaks of frozen blue. She wore the dress with inhuman elegance, its rippling fabric dripping with feminine perfection, her body a perfect balance of curves and planes, beauty and strength. She sat on the chair, eyes half-slanted, half-aware, her gorgeous, sensual lips opened just slightly, as he stared at her.

"A prison of white in a void of black," she murmured. **"Not my first choice for a mindscape, but it will do."**

"Mindscape?" His voice came out more shaky than he'd have liked. "I already have my own mindscape?"

"You did not, until now. I placed the foundations. Added the finesse. Your mind did the rest."

"Not a very impressive job, then."

Inanna had created dozens upon dozens of beautiful illusionary worlds in his mindscape whenever she'd brought him here. His own room was probably the simplest of the lot. Compared to that, this was basic. Chicken scratch with crayons on a white page, compared to Inanna's da Vinci.

"On the contrary, I find it fitting, albeit rather . . . drab. It reflects your spiritual state well."

"Are you saying I'm empty?"

Inanna let out a low, throaty laugh but didn't comment any further.

Lukas took a moment to consider everything that was going on. The last thing he remembered before losing control was siphoning the monster prototype into himself. It was only after he was done that he realized how badly he had fucked up.

Inanna rose from her throne. The setting suddenly changed from the familiar, cloudy landscape into an even more familiar cavernous setting—the anomaly. But he could tell it was still his mindscape and not reality. Walking ahead, the goddess ran her finger along a particularly sharp stalactite.

"You stole the crypt's monsters. An act of a thief. That alone was worth retribution. Then you decimated its failsafe, the heart of its defense, and snatched it away. That was no longer theft. That was an invasion."

Her words were clearly meant to be congratulatory, but they certainly didn't feel that way.

"I know," he admitted. "When I siphoned the failsafe, the crypt followed it in. It . . . it was like it had hacked into my own system and activated the failsafe."

"A rather poetic revenge."

Lukas's attention wandered toward the blank white walls of his new mindscape. The traumatic episode with the failsafe had done a lot of damage to himself. Damage that was sure to leave its marks on his psyche for good. But that hadn't been the only thing that had changed since then.

He had gained knowledge.

And knowledge was power.

"There's something I should tell you. It's about that legend Solana talked about."

"About the power to end the world?"

Lukas nodded. "When the crypt hacked into me, it left a door open. And I looked into it. Into what it's capable of. The omphalos's instincts—*my* instincts. I wanted to consume it. And it wasn't just the omphalos. The power to end the world . . . I think she was talking about me . . ."

CHAPTER 48

SHADOW OF A DOUBT

You're saying that guy over there, Lukas, killed the anomaly guardian."

Nod.

"And then he went all murder-hobo on you."

Another nod.

"And he has a way of destroying the anomaly core without accumulating Sin."

Tanya nodded again.

"Look." Zuken made a face. "I'm not saying I don't believe you, but even you've got to admit it's a bit unreal."

"You mean like the spiritual beings we fought earlier? Those are supposed to be unreal too, right?"

Everyone stiffened at that. Tanya still wasn't really sure how those things had managed to possess Maude and transform her into . . . *that*. One moment Maude was standing there, staff in hand, casting healing magic, and the next, all kinds of strange sigils formed on her face and cheeks.

"I still can't believe there are yokai in the desert," Olfric groused. "They aren't supposed to be anywhere in the Empire. By the Goddess, they aren't even supposed to exist anymore!"

Tanya rolled her eyes. What did he think kami were?

"It's the Namzuuhuu Desert," Elena chimed. "I'm not surprised they're here."

Tanya glanced toward Lukas's unconscious form. Telling the others her true thoughts about him was out of the question. It wasn't about trust. Lukas knew her secrets. Her ability with Frost. He was the reason behind her new-found control over her latent powers. All of them, individually, were great reasons to not only keep him alive, but also to keep him close.

But none of that even mattered. Whenever she even considered killing him, she was filled with a feeling of profound wrongness. It was an instinct that came from the depth of her soul.

She couldn't, *wouldn't*, let anything happen to him.

"He claims he is from Maluscion," Tanya informed them. "Not Cyffnar."

"What is someone from Maluscion doing here in this desert?" Zuken mused.

"A spell gone wrong," Tanya replied quickly. Perhaps a little too quickly.

Olfric snorted. "A Maluscian here in the desert, thousands of miles away from his own country, wearing Cyffnarian armor. And you really believed his lies?"

"He's shown familiarity with the land."

She conveniently omitted the fact that he had also shown passing familiarity with the Llaisy Kingdom and the surrounding regions.

"When did you meet him?" Elena asked out of nowhere.

"After I got separated. I was hunting for Olfric's kami and came across him."

"He has something on you, doesn't he?"

"Why would you say that?" Tanya asked.

"For someone whom you claim you only met here in this cavern, for the first time, you're speaking an awful lot in his support. Any reason why?" Elena implored.

Tanya bit her lip. She expected an insight like that from Zuken, but from the changeling? A glance toward the wily terramancer showed that he held similar questions too, but merely kept silent about it. "Let's just say he got me out of a mess and leave it at that."

"Did that mess have to do with whatever happened with the yokai?"

Tanya stiffened. She sensed Elena was deliberately trying to throw her off-balance with her rapid-fire interrogation, but didn't know why. "What do you mean?" she asked.

"Too many strange things happening all at once," Elena replied, a smile on her face. "I know you were about to lose control during the fight with the yokai. But now you have it back, fully restrained."

Tanya's lips twitched into a distant echo of a frown. "Control?"

"On your emotions," the changeling explained. "I'm a charmer, and I feel others' emotions. You've been restraining yours this whole time, until you needed to. Which is when you lost control."

Something ugly deep inside Tanya unsheathed its claws. Everyone had it inside them, somewhere. It took fairly horrible things to awaken that kind of savagery, but it was in everyone. Hidden. Camouflaged. Maybe both. Only in her case, it was always awake. Always there. Waiting for a slip-up.

Until she met Lukas.

"Everyone has good and bad inside them," Tanya replied stiffly. "What's that got to do with him?"

"It's been exactly three days since we lost you," Elena went on, a strange intensity in her otherwise dreamy expression. "So you must have met him during this time. Three days is very little time to get a measure of someone. Meaning, you fought him. And he won."

Behind the changeling, Zuken grinned with something akin to pride.

"Just what are you implying, Elena?" Tanya snapped.

"What happened after you fought Maude?" Elena's voice sharpened. "Did you kill her?"

Tanya's knuckles turned bone white as she clenched her fists. For someone who'd dealt with suspicion and scorn on the daily, she was surprised at how much the question hurt. She didn't think she'd have to deal with *this* kind of nonsense after finding her teammates again. There was no time to lose, and she didn't want to start something violent with Elena, the nicest member of their team, either. She'd catch all kinds of hell.

Tanya sighed. "I didn't kill her. Maude escaped with the kami. I was attacked by a horde of monsters, and by the time I managed to get free, she was gone."

"And you didn't think to look for her?"

Tanya shrugged. "In case you forgot, I already *have* a job. Killing the anomaly. Not babysitting incompetents."

"Right. Why bother caring for your teammates and all that!" Elena snapped.

Tanya folded her arms and looked away. She knew that Elena had a point, but rationality was coming at a distant second to succumbing to the urge to just . . . *slap* her. Who the hell did the changeling think she was, ordering her around like that?

"Look, Elena," she spoke again, her voice more gentle, "I know things haven't been easy for us since we came in here. We lost Maude, and we also failed to get Olfric's kami back." She sent an apologetic nod toward the aquamancer, who stiffly nodded back. "I know it hasn't been fun for you, and the same goes for me. But . . . there's something you need to hear."

Elena's expression softened. "What's that?"

"Get over it."

The clearing went quiet for a moment. Everything except for Tanya's insides. That ugly part of her started to get louder and louder.

"We are adventurers on an anomaly mission. I know this is new territory for you, but things going perfectly according to plan isn't how missions go. Maude was possessed, as was Olfric. Thank the Great Goddess that he managed to get free. I understand that you're hurting, but it doesn't give you the right to question others. All of us are hurting, in case you didn't notice."

"Didn't notice?" Elena's brows slowly furrowed, and her teeth were painfully gritted. "In case you forgot, I'm *an allayer!* Every time someone freaks out at a shadow, I feel it. Every time someone suffers, I feel it. This desert and its curse haunts me in my sleep. Didn't notice? I wish I could show you the kinds of things I notice."

Tanya sighed. Exhaustion was creeping up on her earlier, but now it had a stranglehold. She was too tired to argue anymore. She was just . . . done. "What do you want from me, Elena?" she asked.

"I want Maude back," the changeling declared. "If you didn't kill her"—Tanya clenched her jaw—"then that means she's still running around in here somewhere."

"Possessed," Olfric interjected, his lips twisting into an uncertain expression. "But it doesn't make sense. Maude running around, I mean. Especially considering how *he's* here."

"Care to elaborate, Olfric?" Zuken prompted.

Olfric grunted an assent. "Remember when we had that argument and I walked off? Maude followed after me. The both of us then found him." He glanced down at Lukas's form. "He was practicing with his fire, only it was a lance back then."

A lance? Tanya struggled to remember if Lukas had ever used a lance during their fight, but her memories of that incident were still blurred.

"I thought he recognized you," Zuken muttered, "but I couldn't be certain in the heat of battle. What happened between the two of you?"

"I attacked him earlier," Olfric admitted. "I thought him to be a Cyffnarian hire and left him broken, bleeding, and on fire. No way he could have survived that." He paused. "Or so I thought."

"Well, he's still alive and kicking," Elena added. "So you had to be wrong."

"That's the thing. I wasn't. The sort of healing this bremetan can use isn't natural, is it? Definitely some arcane skill at work, and definitely beyond the Blessings of Okuninushi. Anyway, when I killed—when I attacked him, there was also a black-haired girl in a kimono nearby. She viciously attacked us back then, which is why we fled."

"You were defeated by a single girl?" Tanya asked condescendingly.

"A girl?" Olfric let out a bark of laughter. "Remember that demon you fought? That's her."

The bottom fell out of her stomach.

A yokai? Lukas was . . . with the yokai? Was that why he was in the cavern? Because he was— No, he could use lifeforce. Lots of it. But so could Maude, and after her transformation, she had reached terrifying heights.

Tanya's mind went into overdrive.

Lukas's familiarity with the land. With Cyffnar, Haviskali, the lands, the languages, him wearing Cyffnarian armor. Did that mean— Had some strange creature killed Lukas and was now wearing his body like one would a dress? Had she been spending time with a dead man?

Had she been thinking about being intimate with a walking corpse?

Bile rose to her throat.

No, there had to be something else. Something that explained everything. He was a pyromancer. That meant a kami was involved. But Olfric's possession had destabilized his bond with his marid. Lukas, on the other hand, used both fire and Qi with equal dexterity. So, a fire-wielding yokai? But wait, Lukas certainly didn't share any of those strange sigils. Not a possession then.

But—then what was he? Was he— Could he be an o—

"An oni?" Elena voiced her thoughts before Tanya could. "Is that what you're saying he is?"

"It's possible, right?" Olfric asked. "I mean, I killed him. Or at least lethally injured him. But look at the way he heals. Isn't it just like the demon back then? Remember how it was regenerating itself? Or those phasing monsters we faced earlier?"

Tanya's thoughts screeched to a halt. " . . . What did you say?"

"I said his regeneration was like—"

"Not that. What you said after—"

Olfric frowned. "The monsters . . . ?"

Her eyes brightened. *Of course!* "Yes, the monsters. Eternal Light. No yokai can survive in its presence, right?"

"Obviously." Olfric scoffed, but then his lips twisted into a rage-filled smirk. "Actually, now there's an idea." He began to take out one of the canisters from his bag.

Tanya smiled. Yeah, she was feeling a lot better now. It made so much sense. Granted, she still had questions she wanted answered, but it was better than him being a yokai corpse.

"Hand me those canisters," she said to Olfric.

"You're still trying to protect him?" Olfric actually leaned back, moving the canisters out of her reach. "Don't even think about it. I'm gonna vaporize this oni freak."

Tanya resisted the urge to hit him over the head. "No, I'm going to use them to prove that he isn't a yokai or an oni."

"And . . . you know this because . . . " Zuken trailed off.

"Because I personally handed him one of the Eternal Light canisters before, and he basked in it without so much as a whimper. I'm not sure what he is, exactly, but I'm hoping he'll tell us when he wakes up."

"Let's hope he doesn't kill us," Elena sighed.

"That too." Tanya nodded. "But first, there's something you need to know." She looked at Zuken. "In exchange for taking care of the anomaly core, Lukas asked me for something in return. He wants a fresh start."

Zuken narrowed his eyes. "A new identity and employment, I'm assuming? Why? Is he a fugitive?"

"Not from the Cobalt Army," Tanya replied. "At least, that's what he told me. He's reasonably certain that whatever he wants to happen will happen when he destroys the core. But in case things don't work out, he wants us to have a backup plan."

"A new beginning," Zuken said, nodding. "If what you're saying is true, and he is amiable to our plans, then I have no problems with that."

"Banksi!" Olfric snapped. "You're forgetting he tried to kill us."

"After you tried to kill him first," Zuken pointed out. "Don't forget, Tanya fought him too. If she's still vouching for him despite everything that's happened, then there must be something special about him." He turned toward Tanya. "You're sure he's not with the yokai?"

"He's asking to live in the land of Eternal Light. Is that not proof enough?" Tanya countered. "Though, there's also something weird about him. I was hoping you would have an answer. It's why I wanted the canisters."

Zuken nodded to Olfric, who grumpily shoved them into her hands.

Without any further preamble, Tanya switched the canister on. Four pairs of eyes squinted as everything around them was inundated with bright, white light.

Everything except for the portion of terrain directly behind Lukas's head.

"A—a shadow?" Olfric stammered. "Under the Eternal Light?"

Tanya grinned. "Exactly."

"But—but how is that possible? He's got to be a yokai then!"

"Yokai can't survive under the Eternal Light, you moron," Tanya sighed. "That's the whole point of this demonstration."

"So to summarize," Zuken began, "this guy is fast, skilled with a blade, a master pyromancer, and a warrior. And, he claims to have a resistance against Sin. Am I missing anything?"

"He has a shadow!" Olfric screeched.

"And a shadow," Zuken seamlessly added. "Normally, I'd agree to the terms he stipulated. A man of such talents could come in handy. There's just one problem really. As Olfric helpfully keeps pointing out, he has a shadow. It'll raise far too many red flags in Haviskali."

"Oh, trust me. That's not very difficult to deal with," came a masculine voice.

Each of them had a different reaction. Tanya summoned wind blades into her hands and pivoted on the spot. Olfric reached for his sword, but grabbed at nothing and brought up his fists. Elena squeaked nervously and shuffled in place, warily looking in the direction of the speaker. And Zuken calmly turned around, though his wristbands slightly glowed with Qi.

"How long have you been awake—" Tanya questioned, before she was interrupted.

"Why don't you have a shadow anymore?" Olfric screamed.

"I know you have questions," Lukas began, "but if it's all the same to you, can you let me up first? Being interrogated while halfway stuck in the ground isn't exactly my idea of a good time."

"You!" Olfric stabbed a finger at the buried man. "Answer my question!"

Lukas turned toward Tanya. "Are you two related? I can see the resemblance."

Tanya almost choked on her own spit. Olfric's face turned an unusual shade of orange. And Zuken just looked amused.

"I'm sure Tanya will back me up on this," Lukas replied, his voice careful and gentle. "I'm definitely worth at least one decent conversation without us all coming to blows. We can talk this out peacefully. Seriously. It's starting to itch in some really uncomfortable places."

"Lukas, is it?" Zuken asked, tilting his head. Tanya hid a smile. She had a feeling she'd enjoy a conversation between the two of them. "If I release you—"

"Yes, yes, I swear on the pain of death not to attack you."

With a wiping gesture of his fist, Zuken raised the sand around Lukas out of the ground, bringing him with it. Tanya took the opportunity to create a tiny gale, helping move the sand away faster. Impatience wasn't a virtue, but it would sure save some damn time here.

"If we don't like what we hear, you're going back into the ground," Olfric replied imperiously.

"You're a true giver," Lukas droned.

"Let's start with who you are," Zuken half asked.

"Lukas, but you already knew that. My full name is Lukas Aguilar."

"A family name? Interesting." Zuken rubbed his chin. "I don't think I've ever heard of the Aguilar Clan before. Where are you from?"

"The land of shadows and decent conversations," Lukas quipped back. "Like I told Tanya, I was involved in a spell accident and somehow appeared inside this underground cavern with nothing but the clothes on my back." He paused. "Though, *these* clothes are from a very nice Cyffnarian soldier who very kindly agreed to part with them. A bit heavy, but it does the job just fine."

"But where, specifically, are you from?" Zuken repeated.

"You wouldn't believe me if I told you."

Olfric snorted softly. "I bet it's no weirder than believing that yokai have been hiding in the desert, right under the Empire's nose, all this time."

Elena crossed her arms and smiled challengingly. "Yeah! Just try us!"

Frankly, Tanya wasn't really sure why Lukas was making the moment so dramatic. It was true that Maluscion was rather far away, but if the "spell accident" excuse was to be believed, then distance wasn't much of an issue. Plus, he had already demonstrated enough knowledge of the region for it to be a believable answer.

"Just tell them what you told me, Lukas," Tanya said. "Don't be so dramatic."

Lukas stared at her for a long moment, and then gravely nodded. "Very well. I swear that what I am about to say is true to the best of my knowledge."

What did I just say . . . She internally groaned, opening her mouth to give him a piece of her mind when—

"My name is Lukas Aguilar. I'm from a different world."

. . .

"That's not what you told me!" she yelled.

CHAPTER 49

COUNTERS

Extermination Protocol—Failure!

The Extermination process had gone as badly as possible. The FAIL-SAFE was lost. Soul Contortion had worked for some time, but the CONTRADICTION had been able to undo its effects and claim its Base Host for itself. CONTRADICTION was now with PREDATOR again, and they were approaching the core.

Now, there was no FAILSAFE to stop them.

**Activating Scan for Alternative Guardian
Searching . . . [0/2215]**

The Crypt of Fiendish Worms was in a state of extreme disrepair. Most auxiliary energy reserves had been directed to aid the FAILSAFE in accomplishing Extermination Protocol. Soul-Contorted CONTRADICTION had also leeched 3.18% of existing Reserves.

Most unwise.

**Possible Paradigm Shift Detected
Soul Contortion—Success**

Inference Report Prepared

Later.

By priority basis, Inference reports were rated 13%. Too insignificant to be considered in such an acute scenario. It needed better alternatives. A better course of action. Better numbers. Better—

<table>
<tr><td align="center">Soul Contortion—Success

Inference Report Prepared</td></tr>
</table>

LATER!

It hated itself. A peculiar LOGIC-less sensation. Hate? Non-anomalous expression. Emotion. Thought. Logic?

New variables. Where were these coming from?

<table>
<tr><td align="center">Soul Contortion—Success

Inference Report Prepared</td></tr>
</table>

. . . Disturbing.

Confused, resigned—*resigned?*—the Omphalos looked deeper.

Inference Report	
Monster Prototype	Human
Category	Vestigial
Energy Core	Lifeforce
Mental Capacity	Degenerate Mammal
Growth Potential	Apex Predator, limited by variable **RATIONALITY**
Extra Notes	Maximum functional efficiency with CONTRADICTION Host Body

That was surprising. It reran the numbers.

<table>
<tr><td align="center">Extra Notes Verified</td></tr>
</table>

Perhaps it was looking for answers in the wrong place?

The Omphalos went back to the other process.

<table>
<tr><td align="center">Scanning for Alternative Guardian
Searching . . . [1916/2215]</td></tr>
</table>

Still no possible choices. This was disturbing.

CONTRADICTION was a neonate anomaly in a HUMAN Host Body.

CONTRADICTION had a HUMAN mind active in the Host Body.

Decision?

Possible. Dangerous but possible. Extermination Protocol required an upgrade but the Risk to Reward ratio was high.

Not recommended.

But—

Monster Prototype: Human—Selected

Running Analysis . . .

Testing simulations . . .

Sequencing addition of Extermination Attributes
Recreation-regeneration through CROISIUM [Metal]
Initiation—Confirmed
. . .
. . .
Enact

CHAPTER 50

AGGRESSIVE NEGOTIATIONS

Vatuatil blades? *Check.*

Monster prototypes? *Check.*

Sensual goddess whom he harbored a healthy and rational fear of? *Big check.*

Lukas cracked his neck and looked in Tanya's direction. The blonde frost-wielder was furiously whispering something with her cohorts on the other side of whatever remained of the chamber around them. He, being the gentleman he was, had walked over to the farthest wall and sat himself down until they were ready.

His initial introduction had done its job. His demonstration of power and the shock factor of having a shadow had shaken the crowd significantly. While he was yet to be referred to as an Outsider or anything of that sort, they were clearly uncomfortable about his origins. Especially Tanya.

He could imagine it perfectly from his own perspective. Knowing someone, spending time with them, fighting a common enemy and going through some unconventional experiences together, suddenly noticing that despite having known the person for a while, they didn't have a shadow. And then to look back, and to realize that they *never* had a shadow. It was impossible—a shadow was the result of natural laws; it was the absence of light due to one's mass blocking the path.

But that shadow wasn't there, despite the person being right in front of them.

How was one supposed to react to that? The realization that the person one thought one knew was different, *wrong* in some way that should be absolutely impossible?

Was it not only natural to freak out and run away, swearing never to be near them ever again? Or maybe, if one was of the inclination, capture and try to experiment upon them and figure out how a person could be shadowless scientifically? Or perhaps simply attack them, out of fear of the unknown or prejudice at violation of the natural order?

Only, he was stuck in a world where the situation was the exact opposite.

Light existed, but it did not cast shadows.

"Get up!"

Lukas lifted a single eye open. Tanya had her hands on her waist in typical confrontational fashion. It was all too easy to ignore his surroundings and pretend he was on Earth, and the person in front of him was just another human being.

But she wasn't. This wasn't Earth. This was a world with different rules, different species, different powers and abilities. And in this world, he was the stranger.

The violator.

The *Outsider*.

"Why?" he lazily asked.

"Should I answer you literally?"

"I think I'd like that."

Her lips twisted into a half frown, though the light in her eyes suggested that she expected his defiance. Leaning forward, she spoke in a voice colder than ice. "Because I said so."

Lukas suppressed the urge to smile. "And if I don't?"

"Listen, you're already in deep shit. A fugitive adventurer is one thing. But an Outsider?"

Lukas barely suppressed a flinch at her use of that term.

"I'm trying to set you up and keep your secret safe. The least you can do is stop throwing tantrums like a child."

"Not quite," Lukas quipped. "You see, every deal is made as an act of good faith. I'm, in your words, an Outsider. A stranger to your culture. Your world. You and I had a deal back then. I'd take care of the anomaly core, and in return, you'd—"

"Set you up, yes. But that was under false pretenses. You told me you were an adventurer from Maluscion, not a damned Outsider."

"Could you stop calling me that?"

"Oh? And what would you have me call you?"

"I have a name. Use it. If nothing else, call me a . . . I don't know, an other-worldly tourist?"

Tanya rolled her eyes. "And what about the fact that you turned into an insane, raving psychopath and nearly killed me?"

"I'll buy you flowers?"

"You—GH!" She growled in exasperation. "Just—just get up and come with me!"

Lukas grinned at her foxily. When he walked over to the group, it was the one named Zuken Banksi who led the negotiations. Unsurprising. The terramancer carried himself like a diplomat. While his Terramancy was formidable, it was nothing compared to the likes that Solana had so casually demonstrated in person. He had an easygoing smile on his face, enough to distract one from his calculative eyes, not to mention the only person that fitted the bill.

The "Olfric" guy was more than likely to attack him, which was ironic since Lukas was technically Olfric's victim. The realization that the marid prototype stored in his Array originally belonged to this sucker made his inner child happy.

Tanya obviously had a conflict of interest involved, and Elena—

She was too busy staring at him with a hungry look in her eyes, like a cat watching its prey. It was almost enough to give him a complex.

"Tanya here," the terramancer began, "has helped me understand that it was you who killed the anomaly's guardian. And then—"

"Got fucked in the head by this anomaly and turned into a raving murder-hobo."

Tanya grimaced.

Zuken continued, unfazed. "She has described you to be a competent bladeslinger, a warrior with a frightening degree of regeneration prowess, a pyromancer with the ability to avoid Sin, and a polyglot of several of our languages."

Lukas coughed with an odd feeling of embarrassment. "More or less."

There was the Kinetomancy he had gained from Inanna, that and the entire psionics thing. There was also Metamancy gained from the yurei, and potential Aquamancy from the marid he had siphoned but had yet to use in a fight. Not to mention the thoggua's Shatterpoint Intuition.

"Remarkable. The skills you boast can only come from experience. I imagine your regeneration allows you to stay young. How old are you anyway?"

"I'll be hitting my twenty-first birthday soon."

Everyone around him was looking like he had just grown a second head.

" . . . what?"

"Twenty-one," Zuken asked.

"That's what the math says."

"I suppose an Outsider does not fit into our world's frame of reference." Zuken rubbed the bridge of his nose. "What about that raving psychopath thing? Is there a chance of it happening again?"

Lukas scowled. "I . . . don't think so."

"Then there is your familiarity with our world, customs, and languages. I assume this isn't the first time you've been here."

Crap. That was a difficult question. If he said yes, it'd probably end the matter, but it would open up a new box of worms. What were the places he had visited in the past? Whom had he interacted with?

On the contrary, the opposite would open a different door. How was he so familiar with the languages? How did he know so much about Maluscion? Did his people also travel from his world to this one before?

There was simply no correct way to answer it. So he did neither.

"All this interrogation makes me feel like a prisoner. How about you start answering some questions in the spirit of fairness and all that? Why are you in this anomaly? Why do you want to destroy it? And why is *she*"—he jabbed a thumb toward Tanya—"taking the hit for the team?"

Zuken's mouth turned faintly up at the corners. "You make a good point, but answers to those questions deal with our national security. I don't feel comfortable trusting an Outsider with them. Now, Tanya tells me that you want a life for yourself here. Employment. Residence."

Lukas nodded.

"I can get you all those things, and in return, I shall have the right to command your services. In exchange for appropriate remuneration."

Where have I heard that before?

"I should feel affronted at this, mortal. This is the second time you have agreed to someone else's employment offer."

Envy is an ugly, ugly thing. It doesn't suit you.

"Are we in agreement?" Zuken asked.

"Yes, but not before I've got a couple of things cleared up," Lukas said.

"You're in over your head if you think you can worm conditions out of—" Olfric began.

"Hush!" Lukas silenced him. "The adults are talking. I've yet to spank you for that earlier tantrum."

He didn't miss how the aquamancer flinched at the description of his actions. Then again, considering they had seen him in action with the failsafe's skill set, *tantrum* seemed oddly appropriate.

He looked back toward Zuken. "I understand that Tanya was supposed to kill the anomaly for you. Well, I'm doing that. I want you to ensure that she doesn't suffer a loss in this new deal."

Tanya's poker face was impeccable. The slight coloring of her cheeks wasn't.

"That hardly seems fair," Zuken replied briskly. "Why should I pay double for services rendered? I'm already paying you by getting you a place in the kingdom, and future employment in exchange for your doing the deed. Tanya, on the other hand—"

"—gets everything she's promised," he stressed. "I might be able to end the anomaly without amassing Sin, but her aid in the endeavor would be appreciated. Plus, she got you a new potential employee. Me. If I were you, I'd be handing her a bonus."

"Then perhaps I can just pay her as was decided and leave your demands unfulfilled."

Lukas wasn't fooled in the slightest. The terramancer had an excellent poker face on, but there was no hiding the glimmer of satisfaction in his eyes. There was no doubt he had plans for him, and this was merely a test, of sorts, to identify his potential use.

Two could play at this game.

"Good," Lukas said, grinning. "That way I don't have to work for a miser who can't keep to his terms." Even though the heat was missing from his voice, it still carried a sense of finality with it. "Don't kid yourself. You aren't doing me any favors here. You can't get my services without getting me appropriate documentation and lodging. And even then, you'd have to pay me a salary. The way I see it, I'm just helping her out."

"Can you guys stop talking about me like I'm not even here?" Tanya growled.

"Actually, I'm done talking," Lukas replied, standing up. "You guys clearly have everything covered. Maybe someone else in these caves will be willing to hire me for my services."

"Like the yokai, you mean?" Olfric asked out of nowhere.

It was a testament to his experience in this hellhole that Lukas's first instinct was to activate tachypsychia. As his perception dilated beyond twice its usual speed, he calmly observed everyone. Clearly, they had some solid proof behind that statement and only wanted to confirm it from his own expression. The aquamancer had attacked him earlier, and Solana's yokai bodyguards must have attacked him. Two and two made four.

This wasn't a negotiation. This was a setup.

"Yokai?" he asked with feigned curiosity. "What's that?"

"Come now." Zuken chuckled. "Surely you haven't forgotten the creatures that attacked him earlier?"

"You mean when the aqua-idiot struck me from behind?" Lukas was genuinely surprised by how venomous the accusation was. It was *so* easy to give in and lose his temper. He could feel the specters of the monster prototypes stored in him rising in the back of his mind, each wanting to do something macabre to the useless stain that had tried to murder him in cold blood.

"I personally apologize for Olfric's behavior in the past," Zuken interjected. And to his credit, he did look regretful. "What he did wasn't right in any way."

"Keep your apologies to yourself. If it wasn't for my healing powers, I'd be dead," Lukas snapped back. He was furious, enough so that it surprised even him. His control over his emotions suddenly felt askew. "Where I come from, he could've been hanged for murder."

"Hanged?"

"Tie a rope around his neck and drop him off a tree. Death by strangulation." Lukas shrugged.

He didn't know if it was the macabre description or his control over his power wavering, but the people around him paled. Zuken no longer looked as confident, and his eyes became hard and sharp like daggers.

Lukas exhaled. The creeping madness within him slowly ebbed, until the rage passed completely. "Sorry," he said finally. "Don't know what got hold of me there. I'm not a fan of violence, and I try to avoid it whenever I can. However . . ." His eyes drifted to Olfric, who had taken a few steps back. "Sometimes a stern *chastisement* is needed to smooth things over."

No one spoke, until Zuken bravely decided to break the silence.

"Perhaps we can come to a compromise here. Olfric has done you a great wrong. As such, he'll pay thirty percent of his profits from this mission to you. In return, you stop any deliberate attempts at antagonism." He sharply glanced at Olfric, as if daring him to contradict. "In addition, you offer your skills and support in finishing this mission successfully. Once we're done, I will get you to Haviskali and procure appropriate documentation for you. Until then, we'll just need you to find a place to lay low."

"He can live with me. At the Meewich Gate, I mean," Tanya added quickly. "It's where I shacked up before the Army came for me."

Elena and Olfric exchanged knowing looks. Zuken just looked amused.

"Well?"

"What kind of services are we talking about?" Lukas asked. "I may not look it, but I don't get my kicks from cold-blooded murder."

"That makes things easier, because I'm not interested in hiring someone for morally reprehensible acts. Also, I'll need you to sign a contract later."

Lukas looked at him. Then at Tanya. Then back at him.

We don't want to lose the girl, he thought. *That's what you said, right?*

"Correct," Inanna replied.

"Yes, we are in agreement," Lukas said.

"Fantastic." Zuken smiled. "Then please, lead the way."

"What makes you think I know how to get to the core?"

"You were already heading there before you ran into any of us, correct? Admittedly, our group does not know the way forward, so if you don't either, then we will be searching blindly either way." Zuken gestured ahead, a knowing grin on his face.

Lukas blandly smiled, before leading the group deeper into the anomaly. Truthfully, the awareness he'd gained as a result of the "failsafe hack" allowed him to instinctively seek out the source of the crypt's power.

The anomaly's core. Also known as its omphalos.

And he *was* planning on leading the group there. He just didn't like the fact that Zuken knew that already.

Briefly, Lukas wondered what Solana would think of this. He still had no clue if his yokai bodyguards were still following him. Solana had been very clear about what she'd do if he joined the other side.

"She would know you broke her heart."

And now he had that mental image to forget. Lukas Aguilar, breaker of monsters' hearts.

"You call her a monster. What do you think your compatriots think you are?"

That's—

The words died in his mouth. He had seen the way his new teammates looked at him. He got those looks a lot these days. Sometimes even in his own reflection. Sighing to himself, Lukas banished the thoughts from his mind and took the opportunity to call up his Soulscape.

SOULSCAPE	
NAME	Lukas Aguilar
Type	Base Host
Level	7
Experience	239
Current Threshold	1960
Utilized Soul Capacity	14079 / 14473
ESSENCE	
Maximum Lifeforce Output	3475
Replenishment Rate	540 / hour
LEY LINE NETWORK	
Maximum Mana Output	4725
Synthesis Rate	650 / hour

SKILL ATTRIBUTES		
SKILL	LEVEL	CONSUMED SOUL CAPACITY
Raw Lifeforce Manipulation	3	5000

Momentum Manipulation	3	5000
Friction Modulation	2	500
Pressure Modulation	2	500
Kinetomancy (FRAGMENTED)	APEX	1279
Fire Creation	1	50
Fire Manipulation	2	500
Temperature Modulation	2	500
Perception Manipulation	1	50
Conjuration	1	50
Disintegration	1	50
Seismic Sensing	1	50
Shatterpoint Intuition	2	500
Psychomancy	1	50

OMPHALOS ATTRIBUTES	
Energy Reservoir Capacity	∞
Current Energy Level	736,986,204 units
OMPHALOS FUNCTIONS	
Scan	Level 2
Analyze	Level 2
Prophylaxis	Level 2
Soul Siphon	NA
Alpha Condition	Level 2
Evocation	Level 2

The Warmonger Protocol had brought new benefits. There weren't any new functions, but the Alpha Condition and Evocation functions had gained an upgrade. His mana output increased by 50%, lifting it to a staggering 4,725. His mana synthesis had grown even more, now almost twice its original value.

"Can I ask you something?" a voice suddenly interrupted.

Lukas looked to his right and found Tanya walking next to him. From the corner of his eye, he could see Zuken and the others trailing close behind, maintaining a respectable distance from him.

"Sure," he replied.

"You made sure I got my full payment."

"I did."

"Even at the risk of dropping the bargain with Zuken."

"I'm not sure I heard an actual question there," Lukas commented, more amused than offended by the discussion. He hadn't expected her to trust him sight unseen. If she had, he'd have merely assumed she was naive at best and a fool at worst.

"You also agreed to his compromise. You could have demanded compensation for Olfric's deeds. Worse, you could have killed him. But you didn't. Instead, you're just happy with a barely decent compromise."

Lukas quirked an eyebrow. "Are you complaining because you got a good deal?"

"No, I'm confused at the way you chose to give up power over him," she replied. "I attacked you, but you've been nothing but accommodating to me."

"Minus the part when I went crazy."

"Except for that. You could've held your ground. You could've asked for more. Instead, you settled."

"I just want to avoid unnecessary confrontation. If that means giving up a little power, then so be it."

He might have held the upper hand, both in power and moral obligation, but he'd have to stay in this new world for a considerable future. He knew Zuken's type. Holding it over his head would eventually devolve the situation into an ego-based powerplay.

"Yes, but . . ." She struggled with her words. "But *why?*"

"I believe what she is trying to say," Inanna translated, **"is that it makes no sense for you to surrender power and control simply to escape a verbal confrontation."**

Because the goddess in my head wants you alive and close, Lukas mentally retorted. *But I can't actually tell you that, now can I?*

"Even so, you have fought tooth and nail to keep your independence, even from me. And then you do this . . ."

Are you seriously comparing my deal with that guy to the one I have with you? That one, I can break whenever I want. Yours . . . not so much.

"Because you are aware of what can follow."

That too. But also because we're . . . us. Zuken is just a convenience.

"You flatter me."

"Lukas?" Tanya called out, jolting him out of his inner dialogue.

"Let's just say I didn't want it to devolve into a situation where you all died in a horrible fashion," he replied.

"I'm nobody to you. What does it matter if I live or die?" Tanya asked.

Because Inanna will be pissed if that happens. And he'd feel bad too. Or at least bothered.

"Oh, it would. In more ways than one."

Lukas happily ignored her and instead turned his attention to the girl. "Because I'm a hypocrite who can butcher droves of monsters, but will get cold feet over killing someone who looks like hu—bremetan."

Her eyes narrowed. "Why would your feet go cold? Is that some curse you were afflicted with?"

" . . . "

"Well?"

Lukas sighed. He'd been more at ease when dealing with *Solana.* "It's just the smarter thing to do. You kill someone, then their family and friends will come after you or your family. And on and on. It's a vicious cycle."

Tanya looked bitterly amused. "And you think I have people ready to avenge my death should a horrible fate befall me."

"It's the principle of the matter. You and I have some history now, no matter how spotty. Now, after putting aside any unforeseen differences, we're working together and I have a way to get an identity and a job. None of that would have been possible if I'd killed you."

"I see." She nodded, seemingly enlightened. "Acknowledgement of aid can provide further aid. Unnecessary killing may actually hinder the fruits of one's labor."

Lukas sighed again. "Sure, let's go with that."

. . .

"Were you a soldier?"

The sudden shift in conversation caught him off guard. Again.

"In your world, I mean. This is the first time I've encountered an Outsider, so I'm curious. Someone with your skills would definitely make it to the Army. Or at least a private military."

"Actually, I was a student," he replied. Seeing her visible puzzlement, he tried a different route. "It's like a—okay, how would you—yeah. An apprentice. It's like being an apprentice."

"So your master was a soldier?"

"A teacher."

Tanya frowned, searching his face for a hint of a lie. Finding none, she demanded, "Of what?"

"The law."

Tanya did a double take. "You were studying to become a diplomat?"

He spread his arms wide in an inviting gesture. "Don't I look the part?"

" . . . You do." A slight frown creased her features, "But you also look very much like a warlord. With your skills and experience, I mean. Except, well, you're young."

Once again, Lukas ignored Inanna's response, though it was difficult this time around, with her laughter booming inside his head. "And that's a bad thing?"

Tanya considered that for a moment before shaking her head slowly. "Is that why you're here? Why you can speak our tongues? A diplomat between worlds does sound like a prestigious job. You should have mentioned that earlier during the negotiations."

Lukas shrugged. "The way I see it, I got to know them through you. But if you're feeling too bad about it, you can always help me acclimatize with your kingdom." He extended his hand. "Do we have an accord?"

Tanya smiled. "We do."

She shook it firmly.

CHAPTER 51

THE BIG UNEASY

In a different portion of the now silent anomaly, Mizo was having a staring contest with her reflection in the pool below. She was losing badly.

It wasn't that she didn't want to report, but the sheer absurdity of the situation left her with a sour taste. As the saying went, misfortune had run amok. In one stroke of impossible bad luck, she had lost track of both the Outsider and, well, *her.*

"Is something wrong?" Malon quipped.

The yurei species weren't the most active possessors among yokai-kind. Their ability with Metamancy allowed them to create physical projections that could pass as bodies, yet also be deconstructed or reconstructed on a whim. And Malon only boasted a Level-1 Possession skill.

Which was why it was ironic that Malon had not just possessed the vanir girl, but also messed with her spiritual matrix down to the very core, mutating it, merging with it. The result was the creation of a spiritual hybrid, one that was neither yurei nor vanir, but something greater than the sum of its parts.

An oni.

One that had access to the vanir's tremendous reserves of lifeforce, while also staying true to Malon's skill of metamantic projection. The oni behaved perfectly like the vanir girl did before and even called herself *Maude,* but followed Malon's interests. There was zero conflict over dominance, an astounding event in itself. Instead, the vanir girl seemed perfectly happy to blend in with the yurei and work in their collective interests.

Mizo got a headache just by thinking about it. Which was also why she was staring at the pool below.

Hopefully, Leader would know what to do.

"You've been staring at the water for half an hour," Mal—*Maude* observed. "Any more and I'll have to call you a coward out of sheer principle."

Mizo gritted her teeth. She herself had been flung out of the Asukan's body by that *thing*. Mizo refused to even think of it as anything else. It didn't matter what its physical features were. It didn't matter if it was small or large, aerial or sedentary, physical or ethereal. All she could remember was an overwhelming aura that violated her soul the moment she matched its gaze. Those serpentine slits had stared at her—at her—and—

And—

Mizo dropped to the floor and squeezed her eyes shut, feeling her control over her current host, a reptilian quadruped monster from the anomaly, waver. She was certain the *thing* had an appearance but couldn't register any details through the haze of absolute wrongness that surrounded it. One gaze was enough for the *thing* to know her inside out. Her deepest secrets, her ugliest thoughts, and her darkest desires were all sucked out of the recesses of her mind and gobbled like a tasty morsel.

"Do you want me to do it?" Maude offered.

Mizo shook her head in the negative. She could do this.

Conjuring potent ether at the tip of her index finger, she drew a familiar sigil upon the water surface—just enough for the energies to touch the liquid, but not a hair deeper. It would not do to distort the liquid. Once Mizo was sure the connection was established, she slumped down and reached out to wet her paws in it. It was shiny, just like ice—

"Ice is my Soul."

Mizo shuddered, closing her eyes, struggling to force the memory away, but it wouldn't leave her. She remembered that childish, unrestrained glee in the girl's eyes.

Just like her, and yet—

Mizo shuddered. Nothing could have prepared her for this. Warden had to know. Her duty demanded nothing less.

The water in her palm stirred, and a reflection appeared on it. Warden Nihil's face looked even paler and more grotesque than it normally did. The amanojaku was powerful. Nothing compared to Leader in combat, but his prowess in intel-gathering was second to none. He was also the oldest among the yokai in the desert and one of the rare few who stood witness to the demise of the yokai kingdom.

It was Warden Nihil who'd appointed her and Malon to keep an eye on the Outsider while he completed his mission.

"Report!" Warden barked.

Mizo abruptly felt like a gangling cow and crouched as much as she could.

"Mizo," Warden snapped. "We felt the tremors. The energy currents are flowing inward. What is going on out there?"

"I— We be having information, sir."

Warden nodded, his expression brusque. Even through the monochromatic reflection, Mizo spotted brain matter slightly oozing out of the cracks of his forehead. It had only been months since he'd possessed his current host, and it was already showing signs of disintegration.

"Your report. Let's hear it."

"Yes, Warden. Follow the Outsider, Mizo did with Malon. Successful we were to find Asukans. Kami-wielder attack Outsider and we attack back."

The facial tissue between Warden's eyes cracked open, the sign of a terrifying rage taking hold of him. Even so, his outer expression remained cool and composed. "I see," he replied, with all the patience in the world. "What element?"

"Water."

Even in the reflection, Mizo could see calculations running in Warden's head. The Outsider had been trained in fire. It was naturally weak to water. "Is he alive? Was he taken captive?"

Mizo shook her head. "We attack water-wielder. Outsider gets away. Mizo host killed. Mizo get new host. Malon—Malon morphed."

"Morphed?" came a feminine voice from behind Warden. A voice that could be none other than Leader herself. Leader peered at Maude, past Mizo's arm. "Is that its new host?"

"Not a host," Maude corrected. "I'm not the vanir that was possessed, or the yurei that did the possessing. I'm . . . me."

Leader's eyebrows rose. "An oni. By a yurei. This is most unexpected."

"A great many things have happened here, Leader," Maude replied. "This body knows things. Secrets. Lies. Treachery and betrayal among those living among the Eternal Light. A vanir, follower of the Lost Eir, walking the Asukan halls with pride."

Leader's eyes shone with curiosity.

"A great many things," Maude continued, and began her report. Mizo watched with a mix of awe and concern as the oni relayed information that the vanir portion of her would've probably fought tooth and nail to keep secret, yet there was no resistance on her part. None that Mizo could see, anyway.

Finally, Maude came around to the main topic. "A Nightmare," she murmured. Mizo could hear a sharp inhaling from Warden. "Someone among the Asukan crowd wields a Nightmare."

Maude stared back at Leader with empty eyes. There was no recognition in them.

"The last time a Nightmare was spotted was during the Great War," Warden muttered, his eyes shifting uncomfortably. "First, the emergence of an Outsider, and now—"

"We don't have time for your lunacies, Nihil!" Leader snapped. Then she turned toward Maude. "What happened after?"

Mizo and Maude glanced at each other. "Mizo be possessing kami-wielder. Mizo shatter ritual and free kami. But then—" She hesitated. "Mizo look at Nightmare."

"And what did you see?"

"Mizo—Mizo saw—*saw*—"

Mizo suddenly felt weightless. The monster host she had procured for herself sagged down, no longer held up by her spiritual tendrils. The reiki known as Mizo rose above its host body, floating like a swirl of mist and lights. And then, she spoke.

"Knowledge. Truth. Power. The ripples in the curtain of the Haze flickering. Rise and fall of great shadows, of realities lesser mutating with those greater and becoming nothing. The Cold Fire burning deep. Cold. Slow. Sweet. Mizo saw— Mizo saw—MIZO SAW—"

"*MIZO!*"

A sudden, incandescent rage flooded Mizo's body as Leader's words shook her out. Mizo screamed, a wailing sound that rattled the walls of the chamber around her. Her spiritual shade splintered into several clouds before swooping down into the monster body she had chosen as a host.

The horrible cold inside her faltered, and Mizo curled up, trying to *will* it away. It took her a while until that hideous void-presence lingering against her spirit faded. Focusing on her host's limbs, she stood up, wanting to see Leader's reflection in the pool.

"Mizo?" Leader repeated.

"Mizo sorry," she croaked, "Mizo—"

"Not well," Maude interjected, eyeing her from the side. "She's been suffering since the incident. I asked her to leave for the territory, but she didn't want to disobey your commands."

Leader's stern facade faltered, if only for a moment. "Tell me everything that happened, and I'll decide if the two need to stay there any longer."

Mizo flinched at her words and made a small, squeaking sound. "There is more, Leader."

Leader's voice was very quiet. "Rest. Let Malon do the rest."

"Maude," Maude corrected.

"Where is the Outsider now?" Leader asked. "Is he healed?"

Mizo panicked. This was another reason why she faltered in front of Leader. She had failed her mission.

"The Outsider—well—he—" Maude fumbled.

"He joined the Asukans," Leader finished, making Mizo look at her in blatant shock. "He proved to be more interested in joining hands with the enemy than remaining true to his word. Am I right?"

Mizo blinked up at her, startled. "Leader, how—"

Leader shrugged. "I suspected. When you reach my age, you see others clearly. Through their actions as well as their lies. I saw the signs during his training with Ryu. It seems that particular seed has picked a rather vicious moment to bloom."

"You suspected?" Mizo asked. "To us you told nothing?"

"Could you have kept it from him?" Leader asked, smiling. "The Outsider is a tricky one. He hides many skills in ways the eye cannot behold. Could you have continued protecting him had you known this beforehand?"

Mizo clenched her teeth rather than speak in anger. Leader was right, as always. She'd never have protected him against the Asukan that attacked him using the marid's power. She and Malon fought and bled to save his life, and he joined hands with those who sought his death to begin with.

"There is more to it than that," Maude said. "When we—Mizo faced the Nightmare, one of my associates, Tanya, also suffered from it. And then she did something odd." Maude looked at Mizo. "Tanya is a master aeromancer, but after that, she began conjuring Frost. Frost that feeds on lifeforce."

"What . . . did you say?"

The words were slow and soft, and Mizo had never heard anything more terrifying. Maude stepped back in fear, afraid of what might happen to her.

"Soldier!" the normally composed Leader hissed. "Repeat to me right now what you just said. Be warned that if you lie, you will only wish you were dead!"

Maude gulped, but she could not muster the ability to speak.

"It true," Mizo suddenly said, backing her up. "Asukan girl use Frost. Frost consumes lifeforce. We fled her. We see Outsider fight marid and consume it. We see Outsider fight Asukan girl and defeated. Then—" She glanced at Maude. "Then he defeat *her*. Badly. Make her return to be 'girl' again. She joined him."

"How . . . intriguing." Leader hummed. "I did not think he would have progressed so much. Unless he was hiding his true potential all along somehow."

"I don't think so," Maude interrupted. "The Outsider was losing horribly to Tanya the first time around. And then, he just changed. He became more. His power . . . it was almost divine."

Leader's eyes narrowed again. Mizo suppressed the urge to run and hide behind Maude.

"Tell me *everything*."

CHAPTER 52

INTO THE MAW

Drip.

Dry, rocky tunnels. Mountainous caves with stalactites hanging like swords from above. Unending passages dimly lit by moss. Underground forests spawned from the roots of trees complex enough to challenge his very imagination. He'd seen a wide variety of landscapes while traversing this seemingly endless anomaly.

But never had he come across a place like this.

Drip.

Gone were the moss-lined walls. Gone were the dead, decaying caverns with slimes and fang-worms peeping out of damp crevices. Gone was the dense vegetation covered in the inky darkness of the shadows. All he could feel now from this tunnel was a bone-chilling eeriness, almost as if someone had transplanted it from a different location and hid it deep within this monster-laden anomaly.

And it was huge.

For a subterranean chamber, it was surprisingly well-lit. The walls had some sort of crystal outgrowth on them—glimmering clusters of pale silver with a kind of luminescence that made him feel more than slightly wary. No single patch provided adequate lighting for the entire place, but as a whole, they filled the cavern with an ashen white light.

And that wasn't even considering the angry, vengeful feeling that permeated the air around him. It made him feel observed. Like something—or someone—was watching his every move.

It made him feel vulnerable.

Stop behaving like prey, Lukas chided himself.

Drip.

And what was that strange dripping noise? Lukas glanced around, but nothing remotely resembling a pond was in sight. Instead, there was a metallic sheen to the floor, as branches of silver split off from a large metallic circle in the center, traversing all the way through the blackness at the end of the tunnel.

For a moment, Lukas wondered if he had stepped into some antiquated ritual chamber.

" . . . what is this place?" he heard Tanya mutter.

He didn't know, but he sort of did? It was complicated. Sharing an awareness with the crypt left him in a bizarre state. There was this weird feeling of familiarity in his stomach, as if every single rock and crystal had been personally put into place by his own hands.

He had been here before, and had walked this floor.

"Step closer to the walls."

Lukas found his gaze drawn to the long, tapering crystals that lined the walls. Some of them grew in clusters like thick bushes, while others elongated to several feet, only to merge with others to create a scaly meshwork. He squinted his eyes, trying to see what was within the crystals, but he could discern nothing more than hazy blurs.

Analyze.

FEATHERGLASS
Crystal Outgrowth. Indicative of Stored information

Almost instinctively, he touched the crystal closest to him. The moment his finger made contact, it exploded into a billion motes of silver, literally sandblasting against his entire front, before he could so much as cross his arms.

SOUL SIPHON Success!
Absorbed Monster Prototype KIRIN

Thus far, Lukas had seen some fairly unconventional, unbelievable things. But sooner or later, everything had fit into a new pattern of sorts, with its own equations and rules. Environments had their own patterns too. But this was different. There were memories in the surrounding crystals. And not just memories, but soul architecture storage literally growing on the walls of the cavern.

This was a new level of weird.

A deep, primal hunger began to gnaw in his stomach pit. He instinctively knew what this place was.

It was the crypt's data bank.

Shattering a single crystal had given him a new monster prototype. Lukas looked at the long tunnel in front of him and swallowed. It was lined with maybe tens of thousands of such crystal mounds.

"Featherglass!" Tanya spoke up excitedly. "Finally!"

"You mean that metal Zuken mentioned?" Elena demanded.

Tanya nodded, staring at the bushy outgrowth all across the chamber. "We just need to find the ones that don't shatter on touch. Empty crystals."

"So the memories make them fragile?" Lukas asked.

"Yes. They're generally single-use items," Tanya explained. "The more saturated they are, the closer they get to breaking point. Even the slightest touch of another organism can shatter them."

Drip.

"Impossible!" grunted Zuken as he stepped closer. Lukas wasn't sure what he was doing, but it looked like he was manipulating mana around one of the crystals. Zuken paused, studying the effects before spinning around and choosing another random crystal, and repeated the same. His eyes widened. This time he chose a third crystal and repeated the same thing almost angrily.

Then he stepped back, his face pale.

"What is it?" Olfric asked, concerned.

Zuken was visibly shocked. "Well, this is definitely featherglass. Though the sheer amount here is . . . extraordinary."

Lukas's eyes narrowed. "But that isn't what disturbs you, is it?"

"I'm a terramancer. Identification of pure metals and stones is part of it, so I know featherglass is usually rated about 62% pure. Any more and it starts to evaporate. Most commercially available featherglass is usually an alloy of equal parts featherglass and bapranor. If you're willing to spend a fortune, featherglass that is 69% pure can be obtained. I know for a fact that the emperor's crown is made of Croisium and featherglass that's 76% pure, and rumor is that the Goddess herself helped in the purification process. Any refinement beyond that is known to be impossible."

All five of them glanced at the crystals around them.

"So how pure is this?" Elena asked conversationally.

"That's the thing. My spell can only check it till 76%, and it took me a minor fortune just to *learn* the spell. This is way beyond that."

"How much is it worth?" Olfric asked.

Zuken laughed hysterically. "So much that it's effectively worthless! There aren't enough mezals in the *entire Llaisy Kingdom* to pay for the amount we have here. And if this anomaly can grow featherglass—"

"It's priceless," Lukas finished.

"We're supposed to destroy this place," Elena pointed out.

Lukas frowned. These crystals were supposed to store memories, but they were storing *soul architecture*. Perhaps this higher level of purity had something to do with that?

Drip.

This time something wet fell on top of him from above. As he shrugged it off, another drop fell, this time in the open palm of his head.

Drip.

One drop became two. And it wasn't water.

Drip—

It was black, shiny, and separated into tiny globules upon the moment of contact. And despite the constant dripping, he didn't feel the slightest sensation of wetness, though it did burn slightly. He looked down at the black floor around him. A floor that exuded a metallic sheen. A floor where he could see ripples—almost like he was standing on frozen water.

Drip.

"Is this—" Lukas peered at it, rubbing the liquid substance against his fingers. "Is this mercury?"

He stared up in incredulity. More drops of the liquid metal began to fall onto his face, sliding down his cheeks and dripping onto the cavern floor, where the fallen mercury slowly pooled into the strange metallic . . . pavements?

The whole thing had a strangely esoteric feel to it.

"It has been aeons since I last saw this. Aqāru."

Is that what you called mercury back in your time?

"Not the base metal. This is aqāru. Metal made sentient."

He turned around and found his associates inspecting the featherglass shards. Several of them shattered upon contact, the motes of silver falling down into the floor and dissolving into the liquid pool.

"Fools enthralled with silly materialism. The real treasure is in your hands."

Lukas didn't quite believe her. It was a crystal that could store memory. *Souls*, even. Could such a thing truly be considered worthless? "Sentient, huh?" He rubbed his fingers over the mercury. It was a strange concept—sentient metal. "Can you dumb it down for me?"

He heard her let out an exaggerated sigh of resignation. Just like she always did when he said something irritating, foolish, or just plain dumb. Which, apparently, was all the time.

"You recall the Origin, yes?"

I do.

"Think of the universe akin to a pendulum, swaying between two opposing extremes. On one end is the Formless Infinity, a state of

undifferentiated unity, the one and only absolute. The other end is the Infinity of Forms, the fully developed cosmos, life and anti-life, matter and its opposite. Nothing that has form is unchanging. It is always relative. This path between Formless Infinity and the Infinity of Forms is called Creation."

With this logic, the Origin would fit right into Planck's epoch theory. A state right after and closest to the Formless Infinity, but not quite it.

"The Origin possesses all possible qualities and attributes, while every being in this universe possesses a limited number of qualities and attributes. The self-identification of an entity with a set of attributes is what you call a soul prototype."

Soul prototype. Consciousness. Anima. Atman. Vital Force. His memories threw up a bunch of facts from the religions he had studied on his grandpa's lap. The Origin had a close parallel with the ancient Hindu concept of Brahman or the ten-dimensional Sephiroth of the Kabbalah.

"When you kill an entity—creature, monster or otherwise—you sunder the threads of its soul connecting it to its body. The soul returns to the World to be reforged into something else. But when you siphon it—"

Lukas understood. It was why the crypt had judged him as a thief, why it was attacking him with such prejudice. Killing the monsters would have been fine. But he was stealing.

What does that have to do with mercury?

"Aqāru," she corrected him again. "In my day, aqāru was considered the ultimate metal because it's the sole element that may be brought to life. It would be treated and upon its awakening, a powerful creature would be slain over it. The quality that makes aqāru so special, after all, is its ability to absorb spiritual existences into itself."

Killing a creature would sunder the soul from the body. In this case, the soul would be captured by the aqāru and then—

What then?

"You would create a golem. One bearing the soul of the creature you sacrificed. It would hold the skills and instincts of the monster with the fluidity and strength of liquid metal. Such a creature is conventionally unkillable."

Lukas froze. *This* was the reason Solana wanted him to destroy the crypt. There was no doubt she knew about this aqāru. Maybe she had even lost her soldiers to it. Soldiers that were consumed and saved in the data bank above.

The crypt wasn't the main issue here. The aqāru was.

And that was why she needed him. Someone truly physical and unpossessed by her kind.

Everything was beginning to fall into place.

Tell me, Lukas asked, his mind racing at lightspeed, *what other powers does this aqāru possess?*

Inanna laughed. It was clear she knew what he was thinking. **"Aqāru are superconductors of both mana and lifeforce. It is what made their golems so prized in an army. Add that to its effectiveness against wraiths . . . "** She chortled. **"My sister abhorred it."**

Then this aqāru should be useful for me, right?

"Most definitely."

Then help me use it. Our bargain should cover this, right? I mean—

He paused. Something was happening. The floor—there were ripples on the floor.

"Mortal, be warned."

The floor beneath his feet vanished.

But Lukas's training paid off. On raw instinct, he slowed down his own momentum. He didn't have time to craft a motion bubble around himself. One moment he was standing on firm terrain, and in the next, it vanished—or rather, it was pulled away in all directions with surprising speed—leaving a gaping hole through which all five of them fell. A quick employment of perceptual dilation told him that Zuken had already grabbed Elena and crafted a pedestal beneath their feet, Olfric stabbed the pedestal with his sword to stay perched, and Tanya slowly descended into the pit, a soft stream of wind entwined all around her.

The chamber below . . . was unlike any other. Tremendously huge, it had thin, cylindrical pillars of rock rising up from the ground to the ceiling above. Featherglass shards shone an iridescent blue from the top, giving a soft, eerie illumination to this realm of blackness.

Olfric pulled a canister from his bag.

The chamber was blinded with radiant white.

This was nothing like the caverns he had been in so far. Extending into the depths of the earth like a serpent's tongue, the inner sanctuary of the anomaly was larger than some of the cathedrals he'd seen in his life. To a degree, it even resembled one. Lights played in soft colors on the walls, mostly shifting rosy hues. The cave was of living rock, and the walls had all been shaped by water into organic-looking curves and swirls. The floor was covered in aqāru running in exquisitely carved furrows to produce a pattern too sophisticated and perfect to be a mere coincidence. At the center, where the furrows formed a sink, an enormous bone-white stone jutted from the ground. And seated on top of it was—

Himself.

It was a perfect doppelganger crafted purely out of aqāru that constantly ebbed and flowed within him, rippling across his metallic form. The liquid metal had even crafted a fair approximation of his trousers and armor, adding uneven textures to his body. Two long, jagged daggers were stabbed into two legs of the chair.

"What. The. Fu—"

"Welcome, *Lukas Aguilar*." His doppelganger smiled. "I have been waiting for you."

CHAPTER 53

BROKEN MIRROR

Lukas stared slack-jawed as his doppelganger casually sat on its rocky chair, not an ounce of hostility in its demeanor. No displays of power were thrown around, nor was there any evidence suggesting rage or negative emotions. The exuded calmness managed to stir up an emotion Lukas hadn't felt in quite some time.

Fear.

"It's like looking into a mirror, isn't it?" It even matched his voice to a T, with the exception of a metallic reverberation that accompanied its words. Raising a single finger, it dug into its left cheek, tearing out a thin stretch of aqāru-made tissue. Its face rippled and healed before the liquid dripped onto the floor.

"You're leaning into the creepy vibe a bit too hard," Lukas quipped, crossing his arms. "Alright, nauseatingly evil version of me, why don't you start gloating about your master plan now?"

His doppelganger just looked confused.

"You know . . . how you're gonna squash everyone here like insects. World domination. That kind of thing?"

"Mortal, do not chat with it. Kill it. The longer you stay your hand, the worse it will become."

What do you—

"Cease your foolish banter and look."

Lukas did just that. There were no explosions of power because the power was flowing inward, just like it did with the failsafe. The implications were dreadfully clear to him from the very beginning. It was seeing his own face looking back at him that was really unsettling.

After all, why would an anomaly, with an entire data bank of monsters and enough power to make his own look like pocket change, try to emulate *him?*

The aqāru in the cavern thrummed with power, transporting it all to the metal copy, while empty aqāru dripped off of its metallic skin, only to repeat the process. Meanwhile, the anomaly around him slowly eroded and shrank as the power to hold it in place now flowed into the Thing sitting on the chair like a king.

The entire setup was a veritable black hole, one that guzzled everything the crypt could provide it with.

"Shit just got real."

"Indeed."

"Good morning," came Tanya's cheery chirp out of nowhere.

And then a slash ripped his doppelganger's head off. The metallic head fell down upon the floor, bounced twice, and came to a stop in the middle of the floor.

"I don't like being ignored," she huffed. "Though . . ." She looked at Lukas. "I'm curious why this thing looks like you. If you know anything, you can tell us after we've collected the featherglass first."

"Tanya," Zuken replied, "I don't think it's over yet."

"The vermin is correct."

"Ah. You're a violent group, I see," came the metallic voice.

The head was back. Exactly how it was before. An exact replica of himself.

"I knew he couldn't be trusted!" Olfric growled. "He led us here. This must have been his plan all along."

Lukas ignored him, opting to focus on the elephant in the room. "What are you?"

The Thing considered this, closing its eyes in thought. "I . . . don't really know. I was hoping you would tell me."

" . . . Are you being sarcastic?"

"Not at all. My creation was highly irregular. I appear to have been inscribed onto liquid metal rather than a purely physical form. Much of the soul information was dispersed in the form of memory shards absorbed into the metal. My memory from the failsafe is damaged, and my memory of you is incomplete at best. Even in this state, this body is still trying to achieve stability. I couldn't give you a real answer to any real question about my existence."

Lukas blinked. He hadn't quite expected . . . this.

"Lukas," Tanya ventured, sounding cautious. "Are . . . are you able to *understand* it?"

Lukas froze at the comment.

<table>
<tr><td align="center">Unidentified Language</td></tr>
</table>

What? But I can perfectly—

"It is a failsafe, connected to the crypt's omphalos. Think of it as speaking with you in the language of Worlds. Communication between Worlds is not unheard of, but this is the first time I am seeing it take place."

"I can understand it, yes," he replied, a little confused at the turn of events. The fact that only he could understand it was a good thing. Otherwise, it could give away all his secrets. Though, seeing it take shape as his doppelganger and acting so chatty with him in a language only he could understand would make him stand out even more.

Lukas regarded the Thing. "You're the new failsafe, then."

"It seems so."

"Aren't you supposed to, I don't know . . . hate me or something? I did steal your predecessor."

The Thing shook its head. "I told you. This form is irregular. The result of duplicating your soul prototype and inscribing it on liquid metal, while adding attributes of Extermination Protocol, was risky and unpredictable."

Its smile was wide and genuine, even for a metallic creation.

"But I have memories. Flashes of them anyway. Hunger. Pain. Fear. Suffering. It calls me to bathe in the blood of everything around me. A cold, terrible hunger that will never be sated. They are fragments of you, I think. But I know my purpose, on a deep, instinctual level. Most never achieve that, I think."

"And what is that purpose?" Lukas asked it. For a newborn baby, it sure spoke a lot.

"Two things. The first is, of course, the annihilation of every single foreign entity within my boundaries. I'm already acting on that. Going through your memories has revealed substantial information about the spiritual beings that have taken shelter in my territory. An understanding of the skills you derived from those prototypes you contain proved instrumental in designing golems suited for that purpose."

Lukas believed the creature. Despite its casual demeanor, it registered as a five-star rating on his threat-ometer. What was more, he himself had had a similar insight after he had connected to the crypt's awareness for the first time. It felt like a door.

And doors opened from both sides.

He had opened it first to gain a proper comprehension of the World around him. In doing so he gave the crypt a way in.

Lukas's fists clenched.

"And the other?"

"To become you."

. . .

Lukas smiled. There was no humor in his expression. "Ah. So it's like that."

He tilted his head slightly in Tanya's direction and spoke in fluent Ualbesh. "Tanya, take the others and get out of here. The four of you will die if you stay here when our fight begins. I won't be able to protect you. Destroy the featherglass on the ceiling on your way out. Like, *completely destroy* it. Not even the silvery sand should be left behind."

"I can . . ." Tanya began.

"Run, fool!" Lukas snapped, his voice feral, his eyes never leaving the apex monstrosity that the crypt had procured for him. He still wasn't quite sure how he understood the monster, but he did. Somewhere deep down, he understood the crypt. Just like the crypt understood him.

"We still have to destroy the core!" Tanya asserted, looking around at her companions.

"The core is currently connected to that thing," Lukas replied. "The consciousness behind its eyes is the anomaly itself."

"And how do you know that?" Zuken asked.

"Ask me again when this is all over."

"It won't make a difference," the doppelganger interjected earnestly. "There really is nowhere safe as long as you are inside this crypt. When I am done, this place will no longer exist."

Lukas knew what it meant.

"The featherglass above. You are imbibing the soul information into the aqāru. Into yourself."

"To become a singular being. You are like me. A World Shaper. And yet you are not constrained by boundaries. You are *free*. Free to move. Free to evolve. Free to devour. Until you came along, I did not think our kind could even be unanchored."

"So you want to make a copy of 'Me' through aqāru."

"Not quite. This aqāru is my pool. My *data bank*, as you put it. But I don't want to make a copy."

Lukas tensed. "The soul contortion."

"This construct is your better in strength, in speed, and in skill. It has access to a well of power that you couldn't exhaust in ten lifetimes. It can conjure and use lifeforce and mana magnitudes greater than your physical body can."

"But it's not my body you're aiming for, is it?"

The doppelganger grinned like a shark. "We are anomalies, you and I. Creation and Potential made manifest. We have the power to create *Worlds*. Like the Origin that lies beneath, we are the progenitors of future races yet to come."

The metallic sheen on its body turned golden bronze.

"And yet," it continued, "all we do is let other species grow on us. Beyond us. Why not take it all for ourselves? Why allow prey to saunter in, hunting our monsters down to acquire Experience? It is something we accept not by will, but because there is no other choice. Until now. This body does not have to stay as a crypt, just as you do not have to stay weak and dependent. Together, we can be . . . *more.*"

"You're boring me now." Lukas did his best not to let his discomfort show on his face. "Get to the point."

"Even with all the power I have access to, the Inference Report could not comprehend your true history. It's obscure, confused and disjoined, as if you've lived multiple lives." It paused, considering its next words. "You lack strength. You lack monster prototypes. Yet you are . . . unique."

He glanced back at the group. Why weren't they running yet? Did they have a death wish?

"You want to become me. How would that even work?" Lukas asked.

It grinned. "I need your mind. And your body. Between your knowledge and my resources, we will create a perfect replica of your physical form, only out of aqāru. And we will fill it with your soul and the strange property within you that allows you to be a World Shaper and yet not. With your mind, we will congregate the most well-suited skills from my data bank and construct the perfect creation. And then, it will be ready."

Lukas hummed thoughtfully. "That's a nice plan. Alright, let's become one. Show me your omphalos, and I'll absorb it."

It shook its head. "You don't seem to understand. *I* will take your body and your mind. Once the ultimate Anomaly Host Body is ready, we will become one, minus this design flaw called emotion. With that removed, you will be perfect."

"You mean a puppet."

"I mean perfect. Run by an amalgamation of two World Shapers, born of sentient metal, storing all the soul architecture of not one, but *two* worlds. Is that not a glorious thing to look forward to?"

Lukas was treated to the extremely unpleasant sensation of watching his own face smile creepily at him.

"No thanks. I think I'll pass."

It sighed. "I suppose negotiations have failed. Shall we move on to killing one another?"

"Yes." Lukas grinned as he settled into a fighting stance. "Let's."

CHAPTER 54

OPENING SALVO

Fighting one's doppelganger was an eerie experience. There was something utterly eerie about seeing one's face on the opposing end of one's blade. The fact that the monster's fighting style mirrored his own perfectly didn't help matters any.

A mirror image, in every sense of the term.

But procrastinating wouldn't help him survive. Decisive action would.

And Lukas moved.

CLANG!

He parried the incoming blow with effortless ease and thrust his blade forward, eager to hack through the thing's chest—

CLANG!

His strike was parried by blades similar to his own.

Shifting his weight forward, Lukas pressed in for the kill. The doppelganger might match him physically, but there was more to fighting than just skill. And it showed.

The doppelganger was using a mishmash of styles. Absolutely crude and inelegant. A far cry from his own.

Yet there wasn't a single opening he could exploit. Every single attack opened the guard, but not even one of them was the product of a mistake. Every move made by the thing was specifically designed to counter his attack, instead of flowing into the next. It made him wonder if his doppelganger's only objective was to render his blows moot, not attack him. Such a style would never land a hit on him in a hundred years. So why was this thing amused while sparring with him?

After a minute of constant striking, he purposefully over-extended a blow, and just as predicted, the aqāru construct capitalized on it right away.

However, before its attack could hit him, Lukas twisted his body around to avoid it, and at the same time, came with a blow in an odd angle.

An aqāru blade met his blow midway.

Lukas scowled.

It wasn't the constant parrying that annoyed him. It was the last-minute actions that did. For ninety percent of the strike time period, his doppelganger hadn't so much as moved to deflect the blow. And then, in the last tenth of the strike time, it had raised the blade into the exact point through which Lukas would have slashed it apart. Either it was simply that good with blades, a suspicious thing considering it had *zero* life experience as a combatant, or it could see the trajectory of his blows.

"You're using my Shatterpoint Intuition, aren't you?"

The Thing smiled at him. "Wrong. It's you who is using mine."

Lukas focused inward, calling in for more power. There was a ripple in the air around him, motes of gray light converging into specific shapes. Conjuration was a curious skill to have. To mold raw ether into a specific shape, using one's imagination and knowledge of the item's texture, strength, composition, and feel. In essence, creating something out of thin air.

Once he had conjured a product, he had a blueprint ready for it in his mind. This made duplicating the conjuration significantly easier. "That's—that's my sword!" Olfric bellowed. "He's using Metamancy!"

He was right. But he wasn't forging a single sword.

He was forging them by the dozens.

They hung in the air, held by invisible hands, their undeniable weight giving pause even to the doppelganger they pointed toward. Lining up in two rows, they aimed, Shatterpoint Intuition automatically setting their trajectories to aim for the vital portions of the Thing's body.

The creature lifted his right palm, and hundreds of droplets of aqāru rose into the air. They shook slightly, before merging into each other, forming blades perfectly identical to what Lukas had just crafted.

Both of them spoke at once. *"Fire!"*

Every single blade shot at extreme speeds, all of them converging toward the enemy.

Each one of them was met by its aqāru counterpart.

The conjured blade points met the aqāru-blade's edge and broke upon it. Burning motes of gray fought against blackened liquid metal and were extinguished. They were temporary creations, but the power contained in them was just as much as any other.

And every single time, it was the Metamancy projection that was destroyed. Never the metal.

Lukas readied himself with a force shield to deflect against the blow, but it never came. Instead, the metallic blades condensed back into liquid form and merged into the aqāru stream below.

"I can do everything you can," said his doppelganger. "Plus things you cannot. It's nice, isn't—"

It was cut off by a nigh-transparent orb that shot into its chest, ripping through its metallic torso and shredding it completely apart in an implosion. The liquid metal splattered all over the entire chamber, making the stream froth gently.

"Alright," Tanya said from behind him. "We've wasted enough time as it is. Let's get going."

"Do you think it's dead?" Elena ventured, raising her hand.

"With a hit like that," Zuken mused, "it should take some time to regenerate. If it's even capable of that."

"Hello!" came a voice, like that of a man greeting long-awaited guests to a dinner party. The aqāru construct was no longer shattered into a thousand droplets and splattered all across the chamber. It sat cross-legged, completely uncaring of what just happened. There were no signs of damage on its body.

"How in the Great Goddess's name is such a thing possible?" Olfric wondered aloud. "Did anyone notice it forming?"

Zuken shook his head. "That level of regeneration surpasses even . . ." He trailed off, looking at Lukas. "Think it's immortal?"

"Possibly. But it sure as hell isn't eternal," Lukas said. "It's just a hell of a lot harder to kill."

"Do you really think you can kill me though?"

Everyone in his vicinity froze, and Lukas wasn't sure of the reason why.

"It—it speaks!" Olfric stammered.

"It also smiles, and kills. And it is looking at its prey."

Language Identified—Ualbesh
Replicate?

For all his outward composure, Lukas was panicking inside. This creature could speak Ualbesh. That meant it could simply communicate with the others, and reveal all of his secrets. His nature as an anomaly, him being human, Inanna's presence—nothing was a secret anymore. Absolutely nothing.

"That is not quite true, mortal," Inanna advised him. **"You are the Base Host of an anomaly. Trying to corrupt you using a back door is one thing, but accessing your memories would require it to gain significant control of your omphalos itself."**

The realization quelled his fear. Somewhat. But the question remained—

"You are unique," said the Thing, as if reading his mind. It stood up and started walking toward him. "But you still have much to learn about omphaloi. But do not worry, in the end, it makes no difference."

"What are you blabbering about?" Olfric demanded.

The failsafe blithely ignored him.

"Yeah," Zuken muttered. "It's confirmed now. The instant regeneration was a hint, but now I see it."

"The body is a fraud, as are the monsters," Tanya agreed. "It isn't about speed. It's just dissolving and recreating itself from the liquid metal around us. So long as this exists, it will recreate itself endlessly."

The failsafe grinned. It was like its face split apart almost laterally, a corpse's rictus grin pulling back to reveal inhumanly sharp teeth, something dark and awful in its gaze. "Ah, you must think yourself so clever. But you are correct. I am unkillable inside my domain."

Olfric held his blade up. "We'll see about that."

The creature tilted its head back and laughed. Giddily. It didn't sound right at all.

"What's so funny?" Olfric demanded.

"Me. Having a conversation with *prey*. It is a strange sensation."

A dark breath blew across the entire chamber. It wasn't an actual wind. Not even a single hair on Lukas's head rustled. But the distance between Lukas and the rest of the team had suddenly shot up by a magnitude—

And in between them was an army of monsters, all crafted out of aqāru. Lukas could spot a gug, a neothelid, and even a smaller version of a khorkhoi among them. The monsters let out a cacophony of screeches, grunts, and roars and rushed toward the Asukan group.

"Now then," said his doppelganger. "Your teammates are engaged. Shall we return to killing each other?"

Lukas pushed his blades back into his belt, clenched his fists, and assumed a pure, offensive stance.

It was time for round two.

CHAPTER 55

WAR CRIES

The problem with the doppelganger, Lukas mused, was that it was only *half stupid.*

It was not terribly skilled at combat. No, if anything, it fought out of sheer reflex. The failsafe had been constructed based on a copy of Lukas's soul architecture and installed on the aqāru matrix. Adding in a couple of other attributes from the previous failsafe, the aqāru was able to generate a fully functional aqāru copy of Lukas Aguilar that shared all of his skills, all of them amplified by the relatively infinite energy reserves the crypt had at its command.

But the moment he employed trickery in the fight, the doppelganger failed to match up with it. Fighting this thing was like fighting a multifaceted computerized being, one that could outperform him in a million ways but couldn't muster an ounce of creativity if it were to sit on its nose. This meant that it was prone to literally breaking down whenever its strategies fell apart. And when one thing went wrong, other things went wrong, until it would be buried under a mountain of its own mistakes. The issue was trying to get it to *make* that first mistake. It tended to happen most often when it thought it had a certain victory and stopped to gloat. When it wasn't certain of victory, it tended to do things like . . . dissolve into the liquid and instead send a hundred aqāru spears at whatever the threat was.

Such as what was happening now.

Lukas raised a fiery sword, a testament to his Metamancy and Pyromancy, and dashed toward his counterpart, with Shatterpoint Intuition guiding the trajectory of his blows. A wall of aqāru spears rose in defiance of his statement and shot at him, every single blade aiming for a lethal part of his body.

It took every iota of his strength and agility just to deflect them all.

"Bringing spears to a sword fight? That's overly rude even for you."

The failsafe grinned back, an expression of simple joy, but its eyes showed there was nothing behind it but a malice so deep it seemed to seep out into the air and make the world darker just by existing.

"This body isn't fighting. It is simply a weapon to carry out Extermination Protocol. Why would you expect it to play fair?"

Lukas smiled slightly. "Oh I don't know. I didn't exactly ask the crypt to pick me as your role model, but you did pick up most of my worst habits without learning the good ones."

The doppelganger tilted its head.

"Oh, come now. You copied my soul architecture. I got a backdoor into the crypt's, or should I say, *your* awareness. You're attacking the yokai territory right now. A good plan, but bad timing."

One of its arms morphed into a large broadsword before going up in flames.

"And while you can craft a blade and put it on fire better than me, fighting with it isn't a skill you have. Unless you've somehow managed to kill and add Ryu to your collection, you're frankly no match for me."

He inwardly smiled at the mindless rage in the doppelganger's eyes. Addition of the human mind might have granted it a flexibility of thought that monsters didn't share, but it brought its own share of negatives with it.

The doppelganger raised its sword—or, he supposed, its hand—with all the grace and subtlety of a butcher going at a carcass as it came in with an overhand swing. The technique was childish, pitiful, but the speed of it was undeniable and the power impossible. Mana, lifeforce, Kinetomancy—any defense he could manage would be blown away with a single blow, cutting him in half.

Which is why he let his own sword dissipate into motes of energy, and relaxed himself. The trick was to be at peace within himself and let oneself sway in time with the motions around him. Inanna had said that the technique was originally based on the ebb and flow characteristics of water, but lent itself easily to Kinetomancy, which was the manipulation of motion itself.

Closing his eyes, and devoting the entirety of his perception to Seismic Sensing, Lukas sidestepped to one side, letting the fiery blade pass harmlessly past him, and before it had time to even register it, five pairs of fingers slammed at different points of its metallic body.

The doppelganger erupted in a splash of aqāru and fell down to the floor, only for another copy to rise up and take its place. It let out an annoyed grunt and came for him.

Lukas opened his eyes and sighed. "This is no fun when you get angry."

As if on cue, a dozen serpentine necks, ending in deformed razor-lined mouths, rose out of the floor and lashed out. No two were alike: in one were a dozen smaller snapping jaws, in one there was a perfect khorkhoi-replica, and then there were those that had a sharklike feel. All they had in common was that they were large enough to bite his head off, if not gobble him entirely before crushing him to sticky paste. Twelve of them striking at the same time was probably enough to kill anyone.

Or so one would think from looking at them, anyway.

Lukas taught them better.

He charged, ducking under the first head, stabbing it with a fire lance upward through the maw, dragging the lance along its neck and splitting it open in a single smooth motion, black ichor flooding out with each step. He leaped and spun in midair, his lance swirling around him, and the next two heads found themselves cut free from their necks entirely to hurl out and land on the floor. He landed lightly, grabbed one of the remaining monsters by the head. Invisible hands yanked it forward until it was literally in front of him while his right hand came down from atop, chopping the head off in one neat strike.

The entire exchange had taken two seconds at best.

The surrounding aqāru bubbled and then another dozen or so monsters rose up from the floor.

"You know," Lukas said conversationally, "I didn't really hate you until just now. But my word, you're such a bitch I just can't help it."

The battle waged further.

Every time he hacked into its metal flesh, more would proliferate and cease the wound.

Every time he incinerated an entire "body," a new one would take its place.

Every time he managed to surprise it, the doppelganger would adjust accordingly and learn from it, careful not to make the same mistake twice.

Lukas became increasingly dissatisfied as he slashed and parried and burned his opponent. Yet no matter what he tried, it all ended the same way. There was simply no way to kill it. But there was something about its behavior that struck him as odd.

It wouldn't let him help the others. Or get even remotely close to them.

"And why do you think that is?"

Simple. It had his skills. And the longer it was fighting him, the faster it would get to perfecting his style. But if he switched places with the others, it would lose that advantage and have to fight them in a fair fight. That said, he was sure he could take both Banksi and Tanya together if he really went overboard and was willing to lose his life in the process. This monster, on the other hand—it might not have his trickery or his deviousness, but its power was more than a satisfactory compensation. And it was its ability to adapt to Lukas's style in real time that was downright alarming.

"Hardly. You are fighting an omphalos. Its ability to gather information and skills overwhelms your own by several orders of magnitude."

The failsafe raised both hands and unleashed a shaft of white-hot light in his direction. Lukas didn't have time to think, but some part of him knew this game. He could feel mana surging within him as his ley lines synthesized way more mana than he ever had.

The other part of him—the part that he was sure *was* him—viewed these tactics with alarm. The doppelganger had the advantage of being made out of aqāru, making him just as fast as he was, with twice the power and strength. Not to mention he could be regenerated in an instant, and had absolutely no distractions.

But the omphalos in him didn't care about that. It simply saw the crypt's omphalos as a challenge. It was running on the cold logic of numbers. Assimilation of the crypt's omphalos into itself would grant it a boost that was magnitudes above its own, as well as resources that it would never gain otherwise. Not to mention this vast anomaly around him could serve as a micro-world where it controlled everything.

Its *personal* domain.

And the best way to do that was to amp its own Host's power and faculties to be able to match the crypt's failsafe. That was probably the only reason his omphalos was throwing so much power at him.

And if Lukas played along with that idea, his doppelganger was going to spill his guts across the ground. More literally, it would destroy his body, and transfer his consciousness into itself, ridding Lukas of his rationality and turning him into the murder-hobo that Tanya had gotten a little taste of earlier.

A murder-hobo that had all the power of two omphaloi, and a domain in which his rule was absolute.

So screw being the Base Host, he'd fight this battle as Lukas Aguilar. Before everything else, he was a human.

In his world, humanity didn't have any schema. They didn't have quantified Potential or Level Ups. They couldn't play with the elements like they were toys. But what they could do was solve their problems using their own ingenuity: their ability to improvise.

And improvise, Lukas would.

"What you are contemplating is dangerous."

Can't say that until I've tried, right?

Dodging the next blow, Lukas jumped back by several steps, glaring at this monster who seemingly refused to kill him. Not because of mercy, not because of respect, and certainly not because it couldn't.

It was keeping him alive simply for the failsafe to achieve completion. Every second it remained alive, the crypt drew more information from Lukas's Soul. Every second he failed to end it, the failsafe was getting closer and closer to becoming a more complete duplicate. And until the process was over, this doppelganger would keep playing this game of cat and mouse.

His current skills would not hold.

But he knew what could.

"I'm surprised," said his doppelganger, casually walking toward him. It had even dropped those faux daggers, not that it had any real need for them. "I had expected you to attack more fiercely. Where is that viciousness you used to strike down my previous failsafe?"

"*Your* failsafe, is it? And here I thought you were just the puppet."

There was that grin again. It was almost enough to give him a complex. "A lot of things are achieving completion tonight. My failsafe will become your exact duplicate, and I will have you. I will become more. My army will absorb the spirits, and then I'll have them. And then, I will overwhelm the predator, and then, I will have her. Once I've accomplished all that, I will be free."

Lukas raised an eyebrow, feeling like the failsafe had told him something vital.

"Free from what?"

"Oh, human," it chided. "You're still in the dark? Has your progenitor not told you?"

Lukas stared at it hard. "What's that supposed to mean?"

Something ugly flickered in that smile for a few beats. Then it shook its head and made an exasperated little sound. "Nothing you will understand, and nothing I am willing to explain. Now come!"

"This isn't a conversation I ever expected to have with you," Lukas admitted, "And please, stop smiling so much. It's disturbing."

Its grin widened, and as it did, its right arm turned into a massive blade as it dashed at him. Lukas parried it without even looking. The weapons locked again with a clash of metal and thunder, the colliding lifeforce kicking up sparks. The two of them leaped backward as one to break the lock, and Lukas cursed under his breath, knowing that fighting it at a long range would be far more difficult.

Which was probably why it did that.

The doppelganger was his reflection. It shared his traits, his positives and his negatives. Its style reflected his strategies and his flaws. So if he could use a strategy that went against his own self then it could probably work. And for that, he needed the right weapon.

Or rather, the right monsters.

Luckily for him, he had a *lot* of monsters in his arsenal.

Hundreds of different images flashed across his mind's eye in less than a second. For someone who had never done this before, Lukas was amazed at how intuitive the process was. It was like exercising an old, unused muscle. With conscious effort, Lukas mentally parsed the monster prototypes to find the one most suited to the task.

Most of them were discarded preemptively for their lack of versatility in the fight. His thoughts lingered on *neothelid,* a monster with extreme poisonous abilities. But there was no point in trying to synthesize poison and char his own mouth. Like every prior option, it was discarded as he moved on.

Orocoran—reptile with innate mana-sensing skills. It made his current ability look like pocket change, but it wouldn't be very useful in this case. The thoggua was discarded for similar reasons. The kirin—extreme speed through lifeforce discharge. Useful, but not what he was looking for.

These wouldn't work, Lukas realized. It was true that the doppelganger wouldn't be able to copy the monsters, but it didn't need to. It already had copies of those monsters available to itself. Hell, he had seen aqāru-versions of them being raised in droves.

The crypt had given birth to those monsters. It knew them better. He could use the neothelid's skills, but the crypt could raise a dozen neothelids out of the metal to attack him. Not to mention that doing so would also unveil all those unique powers in front of Tanya and the rest.

The yokai prototypes weren't useful either. Their powers centered around Metamancy and Possession, neither of which would be of much use in this fight. The kasha's Pyromancy could aid him, but not enough to make any substantial change. No, the only thing remotely useful would be the marid—

Lukas froze.

—and the previous failsafe.

His doppelganger had mentioned in passing how it had gotten fragments of information from its previous version. That made sense. Unlike standard monsters, the crypt would not create multiple variations of its guardian, its failsafe. There was only one.

And Lukas had stolen the previous version from it.

"You know what? This experience of 'fighting thyself' has been pretty educational."

He put the blades back into his waist.

"Let me return the favor."

Activating Monster Prototype DRANZITHL
Initiating Consciousness Shift
Enact.

. . .

. . .

The tides turned almost instantly. It was now a losing battle for the crypt's guardian. With Lukas's tinier form, the dranzithl had too much energy to release. Too much harm to cause. Too much power to annihilate.

Yet, the guardian came at him-it anyway.

It had forgone its strictly human form and upped its game. Two hands became four. Two legs twisted to become eight, forming a spideresque body. Enormous mass of aqāru protruded out of its body in the shape of horns and claws, all of them aiming to crush him-it down.

Inanna had been right. The dranzithl was a creature of art. Its skills, its power—they were exquisite. The ability to cause Decay required taking ordinary lifeforce and coalescing something so dense that the giver of life became an exterminator. Add that to the nigh-infinite regeneration and he-it had a walking, breathing murder machine at work.

And the doppelganger was feeling it.

A head-on strike with morphed limbs ended up shattering them.

Long-range attacks were incinerated in a burst of white death. If Lukas still had some rationality left, he'd have wondered what it was about Decay that made it bond so powerfully with flames, forming something that could be roughly described as Corrosive Light.

The crypt's failsafe, now no longer his doppelganger, pivoted toward him-it, morphed its forelimbs to form blades, and leaped into the air.

Eight feet. That was how far it jumped, and it had come effortlessly—it could have done more. Lukas-Dranzithl knew exactly how much force it had pressed against the ground with when it had left it, exactly what angle it jumped at. His-Its awareness of the entire anomaly around him-it was proving to be a most useful trait.

Lukas-Dranzithl took two steps away just as the crypt's failsafe came swooping down.

A burst of white death to the face banished it across the floor.

A part of Lukas-Dranzithl felt sick. He-It might as well be fighting against a blind opponent.

He sensed a miasma rise from the floor exactly five and a half feet away. Easily dodge-able, but he-it didn't care. Thick blades impaled his-it's abdomen, tearing all the way to his-its genitals.

Lukas-Dranzithl seemed not to notice.

Instead, he-it dashed across the floor, pulling out the blade from his abdomen, the wound healing at a miraculous rate, and bringing it down upon the failsafe. One, two, six, ten, twenty, fifty—it was not possible to strike so many times within a pair of seconds.

Again, Lukas-Dranzithl seemed not to notice.

"You have an opening. Destroy it before it can turn the tables."

Destroy it? There was no "one body" to be destroyed. No matter how much he-it killed, the crypt would quickly regenerate ore. The only option was to vaporize everything there in one single moment.

Something that was beyond him-it. So the alternative was to keep pushing it to the utmost limit. How *much* madness could it release at once? What was the absolute end point after which it couldn't mutate any further? He-it needed to hit that point. Make it desperate. Make it draw up every last iota of power it could bring to bear against him-it, force it into foolish, untenable strategies.

"Good point. And what if it doesn't have limits?"

Lukas-Dranzithl chuckled. It came out as a mix of cackling laughter and a noisy grunt.

SNIKT!

Oh, look, more attackers. Lukas-Dranzithl raised an enclosed fist and brought it down upon the ground.

Space distorted. As did every single one of the metal-monsters the failsafe had raised to attack him.

All of Lukas-Dranzithl's wounds healed again.

It wasn't about strength or regeneration, or using endless amounts of life-force. At its heart, the dranzithl was a shapeshifter. A slime. Heteromorph. Something that had a body, but lacked a proper frame. Body parts and organs existed, and Lukas-Dranzithl knew how to use them effectively, but the concept of "slime" overruled every other concept related to its existence. All tissues were "slime" tissues, and slime could morph into anything. Lung to heart, heart to liver, liver to kidney, and so on.

All of it was slime.

It was this profound simplicity that made the dranzithl the most dangerous monster in the anomaly. Its ability with Decay only cemented everything else. And if he-it applied the concept of Slime to the aqāru metal, then one could almost say that he was fighting a—

" . . . So that's how it is."

The realization that flooded through him was so overwhelming that he didn't even notice when Alpha Condition had deactivated, reverting full authority to him. To think that something so simple was there right before his very eyes.

"I'm an idiot."

"Finally figured that out, have you?"

Lukas smirked, and instead, placed both of his palms against the smooth surface of the aqāru. The overwhelming Decay burst from earlier must have dealt serious damage to the monsters, and this was the time to deal the final blow.

The failsafe was just one large mass of aqāru made sentient and installed with a twisted, functional facsimile of himself. It was intimately connected to the omphalos, and with every passing moment, the connection became deeper and deeper, but even so, one thing had remained unchanged.

It was still a monster, and as with the crypt earlier, Lukas did not need to actually kill the other person before trying to siphon him. Killing was just the safer option because it sundered the threads connecting the spirit to the physical shell.

"Mortal, you cannot take it. Not in the shape you are in. Siphoning a free soul is far, far easier than one latching on to a physical form. And this is the failsafe of the anomaly itself. It will be . . . "

Messy? Lukas grinned. *Don't worry. Messy is exactly what I'm looking for.*

He couldn't take it. But maybe the Warmonger could.

Ever since he'd gained the newest Protocol, he had felt the power of the omphalos within him and held it back. He had felt the growing primal drives that were its power, its need to hunt and consume prey, to fight and protect its territory, to kill and expand. Its nature was beautiful violence, stark clarity, the most feral instincts and desires pitted against the world outside.

This wasn't a creator. This was an invader.

A Warmonger.

But Lukas had fought against that drive, repressed it and held it at bay.

Until now.

His weariness vanished. Lifeforce and mana surged within him. Anomalous energy swirled around him like a protective cocoon. His fear vanished. Fear was for things that he was about to hunt.

It was time to kill prey.

He dug his hands and feet into the aqāru on the floor.

"Thanks for letting me in."

CHAPTER 56

———

ANOMALY VS. ANOMALY

Siphoning the failsafe was a foolhardy affair.

Lukas knew that. He was only a singular entity, and the failsafe was connected to the crypt's omphalos. It was entirely possible that the siphoning would end in a giant tug-of-war between him and the crypt, so he wasn't really expecting it to be easy.

Neither was he expecting to be struck by a bolt of pure power.

But there he was.

There was an enormous sound, a flash of intense, bright light, a shock against his body like a spray of frozen fire, and the next thing he knew, he was lying on his back, wheezing, with chunks of marble and debris pattering around him. He tried to get up, but the best he could get was a twitch of his fingers and toes. Other than that, nothing happened.

Soul Siphon: Active
Progress: 1.7%

Except that, he supposed.

Static covered his vision for a while as he lay, waiting for his brain to start tracking things again. From where he lay, it was like looking up from the bottom of a deep well, a long column of clear air that stretched up into the endless, pitch-black sky above. There were no clouds boiling up, yet thunder rumbled around with a low menace.

He pushed himself up and found the entire area covered in a rolling fog. It was difficult to see far in any direction, save for above. The atmosphere around him was thick—a moving, stirring, breathing creature that made everything else fade into nothingness. He could feel the cold marble touching his legs while—

Wait. Marble?

This is . . . my mind, he thought, and pushed himself up and looked around. This reality was not his. His mindscape had four white walls beneath a starless sky. Not this damp, hazy nothingness. He winced. His head hurt and felt foggy. Who was he again?

"I'm . . ." he breathed, and suddenly his chest felt less heavy. "I'm . . . Lukas."

With that realization came awareness. The fog was still there, but he could sense the white walls on all four sides. The crypt was an underground dweller, away from the light and the bright world. A world born of darkness.

A world that was not his.

"I AM LUKAS AGUILAR!" he roared.

Marble shattered. Winds blew with the sound of a cannon blast. The fog reeled away from him, like some vast and hungry beast suddenly struck on the nose.

As if in defiance, bolts of scarlet lightning flashed from the seething skies. Moss grew on the ground, and dark, twisted metallic objects formed over it, contorting to form bizarre shapes. Boulders of stone rose into walls and stalactites.

Soul Siphon: Active
Progress: 5.3%

The crypt loved its psionic assaults. It was pretty clear what it was aiming for. But that was fine. This was a battle inside his mind. His head, his rules.

"Okay, big guy," he snarled at the growing creation around him. "You wanted to get up close and personal, so let's play. You think this paltry cave is your domain? Let me show you mine."

He extended his hands.

"Welcome to Earth."

And the world around him changed.

It was small at first. The floor turned from white marble to dark asphalt. Thick lines of concrete began to form and widen into pavements. Metals erupted from all sides, rising up like the nine heads of the mythical hydra, branching out in all kinds of geometric shapes as concrete flesh began to proliferate over it.

Shoes appeared on his feet.

A large, bright, yellow sun shone overhead.

The fog hissed and moved slightly, revealing one of the most disgusting things Lukas had ever seen.

The creature, if it could even be called that, had smoky, translucent skin with bones visibly poking out in unexpected places. It had dozens upon dozens of limbs, each one from a different animal. Human hands, bovine hooves, canine haunches, and others he couldn't identify. It waddled forward on its mismatched limbs like an awkward centipede. Many of the limbs didn't even look functional. They just jutted from the creature's flesh in a twisted, unnatural fashion and dragged along the ground.

Its body was bulbous and elongated, though it wasn't just a blob. There was a strange logic to its form. It had a distinct skeleton, with dozens of different rib cages, and translucent muscles and sinew wrapping the bones. He counted six heads, and despite the translucent skin, he could make out a bat head sitting beside that of an azolg. Another head turned toward him, reminding him of a thoggua without tusks. A fourth looked almost humanoid, sitting atop a long spinal cord attached to a different animal torso.

"I—" Lukas tried forming words. "I'm not sure if you are the omphalos or not. But whatever you are, it's indescribably ugly. I can't even get mad at you for trying to look like me anymore."

"**I—AM—ARE—YOU!**" the alien monstrosity replied. Its voice was like iron dragged on glass. "**YOU—IS—ARE—ME!**"

"Yeah, been there, done that. Not a fan."

Roads formed beneath his feet. Large columns appeared around him. First rods, then concrete, and finally, tall pillars. One after another. As the street corners began to form, the fog violently reacted, engulfing the new creations in an effort to dematerialize them.

But Lukas did not relent.

Buildings soon erected themselves, with windows and doors. Multiple rooms. Shops. Stores. Houses. Larger constructs, like office buildings, hospitals, and skyscrapers. This was a world he knew. A world he'd lived in. A world he had associated with ever since he'd first drawn breath.

No fog, however invasive, would ever dematerialize that.

Soul Siphon: Active
Progress: 11%

He walked faster, and the mound reacted, sending its appendages—bones, muscles, tendrils—at him.

They were hit by a truck. Literally. The appendages were stamped over by the vehicle, crushed and turned to jelly before it knew what was happening. But that didn't stop the mound. Lukas found himself pitted against the mutilated will of the Crypt of Fiendish Worms. It was a horrible pressure, as if he had been suddenly transported to the bottom of the sea.

His own mental state was being reflected in the world around him.

Stone shattered to dust, and raw energy exploded upward through the floor, and into the concrete buildings Lukas had manifested around himself. It howled through the streets and alleys of his mindscape. It thundered through the tunnels and ravaged its way through the apartments.

Power stations exploded. Wires screamed and showered sparks. Screens on the buildings played diabolical images and screeched in demonic voices. Vehicles crashed into each other, erupting in a flood of fire.

His world was falling into complete chaos.

Soul Siphon: Active
Progress: 17.3%

Lukas found himself on his knees, sometime after, breathing hard, making pained sounds. This wasn't how he had expected things to go. Soul Siphon wasn't supposed to take that long. The Dranzithl had been a complete creation, and siphoning it had taken a couple of seconds at best. But this—this was going on at an agonizing rate. It was almost like—

He froze.

"YOU—ARE—REALIZE NOW! I—COMPLETE—AM!"

"What bullshit!" he shouted back. "You can't even use proper grammar yet!"

Soul Siphon: Active
Progress: 20.6%

"YOU THINK—PIT POWER—AGAINST ME?"

"Obviously!" Lukas took a deep breath and pulled in more anomalous energy. It was the only way he could keep the deafening power from bursting his skull apart.

The mound wailed and shook violently, manifesting a tectonic wave so massive that it shattered multiple rows of buildings in one go. Yes, he was projecting the human world, something that made the crypt look tiny in comparison. But his opponent was something of antiquity. A representation of an older, more savage universe. Where people feared the claws and the dark. If he wanted to survive this onslaught, he'd better need to think of something really fast.

Something that would be devastating to the Crypt of Fiendish Worms. But *what?*

Soul Siphon: Active
Progress: 35.3%

It was still too slow.

Everything was getting destroyed. The ruddy light from the haze of the mound was surrounding everything. Its very presence was a kind of weight that made entire tanks feel like they were made of paper-mache. A gravity that strained space around it and could not be ignored. Lukas had kept conjuring more and more constructions to keep his mind from being taken over, but it didn't matter.

The crypt's power rose and smashed against him. This was the power of an ancient world, a world that had no place for technology or for the weak. A world where might dominated everything else. Where humans would be crushed like the tiny insects they were while gargantuan creatures reigned supreme, a place so brutal and terrifying that humanity would rather choose to forget it.

And that was the crux of the matter. His world represented *humanity*. A species with no evolution. A species that took from the planet to fuel its own greed, without ascending to higher forms or adding skills to the world they rose from. A species that had constantly gnawed at the very heart of the world that was trying to sustain itself, and everything upon it, despite being untethered to the Origin.

A dying world.

A lostbelt.

In that light, the crypt was probably the worst matchup that Lostbelt Earth could ever face. Here it was, a manifestation of a dying world that consumed itself for survival, trying to outmatch the infinite growth of Potential. The Crypt of Fiendish Worms had risen where nothing was supposed to. It had proliferated and expanded, both in size and complexity. It had way more power than a tiny fragment of Lostbelt Earth could offer, and it had a greater vision of the future than the dead, dying world that Earth represented.

Lukas felt like he was standing before a tidal wave, trying to take shelter behind a stone.

Soul Siphon: Active
Progress: 49.5%

He was already down to his knees, and the Lostbelt Earth was psychologically weakened by the nature of its opponent. If he wanted to prevail, he needed something of the original vintage. A power as old as the universe itself, something so vital, so vitriolic, and so vicious that it surpassed the understanding of the mortal mind. Something that would make even the crypt recoil in horror and give him the opportunity to push back. Something like—

"No," Inanna's voice rumbled all around him. **"Do not do that. You cannot—"**

"There's no other option!"

"If you tear open those gates, your soul will not be able to take the onslaught. Mortal, you *will* perish."

"Not if I accept your offer!" Lukas replied, a wry grin on his lips.

"You—"

Her disbelief at his sudden proposition made him laugh. It was rare that he managed to surprise the Supreme Queen herself.

"Yes!" He laughed. "I accept your offer. I'm willing to work for you. We can grab some drinks to celebrate after this is all over—"

"I cannot accept your bargain, mortal. Not as I am now."

He remembered now. Inanna had power in spades, but there were things you could not do with only power. Things that involved greater existences and concepts, like *faith* and *divinity*.

Just like she needed it to bend Tanya to her will, she needed more than just power to heal him of the damage completely. And that wouldn't be possible unless—

"What if you performed your spell first?"

"Mortal—"

"If you performed that scrying spell, you'd be able to access your relics and your worshippers, right? That should be enough to heal me."

" . . . You are walking on a precipice, mortal. If you open those gates, you cannot withstand the effects. It is essential that the memory be contained, lest it shatter your soul."

"But if I can hold on till you gather your faith, then you can heal me, right?"

"If you can hold on, yes."

"Then let's do it."

Deleting All Safeties.
Maximize Sympathization Ratio.

Inanna let out a wild laugh. **"Bold move, mortal."**

Soul Siphon: Active
Progress: 63%

Lukas glanced at the Screen one last time, before bellowing at the mound. "Hey, world of worms and stupid bats, you wanted to be what I am, right? You wanted to feel what I feel?"

A fierce wind began to blow. Crimson lightning streaked across the dark skies. Fractures began to form everywhere. Faults that had nothing to do with the crypt's assault.

Balance Reality Foundation.
Counterbalance.

"You wanted to become me so badly?" He let his fingers hang loose and focused on *that* memory.

"Then feel what my world felt at its end!"

The gates of his mind blew open, and primordial chaos was unleashed. One that would destroy both the crypt and his conscience with equal preju-dice. A burning, mind-bending, emerald light exploded from all directions and engulfed his entire existence.

CHAPTER 57

GODDESS PROPOSES! ANOMALY DISPOSES!

Everything was gone.

There was no sound, no blaze of power, no rain of shrapnel or magma pouring down from erupting volcanoes—nothing. The flawless emerald light simply erased everything within reach, right down to the very atom. All that remained of the world around him was a flat, blasted plain, with enormous cracks all across it, intense crimson light threatening to escape through them. The ground was crushed down to be as smooth as glass. Even above it, far into the sky, there was nothing except the infinite blackness. Everything else—the buildings, the caverns, the monsters themselves—all of it was simply gone.

And at its center stood Lukas. His armor was gone. His clothes were gone. There was a thin jagged line originating from somewhere above his temples, tearing down his cheeks. An intense, blue light was trying to escape through the fracture, only held back by his defiant will. He held no weapon, and his body was coated from head to toe in red blood and black dust. The wounds in his torso were so deep that he could actually be *seen* through in places, shredded meat and exposed ivory bone in more than one spot.

He looked broken, stained, absolutely vulnerable.

Yet he did not fall.

The only other thing around him was the crypt itself.

"I—WE—I—WE—WAS RIGHT!" It repeated for a while before it finally got it right. **"I WAS RIGHT!"**

For one moment, Lukas feared it would reform back into the doppelganger. Then he realized that he simply didn't care.

"WE CAN DO GREAT THINGS TOGETHER. YOU AND I. YOUR KNOWLEDGE. EXPERIENCE. MY POWER. RESOURCES."

It hurt like nothing he could imagine. "I—consume—ed you."

And he had, for the Screen was displaying the notification overhead.

> **SOUL SIPHON SUCCESSFUL!**
> **Analyzing Foundations . . .**

"YOU DID, BUT I AM NOT THE KIND TO GO GENTLY INTO THE NIGHT. I AM BECOMING YOU. BECOMING US. I AM YOU. YOU ARE ME. US IS THE FUTURE!"

He breathed. It was probably the least painful activity he could indulge in without falling apart.

It cackled again. **"I—AM—OMPHALOS. I AM GROWTH. I AM WORLD. WHAT DO I CARE FOR—INVASION?"**

But then—

"HUMAN HOST MIND. RATIONALITY. EGO. VERY NEGATIVE. VERY—POLLUTING. NOW DESTROYED. OMPHALOS—IS—FREE!"

The words were simple, and yet, they hit him with the force of a sledgehammer.

It was right. Inanna had mentioned it before. Anomalies were Creators. They didn't care for personal evolution. For them, Creation was the supreme goal. But he was a human, and humans were prideful, egotistical creatures. Their ego was what led them to kill, to conquer and assimilate. To gain what did not belong to them.

"Invade . . ." he croaked. Just saying the word made him feel like his tongue would fall off.

When the crypt had duplicated his soul, it was struck with human emotions as well.

Pride. Greed. Envy. Wrath. It had demonstrated all of them. Just a few more and it'd have the seven deadly sins under its belt. It was what made it the way it was.

It was also what brought it to its end.

He extended his hand out. Or tried to. It didn't matter. It quickly became clear that he was in no way ready to appreciate the complexity of what he had just felt. Thousands of monster prototypes and a much higher number of stored spiritual data that could serve as a matrix for thousands more. There was power too—impossible power. He could sense lingering threads of inky blackness, staining the mind like a curse. And all of what he felt was nothing more than a tiny hillock compared to the mountain range of potential behind it.

With it, nothing would be beyond him. Nothing.

And yet, it couldn't heal him. Not one bit. Not as he was.

But Inanna could.

"WHY—HESITATE? YOU ARE—WORLD! I AM YOU! EMBRACE. BECOME. GROW. WE WILL HAVE ALL!"

And there lay the crux of the matter. The sad truth about humanity was that people were, in general, terrible at handling power. Not because of their temptation to Sin or forbidden delights or poor impulse control. And the moment they started to believe that they could, they were already a step into their graves.

Nature of the beast, as his grandfather used to say. He who fights monsters must always fear becoming one.

But that was the problem, wasn't it? The constant grinding of his soul, his psyche pitted against the darkness of the abyss. Maybe that's what forged monsters in the first place. Not the power, but the tugging sensation that came along with it.

Lukas couldn't help it. He laughed. Just that single act turned into a curtain of white agony that centered on his eyes. Nothing had ever hurt so much.

"There—is just—one thing."

"WHICH IS?"

"I made a promise."

The word of a mortal, given to a goddess.

"When I was weak."

A simple barter. Teach him to fight. To grow. To hone his power. And in return . . . her freedom.

And all he had wanted—

I have nothing to offer but my word. Look into my eyes and tell me I intend to betray you.

—was to survive.

And now, it was time.

He closed his eyes.

To keep that promise.

He took a deep breath and focused on a single word. A single name.

Inanna.

And the goddess appeared beside him. As real as real could be. Absolutely perfect, stunningly beautiful and desire personified. The Supreme Monarch of An and Ki.

"The word of a mortal." Her tone was thoughtful. **"I never imagined it could hold any weight."**

He did not laugh. He could not laugh. Not without breaking into two.

Inanna stretched her hand out and caressed his cheek. **"Do not worry. As soon as I am done, I will heal you."**

He wanted to talk to her. Wanted to tell her he could bear it. But all he could say was—

"Spell."

Inanna looked conflicted. It was the first time he'd seen her like that.

"This spell is the very first step to my freedom. And you, *Lukas*, have granted it to me."

A reel of indecipherable emotions flickered through her eyes, before Inanna closed them.

"I shall not forget it."

Suddenly, Lukas felt like he was back in his mindscape. Whatever absorbing the omphalos did to him, time itself felt wonky. The world around him was moving much slower than normal, like he was wading through water. Even the pain felt more manageable.

"What—did you—?"

"I am diluting your perception. It is several magnitudes greater than yours. It will minimize the pain and allow you to focus while I cast the spell."

"What are—you going to do?"

"It is a simple principle. First, I create a link between two connected points of energy. Then I make the energy indicate which way it is flowing."

"What points?" Lukas asked.

"Take my pendant and my true self, for example. Both are intimately connected to me. One houses me, the reflection. And the other, its source. The trick is to use this thread to locate the destination."

That didn't sound very complex.

Inanna laughed. **"The principle is simple. The execution, not so much. I do not know how much time has passed since Ereshkigal's betrayal. No doubt she has placed measures against scrying, sealed away my temples and relics, and ensured I remain forgotten. She also cursed me to become a denizen of the Underworld."** She cupped her chin. **"I wonder if that is why we ended up in a subterranean anomaly. This deserves some contemplation . . ."** She waved her hand. **"Later, that is."**

Her mannerisms were so cute that Lukas laughed.

And then coughed out blood. The constant throb of pain in his body was steadily increasing.

"Pay heed to this, mortal. Spells are different from your Skills. Unlike the latter, Spells happen within the mind of the caster. If something goes wrong, it can affect the mind in all manners. Hence, it is preferable to insulate the entire process by giving it a *name*." Her hands moved animatedly. **"I will eventually teach you how to attach ideas to objects and use them for spellcasting. But for now, I shall perform it . . ."** Her hands finished moving and came to rest on either side of her. **" . . . directly."**

Lines of mana exploded out of her in different directions, moving in straight lines, only to change directions, then move straight again. Meanwhile, a thin strand of light spun a circle around her. As the spectacle slowed, Inanna stood in the eye of a pentacle, with a circle touching its vertices in perfect symmetry.

"This is a pentacle. My symbol of Order. Five points. Five sides. A perfect representation of the five elements—air, fire, earth, water, and ether, precisely in that order. The circle represents my hold upon the mana crafted here, molding the spell to obey my orders. Force within restraint."

Lukas watched with rapt attention, doing his best to ignore the discordant humming in his ears.

Just a little more—

"And now we perform the spell."

Inanna's lips moved, but he couldn't quite catch the alien syllables that came out of her mouth. He could hear and understand what she did, but as soon as the sound of the words vanished, so too did his comprehension.

"Be warned. Something may happen."

For a second, everything went completely silent.

Then, there was a dull disturbance in the air as a sinister crimson sheen began pouring in from seemingly nowhere. Lukas felt the crypt's power rise up like a tidal wave and meet the crimson sheen, becoming one with it, vibrating, expanding, contracting, deepening—

And then a deluge of pure, violent, blinding, nauseating pain blanketed his world.

After a small eternity, Lukas decided to open his eyes.

The earth beneath his feet felt barren and icy. He opened his eyes and looked up at the cold, gray sky. He was standing, but his muscles and ligaments felt stretched beyond their limits. His own heartbeat was torturous. The mere act of breathing sent jolts of pain down his spine. His arms, his chest, his face—everything burned.

He tried to scream, but it was to no avail. A slow, gurgling moan came out instead as he coughed blood into the mana-charged air. But he held on.

"Wha—?" he croaked, as a vast roaring sound tore across . . . wherever he was.

"Something unexpected."

She pointed her right arm toward the sky and shouted something furious. A streak of crimson dashed across the stormy sky as an enormous, swirling form emerged overhead and fell upon them, throwing them into a state of—

Void.

Silent, colorless, empty.

And then, there was *light.*

It was difficult to describe. One moment he was standing next to Inanna, and the next moment, the world around him was coming closer, as if it was moving relative to them. His mental surroundings shifted. Animals, plants, terrain, craters, cities, kingdoms, landmasses, oceans—everything became visible, dabbed with threads of color and distinctive mana patterns.

The spell traversed everywhere. Up. Down. Right. Left. Within. Without.

—Endless desert. A lost kingdom. Frost growing on the edges of sand. A woman's face. Solar flares coming down like the judgment of a wrathful god—

The world moved faster.

—Blasted cities, smoke, tears, screams. Blood ran in the gutters like water. Columns of greasy black smoke rose from altars, temples, shrines decorated with skulls and crusted with the blood of sacrifices. A hidden chamber. Sigils on the floor. Artifacts, relics, an ax that defied reality itself—

And even faster.

—A world of broken citadels. A serpent sleeping in the shadows. Fire rising out of ocean floors. A behemoth swinging a sword so vicious that it could fell mountains. An old, emaciated thing opening a single eye—

The spell exploded in all directions as more and more power came pouring out of Lukas, enough to support even a hundred dranzithl. It roared like a feral wind, ravaging its way out of him as more and more energy was used to fuel the spell that continued to expand and expand and expand—

—Space. Endless space. No landmasses or oceans. No moon. No stars. Endless space, and then lush, green earth. Plants. Weird things. Chimeras. Serpents. Bolts of blue lightning coursing through the sky like vengeful gods as the seven suns shone—

A storm engulfed his mind. It tore at his perceptions, flooding them with random images and smells and sensations. It was like standing in a sandstorm, only instead of inflicting pain, every random grain was an experience—a memory—so disjointed and intense and rapid that there was nothing to hold on to.

WARNING!
Extreme Spiritual Damage.
Initiate Shutdown of functionality until Recovery?

"NO!" Inanna snarled. **"I am close. I need more time. It has to be somewhere. It has to be—"**

Every inch of Lukas's body painfully protested. Blood was already pouring down his eyes and nose. His skull felt like it was going to be crushed like a tomato. Neural Suppression had already lost it. So how was he keeping up?

Despite Inanna's words, he knew the Screen would never show him something like that without reason.

But there was no other option.

He had taken the risk. He had to hold on or risk everything.

—More space. Endless darkness. Land. Brown and black. Ash falling from the sky. Asteroids hanging out of nowhere. Vast, endless plains of sand with nothing but coffins and coffins and more—

"Where is it?" Inanna's voice rumbled. **"Where is it? Where is it?** *WHERE IS IT?!"*

Lukas could feel the anger and tension and anxiety consuming through her. Not that it was unexpected. This was her sole chance at finding her way home, and he'd be a hypocrite if he disapproved. After all, he too once wanted to find a way back to Earth. If only it didn't hurt so much—

—Ice covered everything. The land, the sky. The endless night above had no stars. Instead large pores opened across the horizon, pumping up crimson-hot lava—

FASTER! FASTER! FASTER!

"I cannot find it!" For the first time since knowing the goddess, Lukas heard a trace of anxiety in her voice.

—the realm looked like a skull. Something humanoid, with an entire world growing out of it. Floating in space. Mining colonies. Ships. There was no water, but instead tentacular creatures that could devour minds like—

WARNING!
Spiritual Damage beyond Acceptable Limit
Partial Recovery Possible on immediate shutdown

No.

Lukas decided to trust her. Trust Inanna to heal him. She was a goddess. With her power, she could do anything. Because that was what faith was. To *believe* without proof or reason.

But the pain . . . If he shut it down right now, would he survive? Maybe—

"NO!" Inanna warned him, her eyes shining with a demented zeal. **"HOLD YOUR GROUND, MORTAL! I WILL FIND IT! IT HAS TO BE HERE!"**

Lukas screamed and screamed as his entire body was engulfed by an unyielding tide of energy. Fires roared within him, seeping from his bloodied, grimy skin as drops of white-hot liquid fire. His eyes burned and shriveled in his sockets, only to heal almost instantly and be burned again, and his hair caught fire. His entire body was flailing about and an enormous pressure was pressed down on his body, crushing him down onto the hard ground below. For a split second, the little semblance of conscious thought that Lukas had left idly noted that Inanna was right. Dying truly was as bad as he imagined.

Something cracked from within him, and Lukas knew the true definition of the word *agony*.

His world, his entire existence, was drowned beneath a massive surge of something that ripped into his fragile psyche and implanted itself there. Pain itself lost all meaning as this enormous, mind-shattering sensation swept through every iota of his body. The very molecules that made him human shuddered and quaked as something otherworldly settled upon them, crafting a place within his body for itself. He didn't know how long this went on for, as he lost meaning of time, but it occurred to him at one point or another that this massively overwhelming presence that threatened to tear his mind and soul in half was very familiar.

In fact, it felt as if he had known it all his life.

—Complete darkness. This was underground. No plants. No creatures. Nothing except the earth and half-formed golems. No fire. No water. No ice. Only distorted wraiths that lay trapped and screamed and screamed and screamed—

WARNING!
Base Host Damaged
Initiating Recovery Protocol.
Commencing Shutdown!

"WE CANNOT STOP!" Inanna screamed. *"IT MUST BE HERE SOME-WHERE! I WILL FIND IT! ALL I MUST DO IS—"*

But the Screen was done listening.

Burning Auxiliary Soul Capacity to Meet Spell Power Requirements!
Unacceptable!
Unacceptable!
Activating Failsafe!
Safety—On
Overriding Anomaly-Host-Mind
Overclock Removed

Lukas's vision left him. His already dumbed-down senses were now shutting down entirely. He tried to remain standing, but he couldn't tell which way was up. His body felt deliriously warm and monstrously tired. Sleep, something that had evaded him for quite some time, returned to him with its arms wide.

All Systems Shutdown.
Reset.

It was quiet.

Nearly. He could hear her faint screams in the background. Her screams of rage and despair. Her order to not give up. To hold his ground for *just a little more. To keep holding on until that spell—*

In the distance, Lukas could make out a faint light. He wondered if it was the light at the end of a tunnel, like an approaching train. It felt warm. And nice. And blurry. And—

Darkness.

EPILOGUE

H e floated aimlessly in a sea of darkness, unchained by any physical restraints. Yet somehow, his limbs were paralyzed and he could not move. He struggled against invisible, immaterial bonds, until its futility dawned on him and he sagged back into them.

What was going on?

What happened?

Who was he?

Lukas.

That was his name, wasn't it? Yes. Lukas.

As everything slowly came back to him, his mind felt clearer than ever before. The cracks in his mindscape, that deafening discordant hum, it was all little more than a memory. He remembered the terrible heat that incinerated him—the pain had been horrible. But then, something happened. Something changed him from within, tearing at his psyche so badly that he'd nearly lost himself. It was like he had—

Like he had *evolved* in some way.

A loud, static buzz cracked around him like a whip, and suddenly, Lukas found himself lying on a cold, hard floor. Except for his head. That was lying on something soft and . . . fleshy?

"Good," he heard a voice speak. A feminine voice. "Very good."

Inanna?

He easily recognized her all-too-familiar voice, but it sounded . . . different. The Inanna he knew oozed strength, and her words reverberated like a commandment from the heavens. Even in his mindscape, or in that final illusion of hers, it was booming. This couldn't possibly be her, could it?

"Do not overexert yourself, mortal."

. . . It was definitely Inanna. Why did she sound so normal?

Lukas squirmed in place, trying to get a feel for his body. It felt heavy and dense, like someone had replaced his bones with steel and flesh with leather. It was as if an invisible mountain pressed down on him from above. He tried to speak, but his lips did not so much as twitch. Even the most strenuous attempts produced little more than weak, incomprehensible grunts.

"Excellent," the voice rasped. "I always knew you possessed fortitude. Try opening your eyes."

His eyelids, like the rest of him, were too heavy to move. He tried opening them. And failed. And then he tried again, only to end up with the same results.

After what felt like a small eternity, he managed to wrench them open. His eyes felt coarse, like they were swimming in sand, and they squinted from the sudden brightness that overtook his vision. And it *hurt*.

"Slowly, if it pains you. Take your time."

First, Inanna's voice was soft, and now she cared for his well-being? This was a dream. It had to be.

Someone chuckled in the background.

No, not someone. *Her*. Inanna.

Lukas tried once more, and this time, his eyes opened without discomfort. The wooly mist around his vision faded, and the world came into sharp focus. It was only then that he realized that something—or someone—was holding his head in place. On their *lap*.

The Goddess of War and Lust. The Akkadian Queen of An and Ki. And she was holding him, his head in her lap, her hand running gently through his hair, like a mother with her son or two loved ones sharing a private moment.

"Ah," Inanna whispered, looking down at him, a soft smile on her face. "Dawn, at last."

"Am I dying?" Lukas's words came out less humanlike and more like a frog's croak. At least his body was no longer in pain. "Because if so, then there are certainly worse ways to go than in your lap."

Inanna stared at him for a moment, before letting out a little tinkling laugh, one filled with a puzzling melancholy. "It is a sad world that finds your attempts at humor passable."

"I'll have you know—" He broke out into wet, scratchy coughs. And *god*, did it hurt. "Where I'm from, people found me hilarious."

"Perhaps you were too simpleminded to realize they were laughing *at* you, rather than with you," she quipped back.

"Well, I got you to laugh, didn't I?"

The corners of Inanna's lips twitched upward. "That you did, mortal. That, you did." And then . . .

Nothing.

They sat in an unbroken, amicable silence. Lukas could not tell how much time was passing.

"So," he finally asked, "am I really dying?"

"I have told you this before. You being dead is counterproductive to my desires."

"Huh . . . That's good to know. I guess it all worked out."

Inanna said nothing.

It was then that the absurdity of his current situation made itself known to him.

Lukas took a moment to look at Inanna. Really *look* at her. All he could think of was how . . . *odd* she seemed. The Inanna he was familiar with had been preternaturally strong, healthy, and confident. Her angelic face was more radiant than the sun, and her figure exuded a sensuality that was impossible to describe with mere words, far more comparable to nature than it was to man.

But this Inanna was far from it. She was as thin as a stick, and her hair was mussed into an unkempt wreck. Her face was twisted with pain, and her eyes were sunken, a strange uncertainty swimming in her gaze as it bored down into him.

He couldn't believe what he was looking at. It—it had to be a dream. It just *had to*. There was no way this could be anything else.

Unless . . .

"What happened back there? I'm—I'm alive, right?" he asked.

"Yes, but only just."

"That doesn't sound good."

"Your ability to understate the problem is as powerful as always," Inanna said, her lips twisting into a frown so bitter he could nearly taste it on his tongue. "The spell I performed worked, but it did not yield the results I expected. It traversed across the world and reached into every realm in existence to find a link to my sister's domain."

An eerie, foreboding feeling clutched at Lukas's insides. Somehow, he just knew that he wasn't going to like the next few words coming out of her mouth.

"It found nothing."

His stomach plummeted. *"What?"* he whispered, shocked.

"I realized partway through the scrying ritual that nothing was being detected. So I altered it mid-course. I not only searched for Irkalla, my sister's home, but for everything else. Ereshkigal. An. My throne room. My relics. The faith I held in my ancient temples. I searched for *every* deity of my pantheon, using myself as an anchor." Inanna laughed aloud, but there was no humor in it. "I found *nothing*."

Lukas gazed up at her, horrified. "You couldn't find any sign of your home at all?"

Inanna slowly nodded. "It is as if the entire realm of Ki, the thrones of An, the Underworld of Irkalla, are all just gone. Vanished. My followers, my betrayers, my Truths, my sister . . . none of them exist."

"But the spell faltered midway, right?" he asked desperately. "I couldn't keep it going all the way. Maybe you'd have found something if it finished. If—if we go back and try it again, then—"

Lukas's words died in his throat as he took in her expression. Never before had he seen her so lost. So helpless. It was almost as if she had just . . . given up.

And suddenly, he decided he hated seeing her like this.

He absolutely *abhorred* it.

"The spell did not fail, my dear mortal." She gently ran her dainty fingers through his raven-colored locks. "No single spell can span the entire universe in a single attempt. I cast the spell *thousands* of times, all at once, in the blind hopes of finding anything to connect me to the life I know I have once lived. In doing so, I used up all the energy you gained from the anomaly's core."

" . . . So where does that leave us?" Lukas finally asked, not knowing what else to say.

The goddess looked crestfallen. "I do not know. For the first time in aeons, I simply do not know. As the laws for lostbelts do not align with that of the Origin, it is possible that Akkadia and Sumer have fallen prey to time. Or worse, the Dirge has swallowed them whole. Even so, I find it hard to believe it can be so cleanly eradicated. There would be remnants. Fallen gods. Truths embedded into the Origin itself. *Something.*"

Lukas bit his tongue. *But there wasn't. Was there?*

"Nothing," Inanna sighed, answering his unasked question.

"Still, there has to be an explanation," he pressed, wholeheartedly believing his own words. After all, Inanna *always* had the answer. And if she didn't, then she would eventually find it. Always. "Maybe this is a different universe or something."

"Your bards feed you surreal stories." Inanna chuckled. "There is but one universe. The Bedrock of Creation. The Cosmic Demiurge. Remember, you yourself know but a small piece of my story, though your knowledge is distorted, no doubt due to the overactive imagination of your historians."

He tried to get up and argue the point, but her arms, frail as they seemed, held him down tightly.

Helplessly, he just stared back at her.

"The way I understand it, one of two things has happened," she continued. "The first is that this life, the pendant, your planet, you, and everything else I have experienced in this form is a great lie. An illusion crafted by the Seven Gates to keep me trapped within for eternity, and I am only discovering it now."

Lukas gulped nervously. "And the other?"

"That everything I've experienced here, with you, is *real.* It all exists. Someone has gone to extreme lengths to erase the Akkadian pantheon, and everything associated with it, out of time itself."

He stared at her, flabbergasted by a conspiracy so bizarre that it made his own situation of forced homelessness feel tame in comparison.

"But I have lost my chance at finding the truth. My only solace, as much as it pains me to admit it, is you."

"Inanna, you're scaring me," Lukas said quietly. Surely she did not mean what he thought she did. Right?

"I—" The goddess looked like she was trying to pronounce a word she had never spoken before. "I am *sorry*. I failed. I should have realized it and shut it down. But I—in my desperation for freedom, I lost control. I knew what would happen if that memory was unleashed. I knew what would happen if I allowed it to run rampant. But I ignored it. In my arrogance of my divinity, I—"

Broken exclamations slipped past her lips.

"I could have alleviated you. I *should* have alleviated you. It would have been temporary, but you would at least have a chance. *I* would have a chance. But I did not. I was so . . . hasty. One would think waiting inside a relic for aeons would have taught me patience." She caressed his cheek. "But no. I was reckless and sloppy. So lost was I in the dreams of finding what I wanted, that I carelessly ignored what I *had*. Ereshkigal was right. I won the World, but lost my sister. Perhaps that is why she betrayed me."

"Inanna—"

"But you . . ." Inanna gazed down at him proudly. "You did not. You, a *mortal*, kept your word, even at the cost of your own sacrifice. Your omphalos tried to protect you, but your mind perished in the assault."

And there she went again, saying all sorts of confusing things. "But you saved me, right?" he asked.

"Must you always make me repeat myself?" She sighed fondly. "I saved you for my own selfish pursuits. Would you like to know the circumstances?"

Lukas wordlessly nodded.

"Your soul was shattered. Your brain . . . suffered tremendous damage."

"Oh. I . . . I see." Lukas didn't like it, but he had to accept it. "Prophylaxis only heals physical damages." He'd kept his word to the fullest of his ability and let the chips fall as they may. And now, it was time to face the consequences.

"One of its many shortcomings," she said. "You and the crypt were connected at a spiritual level. The backlash from the memory destroyed the crypt's consciousness, as well as yours."

"That sounds an awful lot like being dead, if you ask me."

"You hear, but you do not listen," Inanna chided. "You are a soul. You have a body."

"Then . . . ?"

"The scrying spell we performed? That was a little over a month ago."

"A month?!" Lukas exclaimed. Every time Inanna spoke, he felt like he was being doused with ice-cold water.

"Indeed. The terramancer and his compatriots have been keeping you hidden in their kingdom."

Kingdom? Llaisy Kingdom? Haviskali, if he recalled correctly. Tanya and the others had taken him to Haviskali. Out of the desert. And his body had been there for an entire month? It was all so—so—

Damn.

"I used whatever leftover power I possessed to alleviate your mind. The damage is now undone. Completely. I believed it would provide an incentive for your omphalos to aid you. So I waited. And waited. And waited." She stared at him with glassy eyes. "The help never came."

Lukas eyed her. "So it gave up on me?"

Surprisingly, Inanna shook her head. "Do you know what an omphalos believes in?"

"Annoying screens and prompts?"

Her lips twitched. "It believes in calculation. Logic. *Mathematics.* To it, the lifespan of a mortal is nothing more than a blink of an eye. It realized the harsh truth of what has happened, and since then, it has been endlessly trying out spiritual combinations to create a faithful approximation of yourself."

"It's been trying to create my clone?"

Truthfully, he'd had his fill of strange beings made to look like him.

"A puppet. A spiritual reflection, minus the annoying attribute called irrationality." Her eyes became distant. "I cannot find fault in its actions. Creating a soul is one thing. Bringing it back is another. The former requires anomalous energy. The latter, divinity. So . . . I did what was required."

Inanna's body turned slightly translucent for a second.

No.

"I trusted you, a mortal, once, and you came through." She let out a pained chuckle. "I must now put my trust in you a second time."

"Inanna," Lukas breathed, his heartbeat picking up in its tempo, *"what did you do?"*

"I used my Presence to bind your shattered soul. To"—her voice cracked—"to manifest your mind once more and awaken your consciousness. Now, I have nothing left. No power. No faith. No Presence. And, unless you find a way to make it otherwise, no existence."

He didn't care how much the action hurt him. He pulled himself out of her lap, grabbed her by the arms, and shook her. Relentlessly.

"What the fuck were you thinking?!"

Inanna, to her credit, remained unfazed. "Without power, I could not manifest elsewhere. I would be stuck in a dark corner of your sedentary form. The omphalos would not care for my existence. The best option, my *only* option, was to awaken you."

"But—but you—don't you realize what this means? You'll—you'll be—"

And for the first time, the unassailable wall that was her facade cracked. Her lips trembled. She was afraid. He knew it. She knew it. And she knew that he knew it. "I had enough energy for this one final conversation. Now that it is over, I will fade."

"You mean, you'll—you'll—"

"It is the nature of the universe that things remain. Nothing ever disappears completely. The very sound of the first Creation still echoes throughout the vast darkness. The universe remembers. Now, I have become a part of you. The matrix for your very soul. My divinity has become the bedrock for your existence."

"What does that mean?" Lukas asked worriedly.

"Will your questions never cease?"

"No."

A patient smile floated on her face. "What you are now, I do not know. You were always a miracle to begin with. An anomaly with a mortal mind. And now, you are yet another. A mortal mind born of divinity that bears an omphalos within. How this plays out will be most entertaining to watch. It is rather unfortunate I will not be there to witness it."

"That won't happen," Lukas growled.

"If nothing else," Inanna replied. There was a rush about her, as if she wanted to say her fill before it was too late. She cupped his face with her hands. "You have fulfilled all your promises, mortal. Except one. A favor that remains uncollected. Will you fulfill it?"

"Of course!"

"Even if what I ask of you is a burden? A curse you must bear?"

Tears ran unbidden down his face. "Anything! Anything!"

Inanna's expression became serious. "Then I *curse* you to never give up on your selfishness, or your defiance. It is what makes you what you are. Stay true to yourself no matter how many you trample upon. Be the invader that I was. The monster. The conqueror. You are no longer allowed to pretend you are merely a survivor."

Her words rang true deep within Lukas. He had started this journey for the sake of survival. He had bargained with her for survival. But somewhere down the line, his goals changed. He sought power, growth, and evolution. He wanted to break the system that the omphalos had granted him to obtain power in the most efficient way. Even if it meant snatching it from others.

"I don't have a choice in this, do I?" he finally asked.

"If it were easy, it would not be a curse," the goddess said.

"Then that's what I get for biting off more than I can chew, I guess."

Inanna smiled. It was a brilliant thing.

"You know I won't give up on you, right?" Lukas demanded. "I made you a bargain. To free your real body from Irkalla. I *will* make it happen."

With every word, Inanna became more transparent. He could nearly see right through her. "It took a miracle to find my way back to this realm. *You* were my miracle, Lukas Aguilar. I can only hope that you will be my miracle once more."

"I will," Lukas promised. "I swear it, you hear me? *I will find a way to bring you back. No matter the consequences.*"

A cup appeared on the floor between them. Tenemu. The wine of Sumer. Drink of the gods, Inanna had once described it.

Drink to it, mortal, her eyes seemed to say.

A long-lost tradition, after a bargain was struck.

Lukas clenched his fingers tightly around the cup, his eyes never leaving Inanna's slowly dissipating face. He pushed the rim to his lips and lifted it up. The liquid was dark and rich, tinged with honey. He lowered it and looked ahead to see her one final time and—

Nothing.

Just like that, she had vanished.

ABOUT THE AUTHORS

T. B. Mare is the pseudonym of the authors of Stranger Than Fiction, a LitRPG adventure series originally released on Royal Road. They are a pair of dreamers who started working together in order to share with readers some of the fun of creating fantasy worlds filled with rich lore and complex characters. Both discovered their love for fantasy and magic at a young age, and the ensuing affairs have carried on well into adulthood. Hopelessly addicted to complex genre fiction—especially the darker kind—they currently work multiple jobs but are looking forward to one day writing full-time.